Kingston Frontenac PL/ARPs

W9-ABV-965

Feb 2017

WITHDRAWN

THE FORGETTING MOON

BRIAN LEE DURFEE

THE FORGETTING MOON

THE FIVE WARRIOR ANGELS
BOOK ONE

SAGA PRESS

LONDON SYDNEY **NEW YORK** TORONTO NEW DELHI

SAGA PRESS

AN IMPRINT OF SIMON & SCHUSTER, INC.

1230 AVENUE OF THE AMERICAS, NEW YORK, NEW YORK 10020

This book is a work of fiction. Any references to historical events, real people, or real places are used fictitiously. Other names, characters, places, and events are products of the author's imagination, and any resemblance to actual events or places or persons, living or dead, is entirely coincidental. † Text copyright © 2016 by Brian Lee Durfee † Jacket illustration copyright © 2016 by Richard Anderson † All rights reserved, including the right to reproduce this book or portions thereof in any form whatsoever. For information address Saga Press Subsidiary Rights Department, 1230 Avenue of the Americas, New York, NY 10020 † SAGA PRESS and colophon are trademarks of Simon & Schuster, Inc. † For information about special discounts for bulk purchases, please contact Simon & Schuster Special Sales at 1-866-506-1949 or business@simonandschuster.com. † The Simon & Schuster Speakers Bureau can bring authors to your live event. For more information or to book an event, contact the Simon & Schuster Speakers Bureau at 1-866-248-3049 or visit our website at www.simonspeakers.com. † The text for this book was set in Absara TF. † Manufactured in the United States of America † First Edition † 10 9 8 7 6 5 4 3 2 1 † CIP data for this book is available from the Library of Congress. † ISBN 978-1-4814-6522-9 † ISBN 978-1-4814-6524-3 (eBook)

FOR ALL

FIREMEN, PARAMEDICS, NURSES,
AND LAW ENFORCEMENT OFFICERS
ACROSS THE WORLD, MUCH APPRECIATION
FOR THE NOBLE WORK YOU DO,
SPECIFICALLY TO ALL MY GOOD FRIENDS
AT THE UTAH DEPARTMENT OF CORRECTIONS

INTRODUCTION AND ACKNOWLEDGMENTS

As someone who was adopted and knows nothing of his biological heritage, I've always been drawn to the heroic quest tales of orphans and bastards. Luke Skywalker was my favorite as a kid. Then came **Terry Brooks'** Shea Ohmsford, **Lloyd Alexander's** Taran, **David Eddings'** Garion, **Robert Jordan's** Rand al'Thor, **Tad Williams'** Simon, **George R. R. Martin's** Jon Snow, and countless others. One might say these stories are in my blood. *Mysterious* blood, that is. I have never met a blood relative. And to always feel unattached and adrift in the world is a unique thing indeed. Sometimes the anonymity is worn with pride, other times sorrow.

Ever since I was a teen, I aimed to explore these themes in a fantasy story of my own. So as you read this series to its conclusion, beware. Assume nothing. Trust no one. For in the end, do any of us know who we truly are? Do any of us ever show our true selves to the world?

I must thank **Bardett and Maxine Durfee** for adopting a son (me). You've always loved and supported me as if I were your own. I could not have asked for better.

Never-ending gratitude goes out to my superhero agent **Matt Bialer**, a dude who is honest and fair and knows how to sell a book. Plus, he's a fellow artist. **Stefanie Diaz** for foreign sales. My editor at Saga Press, **Joe Monti**, deserves all the credit for putting together a spectacular book here. Oh, and thanks for giving a relatively unknown writer a chance! **Justin Landon** of *Rocket Talk* deserves a nod, as well as **Valerie Shea** and **Jeannie Ng** for copyediting. **Chris Lotts**' many notes and initial support helped shape much of the story. And **Amber R. Boehm**'s final critique pushed the manuscript to the next level—huge appreciation to a brilliant writer, editor, and friend. Plus designer **Michael McCartney** and illustrator **Richard Anderson**'s fantastic cover is spot-on gritty, ethereal perfection. Awesome job, guys!

Thanks also to **Stephen King**, **Mötley Crüe**, and the **Oakland Raiders**.

Contents

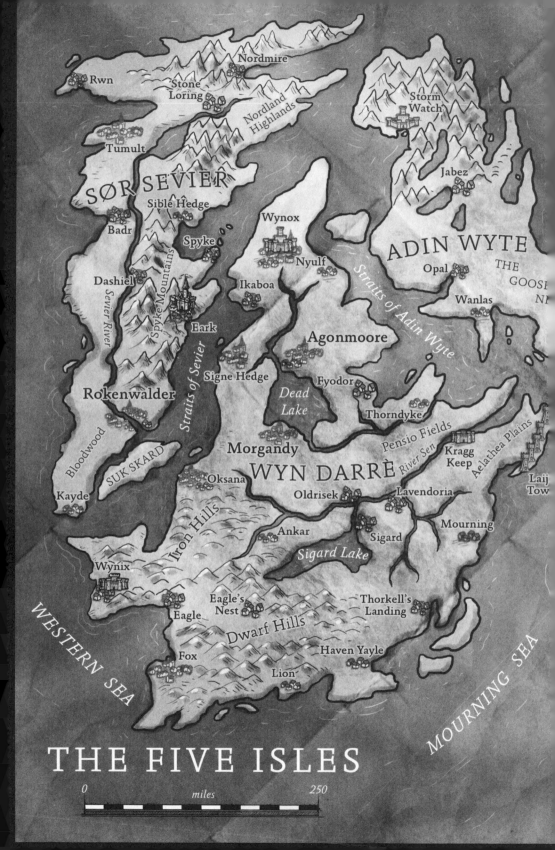

THE FIVE ISLES

0   *miles*   250

THE FORGETTING MOON

Trust is fleeting, while betrayal is timeless. Alas, life is crowded
with lies. So be bloody, be brave, be happy. For at the end of
every tale, nobody is who they seem to be. . . .
— THE BOOK OF THE BETRAYER

PROLOGUE

SHAWCROFT

15TH DAY OF THE FIRE MOON, 985TH YEAR OF LAIJON

SKY LOCHS, GUL KANA

In her panic, the woman had fled with the boy to the very edge of the glacier, a thin boning knife buried hilt-deep in her back. All that remained of her passing: a broad bloody smear that led over the lip of the ice to the loch waters five hundred feet below.

The small boy, kneeling alone on the precipice of the ridge, stared up at Shawcroft with big calf-eyes, piercing green orbs that gaped wide and vulnerable against the seemingly bottomless drop beyond. The boy wore rough-spun breeches, soft woolen boots, and a crude elk-hide coat fit for a child, his tiny hands bare and red from the cold. Wisps of blond hair fluttered in the crisp breeze. Perched against the sunlit backdrop of the loch and the lofty, snow-covered mountains, the child appeared the very essence of innocence and purity. No more than three years old, if that. And despite the horrific injuries of the woman who had carried him this far, there was not a drop of blood on him.

All his life a soldier for the Brethren of Mia's cause, and Shawcroft's heart had never ached more than it did now.

"Don't move!" he called out over the deafening roar of the mammoth glacial river thundering somewhere far below. The sharp ridges of the surrounding crevasses and crags and heaps of ice magnified the immensity of the roiling water's thrum. He could feel the glacier shifting under his leather boots as he carefully moved forward, knowing the ice could shear off at any moment and send both him and the boy plummeting to a violent, crushing death. Struggling not to stare at the red trail of blood that had led him here, Shawcroft stuffed his gloves into the buckled front closure of his fur-lined tunic and adjusted the cloak around his chest, longsword a barely noticed weight in the baldric looped over his shoulder.

As he reached forth and helped the child from the edge, the plunging barrenness of the spacious air beyond seemed to pull at him with an immense, near-irrepressible force as he heard the hollow clomping of the two beasts coming up behind him.

The boy's small hand in his, Shawcroft turned and blinked against the stark brilliance of the mazelike landscape he'd just traveled through, beautiful in its own way, a hard-edged white beauty that tore at the eyes and scoured them raw. And shimmering darkly, two shadowy forms materialized out of that opaque brightness and glided toward him.

He knew what they were.

Bloodwood assassins. Both cloaked in black, riding black stallions. He'd been expecting them. The day's battle wasn't over yet.

Shawcroft imposed himself between the assassins and the boy and drew his sword from over his shoulder—his Dayknight sword, long and cold and sleek with a black opal–inlaid pommel and leather-bound hilt that had molded to the contours of his hand from long use.

Despite the slick ice all around, both horses moved with an unobtrusive ease, sure of their step, seeping through the massive crags and jutting shards of ice like smoke.

Thirty feet before Shawcroft and the boy, the riders reined in their steeds. Large stallions both, their eyes a faint, hazy rose color— the telltale signs of the rauthouin bane the two young assassins had been injecting into the still-growing beasts. Within a year those eyes would glow a flaming red, and both stallions' shoulders and haunches would broaden with corded tendon, muscle, and might. They would be full Bloodeye steeds then, rabid and wild.

The killers atop these brutish creatures were brothers, known by the Brethren of Mia as Hawk and the Spider—King Aevrett Raijael of Sør Sevier's two favorite young assassins.

Lithe and silent, they dismounted and shed their cloaks, both wearing the black leather armor of their craft. The brittle cold seemed to affect neither assassin as they drifted toward Shawcroft. They looked the same. Eighteen years old at the most, with cool narrow eyes, squared jaws and cheekbones, raven-colored hair cropped short. A serene self-assurance evident in their every nimble step.

Shawcroft set his stance. "I do not wish to kill either of you!" he yelled over the waters rumbling deep below.

"Then I promise we won't die," the one named Hawk answered. His familiar voice carried a smooth, indignant lilt that cut across the glacier.

The Spider's eyes roamed the icy ledge behind Shawcroft, pausing on the boy but a moment, coming to rest on the dark stain left by the woman. "Oh, what people won't do to save their loved ones from death at the hands of a Bloodwood. She took a terrible chance fleeing that pathetic mining camp . . . running out here so far." A dagger, black as polished coal, appeared in his hand. He looked at Shawcroft with fierce intent. "And what will you do to avoid death at our hands, old man?"

"I'm not so old I can't handle the two of you. I've killed your kind before. Even today, one like you lies dead in the camp above."

Hawk's flat eyes appraised him. "We only want the boy."

Shawcroft wasn't altogether certain the child shouldn't just die here with him, now. It would at least bring the bleak emptiness of the boy's hard and lonely future to an end. *One swift shove with my boot.* He glanced down at the child shivering just behind him, the rim of the ice so near. *Hardly any effort at all.*

He could feel the glacier moving underfoot again and repositioned himself.

The two assassins launched their attack—like malevolence flowing, daggers seeming to materialize from hidden places in their armor.

With a flash of his blade, Shawcroft blocked the first dagger thrown at his face; the second one cut deep into his right shoulder. From the left, the Spider engaged him first, daggers like snapping shards of glass, striking like lightning. Hawk was on him from the right, his assault just as rapid. In the blink of an eye, Shawcroft was full of holes. He didn't feel the pain. But he knew from experience that numbness was a bad thing, for who knew what foul poisons coated a Bloodwood's blades.

Suddenly all three of them were dashed face-first to the ice as the glacier buckled and shifted violently. The two Bloodeye stallions jumped and neighed, losing their footing as ferocious sound echoed and thundered. Then the horse on the left disappeared into a huge fissure that cracked open underneath, its scream feral and savage as it plummeted into the white yawning violence of the roaring water below. The ice split wider; chunks as bulky and massive as castle towers plunged down while others lanced toward the sky at precarious angles.

On his stomach, clinging to the surface of the glacier, Shawcroft could only stare in awe as the great mountains of ice were thrust heavenward above him with a grinding brilliance. His vision was filled with lustrous deep blues and purples webbed with luminescent streaks of white. And in an instant it all came boiling down, rolling and colliding and splintering into jagged chunks and wicked shards, all of it tumbling away to the left just beyond the Spider, who was now balanced on his hands and knees along the remains of the ledge.

Shawcroft took his chance and scrambled forward, stabbing with his sword. The Spider tried to block the blow, slipped, and disappeared over the rim.

With a burst of speed Shawcroft was on his feet, whirling to meet Hawk, who came at him with fiery purpose. He blocked the Bloodwood's first flurry of blows, the sound of sword on dagger muffled under the riotous carnage of glacial ice sloughing away around them. Shawcroft pressed his attack, forcing most of Hawk's flickering black daggers into superficial slashes and glancing blows, though some struck home. Determined, he advanced, connecting several times with the leather armor of his foe, backing the youth down, driving him toward the growling chasm where his fellow assassin had just vanished. But Shawcroft's injuries were taking their toll. With each heavy swing of his sword, his heart pounded and lungs labored. His throat was dry and raw, sucking in gulps of freezing air.

The glacier rumbled and shook again. Shawcroft lost his sword as he and Hawk were dashed to the frozen surface a second time, both sliding toward the tilting edge. Hawk's lower body slipped over the lip of the glacier. Eyes now wide, the assassin was clawing at the ice with both daggers to find purchase while Shawcroft tumbled uncontrollably straight into him, forcing the youth completely over the rim.

Together they clung there—Hawk dangling by one hand, clutching his black dagger still lodged in the ice, Shawcroft staring over the ledge into a stew of roiling, thunderous water and ice five hundred feet below. To his shock, the Spider had not perished in his fall but had landed on a sizable shelf of flat ice some fifty feet down. He lay unmoving in a growing pool of blood, one arm awkwardly twisted under his body.

Shawcroft's eyes met those of Hawk. "I know who you are, boy."

The youth's eyes narrowed. "To the bloody underworld with you, old man."

"You were meant for greater things than this." Shawcroft punched the dagger out of the ice with the palm of his hand. As Hawk fell, his calm gaze never left Shawcroft's. The assassin landed hard on the outcrop near his Bloodwood partner and rolled, clutching his side.

Shawcroft slid himself backward from the precipice, carefully, or he knew he would be headlong down into the cruel, snarling gorge with the two assassins. He grabbed his sword off the ice and scanned the ledge behind him.

The boy was gone.

Shawcroft clambered to his feet, using his sword as a crutch, still shaky as the glacier around him continued to groan. At least a dozen wounds from the blades of the Bloodwoods soaked his clothes, and he could feel himself weakening fast. Frantic, his eyes searched the glacier.

The remaining Bloodeye stallion nickered somewhere behind him. He turned.

The boy was there, standing directly in front of the horse, one small hand reaching out to touch the lowered snout of the black beast.

Shawcroft staggered toward the horse and child. The Bloodeye's flared nostrils gusted puffs of frozen vapor into the boy's pallid face. A dusting of ice crystals made the child's blond hair glittery in the sunlight. The stallion's red-hazed eyes were ablaze with both fear and uncertainty as the resounding crash and cracking of great blocks of ice could be heard all around.

Shawcroft snatched up the reins of the Bloodeye, and with one twist of the bit and a swift downward pull, brought the horse to its knees. He braced himself, ready to plunge his sword into the beast's neck. To him, this was no regular horse, but an alchemy-induced monster. And he would have no problem killing it.

The glacier shifted violently again. The boy began to cry.

It was then that Shawcroft realized, he *must* survive. Both he and the boy. He could feel the assassins' poisons working on him. If they could get back to Arco—the mining camp in the mountain valley just above the glacier—get back to where all this destruction had started, back to the burnt huts and dead villagers, he could possibly find his own murdered horse in the ruin and the antidotes hidden within his saddlebags.

Shawcroft let go of the stallion's bit. The Bloodeye stood and scampered a few paces away. He sheathed the sword over his shoulder. Weary from his injuries and desperately wanting rest, he let the magnitude and horror of the day's events finally set in. But he would not shed a tear. *Surely my conscience cannot be fading so soon. . . .*

Fighting back all emotion, Shawcroft scooped the boy into his arms, mounted the stallion, and began his long trek back through the arduous maze of the glacier toward the destroyed mining camp, knowing one thing for certain.

For good or ill, the plans set in motion by the Brethren of Mia nearly three years ago were now fully underway.

Be we slave, peasant, knight, or lord, within all of us dwells a craving, a longing
deep in our soul to know our own heritage and to identify the birthright of
our fellow man. For regardless the number of good works and heroic deeds
we achieve in life, the fatherless are by nature deemed unholy, susceptible to
betrayal, and useless in the eyes of the great One and Only.
— THE WAY AND TRUTH OF LAIJON

CHAPTER ONE

NAIL

7TH DAY OF THE SHROUDED MOON, 999TH YEAR OF LAIJON
GALLOWS HAVEN, GUL KANA

W*e become what we think.* Leastways, that was what Shaw-croft was fond of saying. Nail fancied himself a good artist. It was what made him the happiest anyway, charcoal and parchment in hand—that, and dreaming of Ava Shay. He thought about both to an alarming degree. He also thought he was good with a sword.

In fact, despite the pounding rain, things were going well. Nail ducked and raised his blade to parry. Steel cracked against steel. His hand stung with the impact. It felt good. He swung again, his momentum pushing him forward. He slipped, drawing Dokie Liddle's sword harmlessly over his head. With a clatter, Nail fell to his knees, wooden shield plowing into the mud, sword skittering off with a twang.

"Bloody Mother," he cursed, helmet cocked sideways, obscuring his vision. *Fool! Concentrate!* His sword had landed just close enough in the grass that he considered lunging for it, but the tip of Dokie's blade was already poised over him.

"Yield," Dokie ordered, brandishing his sword menacingly. Nail was the strongest seventeen-year-old in Gallows Haven. He wasn't easily beaten. He imagined the grin now spreading over Dokie's face under the helm. Stefan Wayland, Zane Neville, even Zane's brute of a shepherd dog, Beer Mug, watched, all waiting to see him stand and thrash Dokie good. Jenko Bruk was nearest, a look of pure amusement on his face. The Gallows Haven banner hung lifeless, sopping with rain, from the pole cradled in Jenko's arm. The other forty young men gathered on the practice field held similar looks. A grin spread over the gruff, bearded countenance of their trainer, Baron Jubal Bruk.

Frustrated, Nail sat back on his heels. Too much daydreaming about Ava Shay. Tossing his gauntlets aside, he dug grime from under his armor with determined fingers and said, "A lucky twist of fate for you, Dokie. 'Tis only this mud that's bested me." He shoved his gauntlets back on and tried to stand, feet slipping out from under him again. "Rotted angels," he cursed.

The air stirred as a chill wind stung Nail's face. The breath was sucked from his lungs. *Lightning!* His mind screamed in warning as a blinding flash flamed off Dokie's armor. The boy was flung away with a crack of thunder, sliding on his back.

Nail hugged the ground. The air was caustic, his lungs raw, mouth parched. White mist clung about his vision. A shower of sparks spiraled down around him, dissolving in the rain-splattered grass. The back of his sword hand sang with pain.

There were muffled voices, as if he was hearing them from under water. Jenko Bruk and Stefan Wayland were standing over him. "Lucky bastard," Jenko muttered, dark amber eyes shifting between Nail and the others. Zane's shepherd dog was barking up a riot. Stefan held forth a hand. Nail took it, stood on wobbly legs. He spotted Dokie sprawled in the mud, arms and legs splayed out, blank eyes staring up at the rain. Dokie's body had left a path where it had slid through the muck. His helmet was gone and smoke drifted from the soles of his leather boots. Hoarse breaths swelled from his chest.

"He's still alive!" Baron Jubal Bruk bellowed as he made the three-fingered sign of the Laijon Cross over his breast and looked toward the sky. "Let's get him into town." Baron Bruk and his son, Jenko, along with a few others, snatched up Dokie's limp form into their arms and headed for town.

The rest of the sodden troop, clacking and clattering in their armor, quickly gathered their belongings and followed the baron south toward Gallows Haven.

Nail struggled behind the rest, slogging through the muck, still in a daze. He looked skyward, eyes trying to focus as rain peppered his face. The back side of his sword hand still burned under his gauntlet.

"Your satchel." Stefan came up behind him, draping the bag's leather strap over Nail's shoulder. "You almost forgot it."

"Right, thanks." The words felt strange on Nail's dry tongue. He swallowed hard, still trying to regain his bearings. His satchel held his most prized possessions: prayer book, art supplies, collection of charcoal drawings.

Claps of thunder boomed behind Nail and Stefan as they hustled their pace to keep up with the others. Patches of trees added some shelter from the rain, but the road mainly bore them through fields and farmland. Hedges, wattle-and-daub fences, and rows of stone lined their path. The hollow clanking of goat bells sounded in the distance.

On occasion, Zane's dog would bark into the gathering darkness of early evening, as if something were out there following them. Through the fog that still covered his brain, Nail's imagination began spinning with unholy images, images that had plagued his dreams since childhood. The fiery forms of the nameless beasts of the underworld. Red-eyed beasts that seemed to haunt the minds of lonely children, those children born fatherless, motherless, and *alone*. Nail knew he was different. He was a bastard and *unnatural*.

When they tottered by a candlelit cottage, a whiff of woodsmoke swirled past Nail's nose, the aroma clearing his mind of churning thoughts.

Soon the small company of trainees broke through a stand of evergreens and Gallows Haven was a sprinkling of lights before them. To the right of their path, on a low, sloping hill overlooking Gallows Bay, was the empty husk of Gallows Keep. It had not seen use in centuries. Now its leaning crenellated battlements rose over the village, nothing more than the ancient, broken-down remnants of a castle that was once whole.

To their left was the village chapel. Nail felt sudden reassurance in its bulky gray presence. Despite what negative things Shawcroft said about the Church of Laijon and its teachings, Nail felt there was safety held within the chapel's great arches, in the thickness of its walls and its stoic grandeur. Above the door, three large stained-glass windows inlaid with intricate designs threw colorful shadows across their path. As those bearing Dokie's lightning-struck form passed through the front doors of the chapel, Nail looked up at those splendorous windows. On brighter days, with tattered sketchbook in hand, he would sit outside under them and sketch. In the center window was an image of Laijon, five colorful angel stones hanging above him like halos: white, red, black, green, and blue. Laijon wore a coat of shimmering chain mail and hefted a silver battle-ax named *Forgetting Moon*. In the left window floated two white-robed angels, one wielding a broadsword, *Afflicted Fire*, the other a black-wood crossbow, *Blackest Heart*. In the right window were two more heavenly apparitions, one with a horned war helm, *Lonesome Crown*, and the other carrying a mythical shield, *Ethic Shroud.* These were the five ancient weapons of lore.

Once Jubal and Jenko Bruk and the others were inside the chapel, those five angelic images cast ghostlike reflections of white, red, black, green, and blue over them as they laid Dokie on the floor before Bishop Tolbret. The bishop was a plain-faced man, short and balding. He wore the dull brown cassock and black sash of his station with sacred white robes underneath.

In the vaulted apse behind the bishop was a statue of Laijon cut from rough-hewn stone, the muscular carving thrice the size of a normal man, naught but a loincloth about his waist and a wreath of white heather atop his head. Laijon bore a flawless face but for the faint red line representing the fatal wound in his neck. He hung upon an even larger black-painted wooden replica of the Atonement Tree; its twining branches soared, almost reaching the ceiling of the chapel, filling the entire space of the apse.

When Bishop Tolbret saw Nail, muddy and disheveled, he shot him an unfriendly look. Nail dropped his gaze and peeled off his gauntlets. His right hand, his sword hand, stung something fierce. The back of his hand bore a thin burn in the shape of a cross. The fresh wound, so raw and red, almost seemed to glow.

Nail didn't even notice the bile rise in his throat, or the gentle twisting of his stomach, for he'd seen the image of a glowing red cross on the back of his hand before.

As a child, alone and afraid, he'd seen it in his dreams.

† † † † †

Nail and Stefan sat alone, Nail's charcoal drawing unrolled on the table between them. The Grayken Spear Inn's tavern was abuzz about Dokie Liddle. Late winter days along the southwestern shores of Gul Kana were likely to bring sudden bursts of rain that ofttimes turned to snow. But lightning strikes so close to town were rare indeed. Dokie's injury had reined in the normally boisterous mood of the tavern to a somber crawl.

Still, the barmaids were busy doing their jobs. And one young lady who worked here always had Nail's attention—Ava Shay. She was his age, seventeen. Over the past year, when Nail could break away from working the mines with Shawcroft and come into town, they had grown close. At times Nail wondered if they weren't boyfriend and girlfriend. He found it nearly impossible to keep his mind off her.

Thin and delicate as a willow leaf, Ava weaved her way through the tavern toward him, hands laden with two fresh mugs of beer. She wore a simple gray shift tied about the waist with a black sash. Her blond hair fell in rippling clusters down her back, and in the torrid glow of the tavern's many hearths, those silken curls danced about her face like flame. As she drew near, her eyes met his with open interest, deep-green eyes that always left him spellbound. He glanced down at his drawing, a sketch of a long-haired girl in a simple dress carrying a water pail through a knee-high meadow of flowers. Nail imagined the flowers to be white daisies, and the girl to be Ava Shay.

"Sad about Dokie," she said upon reaching their table. "Will he be okay?"

"His parents are with him," Stefan answered. "As are Bishop Tolbret and Baron Bruk. The baron will bring further word, I'm sure."

Ava placed a wooden mug of birch beer in front of Stefan. "One for you." She slid a mug in front of Nail. "And one for you, too, m'dear." She saw his drawing. "I'm not near as talented as you, Nail, but Ol' Man Leddingham displayed one of my fish carvings today." She motioned to the shelf above the bar that stretched along the far wall—her wooden carving sat next to a clear jar holding the rare daggerlike teeth of a mermaid. "If I carve some otters and seals, he said he'll place them on the mantels of the travelers' rooms."

"Your work is terrific," Nail said, happy for her accomplishment.

"You're so sweet." She smiled a winsome smile, then dipped a small curtsy in acknowledgment before making her way back toward the bar.

"I see Ava still sets her charms about you," Stefan said, pulling Nail's drawing across the table. "Calls you m'dear whenever you're in the Grayken Spear."

"She calls everyone m'dear." Nail's eyes followed Ava as she drifted through the crowd. The tavern was fifty paces across and a hundred deep, and tables lined the breadth of it. A bar ran the length of the left side. The scarred surface of the wood floor was covered with a film of soot and ale. Cobwebs hid in the rafters, while the low-hung beams were draped with the pelts of silver-wolf and black bear. The walls were lined with the mounted heads of boar, elk, and stag. Near the door hung the ivory tusks of a walrus and long dried strips of grayken baleen. The owner of the inn, Ol' Man Leddingham, tended to a haunch of venison cooking on a spit in the open hearth in the center of the room.

Every Gallows Haven young man of seventeen and eighteen, most still in some form of armor to impress the girls, was crowded into the tavern. It was tradition. After arms training, the girls working at the Grayken Spear Inn prepared a meal for the conscripts. Nail lived for the arms training with Baron Bruk and the hot meal at the Grayken Spear afterward. It was one of the few times Shawcroft allowed him to come to town—arms training was mandatory; it was the law.

Stefan pushed the drawing back to Nail's side of the table. "Ava seems quite taken with your drawing. She didn't smile once at me."

"You suffer from no lack of attention." Nail noticed Gisela Barnwell approach, her eyes fixed on Stefan, who was now blushing. Gisela set two steaming plates of food on their table, curtsied, and said, "Poor Dokie," before heading back to the bar. The dainty girl, two years younger than Nail and Stefan, wore a wreath of blue heather on her head. She had recently been crowned Maiden Blue of the upcoming Mourning Moon Feast, the annual honor bestowed upon the fairest young girl in all of Gallows Haven.

It was clear Gisela liked Stefan. But Stefan Wayland didn't see it. Nail's friend had the beginnings of a strong jaw and hawkish nose. Dark hair fell in a tumble over his shoulders. He had the hard eyes and tanned skin of one who had spent the last few years on Baron Bruk's grayken-hunting ship. Where Nail was strong and fast on the practice field with a sword, it was the longbow where Stefan excelled. He was a lock to win the archery competition against the conscripts from Tomkin Sty and Peddlers Point during the annual tournament between the towns. After all, he'd won every Mourning Moon archery competition since he was ten. And from the look on Gisela's face when she'd brought them their food, Stefan had likely won her, too.

Nail knew how he himself looked to others. At seventeen he was bigger and stronger than most men in Gallows Haven. He had grayish-green eyes, a thin nose, and a pleasant smile on a youthful face under locks of blond. He continually flicked wild strands of hair from his face, a habit he couldn't shake, but a habit that made the girls notice him even more. Nail kept his hair just long enough to cover his ears—thin ears that he felt poked out from his head a bit too much.

Stefan had stopped eating, eyes staring into space.

"Eat," Nail said. "Don't mope; Dokie will be fine."

"I know," Stefan muttered. "It's not that."

Nail set his fork down. "You'll soon be dancing with Gisela at the Mourning Moon Feast like man and wife." He pointed a finger at his friend. "And you'll ask her to dance even if I have to force open your mouth and move your lips about for you."

Stefan smiled weakly. Zane Neville walked up.

"I'll have that beer if you're goin' to do naught but stare at it." Zane plunked himself down on the seat beside Stefan, a heaping plate of food in hand. He snatched Stefan's beer as promised, and in two gulps, it was gone. Zane's shepherd dog, Beer Mug, sat next to him, long snout resting on the table. Zane slid a piece of smoked salmon the dog's way. Beer Mug gulped it down, tail thumping the floor. Zane's large dog reminded Nail of the stealthy silver-wolves that roamed the mountains near the gold mines above town. But unlike those wild wolves, Beer Mug was a good-natured fellow.

Zane's round face boasted a plump nose, a smattering of freckles, and a bush of carrot-colored hair that stuck up from his head like a big lit torch. He was tall yet portly, and his sloping shoulders and pear-shaped body defeated his best attempts to squeeze completely into his training gear. Still, despite his plumpness, Zane was one of the best new grayken cutters on Baron Bruk's crew.

"You two talkin' about Gisela Barnwell?" Zane asked, chomping a mouthful of potatoes. "She made mention she was glad to see you here tonight, Stefan. As Laijon is my witness, I swear it's true. She was glad you weren't lightning-struck, as was Dokie."

"Stefan's frightened to death of Gisela," Nail said. "Wouldn't acknowledge her if she came up and slapped him in the face or grabbed him by the pecker."

"Well, he's blushin' redder than a billy goat's arsehole now," Zane said. "I'll wager he's probably already took her up in Farmer Wetherby's hayloft and buried his face under that skirt, her pretty little legs wrapped around his—"

"It ain't like that," Stefan snapped. "I would never—"

"Well, spank me rosy, someone's bound to. All you ever do is moon over her like a heartsick pup. Act now lest some other fellow snatch her up. I swear it, as Laijon is my witness, someone will snatch her up right from under you." Zane had the irritating habit of saying *as Laijon is my witness* a half-dozen times in every conversation.

Zane stood. "Perhaps I'll just throw Gisela to the floor and dry-hump her right here in front of you." He leaned over the rear of his dog and mimicked a humping motion, tongue out, moaning.

"Don't be crude." Stefan looked around frantically. "She might be watching."

"Humorless as always." Zane sat and chomped a mouthful of salmon, spitting bits everywhere. Beer Mug eyed the food as it tumbled from Zane's chest-plate armor to the floor, then licked it up.

Zane's hefty older sister, Liz Hen, set a bowl of stew in front of each of them—the Grayken Spear was generous with its many courses of food. She was nineteen, tall, broad of shoulder, thick of gut, and bore a thatch of hair wilder and redder than Zane's. Beer Mug was glad to see her, tail wagging, ears alert.

"I can't eat this." Stefan sniffed the steaming bowl. "Chunks of turnip, radish—"

Liz Hen swatted Stefan upside the head with a beefy backhand. "Feed it to the dog then, you clodpole."

"Ouch," Stefan exclaimed, poking at the stew. "I'm only saying—"

"Does it look like I give a goat's fart what's in the stew? Could be pigeon shit for all I care. I'm only the innkeeper's big fat errand girl." With that she stomped away.

"Don't anger her so." Zane watched his sister waddle off. "I swear she'll take it out on me later. As Laijon is my witness, she thinks she's the most important person in the whole Five Isles. You're so damned dour tonight, Stefan. Dokie'll be fine."

"I've other news that weighs heavy on my mind," Stefan said. "My uncle Brender sent word from Bainbridge this morning. The rumors are true. The White Prince's armies have almost reached the Laijon Towers. They're almost to the eastern shores of Wyn Darrè."

A chill traveled through Nail. Rumors of the White Prince's complete victory over Wyn Darrè were true. It was dire news indeed.

"Absolution is near," Stefan said. "Fiery Absolution, as prophesied in *The Way and Truth of Laijon*. On a clear day, from atop the walls of Lord's Point, you can see all five Laijon Towers lit up across the straits.

Soon they'll be completely dark, extinguished by Aeros Raijael. Adin Wyte is conquered. Now Wyn Darrè. The armies of Sør Sevier are coming. Soon Sør Sevier will own all the Five Isles."

"What of the beacon atop the Fortress of Saint Only?" Zane asked, patting Beer Mug.

"Still afire," Stefan answered. "But only at the sufferance of the White Prince. My uncle says Aeros Raijael will attack the coast of Gul Kana with his full might. Gul Kana is Aeros' ultimate prize. Sør Sevier men are bred to war and hunt. I'm for getting out of Gallows Haven. Come with me to Bainbridge. We can join a real fighting company there. My uncle will sponsor us. If he sponsors you, Nail, you'll no longer be ward to Shawcroft."

"You're smack full of ideas tonight," Nail said, though he did like the idea of no longer being beholden to Shawcroft—the man had a cruel streak in him that was unpredictable at the best of times. Stefan always kept abreast of the goings-on in the realm. Nail admired his friend for that. But though he was full of lofty ideas, Stefan was wrong about a few things. "We'd hang for sure if we abandon Baron Bruk and our duties to Gallows Haven," Nail said. "Two years' service to the church and the Silver Throne. We are all called to serve. We must all put in our time. Who would defend Gallows Haven if we up and left? Who'd protect the women and children?"

"Nail's right," Zane added. "Conscripts like us can't just skip from town to town." He nodded at Nail. "Even bastards are not excused from service to Laijon."

Nail was not offended. Zane meant no harm. What he'd said was true: even bastards served Laijon and the Silver Throne. Everyone in Gallows Haven knew Nail's heritage. His master, Shawcroft, was the closest thing to kin he had, save a sister Shawcroft mentioned on occasion—a lost twin sister Nail dreamed he would someday find. Never having known his real mother or father, he wondered if they'd ever existed at all. Those vague but real memories of the tender touch of the nurturing woman from his childhood were fading more each day.

"If we flee to Bainbridge, Baron Bruk will hunt us down," Zane said. "Bishop Tolbret would see to it. Your uncle would be hard-pressed not to turn us in himself. Why must you always see things so contrary to *The Way and Truth of Laijon*?" Zane snatched Nail's beer away this time and stole a long drink. "Stefan the Skeptic, I name you. Always thinking too much. To question the laws of Laijon is to show a weak mind."

Nail felt stuck somewhere between Zane's blind devotion to the tenets of *The Way and Truth of Laijon* and Stefan's cynical view of things. Master Shawcroft was no help in matters religious. Seemed he had a huge dislike for all things to do with the Church of Laijon. But the man rarely explained himself. For his part, Nail enjoyed the church and its Eighth Day services—mostly for the social aspect, and as an excuse to get out of mining with Shawcroft and the tedium of swinging a pickax with the exacting precision his master required. Attending the weekly Eighth Day services brought Nail closer to his friends, closer to Ava Shay. Plus, the ritual Ember Lighting Rite was this spring. Nail had committed the Ember Lighting Prayer to memory, repeating it in his head daily to the point that he could recite it forward and backward.

"Stay here and die by the blades of an invading army, or leave and become hunted by our own countrymen." There was frustration in Stefan's voice now, a resignation echoing the futility of their situation. "That's if Baron Bruk doesn't get us killed. Can't he see our helms are lightning rods out there? We're likely to be fried like chicks in a kettle. I daresay, even Bishop Tolbret's white priesthood robes would offer more protection."

"Don't joke," Zane said. "The silk robes of Laijon are anointed by the grand vicar himself and rendered stronger than armor. Tolbret would be well protected in any squall."

"Tolbret's priesthood robes are woven of *silk*, not iron, and certainly not *magic*. Tales of their holy properties are only fables meant to impress the children."

"*The Way and Truth of Laijon* speaks of their sacredness and strength."

"All I am saying is our armor is naught but rusty relics dug out of that old keep. We can't stand against Sør Sevier with but forty of us village conscripts and a few codgy sailors and farmers with rakes. Jubal Bruk. I know he's the baron of our lands, the owner of the grayken-hunting ship upon which I work, but sometimes I think the man's brain has been addled."

"Addled?" Baron Jubal Bruk materialized from the crowd and stood over their table, his son, Jenko, at his side. The baron was wrapped in a rain-soaked cloak that smelled of wet horse. Beer Mug sniffed the man and backed away.

"Baron." Stefan stood abruptly, bowing, looking like he'd just swallowed a frog.

"How goes it with Dokie?" Nail stood also and bowed. Despite what Stefan claimed, Jubal Bruk was no dribbling fool. His eyes darted angrily over the table. The baron had broad brows and deep-set eyes that always appeared fixed in a fearful squint. With a bearded face and forehead sloping back to a scruff of gray hair, the baron intimidated all in town—especially with his huge sword and its thick, leather-wrapped hilt and black opal–inlaid pommel. Rumor was, before he had settled in Gallows Haven five years ago, he had served as one of Amadon's famed Dayknights. Most in town thought him a good fighter, but ill-equipped as a leader of men.

"Dokie is burnt, but not bad." The baron motioned for Stefan and Nail to sit. "Bishop Tolbret watches over him. With the blessings of the priesthood, Dokie'll recover."

"A lucky slip in the mud, Nail." Jenko smiled. "Otherwise it would be you cooked instead of Dokie." Still wearing most of his battle gear, the baron's son had a leather scabbard at his hip and a black shield slung across his shoulder. Jenko was a strong, swaggering fellow of eighteen. Tousled brown hair crowned his head and fell to just above his shoulders. Towering even over his father, arms stacked with muscle, Jenko was probably the stoutest man in Gallows Haven.

"In battle, you need to keep your feet," Baron Bruk said. "Lying facedown in the muck whilst garbed in heavy armor is a horrible position to find oneself in. Truth is, I don't think any of you boys have a holy prayer's chance against the White Prince's army. Regardless, the Silver Throne requires land barons to train all conscripted young men the length and breadth of Gul Kana in the art of warfare. That's my charge. Believe me, if for some reason Sør Sevier should ever reach Gallows Haven, I guarantee, they won't wait for a sunny day just so you fellows don't have to get your feet wet. I was in the Iron Hills with King Borden when Sør Sevier first invaded Wyn Darrè. A snowstorm and freezing wind struck the walls of Oksana like needles of ice. Did that stop Aeros' slaughter? No. Our legion of Amadon Silver Guards and Dayknights lent Wyn Darrè what aid we could, but our numbers were few. The White Prince marched straight through the snow and straight over us. Very few of us were lucky to escape that day. I saw King Borden fall with my own eyes. I have seen war."

The baron leaned over, planted scarred and calloused hands on their table. His steely gaze, angry and filled with purpose, cleaved through Stefan like a sharp knife. "In battle, not all die gloriously. Not all die instantly. Lest you forget your lessons, when armies face off, there first comes an onslaught of arrows. A Sør Sevier longbow is a six-foot-long affair. And their archers can launch near twenty arrows a minute. And when armies finally do clash, be glad for what plate armor you have, even if you it's naught but rusted junk from that old keep. It will block most attacks. A well-placed sword thrust may not cleave chain mail. But it can drive the links down into your flesh. Then you've got yourself a real mess of a wound to deal with.

Try running around the battlefield with chunks of your own mail lodged in your gullet as you slowly bleed out. Take your training seriously, all of you."

"I'm good with a sword," Nail interjected. "Getting better with the—"

"Where is Shawcroft?" Baron Bruk tersely asked. "Still pissing his time away at the mines, I wager?"

"He went to the mines early this morning," Nail answered, stung that the baron had so casually dismissed his swordsmanship skills. "He made mention he would be gone digging for a week. I'm to stay with Stefan's family whilst he's away."

The baron met Nail's gaze. "I was hoping your master would see fit to help me with you conscripts. But, Laijon knows, everything *that* man does in those gold mines is of utmost import." With that, Baron Bruk withdrew from their table and made his way toward the tavern's front door.

What does Shawcroft know of swordsmanship or archery? Nail knew there had been some tension between his master and the baron as of late. It had something to do with the gold mines. Nail thought it of little import. But Jubal Bruk had just now said his master's name like it was poison on his tongue. That the baron wanted Shawcroft's help with the conscripts seemed laughable in many ways.

Jenko Bruk remained. He sidled up to their table, looking at Nail unflinchingly. "My father's right, you know. All the gold was stripped from the mountains centuries ago. No Mourning Moon Feast was ever held for gold digging. Grayken hunts are what Gallows Haven was built upon. The grayken are what sustains Gul Kana. Spend your days at sea doing men's work, Nail. Bring home a grayken or a load of salmon. Feed the entire town. Now that's a true living. When is your master going to realize that?"

Nail cared little for Jenko's tone. Jenko's two-year conscription to the church and crown was nearly over. It was well known that he would soon inherit his father's grayken-hunting vessel. Jenko's position in Gallows Haven was firmly set. Nail, on the other hand, was heir to nothing. Still, as much as he agreed with the baron's son that mining was a waste of time, Nail knew the hard work Shawcroft had set him to all these years had built him up as a man. Swinging ax and pick had made him strong. He took some pride in that and was loath to see Jenko slander it.

"Nail means to join us on your father's grayken hunt," Stefan said.

"Is that so?" Jenko Bruk gave Nail a sharp look.

"I've Shawcroft's permission, of course, to learn the fishing trade whilst he's at the mines," Nail answered, knowing his words were a lie. Shawcroft would have no clue if he went grayken hunting and would disagree with it strongly. But the man was working the mines for the week. The average grayken hunt took less time than that. Nail knew he would be in open defiance of his master. But he didn't care. The man could be demanding, stubborn, disagreeable, and cruel. Nail was completely dependent on Shawcroft, yet at the same time, to be free of the man was his greatest desire.

"You wish to be a grayken slayer?" Jenko asked. "You'll more likely get shark bit or gill-fucked by one of the merfolk than become a hero."

"Nail will come back a hero all right," Zane piped up. "A hero covered in grayken blubber. Ava Shay can do naught but fall more in love with him then."

"Ava Shay, huh?" Jenko raised an eyebrow. "Indeed, she's one ripe skinny lass."

Nail looked over his shoulder toward the bar, where Ava was wiping her hands on a towel. She glanced at their table and smiled. Jenko threw her a nod. Nail's heart leaped in his throat. That the baron's son might see the same in Ava as he had never crossed his mind. But the look that crept into Jenko's eyes was alarming, and challenging. In fact, the baron's son was staring at Nail. A smile played at the corners of Jenko's mouth, and there was a smoldering, fierce squint to his eyes. "What say we spar for the right to Ava Shay's hand at the Mourning Moon Feast, Nail?"

"Well, kiss my pickle." Zane Neville slapped Jenko on the back. "The gauntlet thrown. A bit of fun to top off an otherwise sorrowful evening, right? Dokie would love it were he here!" Beer Mug even seemed excited by the prospect, tail thumping the floor.

Jenko was grinning now, fingers poised at the hilt of his sword. His gaze never wavered from Nail. "What say you, a spar in the street? Like Zane said, a bit of fun to lighten the mood around here. Or do you dare not draw swords with me?"

On the training field, Nail had bested Jenko on occasion. Jenko had also beaten him. Every conscript knew he and Jenko were evenly matched. But to spar in the village street was another matter altogether. In front of the Grayken Spear, Ava Shay could finally witness his prowess. At the same time, he could put Jenko in his place.

"Do you lack courage, Nail?" Jenko said, his smile growing. He snatched Nail's charcoal drawing from the table, crumpled it, and tossed it to the floor.

Nail looked at his ruined drawing through the stray strands of blond hair that now covered his face. Anger welled. The back of his right hand flared in pain, the cross-shaped mark stinging. He knew the baron's son was only goading him. Until now, he had never harbored any ill will toward Jenko Bruk. Sure, he was the son of the richest man in town and could behave boorishly at times, but it was all talk to be ignored. However, this time his insults had done their job. Jenko's cocky grin was now poised above Nail, and Nail wanted to smack it from Jenko's face. A challenge followed by a friendly spar was normal fare at the Grayken Spear once the beer took hold. The only problem was, Jenko wasn't drunk and this challenge had grown personal.

Nail brushed the hair from his eyes, stood, and gathered his blade. "It's not lack of courage." He met the baron's son eye to eye, then jammed his sword into the table, point first. At the sound, Zane's dog jumped, as did the village conscripts sitting nearby. Nail kept his eyes trained on Jenko. "It's because we are not yet outside that I haven't knocked that smile from your face."

Zane yelled, "Nail has just accepted a challenge!"

The Grayken Spear erupted in cheers. Soon the tavern began to empty, the eager spectators spilling out onto the street. "No steel," Stefan said, looking nervously at both Jenko and Nail. "We wrap the blades in sackcloth as usual."

Jenko nodded, smile gone, eyes no longer fixed on Nail. The baron's son strode from the tavern without looking back. A snub. As if Nail was of no account.

† † † † †

A circle of spectators had already formed outside in the dark. Many bore torches, lighting the puddle-stained street in front of the Grayken Spear and the blacksmith shop next door. The rain was just a drizzle now. Still, footing would be treacherous in the mud. Nail stepped from the wood-plank porch of the tavern down into the sludge. Zane stood there with his dog. Stefan wrapped Nail's sword in a long strip of sackcloth and handed it over.

The crowd parted. Jenko waited in the middle of the circle, cinching his armor. His sword, already wrapped in strips of cloth, was near his shield at his feet. He donned his helm, snatched up his shield and sword, and stepped forward. Nail looked toward the Grayken Spear. Several of the tavern girls were on the porch among the onlookers— Tylda Egbert, Polly Mott, Gisela Barnwell, Liz Hen Neville, even Ava Shay.

"I'm over here!" Jenko banged his sword against his shield.

Nail put his helm on, wincing as he slipped his gauntlet over the cross-shaped wound on his sword hand. Once geared up, he felt outmatched before his foe. Jenko's sword was long and sleek with a fine leather-strapped hilt. His iron-bossed shield was painted with a silver-wolf's head. Nail's shield was all wood and painted with nothing, his sword an old blade found in the catacombs of Gallows Keep. Baron Bruk had scraped it free of rust before giving it to him last year. It was a solid blade, if a tad stumpy, and came with a crooked hilt and a patched leather scabbard lined with rotted fleece. Overall, it was thick, clumsy, ill-weighted, and terribly unbalanced. Still, ever since the baron had handed it to him, Nail had worshipped the thing and slept with it near his pillow.

Stefan stepped between Jenko and Nail and yelled for all to hear, "You spar in the normal fashion, as if the baron himself watched. Slash and counter. No thrusting. First with three strikes wins!" Stefan moved back and the way was clear.

Jenko swung. Nail thrust his shield forward, and there was a clash of sackcloth-wrapped iron on wood. Nail stumbled back and Jenko's next swing whistled over his head. Jenko swung four more times with rapid ease. Nail blocked each, but his shield arm grew weary. Jenko's next blow struck heavy and hard. Jenko then faked high. Nail raised his shield and Jenko stabbed under it, striking the armor covering his stomach. Nail reeled back. "No thrusting!" Stefan yelled. "That strike doesn't count! Slash and parry!"

Jenko backed away. A good ten paces separated them now. Nail was embarrassed. He hadn't swung yet, to Jenko's flurry of blows. Nail used the time and space to get a much firmer grip on his sword and shield and, more importantly, his confidence. He was wheezing for breath under his helm and tried to calm down. There were cheers for him, the loudest coming from Stefan and Zane. Their cheers bolstered him. He advanced with his head down under the rim of his shield, peering over it, sword poised. Jenko lunged, swinging for his legs. Nail lowered the shield, spoiling the stroke, and slashed at Jenko's helm. His sword connected with a thud, snapping Jenko's head back. The baron's son stumbled sideways. Nail hammered Jenko with his shield, and his foe fell to the ground.

"One strike for Nail!" Stefan yelled, and a smattering of applause sounded from the crowd as Jenko scrambled away on hands and knees, mud sloshing under him. Nail, with the advantage now, swung again and connected with Jenko's back. "Strike two!"

Before Nail could finish him, Jenko sprang to his feet and lunged with two quick blows. Nail blocked them with ease. Now that Nail had gotten in two good hits, there was a bounce in his step. Jenko backed off, and there was space between them again. The baron's son plunged ahead with two more strikes that landed fast and hard against Nail's midsection. "Two for Jenko!" Stefan yelled. Nail reeled back, angry, side throbbing. He came up swinging as Jenko's third blow connected the same time as his.

"Both strikes count!" Stefan yelled. "It's a tie!" Everyone cheered.

"Rotted dog shit!" The baron's son ripped off his helm and threw down his shield. "A bastard is no equal of mine." No sooner had his shield and helm hit the mud than Jenko leaped forward, gripping his sword in both hands now. His high swing came crashing in. The blow knocked Nail's shield spinning away. His second blow planted Nail's butt firmly in the mud. Instantly, Jenko loomed over him, raining blows. Nail scrambled back on his haunches, mud plowing up behind him. He kept his sword up in defense, but it was beaten back swiftly. Then it wasn't in his hand anymore. It spun off and lit in a puddle. Then Jenko was striking him about the shoulders, arms, and chest.

"Enough! Enough!" Stefan yelled, but Jenko's blows were relentless. "It was a tie, you bloodsucking oghul! You're likely to kill him behaving like that!"

Nail felt the breath pounded from his lungs as he tried to crawl away, at the same time groping for his lost sword in the puddle, finding it, turning, holding it aloft. He would not retreat. But the blows from Jenko kept coming.

Stefan tackled the baron's son from behind and both dropped in the mud. In a heap, they struggled. Jenko threw Stefan off and stood, sackcloth-wrapped sword still in hand. He came at Nail again. "Stop!" Stefan bellowed. Zane was there, and with Stefan, the two wrestled Jenko to the ground a second time.

"Get off!" Jenko snarled, eyes blazing at Nail from under dark, wet locks. Nail, kneeling in the mud, the percussion of Jenko's crushing blows reverberating through his armor, could feel the fresh dents in the iron plate pushing in. There was a dull ache throbbing deep in his chest. He wasn't certain he could stand if he wanted.

"Let me up, you pox-scarred scum!" Jenko fought against Stefan and Zane.

"The wraiths take you if you don't stop fighting," Stefan said, breathing heavy.

"Turn him loose," Nail snarled between hard-fought breaths. "I'll still fight him! I ain't dead yet!"

"That's right, lemme up! Let me finish him like he wants!" Jenko yelled.

Zane whistled for Beer Mug. Soon the big shepherd dog was snarling and barking at the pile of struggling bodies. With the threat of the dog, the fight died in Jenko and he gave up, head hanging. "I'm done then."

"Let him up," Stefan said, motioning Zane to hold his dog. "Be wary." He released the baron's son. Jenko stood, brushing the mud from his greaves, smiling, his teeth stark white shards in the lamplight as he walked toward Nail. Nail didn't know whether Jenko was going to help him up or what. Either way, he wouldn't allow himself to accept any help. He'd stand on his own no matter how much his body ached.

Jenko plucked the sword from Nail's hand and threw it. It sailed over the crowd and into the darkness, landing near the narrow alley between the inn and the blacksmith shop. "Fetch that, you goose-shit-eating bastard." Jenko stepped around Nail, shoving his way through the crowd and back up onto the porch of the Grayken Spear Inn.

Nail growled and scrambled to his feet, his mind set on tackling Jenko and ending the fight with his fists. But his foot slipped and down he went again, face-first.

"Hold steady now," Stefan said, grabbing him by the arm. "Don't know what you did to piss Jenko off so, but I reckon it's got something to do with Ava."

Nail's gaze followed the baron's son. Under the torchlight, he saw Ava Shay leaning against the porch railing. Jenko stepped up to the girl and whispered something in her ear, his hand brushing lightly over her shoulder before he entered the tavern. Nail was humiliated more by the small interaction between Jenko and Ava than any blow the baron's son could've dealt with his sword.

"Pay him no mind." Stefan helped Nail stand. "You'll be stiff on the morrow. Bruises for a moon or more. You put up a real fight, though. Gave us all a grand show."

The crowd was dispersing. Some back into the Grayken Spear, others wandering off into the darkness and home. Zane trundled back into the inn, Beer Mug bounding happily behind. Nail didn't know how far he could walk on his own. He hunched over and clutched his stomach. Soreness blanketed his body. Despite all his hurts, he was most of all embarrassed.

Stefan ducked under Nail's arm, propping him up. "My pa can send word to Shawcroft if you'd like. He'll let your master know you're hurt."

"I ain't hurt," Nail mumbled. "Besides, Shawcroft's never been concerned about me. Jenko's right, his only concern is those gold mines." He was envious of Stefan's family and the comforts of a warm home, surrounded by loving parents and siblings. Nail lived on the outskirts of town in a small, cold, one-room cabin with his master. He put on a strong front, but deep down he knew how lonely his life really was. "I'll sleep in the coop tonight. I'm sure your mother hasn't the room inside."

"You needn't sleep with the chickens," Stefan said. "We've the room."

Nail had managed to hobble only a few steps when Ava's soft voice sounded from behind. "You fought well."

He turned. She held his sword. It was covered in mud. Nail slid from under Stefan's arm and took the weapon from her. Mud remained on the palm of her hand. In her other hand was the drawing Jenko had crumpled. "I'm sorry it got ruined," she said, handing it over. "It was pretty." Ava hesitated as if wanting to say more, then pulled a leather-thong necklace from the folds of her linen skirt. She reached up and slipped it over his head and around his neck and quickly backed away.

"A gift," she muttered shyly. "To make amends for the drawing Jenko ruined."

Hooked to the leather thong was a small carving of a turtle no bigger than the end of Nail's thumb. He held the carving in his hand, admiring Ava's delicate workmanship. Every display of her talents filled him with desire.

"Thank you," he stammered, meeting her soft gaze. That she had made this wooden trinket for him set his heart soaring. Ava kissed him lightly on the cheek and made her way back toward the Grayken Spear Inn.

And as she stepped back up onto the inn's porch, Nail saw it.

At the back of the alley between the Grayken Spear and the blacksmith shop.

A cloaked figure astride a red-eyed horse, silhouetted black and hollow against the glittering waters of Gallows Bay beyond. The glowing eyes of the horse were fixed on Nail like stark smoldering coals.

Other than within the darkness of his own worst dreams, Nail had never seen such a demon-eyed creature. His blood ran cold. "Do you see that?" He turned to Stefan.

But Stefan Wayland was already walking toward home. And when Nail looked back into the blackness of the alley, the cloaked horseman was gone.

The lost and lonely ship finally berthed in Avlonia, thousands of days adrift. What few were left stumbled ashore, the Firstlands lost to them forever. Desperate souls all, starving and weak, half-naked, garbed in animal skins, still these newcomers to the Five Isles offered up alms and blood sacrifice to the gods of their Firstlands.
—THE WAY AND TRUTH OF LAIJON

CHAPTER TWO

NAIL

11TH DAY OF THE SHROUDED MOON, 999TH YEAR OF LAIJON
THE MOURNING SEA SOUTH OF GALLOWS HAVEN, GUL KANA

They had finally found the path of the grayken—two and a half days' journey south of Gallows Haven in the great vastness of the Mourning Sea. To the south and west lay the Firstlands, storm-shattered lands beyond the farthest reaches of the seas, where humans had first sprung. The Firstlands, continents rumored to span tens of thousands of miles, were also rumored to be barren of all humankind, shrouded in gray mists, inhabited by naught but ghosts. Those who foolishly sought them never returned.

Thick storm clouds roiled overhead. Occasionally, thin shafts of morning sun poured heedlessly through breaks in the clouds, bouncing off the waves as the *Lady Kindly* cut a jostling path. Nail wobbled as he hustled across the deck of the grayken-hunting ship toward Stefan Wayland and Zane Neville. He hadn't stood on solid ground for days now. The ship dipped to the left as a gust of wind caught her sails, and he clutched the railing. A hundred feet up, the canvas stretched and cracked.

Those aboard the *Lady Kindly* had spent the bulk of the journey trailing nets and catching salmon. Bishop Tolbret, an integral part of any hunting voyage, had spent his hours anointing various parts of the ship with vials of consecrated holy oils. Now the ship floated among a school of fifteen grayken and Tolbret prayed, offering up fervent thanks to Laijon as the monsters of the sea rolled their barrel-like bodies up out of the water and plunged beneath. They were larger than Nail had ever imagined. Most looked fifty to seventy feet in length. The closest one to the ship was gray and sleek—it skimmed the surface of the sea for a while, half-submerged. It had a long slit for a mouth, two round eyes and flat fins on either side of its head, a blowhole on top, and a tail of six long tentacles that bunched and coiled in unison, pushing through the water.

At the first sighting of the school of grayken, Baron Jubal Bruk shouted a torrent of orders and a flood of men scurried up ratlines and over the deck. Large barrels were brought forth, the hanging skiffs uncovered. "Do your jobs!" the baron spewed forth. "Any man goes overboard fends for himself or he's lost to the sea!"

With nothing to do, Nail had found this spot near the starboard railing with Stefan and Zane. Before they'd set sail, the three of them had ventured into the chapel's catacombs to visit Dokie Liddle. The musty stone room under the nave had seemed a gloomy place to keep the lightning-struck boy. Dying embers smoldered in a fire-place. Bishop Tolbret sat on a stool next to Dokie's bearskin-covered bed and dabbed at the injured boy's head with a warm, damp cloth. He pulled the bearskin down, revealing the boy's chest and arms. A cloverlike pattern of red burns dotted Dokie's skin. The boy's chest rose and fell to the slow rhythm of his breathing. "His fingers and toes were black," Tolbret said, "just like that frostbit man from

Peddlers Point who stumbled into the Grayken Spear last winter. But the many priesthood blessings I gave the lad seem to have cured him of that." It was too bad Nail couldn't share the voyage with Dokie, too. To hear the others tell it, Dokie had a sharp eye and was the best grayken spotter Baron Bruk had ever seen. But now the grayken were easy to see, wallowing in the sea, spouting air and water high. Seagulls circled above them, lonesome cries sharp and harsh.

Then the sharks came. Nail couldn't explain it, but there churned in his gut an ominous feeling before the first shark arrived. He lost his breath as if a hush fell over the *Lady Kindly*. There was a boil and swell of water just before the shark's fin broke the surface, pale as bone. Nail took a step back from the rail as the grim white creature dipped below the water and glided under the ship. Soon there were more sharks weaving just under the surface, fins ducking in and out of the water. Though considerably smaller than the grayken, these stark, graceful ghosts of the sea left a deadly aura in their wake.

A burly sailor ran up and tossed a salmon overboard. One shark lunged straight up. Its jaws opened, lined with rows of teeth, its great bulk suspended there momentarily just above the water. The shark bit the fish in half, then slipped back into the sea and slithered away. A second shark stabbed the remaining half salmon from the water. *Give these sharks red eyes and leathery, clawed wings along with serpentine tails and they would easily pass as nameless beasts of the underworld.* With that thought, Nail's mind jumped to the cloaked figure he'd seen in the alley between the Grayken Spear and the blacksmith shop. The gaze of the red-eyed steed had burned a hole in his soul, bringing back a flood of terrifying memories. Memories he'd suppressed over the years, memories that clawed their way to the forefront of his mind now.

But he'd fight off those dreams and memories as he'd fought Jenko Bruk. Cramps still ached throughout his chest, and a knot the size of a seashell was lodged under his ribs somewhere—the lingering physical pains garnered from the drubbing at the hands of the baron's son. But he would not let thoughts of the dark-cloaked horseman or the physical evidence of Jenko Bruk's thrashing get him down.

In fact, despite the brewing storm above, and the sharks below, the last few days seemed sunnier than any he'd ever known. On every place aboard the ship was the surrounding scent of heavy timber, which lightened his soul. And the ocean smelled fresh in comparison to the rocky shoals around Gallows Haven. Today Nail observed and listened more acutely than he ever had before. The very breath and whiff of the wind against his face filled him with a happiness he'd never experienced. He felt the thrill of the ship, the rhythm of its life, listened with rapt attention to each prayer of the bishop. He had wanted to know everything about the ship, the name of every sail, brace, bowline, and rope, and how each worked, even going so far as to pull out scraps of parchment from his satchel and sketch each new thing shown him.

Things had been different at the start of the voyage, and Nail had wondered if he hadn't made a terrible mistake by joining the crew of the *Lady Kindly*. That first day, he had recalled doing little else but leaning against the railing, fighting the seasickness. Jenko Bruk had noticed him against the railing and informed him that vomiting was a sure sign of weakness in a seaman, and anyone caught vomiting on deck would be pitched over the side. Zane Neville had waddled up, looking half-hazy about the eyes himself. "Pay no head to Jenko. Seasickness is nothing a cheerful disposition can't cure. Just do like this." Then Zane leaned over the railing, jammed his finger down his own throat, and puked a green stream over one of the canvas-covered skiffs hanging below. "You'll feel better in a jiffy," he said, wiping slime from his chin. "I always feel grand after a major spew. My stomach's emptied and I can eat more later. Got to keep up one's strength. Seasickness will dehydrate a fellow. Make your mouth feel as dry as a fat man's titty."

Jenko leered at Zane. "If my father sees that skiff all covered in vomit, he's gonna make you climb down there and lick it clean yourself."

"The birds will take care of it," Zane said. Indeed, the seagulls were lighting on the white canvas, pecking at Zane's spew.

In the end, Nail had not puked that first day aboard the *Lady Kindly* and was the prouder for the accomplishment. By nightfall, his seasickness had dissipated completely. After knighthood or the clergy, grayken slaying was considered the grandest of all trades in the Five Isles. *The Way and Truth of Laijon* spoke of grayken hunting as a much simpler thing in ancient days, men doing nothing more than waiting for a grayken to drift ashore, dead. But that had been over a thousand years ago. The Book of the Great Hunts in *The Way and Truth of Laijon* told of how Laijon, as a teenager, would spear the grayken from the rocky shoals just southwest of Mont Saint Only, jumping from rock to rock, leaping over the merfolk who tried to snare him, thrusting and jabbing with his many spears until the great grayken were tired or dead, sometimes even jumping onto the backs of the leviathans themselves. Legend was, he would tie the beasts up and pull them ashore by the strength of his own arms. It wasn't long before grayken hunting became almost a religion unto itself, the launching of voyages and ships in hundreds that would last all day and bring in two or three grayken per ship. But over time, the grayken grew scarce. Now a normal hunting voyage lasted about a week, sometimes two. Some hunters predicted, come a thousand more years, it might take a year of sailing to find but one grayken.

For Nail's part, to be working alongside a crew of hardy men aboard the *Lady Kindly* was far better than traipsing through dark mines or toiling away with the sluices and pans alongside a lonely stream high in the Autumn Range. Jenko had been right when he'd said there was freedom at sea. After scarcely a few days on the water, Nail agreed: no good ever came of gold digging with Shawcroft. Here on the ocean, Nail could be with his friends.

And now that they were among the grayken, Nail wondered what his role would be. As if reading his mind, Stefan handed him a small dagger and said, "Let's watch from above," and bade him follow. Stefan, with his bow and a quiver of yellow-fletched arrows strapped to his back, scrambled halfway up the fore-topmast rigging. Nail slipped the dagger into his belt and scurried up behind his friend. Once perched upon the slender spar, hands grasping the cold rigging, he prepared to watch the great hunt. Stefan, more sure of himself, boldly straddled the rigging and strung his bow.

A crack of thunder boomed over the ship, and the sea became more agitated. The *Lady Kindly* was brought to a slow halt in the water by backing the mainsail. The canvas tarps were quickly pulled off the three white hunting skiffs tied to the side of the ship. Harpoons, killing lances, and barrels of harpoon lines were placed into the skiffs as the bishop prayed over each vessel. The skiffs were lowered into the water carefully. Men descended by rope into the skiffs, until each boat had a crew of eight, but not before every man of the fifty aboard had knelt before Tolbret and received a blessing. Once the men were blessed and safely in the hunting skiffs bobbing beneath the *Lady Kindly*, the three skiffs struck off, the men rowing madly out to sea. Baron Bruk was harpooner on the first boat, a man named Brutus Grove on the second boat, and Jenko Bruk was harpooner on the third. Each harpoon was fashioned from hardwood, rough-hewn to provide a solid grip.

From his perch in the rigging, Nail watched the skiffs as they cut through the water, each with a single harpooner, a helmsman, and six rowers. The three boats swept in among the large school of grayken, the baron's skiff leading, sneaking up on a particularly massive monster billowing blasts of air from its blowhole.

"A grayken will blow once right before it plans on diving under water," Stefan said, readying some arrows. "Once submerged, they can resurface anywhere, ofttimes straight under a boat, capsizing it.

Baron Bruk better strike quickly, because that grayken is about to go under."

The baron's skiff hove to, right beside the beast. Baron Bruk launched his harpoon, a rope tied to its end. It flew short of the mark and the grayken moved away, sinking below the surface. The baron reeled his harpoon back aboard by its rope line.

"The real show starts once a grayken is struck, fins and tentacles thrashing, sharks swarming," Stefan said. "Let's pray no merfolk show up. They're apt to help the grayken, cut the harpoon lines with sharpened fish bones. Tear at our ship. A huge bloody nuisance they are. But if they do"—he held up his bow—"I've got this for 'em."

Jenko's skiff peeled away from the other two, sneaking up on a different grayken from the rear, an even bigger beast than the first. The helmsman nimbly directed the boat until the prow was thudding right against the beast's flank. Jenko had his rope line and harpoon ready, his left leg planted in the bottom of the boat, his right knee securely fixed against the sidewalls. Jenko's harpoon rose up in his hand and his arm stretched back.

A tense moment passed, and for Nail there was never a more incredible sight. As if he were carved of marble, the baron's son, with long harpoon held aloft, stood perilously poised there on the lip of the tiny bobbing boat like a glistening sculpture of Laijon himself, the sun shimmering off the tip of his harpoon's clover-shaped blade.

Jenko struck with astonishing speed and power, the shaft sinking deep into the grayken's thick side. Quickly, once the beast was struck, Jenko leaned his weight onto the harpoon, pushing it farther inward until the entire shaft was almost buried, only the thin rope sticking out from the dark flesh. The beast leaped halfway out of the water and slammed back home. A great wave almost swept Jenko overboard, nearly swamping his boat. The grayken disappeared into the ocean, tentacles thrashing, rope trailing. A huge cheer rose up from the men on the *Lady Kindly*.

"Lucky Jenko wasn't sent straight to the underworld with all that thrashing," Stefan said. "They'll have to row away from the beast if they can."

Jenko's harpoon was not meant to kill the grayken. From Nail's vantage point, it was clear: the harpoon was merely the easiest way for the helmsman and his crew to link their small boat to their now quarrelsome large quarry. The grayken lurched above the surface again. Quivering in its gray flesh was the harpoon line, trailing the beast like a darning needle and spool of thread. Rivers of bright blood from the harpoon raced along the grayken's sleek surface. The beast blew air, and then plunged in an attempt to shake off its tiny tormentor. The rope snaked out of the barrel fastened in Jenko's boat, uncoiling and whipping down into the boiling darkness of the sea, following the grayken into the bottomless depths. The helmsman now held a hatchet over the rope, ready to chop it in twain if the grayken were to dive too deep, dragging their boat down.

The two other skiffs sped toward Jenko's boat. And for a span of time, there was no sign of the grayken—or any grayken. It seemed the entire school had beaten a hasty retreat into the far reaches of the sea. The rope ceased its whirring dance down into the blood-flecked ocean and went slack. There was silence but for Bishop Tolbret's rhythmic, prayerful chant. Nail thought the grayken had snapped the line and freed itself, or perhaps down in the depths unseen merfolk had cut through the line as Stefan had warned. But the grayken came roaring upward. A sweeping surge of water nearly overturned all three boats as the monster flew high. Nail's heart lodged in his throat as the full length of the beast's massive body hung above the ocean's surface, glistening red sheets of water streaking its flesh. He gawked in mute wonder as the beast twisted in midair, blowing out a fountain of red, then splashed back into the sea, great fins and tentacles lashing the water with bloody foam as it disappeared.

"Jenko stuck 'im good!" Stefan shouted. "And his line's still attached!"

Rolling waves rocked the three skiffs. The helmsmen of Brutus Grove's boat steered into position, the skiff bobbing in the dying waves. A throng of sharks circled the area now, weaving ominously just beneath the *Lady Kindly*. When the injured grayken surfaced again, it rose up in a swell of water nearest to Brutus' boat. He struck the beast with his harpoon. It thrashed with less vigor now.

"Merfolk!" Stefan, alert now, nocked an arrow to his bow. Nail saw them too. Three spun up from the sea near the grayken, half-human and half-fish, two male and one female, launching themselves so high their full forms were briefly suspended above the water. From head to fin, all three were taller than a man, all wielding long, sharpened bones in their webbed, clawed hands. Nail was stunned by the pale beauty of their skin and sparkling brightness of their scales. Almost white was their human half; their fish half was like polished steel. The rippling muscles on the two males were magnificent. The full breasts on the female caught Nail's eye while the shimmering scales of her lower half shone like gems of emerald, copper, and silver.

As the merfolk silently splashed back into the sea, Baron Bruk roared, "Bloody rotted merfolk! Be wary, Brutus!" And when the three merfolk spun up from the water again, screeching and shrill, they slashed at Brutus Grove's rope with their fish-bone weapons. Just as quickly, they fell back into the sea, Brutus' rope severed in twain.

One of the mermen came back up, head bobbing in the ocean, shrieking. Stefan loosed an arrow. Over a hundred feet it sailed true, then struck the merman in the face, and he dropped below the water. Nail had had no idea how deadly with a bow Stefan really was. The arrow shot afforded Brutus Grove the time to launch a second harpoon straight into the grayken's side. Another cheer rose up from the *Lady Kindly* as the beast dove again, the rope uncoiling from Brutus' skiff. The rowers scrambled and ducked to avoid being swept up in its twining path.

The ropes from both skiffs went taut, slack, taut, then slack. The grayken resurfaced quickly this time, blood bubbling from its blow-hole. Several sharks lunged at it then, their toothy mouths carving chunks out of the grayken's flesh. One shark even sailed forth and latched onto one of the grayken's six tail-like tentacles, but the mighty monster flung the shark back into the cold ocean as if swatting at a flea.

The merfolk, a dozen of them now, slithered up from the sea, occasionally hacking at the ropes and harpoons attached to the grayken. Nail noticed that some of the merfolk were small, children—some so tiny they might be babies. All of them fought and tore at the ropes attached to the grayken, some with sharpened bones, some with naught but their webbed, clawed hands. The shrieks that accompanied their fight pierced Nail's ears. The merfolk fought a losing battle as more harpoons from both Brutus' and Jenko's boats were launched into the grayken. And several more merfolk now floated in the water, dead, pierced by Stefan's arrows.

This crazy, frothing battle between men and beasts sent a peculiar shiver through Nail. It was the most terrifying yet awe-inspiring experience of his life. The injured grayken drifted toward open sea. More harpoons slammed home. The leviathan slashed with its six powerful tentacles and shot another pillar of bright crimson water skyward. Four times it spouted, its dying lungs purging blood, choking, spouting, and spewing, flapping fins and coiling tentacles beginning to tire.

Baron Bruk clapped wildly at his harpooners' efforts, and so did the men aboard the *Lady Kindly*. The screaming merfolk had disappeared altogether as the grayken fought on, biting at the air, bleeding copiously into the sea, sharks in a frenzy circling, gouging out bits of its flesh. The beast slowed and stopped moving altogether, the skiffs bobbing. Harpooners on all three boats started hitting the grayken with the killing lances until rushing rivers of bright blood poured from its many wounds. The beast slapped the water with its tentacles one last time. But it was a weak gesture, and just that quickly, the grayken rolled over and died, floating in a stew of its own oily blood.

† † † † †

A sprinkling rain began to fall as the three skiffs towed the dead beast, tentacles first, toward the ship, a T-shaped wooden toggle attached to a hole in one long tentacle. Sharks circled, looming under the small boats, drinking in the trailing wake of blood. Below Nail, along the starboard side of the ship, a wood-plank platform was lowered into the sea by the same block-and-tackle system used to lower the three skiffs. Men lugged huge iron hooks across the deck, each sharp as an ax and half as large as a man. They hauled them to the starboard side, and thick ropes were attached to all.

Nail was alone in the rigging now. Stefan had climbed down and was scurrying around on the deck with Zane. The three skiffs were near enough to the ship that the harpooners had pulled their harpoons loose, raindrops peppering their faces. Soon the beast's heavy body was thumping against the side of the *Lady Kindly* as waves swelled up around it. The water along the starboard side of the ship was a swirl of red. Occasionally, a shark would emerge ghostlike from the frothy pink and take a hunk of grayken flesh back down into the deep with it. There soon came a wooden *tap, tap, tap* from somewhere under the water, and Baron Bruk cried out, "The damn rotted mermen are tearing at the bottom of our ship! Let's make haste, lads! The sooner we get this thing up and outa the water the sooner them ghastly fish men will leave us be!"

There was a flood of movement on the deck below, and Zane pulled a long knife from his belt, grabbed a rope, and swung over the railing, straight down the side of the ship and onto the massive back of the grayken. Stefan followed Zane's plunge over the side, and soon both were running, balancing along the great leviathan's barrel-like body, slicing deep gashes into the back of the grayken's flesh with their knives. It was their job as grayken cutters to cut slits into the blubber where massive hooks could be inserted—their work accompanied by the wooden *tap, tap, tap* of the merfolk under the ship.

Soon other men were down upon the grayken with Stefan and Zane, and the iron hooks were lowered. The hooks swung wildly as the *Lady Kindly* jostled in the waves, the dead beast's girth hammering against the side of the ship. The men began securing the grayken by inserting the hooks into the gashes Stefan and Zane were opening with their cutters. Two hooks were inserted just above the grayken's fin in the deep slits the boys had previously made. More thick ropes, suspended from the lower masthead, were attached to each hook. Then the tremendous muscle of the windlass was put to the test, heeling the *Lady Kindly* onto her side using the weight of the great grayken as a counterbalance.

Nail was surprised as he slowly descended out in a great arc, the creaky wooden crosspiece he hugged was unsteady and difficult to grasp with his arms and legs. The sudden drop caused a swooning light-headedness, giving him a fright for several heartbeats. His perch high in the rigging was no longer a perch. As the *Lady Kindly* turned onto its side, he now feared being lowered almost to the level of the sea itself. The mast quaked with the strain. The ship trembled and creaked as more and more it leaned over toward the grayken. Nail clung to the crosspiece with a knuckle-white grip. He slipped and fell, catching himself in the rigging below as it swayed and twisted under him. Legs scrambling, he managed a quick reorientation, gripping the ropes fast, remaining securely suspended over the water. Only the strength in his own arms had saved him.

Zane, on the back of the beast, gave a hoot of surprise when he saw Nail, hanging in the rigging, pass overhead. Actually, Nail was passing over the flank of the grayken and sailing onward beyond it. The helmsman of Jenko's skiff had to scramble to turn his small boat, and all aboard rowed vigorously, not wanting their vessel to become entangled in the wood and rope rigging of the bigger ship's foremast and topsails. Nail was soon suspended a mere twenty feet or so above the ocean's surface. He was ripe with fear at the thought of being dunked in with the sharks and merfolk. But the *Lady Kindly* heeled as far as she was going to heel, and Nail found himself staring straight down into water red and thick with blood. "Having fun?" the baron's son said, standing in the bobbing skiff not fifteen paces away. Nail nodded with enthusiasm, and Jenko laughed.

There was a sudden shift in the wind, a brisk gust of rain, and a rolling of the ship upon the water. Men shouted. One of the great iron hooks tore loose with a snap and rending of grayken flesh and spun through the air, striking Zane Neville square in the chest and launching him from the security of the grayken's great flank straight into the rain-pattered sea. With a huge splash, the bloody water engulfed Zane. His hefty body vanished among a tangle of the *Lady Kindly*'s foremast rigging and was immediately swallowed up by the frothing darkness of the water.

Nail stared in horror at the scarlet bubbles below, all that remained of Zane's passing. He looked to the nearest skiff. Jenko Bruk was there, standing in the small boat not twenty feet from where Zane had disappeared. Their eyes locked. They stared at each other a moment, and the look in Jenko's eyes was not one of concern for Zane, but a look of resigned callousness, knowing there was nothing to be done. The severity of the situation dawned on Nail. Many aboard the *Lady Kindly* had seen Zane fly from the body of the grayken and sink like a stone beneath the water's surface. Even Bishop Tolbret's face was impassive as he stood at the railing.

At that very moment, Nail realized no one was going to do anything about it. *Any man goes overboard, he's lost to the sea!* Baron Bruk had said. It was clear. Zane would have to fend for himself. Nail's eyes sought Stefan and found his friend still planted on the grayken's back, horror etched in every line of his face. The hook man grabbed Stefan by the arm and forced him to help resecure the swinging hook under the grayken's fin.

Nail's gaze flew back to the spot in the red churning sea where Zane had vanished. The rope rigging jerked back and forth in the water, then went still. Nail waited. Staring. Hoping his friend would resurface. But as the moments passed, he realized Zane was truly lost, tangled down there somewhere amongst all that rigging.

Pale shapes hovered below the surface. The thought of a shark biting his friend in half like a salmon sent a shudder through Nail, and suddenly this grand grayken-hunting adventure wasn't so fun. Seabirds shrieked in joy around him. The tangled rigging where Zane had disappeared thrashed about wildly, as if someone beneath was struggling within it. Nail thought he saw the metallic sparkle of one of the merfolk down there too. The rain picked up. Thick droplets splashed the water. Lightning flashed above. And with all the blood, it seemed as if fire danced along the surface of the sea.

Without thinking, Nail pulled the small dagger Stefan had given him from his own belt, gripped it firmly in hand, and dove from his perch. Twenty feet straight down he flew. Headfirst he knifed into the ocean.

Water spewed over him, and a deep-red darkness pressed inward. At the water's bitter touch, the crosslike burn on the back of his right hand flared with pain. The bloody sea was icy and stole his breath, the water seeming to constrict inward, paralyzing his muscles. He spun and clawed to the surface, crimson bubbles churning. His head broke the skin of the ocean. He choked. The taste and smell of the grayken's blood gagged him. Chunks of regurgitated grayken bile were floating everywhere in the rain-splattered sea. Water closed in around him as he bobbed below the surface a second time. When his head surfaced again, he could scarcely see through the film of red seawater blanketing his eyes. The men on Jenko's skiff stared down at him. One man held an oar out to Nail. "Fool! He'll pull you down with him!" Jenko yelled, and slapped the oar away. Nail sank below a third time, his vision awash in red oblivion. Panic set in. He kicked wildly, his foot striking something. *Sharks!* He resurfaced one more time and floated there. His limbs couldn't move. The water was too cold.

Wind gusted. Stinging rain raked over Nail's face. The cold hurt, dreadfully, like needles racing under his skin, like molten metal poured over his bones, driving bolts of pain from muscle to muscle. Agony encompassed him as he gazed pleadingly up at Jenko Bruk and the seven other men, who were slowly rowing away. Something brushed against his foot and he spun, kicking slowly, legs numb, the sudden surge of adrenaline spinning him, all limbs flailing, useless. He now faced the grayken, not five feet away. Bloody water lapped lazily against its massive bulk. Rainwater washed down its side. Stefan was crawling down the slippery slope of the beast, a rope line tied around his waist, one hand reaching for Nail. Lightning ripped down from the sky, hitting the water between them. The blinding flash was followed by a thunderous clap that set the sea to buzzing and dancing with an eerie light.

Nail's skin tingled so sharply that all other senses were drowned out and he couldn't move. Every nerve in his body felt pinched and frozen in pain. Something caught him by the leg, and he was jerked beneath the sea. He swung out in defense, but his knife only sliced through water, slowly, ineffectively. It must be Zane clawing at him from below. His friend's grabbing hands were a mad thrash, clawlike, pulling Nail farther down into the darkness. Soon Zane's arms were beating wildly against him, and the small dagger was knocked from his hand. Zane's limbs found purchase, clutching, squeezing the breath from Nail in one great hug, pinning both of his arms to his side. Zane's clenching bulk was going to drown them both. Nail felt his lungs burning. Pain stabbed through his straining chest as he tried not to gasp for air.

Then he realized it wasn't Zane who had hold of him.

His eyes flew open. And he saw her pale, ghostly visage—the mermaid who held him tight. Inches away, her face floated in the deep. She had a delicate chin, thin lips, thin nose, and eyes that were as wide and crystal blue as the summer sky. Her eyelids blinked ever so slowly. A serrated row of gills fluttered open and closed along her slender neck. He felt her breasts against his chest, her slithery scaled tail coiled around his legs. She tilted her head and opened her mouth, revealing long fangs that were shockingly sharp and grotesque in comparison to her overall glamour. Nail mustered what strength he had and wiggled one arm free of her. He attempted to push the fearsome mermaid away, but the pointed claws tipping her webbed hand raked across his right bicep, tearing shirt and flesh.

Lightning struck the surface of the sea above again. Soul-shattering sound flashed down through the blood and water, engulfing Nail and the mermaid in a flame of crimson light. Pockets of redness pulsed in waves around them whilst runnels of red seeped and flashed. It felt as if the ocean was slowly twisting over on itself. The bands of sparkling ruby light that streaked the water throbbed like veins along a monstrous scaly arm, in, out, in, out. Then the deepening red light was gone. Dark. The mermaid shrieked, her eerie voice muffled and ghostlike underwater.

Another lightning blast. Light and sound blossomed brilliantly, illuminating everything under the sea in crystal-clear, bloody redness: the underside of the ship, sharks, mermaids, the grayken and its dangling tentacles, and most startling of all, symbols. Emblazoned like pockets of flame in every direction: squares, circles within circles, crosses, all twinkling like shooting stars. The glittering veins of light intensified into a flaming red, blooming and running like spiraling streams of flowing fire.

Even the cross-shaped wound on the back of his hand was pulsing light and pain.

The mermaid jerked violently in front of him, and the ocean seemed to spin inward on itself again. The gleaming ribbons of fire wrapped around them both, then faded to a dull red—then dwindled and washed away to nothing. The water was pitched in black.

Nail could feel himself drowning. Eyes open, or closed, he knew not. But deep down somewhere below in the darkness, he saw something, hazy, fluttering in the water. It slowly solidified. He saw *himself*—standing under a large burning tree. There was a knight with glowing white shield and horned helm astride a brilliant white warhorse, a blond girl on the saddle before him, her hand a metal claw. And *green* glowing eyes!

Something slammed into him then, hurtling him from the mermaid's grasp and up through the water and to the surface. "There they are!" Nail heard Stefan yell.

Nail took one blessed breath before a bloody swirl of churning water enveloped him again. When he floundered to the surface a second time, he realized Zane was there with him, eyes wide and rivulets of crimson water streaming from his sopping red hair down over his terrified features. They were face-to-face, Zane coughing, choking, spewing forth gouts of chunky water.

The pale head of a shark broke the surface and eyed Nail from just beyond Zane. Nail found himself in the grip of utter terror. It screamed through his mind, drowning out any thought. Time seemed to freeze in that moment. His heart thundered. The sounds of Stefan's yells were silenced. The clap of the water beating against the hull of the *Lady Kindly* ceased. Even the shrieks of the seabirds were gone. Nail couldn't break his gaze from the milky dark eye of the great white killer before him. At that very moment, he would've given anything to be back home, safe in the mountains with Master Shawcroft, calmly panning for gold by a cool gurgling brook under the green pines and warm sun.

A spear was thrust into the shark's head, and it calmly dipped below the red skin of the sea. And like a burst of thunder, Nail was aware of someone shouting, yet it seemed so far away, and he felt firm hands grasping at his shirt. He was roughly hauled from the ocean and dashed into the bottom of Baron Bruk's skiff with brutal force, instantly coughing out what scant air remained in his lungs.

Soon, and with great effort by all the men in the skiff, Zane was pulled up and plopped on the deck next to Nail. Crystal-clear tears streaked Zane's cheeks as he raked madly at the bloody seawater coating his face. One of the merfolk was attached to his leg. It was a small one—a baby, its arms around Zane's calf, teeth buried in his leg just below the knee. Zane frantically batted it away. It flipped and flopped at the bottom of the skiff on its back, the gills on its neck splayed and heaving, mouth wide and round, spitting and screeching an ungodly racket. Its lips pulled back in a grimace and its gruesome teeth were exposed, gnashing. Little arms thrashed and tail slashed as Zane kicked wildly at it.

"Get that gill-fucking creature outa here!" Baron Bruk roared. One of the rowers deftly scooped the wiggling little demon onto the flat of his oar and tossed it out to sea.

"Bloody beasts of the underworld." The baron knelt above Nail and Zane, eyes dispassionate and cold, the sky gray and rainy behind him. He seemed almost distracted, bored, as if his mind were on other things. "Back to it!" he yelled. "There's work to be done!" Just like that, every man aboard the *Lady Kindly* sprang into action.

Once rescued, Nail now felt the sodden blood-covered weariness of his own body. He also felt he had just been awakened from some long, bizarre dream. His eyes stung from the salty water still dripping from his matted hair. Pain clawed at his lungs. The taste of death clung to his tongue. *And the eye of the shark, staring right through me mere moments ago. By the Blessed Mother Mia, the thing was a terror! And the merfolk! Demons all!* His mind couldn't shake the red-hazed horror of what he'd seen under the water. *Visions! Symbols!* He would not think of it. He would lock it away.

The claw marks on his bicep were not deep at all, barely having broken the skin, but they were ragged and bleeding and stung something fierce. The leather-thong necklace Ava Shay had given him was still around his neck. He was dimly aware of the curious faces peering at him as the baron's skiff cast free of the grayken.

Zane remained curled at the bottom of the skiff, coughing, eyes on Nail. "I thought I'd never see my poor dog, Beer Mug, again." He managed to do the three-fingered sign of the Laijon Cross over his breast. "Blessed Mother, have mercy upon my soul. Buried under all that red water like that, the only thing that crossed my mind was that if I died, my dog would surely miss me. As Laijon is my witness, I swear it, Nail."

Still trembling, Nail watched in a daze as Stefan, still on the grayken's back, finished refastening the large hook that had struck Zane under the grayken's fin. Soon all the men on the grayken began climbing up ropes to the deck of the *Lady Kindly*.

The men handling the lines leading to the heavy hooks began to haul, the ship gradually began to right itself, and the grayken slowly spun in the water. There were now men standing on the wooden planks above the grayken. They carved at it with long scythes. As the grayken's barrel-like body spun over in the water, they began peeling a layer of blubber away from the beast in a giant spiral. It reminded Nail of how Master Shawcroft would peel the skin from his apples with a hunting knife. The first strip of blubber fell to the deck and was chopped into strips and pieces by stout ax and sword and shoved down through the ship's main hatchway. This process of heeling the ship and spinning the grayken and slicing rinds off its flesh was repeated for about an hour. Soon the deck of the *Lady Kindly* was awash with slaughter and huge chunks of flesh.

The rain stopped. Nail and Zane were eventually put back aboard the *Lady Kindly*. Zane immediately sought the bishop and knelt before him. Tolbret laid his hands on the boy's head and offered a brief blessing. Seeing what comfort the blessing had given Zane,

Nail knelt too, but the bishop grunted, "No," and ordered him to stand. Nail, hurt, wondered why the bishop had so coldly refused him. Tolbret bandaged the wound on his bicep, if a trifle reluctantly, then set him to work hauling strips of blubber to the hatchway. Zane helped too, but soon collapsed from exhaustion and was carried away to Jubal Bruk's quarters. For the next few hours, caught in a dull haze, Nail hauled blubber. It was not soft and flabby as he had imagined, but rather tough as leather. The work wore his hands raw and left them stinging in pain.

Once the grayken was stripped of its blubber, a giant saw was brought out and two men began sawing at the monster's mammoth head. The beast's head, a third the size of its entire body, was hoisted aboard the ship. It thudded to the deck amidst a great cheer. It was then harvested of its oil with shovels. Men began to shear strips of baleen from the roof of its mouth. Soon the deck ran slick with a mixture of ghastly white brain fluid and blood. The savagery in the looks of the blood-soaked sailors who hacked at the leviathan's head gave Nail a fright.

What remained of the corpse was turned loose from the ship. Despite having just been beheaded and stripped of its most valuable flesh, the grayken was still a colossal mound of ivory meat as it floated away. The frigid water soon became a boiling mass of swarming, feasting sharks. Even the seabirds swooped down and began pecking at it. Cries of the merfolk could be heard in the far distance, their shrieks harsh and shrill.

† † † † †

"I've seen a man bitten in half by a shark." As he spoke, Baron Bruk gazed out at the tranquil, dark sea moving calmly by, his fur-rimmed cloak thrown carelessly over his broad shoulders, snowflakes gathering upon it. Nail, Baron Bruk, and Jenko stood together under the mizzenmast whilst the rest of the crew partied on deck between the main mast and fore. The baron continued, "I witnessed the horror in that man's eyes as the shark rose from the water to engulf him, teeth grinding up his body as the shark swallowed his legs down whole, teeth engulfing his chest, then, snap! Half of him was gone. And when I was a boy, I watched an enraged Dyrwood Rutherford wade out, waist deep, into Bainbridge Bay dressed in full armor, complete with helmet, greaves, chest plate, and sword, to do battle with a great white that had been wreaking havoc with his crab traps. He lasted, oh say, two minutes before the shark shot forth and swallowed him whole. Odd thing was, in the end, Dyrwood did kill that shark. Armor, as it turns out, is none too digestible. Six days later, we heard tell of a great white washed up in the shoals near Tomkin Sty. When the fishermen cut the beast open, imagine their surprise as a dead Dyrwood Rutherford spilled out in full armor, sword still in hand."

Baron Bruk turned his gaze from the frosty sea and looked at Nail. "What I'm getting at, boy, is that it was a damn fool thing diving in after Zane like that. Not only for the sharks, mind you. But especially for those merfolk in the water. Once they catch a grayken slayer, they'll give him one grim, slow death."

Jenko added, "Lucky my father's men disobeyed his orders and rescued you."

Nail shuddered at the thought of a suffocating death at the hands of the merfolk. He'd figured a tongue-lashing was coming when the baron pulled him aside after the deck was swept and swabbed. He didn't want the baron's son to hear the scolding, though. Nail stared out at the placid sea and drifting snowflakes, figuring if the baron was going to tell him he was not wanted on any other voyages, he would just remain quiet.

The air was crisp. Luckily, he was wearing an extra pair of sailor breeches and shirt and jacket, clean and warm. His own clothes stank of blood and salt water. The pain from where the mermaid had clawed him was mostly gone. But as he stared at the ocean, the moon a shimmering gleam on the black of the Mourning Sea, he thought of the mermaid and the visions he'd seen. As the sullen waves splashed away from the hull of the ship in lines of glistening white foam, he imagined the ghostly horror of a mermaid was following him still, clinging, trying to pull him under, forcing his eyes open wide so that he had to see the glowing red symbols again.

"I could legally have you flogged for disobeying my orders," Baron Bruk said. "But if I have you flogged, I'd also have to flog the seven good men on my skiff who insisted on rescuing you."

Nail still stared out at the sea and growing snowstorm. As he listened to the baron, he could feel the anger building inside, throbbing like muffled drums in his head. He'd seen terrible things in the water.

"The truth is, Zane Neville was standing in the wrong spot," Baron Bruk said. "It was no accident that sent him spinning into the sea. If anyone is to be flogged, it is he."

The baron paused. "Look at me, boy," he said curtly. Nail looked up, defiant. But he could feel himself growing more and more cautious, withdrawn.

Baron Bruk continued, "Shawcroft doesn't know you stowed aboard the *Lady Kindly*, does he?" A sudden pang of guilt touched Nail. He didn't answer, just turned his gaze from the baron to the sea. It was true. He had not told Shawcroft his plans. It was an act of defiance. On the one hand, Nail feared how his master would react upon the *Lady Kindly*'s return. On the other, he didn't really care. He had found a kind of peace with his decision. If Shawcroft wanted to spend an entire week in the gold mines alone, then Nail figured he himself could do as he pleased. He would get scolded either way.

"Had you died today, boy, I would've had to answer to that man. Informing Shawcroft that his ward had perished under my command is not a thing I would take lightly. May the wraiths take me, but I know who Shawcroft is."

Who Shawcroft is? Shawcroft was, well, just Shawcroft. A mean, gold-digging fool. *What could Baron Bruk know of Shawcroft?* Nail took a deep breath and looked out to sea, composing himself. When he decided to turn and question the baron about Shawcroft, it was Jenko who caught his attention. Nail found, to his immense irritation, that the baron's son was leering at him with an expression of complete insolence.

"I know what Shawcroft is capable of." The baron's hard eyes softened, but only a little. "Truth be told, I approve your desire to find your own way in the world. Rooting around those dead gold mines is a waste of time. You already know that, don't you?"

Baron Bruk was looking straight at him now, eyes unwavering. "I may have need of a fourth harpooner, someone with a true set of balls, someone with balls enough to defy his addled, gold-digging master and go a-grayken hunting, someone with balls enough to jump into bloody, shark-infested water." The baron took a step back and held out his hand toward Nail. "You are welcome on the *Lady Kindly* anytime she sails. Upon our return, I shall inform your master of my intentions for your employ."

Stunned, Nail knew not what to do. Had Baron Jubal Bruk just proffered a formal offer of employment? *Am I now freed from Master Shawcroft?* He looked from Jenko to Baron Bruk and back. Jenko looked like he'd just eaten something sour. And that sour look on Jenko's face pleased Nail. So he reached forth and shook Baron Bruk's hand.

"It was a foolish thing diving in after Zane." The baron shook Nail's hand vigorously. "But a braver thing I have never seen." As Baron Bruk grasped Nail's hand, he looked at his son. "Jenko, my boy, you are stout and hardy and hardworking, but you need to show true bravery, bravery like Nail has shown us today."

Nail looked at the baron's son. An angry, jealous glint formed in Jenko Bruk's moody eyes before he whirled and stalked away.

† † † † †

Later that night, Stefan Wayland snatched Nail away from his game of cards with Zane in the crew quarters and hauled him onto the snowy deck to the cheers of the rest of the crew. Once on deck, Stefan stripped Nail of his jacket and shirt, removed the bandage from his right arm, and brought forth the ink and tattoo needle. The ink, Stefan explained, was the best of its kind, made from the soot of grayken oil lanterns and mixed with Avlonia molasses. "No weak squid ink is ever used for a true grayken hunter's tattoo," he claimed. "Only pirates and outlaws use the cheap stuff."

When he was done, Nail couldn't have been more pleased with the result. Stefan's artwork, placed just above the mermaid's claw marks on his bicep, was the perfectly fitting image for Nail's maiden voyage. He was a full-fledged grayken slayer now.

He had never felt more contented in his life.

The Five Isles are drenched in secret history, every castle smothered in intrigue and steeped in lore, and every carving on every standing-stone has roots in the past. Hence, that secret past survives, always clawing to the surface, breathing, growing, like a living thing, never resting, always clawing, clawing in the deep.
—THE WAY AND TRUTH OF LAIJON

CHAPTER THREE

NAIL

15TH DAY OF THE SHROUDED MOON, 999TH YEAR OF LAIJON

GALLOWS HAVEN, GUL KANA

A rudimentary latticework of wooden flumes, ditching, damming, and aqueducts had diverted most of the water off to the side, leaving the streambed full of dry boulders for a lengthy stretch. With little enthusiasm, Nail unslung his satchel and tossed it to the ground near a mossy tree trunk. Shawcroft handed Nail the tools, a pickax, copper bowl, and a knife. Nail bemoaned the fact that he was here again. Like the lines on the palms of his own hand, he knew every pond, creek, canyon, trail, and meadow in these peaks, panned for gold at every watery twist and turn. In all that time, they had found scant color, just a handful of nuggets and a cupful of gold dust—enough to eke out a meager living. But what was most bothersome—it had been days since the grayken hunt, and Baron Jubal Bruk had still not made the formal offer of transference to Shawcroft or officially offered Nail a place on the *Lady Kindly*.

"Let's get to it." His master released the water through the sluice, shoveling sand and gravel along with it. The water rushed down the streambed, crashing against the dry boulders. Nail stood just as he was trained to, feet set, balanced, left one slightly in front of the right, shoulders straight, front knee bent at just the correct angle, and swung the pickax down with all his might. The pike sank deep into the ground, and then he raked back, loosening the soil and stones in the streambed. He did this three times in succession, the same each time, for he knew Shawcroft would make him do it over if it wasn't done just right.

Once the soil was loose, he set down the ax and filled the copper pan with heaps of sand, water, and rock. With little enthusiasm he shook the pan back and forth in his hands, allowing the slurry to spill over the sides, carrying with it silt and dust. *Hold the pan and swirl just right or you'll make him mad!* He completed the sifting by halfheartedly blowing on what remained in the pan, causing it to dry some. It wasn't long before his fingers were numb from working the cold water. Just like swinging a pick at the ground or in the dark mines. *All your body weight into the blow. Crush that rock, Nail!* Ever since he could remember. It was all so useless. He hated this dreadful work more each day. *When will Baron Bruk come and save me from all this?*

He sat back and looked up the bank toward Lilly and Bedford Boy. A circle of standing-stones, weather-beaten and overrun with ivy, rose up regally behind the two chestnut-colored ponies. Beyond that, breaks in the thick pine forests offered up glimpses of the steep, rocky slopes across the canyon and the hundreds of black dots marking the Roahm Mines and their tailings. He had spent the last five years working inside those mines with his master. Always panning streams and toiling in mines. Always swinging an ax at rock and tree, digging pits to snare game with the ax, perfect footwork, left, right, left, hold your stance, grip like this, swing just so, swing from the left, swing from the right, never use your hands to grab at the rock, always rake with the ax, pry the rocks loose with the ax, let the tools do the work for you. Swing. Pull. Swing. Pull. Rake. Even before Shawcroft and Nail had relocated to Gallows Haven, they had worked the mines near Sky Lochs, Nail a mere child, and later, the mines north of Deadwood Gate. He had no memories of Sky Lochs and the huge glaciers rumored to dominate the landscape. Deadwood Gate he remembered well. His master would go off into the mines alone to work, same as now, leaving Nail to pan a stream like this. Or, toward the end of their stay at Deadwood Gate, Shawcroft began to work the mines with a young fellow named Culpa Barra, whilst Nail was set to some other chore, usually involving a pickax and hard stone and the repetition of swings. Nail thought of Culpa and the sleek longsword the young man always wore at his side, how his master continually complimented it and Culpa.

"Get to work," Shawcroft, standing on the slope above, leaning on his shovel, grumbled down at him. "Enough woolgathering."

Nail stared at the mines in the distance. His master had been keeping him out of the mines a lot lately, preferring to work alone, leaving Nail to pan the streams like this. The man was growing more and more distant as time wore on. "We're not going into the mines today?"

"Nope," Shawcroft answered curtly. The man was shorter than Nail, but stout and broad of chest. He had a thick neck and hard brown eyes that held an air of sturdy self-control. His black hair was shaved to stubble on his scalp.

"So I can meet up with Stefan later and help him practice the Ember Lighting Prayers?"

"Seems pointless, but if you'd like."

"It's pointless to sift this stream," Nail said just loud enough. "Why bother?"

"We will work all the streams this coming summer. Together."

"Why?"

"Don't question. Just respect my decision. The mines are becoming too dangerous."

Too dangerous? Nail did not believe that. There was always something of the mysterious about the man. Shawcroft was the only family he'd ever known. But they were not blood kin. All things considered, beyond the gruffness and ofttimes cruel words, the man had treated him well enough. Though he had never truly felt like a son to Shawcroft, Nail had often wanted to hear that one word from the man. *Son.* Even the word *friend* would suffice. *Or was that fellow from Deadwood Gate, Culpa Barra, Shawcroft's son?* One thing was certain: Shawcroft had never concerned himself with any of his wants or hopes or dreams, nor acted the least bit curious about his drawings. And perhaps those were the reasons Nail wanted away from him so bad. With Shawcroft it was nothing but mining, hard work, perfection with a pickax, and obey. Gold was Shawcroft's life. It always had been. And in all the years they had found scant color.

Just respect my decision. He'd show his master respect, all right. "In town they say you're naught but a gold digger and a lack-wit."

Shawcroft barely looked up, kept working.

"Jubal Bruk asked about you a while back."

"Did he now?" Shawcroft's stiff brow furrowed as he shoveled.

Nail continued, chuckling, "Said you might could help us conscripts with some sword training."

There was a moment of silence. "Get back to work, boy."

Nail knew the taciturn man had scant use for pointless conversation or sarcasm. He also knew Shawcroft would only be pushed so far. As he grew older, Nail liked to see how far he could push. He knew any mention of Baron Jubal Bruk would not sit well with his master. There was a history between the two Nail was not privy to. He figured Shawcroft must already know he'd stowed aboard the

Lady Kindly. But the man was silent on the subject. Cruel words and punishment would come at some point, though.

Better now than later. "I'm sick of digging for riches that we are never gonna find. Never *have* found."

"Patience, Nail." Shawcroft glanced his way, still shoveling. "Patience."

"Patience," Nail repeated in disgust. "It's always patience with you. Stand this way when you swing an ax, set your feet just so, turn your hips, shoulders up, grip just so, use the ax to pry away the rock, over and over. Always tedium and patience. All for nothing."

Shawcroft stopped working and stared down at him. "The mountains hold music and magic for those who listen. And someday you will learn there are curious things hidden in the dirtier and darker places of this land. So keep sifting."

Nail shrugged. "I'd rather do something else with my life."

"Like most men, you would prefer a life of leisure. Hard work and precision in all things builds strength, character, and pride. Your mother wanted me to instill those things in you more than any other. She never took things such as hard work for granted, nor should you."

Nail's ears perked at the mention of his mother. "What do you remember of her?"

"Nothing new since you last asked." Shawcroft went back to his shoveling.

"Nothing at all?" Nail hung his head, letting the hair fall into his eyes.

"She was only fifteen when she bore you and your sister," Shawcroft said, still working. "She didn't live long after that. I only knew her a short while."

"Before she died in that mining camp, the one the oghul raiders destroyed?"

Shawcroft shot him a dark look. Nail knew nothing of his mother, aside from the fact that she'd died in a place called Arco, a long-deserted mining camp high in the Sky Lochs, a humble community destroyed by oghuls, or so his master said. In fact, that was the sum total of the information the man had ever offered on the subject.

"I only want to know my heritage," Nail said. "What of my father, was he—"

"I know nothing of your father to answer with any certainty what he was like."

"What of my sister?" Shawcroft had answered these questions the same many a time—with silence. Still, Nail charged ahead. "Where is she? We were twins, right?"

"We've gone over this before." Shawcroft's voice was strained with impatience. "I know not if your sister even lives. I rue the day I ever mentioned her to you."

"There seems to be much you won't tell me . . . about a great many things."

Shawcroft planted his shovel in the dirt and leaned into it and for once looked thoughtful. "I daresay we're the same then. There are secrets you hold from me." Nail's heart hammered. *So he does know I went grayken hunting with Baron Bruk.*

"Back to work." The heavy tone of Shawcroft's voice brooked no argument. "I've had enough questions for one day." He took his shovel and hiked up the streambed.

Nail wouldn't let it be over so easily. "Like what secrets do I keep?"

Shawcroft turned. "There's been talk in town of how you saved Zane on that grayken hunt." A hint of pride seeped into the man's voice as he spoke. But that only confused Nail. He didn't understand how the man could be so inconsistent with his emotions. Shawcroft continued, "They claim he would have drowned had you not been on that ship." His face turned dark. "The problem is, you should *not* have been on that ship. You were supposed to stay at the Waylands' after your arms training."

"It's my right to work for Jubal Bruk. He'll make an offer soon, freeing me from you. He's a baron."

"I'll refuse his offer. I will inform Jubal Bruk that you will not be allowed back aboard the *Lady Kindly* again." The man turned and walked away.

"You're wrong! I will join the grayken-hunting crew! I will go to sea when they next launch."

Shawcroft whirled, fists clenched. "In all these years I've never whipped you, boy. But I just might."

"Just you try." Furious, Nail snatched up the pickax, wielding it like a club. Shawcroft was a stout, hardy man. But Nail knew he was big enough to take his master down. After all, he had training with swords, while his master had none. Shawcroft was naught but a dirty gold digger—a stout dirty gold digger—but a gold digger all the same.

"Lest you forget, I am charged with your safekeeping till the day you die." Shawcroft's face was harsh, scowling. "Now drop that ax before I snatch it from you and whip you with it good. A ward can be legally put to death for threatening his master."

Nail simmered. The man was right. He dropped the ax. Shawcroft walked up forcefully. Nail backed away. But his master grabbed the leather thong around his neck and pulled Ava's wood carving out of his shirt. "What's this?"

"A gift," Nail said with as much defiance as he could muster. "It's mine."

"From a girl?"

Nail said nothing.

"Don't grow too attached to any one person." Shawcroft yanked up the sleeves of Nail's shirt to his elbows. "Bruises." The man's gaze traveled the length of Nail's black-and-blue forearms, eyes lingering on the thin, crosslike burn on the back of his right hand.

"I sparred with Jenko Bruk." Nail brushed the man's hand away. The cross-shaped burn on his hand was still as red as the day Dokie had been struck by lightning.

"Looks like Jenko thrashed you good then" was all Shawcroft said.

Nail felt his face flush. He certainly wasn't going to show the man his tattoo or the scars on his bicep from the mermaid. He pulled his shirtsleeves over his bruises and stuffed Ava's carving down the neckline of his shirt.

"Jubal Bruk never was much of a swordsman," Shawcroft said. "You will need proper training. I should've taken it upon myself to teach you more about swordsmanship long ago."

"More about swordsmanship?" Nail laughed hollowly. "You've never taught me *anything* about sword fighting. What do you know of it?"

Shawcroft motioned for Nail to get back to work. "We're done talking."

† † † † †

"All the chatter about town is of how you saved Zane," Ava Shay said. "Zane especially mentions it often." Nail felt pride well up. After his earlier conversation with Shawcroft, it was good to hear anything positive. Far below, the waves in Gallows Bay rolled in from the west. It was near dusk, and Nail and Ava sat next to each other on a flat boulder near the edge of a sloping cliff high up the Autumn Range. She carved a small wooden duck whilst Nail drew the scene below with sharpened charcoal. Stefan Wayland was shooting yellow-fletched arrows into a makeshift target he'd set up along the Roahm Mine Trail, which wound up the mountainside behind them.

Nail had met Stefan on the trail as they ofttimes did in the evenings with Dokie Liddle. Stefan had brought Ava with him instead. Dokie's recovery from the lightning strike was going well; he was up and walking some, but not up to hiking steep trails. Nail, Stefan, and Dokie would usually study their Ember Lighting Prayers up here after Nail's work with Shawcroft was done, or practice with swords or bows.

Their solitary perch was so high that seagulls circled beneath them. Far under the gulls, the distant, green-tinged shoreline was thick with the first growth of spring. Patches of lush meadows, fields, woodlands, and rock-fence-lined properties randomly dotted the landscape north and south of Gallows Haven. From so high up, the chapel and abandoned keep north of town looked like children's playthings. An armed silhouette paced atop the keep's western wall, some poor sod Baron Jubal Bruk had put to the watch. The court-yard of the keep was a clear swath of grass, soon to be packed with Mourning Moon Feast goers. There were a handful of carts moving along the pathways. In the center of town near the docks, some-one was sweeping the front porch of the Grayken Spear Inn. On the beach just north of town, streams of black smoke rose into the sky, billowing from hundreds of black cauldrons filled with grayken blubber. Wood fires under the pots were melting down the leath-ery blubber. Baron Bruk would sell the oil to traders. Fishing boats bobbed in the waters beyond the pots, the tiny forms of men casting nets into the ocean.

Nail pulled up the sleeve of his shirt to his bicep, showing Ava the tattoo Stefan had given him just above the claw marks of the mer-maid. "Three shark's teeth. Most grayken hunters get a mermaid or a sea serpent tattoo. Some get an anchor. A lot get crossed harpoons."

"It's wonderful." Ava ran her fingers gently over the tattoo. "But what's this?" she asked, touching the still-visible scars from the mer-maid's claws.

"One of the merfolk tried to drown me while I was in the water."

"How ghastly." She immediately withdrew her hand, revulsion on her face.

Nail sat up straighter. "I fought my way free. Saved Zane. Baron Bruk said it was the bravest thing he'd ever seen." His eyes darted to Stefan on the trail behind them—his friend was fussing with his quiver of yellow-fletched arrows, oblivious to their conversation.

Nail had never mentioned his encounter with the mermaid to anyone; he'd told Bishop Tolbret, who'd wrapped the wound with bandages, that it was just the ratlines that had slashed his arm. The lingering image of the mermaid's pale face in the bloody water and the feel of her scaly tail wrapping around his legs had become a nightmare fixed in his mind that he would not soon forget.

"It's why Baron Bruk offered me a place on his ship, for saving Zane," he finished.

"Grayken-hunting ships are magnificent indeed." She ran her fingers over his bicep again, tracing the lines of the tattoo over his muscles. "The town is a-talk of how you snuck aboard the *Lady Kindly*. But they also say Shawcroft most likely won't let you sail with Baron Bruk again. It must be sad, always belonging to people."

Her words hurt. But the pain was brief as she leaned into him and rested her head on his shoulder. Even in her drab hiking clothes—brown jerkin over tan shirt and plain, rough-spun pants—her beauty kindled a flame that flared in his heart. He felt the turtle carving she had given him resting against his chest under his shirt.

It must be sad, always belonging to people.

Nail's world was a small one, and he knew his place within it. Along the coastline as far as he could see, between mountain range and ocean, his entire world was spread out below. The social order of Gul Kana and its peoples was broadly similar to that of Wyn Darrè. The king in Amadon ruled alongside the holy vicar of the Church of Laijon. The land was divided into shires. A local bishop along with a sheriff or baron ruled the largest town within the shire. Together they collected the king's taxes and the church's tithes, and oversaw justice. It was these two leaders, under the direction of Amadon, who made sure every Gul Kana male, be they peasant, freeman, or baron's son, serve church and crown as a conscripted soldier in training for two years, starting at seventeen.

The rulers of the larger cities like Avlonia, Rivermeade, Eskander,

Lord's Point, and the like were titled lords. Large estate owners near the smaller towns were titled barons. Peasants and freemen were tied to business owners or large estates and were subject to the barons. One's station, high or low, fortunes good or bad, was established by one's parentage. Whatever your lineage, you had security in your station.

As a bastard, Nail was free only to follow his master's bidding unless a formal offer of legitimate employment was made by another of higher station—just as Jubal Bruk had offered Nail a place aboard the *Lady Kindly*. Nail knew he relied entirely on the goodwill of others. Still, he had always known he was different, creative, and strong, better than others of no birthright. If a girl as enchanting as Ava Shay could see something in him, then anything was possible.

Gazing down the mountain, he found the familiar shape of her home near the center of town. It was half-hidden under a large oak, a small two-room affair she shared with her five younger siblings, its thatched roof no more than a brown dot below, a curl of wood-smoke twirling up from the chimney. Ava lived with her brothers and sisters in a house near the Grayken Spear Inn that Ol' Man Leddingham had set them up in. She'd helped raise them since her parents had died. A sickness had taken her mother. Shortly after that her father had been killed in a logging accident above Tomkin Sty. Nail admired Ava's hard work and resolve in dealing with life's challenges.

"Your house looks so small from up here," he said.

A dog ran past Ava's home, a pinprick on the landscape as it sped through town, Zane Neville chasing it. Even from so far up, Nail recognized Zane's awkward gait. The two specks ran past the harbor, where Baron Bruk's grayken-hunting ship was nestled. Nail could see people scurrying about on her riggings like spiders on a web. Beer Mug kept going, shooting past the harbor up the road, followed by Zane, chugging along behind. They both charged into a small field

north of the chapel and ran in circles, Zane chasing, Beer Mug leading. Nail could imagine Zane's laughter and the dog's barks of joy.

"Who are you?" Stefan's shaky voice said from behind.

Both Nail and Ava turned to find Stefan Wayland with his bow
taut, yellow-fletched arrow pointing up at a dark-cloaked horseman
on the road behind them.

Ava squealed. Nail lurched to his feet.

The horse on the trail was straight out of his childhood nightmares: a mare, sleek, black, and powerfully built, with feverish eyes
like red-glowing holes in its wedge-shaped head. Arteries and corded
muscle pulsed beneath its glistening black hide. The rider was darker
still, bathed in midnight against the greenery of the mountainside, a
hint of black boiled-leather armor under the cloak, pale face mostly
obscured beneath a hood.

But when the rider pulled back the hood, Nail was startled even
further. For it was not the face of a man hidden underneath, but that
of a young woman. And she was not just pretty, but beautiful, arrest-
ing even. Hair of exquisite silvery-white waves framed her face. She
had slanting eyebrows above striking green eyes, high-boned cheeks,
and full lips. Some pale light glowed just beneath her skin, as though
through a thin veil.

And there was something achingly familiar about the way she
spoke, her voice dark, musical. "My blade thirsts," she said, eyes on
Nail. Then she produced a black dagger from the folds of her cloak.
A smile played at the corners of her mouth. Not quite a smile, but
something *fierce*. In fact, there were things not at all human about the
way this thin-faced woman moved. It was something ethereal, almost
akin to the mermaid who'd nearly drowned him. And there were her
perfect narrow ears, pointed, just visible through the strands of lustrous blond hair.

She was no human, but a creature, a fey, a *Vallè!*

Nail had never seen one of the Vallè up close, only from ashore when the occasional Vallè trading ship docked in Gallows Bay. Two things were certain, though: her bearing was commanding, and the dagger in her hand seemed to swallow all light.

Her eyes were locked on his, large, almond-shaped pupils more brilliantly green than anything he'd ever seen. They tugged at him, drew him in, as if she were searching, pulling something, *his thoughts*, from his mind, as if she wanted to devour his very soul.

"You are not of my blood." Her smile disappeared as she slipped the knife back into the folds of her cloak. "Still, they will be coming for you."

And with a rustle of leaves, the frightening black mare and ghostly Vallè woman vanished into the thick green bracken above the trail.

Stefan let down his bow. "She had an ill-favored look," he said, pale-faced.

"Let's go before she comes back," Nail said, heart pounding. He gathered his drawing supplies and satchel.

"She seemed to know you." Ava Shay was looking at him. "Who was she?"

"A Sør Sevier spy," Stefan offered. "An emissary of the White Prince, scouting our lands, I wager."

Nail was too haunted by long-forgotten dreams to say any different.

In life, as in war, more is lost when hope dies, than by a cold steel and slaughter.
—The Chivalric Illuminations of Raijael

CHAPTER FOUR

GAULT AULBREK

15TH DAY OF THE SHROUDED MOON, 999TH YEAR OF LAIJON
AELATHIA PLAINS, WYN DARRÈ

Gault Aulbrek had walked among the dead for so many years he had grown hardened to the horror. The enemy blood that coated his chain mail had also splattered his face. He could feel it stiffening on his bald head in the frigid air.

As his gaze ranged over the landscape, dusk leached daylight from the foggy air, adding a measure of unwanted difficulty to his search for the body of the rival Wyn Darrè king. Gault led his white destrier, Spirit, by the reins, the stallion's dark eyes wide and aflame. In the sullen mist that hung over the battle, the ground was boggy with horse entrails, vomit, and blood. And the stench was gathering strength. No Wyn Darrè fighter had escaped the massacre this time. Even those who attempted surrender had been slaughtered without mercy. Over five thousand Wyn Darrè knights and half as many warhorses were strewn across the Aelathia Plains.

What few still moaned, Gault silenced with his sword.

He considered himself a hard man born of a harsh and lonely land. Still, his body begged for respite. How long ago was it he could run like a silver-wolf and scarcely feel his heart race? Perhaps not since before he last saw his stepdaughter, Krista. Maybe not even since before her mother, Avril, had died. *Where is that hard-earned stamina I once possessed?* Gone with his youth, he reckoned. After years of endless soldiering, it was a wonder he could walk at all. *And I daresay I've done more killing than most.* But to be so bone-weary and tired, now, after his lord's greatest triumph, was a disgrace.

Gault was one of the five Knights Archaic of Sør Sevier. A vaulted member of the Angel Prince's personal guard. Weakness was not an option.

As he and Spirit picked their way through the corpse-strewn gauntlet of blood-splashed boulders, through the leaning thickets of shattered spear and halberd shafts, Gault focused on the faces of the dead. A stick-thin boy scarcely old enough to wield a weapon lay legless in the mud. A grizzled Wyn Darrè veteran listed awkward and broken against the split belly of his roan destrier, beard befouled with grime, helm cocked sideways over bulging dead eyes, rusted links of a chain still wrapped around his neck. Evidence of one of the many lonely struggles that had played out in this swarming morass of screaming humanity, this crazed havoc of slash and parry. The ground was a-littered with the drift and crimson carnage of a human storm. Amongst this stillness and destruction, Gault and Spirit searched for the enemy king.

They made their way up a grassy slope toward a patch of yellow atop a standing-stone, both man and horse wary of the treacherous footing. The blood-soaked ground was slicker even than wet clay. The standing-stone, its lichen-covered carvings weathered and crumbling, was shoulder high. A yellow Wyn Darrè banner with a black serpent crest was draped over it, damp to the touch. When Gault stepped around the stone, he let go Spirit's reins. He had found the adversary the Angel Prince had tracked these last five years.

Torrence Raybourne, king of Wyn Darrè, lay on his back, legs crushed beneath the bulk of his dead warhorse. One arm twisted awkwardly. The splintered bone, showing through a joint in his armor, was shockingly white against the stain of war. Clutched in Torrence's gauntleted fist was the hilt of a broken sword. His other hand, smeared with blood, gripped the tattered corner of the yellow banner. An ox-horned helm, burnished bronze with intricate gold and silver inlays, rested in the grass near his head. It sparkled despite the surrounding fog.

Something about the helm struck Gault as odd. It was the two horns sprouting from it. Not oxen at all, but something else entirely, something . . . unrecognizable.

The king's eyes were closed, face blackened with blood. Many Sør Sevier barb-tipped arrows and crossbow bolts lay scattered around his body. Two thick quarrels jutted from the ridged steel cuirass over his sternum; two more pierced the ring mail covering his stomach. Gault turned and yelled for his prince.

Aeros Raijael, scarcely visible in the fog and searching the battlefield not more than a hundred paces away, came running. His white cloak billowed behind, revealing a sheathed longsword at his belt, holding the blue shimmering blade of Raijael lineage named Sky Reaver. So fine was the pearl-colored chain mail of the Angel Prince that it rippled like water as he ran. There was not a spot of blood upon him.

As his prince approached, apprehension gnawed at Gault. The vague, unsettling feeling struck him more frequently now than it used to, and only around Aeros. In Wyn Darrè and Gul Kana, they called Aeros the White Prince. It was meant as an insult. But in Sør Sevier, he was the Angel Prince—for he was King Aevrett's son, the heir of Raijael.

Upon Aeros' arrival, Gault sheathed his sword, bent his knee, and bowed to his lord. The Angel Prince was only twenty-eight, ten years younger than Gault. He always appeared ghostlike, with bright blond locks of shoulder-length hair, skin as pale as a walrus tusk, and bloodshot eyes with irises and pupils as black as obsidian.

"You've a knack for sniffing out fallen kings," the Angel Prince said, motioning for him to stand. Indeed, Gault had also found King Borden Bronachell of Gul Kana buried amid the carnage after the Battle of Oksana.

Aeros bent down and snapped the yellow banner from King Torrence's clenched fist. "He must have it with him," he said, pulling at Torrence's ribbed steel cuirass and the boiled-leather vestments and ring mail underneath. But the armor was battened down, effectively nailed to the king's body by stout quarrels. "Help me pull him from under his horse."

Before Gault could move to help, the king of Wyn Darrè sucked in a deep gasp of air. Frothy blood welled from his mouth. The Angel Prince grabbed the king by the shoulders. "Where is it?" Aeros shook him. Torrence stared blankly up into the fog. "Where is it, you goddess-worshipping fool?" Aeros latched onto one of the quarrels lodged in the king's sternum. "Speak, damn you."

Torrence reached out with his uninjured arm and grabbed Aeros' wrist with a strength seeming impossible in one so near death. "You killed them, my wife . . . the daughter I'd"—blood bubbled between his lips—"promised to King Jovan."

"Karowyn was as ugly as you." Aeros jerked away from the man's grip. "I did Jovan a favor ending her life. Now where is *it*?"

"It will do you no good," Torrence choked. "A useless trinket . . . nothing more."

"Then where is *he*?" Aeros demanded. "The boy your brother *stole* from us?"

"A ghost you chase, that one. You don't even know what you've brought upon yourself." Torrence's voice trailed off. "You will never destroy . . . the Brethren . . . of Mia." A bloody wet hiss escaped the king's throat, and his eyes rolled up.

"He may not know where the boy is." Aeros stood. "But he has *it* with him."

The Angel Prince bent over the king's dead warhorse, rummaging through the leather saddlebag, throwing the king's possessions to the ground with a barely suppressed hunger. Finally Aeros pulled forth his prize—a smallish object, wrapped in black silk.

"A distrustful lot, the Brethren of Mia," Aeros said to Gault. "Torrence didn't even trust it with his own Wyn Darrè countrymen who fought and died at his side. He'd sooner place his faith in goddess-worshipping traitors and demented dwarves."

Aeros slowly unfolded the cloth. Buried within was a green stone of curious make. It was somewhat flat and oval with polished round edges. It rested graceful and perfect in his hand. By some trick of light, smoky waves of changing green color passed over the stone's smooth surface, and its translucent innards appeared to dance and glow.

"Tell no one of this, Gault." With that, Aeros Raijael covered the stone with the black silk and slipped it into the folds of his cloak. He picked up Torrence's horned helm, cradled it in the crook of his right arm, and walked past Gault's stallion and into the fog.

Gault was left alone among the dead. He stared into the swirl of vapor beyond his stallion where the prince had disappeared, and tried to catch his breath, not even aware he had been holding it in. *The stone's brilliant radiance . . . that was no trick of light!* After all, the world around him was shrouded in an ever-darkening mist. But the stone had *glowed. The Chivalric Illuminations* spoke sparingly of the stones, vague hints that they were cursed, but that they—along with the weapons of the Five Warrior Angels—would find their way into the hands of the last heir of Raijael before Fiery Absolution. *And the helm! Could it be? Lonesome Crown!*

Gault hearkened back to his youth. Born into royalty, he'd had a blessed childhood, for a time. As a youngster, he had imagined myth and legend were part of his destiny. Whereas most in the Five Isles believed the angel stones had been translated into heaven at the time of Laijon's death, Gault's mother, Princess Evalyn Van Hester of Saint Only, had taught him different. Before her marriage to Agus Aulbrek, lord of the Sør Sevier Nordland Highlands, Gault's mother had lived on the isle of Adin Wyte among the worshippers of Mother Mia, a religious faction who believed the five angel stones still existed. Before her death, Gault's mother had told him stories of the angel stones and their powers. Daydreams of quests to find lost stones had filled Gault's head as a boy.

He was born in Stone Loring of the Sør Sevier Nordland Highlands in 961. Ten years after his birth, after a series of savage winters, the great Spyke famine struck, and the landscape of his childhood soon became a hollow and haunted place. The countryside was so crushed with cold and starvation it was said that in places such as Rwn and Tumult, once the sheep, cattle, and horses were gone, some women cooked their own babies, scooped the steaming vitals from their bellies, and ate. After that, Adin Wyte raiders continually attacked and pillaged the northeastern shores of Sør Sevier. Most claimed it was the unholy union of Gault's parents, Agus, a believer in Raijael, and Evalyn, a worshipper of Mia, that had brought on the famine and merciless Adin Wyte attacks.

During that time, myth and legend seemed to wither away for Gault. Within the span of three short years, his entire family was dead. Hunger took his three younger sisters. Assassins claimed his parents. At the tender age of fourteen he was left completely alone. But over the years, Gault had rid himself of what youthful tenderness assailed him.

Now, here he was, standing triumphant on the Aelathia Plains, a mere few miles from the five famed Laijon Towers, on this, the last battlefield for Wyn Darrè. His homeland, Sør Sevier, had finally retaken another one of the lands stolen from her so long ago, conquered another one of the kingdoms that had plagued the northeastern shores of Sør Sevier with continuous, vicious raids for ages.

"And what was that all about?"

In one fluid motion Gault pulled his sword, whirled, ready.

It was Enna Spades. She sat high and regal astride her own white stallion, Slaughter. Cursing himself for woolgathering, Gault sheathed his blade and looked down at King Torrence and the crossbow bolts bristling from his body.

"Well, Gault, have you no tongue?" Spades wore a silver cuirass over a long tunic of sparkling chain mail, and leather greaves also studded with silver. The dark blue cloak and pure white stallion she rode marked her, like Gault, as one of Aeros' five Knights Archaic. A wooden crossbow and a quiver of quarrels were strapped to her back. Her battle helm dangled from her left hand, and she gripped a bloodied longsword in her right. Spades was a tall, thin woman whose flowing hair hung in damp red curls around her face and shoulders. Her ivory skin bore a dusting of freckles about her straight nose and high cheekbones. Though she had fooled many a foe with her innocent looks, Spades was a deadly warrior.

She now held her head high and proud as if she were looking down her nose at Gault. "Are you like the Bloodwood?" she asked, her voice filled with contempt. "Has our Angel Prince taken you into his secret councils?"

Gault felt himself grow rigid. He didn't want to be goaded by her now, or reminded of the Bloodwood. He remained silent under her withering stare.

Spades looked past him to Torrence. "Or perhaps the dying Wyn Darrè king keeps council with our blessed Lord Aeros." She planted her helm on the pommel of Slaughter's saddle and dismounted, sheathing her sword. She drifted toward the king's dead warhorse and, finding the saddlebag, discovered its emptiness and the scattered contents strewn about. "Someone's already been at this." She tossed the bag casually aside, eyeing Gault as she reached down and pulled one of the quarrels from the belly of the king.

"This could very well be mine," she said, flipping chunks of flesh from the bolt's barbed tip. "Bears a certain familiarity. Their fickle flight in battle. Could strike anyone." She yanked all the quarrels from the king's midsection save one lodged in his sternum, which broke off in her hand. "A shame." Her gaze slid from the king to Gault. "I believe Lady Death has finally taken another of her followers." She swiped the ropy-red flesh from the quarrels, keeping her eyes fixed on Gault. She tucked the bolts into her own saddlebag and remounted Slaughter. "Shall we make a deal, Gault?"

He remained quiet, stoic, as she took up the reins of her charger. "I'll let you into my tent again," she said, "if you tell me what Aeros found in that saddlebag."

Continuing his blank stare, Gault refused to show any trace of emotion. "I care little for your deals, your *games*. They always end poorly."

Spades glowered down on him a moment, then whirled her mount. Gault wasn't cold, but he shivered as he watched her ride away. Sometimes the flinty look in her eyes could freeze his blood. He watched as Spades pulled a copper coin—a trinket she kept with her always—from her leather greaves. She flipped the coin up, caught it, then made it dance lithely between her gloved fingers. Before she disappeared into the gloomy mist, Gault saw her turn in her saddle and throw him a coy, curling little smile.

Somewhere in the distance came the lone shriek of a crow. Gault's gaze followed a few lazy flakes of snow as they floated to the ground, melting as they landed gently on the dead king at his feet. Gault dipped his head to the rising wind. He blinked against snow that now blew into his eyes, took Spirit by the reins, and followed Spades.

His mind was consumed by thoughts of a small green stone.

Soon men found that others dwelt upon the Five Isles: half-men, stout and hardy;
fey creatures, cunning and cruel; oghul and merfolk, monsters of both land and sea,
ferocious and bloodthirsty. But 'twas the tremor of the winged demons' fiery cry
that rang like a hammered anvil upon the Five Isles. Primeval they ruled the skies,
flame and power wreathed in iniquity. Man could naught but flounder before them.
—THE WAY AND TRUTH OF LAIJON

CHAPTER FIVE

TALA BRONACHELL

15TH DAY OF THE SHROUDED MOON, 999TH YEAR OF LAIJON

AMADON, GUL KANA

Tala Bronachell and Lawri Le Graven stole through the silence that shrouded the forgotten corridor of Amadon Castle. The passage was hung with tapestries, decorative shields, and crossed swords. Empty sconces hung high on the walls. Glowing light warped through a stained-glass window far above, and from it, a web of color danced on the floor. Swathed in soft leather boots, their feet made scarcely a sound as they ran, hair rippling behind. Tala, sixteen, had long straight locks of midnight. Lawri, seventeen, was tawny-haired with sharp bangs that grazed her brows. Both wore tunics over black silken shirts and brown woolen leggings.

They slid to a stop at the end of the hall under the last velvet tapestry. Tala brushed strands of hair from her face and pulled a small dagger from her leather belt. Its jeweled hilt was bone-thin and fit snug in her fingers. "No danger here. I've this to keep me safe." She flipped the dagger up. It spun. She snatched it out of the air by the hilt and slipped it smoothly back into her belt—a trick the dwarf, Roguemoore, had taught her.

"You'll cut your fingers with that," Lawri said. When she and her cousin were little girls, Lawri had always been overly protective. But now that they were older, Tala was taking more of a leadership role in the friendship. She wondered if it was because she was sister to the king that Lawri allowed it. Growing up, Lawri had organized their childish games and wanderings into the castle's "secret ways." Now it was Tala's turn, and she had a mind to turn their wanderings into *actual* adventures—like her older sister, Jondralyn, might do.

Many hallways now separated them from Dame Mairgrid and the king's chamberlain, Ser Landon Galloway. Tala had dismissed her tutor, Mairgrid, then merely walked out her chamber door, informing Galloway and the two Silver Guards that she and Lawri were off to visit her older sister, Jondralyn, whose chamber was just down the hall. But instead of entering Jondralyn's room, the two girls had continued on down the corridor. And the sleepy guards, ever apathetic at their stations, hadn't noticed a thing. Tala felt a pang of guilt knowing that Galloway and the guards would come under harsh discipline when the captain of the Silver Guard, Ser Lars Castlegrail, discovered they had lost sight of both the princess *and* her royal cousin.

Tala drew aside the corner of the heavy gilt-worked tapestry that stretched from ceiling to floor. "A new passage Lindholf told me about."

Behind the tapestry was solid block and mortar but for one missing stone roughly a foot and a half high and two wide, a floor-level opening just big enough for a person to crawl into. Tala lay on her stomach and wiggled her head and shoulders into the hole until her upper body was beyond the wall, then pulled her way through. Lawri squirmed into the hole too, and the corner of the tapestry fell back into place behind her, hiding all trace of their passage. The small chamber they'd entered was scarcely big enough for two. "A dead end," Lawri said, "an empty room leading no place."

Lawri had dark eyes that held an innocence Tala found charming. Her cousin was stunningly beautiful, with straw-colored hair that almost appeared to glow in the narrow beam of sunlight raining down from a crack up high. Dust sparkled in that tiny ray. There were many cracks in the stone walls around them, cracks where ivy crept in. Tala imagined the vines coming alive to strangle her and burrow into her skin. She shuddered, then grinned. *The thoughts that sometimes come a-creeping into my head.*

"Lindholf told me of a secret latch he and Glade found last year." Tala felt along the stone wall until she located the outline of a wooden door just above her own head. She found the bottom corner of the door, pulled forth her dagger, and slipped the blade into the crack. Fishing around with the blade, she heard a click and then the rasp of a hinge, and the door pushed inward. She pulled herself up and into the opening. A short, narrow corridor appeared before her with a ladder at its far end. "There's better light up here," she called back to Lawri.

Soon her cousin was up and into the new passage too, a worried grin on her face. "Aren't we getting a little old for this?" Lawri asked. "Sneaking about the castle with Lindholf and Glade was fun when we were children. It seems silly now."

"It's never silly," Tala said, bothered by her cousin's attitude. After all, there were many secret things to be discovered whilst sneaking about. Like when she'd spied on her sister one recent evening as Jondralyn had squirreled away a folded parchment within which was a hidden sapphire necklace behind a removable panel built into the wall behind her bookshelf. *Third book to the left on the top shelf, to be exact!* Later Tala had snuck into Jon's room, admired the glittering necklace, and read the scroll—nonsense their late father had written about something called the Brethren.

Exploring the hidden passages of Amadon Castle kept Tala from growing bored with life as the pampered youngest daughter of the late king, Borden Bronachell. After all, the drudgery of leisurely castle life under the cumbersome tutelage of Dame Mairgrid could grow unimaginably tiresome. Adventuring was the only time she could put aside the facade of the highborn princess everyone expected her to be. In fact, the only moments in life Tala felt normal were those precious few she'd spent with her older twin cousins, Lawri and Lindholf Le Graven. But it seemed lately all Lawri was concerned with was what young noble had been given what lands and title or what dashing young prince had been newly knighted. Her father was Lord Lott Le Graven of Eskander. Her mother, Mona, was Tala's aunt—sister to Tala's late mother, Queen Alana Bronachell. The Le Graven family and their Lion Court had journeyed from Eskander to enjoy the coming Mourning Moon festivities and watch Lindholf perform his Ember Lighting Rites in the Royal Cathedral, an honor only bestowed upon the sons of royalty. Other young men performed their Ember Lighting Rites in their local chapels. Lawri and Lindholf weren't the only set of twins in the Le Graven family—there were also twelve-year-olds Lorhand and Lilith.

"Let's go," Tala said, beckoning. The two of them crossed the length of the corridor. Pink light began to filter in at regular intervals. Wind whistled through arrow slits in the walls. Tala paused at one of the slender openings and peered through. It took a moment for her eyes to adjust to the brightness of the outside light, but once she did, beyond the pigeons perched on the battlements below, she could see the panorama of the city.

Amadon—the largest city in Gul Kana—spread out before Tala as far as her eyes could see. The rotund Royal Cathedral, shaped like a crown, the sanctuary where the Blessed Mother Mia was buried, dominated the skyline. Next to the Royal Cathedral was the Temple of the Laijon Statue, equally as tall. The cathedral and temple were the physical monuments of the great Laijon and the Blessed Mother Mia. Pilgrims from the breadth of Gul Kana flocked to worship at these two massive edifices. Beyond the crenellated bastions marking the inner wall of the old city lay the exquisite, ethereal Hall of the Dayknights and the circular, columned gladiator arena. Even farther out, like a barely visible kiss of green, lay the Hallowed Grove, a patch of sacred forest on the outskirts of the city, where the thousand-year-old Atonement Tree still stood. Beyond that was the marbled mound that was the slave quarry at Riven Rock.

Amadon's population had swelled in recent days. Royalty from all corners of Gul Kana had flocked to the city, along with free-men, peasants, and farmers. All had come to partake in the three-week gladiator spectacle and annual Mourning Moon Celebrations. A myriad of tents had been pitched in the outskirts of the city to accommodate the eager throngs.

Tala looked down upon the warren of crooked and cobbled build-ings and streets with their narrow winding pathways with two parts revulsion and two parts excitement. The River Vallè wove a sluggish pale path through the center of Amadon. The distant barks of a dog echoed off stone walls, mixing with the sounds of vendors hawk-ing their products. Tala could imagine the teeming masses filling the marketplaces. Sailors, dwarves, oghuls, urchins, bloodletters, and thieves milled through it all. Tala both loved and hated her city, as she both loved and hated the massive castle she called home.

Completely engulfing what were once the steep cliffs of Mount Albion, high above the mouth of the River Vallè overlooking Memory Bay, was the grandest structure in all of Gul Kana: Amadon Castle. It brooded over the city like an ominous storm cloud. Tala had lived her entire life within its walls. Skirted by a wind-tattered patchwork of outer buildings and hundreds of add-on structures, the castle boasted a daunting legion of crenellated battlements, spires, towers, baileys, courtyards, palisades, barbicans, and connecting causeways all hewn of the grayish-black lava stone of Mount Albion and dotted with flags of silver and black. The sun was going down, and the castle's many spires stood rose-tinted against the cloudless sky. There was Blue Sword, Black Spear, and Confessor Tower, along with Martin's Spire, Sansom Spire, and a dozen or so more named after dead grand vicars: Coye, Styne, Rion, Dairehne, Swensong, Cember, and the like.

A shaft of cool air brushed Tala's face, and she pulled away from the opening.

They moved on, passing through another corridor, down twisting stairs, and into a red, high-ceilinged, spacious room lined with gritty wooden benches and a stone altar in the shape of a cross smack in the center. The altar frightened Tala. High on the near wall was a large stained-glass window, each pane such a deep shade of red it cast a gloomy, scarlet pall over everything. Along the far wall hung a tapestry, graced with a beautifully stitched likeness of the Blessed Mother Mia. This ruby-hazed room looked big enough to hold near twenty people, yet none of the furniture appeared to have been used in years. Its white-plastered walls were so discolored and streaked by smoke they were almost black. There were ashes and fragments of bone strewn around the base of the cross-shaped altar. Its surface was stained with a dark substance. Dried rivulets of blackness ran down the altar's sides, as if someone had poured tar over it. *Or blood.* Tala shuddered.

"Let's go back," Lawri said.

Tala's gaze roamed back to the tapestry of Mother Mia. She recalled her father saying the Raijael worshippers of Sør Sevier never referred to Mia by name, but called her Lady Death. Tala did not like to think too long on things her father had taught her. He'd hurt her deeply going off to Wyn Darrè to fight against Sør Sevier and never returning. She had loved him more than anything, and he had almost destroyed her in dying.

She continued searching the room. Rags and furs were jammed

into the many cracks lining the far wall to keep out the wind. Two wood-plank doors were on the right. Neither was locked. Both doors yielded easily and, with a creak of rusty hinges, opened. Behind both doors were stairs, one set leading up, the other down.

"Upward, I say." Tala climbed the stairs. Lawri followed.

They soon found themselves in a long, peculiar corridor. The ceiling was lost in darkness, the floor was flat. To their right a rough stone wall rose straight up into black nothingness. But to their left, the wall was smooth and arced outward away from them at an angle, also disappearing into darkness. Atop this curved wall was a system of counterforts and flying buttresses, like the roof of a grand cathedral. Row upon row of these buttresses receded away into the darkness. Blots of shadow dwelled in the angles and alcoves. There was a faint orange glow in the distance. Tala and Lawri proceeded. It was as if they walked along the edge of a cathedral roof now, only this cathedral was enclosed within the confines of the great Amadon Castle. Ahead, cracks in the sloping wall shot spears of yellow light upward as if lit with fire from underneath.

Tala heard voices coming from below and quickly realized where she was—above her father's study. She leaned over the curved wall until she lay flat against it, ear pressed to the cold stone. The voices were muffled. One was her older brother, the other her older sister. There was a stream of brighter light above, so she climbed. Once at eye level with the beam of light, Tala wedged her feet against a nearby buttress. Feeling safely perched on the curve of the wall, she peered through the crack.

The study below was large, windowless, stone floor worn smooth. Four pillars held up the arched roof, and each pillar carried a burning torch. Deep rugs lined the room's center. Iron double doors at one end were emblazoned with the royal crest: a silver tree. There was a stone hearth fireplace at the other end, crackling with flame. Weapons and armor were piled in one corner. From their crude workmanship,

Tala figured the weapons were oghul-made. The room's lofty, curved ceiling was adorned with intricate carvings above a maze of wooden rafters. Next time she was in the study, Tala would make it a point to look up and find the crack she peered through now.

"What can you see?" Lawri asked. Tala turned, shushing her cousin with a wave, then planted her eyes to the crack, watched, and listened.

"You don't understand the costly undertaking of a war in a distant land, Jon," said Tala's oldest brother, King Jovan Bronachell. Twenty-eight years old, he was wrapped in a fur-rimmed cloak fastened with a brooch of Vallè-worked silver. He wore decorative ring mail under the cloak, and his hair was thick waves of shoulder-length brown confined by a simple silver band about his head—the royal crown. Despite his relative youth, he was tall, imposing, and radiated power. When he spoke, the timbre of his voice was deep. "The time-consuming cares of palfrey and charger alike, the provisioning of an army of men and beast, the food, logistics? It's not the overnight picnic you imagine it."

Tala's older sister, Jondralyn, shook a sheaf of papers before Jovan. "Gul Kana should have stayed by Wyn Darrè. Instead you fled the battle five years ago after Father was killed, leaving Wyn Darrè to ruin and your betrothed to die at the hands of Aeros Raijael."

"Do not lay that cow's death at my feet, lest you forget your own betrothal. A gross blunder and misjudgment Father ever matched you with that thief and killer."

"I will *not* have you bring Squireck into this."

Jovan laughed hollowly. "If not for the White Prince's war, you'd be married to that thief for nearly ten years now, his traitorous little babies bouncing on your lap."

"And you'd be married to Karowyn Raybourne . . . eternal bliss for one like you, I'm sure."

Jovan's sharp brows narrowed at his sister. At twenty-five, Jondralyn Bronachell was nearly ten years older than Tala. Most deemed her the most beautiful woman in all the Five Isles. Four years ago, the mint in Avlonia had changed the image on its copper coin from the fabled Val Vallè princess, Arianna, to a likeness of Princess Jondralyn Bronachell of Amadon. Tala knew her older sister was a beauty. She was compared to Jon every day and in every way. Jondralyn, tall as any man, had long legs, a perfectly formed athletic body, full lips, and frosty blue eyes set beneath delicate brows. Her shoulder-length hair matched Tala's in color, but seemed more alive and lustrous. Jondralyn was dressed in a flowing blue, richly brocaded gown tied at the waist with a silver belt, a casual forest green cape thrown over one shoulder.

"I know you wish to act the crusader." Jovan made a crisp gesture at Jondralyn's outfit. "I know you wish to throw that gown aside and prance around the castle dressed like a man, Hawkwood teaching you sword fighting. It flies in the face of your Ember Gathering Rites. You're no warrior. You're not even fit to be a squire. You need to act more like a lady. Mother would be mortified. I've seen battle. A lady does not belong there."

"In Sør Sevier, women fight alongside the men, doubling the size of their armies. Hawkwood has trained many women to fight."

"Sør Sevier is full of crudeness and idolatry."

"Be that as it may, Sør Sevier is at our doorstep. You placed too much faith in the advice of Grand Vicar Denarius and that Vallè you keep council with."

"The Silver Throne keeps council with whom it chooses!" Jovan's voice thundered through the room. "I don't need my sister telling me how to govern my own kingdom."

Jondralyn threw the sheaf of papers at his feet. "There is growing unrest throughout your kingdom!" In that one act Tala saw the fire of their late mother, Alana Bronachell, in her sister. Queen Alana had died whilst birthing Ansel five years ago. Alana would argue politics with their father with the same fervor as Jondralyn argued with Jovan. "These are the letters from starving, war-ravaged, plague-ravaged villagers of Wyn Darrè. Hundreds more letters arrive on Roguemoore's doorstep every day. Letters from Agonmoore, Oldrisek, Morgandy. Everywhere Wyn Darrè people suffer, as Adin Wyte did before them. And now that the Laijon Towers are under final threat, our own country fears invasion. We've even reports of oghuls trying to hasten their own Hragna'Ar prophecy by raiding northland towns here in Gul Kana! Hragna'Ar! And you do nothing. We've naught but ill-trained landowners and barons out giving farm boys two years' training in naught but how to fight with rakes and shovels. The White Prince from the west. Hragna'Ar oghuls from the north. The oghuls live for their Hragna'Ar prophecies."

"The oghul raids are hearsay."

"We need to bolster our armies. We need real warriors. We need to forge weapons and armor. Lord's Point abbeys are overflowing with Wyn Darrè refugees—"

"We are in the last minutes of the eleventh hour before Absolution," Jovan cut her off. "The great and last battle will be fought in Gul Kana, as was prophesied in *The Way and Truth of Laijon*. Neither you nor Roguemoore can change the will of Laijon. There was nothing to be done in Adin Wyte, and there is nothing to be done in Wyn Darrè."

"Nothing!" Jondralyn snapped. "Fiery Absolution need not happen. The prophecies in *The Way and Truth of Laijon* are false."

"The dwarf brainwashes you with that kind of talk, as he did Squireck!"

"You could have fought off the White Prince on Wyn Darrè soil as Father willed. He gave aid to Adin Wyte and Wyn Darrè against those earliest Sør Sevier raids. You yourself fought alongside Father to defend Wyn Darrè's western shores against the initial Sør Sevier attack. Do you not remember your own two-year conscription to church and crown? Or have you now grown so complacent, so far removed from threat that you do not care? You could have beaten back Sør Sevier before they ever threatened our shores."

"We are sufficiently garrisoned," Jovan answered. "There are many who believe Wyn Darrè and Adin Wyte now pay the butcher's bill for the centuries of turmoil and death their pirates and raiders caused Sør Sevier. There are many who say Sør Sevier is merely taking back what it is owed. The wars and battles and back-and-forth between those three kingdoms have gone on for a thousand years. Gul Kana will endure until the time of Fiery Absolution. Once Father died, I was right not to further waste our armies in Adin Wyte or Wyn Darrè. Father once told me he wished all leaders of men could walk a battlefield and witness the horror of mutilated bodies and cries of the dying. Leif Chaparral and I did fight in Wyn Darrè—"

"You retreated from Wyn Darrè after Father's death."

"We should be rejoicing that Laijon's return is nigh. Adin Wyte and Wyn Darrè's ruin was foretold in *The Way and Truth of Laijon*."

"We could have staved off that ruin. Absolution need not happen."

"Do not speak against holy scripture. When Absolution comes, the Silver Throne will fight, and not a moment sooner. We will defend our own shores. 'Keep your swords honed,' wrote the Fourth Warrior Angel. Battle readiness has been built into the very fabric and culture of this land. Every village in Gul Kana is filled with men who have spent two years in training, preparing for the great and glorious day of Absolution. Tradition has sustained Gul Kana thus far."

"Those are the words of Grand Vicar Denarius," Jondralyn snarled. "He *wishes* for Fiery Absolution—"

"We all seek the return of Laijon!" The king spun away from Jondralyn, drawing his sword. He moved to the hearth and poked at the fire with it. Tala knew her brother would brook only so much from his siblings. He could be a miserable, pious, rigid king who distrusted everyone one minute—and affable, congenial, and taking advice from all the next. He was loath to discuss Aeros Raijael's war in Wyn Darrè, the death of their father, or Absolution. *The Way and Truth of Laijon* spoke of the war before the return of Laijon. It was prophesied that all armies of the Five Isles would gather in Amadon and engage in battle. The streets would run with blood and fire."

Jovan turned, glaring at Jondralyn. "Roguemoore has set you against me."

"He is my dearest friend, and one of your own high councillors."

"He is not your friend. You think he will make you part of his secret *brethren?* He keeps you in the dark on a great many things, Jon. He would have you believe the Brethren of Mia are all about defending Gul Kana. But there is more of the sinister to them than you know. He's already turned Squireck Van Hester against me. Because of that dwarf, I know not who to trust in my own court. In due course I'll have the Dayknights root every last one of the Brethren from their hidey-holes—"

"I've heard Denarius say much the same. Does he now speak for you?"

"We *all* swear fealty to Denarius! Even I, the king who sits the Silver Throne, am to heed his counsel above all others. Or did you forget your studies? Do you not attend worship service every Eighth Day? Or are you now buried too deep in the clutches of that dwarf and his goddess-worshipping cult?"

"The grand vicar just regurgitates the same worn-out platitudes of the vicars before him." Jondralyn sounded exasperated.

"Denarius believed Sør Sevier played a part in Mother's death when Ansel was born. Father believed it too. And now this foolish Brethren of Mia business lands your once-betrothed in prison. Squireck *murdered* one of the Quorum of Five Archbishops of Amadon because of Roguemoore's *lies.* The dwarf and his wretched *Moon Scrolls* have turned you against me. The Church of Laijon has clearly deemed *The Moon Scrolls of Mia* unholy and had them hidden in the vaults. Squireck stole them for Roguemoore and then murdered Archbishop Lucas. As if his father hasn't been humiliated enough having already been conquered by the White Prince. Squireck's crimes have plunged the entire kingdom of Adin Wyte into further shame. Or have you forgotten his sins? Have the dwarf and that Sør Sevier traitor, Hawkwood, clouded your mind so?"

"Squireck did *not* slay Archbishop Lucas as Denarius and the quorum of five would have you believe. He is a peaceful, innocent man, wrongfully imprisoned."

"I'm sure your heart just bleeds for him, now that he has chosen death in the arena. The dignity of a quick death by the noose would be far more than he deserves—"

Tala's foot slipped and she slid from her perch. She hit the floor hard, smacking the back side of her head against the opposite wall. "You okay?" Lawri whispered.

Tala rubbed her head. Talk of Fiery Absolution scared her. But to hear that Squireck Van Hester, the Prince of Saint Only, the fallen prince of a conquered country, the man once betrothed to Jondralyn when the two were but children, a man whom Tala adored like an older brother, had chosen the arena put a lump in her throat. Of all things, Tala hated the arena most. Squireck, though decent with a blade, was not gladiator material. She remembered herself at five years old, sitting on Squireck's lap, him eighteen, tall and lanky, entertaining her and Jondralyn with stories of Mannfrydd the dwarf jester. Such an innocent, simple, and happy young man Squireck had been, and that good-natured quality had followed him into adulthood. But that was before his kingdom had come under war. That was before he'd been convicted of murdering Archbishop Lucas. At the time it had been the most infamous crime in all the Five Isles. It was said that Squireck's father, King Edmon Guy Van Hester, conquered ruler of Adin Wyte, lord of Saint Only, was so overcome with grief over his son's crimes that he moped about the halls of Saint Only in rags and a broken crown, his throne abandoned to ruin, his Lancer Guard destroyed or scattered to the winds by Aeros Raijael's armies. So deranged with grief that he'd cast his family and advisers aside and now supped with curs and swine, lounging in his own filth at the foot of his empty throne. Rumor was, he'd professed that he'd rather have died at the hands of the Sør Sevier fighters than live under the shame of Squireck's murderous betrayal.

Tala's heart sank with the weight of knowing her family was fractured. Her older siblings hated each other—Jondralyn, increasingly full of honor and chivalry, tried to bridge the gap between them when she could, but Jovan trusted the grand vicar and quorum of five more than his own kin. Tala wished her parents were still alive for a few reasons: first, to bring their family back together; and second, to keep their country from crumbling under Jovan's rule. She knew Jovan's unshakable, rigid faith gave his character its hard, unforgiving side. He could be narrow-minded, stubborn, and uncompromising where religious principles were concerned—and because of it, he was losing control of his court to the grand vicar.

"Let's go," Lawri urged. "It's getting dark. Our path will not be as well lit."

Tala noticed her cousin's shoulders were covered in dust. "You're filthy." She brushed the back of Lawri's tunic, then brushed herself, too, and quickly realized something was missing. "I dropped my dagger." It was not at her belt.

"Leave it." Lawri turned, heading back the way they had come. "It's too dark."

"It was a gift from Roguemoore." Tala dropped to her hands and knees, crawling back to where she had slid from the sloping wall, carefully feeling along the floor. It was carpeted with dead bugs and who knew what else under her searching fingers, but she didn't want to leave the dagger behind. Finding it, she stood quickly, relieved. The dagger with its thin jeweled hilt felt snug and proper in her hand. "Here it is," she announced. But Lawri did not answer. "Lawri?" she called out for her cousin. Lawri was gone.

A chill wind blew across Tala's face, and she felt the hairs prickling at the nape of her neck. Either her mind was playing tricks on her or the shadows, a few paces beyond where she stood, now moved. "Is that you, Lawri?"

Something rustled softly, a movement in the dark.

"Lawri?" Tala kept her eyes fixed on the place where the shadow hovered, a clot of blackness, like a hole had been punched into the dark.

"Answer me, Lawri." Tala felt the menacing glare of unseen eyes, as if the darkness were taking solid form. Then next to her was a shapeless, shadowy blur. Tala twisted her slender body to avoid the phantom's clutch. Then it had her. Trembling in every limb, Tala tried to squirm away. But the shadow held her fast by the wrist.

"The secret ways of the castle are my lair." A voice of low and subtle tone issued forth, the sound neither male nor female, but soft and hissing. Tala thought about stabbing at the apparition with the dagger, yet fear gripped her. She could hear her own heavy breath as she struggled to free herself. "Lawri!" she cried out.

"Be still," whispered the shade, its tightening grip now painful. "My blade thirsts." The shadow pulled her close as if reading her thoughts. "Alas, killing you now would serve us not. So get from these passages, girl. Never venture here again."

Tala couldn't breathe. She could barely make out the outlines of the one who held her. The dark figure wore all black and a black hood. A wan beam of light crossed over the hood and brushed the figure's eyes, which glittered faintly like water shimmering under the moonlight. It seemed those two sullen slivers of light glinted with malice.

"Heed what I say." The voice was silky from under the hood. "A warning, this, and you won't feel it for some time, but I just stabbed you."

Tala felt leather armor scrape against her arm, and the shadow was gone like the wind through the leaves. She whirled and fled. She reached the stairs and careened down them, nearly falling, leaping two at a time, until she stumbled out into the spacious red room with the bloodstained altar and benches. The faint pink light of dusk spilled through the windows above, illuminating her cousin's golden hair at the opposite end of the room.

"What kept you?" Lawri asked as Tala drew near. "I thought you were behind me—" Her cousin's face turned ashen. "Blessed Mother, Tala, you're bleeding!"

Tala looked. Her tunic and shirt were blood-soaked.

And thick redness welled from a small hole in her chest just above her heart.

For the Time of the Fiery Demons was a dark time, full of strife and much peril. It is thus commanded that from this moment henceforth, their true name shall never be uttered by the mouth of man. Nor shall any likeness of them be painted or carved. They are to be forever known as the Nameless Beasts of the Underworld. And any who bear the Mark of the Beast upon their flesh are especially cursed.
—THE WAY AND TRUTH OF LAIJON

CHAPTER SIX
TALA BRONACHELL

15TH DAY OF THE SHROUDED MOON, 999TH YEAR OF LAIJON
AMADON, GUL KANA

The man dropped. The rope snapped. *Squireck Van Hester, the Prince of Saint Only, executed!* Tala jolted awake to a profound sensation of horror and dread. She jerked up in bed, heart thundering, dark memories returning in a mad rush.

It seemed all hope and happiness were now stanched by the vivid recollection of a dark-cloaked figure and the all-too-real wound in her chest. *Blood and death everywhere!* A haunting panic had rendered her all but helpless since she was stabbed in the secret ways. She searched with trembling fingers for the small scab newly formed above her breast. Her heart quickened at the discomfort she felt of being watched—always watched.

She searched the darkness of her chamber. A space between the heavy curtains let in a slice of moonlight. She could just make out the familiar shapes of the room and the vague contours of her dresser, chairs, and chest, along with the form of her cousin, Lawri, curled on the divan near the door. A giant stone hearth was built into the far wall. Double doors, barred and latched securely, were at the near wall. Two Silver Guards were always posted beyond those thick wooden barriers. But they were of little comfort.

She kicked the covers from her bed and padded barefoot across the cold stone. She felt naked in her sleeping garment, a light, loose-fitting pullover shift of dyed silk. But she feared changing clothes. She might wake Lawri in the process. Carefully opening the chest near her desk, she pulled out a length of twine along with the thin dagger Roguemoore had given her. She tied the twine around her waist and fitted the dagger snugly into it. She closed the lid of the chest and snatched the wooden stool from her desk, crossed the room quietly, and placed it directly into the cold stone hearth. The floor of the hearth was swept clean of soot. A fire hadn't been lit in the fireplace in her memory. Her quarters, so near the center of the castle, stayed warm, even in the harshest winters.

She stood atop the stool and felt inside the chimney with her hands, searching for the bottom rung of the ladder hidden there. Once firmly grasping the iron rung, Tala quietly pulled herself up. Hanging, she felt around with her toes until she located the under-side of the stool's round seat. Once she felt the tops of her feet were secure enough under the wooden seat, she lifted the stool, bent her legs at the knees, swung back, and flipped the stool onto her bed. The stool was not heavy and landed softly on the thick quilts.

Flinging the stool to the bed with her feet was a move Tala had performed a hundred times. It was a risk leaving the stool so obviously placed within the hearth. Anybody—in particular Dame Mairgrid —who came calling might find the stool, which would lead to the ladder, which would lead to the discovery of the passageway that joined with the many secret warrens crisscrossing Amadon

Castle. And Tala didn't want that; this passage through the hearth was her only escape from her chamber.

As she climbed, Tala passed several dark openings in the wall behind her, one a flue, the others tunnels leading to more hidden passages. As she ventured farther, the sounds of mice scurrying about the dark holes sent shivers racing up her spine. She imagined a shadowy figure, wicked blade ready to strike, lurking in every alcove.

When Tala reached the thirty-second rung, she felt with her hand along the wall to her left. There was a wooden door, closed and securely latched. With a flick of her fingers, it was easily unlocked. The small door swung inward and she slithered through, letting it swing shut behind her. Blackness surrounded her on every side now. Still, she crawled forward, counting the rough stone tiles beneath her. When she reached the twentieth tile, she dug her fingers into the cracks, lifted up the tile, and slid it aside. Underneath was another trapdoor. Tala lifted it up and over, its rusty hinges faintly squealing. The dagger was still pressed tightly against her hip, and at the moment, it felt of little use against whatever dangers lurked in these dark warrens. Tala could see nothing down the new hole, yet she could feel its yawning presence. But she knew from years of experience that this ladder would eventually empty her into the stone hearth located in the bedchamber her older cousin, Lindholf, used when the Le Gravens came visiting. Fishing with her toes, she felt for the comforting cold iron rung. Finding it, she descended. Once at the bottom, she wiggled free of the fireplace and stepped into her cousin's room, silken nightgown a complete dirty ruin.

"That was the loudest clatter I've ever heard." Lindholf's face peered from under his bedcovers, lit candle on the wall behind him.

Tala crossed the room and sat on the end of his bed. He slid his feet aside, making room for her. "Why are you sneaking around so late?" He wore a bright red sleeping gown and a red cap with a white tassel.

"You look foolish," she giggled.

"It's warm for nighttime," he said, tossing the sleeping cap to the floor. "No one can see me anyhow, unless the Silver Guards step in, which they might, after hearing you knocking about so." He looked to the double doors of the bedchamber. "Let's hope they don't summon Dame Mairgrid. I'd be loath to answer to that old crone now."

Lindholf had a way of always appearing worried. He only partially had the look of his twin sister. Lawri was pretty and graceful, Lindholf awkwardly thin and gangly. Even the other set of Le Graven twins, twelve-year-olds Lorhand and Lilith, were blossoming into unbearably cute teenagers. Not Lindholf, though: he had a head of short blond curls and a terribly sunken, deformed face. The deformities were the result of severe burns he had suffered as a baby. The scarred flesh covered one cheek up to his forehead and down his neck and had mangled both of his ears. Half the flesh on his face was stiff and dead, the skin cracked, flaking, mottled purple and yellow.

"From now on, do not go into the secret ways," Tala whispered. "They are no longer safe. And do not let Glade talk you into any sneaking around when he gets here. I know you've planned many adventures for when he arrives. But I don't think it wise."

"Why?"

Tala pulled the neckline of her silken shift aside, revealing the tiny dark scab just above her breast. "I was stabbed."

"Stabbed?" He reached out and touched the wound, worry in his voice, fingers cold against her skin. "How so?"

"I was in that passageway you told me about near the western wall between the armory and the abandoned rookery, just above the queen's pantry. I met a cloaked stranger there who ordered me to stay out of the passages, then stabbed me as a warning. I fear some sort of witchcraft was used. I never felt the blade. Your sister was with me. She saw nothing. I made up a story about falling on a nail. I don't think she believed me."

"Did you see his face, this person?"

"No." Goose bumps tickled her flesh as she tried to recall anything of the dark stranger. "I know nothing of the cloaked person or how to find him again."

"You should not have gone off a-wandering without me or Glade." Lindholf was clearly shaken. "We should tell Jovan."

"And have him question why I am sneaking about?" Tala asked.

"He could have the Dayknights hunt for this cloaked fellow."

Tala shook her head. "No. He'll just have the Dayknights and Silver Guard watch me more closely. And that's the last thing I want."

"Probably so."

"There's something else I need to tell you. I heard Jondralyn and Jovan speaking about Squireck Van Hester. He's chosen the arena."

"*Arena?*" Horror washed over Lindholf's face. "Squireck has some training, but not the stomach to kill as the gladiators do. He is like me, but twice as tall and frail. I fear he will die horribly, begging in the end."

"I pray Jovan will put a stop to it," Tala said. She stood and moved toward the hearth, feeling the tears well in her eyes. "I cannot bear the thought of watching him be stabbed or, worse, dismembered or beheaded." She hadn't seen Squireck Van Hester since he had been imprisoned, but she wanted to go to him now and pray at his feet, pray that Laijon spare him this fate. But he was being kept in the dungeons of Purgatory.

"Just stay out of the secret ways," she said. "I beg you. This is the last I'm using them. Ever."

† † † † †

As she lay comfortably in bed, moonlight from the window fading, Tala felt at peace. Warning Lindholf of the danger in the secret ways had lifted a load from her mind. Relaxed now, she felt sleep overtake her. But just before she dozed into sweet oblivion, an awful thought struck her and she shot up in bed. Her eyes flew open, sweeping the room. *How could I have missed it?*

She'd come straight down the chimney and crawled right into bed, wrapping herself snug in her blankets, welcoming the comfort. Yet in her haste to curl up under the warm covers, she had overlooked one gigantic detail. *The stool!*

When her frantic eyes fell upon the stool, cold reality struck. Her blood froze and everything in the room came into clear focus. Wide awake, heart pounding, Tala could only stare at the wooden stool as it now sat smack in front of her desk.

She hadn't put it there.

And there was a small slip of white parchment pinned to the center of the stool's round seat by a thin black dagger. *Lawri!* Tala sprang from her bed. Her older cousin was still on the divan, lying in the same position as when Tala had left her. Dread filled Tala's heart. "Wake up!" She shook her cousin.

"What is it?" Lawri moaned sleepily, yawning and rubbing at her eyes as she sat up, her golden hair tousled. Tala breathed deeply, relieved that Lawri was alive. She crossed the room, lit a candle, then held it over the stool with the dagger sticking from it. "What's that?" Lawri asked, still not quite awake yet

Tala focused on the dagger. She dared not touch it. Yet as she leaned down to study the thin blade, she couldn't help but read what was written on the parchment. The ink was black as night, the writing small, yet beautifully executed.

> *I warned you once. Stay out of the secret ways. If I have to warn you again, you will surely die. I stabbed your cousin with this very knife. She will not feel the pain for some time. But feel it she will. This is your last warning.*

Tala whirled and stared at Lawri. A small spot of blood welled from under her cousin's nightshirt, just above her heart. Lawri followed Tala's gaze and clutched her hand to her own bloody chest, dark eyes wide with confusion and panic. Tala's eyes flew back to the note. The ink slowly faded, then was gone entirely. She flew to the doors and threw them open, startling the two Silver Guards posted outside.

"Fetch Jondralyn immediately!" she shouted.

"This time of night," one of the guards chuckled, "I think not. But I will get that old bat Mairgrid. She'll set you straight."

"Get Jondralyn!" Tala screamed. "Or I'll have your head! I swear it!"

† † † † †

"It's definitely Bloodwood." A worried look was set into the deep creases of Roguemoore's leathery face as he examined the dagger stuck in the stool. He ran short, thick fingers through his grizzled beard. "It's coated with some sort of numbing agent—most likely lavender deje. A Bloodwood never parts with his blades. I fear this dagger is a dire message indeed. Meant for who, though?"

The dwarf pulled the blade from the stool and held it up to the candle flame. It looked to be one single-molded piece of polished, hewn glass, black as the underworld and twice as scary. Candlelight didn't even flicker in its inky blade; its very surface seemed to swallow all light. He set the blade on the stool again and looked at Jondralyn.

Tala's older sister, even having just been woken in the middle of the night, with mussed-up hair, wearing naught but a maroon jacket over her nightclothes, looked radiant in the dim candlelight. Tala, always self-conscious around Jondralyn, straightened her own dirty nightshift, grabbed a comb, and nervously began brushing her own hair.

"You were smart not to touch it, Tala," the dwarf said. With his beard, squat and stout stature, and sunken-eyed face, Roguemoore always reminded Tala of an angry boar. Yet despite his rough and coarse look, the dwarf was one of the few ambassadors in Jovan's court who Tala even remotely liked.

"Was also smart to call for your sister, and not Jovan." Roguemoore turned and examined the wound above Lawri's heart. Tala's older cousin held the neckline of her nightshirt low enough for the dwarf to examine the wound.

"What's a Bloodwood?" Tala asked.

"The most deadly of creatures," Roguemoore answered gravely. "A trained assassin from Sør Sevier. That we've one lurking about the castle amuses me not."

"Someone from Sør Sevier tried to assassinate me?" Lawri looked horrified.

"Had a Bloodwood wanted you dead, you would be dead. Your wound is meant as a message. This assassin wants us to know of his presence. Hawkwood could answer many questions for us. I will speak to him later about this."

"What do we do?" Tala asked. "How do we get rid of this assassin?"

"We can't," the dwarf answered. "I've only ever known one man who could kill a Bloodwood." He reached for the slip of paper previously pinned to the stool by the assassin's dagger. The paper was blank now, useless, its writing completely faded.

The dwarf pulled forth a small round tin from his pouch, opened it, dipped his fingers into the fine black powder within, then rubbed his fingers over the blank slip of paper. Soon the assassin's words were legible again through the smeared black powder. Roguemoore read the note and looked up at Tala. "You've been skulking about the innards of the castle again, haven't you?"

"What did you put on there to make the words appear again?" Tala asked, hoping to redirect the dwarf's hard gaze.

"Ink from the squid of the Sør Sevier Straits was used to write this note." The dwarf studied the writing, brow furrowed. "Rare and expensive. The ink fades quickly but the writing remains intact." The dwarf paused, his eyes boring into Tala's. "Tell me what you're hiding from us, girl. What have you seen?"

"Nothing," Tala answered.

"Don't think me daft. I've the silver-wolf's eye. You've been jittery since we arrived."

"Lawri was just stabbed." Jondralyn leaped to Tala's defense. "Someone snuck into her room. They could've both been killed."

"You are right." Roguemoore's face softened. "I can be gruff and ofttimes insensitive." It seemed Jondralyn's beauty bewitched even the dwarf as he gave his apology. But his eyes quickly fixed on Tala. "Still, Jon, your sister hides something."

"Tala was stabbed too," Lawri blurted. "Remember, Tala? You said you fell into a nail. But I knew it was no puncture from a nail. What happened when I left you?"

Jondralyn's gaze shot to hers. "Did you see a Bloodwood in the secret ways?" Tala shrank away from her sister's searing look.

"We must know any information you have of this Bloodwood," the dwarf said.

Tala felt unseen eyes watching her. She dared not speak. This Bloodwood assassin from Sør Sevier could be peering in on their conversation now.

"Prove you were not stabbed and I will drop the subject," Rogue-moore said.

Tala had no choice. She pulled the collar of her own nightshirt down, revealing the still-raw scab just over her heart. Jondralyn gasped. The dwarf leaned in, examining the wound. His breath smelled of stale pipe smoke. "I daresay you never felt the blade either." He ran the tip of his calloused finger over the wound. It was true, Tala had not felt the knife slip in and out of her flesh, yet she shivered at the dwarf's cold touch.

"Tell us what happened," Jondralyn ordered.

Tala described the encounter with the cloaked figure earlier that day in the passage above their father's old study and how she had been stabbed. At the behest of Roguemoore, she also recounted the conversation she'd heard between Jondralyn and Jovan.

"An innocent conversation, that," Jondralyn said, worry etched in her voice. "Things my brother and I argue about all the time."

"But who knows what other conversations might have been overheard, between who and about what." The dwarf picked up the dagger and held it to the light again. "The next knife we see may not be a warning."

"Did a beast of the underworld make that knife?" Lawri asked. "It scares me."

"Better a demon had forged it." Roguemoore set the blade into his satchel. "But alas, was Black Dugal who helped craft the blade. Forged from the sap of a Bloodwood tree."

"Bloodwood tree?" Tala asked.

"They grow in the southern mountains of Sør Sevier between Rokenwalder and Kayde. Like aspen or birch, only black as pitch. Take an ax and chop into the leathery black bark of a Bloodwood tree and its sap runs thick and red and sizzles to the touch. Black Dugal and his Caste harvest the sap in a ritual called the Sacrament of Souls, then forge the daggers using a mixture of Sør Sevier steel, Bloodwood sap . . . and the souls of the condemned pulled from the dungeons of Rokenwalder. This makes the blades light and hard and indestructible. Only a select few are chosen to wield them."

"You mean only a Bloodwood assassin can wield them?" Tala was hoping for more information on her silent tormentor, shuddering at the thought of her brush with a Sør Sevier assassin.

Roguemoore did not answer. He pulled a small glass jar and bandage from his satchel, dunked his fingers into the jar, and placed a yellow, pasty salve from the jar onto the bandage. He put the bandage over the small wound on Lawri's chest. "That's sylwia root. It should help the wound heal. Bloodwood assassins are a dangerous lot. Resin from the lavender deje plant is boiled and then spread over the Bloodwood's blade to numb the flesh instantly upon the blade's entry. A flea lighting on your skin would cause more commotion than a Bloodwood dagger coated with lavender deje." He rubbed some of the salve onto Tala's wound too.

"How many Bloodwood assassins are there in Sør Sevier?" she asked.

"Nobody knows." Roguemoore looked at Jondralyn. "Hawkwood could shed light on the subject, though it's been a while since he lived in Sør Sevier. I'm curious to see what he knows of the dagger and what this Bloodwood may be up to."

Whenever Tala thought of Hawkwood, she also couldn't help but think of Jondralyn's previous betrothal to Squireck Van Hester when the two were youngsters and Adin Wyte an unconquered land. As for Squireck, the Prince of Saint Only had been imprisoned for a year now. Over the years, things had changed for Jondralyn. It was clear she was falling for Hawkwood, an ex-soldier from Sør Sevier. He was tall, gorgeous, charismatic, and, as it turned out, one of the most graceful sword fighters in all of Amadon. When Aeros Raijael had first attacked Adin Wyte, many from Sør Sevier had disagreed with the crusade, and feeling betrayed by their homeland, they'd fled to Gul Kana. Hawkwood was one such ex-soldier. Tala did not know everything about the man, but she had gleaned some information over time: Hawkwood, having successfully gained favor for his fighting skills, eventually worked his way into the graces of Jovan's court and had become friends with Squireck, Jondralyn, the Dayknight captain, Ser Sterling Prentiss, and the dwarf ambassador, Roguemoore, all to the consternation of Jovan.

As the dwarf rubbed more sylwia root on her wound, a sudden and unpleasant thought dawned on her.

"Was Hawkwood once a Bloodwood assassin?" she asked.

Jondralyn looked up at the question. Roguemoore met her eyes briefly, placed the tin of sylwia root back into his satchel, and left the room.

*There is scarce to write about the dwarves, other than that man is
commanded to consider them naught but stupid farmers. Stubborn, yes.
Bold, indeed. But mostly stupid. And what can be said of the oghuls?
Not eloquent like the Vallè, nor hardworking like the dwarf, but slothful
and slow of tongue. Man is commanded to consider these foul drinkers of
blood naught but wild creatures, one step away from savagery.*
—THE WAY AND TRUTH OF LAIJON

CHAPTER SEVEN
TALA BRONACHELL

17TH DAY OF THE SHROUDED MOON, 999TH YEAR OF LAIJON

AMADON, GUL KANA

I don't feel well." Lawri's face was pale. The arena orchestra, just
a few rows below the king's suite, played a soothing song during
the break in the action.

"Jovan will not allow any of us to leave," Tala said. "A contingent
of Silver Guards would have to escort us back to the castle, and they
would be most unhappy to miss the final match. I doubt Mairgrid
desires to waddle back there with us in tow either."

Dame Mairgrid whirled, an unhappy expression on her broad face.
Tala's tutor sat in the row in front of them. She was a big woman
with bulging eyes on a perfectly round head topped with a nest of
gray. "Quiet," she ordered with a stern look.

Below, slaves restored the arena floor to its original state, raking
the bloodstained dirt from the previous bout into iron grates in the

ground. More than thirty gladiator matches had already taken place today. The last bout of the afternoon was drawing nigh.

A looming dread consumed Tala's soul. She did not want to see Squireck down there. During the fights, she had not only shut her eyes, but held Lawri's hand for reassurance. Dame Mairgrid would turn and slap their hands with her sweaty palms, admonishing them to act like proper court ladies and watch. Even with her eyes clamped tight, Tala could still hear the agonies of the condemned, abandoned and alone in the dirt, fighting for their lives. Their horrid screams had a way of rising above the sound of the orchestra horns and drums and roar of the crowd.

Tala and Lawri sat in their uncomfortable dresses at the end of the row next to Tala's younger brother, five-year-old Ansel. Next to Ansel sat Jondralyn. Tala's older sister wore calf-high black leather boots, woolen horse-riding pants, and a buckled leather vest over a billowy white silk shirt. Many in Jovan's court did not approve of her unladylike attire but were loath to voice their opinions. When asked why she'd not come in her gown like the other ladies of the court, Jondralyn had professed that she'd been out riding earlier and hadn't had time to change. Beyond Jondralyn sat Lawri's twin, Lindholf, the Vallè princess, Seita, and seventeen-year-old Glade Chaparral of Rivermeade.

Tala found her eyes were continually seeking out those of Glade. He'd just arrived yestermorn with his family to participate in his royal Ember Lighting Rite in the cathedral. Jovan had been hinting of a betrothal between Tala and Glade for moons now. The notion of an arranged marriage bothered Tala not at all. For Glade Chaparral had the dashing looks of his older brother, Leif, who at the moment was stationed in Lord's Point with a garrison of Dayknights watching for Sør Sevier raiding ships. Glade, on the other hand, was here in Amadon, not ten paces from Tala. Though they'd been friends since childhood, Glade had, over the years, developed a regal aura about his bearing that currently left Tala a trifle unbalanced in his company. His father, Lord Claybor, was a man of height and bulk. But rather than growing thick around the gut like Claybor, Glade was filling out in a more pleasing way. He had well-chiseled muscles along with a square-jawed face and auburn curls atop his head that glistened in the sun. The scullery maids and court girls were hard-pressed not to notice Glade. Tala flushed as red as a turnip whenever she was in his presence.

But today, Glade, in Amadon Silver Guard training attire, only had eyes for Seita. The Vallè princess pulled forth a curious, small ball-and-chain weapon from some hidden place within her white cloak and began spinning it around her arms and shoulders deftly. It made a loud whirring noise. Both Glade and Lindholf seemed delighted by the weird weapon. Seita handed it to Glade and he attempted to spin it, his efforts awkward.

"My dear, you're doing it wrong," Seita giggled, placing her delicate hand atop his, helping him hold the chain correctly. "You must roll your hand like so"—her fingers interlaced with his—"to build up the muscles in your forearm." The Vallè princess leaned into Glade's shoulder, the two squeezing and twirling the chain together slowly.

Tala felt her entire body stiffen in jealousy. Seita was smooth of skin and bright of eye, with flowing blond hair of such a white hue it was almost blinding. Today she wore a formfitting light gray gown of Vallè make under a shimmering white cloak.

After a five-year absence, Seita had just returned to court in Amadon. She had an older sister, Breita. The two Vallè princesses were nearly identical. Breita had also been gone from court for five years. But she had not made the trip back.

Seita was young; still, older than Glade by at least a few years, and a good deal more experienced in courtly flirting than Tala. Along with their green eyes, upturned ears, needle-thin brows, and catlike grace, the Vallè were renowned for their silken tongues. In fact, Seita was just now complimenting both Glade and Lindholf on how much she was looking forward to their Ember Lighting Rites and how handsome they would both look in their white robes whilst passing the Ember Lighting flame.

Lindholf Le Graven handsome? Tala's cousin was anything but. Whenever she looked upon the scarred flesh that covered his neck, cheek, forehead, and ears, it was ofttimes with pity. Though she loved him dearly, she couldn't help but wonder what unfortunate court girl would find herself one day so unluckily betrothed to him.

Just beyond Seita was Hawkwood. The Sør Sevier man wore dark leather riding breeches and a billowy shirt like Jondralyn. With a graceful gesture, he drew aside a strand of black hair from his face and threw a nod of greeting toward Tala, eyes lingering a moment. There was a mysteriousness within those eyes as they sliced through the air, piercing into hers. That Hawkwood was once from Sør Sevier, perhaps even a Bloodwood assassin, gave Tala a smidgen of a fright. She didn't mind admitting that to herself. Hawkwood smiled at her, and in that one look, apprehension faded away. Tala could see why Jondralyn, now that her childhood betrothal to Squireck Van Hester was long over, was falling in love with this captivating man.

A breeze bit into Tala's skin, rippling the awning over the king's suite. The vastness of the arena surrounded her: tall columns, crenulated balconies, grandstands, a warren of grates and tunnels under a dirty battlefield, and intricately carved stonework palisades that rose up in a glorious circle around the crowd of over ten thousand spectators. During the bloody bouts, the nobility and those in the king's suite did naught but laugh and carry on, pretending to admire one another's clothing and acting like fools, all while condemned men hacked away at each other in the bloody battleground below.

To Tala, the annual gladiator event was, in a word, *wrong*, lasting for three weeks until only one was left alive. Hundreds of criminals fighting for freedom. The last four invited to dine with the nobility in the grand Sunbird Hall in Amadon Castle during the Mourning Moon Celebration. The citizenry of Gul Kana rejoiced in the shed blood of the lawless who waged battle in the arena. After all, to die in the arena was a shameful death—for it proved one's guilt.

Royalty from the breadth of Gul Kana surrounded Tala, blood-lust in their eyes. On the row directly behind her, bearded and hefty, dressed in the white-and-silver-marble colors of the crest of Avlonia, sat Lord Nolan Darkliegh. Next to him was Lord Kelvin Kronnin of Lord's Point. Lord Kelvin was tall and angular and dressed in leather leggings and a doublet of bright blue, representing the ocean near his homeland. His wife, Emogen, had remained at Lord's Point, pregnant with their first child.

Next to Kronnin was Glade's father, Lord Claybor Chaparral of Rivermeade. Thick-chinned and stalwart, he wore the maroon raiment and silver-wolf crest of Rivermeade thrown over his shoulder. He sat with his wife, Lady Lesia.

Lawri's father, Lott Le Graven of Eskander, thin, pale, and freckle-faced, sat next to Claybor. Lord Le Graven wore the yellow colors and lion crest of Eskander. Tala's aunt, Mona Le Graven, looked truly splendorous next to her husband. She was draped in a richly brocaded gown, her neck and arms bejeweled in ruby and pearl. At fifty-three, she appeared as radiant as her sister, Tala's mother, Alana, once had. Mona's youngest twins, Lorhand and Lilith, sat nearby, faces pale with shock at the arena events.

Next to Mona, two spear-wielding Dayknights stood on either side of the king's chair, shielding Tala's older brother, Jovan. Grand Vicar Denarius and the Quorum of Five Archbishops of Amadon—Vandivor, Donalbain, Spencerville, Leaford, and Rhys-Duncan—were seated behind the king, all in their most opulent finery. The holy vicar wore the burnt-orange cassock of his position, silken priesthood robes underneath. From neck to belly, Denarius' chest was hung with chains and necklaces of every shade of gold. He was bald on top but had a strip of brown hair running around the back of his head. He also had a round red face, puffy jowls, and a large, paunchy stomach.

The vicar had opened the arena matches with a blessing of peace, then spent the remainder of the day gorging himself at the banquet table not twenty paces behind the king's suite, discussing trivialities and court gossip with the Dayknight captain, Ser Sterling Prentiss, and four others: the commander of the Silver Guard, Ser Lars Castlegrail; the king's steward, Ser Tomas Vorkink; the king's chamberlain, Ser Landon Galloway; and the stable marshal of Amadon Castle, Ser Terrell Wickham. At the moment the vicar whispered conspiratorially with the Dayknight captain. Sterling Prentiss, tall and broad, was an imposing figure in the silver surcoat and black-lacquered armor of his station.

Seita's father, the Val Vallè ambassador, Val-Korin, stood near the vicar too. He respectfully bowed when he met Tala's gaze. He was ever watchful. With their delicately sculpted features, Val-Korin and Seita stood out in the king's entourage like statues of polished ivory in a thicket of moss-covered boulders. All looked upon the Vallè with a certain measure of reverence. The Silver Throne had a long-standing relationship with their neighboring island of Val Vallè. Val-Korin was one of Jovan's most trusted councillors.

"I know Jovan will let us go back to the castle," Lawri said, pulling Tala's attention away from the Val Vallè ambassador. "Must we stay even a minute longer? Ask him?"

"I'd likely get yelled at for asking."

There was a rattle of chains as the wrought-iron gates on either end of the arena rose up, followed by a thunderous sound as all ten thousand spectators lurched to their feet. The immensity of the crowd's roar never failed to leave Tala shaken. The last two combatants of the day strode from under the gates and into the arena. Tala's heart was instantly in her throat. One of the fighters looked familiar, yet vastly different.

Squireck Van Hester.

He was twice the size she remembered. Still tall. Six and a half feet. But not lanky. Not awkward. He was all might and muscles now. His blond hair was long and rested in sweaty strands down his bare back. He wore leather greaves over his pants and a thick leather belt around his waist and little else. A sheathed longsword was strapped high on his shoulders, with leather straps crisscrossing his back. His chest was totally bare but for the square gladiator brand showing red and raw upon the flesh of his shoulder.

The herald above the king's suite approached the copper tubes that magnified his voice and bellowed, "The Red Demon of Wyn Darrè versus the Prince of Saint Only!" His announcement was met with silence, for the Prince of Saint Only was the most notorious and hated criminal of an age. To slake their thirst for justice, the crowd had come to see him die a painful death. Like a pack of baying dogs, they began to boo.

Tala knew everyone in Amadon hated the Prince of Saint Only, fallen son of a conquered king, the one accused of murdering one of their beloved five archbishops, DeVon Lucas. She remembered herself at five years old, just before Sør Sevier invaded Adin Wyte, marveling at the shiny trinkets from Saint Only Squireck spoiled her with. But the Squireck Van Hester that Tala saw now had changed. At twenty-eight, and after over a year of imprisonment, the Prince of Saint Only had grown in stature. Great muscles in his arms coiled and bunched as pulled two long daggers from his belt. He held the daggers by their blades, testing their weight in his hands. That Squireck had chosen to wear so little armor made Tala even more afraid for him.

The fighter from Wyn Darrè prepared himself too, swinging a curved sword above his head in wide, sweeping arcs. He wore red armor, shined and polished, and the sharpened spikes jutting from his helmet and arm guards made him appear more oghul than man. His armor gleamed like molten stone, his black shield twirling in his hand for show. When the shield stopped twirling, the Wyn Darrè fighter screamed and shouted. He swung his great sword up and then down, swinging it so low it dug into the ground, throwing a spray of dirt high into the crowd. The crowd loved him instantly and chanted, *"Demon! Demon! Demon!"* The orchestra struck up a big bass sound like thunder set to the rhythm, *deh duh, deh duh, deh duh.* A little girl leaned over the railing just above the Wyn Darrè gladiator. She was grabbing handfuls of bright flowers from a copper ewer and tossing them gaily into the air, where they fluttered down about the fighter's feet.

Roguemoore came waddling up the aisle toward Jondralyn, panting as his short legs churned. "I'm sorry, Jon," he said upon arrival, his rough voice barely heard over the crowd's roar. "I've been working to put a stop to this. The quorum of five has matched him against this Wyn Darrè brawler, a murderer of women and children and several of King Torrence Raybourne's personal guard. The grand vicar and quorum are not gonna make it easy on Squireck for killing one of their own. Thing is, I don't rightly know who to blame: Jovan, Denarius himself, or Squireck's own father—"

The crowd erupted. A wave of sound washed over them, drowning out the dwarf's voice. The red-armored gladiator charged across the arena toward Squireck with a shout, a rousing *Deh! Duh! Deh! Duh!* crescendo from the orchestra spurring him on.

The Prince of Saint Only stood his ground, aimed one of his daggers, pulled back his arm, and let throw. The silver blade cleaved the air with a snap and bounced from the charging fighter's helm. Still the devil ran—his shield up and his sword poised for the killing stroke. Instantly Squireck aimed the second dagger. The raging Demon closed in and swung, his great sword whistling downward in a crushing path toward Squireck's neck. But the sword never reached its target. Instead, it spun from the Demon's hands to land in the dirt as the Wyn Darrè man staggered, the hilt of Squireck's second dagger jutting from under the faceguard of his spiked helm. The man in red stumbled on wobbly legs, triumphant no more. The rising tide of music silenced.

In one smooth motion Squireck pulled his own longsword from its sheath and swung downward, burying the blade into his opponent's neck and shoulder. The red helm flopped from the gladiator's head as a great gush of blood spewed upward from the wound, obliterating the Wyn Darrè man's face and chest in a thick crimson spray. As he toppled to the ground, there was a smattering of cheers, then silence. Only a handful of flowers rained to the arena floor at the herald's cry, "The victorious Prince of Saint Only!"

Then, in a brutal display, Squireck swung his sword as if chopping at a fallen tree and cleaved the head from the Wyn Darrè fighter's body. Jondralyn gasped and turned away. Tala could barely contain the sense of horror rising within her—horror of a sort that blocked everything else out. Lawri Le Graven was vomiting in the seat beside her.

"May the wraiths take us," Roguemoore said as Squireck snatched up the severed head by a bloody mat of hair and flung it in the direction of the king's suite.

"A gift for Denarius and the quorum of five!" Squireck shouted as the head sailed over the throng. The king's suite was too far above the orchestra box, and the head landed among the cellists and bagpipes below—musicians scattered as it bounced down the aisle. A crowd of gawkers circled around the head, stopping its path.

"His blood be upon the grand vicar and quorum of five!" Squireck spun slowly on the arena floor, both arms held aloft, sword still gripped in his right hand. "His blood be not upon me! Laijon is on my side! His blood be not upon me! I am innocent!"

And there was no blood on Squireck. His skin glistened with

naught but beads of sweat as he began stripping the red armor from the headless gladiator at his feet.

Muttering amongst themselves, the Quorum of Five Archbishops of Amadon looked to their leader. The grand vicar remained stoic, face unrevealing.

"A flower to throw to the victor?" There was a small, dirty-faced boy standing there in the aisle, holding a yellow flower out to Tala.

"No," she answered, wondering how the boy had slipped through the Silver Guard and into the king's suite unseen. "No. Please. Go away."

"Take it, m'lady." The urchin grinned and held forth the yellow rose. "It's a special flower, meant just for you." Before she knew it, the flower was thrust into her hand and the boy was gone, running up the aisle.

"Who was that?" Dame Mairgrid asked with a disapproving frown. The sour smell of Lawri's puke wafted up from under their feet.

"Just a boy." Tala examined the flower, a chill crawling up her spine. It was no flower, but a thin sheet of yellow parchment folded into the shape of a flower. There was something written on it.

She turned her back to Mairgrid, unfolded the flower, and read.

Tell no one of this note or your cousin Lawri will die within a heartbeat, pierced by a poisoned dart from my own hand. Bear in mind, the knife I stabbed Lawri with was not the same knife I left on your stool last night. The knife I stabbed Lawri with was coated with a slow-working poison. She will die from this poison in the turning of a moon if you do not do exactly as I wish. Only I know where the antidote can be found. It will be hidden somewhere within Amadon. I will give you clues to its location from time to time.

Lawri will grow more ill by the day. Delusional. In a few weeks completely mad. Bedridden. Within a few weeks of that she will be dead unless you follow my every instruction and complete every task I set upon you, tasks that are important not only to Lawri's survival but also the very survival of Gul Kana. Think of it as a game. With each task you complete, the closer you will get to the antidote and saving Lawri, and the closer you are to fulfilling your destiny as the Princess of prophecy. Your first clue is this:

Retrieve the red helm of the dead demon and read what is inscribed therein.

The red helm of the dead demon? Tala's eyes flew to the dead gladiator. The note couldn't possibly refer to the spiked helmet worn by the Wyn Darrè gladiator.

On the arena floor, Squireck was tearing the red armor from his vanquished foe. Once done, he gathered up the decapitated man's sword and shield, placed the dead man's red-spiked helm on his own head, and walked through the northern gate.

Another man strode forth from the southern gate with a hot iron and branded the flesh of the corpse with the mark of Laijon— the four-pointed cross. Tala knew the branding served a threefold purpose: first, the Cross of Laijon brand was meant as a heavenly seal representing the criminal's blood penitence for his crimes; second, it served as a conduit through which his soul could be escorted into the afterlife; and third, the hot iron was a means by which those faking death would be sufficiently roused back into battle. Yet in this instance, the severed head lying in the orchestra pit was proof enough that this particular gladiator was sufficiently dead.

A horseman rode out from the southern gate, his sorrel charger long of mane, a thick rope and meat hook tied to the saddle horn. The rider dismounted, uncoiling the rope. He sank the hook into the flesh of the headless gladiator, climbed back upon his sorrel, and dragged the body away.

With that, the crowd began to disperse in ferocious high spirits. But to Tala, it now seemed the world had somehow gone temporarily mad. *Squireck a gladiator? Lawri poisoned? Retrieve the helm of a dead man?*

A brisk wind blew. The black-and-silver banners of Amadon snapped to attention and the petals of a thousand flowers kicked up and drifted about the arena like snow.

We journey most naturally in the state of deceit. Oh gentle and naive reader, so trusting and kind. I, your Blessed Mother Mia, beg of you, do not put faith in the writings of the Last Warrior Angels, for they set out to deceive the hearts of men after Laijon's death. Like unto the mad illuminations of my son Raijael, The Way and Truth of Laijon—*that whoredom of perverted history and falsehood the Last Warrior Angels have penned—is rife with lies.*
—THE MOON SCROLLS OF MIA

CHAPTER EIGHT

JONDRALYN BRONACHELL

17TH DAY OF THE SHROUDED MOON, 999TH YEAR OF LAIJON

AMADON, GUL KANA

Jondralyn immediately loved the place. Despite the confines of the hood she kept pulled over her head, she saw enough. The first thing she noticed about the Filthy Horse Saloon was its sour stench and the wretchedness of its patrons. It was a dusky, smoke-filled place with low-slung beams complete with a motley collection of sailing decor: wheels, flags, oars, nets, planks, harpoons, hooks, anchors, and the like. It reminded her of being inside the bulwarks of a heavy-timbered sailing vessel.

Hawkwood had chosen a table in the back corner of the tavern with a clear view of the entrance. He placed his hand in the small of her back and guided her to a seat opposite the dwarf. She was both irritated and thrilled at his touch. He sat to her left, eyes on hers. Sometimes she found she could not meet Hawkwood's dark, devouring orbs. As if the very moment her eyes met his, he would somehow gain the upper hand. She wanted the control in the relationship. And she feared she'd been slowly losing that advantage over the last year with his every mysterious look. *What are you thinking?* She wondered if she would ever plumb his depths. *Who exactly are you?* She knew there were many types of suitors, and Hawkwood seemed the wrong type for her in every way.

"You have a way of locating only the finest establishments." Her comment was directed toward Roguemoore, who was sitting at the table opposite her. "And it stinks."

"It's a trifle unfair to single out this locale," Roguemoore said with a smile, "when this entire city stinks of rubbish. Besides, I didn't choose it."

The dwarf had drawn unfriendly stares as they'd entered the tavern. Perhaps it was the heavy mace bristling with sharp spikes strapped to his back. They were all well-armed. Jondralyn bore a shortsword under her cloak. Hawkwood had two cutlasses slung over his back, the hilt-guards of each sprouting a profusion of serrated spikes.

Several burly sailors, looking none too sober, beards as woolly as unshorn sheep, crouched around a stew pot hanging over a fire pit in the center of the tavern. They eyed Roguemoore still. The unkempt men were roasting strips of salmon on sticks, the crackling light of the fire dancing over their crude tattoos and body piercings.

Indeed, at a glance, the Filthy Horse was certainly a sight, what with its food-stained bar, unswept floors, nasty spittoons, vulgar sailors, plump and ugly serving wenches, and underlying smell of tar and grayken oil. This establishment would never suit the king's councillors, or, more importantly, Jovan. Nobody of the court was liable to recognize them here. And just to be safe, Jondralyn, the most recognizable of the three, kept herself covered under cloak and hood. After all, her likeness was on every copper in Gul Kana.

"I have the uneasy feeling we were followed," the dwarf said.

"Someone was indeed skulking behind us," Hawkwood said, "for a time."

That surprised Jondralyn. She had been unaware of anyone lurking about. Still, she wanted to add something to the conversation. "Perhaps it was the Bloodwood who attacked Tala and Lawri who now stalks us."

Hawkwood shrugged. And in his casual shrug, she glimpsed what he might have looked like as a young man. Jovan had once snidely called Hawkwood "beautiful," and he was. There was something both manly and lovely about his face, the angles, the shadows, the way his long, dark hair framed his cheekbones. And the tone in his voice when he said her name would set wing to her heart. Hawkwood was a distraction for her; sometimes it was enough just to be near him and hear him speak. It didn't matter about what, be it danger or assassins following them. Anything he said could arouse her interest.

"Much of what a Bloodwood does is mere deception," Hawkwood said. "Every move is calculated. Leaving that dagger in Tala's room was just a ruse in a bigger game. But I can't make sense of it. If indeed a Bloodwood followed us here, it could mean nothing, or more than nothing."

"That's reassuring," Roguemoore said.

As the three had journeyed to the docks, the air had been brisk, with only a few torches lighting the dark streets. The cobblestone lanes of Amadon proper had turned to mud the nearer they got to the bay. Ramshackle buildings closed in, hovering one atop the other. If someone *had* lurked in the shadows, Jondralyn hadn't sensed it.

She was in a good mood. Hawkwood wasn't the only one on her mind tonight. Squireck's victory in the arena had put her in jocular high spirits. His victory had stirred something deep within her. *Could I still love him, too?* She'd thought she loved him when they were first betrothed as teens. He'd been in prison for over a year. To see him again after so long, to see how large and powerful he'd made himself, to see him fight, had changed her. She was conflicted. She had always prided herself on her strong sense of fairness, of knowing right from wrong. Her mother, Alana, had instilled that in her—compassion and empathy to always go with fairness. But Jondralyn wanted to be like Squireck. Strong. In control. Her beauty gave her control, to a point. But what she desired most in life was *real* control. Power. So she could see the injustices in the world around her set right.

Another thing that had put her in a good frame of mind was that this would be her first secret council as a member of the Brethren of Mia. It was Squireck who had first mentioned the Brethren to her, hinting at the Brethren's interest in *The Moon Scrolls of Mia*, hinting that her mother and father had been studying them. That had been more than five years ago. She'd asked her father about the Brethren, and he'd confirmed his involvement, though reluctantly, offering little detail . . . then he'd gone off to war and died. To be involved in the *Moon Scroll* histories that had so consumed her parents—the histories that her older brother, Jovan, had shunned as heresy—was exciting. In fact, to be a part of anything *not* involving Jovan was part of her quest for control, part of her quest to see both her family and the Five Isles at peace, to see the wrongness of Aeros Raijael's brutal crusade put to an end.

But lately she harbored a seething dislike for her older brother. Sure, as a youngster, she had idolized Jovan. But when they'd reached their teens he'd turned surly, cynical, bitter, abusive. She recalled a time when she was thirteen, Jovan sixteen. She'd memorized a certain prayer from *The Way and Truth of Laijon* quicker than he. It had spun him into a rage unlike any she'd seen before. To escape his abuse, she'd hid. Alone, she'd cowered behind a tapestry at the top of the stairs of Sunbird Hall. He found her and tore the tapestry down, then stripped her naked. She had struggled, especially when he tore at her clothes, but he was too strong. She was mortified that he'd seen her nude. Her breasts were just starting to form, and she was embarrassed enough. But he made it worse when he hesitated and stared right at them before dragging her onto the fallen tapestry. She would always remember that look of both rage and twisted lust on face as he rolled her up into the tapestry and pushed it down the stairs, with her trapped inside. The tumble down the stairs of Sunbird Hall wasn't the worst of it. As she lay rolled up tight in the stiff fabric, she struggled for breath, struggled to find light. But the tapestry was too heavy, too constricting around her body, neck, and head. He'd left her there, naked, fighting for air. She eventually slithered free of his cruel trap. But she began to hate him from that day on, and the bullying and abuse only continued.

Now she was learning sword craft from Hawkwood. And becoming quite good. It bolstered her confidence in many ways. Plus, he was sharing history books with her. Secret books that were opening up her mind about a great many hidden things. She was glad to finally be a part of the Brethren of Mia, a group led by a dwarf who she loved like a father. She wanted to prove herself to Roguemoore and Hawkwood in any way she could. But she wanted to prove her mettle to Jovan more than anything.

She shrank behind the hood of her cloak as a tavern girl—a surprisingly fetching young thing in a low-cut corset with a close-fitting jacket that revealed an ample portion of pale flesh—brought three mugs of mead. The deep cleft of her cleavage bobbled above the fabric of her corset as she bent in front of Jondralyn and set the mugs upon the table.

"Get an eyeful, lassie?" the tavern wench said. "Perhaps you'd prefer I just pull down my top and smacked you about the face with 'em, huh?"

"Are you always so crude?" Jondralyn was embarrassed at the girl's forwardness.

"I'd gladly smoosh my titties in that warm spot betwixt your legs, then lick you head to toe, if that's what you mean by crude, or if that's what your men wanna see."

"It's quite all right." Roguemoore smiled. "Just three plates of salmon, please. And perhaps your name. So we can inform the proprietor how helpful you've been."

"Name's Delia. And I'll get you all the salmon you want." She looked closely at Jondralyn. "You've a familiar face under that hood. Do I know you?"

Jondralyn lowered her head.

"Just the salmon, please," Hawkwood said, diverting the girl's gaze. The serving wench winked confidently at Hawkwood, twirled, and sauntered away. Jondralyn felt her cheeks flush. That another woman would flirt with Hawkwood in front of her rankled. Yet it seemed he hadn't even noticed the girl. But that wasn't so surprising. Hawkwood was a man who carried himself like he was comfortable around any type of woman, from the fairest princess to the crudest dockside whore. *In fact, he carries himself like the type of man who might one day make love to me rough and proper.* Not like Squireck as a teen, full of doting duty and awkward, formal watchfulness, never daring to overstep the bounds of their betrothal, always chivalrous. She knew Squireck had loved her back then. And she'd grown to love him. But Squireck's young love was a possessive love, all gushing emotion and timidity. He'd worn his heart and jealousy out in the open. But wasn't all young love full of awkward insecurity? They were all grown-ups now. And Hawkwood treated her in a way that made her feel confident and free. He was quiet, calm, as if there were some hidden part of him she would never know, no matter how close they became.

She'd never wanted a forced marriage, a betrothal at fifteen for political advantage. It went against all things fair and right. Even her mother had voiced her displeasure at the arranged marriage. But her father had insisted. Jondralyn wanted to be caught off guard by love, caught unawares by her feelings, swept away in a moment. And Hawkwood's timing had been perfect. He'd entered her life right as Adin Wyte was being conquered by the White Prince and Squireck's kingdom was being destroyed, their betrothal crumbling to ashes. And then after Squireck had been accused of murdering Archbishop Lucas, right when she'd been forced into the part of the bereaved princess, Hawkwood's strength had comforted her in just the right doses, never overbearing, and with no judgment. Yes, his timing had been perfect.

Yet seeing Squireck again today, all solid muscle and force, had stirred something deep within her again. *Can a woman love two men at once?*

"This *friend* from Val Vallè we're to meet." Hawkwood leaned in, voice scarcely above a whisper as he addressed the dwarf. "You say you've never met him before?"

"Might not even be a *him*," Roguemoore answered. "But others in the Brethren I trust vouch for this Vallè. Our dear departed king and queen vouched for this Vallè. This Vallè is the truest of friends, they say."

"I admit I am nervous about this."

"Hawkwood nervous?" the dwarf chortled.

"For a Vallè to belong to the Brethren of Mia is strange indeed. And for a Vallè, be they male or female, to show their face in a sailors' tavern like this is stranger still."

"Well, this tavern was of the Vallè's choosing. The note was specific."

"Trust no one." Hawkwood turned to Jondralyn. "That is the Brethren's creed."

Roguemoore looked grave. "Hawkwood's too cautious. Sometimes we must trust. In fact, there is one we *have* trusted, one in whom we've all confided. One who is not with us today, yet plays his part. Let us not forget about Squireck."

"I had not thought him capable of killing," Jondralyn said, her mind in instant turmoil. Squireck *had* changed. He had definitely shown something to her today. *How do I explain my sudden feelings for him again?* "How did he get so strong, imprisoned so?"

"The dungeons under the arena can be a complex place," Roguemoore answered. "Alone, in a cell, with naught but time, one can fill water skins as weights for strength training. And for the right price, one can even purchase oghul fighters to escort you to the prison yards and train you in the more brutal forms of sword fighting whilst the turnkeys you've purchased look the other way. Squireck has been preparing to win his freedom."

Her heart was hurting. "I worry he's going to die, and I'll be forced to watch his slaughter." She did have feelings for him. And those feelings had caught her unawares.

"Everything serves a purpose," the dwarf said. "Another of the Brethren's creeds. Squireck is where he is meant to be. He's prepared for this. All we can do now is pray for him. My only fear is that the quorum and grand vicar have the games rigged against him."

"From what I've seen," Hawkwood said, "Squireck seems quite capable of surviving whatever the quorum has planned. He's become a strong warrior."

"We must trust in fate," Roguemoore added, yet he looked worried. "But I must admit, I do fear for his safety. He is like a son to me."

Jondralyn's eyes sharpened as her gaze traveled to the front of the tavern, where the double doors swung open. A cloaked figure stepped in. Her back stiffened at the sight. A whisper of dread billowed through the room toward Jondralyn as the doors swung shut and the figure moved toward the bar, face and hands concealed within the hood and sleeves of the black cloak. "Is that our friend?" she asked in a hushed tone. "Our Vallè friend we're to meet?"

"I know not," the dwarf answered, taking a swig of his mead.

"Watch him, Jon," Hawkwood whispered. "Every third sailor he brushes against, he picks their pocket. It's subtle, but notice how the sleeves of his cloak ripple."

If the cloaked figure was pickpocketing his way through the room, Jondralyn could not detect it. The person almost floated through the crowd, effortless.

"He is brazen indeed," Hawkwood said as the newcomer reached an open spot at the bar near an old man whittling a grayken bone. Once seated, the newcomer threw back his hood, revealing the unmistakable green eyes and sharp face of a Vallè—a face that seemed like any ordinary man but for the upturned ears visible through strands of inky black hair and facial features appearing to have been stretched back a bit beyond human shape to form something more unblemished and refined. The sailors around him looked brutish and coarse by comparison. The tavern wench nearest the Vallè gasped when she realized what had sat next to her. Sailors backed away, glaring darkly.

The Vallè untied his cloak, revealing supple black leathers studded with fine layers of ring mail about the neckline. No weapons were visible. The newcomer's gaze swept the tavern, yet never focused on one thing—though a shudder swept through Jondralyn when the Vallè's eyes fell upon their table momentarily.

"Is it him?" she asked.

"Or is it the Bloodwood?" Roguemoore whispered. "The one who's followed us here? The one who stabbed Tala and Lawri?"

"A Bloodwood wouldn't bother pickpocketing a roomful of sailors," Hawkwood answered softly.

"Unless it's a ruse to throw us off."

"A Vallè trained as a Bloodwood would be rare. No one knows who Black Dugal recruits or why. Anyone could be a Bloodwood. One of these sailors, our server. We may be being played in some grand scheme."

"Once again, reassuring to the last," Roguemoore said.

"The Vallè has seen us sitting here, yet hasn't approached."

Hawkwood sat forward on his chair, elbows on the table. "This worries me."

It wasn't long before everyone in the tavern was staring at the newcomer. For a Vallè to enter a dockside tavern in Amadon so casually was tantamount to starting a riot. Jondralyn gripped her chair for what she knew was soon to come, figuring this particular Vallè would not last long here, Bloodwood or not. The unfairness of the way the Vallè were ofttimes treated in Amadon made her seethe.

Sure, Jondralyn was used to the Vallè. The Val Vallè ambassador, Val-Korin, and his daughters, Breita and Seita, had lived in Amadon Castle on and off for many years. The Vallè bore much more of a resemblance to humans than did dwarves or oghuls, but with an added flawless, otherworldly, catlike grace. Jondralyn had never been around Val-Korin or his daughters without being reminded by their large, perfectly formed eyes, elegant pointed ears, and almost see-through skin that it was a Vallè she was near, not an ordinary person. As a race, they possessed an acute, almost wolflike sense of hearing, along with an uncanny, clairvoyant nature. Vallè were so perceptive it was as if they could read one's mind.

Like the dwarves and the oghuls—according to *The Way and Truth of Laijon*—the Vallè had roamed the Five Isles long before humans arrived from the Firstlands. As the humans slowly conquered the Five Isles, the dwarves were pushed into the Iron Hills on the isle of Wyn Darrè, the oghuls were beaten back onto the Jutte peninsula north of Crucible, and the Vallè fled to the most eastern, most barren, of the Five Isles. Now the Vallè were the sole inhabitants of that isle, Val Vallè. On a clear day, their island was visible from the top of Amadon Castle just across Memory Bay. Few humans ventured there.

Most folk in Amadon were not used to mingling with such creatures. So rare were the Vallè, so sublime their aspect, so disconcerting their air of superiority, that no human in Gul Kana was likely to welcome one with open arms, but rather with abhorrence and anger, unless it was King Jovan, who bore an unwarranted affection for his Val Vallè ambassador, Val-Korin. True, a lot of this distrust was brought on by their own arrogance, but this radical hatred of the Vallè among the commoners was wrong, and Jondralyn did not like it.

Sailors in particular hated the Vallè. In fact, a handful of grinning sailors approached the black-haired Vallè now. The tavern was silent.

"Pointy-eared foreigners are not welcome here," the largest sailor sneered. He had a ragged mass of red hair jutting from his head, and a wild beard covered his jowls like a shrub afire. "Best you swim back across the bay from whence you came."

"And if I don't?" The Vallè's tone was casual.

"I'll chop off your head and toss it into Memory Bay myself."

"I'd think a scab like you would find it hard to locate Memory Bay."

"Do you wish for a quick death?" the man snarled.

"As much as I'd like to bandy insults about, I should probably just order a drink."

"As I said, you'll find we don't serve your kind here. Are you deaf as well as pointy-eared?" Many in the tavern laughed at the pirate's witticism.

Rage at the sailors' ignorance and prejudice was simmering within Jondralyn. These were issues her mother, Alana, had fought against her entire life—issues her mother had warned her to never tolerate. Shunning anyone was not the way a daughter of Alana Bronachell was ever to behave.

"I have come here unarmed." The Vallè removed his cloak and set it over a stool. Indeed, the lithe Vallè looked unthreatening among the burly seamen.

"The sailors of Gul Kana will forever hate the Vallè!" someone yelled from the crowd. "What with the tolls you make us pay to pass through the Valea Channel!"

"A channel the Vallè dug for Gul Kana's purposes." The Vallè appeared to be growing bored with the conversation. "The treaties and fees were set in place ages ago. However, I daresay you all know nothing of true sailing. The sailors of Gul Kana are more like a bunch of bloated children mucking about in boats."

With two hands, the red-haired sailor shoved the Vallè against the bar and drew his sword. "I'll be chopping your head off now, child."

The Vallè moved with astonishing speed. He lunged forward, spinning in midair, kicking out. There was a meaty thump, and his leather shoes slammed into the sailor's crotch. The man instantly vomited a smear of half-digested stew and salmon onto the floor. The Vallè landed firmly on two feet, a dagger in his hand. Another sailor scuttled toward him, raising a long serrated knife, strips of salmon clinging to it as he swung. The Vallè's blade slashed out as he stepped back, slicing through the sailor's neck, opening a great streaming gash beneath his jaw. The room was plunged into shadow as the man fell into the fire pit with a hiss. Grasping at his frothing neck, the man thrashed in the middle of the glowing coals and billowing smoke like a beetle on its back.

Jondralyn's heart pounded with anger as every sailor in the room boiled toward the Vallè, their curved cutlasses ringing from their sheaths. The wenches and old men remaining at the bar scattered out of the way. The Vallè withstood the first few blows, then took a wicked slice to the upper arm. He did not cry out, but effortlessly leaped onto the bar, feet dancing, as swords cracked and clattered around his legs. He bled from the gash in his shoulder now as he kicked back at the mass of swords swirling under him. With naught but his kicking feet, the nimble Vallè managed to disarm most of the attacking sailors.

"We can't just let him die." Jondralyn stood, incensed at the lawlessness.

Hawkwood already had his two cutlasses in hand. In a flash, he sprang over their table and plunged into the fray. Jondralyn's stomach leaped into her throat. But with a few deft sword strokes, Hawkwood knocked sailors aside and soon stood between the mob and the Vallè atop the bar. A thrill ran through Jondralyn as she watched him, all deadly confidence and calm, standing up for justice.

"Out of my way," the sailor who had started the fight snarled, glaring at Hawkwood; chunks of vomit still dripped from his tangled red beard.

"Would you like me to kick you in the balls too?" Hawkwood swung his boot up, then instantly pulled back, the move a mere feint. But the sailor covered his groin with burly hands. Hawkwood grinned—a cocky grin in the face of overwhelming odds that made Jondralyn's heart race with excitement and desire, not just for him, but for the just cause he fought for. The rush was more intoxicating than mead. She pulled her shortsword from under her cloak, Hawkwood's training fresh in her mind. She wanted part of this fight against inequality. She wanted to feel *power*, too. With confidence, she strode through the bar toward the fight.

The fire flared up as someone pulled away the body of the dead man. The tavern was aglow again, but silent. The air was rank with the odor of burnt flesh.

"Let's kill this Vallè lover too," the red-haired man growled, and lunged bare-handed toward Hawkwood. Hawkwood thumped the sailor on the head with the flat of his blade and the man staggered. Bloodlust swelled up in the tavern, death firmly planted in the eyes of the rest of the mob. As one they rushed Hawkwood.

Jondralyn leaped to his defense. The man nearest Hawkwood fell dead, face pulverized by Roguemoore's spiked mace, his drawn sword clanking against the floor.

"Stop this madness!" the dwarf roared. "I refuse to have my dinner interrupted by the squabbles of the degenerate!" His mace came back up fast, bloody, and poised for another blow. Jondralyn pulled up, stunned at the brutality of the sailor's death. So close. She'd seen men slaughtered in the arena and not so much as blinked. But this fellow had just been standing right next to her. Her hooded cloak was splattered with his blood.

The room was silent save for the wretched gurgles coming from the faceless man who now twitched on the wood-plank floor under the dwarf. Roguemoore's attack had been blunt and fierce and far less intoxicating than Hawkwood's smooth fighting. Jondralyn's heart thundered.

"Now a dwarf fights us?" the red-haired sailor growled. "I suppose a bloodsucking oghul will come a-traipsing in here next?" He still looked convinced that the remaining sailors could rout these interlopers who had ventured unwelcome into their tavern. Hawkwood, Roguemoore, and the injured Vallè held their weapons up, ready.

Jondralyn felt the blood roar up within herself as she moved toward the bar and joined her companions and the injured Vallè, her sword wavering before the sailors too. Now they were four. Roguemoore grabbed her by the arm and pulled her roughly behind him.

The hood fell from her face.

A murmur ran through the crowd as someone muttered, "It's her." Someone else stated loudly, "Princess Jondralyn." A somber mood struck the room as all came to realize who she was. The red-haired sailor looked green as he bowed. "Pardon, m'lady."

"No pardons will be granted tonight," Jondralyn said. Mustering her courage, she shrugged the dwarf's hand away and stepped forward, feeling every eye upon her. There was real danger here. There was a man with a brutally smashed face lying right in front of her. But her mother had taught her, *Face all challenges. Never run away from them. Especially if you are in the right.* "Seems this Vallè was accosted for no reason within my brother's city," she said.

The injured fellow atop the bar held his hand over his right arm, blood welling from the wound. "Come down." She sheathed her weapon and held forth her hand. "The way is safe now." She helped him down.

"Thank you." The Vallè bent his knee to her and sat gingerly on a stool. There appeared to be a hint of mockery floating behind his luminous green eyes. Hawkwood handed him a rag, which he used to stanch the flow of blood from his wound.

Jondralyn turned. Her eyes were now trained on the sailor. "Foreigners, even Vallè, are welcome in Amadon. They are free to go about their business, unmolested."

The red-haired sailor quivered in anger. "Two of my friends lay dead, one from the Vallè's dagger and one from the dwarf's mace. Blood Price must be paid. Even kin to royalty are not immune to Blood Price. Murder was committed here tonight."

"Blood Price?" She stepped dangerously within the reach of the sailor, but on purpose. "I think not." She was used to most men cowering in her presence, intimidated by her looks alone—it was the one distinct advantage of being beautiful and tall. Her height and looks served her well. But more importantly, she wanted to intimidate this man with her station, confound him with the validity and virtue of her words, threaten him and show him she was not afraid. She had trained with Hawkwood for a year. She knew if it came to a sword fight, she could take him with ease. Plus Hawkwood, Roguemoore, and the Vallè fellow were behind her. The question was, could the four of them take on an entire tavern of angry sailors?

She stared down the man before her. "You will treat all who enter this tavern as if they were royalty, be they Vallè, dwarf, or oghul, understood? Or do you dare question my authority?"

Her gaze met that of Hawkwood. She could see the pride in his eyes at her words. She faced the rough patrons of the saloon a little taller now.

The sailor looked for help amongst his friends. There were a few nods between the sailors. When the red-haired man turned back to her, a wide grin lit his face. "I challenge the Vallè to a pirates' duel. Blood Price to make amends for the death of my comrades. That is how fairness is meted out." A buzz of agreement traveled through the tavern.

Pirates' duel? Jondralyn had never heard of such a thing. She fought down a gust of anger at the sailor's brashness. "Explain this pirates' duel," she demanded.

The sailor only smiled at her, a rust-colored, toothy grin that rankled. She couldn't fight her anger. "The Vallè is too injured for any duel." She drew her sword a second time. The moment had come upon her so suddenly she was not quite aware of what she herself was even saying. "I shall fight you in his stead!"

"Fight a *woman!*" the sailor sneered. There were guffaws and hoots from the onlookers. "I dare not kill the king's sister. I will be a hunted man."

Roguemoore grabbed her arm again. "You do not know how to fight as they do."

The Vallè stood, pulling his dagger from the folds of his black leather armor, eyes trained on Jondralyn. "With all due respect, I can fight my own battles, thank you very much." The entire room was staring at her now, waiting. She was shocked to her core by the look of cold anger now on the Vallè's face. "It was kind of you to procure a duel on my behalf," he said. "But now that you have, please stand aside. I fight my own battles, m'lady." His words had a sharp, danger-ous edge. His brow narrowed and he stared at her, eyes unwavering. The Vallè smiled, but it was an angry smile, dark green gaze fixed on her. The look the Vallè gave was startling, really, as though she had been playing with a harmless kitten that swiftly revealed it was a full-grown saber-toothed lion.

"He's right," the red-haired sailor said. "The Vallè can fight his own battles."

"It's settled then." Roguemoore shoved himself between Jondralyn, the sailor, and the dark-haired Vallè, separating all three. "A pirates' duel it is. Blood Price."

Jondralyn was swallowed up into the background as the crowd formed a circle and the two combatants prepared to fight. She couldn't help but feel that something important had just happened here and she had missed it. Just moments ago, she had felt so sure of herself, felt the anger and the readiness for a fight burning within her, the *power*, and firmly believed in the justice behind it and her skill. Now she felt she'd just suffered a swift and humiliating defeat in the eyes of Roguemoore, and perhaps even Hawkwood. She'd made a mistake in letting the hood fall from her face and compounded it by acting a fool.

Roguemoore tied a bar rag around the Vallè's wounded arm and cinched it tight. The red-haired sailor removed a rope belt from around his waist and handed one end to the Vallè, who placed it in his mouth, clenching it between his teeth. The sailor placed the other end of the belt into his own mouth and stepped back until the rope was pulled taut between them. Roguemoore stepped away from the combatants and said to Jondralyn, "Witness the pirates' duel and be glad you are not part of it."

"Ready?" the sailor growled between tightly clenched teeth, flipping his dagger from hand to hand, a gleam in his eyes. The Vallè nodded, but from shoulder to fingertip, his right arm was slick with blood and dangled near useless at his side. Still, he held his dagger low in that hand.

"As they fight"—Roguemoore leaned toward her—"if one of them fails to keep the belt in his mouth, the other wins and gets free rein to finish the fight however he sees fit." The dwarf drew his hand across his own throat. "Quick and easy, otherwise they hack away at each other with that belt stretched between them and nowhere to retreat. If the Vallè's got any fight left in him, they'll both be hacked to ribbons. And that's a bloody long and painful way to die. Be glad this fellow likes to fight his own battles."

Jondralyn could feel her face flush. She'd never admit it, but indeed, this pirates' duel was beyond anything Hawkwood had taught her. She could see no honor in it.

It started quickly. The sailor lunged, his dagger looping out in a wild arc. The Vallè danced aside. The crowd urged the sailor on. He swung again. The Vallè ducked and the blade whistled over his head. The Vallè swung, wincing visibly in pain. The sailor laughed through clenched teeth, jerking away from the Vallè with force, thrashing his head around, yanking violently on the belt. The much bigger sailor effortlessly whipped the Vallè about. Yet the lithe fellow managed to keep his feet, managed to hold fast to the belt with his teeth, his neck straining with the effort.

Seeing he couldn't shake his foe from the belt, the sailor stabbed out again. The Vallè leaped aside, swinging his own weapon, but to no avail; his swing fell woefully wide. The injured right arm was clearly hampering the Vallè's fight. He was panting for breath, all limbs dragging. As the two fighters circled each other, rope belt taut between them, Jondralyn could see triumph in the sailor's eyes and weariness in the Vallè's.

Another lunge by the sailor caught the Vallè by surprise. The dagger slammed into his already wounded shoulder with a meaty smack just above the bloody rag, and he folded to his knees. The sailor waggled the blade in the wound before jerking it free and striking again, aiming for the Vallè's throat this time. But the Vallè jerked back and the blade plowed a shallow furrow into the black leather armor covering his chest. The sailor stabbed out again, nicking the Vallè's armor a second time. The Vallè, still on his knees, swung in response, his blade scarcely rising above waist level. The Vallè's attack was so slow and awkward the sailor easily clubbed the dagger from the Vallè's hand. The weapon spun to the floor with a twang and skittered under a nearby table.

"Pick it up and fight," the red-haired man snarled, rope still clenched in his teeth. He kicked the dagger toward the Vallè, who scooped it up. As he slowly stood, the Vallè now gripped the blade firmly in his left, uninjured hand.

Then the Vallè grinned, eyes now icy and sharp with a killer's keenness. Any trace of weariness had instantly vanished. With a flick of his left arm, he lashed out, and a ribbon of blood opened up along the sailor's forehead. A startled gasp rippled through the crowd. The Vallè no longer moved like one injured, sluggish and slow. There was now a bounce in his step, and his eyes burned with bright vigor. His left hand holding the knife flitted around in a blur, shaving a swatch from the sailor's beard clear to the skin. With another flicker of the blade a second chunk of hair was gone, and another, and another. Soon the sailor stood stock-still, not even trying to duck the blows, blinking wild and nervous. He went quite pale, realizing his death was nigh.

The Vallè planted the dagger straight into the sailor's ear hole, burying it to the hilt. When he yanked the blade free, blood spurted from the sailor's head and nostrils, splattering a nearby serving wench. An expression of astonished horror was on the man's face as he crumpled to the floor, dead.

"It's over!" Roguemoore leaped to the Vallè's side, his mace at the ready. "He won the duel fairly, we all saw. Blood Price is paid."

The dwarf led the Vallè through the tavern, shoving his way through the crowd and out the door into the dark street. Jondralyn followed, Hawkwood retrieving the Vallè's cloak. Soon they were all hustling from the Filthy Horse through the cool night. Amadon Bay, a choppy glitter just a stone's throw away, could be seen between the Filthy Horse and its neighboring, staggered buildings. The masts of many ships rose up just beyond. The Vallè stumbled and leaned into Hawkwood for help.

"We must make haste," Roguemoore said. "Just because it was a fair fight doesn't mean they don't still wish to thrash us. We've got to get him to the castle and properly dress these wounds before he bleeds to death."

"Do you think it's a good idea to haul him to the castle?" Jondralyn asked. "He hasn't even told us who he is." She looked at Hawkwood. "Trust no one, right?" Then she recognized her own hypocrisy. Now she was being the suspicious one.

"Good idea or not, we take him to the castle," Roguemoore said. "We owe him at least that. Of all of us, you owe him the most, Jon."

Despite all the abuses Jovan had heaped upon her over the years, there were few times in her life when Jondralyn had felt less significant and more foolish than now.

She hurried her pace and stepped in front of the injured Vallè. "Who are you?" she demanded. "You are welcome in my family's castle, but I must know who you are."

The Vallè hung his head. Blood flowed freely from his injuries, and his large eyes were fogging over. "I fear I've fouled up my own plans and become fatally wounded here. I do admit I need help with these injuries."

"What is your name?"

When the Vallè answered, his eyes never wavered from her. "I hail from the Val Vallè village of Vitali. I have come to Amadon to find Val-Korin's daughter Breita. We were to be betrothed. Yet I have not seen her in five years. My name is Val-Draekin."

"An inauspicious name." Roguemoore's thick brows furrowed. Then he let out a big, hearty guffaw. "Breita, huh? Foolish behavior becomes the heart. But you will be sorry to hear, lad, that Breita did not return with her sister, Seita. She is not at court."

The Vallè smiled weakly. "That is what I feared. Perhaps Val-Korin can tell me where she went. Where she's been. I am most desirous to know."

"Perhaps you're telling the truth. But what if we had not come to your rescue?"

"Had you not come to my rescue, dwarf, many questions would have been answered for me." Val-Draekin met the dwarf's gaze, unflinching. "And then I would've been forced to kill every sailor in there, I suppose."

"And then you'd have been thrown into the dungeons under the Hall of the Dayknights for the effort. Most likely."

"Not even Purgatory can hold me long."

Roguemoore laughed. "I'm beginning to like you. You remind me of Hawkwood. Life's a game to the likes of you two." But the laughter quickly drained from his face, as if he could mask his irritation no longer. "No. All is a *ruse* with the likes of you two."

"You misunderstand my motives, dwarf," the Vallè said. "I realize I've caused much trouble for you tonight. I promise to repay your kindness."

"It's more like those sailors from the tavern will repay us," the dwarf said, shaking the Vallè's cloak. The pockets jangled with coin. "Now, what is your *real* purpose in coming to Amadon?"

The Vallè gingerly reached into the folds of his cloak and pulled forth a gold coin, handing it to Roguemoore. "This should assure you of my true purpose, dwarf."

The dwarf looked the coin over and fixed his cold eyes upon the Vallè. "Borden was wise when he chose you. Laijon save us. Be it ill fate or Mia's fortune that has brought you to us, Val-Draekin, Laijon save us."

Frustrated, not understanding much of what the two were going on about, Jondralyn pulled the hood of her cloak over her head and cinched it tight around her neck. Her hands came away slick with blood—splattered blood from the sailor's head Roguemoore had earlier smashed. She unhooked the cloak and tossed it away into the gutter and followed Hawkwood, Val-Draekin, and the dwarf back to the castle.

As with the fairy and fey creatures of the Firstlands, man is commanded to consider the Vallè of the Five Isles an indolent race full of mischief and guile. Some claim the Vallè are like unto witches that can pull at a man's will and read a man's mind. Some say a Vallè maiden of royal blood can foretell signs and prophesy the future. But who would dare believe such foolishness?
—THE WAY AND TRUTH OF LAIJON

CHAPTER NINE

NAIL

17TH DAY OF THE SHROUDED MOON, 999TH YEAR OF LAIJON

GALLOWS HAVEN, GUL KANA

C ome." Shawcroft beckoned. "There's something you need to see." His face disappeared as he let the cabin door swing shut. Nail rose from his bed of straw in the loft, grabbed his sword from under his pillow, and descended the ladder to the bare stone floor. There was one window to the left of the door and another window in the loft where Nail slept under a deer-hide blanket. Both windows were covered in oilcloth. A brazier filled with coal, its smoke drifting to the thatched roof above, sat by the cupboards near the door. Shawcroft's bed was under the loft and framed in logs, upon which lay blankets of silver-wolf fur and elk hide.

The first thing Nail noticed when he stepped out of the cabin was the bonfire raging in a clearing just beyond the corral. Its glow illuminated the yard in an orange haze. He'd heard his master hacking away at deadfall in the woods earlier that evening. The man had since piled the wood and set it ablaze. Despite the nearby fire, it was a cool evening. Nail was glad for his shirt and woolen breeches.

Their one-room log cabin sat in the foothills above Gallows Haven in a small meadow between rolling mounds of grass and aspen and was made of pine logs and covered with shingles of cut cedar. Outside were two small sheds filled with mining tools. An apple orchard and a garden were situated on either side of the cabin. A corral where Shawcroft kept Lilly and Bedford Boy was behind the cabin. In the trees above the corral was a small wood-and-wire-framed cage where Shawcroft kept two carrier falcons.

Nail's master held one of the falcons atop an arm gauntlet of black polished leather. Shawcroft opened a satchel slung at his hip. Made of dark-umber leather, the satchel had a flap that wrapped over the top and buckled on the side. The curving scrollwork inlays stamped into the leather were of a strange design. Many a time Nail had run across Shawcroft hunkered under a tree or lazing near a stream, studying the books and scrolls he kept in the satchel. Now Shawcroft sprinkled some gold dust in a tiny pouch, then tied it, along with a tube in which a rolled note had just been inserted, to the leg of the falcon. The bird, flecks of yellow and ebony in its plumage, fixed amber eyes on Nail.

"She knows what lies at our feet," Shawcroft said. "She's spooked."

It was then that Nail noticed the rolled-up elk hide on the ground. It was tied with rope on either end and looked larger and heftier than any hide Nail had seen before. Something moved within it. He took a step back, gripping his sword. His eyes flew to Shawcroft questioningly. The man whistled and the falcon took flight and soared away eastward. The sun was going down and the falcon disappeared into the last streaks of sunlight carving through the jagged peaks of the Autumn Range.

Nail marched forward and kicked the elk hide, then prodded it with the tip of his sword. "Don't do that," Shawcroft said sternly, pulling him away.

"Something in there moved. What is it?"

But the sound of a heavy horse clomping hollowly up the path behind them stole their attention. Shawcroft bade Nail follow as he made for the approaching steed. Nail was half expecting to see a horse with red-glowing eyes appear out of the dusky night air. He gripped his sword, feeling the cold reassurance of the blade. But the mount was a familiar dapple-gray draught mare, its mane braided with ribbons of white. Its broad chest and powerful hindquarters glistened in the firelight. Baron Jubal Bruk sat tall upon it. He wore his sword with the black opal–inlaid pommel at his side. Nail's heart thumped with anticipation, the sword in his right hand forgotten, left hand nervously caressing Ava's turtle carving, which lay under his shirt against his thudding chest.

"I've come to ask permission to employ your ward." The baron's voice cut through the stillness of the night as he reined his stout mare up before them.

"Nail stays with me." Shawcroft's answer was quick in coming.

At his master's casual dismissal of the baron's offer, rage blossomed in Nail's heart. "Do I get a say in this?" He looked at Shawcroft accusingly.

"You do not," the man answered.

Jubal looked at Shawcroft. "Nail deserves more than the pointless toil you offer."

"Even so, he stays with me."

The baron sat up straighter in his saddle. "There's been talk of a dark-cloaked stranger on a curious-looking charger seen about town."

Shawcroft met the other man's gaze without speaking.

Jubal Bruk leaned and spat on the ground. "Curse you, Shawcroft. Have you brought danger to Gallows Haven? Don't think I cannot tell who your ward resembles. Nail bears *their* look about him. Don't forget, I fought in Wyn Darrè at Borden's side. I know what I saw there, *who* I saw there."

I look like who? Nail felt his whole body shiver as if he'd just crawled out of an icy river. *I look like who?*

"You *fought* at Borden's side?" Shawcroft said coldly. "Or did you run like Jovan and Leif Chaparral?"

"Unlike you, Shawcroft, I've seen war. I haven't been wasting my days away digging for treasures that don't exist. Need I remind you of your duties as an—"

"You know naught of my duties," Shawcroft cut him off.

"The dwarf has seduced your brain with goddess worship and relic digging, as he's done with Squireck Van Hester, as he now does with Princess Jondralyn. As he did with your brother."

"Roguemoore is the only one with a reasonable plan for fighting off the Sør Sevier invasion, while King Jovan does nothing."

"Nonsense!" the baron shouted. His horse skittered to the side. He gained control of the dapple gray and reined around. "What would help against the Sør Sevier invasion is if Ser Roderic Raybourne was to cease his treasure seeking and teach these Gallows Haven conscripts what sword craft he knows."

Ser Roderic Raybourne? Nail looked at his master.

"That's right, Nail, how much do you really know of 'Shawcroft'?" Baron Bruk snarled Shawcroft's name this time as if he loathed hearing it even pass through his lips. Nail was startled at the venom in the baron's next words. "To think Borden Bronachell trusted so much to a traitor like you. I should behead you myself here and now." The baron threw back his hood and drew his sword—the weapon threw shards of orange from the light of the nearby bonfire. His dapple gray neighed and took a few steps back.

"Our disagreement need not come to blows." Shawcroft's voice commanded the night as he stepped toward the baron's horse. He grabbed the reins near the mare's jaw and pulled the animal's head straight to the ground. As Baron Bruk tumbled forward, Shawcroft snatched the sword from the man's grasp. The baron hit the ground with a clatter. Shawcroft calmed the dapple gray with a soft word in its ear. The draught mare knelt there, head pressed to the turf for just a moment before Shawcroft let go its reins. The horse jerked upright and galloped down the path.

Nail found it hard to believe, but in one fluid motion his master had brought the thick-necked mare to her knees and disarmed the baron. *How well do I really know him?*

Sputtering, the baron scrambled to his feet. "Perhaps you forgot, Ser Roderic, I was once a Dayknight too. I am not impressed by your tricks."

"A good Dayknight would've been ready for my tricks." Shawcroft threw the sword down at Jubal's feet. "And you were hardly a good Dayknight, Jubal."

"At least I was discharged with honor." The baron's voice had lost its edge and was bordering on a whimper now. Still, he snatched his sword and held it out, steady, poised to strike at Shawcroft, who was unarmed. "At least I was given lands and title and a ship."

"And with those lands, orders to spy on me."

"Jovan knows of the Brethren of Mia. He knows of your heretical beliefs."

"This is a battle you cannot win," Shawcroft said, seemingly unconcerned with Baron Bruk's weapon. "If you swing that sword, I will kill you. And what purpose would that serve the village? They need your training. Don't waste your life because of our differing views. Don't find so much offense in Roguemoore and his followers. The dwarf made many promises to Borden, as did we all. The vagaries of *The Way and Truth of Laijon* have always been a problem between some. We in the Brethren of Mia, what we do, what we seek, are none of your concern." He turned away and dusted his hands.

Baron Bruk pointed his sword at Shawcroft's back. "I only want you to fulfill your duties as a former Dayknight and help these boys learn to fight. Aeros Raijael is aiming for Gul Kana! These young men are under my charge. I must train all of them. Including Nail. That alone should make you see things as I do."

"Nail is no longer your concern." Shawcroft turned toward the baron. "I will train him myself."

"Will you, *Ser Roderic*?" Baron Bruk snarled. "You treat Nail with an indifference bordering on contempt. You're not half the man your brother was. A real warrior was King Torrence. He would have raised Nail proper." The baron sheathed his sword. "Do what you want, *Shawcroft*. But as a sworn Dayknight, it's my duty to help train these young men, Nail included. I will expect him on my training field with every other boy in Gallows Haven." With that, Baron Bruk trudged down the path toward his horse. And with him went Nail's chance to join the grayken-hunting crew.

"Fellow's had a bug up his arse ever since we arrived in Gallows Haven," Shawcroft muttered. "He is hot-blooded and far too quick to anger. He is no leader of men."

Resentment and confusion grew within Nail. "He called you Ser Roderic. What did he mean? He talked of King Borden Bronachell. Isn't he dead? Who are you?"

"We've more important issues at hand," Shawcroft said. "I've something you need to see." He led Nail back to the cabin, stopping short of the bonfire near the rolled-up elk hide. "Help me untie it," Shawcroft ordered.

He'll never answer any question I ask. Nail, not in the mood to do anything his master wanted, scowled. Still, he jammed his sword into the dirt and reluctantly knelt before the tanned hide. It took some work, but he loosened the rope, pulling it free. Shawcroft threw back the flaps of stiff hide. Hidden within was a person. Nail scrambled back in fear.

It was the shadow from his nightmares. *The Vallè rider on the trail!*

He could tell it was her from the black leather armor, pale young face, and astonishing silken hair. Her eyes opened, almond-shaped green pupils darting between Shawcroft and Nail. There was not a hint of fear in those cold jade orbs. Her mouth was bound and gagged with a bloody gray rag. A thick-twined rope was spiraled tight around her body from head to toe, keeping her secure. There was an arrow jutting from the top of her shoulder, most of its shaft buried straight down deep in her leather-clad body, the side of her head almost resting against its blue-feathered top. Another arrow was lodged in her chest, its shaft bloodied and broken off a few inches above her black leather armor. Even injured, there was a serene beauty to this creature that left Nail breathless. *Where's her demon-eyed steed?* Nail looked around frantically.

"A Vallè Bloodwood," Shawcroft hissed. "Black Dugal's Caste is long reaching if he's trained a Vallè. Some prophecies are coming to fruition, Nail. There are things you may see and hear tonight you best keep to yourself."

Nail stepped up to the elk hide. In the light of the nearby bonfire, he could detect a hint of pointed ears under the silvery nest of the Vallè woman's hair. He recalled her words to him on the trail. *You are not of my blood. Still, they will be coming for you.*

"Her daggers," Shawcroft said, "her cloak, all of it I left with her horse, dead and rotting at the bottom of that old elk trap we dug years ago." A hint of pain filled the Vallè woman's eyes as Shawcroft touched the broken shaft of the arrow lodged in her chest. "Luck and fortune that I was able to capture her at all. One does not simply catch a Bloodwood. Foul demon-spawned filth." Anger flared in her pain-drenched countenance.

"Still, a Bloodwood *can* be killed." Shawcroft pulled the small boning knife he used on salmon and muskrat from his belt and knelt at the Vallè woman's side. "They're not invincible." He cut through the gray rag tied over her mouth. "I've killed them before."

"Killed them before?" Nail's heart was beating a little faster now.

"I doubt I can get her to talk." Shawcroft pushed the hair away from the Vallè woman's face and placed the blade of the knife to one of her ears. "But I aim to try." The Vallè woman's eyes changed from angry to fearful. And with that fear Nail realized how young she was, perhaps not much older than he.

"Ears are the one thing that makes a Vallè a Vallè." Shawcroft pressed the edge of the boning knife against her flesh, pushing. "Tell me your name and you can keep yours."

The Vallè woman said nothing as Shawcroft pressed down with the knife. Dark redness welled from under the blade and soaked downward into her white hair as she struggled against her bonds, trying to pull away from the pain. From the rapid rise and fall of the leather armor, Nail could see she was panicking now.

"Stop!" he shouted, never imagining Shawcroft capable of such cruelness. In a lifetime spent with the man, he'd never seen such brutality. "Leave her alone!"

Nail lunged for the knife. But in a flash, Shawcroft tossed the blade aside. Nail felt his arms instantly pinned to his chest as his master picked him up in a barrel hug and then dashed him straight to the ground. Air whooshed from his lungs as he hit hard. Dazed, he tried to stand. The old man was stronger than he would have ever imagined.

"We must see this through, boy!" Shawcroft roared, eyes ablaze. "This creature before us is pure evil, a Bloodwood, deadly and fierce. She must not be allowed to live."

Nail lunged at Shawcroft's legs and they both hit the ground. As they wrestled in the dirt, the rage against the world's many injustices boiled within Nail's heart, feeding him. Shawcroft had denied him his due on Baron Bruk's ship. Now the man was going to mutilate a Vallè woman for no reason. Nail drew strength from his anger and pinned the man to the ground underneath him. But Shawcroft threw him off and stood. Nail rose to engage him again, only to be met by a hard slap to the face that sent him reeling against the cabin, head throbbing as he slid to the ground, vision blurred.

"Bloodwood assassins have hunted us your entire life, boy!" Shawcroft hauled him to his feet and forced him to his knees beside the Vallè woman. His hand on the back of Nail's head, he made his ward look. Her eyes were wide as she stared back at him. Blood swelled from the cut under her ear and pooled under her hair. Dazed, Nail could feel his own warm blood trickle from the lip his master had split. Shawcroft had never struck him before. That was shocking enough, but it was the man's words that had their effect. *Bloodwood assassins have hunted us your entire life, boy!* His head pounded. It felt as if the back of his skull had been caved in. His chest felt on fire— the same feeling, he imagined, as when Dokie Liddle had been struck by lightning. Agony coursed through his body, and his lungs felt raw, mouth parched. As Shawcroft's words churned over and over in his head, the inside of his skull began spinning with unholy images he'd thought long forgotten: fiery forms of the nameless beasts of the underworld, mermaids in the deep, red eyes and red-glowing symbols, a pale-haired girl on a white stallion, her hand a metal claw.

There was danger here. *Is this Vallè Bloodwood evil?* Nail felt his entire body grow slack in Shawcroft's hands. He slumped against his master in exhaustion, head swooning, aching.

"Has the fight gone out of you yet?" Shawcroft released his grip on the back of Nail's neck.

"Why torture her?' Nail breathed heavily, face beading with sweat as he fell forward to the ground, struggling to rise and giving up.

"You are right." Shawcroft's voice was strained, growing hazy and seemingly distant. "She will never divulge her secrets. And we must set off for the abbey and Bishop Godwyn soon. It's only by chance this Bloodwood lies at our feet. Who knows what information she's gathered? There are some who wish this farce to be over." Deep breaths filled his lungs. "I too wish this farce to be over. It has cost me dearly and has gone on too long. There are some who still wish you dead."

Face pressed sideways in the dirt, Nail felt his heart plunge to the depths of his gut. It was all hazy, though. Shawcroft was speaking of him, and people who wanted him *dead!* He couldn't move. The slap from Shawcroft. The blow he'd taken to the back of the head when he'd struck the cabin. Both had rendered him immobile, nauseous. He couldn't even sit up and ask the questions he wanted to ask.

Nail bears their look about him, Baron Bruk had said earlier.

As he rose up and looked at the Vallè woman next to him, Nail realized much had been opened up to him now. Yet at the same time, more questions arose. *We must set off for the abbey and Bishop Godwyn soon.* Bishop Godwyn was the old hermit who tended to the Swithen Wells Trail Abbey high in the Autumn Range. Feeling hollow, sick, Nail knew he should pose more questions to Shawcroft, but it would likely get him nowhere, and then the man's lips would become even more tightly sealed. *Why was Shawcroft doing this? Why was he taking care of me at all? Or is he taking care of me? Perhaps he is keeping me from the family I never knew? Or perhaps it is the Vallè woman wrapped in the elk hide who knows my true parentage!*

"I daresay I've lost more to Black Dugal and his Caste of Bloodwoods than any man alive." Shawcroft jerked the white arrow lodged in the Vallè woman's shoulder straight out. Her mouth opened in silent agony as the arrow's barbed tip pulled strands of muscle and sinew from her wound. Dark blood blossomed and gushed. The barbed arrow had severed an artery in its removal. Shawcroft left the broken arrow in her leather-armored chest. He then folded the stiff elk hide back over the Vallè woman's bound body, lifted her up, and carried her straight to the bonfire and tossed her in.

Nail sat there on the ground and watched him do it—watched her burn.

Before he passed out completely and remembered no more, he heard the Vallè woman's screams above the crackling of the flames.

For the sword of Raijael is bathed in heaven. There are some sins unforgivable in the eyes of Raijael. Grace is not sufficient. Only by the shedding of one's own blood can forgiveness be attained. 'Tis only by the Chivalric Rule of Blood Penance that one's station can be restored at the side of Raijael.
—THE CHIVALRIC ILLUMINATIONS OF RAIJAEL

CHAPTER TEN
GAULT AULBREK

17TH DAY OF THE SHROUDED MOON, 999TH YEAR OF LAIJON

AELATHIA PLAINS, WYN DARRÈ

The storm was one of those quiet hammerings, the snow so thick it felt as if the cloudy sky might cave in under the burden. But the heavy squall had mostly passed over them now. Gault and Beau Stabler lingered near the fire, awaiting their turn at watch. Gault's destrier, Spirit, tied in the birches behind them, nickered in the cold. Shine, Slaughter, and Battle-Ax, the white Archaic stallions belonging to Stabler, Spades, and Hammerfiss respectively, stared out into the snowy darkness beyond the camp.

Fifty paces to the north, near the southernmost Laijon Tower, was Aeros' tent; large as a good-sized cottage, complete with partitioned rooms, a bath, closets, cabinets, bookshelves, and a four-post mahogany bed. Hammerfiss and the Bloodwood stood just outside the tent's entry. Enna Spades was inside with Aeros. The flicker of candles lit up the tent's far end. The rest of the army encampment, some fifteen thousand Hound Guards, Rowdies, and Knights of the Blue Sword, and more than five thousand archers and squires, were sprawled out to the northwest. Their fires, twinkling clusters in Gault's periphery, receded away into the cold distance. An air of exhaustion still encompassed the army, but their victory over Wyn Darrè near two days ago certainly lightened the fatigue. They were itching to fight again. Ten miles to the west, King Torrence Raybourne and the last of the Wyn Darrè army lay as they had fallen, rotting. Snow covered them now. Their bodies would be left to freeze, then rot, freeze again, thaw, rot, bake in the sun, until naught remained, never to be given religious rites or a proper burial, fated to become food for the nameless beasts of the underworld.

A hundred paces to the east, beyond the Laijon Tower, lay the Aelathia Cliffs and a sheer drop to the Mourning Sea below. The Laijon Tower itself was five hundred feet of quarried granite soaring above them. The circumference at its base was impressive, the size of four to five horse stables clustered together. Vines of ivy, brown from the late winter chill, grew up the tower's base in a twisty maze. Its northern side was thick with moss. The four other Laijon Towers rose up into the darkness to the north, ten miles separating each.

Hammerfiss walked up to the fire. "There are good ways to die and bad ways to die," he said. His skin was colored with anger beneath the blue Suk Skard clan tattoos spanning his face. The small fetishes tied in the tangled mass of his red hair and beard seemed to quiver with anger too. His battle armor thunked heavily as he plopped down on a birch stump directly across the fire pit from Gault and Stabler. The bark of the stump splintered under his girth. "That's exactly what that sneaky little bastard over there said. Good ways to die and bad ways. Quoting the *Illuminations* right to my own face."

Gault shrugged, drawing his cloak tighter around himself.

"Best leave that man be." Beau Stabler pulled the hood of his own

blue cloak away from his face, revealing a dark mane of hair and a black eye patch over his right eye. A legion of battle scars crisscrossed Stabler's face, but most were hidden under his beard, a scraggly, unkempt bushiness, rarely trimmed. The only hair on Gault's head was a finely carved goatee. He kept the hood of his cloak pulled tight over his bald head.

"Gives me the creeps, he does," Hammerfiss said. "What do you make of the Bloodwood assassins, Gault?"

Gault looked toward the Bloodwood—Aeros' newest member of the Knights Archaic—who was now writing in a small book and reclining against the base of the Laijon Tower. His gaunt Bloodeye stallion stood watch over him. The horse's ribs gleamed with the oils rubbed into its velvety-black hide, and the beast's eyes glowed red. The demonlike steed, different in both color and temperament from the other four steeds belonging to the five Knights Archaic, was named Scowl. Enna Spades had the first two hours' watch over the Angel Prince tonight. Normally, she would be standing watch at the door of the tent. But Aeros had earlier ordered her inside. The Bloodwood would soon take second watch, Gault third.

"True, I suppose," Gault answered. "There are good ways and bad ways to die."

Hammerfiss chuckled, fetishes jangling in his beard. "Aye, nothin' but nonsense, that, and after spoutin' such foolishness, he went and claimed to have just stabbed me."

"He claimed to have stabbed you?"

"Aye. The wicked sneak."

"You'd think a stabbing would be something you'd notice."

"Indeed."

Gault looked back toward the Bloodwood again. Everything about the man seemed dark, treacherous. Wrapped in tight-fitting black leathers, no weaponry visible, the Bloodwood looked—as Hammerfiss would say—wicked sneaky. The entire camp knew of the dozen or more daggers hidden within the assassin's boiled-leather armor and how rapidly those thin blades, black as smoke, could slice and fly at a moment's notice. Gault and Stabler, once finding themselves surrounded by Wyn Darrè knights at the Battle of Kragg Keep, watched amazed when the Bloodwood swooped into their midst, knives seeming to scarcely graze everything they came near. Before Gault or Stabler could even draw their swords, there was naught but corpses. The air was a mist of blood, every throat severed and every assailant dead before they hit the ground. Yes, the Bloodwood was deadly. Spiderwood was the name given him by Black Dugal, leader of the Caste of Bloodwood Assassins. Spiderwood's real name and age, no one would ever know. Most in camp avoided him, most but for Hammerfiss, who felt the need to incessantly prod at the Angel Prince's newest Knight Archaic. Most in camp just called him the Spider.

"Quite a trick to stab a man clean through his armor without him even noticing it," Gault said with a grin. "Quite a trick indeed."

Hammerfiss smiled at that. A big, yellow, toothy smile, which, in spite of his tattooed and wildly bearded ruggedness, made him look a trifle childlike. "Like ya said, mate, I'd likely notice something like that."

"Well." Stabler pointed. "You do have a bit of blood about to drip from under that armored plate." Despite having but one eye, Beau Stabler was Aeros' best tracker; he possessed an uncanny ability to see things normally unnoticed. Sure enough, a tiny dot of red had seeped from under the big man's chest-plate armor and now dripped to the ground.

Hammerfiss looked down and ran his hand under the armor. His fingers came up bloody. "Lady Death, take me!" He jerked to his feet, unbuckling his plate cuirass, stripping off his leather tunic and undershirt. Both tunic and shirt sported a small hole and fresh bloodstains. Under the armor, Hammerfiss wore a peculiar-looking necklace of thin, pointed mermaid teeth adorned with jewels. The necklace looked right at home set against the wild red curls and muscular grandeur of his bare chest. He quickly parted the mat of hair above his heart, locating the pea-sized wound just under his collarbone, probing it with his meaty forefinger. "The wicked sneaky bastard."

"A bad way to die, that there," Stabler said. "I hear his knives are poisoned."

"Forged of some foul witchcraft, they are," Gault added. Hammerfiss looked up from the wound, genuine fear set into his eyes.

"He was King Aevrett's favorite torturer for a time, you know," Stabler pointed out. "Probably practiced that trick on some poor sod pulled from the dungeons of Rokenwalder. Perhaps you're next in line for Dugal's Sacrament of Souls."

"I'll show him a thing or two about torture." Hammerfiss turned toward the Bloodwood and yelled, "Hey, you, sneak thief! Come over here and answer for this!"

Spiderwood scribbled in his book a moment, then sheathed both book and pen and rose. He casually brushed snow from his cloak and walked toward them, his steps soundless. Gault stood. As did Stabler, who rested his hand on the hilt of his sword. The Bloodwood dipped his head in greeting as he stepped into their midst. He looked at them through cold, narrow eyes—eyes blood-shot with red. He had a chiseled set to his jaw and cheekbones. Brows were sharp. Hair was cropped short and glistened with the same bluish-black hue of a raven's wing. A quiet, icy confidence clung to him like a vapor.

Still, at seven feet, Hammerfiss towered over him. With thickset, immensely powerful shoulders above a barrel chest, massive arms, and stout legs, Hammerfiss had the look of a man who could uproot trees with his bare hands. "If you value your life and want my respect, you'll have to earn it in some other way," he said, chest puffed out, bright blue eyes looking down on the Bloodwood as he pointed to the wound on his own flesh. "Respect you earn on the field of battle with hard steel. You can't cheat your way into it with black daggers and your sneaky assassin ways."

"No." Spiderwood's eyes strayed toward Aeros' tent. "As I see it, there are a great many ways in which one can earn respect. I kill how I please. As do you, clumsily I might add, with scant style or grace. But you are Hammerfiss." He bowed. "I am Bloodwood."

"Clumsily." A flush of rage spread over Hammerfiss' face like a rash. "You tread on dangerous territory."

"Ofttimes your great bulk crowds me." Spiderwood motioned to the wound in Hammerfiss' chest and shrugged. "A mere warning, that. Next time you venture *clumsily* within my reach, I make it painful."

"If it weren't for Aeros' misplaced affection for you, I'd flog you right now."

"I think not." The Bloodwood took a step back. With a flick of his arm, a dagger appeared in his hand. "My blade thirsts. If you made such an attempt, you would be dead between heartbeats."

Gault slipped between Hammerfiss and the Bloodwood. Stabler drew his sword, saying, "I like not the tone of this conversation."

Hammerfiss grinned at Spiderwood, pushed Gault aside, and stepped easily within the Bloodwood's reach. "I see your true heart now. Full of weakness. Lacking in courage. That's why you rely on your sneakiness, your devilry, and your childish acrobatics. It's all a ruse with you. The truth is, you'd like to fight me now that I stand mostly naked before you, my gear scattered at my feet."

"Do not mock my ways," the Bloodwood said.

"No, do not mock ours. What have you and your black-hearted Bloodwoods done to help this war effort? Where were you when Felisar Gannon yanked a dozen Wyn Darrè arrows from his own chest and then flung himself back into the Battle of Agonmoore?"

"I've heard the tale a dozen times. Wasn't Felisar crushed by his white destrier moments later, his death opening up a vacancy in the Knights Archaic for Stabler?"

"Where were you when Wolfmere Lohr, still impaled by a spear, staggered into camp after the Battle of Oksana and tossed the severed heads of his foes into the fire pit?"

"Then he keeled over dead, right? Now I have replaced him at Aeros' side."

"He died proper," Hammerfiss said, voice rising. "A glorious death. With honor."

"Perhaps," Spiderwood drawled. "But I see nothing before me but a brutish idiot practiced only in the fine art of clumsily swinging an unwieldy spiked ball about. True, you've won battles. Smashed the heads of the blindly unaware. You recount the same barbaric stories to your fellows here every night."

"I've helped conquer an entire kingdom. The *Illuminations* record my deeds."

"Oh, yes," the Bloodwood said. "Bloody violence will save you."

"Don't quote the *Illuminations* to me. I was reading them before you were born."

"Did your *Illuminations* record Hollis Berne's death? Is it written how this fool charged straight into the fray along the River Sen, leading a cavalry of a hundred Knights of the Blue Sword behind him? Does it tell of how Sør Sevier lost many good men that day, most sinking like stones while the rest, floundering in the river, were crushed to death when five hundred Wyn Darrè foot soldiers fell upon them? Do your *Illuminations* tell how Hollis' compressed corpse was dug from under the mass of dead and returned to his homeland in shame accompanied by the severed head of his destrier? Does it tell why he was not burned as a hero? Does it tell why his soul was not allowed to take wing with the smoke of a holy pyre and rise into heaven to dwell in service of your precious Raijael but was instead banished to the underworld and the dreadful abyss of the dishonored? Your *Illuminations* are selective in who they speak of."

Stabler jumped in. "Victory is a gift from our Lord Aeros, a lord who communes with both Laijon the Father and Raijael the Son. Our success is not carved by the skill of our weaponry and bravado alone. 'Slay all' is our creed. 'Raijael will know his own.'"

"Again, you quote the *Illuminations*," the Bloodwood said.

"Better to read the *Illuminations* than those black words of a non-believer you must scribble in that secret little book," Stabler said, his anger now matching that of Hammerfiss. "Why are you even here?"

"My reasons I keep secret," Spiderwood said. "In my little book."

"Again you continue to think us idiots," Stabler said.

"With respect, you know that we Bloodwoods pay scant homage to Raijael or Laijon, or even Mother Mia. Still, Black Dugal and my fellow assassins have much business in Gul Kana. All has been sanctioned by our blessed King Aevrett."

This last statement brought with it a moment of silence. Gault knew that Black Dugal, his Caste of assassins, and their relationship to King Aevrett were all hard to define. It had been a mystery to the other four Knights Archaic why this particular Bloodwood was counted among them.

"So you hunt your brother?" Stabler asked. "You hunt Hawkwood?"

"You will not speak his name around me." There was challenge in Spiderwood's eyes as they raked over Stabler. "There are many I hunt in Gul Kana."

"Enough!" Enna Spades yelled. They all turned. Spades let the flap of Aeros' tent fall shut behind her. "The tone of your blathering disturbs the prince."

Snow crunched beneath the red-haired woman's boots as she strode toward them, purpose in her gait. The four men, Gault, Stabler, Hammerfiss, and the Bloodwood, parted as she stood among them. They lapsed into an uncomfortable silence. Spades appraised Hammerfiss first. He was still naked from the waist up, a trail of blood running down his chest from the small hole. She eyed the Bloodwood—his dagger had vanished.

"Idiots," she said, glaring at them all.

More silence followed her withering stare. "Aeros' wishes are known," she began. "We strike at Gul Kana. We aim for the small fishing village of Gallows Haven." She turned to Spiderwood. "Your fellow Bloodwood has gathered evidence that one of the Brethren of Mia, Ser Roderic Raybourne, King Torrence's younger brother, resides there under a false name."

Spades paused, her gaze roaming toward the Aelathia Cliff and its three-hundred-foot drop to the Mourning Sea below. "With Ser Roderic may be the one thing Aeros desires most . . . the boy who was stolen."

It was faint, but Gault saw it. Spiderwood had narrowed his eyes just slightly at the mention of Ser Roderic, tightening them into something fierce and cold.

† † † † †

Gault, Stabler, and Hammerfiss slumped back down in front of the fire, the quibble between the Bloodwood and Hammerfiss forgotten, anxiety building within each as they thought upon the upcoming siege of Gul Kana. The Bloodwood was standing watch before Aeros' tent.

In the silence, Gault's mind wandered back to his childhood and the famine that had left him an orphan. Home. Stone Loring. Those words held scant meaning for him now. Starvation, squalor, and assassination—the ways in which his family had all died—were not honorable deaths. According to *The Chivalric Illuminations of Raijael,* the ideal death was in war. The ideal death was not a tame one. A peaceful death in bed, lovingly embraced by family, was a humiliation to any true warrior of Raijael. An ideal death needed to satisfy the *Illumination*'s code: "Bloody violence will save you; awaiting survival won't." In death, a warrior's soul was taken up into heaven to serve the one and only son of the First Warrior Angel, Laijon, in the Court of Raijael.

The Chivalric Illuminations of Raijael—a ten-volume and growing manuscript housed in the Rokenwalder Castle library—was a detailed history of Sør Sevier warfare to be read as holy script. Warfare was Sør Sevier's heritage. And Gault knew war. Almost his whole existence had been honed in violence. It was simply a way of life. He knew no other. Five years conquering Adin Wyte, and then five more raiding and pillaging across the island of Wyn Darrè, had led the armies of the Angel Prince to this point under the southernmost of the five Laijon Towers. In their wake, the armies of Sør Sevier had left behind a mournful collection of burned cities, smoking ruins, deserted hamlets, scarred fields, empty churches, and penniless marketplaces. The once fruitful and mighty Wyn Darrè was now no more than a wasteland of scattered rubbish, her people a simpering, beaten-down lot. Just like Adin Wyte before, Wyn Darrè was now full of naught but criminals, poverty everywhere. The plague had sprung up from the squalor and was spreading. Roads were unsafe. Murder was rampant. Robbers and thieves now ruled with scant regard for life. All was now exactly as it should be—exactly as both Adin Wyte and Wyn Darrè had deserved. The decades and centuries of savage attacks on Sør Sevier shores were finally avenged.

Slay all. Raijael will know his own was the *Illuminations'* creed.

Yet the truth was, in battle, most men, some even fully knighted, were a disgrace. They pissed themselves, shat themselves, then found themselves stuck to the pointy end of a better man's sword. Some warriors, the green ones usually—the Hound Guard and Rowdies—cried for their mothers in the end. Seventeen-year-old Konnor Riddle, lying facedown in the mud of Pensio Fields, encased in fifty pounds of armor, blood spurting from two severed legs, had cried for help before Gault's merciful killing stroke took his head. Then there was young Salisan Lusk. As the surgeon pulled chunks of chain mail from the gruesome wound done to his groin, Salisan had squalled like a babe. He begged Gault to deliver a copper trinket to his girlfriend in the case of his passing. Salisan did die. Gault pitched the trinket into the River Sen. Both he and Spirit had watched it sink.

Ten years of war. Now here they sat, the Angel Prince and his five Knights Archaic: Gault Aulbrek, Beau Stabler, Hammerfiss, Enna Spades, and the Bloodwood, camped smack under one of the five Laijon Towers, its ever-burning fire put to sleep forever, smothered with the bodies of the enemy knights guarding it and left to dwindle down to naught but smoldering coals and fetid smoke. Their crusade to retake the Five Isles had now reached this point, the easternmost edge of Wyn Darrè atop the Aelathia Cliffs, the Mourning Sea the only thing now separating them from their ultimate goal—the island of Gul Kana.

Gul Kana, the *Illuminations* claimed, was a rich and fertile land, infested with nothing more than gluttonous wretches who worshipped Laijon in blasphemous gaudy cathedrals and temples, a place where the people would wail and flagellate themselves before a enormous sculpted statue of Laijon, hailing it as an effigy of the great One and Only. *The Chivalric Illuminations of Raijael* spoke of Gul Kana and the ghastly harvest of carnage and bloodshed Church of Laijon zealots had reaped in the name of their perverted view of Laijon when they had taken and lost and retaken time and again both Wyn Darrè and Adin Wyte from the heirs of Raijael over the centuries. Aeros Raijael would take Gul Kana as he had retaken Adin Wyte and Wyn Darrè. He would give Gul Kana its Fiery Absolution. *For that which was taken in blood, can only be regained in blood*, spoke the *Illuminations*. As the prophets foretold, on that day of Absolution, the Angel Prince of Raijael would reign as the true One and Only returned. King Aevrett Raijael had raised his only son, Aeros, for just this purpose. And Aeros had fought these last ten years for just this goal. To the armies of Sør Sevier, Aeros Raijael was not only their fellow warrior, but their prince, their lord, even their One and Only returned.

In Sør Sevier, to be saved, one must only proclaim Laijon as the true One and Only and swear fealty to Aeros Raijael as Laijon's living heir. There was no vicar or Quorum of Five Archbishops in Amadon to pay homage and tithes to. There were no temple prayers, lists of good works, flagellations before holy statues, or ceremonies of ember and ash to earn your way into heaven. In Sør Sevier, belief was simple: study the *Illuminations* and believe in Raijael, Laijon's only son, and Aeros, his living heir and warrior for the faith.

And Aeros had more than proved himself in battle these last ten years. He was a keen and brave fighter, at the forefront always, seemingly indestructible, glorying in the savagery of battle. Never injured once. He'd been trained by the best warriors and killers King Aevrett could offer. Aeros was Aevrett's prize, his pride, his joy. And both were driven by this one goal of ushering in Absolution.

All of which brought Gault's mind around to something else.

Thoughts of the brilliant green stone Aeros had found on the battlefield had lately consumed him. *To see it one more time is all I'd need.* He looked to the soaring height of the Laijon Tower. Its witch-born flame had been extinguished nearly a moon ago, doused forever as was prophesied. But Gault took little solace in that final act of triumph. Years ago, the very thought that he himself might be an integral part of fulfilling that ancient *Illuminations* prophecy would have thrilled him no end. But now, after so much war and death, he scarcely cared. Now all he could think of was a small green stone. And that frightened him. *Was it really an angel stone?* That was the question he'd been mulling for the last few days now. He wondered if his mind hadn't played some trick on him—wishful thinking combined with the stories of his mother. He pulled his cloak tighter over his shoulders like a mantle. It would soon be his turn at watch. The snowy Wyn Darrè night would soon grow bone-chilling.

The flap of Enna Spades' tent folded aside. She stood there, still wearing most of her armor, tossing a copper coin in her hand—her special coin, a trinket that had a history. Spiderwood, still standing watch, looked at her briefly, then turned away. Spades showed no emotion.

Gault knew her well. She'd described her childhood to him once, traumatic, full of pain and betrayal—horrific things he himself would rather not think of. She'd never felt much power in her life. But in the hideousness of war she'd discovered a way in which she could gain it. She'd joined Aeros' army in her late teens and, through sheer skill and ruthlessness, had risen through the ranks: squire, Hound Guard, Rowdie, Knight of the Blue Sword, and she'd rightly earned her spot at Aeros' side as Knight Archaic.

She faced Gault with a curious tilt to her chin. He knew that look and wanted to turn his eyes away. In matters like this, she had nurtured her icy lack of facial expression to an art. He could read nothing in her but knew what she wanted. He purposely looked away. She pocketed her coin and retreated into her tent. Both Hammerfiss and Stabler chuckled. As much as Enna Spades tempted him still, Gault knew nothing good would come of their coupling. Let the Bloodwood pleasure her if he so desired. They'd been together as of late. After all, the two shared a common bond. Spades and Spiderwood both hunted the same man—a former Bloodwood assassin known as Hawkwood.

Hawkwood had betrayed his homeland for the love of a woman: Jondralyn Bronachell, sister of Sør Sevier's greatest enemy, King Jovan Bronachell of Gul Kana, and daughter of the woman he had been sent to assassinate—Queen Alana Bronachell. Most believed Alana had died in childbirth. But there were some, like Gault, who knew the truth. Alana Bronachell had died at the hands of a Sør Sevier Bloodwood assassin. And that assassin had been Hawkwood. And that assassin had fallen in love with the woman's eldest daughter, Jondralyn, the fairest woman—it was said—in all the Five Isles. So fair her face was minted on every copper coin in Gul Kana. Now Hawkwood was known in Sør Sevier as a betrayer, a turncoat. Many wanted him dead. For he was to have killed Jondralyn, too—but had not.

Hawkwood was not only a former Bloodwood assassin, but also Spiderwood's brother, and Spades' former lover.

A Bloodwood was not allowed to fail in his duties.

And one did not just leave Black Dugal's Caste of assassins for a woman.

And one certainly did not leave Enna Spades for *anything*.

And now Spades kept a Gul Kana copper with Jondralyn Bronachell's image emblazoned on it with her always—she kept it so she would know the face of the woman she most desired to kill.

In this embattled world, man held faith in invisible forces and hostile
spirits, ofttimes doing the bidding of the wraiths that fed in his soul.
To appease the winged demons who ruled with fiery death, man erected
altars of sacrifice. It was a time of selective loyalties, a time of great
betrayal. A time of celestial divinations that one holy and pure and strong
of mind would be born by the sea, blessed with the Mark of the Cross.
—THE MOON SCROLLS OF MIA

CHAPTER ELEVEN
JONDRALYN BRONACHELL

18TH DAY OF THE SHROUDED MOON, 999TH YEAR OF LAIJON

AMADON, GUL KANA

Squireck Van Hester circled his foe, a stick-thin man in rusted chain mail, wooden breastplate, and dented helm, bearing an unwieldy-looking longsword.

The orchestra bell gonged a deep *Boom! Boom! Boom!* whenever the Prince of Saint Only stepped onto the arena floor. The crowd booed to the cadence, the bells heralding the inevitable. The air was ripe with the stench of death. But that was the way of the arena: ancient, gray, pitted, rancid, and stained.

Today the king's suite was crammed with the entirety of Jovan's court; only Lord Kelvin Kronnin was absent. He had taken leave of the festivities yestermorn and journeyed back to Lord's Point to attend to his wife, Emogen, and their newborn daughter.

Tala held hands with Lawri Le Graven, both with heads bowed

and eyes clenched shut. Occasionally Dame Mairgrid would reach back and slap the top of their hands with one of her own beefy palms. Jondralyn knew her sister and cousin merely wished to have their delicate sensibilities unsullied by the arena horrors. But Jondralyn saw things differently: she figured a princess must look unflinchingly at the world, soak it all in without abhorrence. Those were things her mother, Alana, had instilled in her. Though her mother had hated the arena as much as Tala seemed to now, she'd taught Jondralyn to see it for what it was. She worried for her younger sister. Tala hadn't spent as much time under the tutelage of their mother as she had. Now it seemed Tala wandered about the castle full of naught but idle mischief. But soon Jovan would have her marry Glade Chaparral, and her standing in the court would be firmer and she could avoid the arena if she so desired. Jondralyn elbowed her. But Tala refused to look. Jondralyn turned her own attention to the arena floor. She would look. Though she still feared for Squireck's life, watching his brute power in action was magnificent. To her, there was a quiet accuracy in Squireck's movements, a clean efficiency.

He swung his longsword only once; it flashed fiercely in the sun. And his foe fell dead at his feet, chain mail and wooden breastplate torn asunder, chest split open and weeping sheets of scarlet over the dirt. *Boom! Boom! Boom!* went the bells. And a great chorus of boos rained down upon the Prince of Saint Only. Squireck held his bloody sword aloft.

He stood there below the king's suite in naught but his leather breeches, frozen in place, bare-chested. Wearing no armor, beads of sweat glistened on his tanned, rippling torso. He was fearsome, eyes wide and inflamed. Golden hair just a wild tangle down his neck and back. Except for the quivering of his forearm held high, Squireck was quite still, elegant even—as if forged of marble. Jondralyn knew her feelings for her once betrothed were deepening. Sitting here next to

Hawkwood, watching Squireck kill in the arena, she had never felt more vibrantly alive.

The Prince of Saint Only had scarcely taken his eyes off the king's suite. Even in the midst of slaying his latest challenger, Squireck's eyes almost never wavered from the spot where Grand Vicar Denarius and the quorum of five sat. Archbishop Spencerville, squat and round, seemed especially to squirm in his seat.

"The victorious Prince of Saint Only!" The herald's voice swelled through the arena once the ravenous boos of the crowd and thunderous booming of the bells ceased.

"Blessed Mother," Roguemoore said. He sat near Jondralyn with Hawkwood. "What a specimen. I daresay his arms have grown two sizes bigger since his last fight."

What the dwarf said was true. Squireck's body was as chiseled as the sculpture of Laijon that graced the rotunda of the temple. Down on that arena floor was a true fighter, a true warrior, a real man, all sculpted muscle and confidence.

A feeling of complete and utter inadequacy filled Jondralyn then. A desire to build up her own physique to match that of Squireck's instantly consumed her—she too wanted a warrior's body. But as a woman in Gul Kana, what chance was there of that?

I will find a way!

Hawkwood was looking at her curiously. She wondered if he knew what she was thinking. On the floor of the arena, Squireck swung his sword and chopped the head from the dead gladiator, then picked it up by the hair and flung it high into the air. It sailed over the bulk of the orchestra, landing among the drum section just below the king's suite. The musicians gasped and scrambled away.

"This man's blood be upon the grand vicar and quorum of five!" Squireck yelled, holding his arms wide in supplication. "His blood is not upon me!" He turned and stalked away. The arena crowd booed with more vigor and flame. Once again, Squireck Van Hester exited the arena, his body free of blood. This had been his fourth win without suffering so much as a scratch. The headless corpse was branded with the cross of Laijon and the body dragged away. As the dirt of the arena floor was raked, the orchestra struck up a soothing melody, and the crowd patiently awaited the next match. A Silver Guard pikeman leaped down into the orchestra pit and snatched up the head of the gladiator. He flung it back onto the arena floor, where it landed in a spray of dirt for the sand rakers to gather.

"Someday," Roguemoore said loud enough for all in the king's suite to hear, "one of those heads is bound to reach the lap of one of our beloved archbishops." There was a defiant challenge in the dwarf's stance and a dangerous rising of his bushy brows.

"Best watch your mouth, dwarf," Grand Vicar Denarius chortled, staying seated. His thick hands were folded over the lump of his stomach. He took a deep breath that sounded more like the grunt of a boar. His eyes, prickly and wandering, appeared to miss nothing as he continued. "Yes, best watch your mouth or you'll soon be down with Squireck, running about in that arena on your stumpy little legs, begging for your life."

"Is that a threat, Denarius?" The dwarf faced the quorum of five.

Archbishops Leaford and Donalbain stood as if to protect their leader, the latter tall and sticklike, always reminding Jondralyn of an old scarecrow she'd once seen. Vandivor, Spencerville, and Rhys-Duncan stayed seated—but they were the more heavyset of the five, Spencerville particularly round of gut.

The grand vicar's scrutiny of the dwarf was unwaveringly long. It seemed as if the dwarf was momentarily taken aback by the intimacy of the unending look from Denarius.

"Fools," Jovan snarled, leaning forward in his chair. "Can't you see, the Prince of Saint Only makes us all look like simpletons." He looked to the Dayknight captain, Ser Sterling Prentiss. "See to it that Squireck is imprisoned separately from the other fighters." With strained impatience etching his face, he stood and addressed the entire suite. "The Prince of Saint Only's training is at an end. He is to be given naught but bread and water by the guards. On pain of death, nobody is to visit the arena prison without my leave. Or perhaps I will just have him moved back to Purgatory."

"That is unfair!" Jondralyn shot to her feet.

"I won't have my sister questioning me in public!" The king snapped his fingers and pointed to the exit. "Have her removed, Prentiss."

Since Jovan had grown up and become king, his childlike bullying had only become worse, but in a different, sinister, more official kind of way. Now he had other men, like Sterling Prentiss, do the dirty work. Prentiss motioned to the four Dayknights standing guard behind the king. They moved toward her with purpose. Hawkwood stood, hand on the hilt of his sword. Each of the four Dayknights drew his weapon. Everyone froze. The tension was thick. Jondralyn was at once flattered that Hawkwood would risk so much for her, and irritated that he just assumed she could not take care of herself.

"Please, Jovan, Your Excellency." Jondralyn's aunt, Mona Le Graven, stood and bowed deeply. "Don't quarrel. Grant us leave to just sit and enjoy the—"

"Do you wish to be removed too?" The king's face was lit with rage. Mona slunk back into her seat next to her husband, Lord Lott Le Graven, who now looked ill.

Jovan shot an icy stare at Hawkwood. "Remove your hand from the hilt of that weapon or else my Dayknights will cut you down where you stand."

Hawkwood kept his hand where it was, cool gaze unwavering.

"Do not do this, lad," Sterling Prentiss said to the Sør Sevier man. "You've been a great help in training my men. That I appreciate. But I must do as my king commands. My men will slice you to ribbons on my orders. Make no mistake."

Everyone looked between Hawkwood to Jovan. The king stood

tall and sure, rage on his face. As a young girl, Jondralyn had always been reassured by the breadth and firmness of her older brother's shoulders, the rigidness of his posture, the squareness of his young jaw. But when they'd reached their teens, those attributes turned Jovan into a more formidable tormentor to her. That rage everyone now saw on his face, she'd seen before. Again she recalled when she was only twelve and he fifteen: Jovan, having become enraged over some triviality between them, cornered her in a dark corner of Tin Man Square. He ordered her Silver Guard watchmen away, then threw her to the ground and stomped her arm and leg muscles beneath his heavy boots as she lay helpless on the ground. He made her promise to never tell their father or he would scar her face until she was so ugly no man would want her. Jondralyn, fearing he would follow through on his threat, obeyed. She had seen the determination for cruelty in his face. Yes, today he stood tall and sure. But now those attributes just added to the crazed look of him. Everything he ever did was full of brute unfairness and spite. Where had he learned such unkindness? Their father had never been like that. Alana Bronachell had not been totally blind to her son's meanness as a child and had tried her best to correct that in him, but she would hate who he had become, as Jondralyn did now.

In fact, Jondralyn hated him more than ever before as he motioned to the captain of the Dayknights. "Remove her from my sight. Kill anyone who tries to stop you."

Jondralyn shoved away the first Dayknight who attempted to grab her. "If I'm to leave the arena, it will be under my own power."

The captain of the Dayknights appraised Jondralyn with a heavy-lidded gaze. "The order was given to me. I aim to fulfill it. I will escort you from the arena whether you like it or not." There was purpose behind his words. He had once been Borden Bronachell's most trusted knight. But since her father's death, the Dayknight captain had been a bulky threat looming at not only Jovan's but the grand vicar's side. When she was a child, the grim look of Sterling Prentiss could send Jondralyn scurrying away in fear. He was looking down on her now with those squinty, steely eyes of his. She wondered if the man sat up at night practicing intimidating looks in front of a mirror. The thought made her giggle. This earned an even darker look from Jovan. Sterling's thick hand went to the black opal on the pommel of his sword. The man followed her brother's orders to a fault.

Grand Vicar Denarius spoke. "You should take little offense at your sister's words, my king." He was puffed up like a toad in his seat. "Though she is one most beautiful, she is only a woman. Barely more than a silly court girl, really. They never grow out of it, the court girls. It is why you don't see them in the bishopric, or as lords or nobles or kings. They know not what they do. And Jondralyn knows not what she says. It's the dwarf who fills her head with such folly, having her believe she is more than she is. And that Sør Sevier turncoat who teaches her sword craft does her no favors either. Just look at how she dresses. She thinks she's a real warrior. Thinks it unfair that Squireck go without training and food. But what does a woman know of the arena and its workings?"

"I know exactly of what I speak," Jondralyn snarled.

The vicar sat back in his chair, chubby and self-contained.

"I agree with our holy vicar," the Val Vallè ambassador, Val-Korin, said in his very peculiar taut voice, just above a whisper. Everyone had to strain to hear what he said next, his words directed at Roguemoore and Hawkwood. "Ever since the dwarf council in Ankar sent you to Borden's court, you've stirred up nothing but trouble for the Silver Throne, Ser dwarf. And you, Hawkwood, are naught but a dirty Sør Sevier turncoat and assassin."

"I'm no assassin." Hawkwood's retort was dismissively casual, eyes narrowing at the Vallè ambassador. "Nor am I a traitor."

"You're both a traitor and an assassin," Val-Korin said. "You know it. I know it."

Jondralyn looked closely at the long-eared Vallè. There was a certainty in the way he spoke that brooked no argument. His eyes were a light green, and in that moment she was able to see the flecks of gold dusted through them. His daughter, Seita, sitting next to the injured Val-Draekin, appeared amused by the entire conversation. That angered her.

"Remove my sister, the dwarf, and Hawkwood from my sight, Prentiss," Jovan ordered with impatience, his eyes fierce and commanding. "Now!"

Sterling Prentiss and his four Dayknights moved forward, wary.

Hawkwood spoke calmly. "I daresay it will take more than just you and four Dayknights to *escort* me anywhere, Prentiss." His sword rang the rest of the way from its sheath. Jondralyn's heart leaped straight into her throat as two of the Dayknights advanced to defend their captain. But Sterling stayed them with an upraised hand. The Val Vallè ambassador was smiling now too. To Jondralyn, it felt as if the entire episode had been orchestrated by Sterling and Val-Korin for just this purpose—to catch Hawkwood, and possibly even her, in this very position. She took a step toward her brother but was immediately blocked by the bulk of Sterling Prentiss, who grabbed her roughly by the arm.

Hawkwood raised his blade. "Take your hand off her."

"Are you calling me out?" Prentiss growled. "Are you issuing challenge to a Dayknight?"

Hawkwood's eyes lanced into those of the Dayknight Captain. His sword did not waver.

"I've a proposition to make." Val-Korin weaved his way between everyone, commanding the attention of all. He looked at Jovan. "Sterling Prentiss has stumbled upon a grand idea. If Hawkwood is so insistent upon defending Jondralyn's honor, Your Excellency, I say we let him. We are nearing the Mourning Moon celebrations, after all. What better way to celebrate than a duel to settle a point of honor?"

"Yes." Jovan clapped. "I like the way you think, Val-Korin." A smile played at the corners of his mouth. "The four Dayknights against Hawkwood. A week from now. Black Glass Courtyard. A duel to the death to settle this."

"No, please, brother," Jondralyn said, weary, truly expecting nothing to come of this save more suffering. "Is there no other way? This is all a misunderstanding."

"Hawkwood and the dwarf have poisoned you against me long enough," Jovan snarled, rage etched on his face. "Even turned you against our holy vicar. Against Laijon. It is a father's job to raise his children in the truth of Laijon or be damned. But our father is dead. It's now my duty to keep you in step with the church and its teachings. I merely do the will of Laijon, ridding you of those who turn you against me."

In the background, Grand Vicar Denarius nodded his approval. Jondralyn knew Jovan was set in his ways—there was no arguing with him, especially in the vicar's and quorum's presence. When her mother was pregnant with Ansel, she had spoken to Jondralyn of her fear that if Borden was killed in war, and Jovan took over as king, her son would fall prey to the political machinations of both the grand vicar and the Val Vallè ambassador, Val Korin. And she'd been right. Jovan was beholden to both to an alarming degree. And Jondralyn found her brother's constant piety and bullying in the name of Laijon ultimately dangerous for Gul Kana. Ever since hearing some of the Brethren of Mia's interpretations on Laijon, the Blessed Mother Mia, and the baby Raijael, Jondralyn wasn't sure she believed in the Church of Laijon's infallibility anymore. She hadn't prayed of her own accord in moons. There were tiny effigies of Laijon throughout Amadon Castle, but she no longer paused to kneel before them as she once had.

"You four Dayknights"—Jovan pointed to the four surrounding Hawkwood—"make yourselves ready for the duel. I will bestow treasure and holdings near Knightliegh upon the one who strikes the head from the villain before you."

"Four against one!" Jondralyn shouted. "It is not fair!"

"And when I win?" Hawkwood asked, sheathing his sword, as if in acquiescence to the coming fight, eyes on Jovan. "What holdings and treasure do I get?"

"When you win?" Jovan laughed. "What could you possibly want besides your feeble right to live a short time longer than you normally would have?"

The arena herald's voice sang out through the stadium, announcing the next match. The orchestra struck up a wild chord as the next fighters strode onto the field. One was Shkill Gha, the killer-oghul from Jutte, a seven-foot-tall, leathery beast of a fighter in rusted mail armor who lumbered into the arena to the beat of the orchestral drums. He slowly swung his heavy war hammer to and fro above his head. The crowd booed the oghul voraciously. He answered with a smile, baring teeth like yellow-rusted knives.

"When I win!" Hawkwood demanded over the roar of the crowd.

Jovan scrutinized the other man with a scowl. "The matter is settled! You win your right to live but a moment more by my leave!"

Jondralyn pleaded, "That means next to nothing—"

"Shut up!" Jovan bellowed. "I don't wish to miss watching this bloodsucking oghul crush his opponent." He then clapped loudly. "This foul beast is my favorite!"

Below, Shkill Gha pulverized his foe beneath the weight of his massive war hammer. His victorious roar was so loud it drowned out the chorus of boos from the crowd and swallowed up the sound of the orchestral horns and drums. "*I fuooking'a shite on yo all'a!*" he bellowed in his thick oghul accent, booming voice deep and jarring. "*I fuook on'a yo muothers!*" The oghul's thunderous shouting brought the entire arena to silence. Shkill Gha tossed aside his war hammer and grabbed the fallen gladiator under both arms. The oghul lifted the limp corpse so he was face-to-face with the dead man. He bared his teeth, lips curling back, drool running from the corners of his mouth. He bit into the mutilated flesh of the dead man's pulverized neck and sucked the still-warm blood from lifeless veins. That was the last thing Jondralyn saw as the Dayknight captain escorted her, Roguemoore, and Hawkwood from the arena.

† † † † †

An iron-gray sky heavy with clouds boiled above Jondralyn and Roguemoore as they stood upon the battlements. The arena matches had ended earlier that afternoon. Below, Tala and Lawri, along with Lindholf Le Graven and Glade Chaparral, watched Val-Korin's daughter spar with Val-Draekin in the center of Greengrass Courtyard. Val-Draekin's injured arm was in a splint and heavily bandaged; still he fought off Seita's flurry of attacks with ease.

"Look how fluidly the Vallè fight," Jondralyn said. "Even with one arm in a sling, Val-Draekin can beat back any threat Seita poses."

"Indeed, the Vallè are a different breed in many ways," Roguemoore followed.

Jondralyn could hear the Vallè princess's lilting laugh even from her perch overlooking the yard. Greengrass Courtyard was a private royal garden roughly three hundred paces long by a hundred wide. It was located about three-quarters of the way up Mount Albion near the center of Amadon Castle, directly below the King's Gallery and the great Sunbird Hall. There were perhaps two dozen such courtyards scattered about the many levels of Amadon Castle. The largest—Tin Man Square—was nestled between the two towers of Thesua just below the Great Gatehouse about halfway up Mount Albion.

The sight of Val-Draekin's skill with a blade left a somber residue of bitterness in Jondralyn. She'd blundered miserably in the Filthy

Horse Saloon. It made her feel inadequate in every way. "To me it seems Val-Draekin let those sailors in the saloon injure him intentionally. Someone with the Vallè's skill could have beaten them back." She turned to the dwarf. "Have you met with him since he came to the castle last night?"

"He's saddened that Breita is not at court with Seita. But he's brought news from his homeland. He claims Val-Korin has fallen out of favor with the Val Vallè royal family. I will leave it at that for now."

With two flicks of his wooden blade, the injured Vallè disarmed Seita. Her wooden sword spun off into the grass, but cat-quick she dove and caught it before it touched the ground. Tumbling, she sprang to her feet and launched her own wave of blows. Val-Draekin was soon retreating under her onslaught. The two Vallè looked like dancers as they sparred, yet there was something almost barbaric about them too, some savage quality that was both lethal and serene. As they fought, Val-Draekin's face remained beautiful, yet devoid of passion. Seita always appeared at ease with the world. Indeed, pleasant laughter lived within her eyes and voice. She disarmed Val-Draekin. His wooden sword arced away and he nearly dove for it, then pulled up short, motioning to his injured arm. Vallè flesh healed thrice as fast as a human's. Injuries like Val-Draekin had suffered in the Filthy Horse Saloon would normally take a man six moons to recover from fully—it would take the Vallè about two. Still, even injured and in defeat, Val-Draekin moved with a languid grace few possessed and many envied. Jondralyn knew she would've been slain in that pirates' duel had Val-Draekin not fought in her stead.

"Don't feel so sorry for yourself," Roguemoore said. "Don't think I can't tell what you are thinking."

"How do you know what I think?" she snapped, then realized the dwarf did not deserve her wrath. Still, many things had upset her today. "True, I am unhappy. Hawkwood is now under guard of the Dayknights, awaiting the duel."

"Everything has a purpose," Roguemoore said. "Another of the Brethren's creeds. I know you worry for both Hawkwood and Squireck. But everything has a purpose."

"Everything has a purpose?" She was beginning to think the dwarf was not telling her all he knew about Hawkwood, Val-Draekin, the Brethren of Mia, and their plans. She saw the honor in Hawkwood's defense of her at the arena. But the whole episode seemed entirely pointless; it felt almost staged by her brother to catch Hawkwood in just such a dilemma—defending her. She wondered why Jovan hated Hawkwood so. "I see no purpose in the duel. Surely Jovan knows Hawkwood will kill the Dayknights."

"Don't be so sure he will, Jon."

"You doubt his skills?" she asked harshly.

"You remind me of your mother, headstrong and foolish, the both of you. Your brashness at the Filthy Horse bears that out. You want to challenge and threaten and fight and out-argue everyone, including your brother. Everything to you is a crusade for fairness. In a great many ways you remind me of Alana. She acted as such with your father. She challenged him, as you challenge Jovan. But she was far more cautious than you."

"Me challenge and threaten and fight and argue? It was you who mocked the grand vicar, you who initiated the entire argument that led up to this pointless duel."

"Jovan's court is much like the arena. You have the quorum, the grand vicar, the Vallè ambassador, countless other lords and barons, all vying for Jovan's attention and favor. Jovan senses you are smarter than them all. He fears you."

"Fears me?" She felt herself swell with pride.

"Hawkwood says you have potential as a fighter. But you attack too quickly with too much attention spent on cutting and slashing, with no attempt to defend. You could do well in the arena fighting in such a brash way against untrained criminals. Perhaps you could have taken that old sailor in the Filthy Horse had the fight not been a 'pirates' duel.' But in reality, you haven't the patience to find your opponent's weaknesses. You shoot your mouth off in the same way. Think before you speak or threaten or challenge. Unlike your mother, you wear your emotions too visibly, Jon."

"*You* advise *me* to think before I threaten or challenge?"

Roguemoore looked directly at her, eyes unyielding. "Ask yourself this. Why was your father in Oksana when the White Prince first attacked Wyn Darrè?"

"I don't know," she answered, feeling the dwarf was just running her around in circles. "It was nearly five years ago when he died."

"Is he dead?"

The abruptness of the question stunned her. "Ser Jubal Bruk saw him die, as did Jovan and Leif Chaparral and a host of other survivors of the battle."

"Jubal Bruk claimed he saw your father *fall*, and from a distance of several hundred yards, mind you. And I doubt Jovan or Leif saw a thing. But more importantly, why was Borden on the far side of Wyn Darrè at that particular moment in time?"

"Under Father's rule, Gul Kana always lent what aid it could against Sør Sevier's crusade. He was there in Oksana to stop the White Prince's invasion in Wyn Darrè before it reached Gul Kana."

"Yes and no."

She looked at the dwarf, expecting more, but she could read nothing in his gaze.

"There are such things as prisoners of war," Roguemoore stated, turning away.

"Sør Sevier would have bragged they'd captured Borden, held him for ransom."

"Not if they wanted us to keep Gul Kana's armies out of Wyn Darrè. A dead king is easier to reconcile than a captured king. A captured king needs rescuing. And Sør Sevier did not want Jovan rushing to the aid of Wyn Darrè. Their spies and influence run deep. Sør Sevier knew that Borden's councillors would pull Gul Kana's armies out of Wyn Darrè at his death."

"If what you say is true, and Sør Sevier influences our court, and if the White Prince indeed captured my father, then in all likelihood he killed him soon thereafter."

"Not if he wanted to bring him out later, for some other purpose."

"You are like Jovan. You see a conspiracy in everything, dwarf." At her words, she detected a measure of hurt behind those dark, unrevealing eyes of his.

"The Five Isles are thick with conspiracy, Jon. I just told you. Trust no one. Your father was a clear thinker. He would have marched the entire might of our armies into Wyn Darrè and fought off Sør Sevier on foreign soil had his councillors and lords allowed it and backed him in his plan. He was not enamored of the idea, but he knew that if an enemy comes, you fight. For, if they keep coming, they may destroy you. He knew that the only way to utterly conquer an enemy is to go to his kingdom and burn his lands, kill him, kill his wife, his children. He believed one does not negotiate with a butcher. With a butcher, the only way peace is achieved is with the honed edge of a blade and the spilling of blood. And the White Prince is a butcher. As, I fear, Gul Kana will soon learn."

Roguemoore paused before continuing. "Your father believed a Sør Sevier assassin was responsible for your mother's death when Ansel was born. Most chalked Alana's death up to the complications of childbirth. Not your father. His desire to strike against the White Prince was spurred not only by practicality, but by his emotions, too. He fought Sør Sevier despite what others thought. There were barons, lords, archbishops, and even a grand vicar along with scores of others in Gul Kana who did not approve. Their case was that Wyn Darrè's problems are not Gul Kana's. Let Wyn Darrè fight its own battles. After all, Sør Sevier is no direct threat. The entirety of the king's court thinks the prophecies in *The Way and Truth of Laijon* are about to be fulfilled and Fiery Absolution is inevitable, so why send good men to fight against prophecy and destiny? These notions, in part, were planted in their heads by conspirators, emissaries of Sør Sevier. But your parents and others in the Brethren of Mia swore many oaths together, promising to never allow Absolution to happen. That is our focus, the prevention of Fiery Absolution. Now that fighting the White Prince on Wyn Darrè soil is no longer an option, we must proceed by other means. The Brethren have been preparing for near two decades. We've a way to defeat Aeros and his armies that does not involve the deaths of tens of thousands of Gul Kana soldiers."

"What are you getting at?"

"Trust no one, Jon, not the vicar or the quorum, certainly not Val-Korin or his daughters, and as I see it, perhaps not even Val-Draekin. I have not made up my mind yet, though your father spoke highly of him." His words only added to her confusion.

"Indeed, you *are* like my brother." Jondralyn was growing tired of the vagueness in parts of their conversation. "Everything *is* a conspiracy with you two. Why is Val-Draekin here?"

"We must keep him close. The information he carries is important to the many oaths I swore to your father so long ago. Val-Draekin has the potential to become either one of our greatest allies or our worst enemy. It depends upon how we treat him. No. How *you* treat him, Jon. You are tied to him in a way. He is important to the plans of the Brethren of Mia, more so than your father initially believed. If something should happen to Hawkwood during the duel with the Dayknights, do not lose sight of Val-Draekin."

The dwarf had earlier hinted that he did not expect Hawkwood would kill the Dayknights, when she knew he was more than capable. Her brother was setting Hawkwood up for something worse, she feared. "It is clear Jovan wants the Brethren of Mia eliminated. You should escape the city, Roguemoore, now, while you can, before my brother sets you up too. Flee from this place if you value your life. There is something about this duel that doesn't seem right. We fell right into Jovan's trap."

"Indeed." The dwarf smiled, and his deep-set eyes now sparkled. "Sometimes it is best if you make them believe the trap is theirs."

With an icy rattle along the nape of her neck, Jondralyn had the sudden stark sensation of falling into a brisk rolling river, of being hurled about by unseen currents. Around Roguemoore she often felt she was an unwilling participant in a very large game, a game so far beyond her she was helpless in it. Yet, still, within the midst of this spinning battle, she was both frightened and thrilled. Like her father and mother before her, Jondralyn wanted to be part of the Brethren of Mia. But who were her allies? Hawkwood? Squireck? Roguemoore? She had made her bonds with each them, for sure. But had she chosen them? Or had they chosen her? And what was the Brethren's true purpose that Roguemoore had just spoken of? *We've a way to defeat Aeros and his armies that does not involve the deaths of hundreds of thousands of Gul Kana soldiers.* How? This question ran around her head like a rat trapped in a cage.

Roguemoore's gray eyes met hers. "Hawkwood and I both agree. Val-Draekin was not the only one who followed us into the Filthy Horse Saloon. There are others, many in fact, who are watching us from every angle."

With those parting words, Roguemoore turned and strode away along the battlements of Amadon Castle. Jondralyn looked toward Seita and Val-Draekin in the courtyard below, confused, uneasy, and afraid.

But something the dwarf said earlier had given her an idea.

Jovan senses you are smarter than them all, Jon. He fears you.

But worst of all creatures found in the Five Isles are the merfolk—beautiful and shocking to behold, dangerous beyond measure. They will rape you and they will eat you. For they are the most vile of all living things.
—THE WAY AND TRUTH OF LAIJON

CHAPTER TWELVE
TALA BRONACHELL

18TH DAY OF THE SHROUDED MOON, 999TH YEAR OF LAIJON

AMADON, GUL KANA

Glade Chaparral's eyes were dark and bold. Whenever he removed his helm, his golden-brown hair was a careless, but glorious, tangle. His armor glistened in the sun like shards of lightning that pierced Tala's heart. And when he looked her way, she felt an invisible cloud of warm air, luxurious and heavenly. Yet today in Greengrass Courtyard, Glade only had eyes for the Vallè princess.

Glade and Lindholf gave Seita and Val-Draekin their full attention as the two demonstrated how to block and parry with wooden swords. To most in Gul Kana, the very notion that a woman would want to sword fight was heresy. But Tala secretly desired that someone would teach her such things, as Hawkwood taught Jondralyn. She wished to be acknowledged in just the way Glade acknowledged

Seita. She longed to be treated with fondness or even respect. It was because the Vallè girl *could* fight as well as a man that she was treated so. But Tala lacked patience. That is, she lacked the patience to wait contentedly, or patience to practice her knitting, or memorize her Ember Gathering prayers, or patience to learn the craft of sword fighting—everyone knew Jondralyn practiced with Hawkwood against Jovan's wishes. But Tala had nobody to champion her cause, to defend her honor. She'd like Glade to take that role. She felt her impatience with everything was always there, simmering beneath her graceful poise and polite veneer. *Ah, yes, poise and grace . . . the quality and high breeding of a princess.*

Tala had never before seen a couple of boys eye a woman as attentively as Glade and Lindholf eyed Seita. Vallè women had a way of turning men into slobbering, blathering fools, mostly because it was well known that a human male could have as much sex with a Vallè female as he wanted and never get her pregnant. And what human woman in her right mind wanted to contend with that?

As Seita leaned into Glade and helped him with the grip on his wooden sword, Tala imagined bitterly that the two were not talking of weapons but pledging eternal affection or sharing little lovers' jokes. It made her stomach churn to see Glade so near such an exquisite beauty. It further sickened her that she felt such jealousy over a boy who until just recently had paid her scant romantic attention. They had been friends since childhood. But things *were* slowly changing between them since Jovan had hinted of their betrothal. There was a strained awkwardness now.

Tala stood with Lawri near the inner wall. Atop the battlements were a dozen Silver Guards, keeping watch over the courtyard and the safety of the king's sister and cousins. Normally Tala would be thrilled to be spending time with Glade and her twin cousins, but today was different. It had been almost an entire week and still she'd done nothing about the assassin's note, *Retrieve the red helm of the dead demon and read what is inscribed therein.* She refused to believe the Bloodwood's intent to poison Lawri was real. After all, her cousin did not appear the slightest bit ill. She still radiated beauty.

"M'lady, Tala, would you care to join us?" Seita bowed toward her. "It would do me great honor. I wish to show you and Lawri something."

As Tala made her way toward Seita, she crinkled her nose. The smell of Glade and Lindholf in their battle gear was that of damp leather and old, mildewed stockings.

"You seem troubled today, m'lady," Seita said. The statement came out pleasant, yet in a way, there lurked a cold indifference in Seita's congenial concern.

"It's nothing," Tala responded.

The Vallè princess wore formfitting leather breeches laced up the sides, a black belt, and a tan tunic. Her lithe legs fit perfectly in the pants. And her silvery hair was the color of fine-spun silk—sleek and clean and hanging a little loosely over the sides of her face and ears. She might be eighteen years old, Tala figured, or perhaps twenty. Over the years, all in Amadon had been charmed by Seita and her sister, Breita. However, Breita had not returned to court with Seita, which, Tala supposed, was a good thing—she had a hard enough time competing with just one Vallè princess.

Tala considered her own yellow dress and frilly shawl, wishing she'd worn something more befitting the courtyard. Every time Glade and her cousins visited Amadon, the visits would start as dress-wearing, formal affairs, with all the pageantry of royals of the opposite sex getting together. But after a few days, the formality would wear off. They would soon relax and begin conversing as real people, as real friends.

Seita pulled forth a thin dagger from her belt and held it hilt-first toward Tala. "I would teach you something Breita and I learned when we were your age." She motioned for Tala to grab the dagger.

She took it by the hilt. Seita continued, "Hold it firmly, threateningly. And look me in the eyes as if you truly mean to slay me."

Tala did as instructed. Seita clapped and the blade went flying from Tala's hand, landing in the grass at Lawri's feet. Lawri picked it up. The back of Tala's hand stung, as did her inner wrist. She rubbed the tender flesh. Seita took the dagger from Lawri and handed it back to Tala, saying, "Hold it out again. Grip it as tight as you can this time."

Tala clenched the dagger's hilt and glared at the Vallè. This close, she could see that Seita's face was indeed narrow and sharp, with the flawless beauty of porcelain, and green frosty eyes, but gorgeously exquisite. *Oh yes, if I could slay her now.*

Seita clapped. The dagger spun from Tala's hand. Skin blossomed red along the underside of her wrist. She looked at Seita, quickly realizing that the Vallè princess standing before her was not only a beautiful creature but a dangerous one as well. She found herself shrinking back from Seita's quiet gaze. She was also worried that this princess was purposely making her look a fool in front of Glade.

"Part of the trick is speed." Seita retrieved the dagger from the grass herself this time and handed it to Lindholf. "It's a simple trick, really. Most who attack with a knife are not usually looking at their own hands, but into the eyes of the one they are attacking. So look me in the eyes and attack me with the blade, Lindholf."

Tala's cousin removed his helm with one hand and held the dagger out before him in the other. Lindholf's hair was a matted, corncob-colored mess. His every attempt to look manly took on a certain magnitude of foolishness, and his misplaced attempt to grow facial hair did little to help his cause. A mere wisp of a goatee clung to his burn-scarred face.

Lindholf crouched, planting his boots in the turf and bracing his legs. He clenched the blade so tightly his face strained with the effort and his protruding brow furrowed, making his freckled forehead bulge unnaturally like a deformed potato.

He lunged. Seita clapped. "Holy Mother Mia!" Lindholf exclaimed as the dagger spun away. He waggled his hand as if injured. "May the Blessed Mother show mercy on me." He made the three-fingered sign of the Laijon Cross over his breast.

Seita picked up the dagger and handed it back to Tala. "I'll show you where to strike and why it works." Tala held the dagger out, and Seita touched the inner part of her wrist. "If you strike hard on the inside of the wrist here, just below the palm, at the same time striking the back of the hand . . ." Seita put pressure on both spots against Tala's hand and pushed. Involuntarily, Tala's fingers slowly folded open and the dagger slid free, dropping to the ground. "The hand has no choice but to release the blade."

Tala picked up the dagger and held it out again with a bit more enthusiasm. Seita clapped, not as hard as before, but still the blade was forced from Tala's grip. She looked at Seita with new admiration. The fact that someone, anyone, was taking the time to teach her something—especially of weaponry—meant a great deal.

"Your turn." Seita held the dagger out tightly in her own hand. With a well-placed clap, Tala disarmed the Vallè princess.

"You're good at it, Tala," Lindholf added with a pleasant smile. "We should all thank her for teaching us her elfin tricks."

"What did you say, boy?" Seita's eyes darkened. A gravelly, strained tone was now set in her normally silken voice. Her posture was tense, limbs seeming on the verge of uncoiling in fury. The sheer coarseness of her question evoked an awkward silence.

Lindholf appeared stunned at the stark look in Seita's eyes. "I merely wished to express to you my thanks for teaching us your elf trick."

"Elf trick," Seita snapped. "Have you learned nothing from your history studies? Do you think Val-Draekin and I are naught but fairies, tossing magical trickery about as if we've nothing better to do than prance about in some sort of fairy tale?"

"I merely meant—"

"Fairies are stupid," Seita said forcefully. "To call a Vallè an elf or a fairy is an insult. It only reveals your own ignorance. Just because we have ears unlike your own, and clearer skin, does not mean we are *mere* elves. We are just like humans. Well, I suppose we can run faster, and perhaps jump higher. After all, can a fairy do this?" Seita whirled, throwing a dagger across the courtyard, where it stuck point first into the stone wall. Lindholf took two steps back from her, averting his eyes, clearly frightened.

"For centuries, the very word *fairy* denoted weakness to you humans," Seita continued. "It recalls the ancient tales of fey devil worshippers, who talk to animals and breed with dragons and other such nonsense. Let me tell you something. There are no such things as talking animals. It's a stupid notion. So mind your tongue, boy. We are no dragon breeders. We leave that filthy practice to the oghuls."

A fearsome silence fell upon the group. Seita had just dared speak the forbidden word—*dragon*—the most damning of all curse words. That she had uttered such foulness in front of royalty belied the seriousness of Lindholf's insult.

Val-Draekin held a dagger under Lindholf's chin, forcing his head upward, so the boy had to look him directly in the eyes. Tala was instantly gripped with light-headedness. She looked toward the battlements. The complacent guardsmen seemed oblivious to the goings-on below. Beyond the guardsmen, dark clouds roiled, cresting the battlements, blocking out the sun, setting a chill into the air that cut straight through the thin fabric of her dress. Tala shivered as Val-Draekin, jade eyes smoldering, made a shallow nod before lifting a knowing eyebrow and saying, "She's only joking, you know."

Realization dawned in Lindholf's eyes first, and he backed away from the knife, caressing his throat—and clapped. The dagger spun from Val-Draekin's hand.

"Nicely done." Seita smiled. "But I must say the look in your eyes was precious."

"Bloody rotted Mother," Glade said, as if expelling a lifetime's worth of pent-up air from his lungs. "I seriously thought I was goin' to have to take up my wooden sword and wade in between you three."

"Well, I should've kept up the ruse a while longer." Seita sounded dryly amused.

"You doubt my skills, m'lady?" Glade puffed his chest out, his tone quite jovial. "I daresay you and your one-armed Vallè friend would be hardly a match for me."

"Perhaps," Seita said, then addressed Lindholf. "If you can pull your dagger from the stone wall, I'll personally give you three hundred gold Vallè medallions."

All eyes turned to the dagger Seita had thrown, the dagger that was now protruding from the solid stone wall of Greengrass Courtyard.

"My dagger?" Lindholf, confused, reached behind his own waist. "My dagger's right here at my belt . . . wait . . . how?"

Glade laughed. "She lifted it right off you, man."

"Aye." Val-Draekin handed Glade the dagger that he had previously held up to Lindholf's throat. "And here's your knife back too." Glade took the dagger, brow furrowing, one hand feeling for his own sheath behind his back, and when he found it empty, a smile spread over Val-Draekin's face. "Even one-armed, a Vallè is dangerous."

"Elf tricks indeed." Glade bent his knee before Seita, smiling. "However, my good friend Lindholf Le Graven offended the daughter of the ambassador, inferring she was naught but a fairy." He brandished his wooden sword. "Must I defend her honor?"

"Defend my honor." Seita tossed back her head and laughed. "Don't bother."

Tala found Seita's lighthearted laugh quite pleasing. Overall, she was enjoying her time spent under the tutelage of the two Vallè.

"My honor will never need defending," Seita said, a distant tone in her voice. "But I fear the arena changes every man in Amadon. The whole city has gone gladiator mad; every man wants to defend *honor*. Every man wants to prove the rightness of his cause by throwing a challenge. They have more regard for a bit of honor than any hundred lives. To place personal honor or the defense against insult above the safety of those around you is the behavior of an oghul raider—or worse yet, the behavior of kings, princes, councillors, and archbishops. As if Laijon truly cares who wins."

Glade countered, "*The Way and Truth of Laijon* deems dueling to be sanctioned by Laijon. The gladiator pit is full of glory, a way to prove one's innocence before Laijon, and a way for the guilty to suffer pain. It's the most honorable event in all Gul Kana."

"You're being a bit hypocritical, Seita," a familiar voice interjected. "Wasn't it your own father, Val-Korin, who first suggested that Hawkwood duel the Four Dayknights?" Jondralyn looked both wild and beautiful as she approached. She wore a long coat of silver chain mail, an old Amadon Silver Guard shortsword strapped to her back, silver shield and helm in hand. When Seita did not answer, Jondralyn carried on, "Even the knights of Sør Sevier follow their own Rule of Blood Penance—a fight to the death to defend one's honor. We all must learn to fight, even me. Even you." Jondralyn met Tala's gaze and then both Glade's and Lindholf's too. The boys looked at her like they couldn't believe she was dressed like a man, in actual *armor*.

Jondralyn's eyes turned back to Seita. "Unlike our vigilant guards, I was watching Seita teach you those tricks with the dagger. Impressive, for one so set against dueling."

"Though I am trained with a blade," Seita said, "I see no honor in dueling."

"Our histories are rife with the glory of dueling," Glade interjected, eyes still trained on Jondralyn's garb. "Some of the most worthy combatants who've risen gloriously from the arena matches have gone on to become some of Gul Kana's most worshipped men. The gladiator matches are a religious occasion to celebrate Laijon's great sacrifice. The arena is a way in which criminals can atone for their own sins in combat. And when the guilty die, their spilt blood mixes with the soil of the arena floor and is considered sufficient sacrifice."

"As you've said." Seita nodded.

"If I may speak, Ser Glade?" Val-Draekin stepped forward. "There are plenty of unbelievers who have won duels. How is this reconciled in Laijon's plan?"

Glade nodded in acknowledgment. "In such cases, *The Way and Truth of Laijon* says that we must pray for the wisdom to know what holy lesson can be learned by the victory of an unbeliever. Perhaps the *supposed* righteous loser of the duel was not true in his faith, or perhaps he was an unrepentant sinner. Or more simply, perhaps Laijon's divine plan was for him to lose. Laijon's ways are not our ways." Glade looked skyward as the first few sprinkles of rain pinged off his armor.

Jondralyn again took up the debate. "Even nobility has joined in the arena matches for sport—and won, mind you. King Laban Bronachell, in the year 324, renounced the kingship and fought in the arena, claiming he would take up the crown again only if he could prove his mettle. He slaughtered every foe and became one of Gul Kana's most revered kings. There were even women gladiators for a time. One became queen who ruled."

"You seem to have been thinking on these matters quite carefully." Val-Draekin bowed before Jondralyn. "Does your interest in the history of the arena have something to do with the pirates' duel?"

Jondralyn shot the Vallè an angry look. "That matter seemed to resolve itself just fine."

"My pardon." Val-Draekin bowed one final time, truly seeming contrite. "I only bring the subject to your attention again in the hopes that perhaps you might allow me to teach you how to fight such a duel . . . and never lose."

Tala had no idea what a pirates' duel was, but her older sister's countenance softened for a moment, only a moment, and then her brow sharpened darkly.

The sudden rumble of heavy steel-toed boots and the clamor of armor sounded above. Silver Guards were running across the battlements, taking positions surrounding the courtyard, crossbows drawn and cocked. The ponderous bronze doors under the battlements creaked open and Jovan stepped from the inner bailey into the courtyard.

The king, dressed in the silver surcoat and black-lacquered armor of the Dayknights, walked toward them; Sterling Prentiss was by his side, carrying a black shield with the silver-painted Laijon tree centerpiece and a long Dayknight sword with black opal–inlaid pommel. It looked freshly sharpened. Everyone bent their knee as Tala's brother strode into their midst.

Jovan took the sword and shield from Sterling. He thrust one arm through the strap of his shield and hefted the sword, feeling its weight. He met Tala's eyes for but a moment, and she saw something she hadn't noticed in Jovan before. Her brother's face looked tired, older, drained. The once-boyish cast to his features had faded. He stared at Jondralyn in her armor for a moment, then turned from her.

"You shouldn't worship Hawkwood so," he said casually to Glade and Lindholf, who now stood at attention before him. "I have been watching you from above, dueling, using Hawkwood's Sør Sevier tricks. The techniques of that Sør Sevier bastard are no longer a part of your training."

"With all due respect"—Seita bowed before the king—"those were Vallè tricks I was teaching, with just a sprinkling of Sør Sevier blade work intermingled."

"And Hawkwood's the best fighter in Amadon," Lindholf said. "We've learned so much from him alread—"

Lawri let out a sharp gasp as Sterling Prentiss slapped her twin brother's face hard with the back of his gauntlets. "Don't argue with your king, boy."

Lindholf's head snapped back. Cuts from the gauntlet welled red along his cheek, and his nose was bloodied. The rain had picked up. It quickly washed the blood away. For some reason, Lindholf glanced at Tala. It seemed he was more embarrassed that she, of all people, had seen him get slapped. Tala took pity on her cousin and sent him what she thought was a warm look. It didn't seem to help matters, though. When Lindholf looked back at the captain, both hurt and rage glinted in his eyes.

"Yes, be mad at me, you sniveling arse-wipe," Sterling said. "But mind your manners, too. I will remember this day and your ill-advised words." He turned and addressed all the soldiers gathered around. "The king is right. We should be wary that a scoundrel such as Hawkwood has been allowed to live and train among us for so long. You are henceforth forbidden to practice any sword craft he has taught you."

Jondralyn stepped in front of the Dayknight captain, anger on her face. "Hawkwood is my friend."

Tala was stunned when Jovan swung his sword. Jondralyn pulled her own short blade, barely in time to block the blow aimed at her head. Tala's ears rang with the sounds of steel on steel. The sharp twang and clank of Jovan's naked blade striking against that of Jondralyn carried with it a certain foreboding and reminded Tala of the real sounds of death and battles in the arena.

"What's the meaning of this?" Jondralyn stammered, backing away from her brother, sword at the ready. Tala sensed that every crossbow bolt in the battlements above was raised and aimed straight at her sister. Rain fell harder now, the drops dampening Tala's dress and streaming across her cheeks. She was assaulted by a gloom that settled into her heart. The courtyard had now become a joyless place.

"The folly of Borden's eldest daughter is at an end," Jovan said. "I am your older brother and I am your king." He thrust his shield out and readied his blade for another strike at Jondralyn. "If you love Hawkwood so much, then let us fight, sister. It is what you want, after all. To prove your *manhood*. Disarm me and I call off the duel between your *friend* and the Dayknights. You lose, the duel goes on as planned. One week from now."

Jondralyn's answer was quick in coming. With surprising speed her sword lashed out in a wide swing aimed beneath the king's shield, meant to sweep his feet away. Jovan jumped backward and thrust his shield to the ground. Jondralyn's sword clacked against the shield. They backed away from each other, swords poised.

As her older siblings circled each other, Tala found it hard to believe they were actually fighting with bare steel. Neither wore a helm, and rain plastered their hair around their heads and ran in rivulets from their faces. Tala shivered from the biting squall that poured down. How had it so quickly come to this, a duel between siblings to settle other people's problems? Seita was right about the folly of dueling. Something had definitely changed in Jovan since the kingship had been thrust upon him. The older brother Tala had once admired was becoming more distrustful of everyone, including his own sister. Tala wanted to shout at them to stop. But as the younger royal sibling, she knew she must act normal, appear unconcerned, remain stoic, as if a duel between brother and sister were a mere diversion from her normally uneventful, solitary, routine-dominated life.

It soon looked as if the early blow Jondralyn had delivered would be her only one. Jovan blocked the rest with his upraised shield; at the same time, he was attacking repeatedly with his own sword, beating Jondralyn about the arms and shoulders, quickly wearing her down. Jondralyn's chain mail was the only thing saving her from serious injury. The weight of her sword was becoming a disadvantage now. Even though she wielded a short sword, her every swing was more labored than the last. Jovan was thrusting his shield up under her guard, pushing her backward. Jondralyn had no choice but to retreat, winded. Once they were separated by a few yards of turf, Jondralyn bent and sucked in air. But Jovan allowed her no respite and lunged. Jondralyn raised her sword to block, but it was knocked from her hand. She fell to her knees from the impact.

"Done!" Jovan placed his booted foot against Jondralyn's chest and shoved her backward onto the muddy grass. "It appears Hawkwood will duel the Dayknights as planned." He handed Sterling Prentiss his shield and sword. Both men walked from the courtyard in silence, and the crossbowmen along the battlements retreated from sight.

"Well," Seita said as Jovan and Sterling disappeared through the far tunnel. "I see the pecking order has clearly been established. As if we didn't already know."

Jondralyn gathered up her fallen sword. Still kneeling, she dropped back to her haunches, the shortsword now gripped in both hands, resting on her legs. Her head hung low. Matted strands of hair partially obscured her face. Rainwater ran from the chain mail in sheets. Tala took two steps toward her sister but stopped as Lawri Le Graven slowly folded to the ground directly in front of her.

"She's fainted." Lindholf rushed to his sister's side.

Seita and Val-Draekin knelt over Lawri. "We must get her out of the rain." Seita felt Lawri's neck for a pulse, shielding Lawri's body from the rain with her own.

Tala's heart was pounding. She tried to take hold of her deeply rooted emotions, a breath, another, yet there remained a puddling warmth sinking within her chest, a faint swirl of dread growing in her gut.

Could it be the assassin's poison was truly eating at Lawri?

"We should carry her to the infirmary." Lindholf cradled his sister's head. "Help me lift her, Glade. She's been hiding some terrible bouts of sickness lately. Looking pretty for the court but puking her guts out in her chamber in secret."

Seita pulled a small wooden box from the pouch at her waist, stuck two of her fingers into it, and rubbed her fingers under Lawri's nose. Lawri's eyes darted open as she shot to a sitting position, sneezing and coughing.

"What was that you wiped under her nose?" Lindholf asked.

"Just a little fairy dust," Seita answered, smiling. "A magical elf concoction my pet mouse taught me how to make." But her attempt at humor was lost on Lindholf as he put one arm around his sister's shoulders whilst his other hand held wet hair out of her face. Lawri sneezed. With Glade, Lindholf helped his sister to her feet.

"I'm taking her in," he said as Lawri's sneezing turned to a hacking cough. Then she vomited. "Rotted angels," Lindholf muttered, looking up at Seita. "Bloody Mother Mia, what did you rub under her nose? It's made her spew."

"Its purpose was to make her spew," Seita said. "It all has a purpose, Lindholf. Everything I do."

Tala felt a tug at her arm and turned. It was Jondralyn. Her older sister was sodden with mud from the field. As Tala looked upon Jondralyn, a vague weight of unease was burrowing into her heart. The cause of her consternation was in the look that her sister gave her, an almost pleading look.

Jondralyn's eyes traveled slowly, deliberately, from Tala to Lawri and back. "I'm going to need your help," she said, moving closer. There was a splattering of rain across her shoulders, and she smelled of wet leather and cold armor. She whispered in Tala's ear. "Yes, Tala, I think you're the only one who can help me now."

Whoso believeth that hostile spirits dwell in the totems, let them be accursed.
Whoso believeth the standing-stones guard buried treasures and the holy
weapons of Laijon, let them be accursed. For we the prophets of old say unto you
now, the weapons of the Five Warrior Angels were taken up into heaven.
—THE WAY AND TRUTH OF LAIJON

CHAPTER THIRTEEN

NAIL

2ND DAY OF THE MOURNING MOON, 999TH YEAR OF LAIJON
GALLOWS HAVEN, GUL KANA

There are those in Gallows Haven who expect me to be perfect," Ava Shay said with a touch of sadness, her face a golden silhouette against the starlight twinkling off the ocean waves beyond her. "I fear I may never be able to live up to their expectations. Living alone, raising my brothers and sisters, takes its toll."

"I think you're perfect," Nail said simply.

"You're so nice."

They sat in the sand, gazing at the ocean. Nail's sword and armor rested nearby. All the day's Mourning Moon Feast competitions were now over. Nail wore a rough-spun shirt, pants, and leather greaves. Smoke from Jubal Bruk's black cauldrons billowed up into the darkness to the north, the boiling of grayken blubber still ongoing. A few scabby chickens pecked in the dirt just to the south. The sound of dogs barking in the distance and the natter of the village women preparing food for the revelers of the Mourning Moon Feast were a blur of noise near the keep far behind them. So conscious was he of the nearness of Ava Shay, Nail was only dimly aware of any of it. The turtle necklace she'd made for him was still around his neck, its presence a burning reminder of his want for her.

"The future can be frightening," she continued. "Some prospects seem exciting, overwhelming even. Things may open up for me and my siblings soon. I mean, my parents have been dead a while now. I'm so conflicted, most times." Ava trailed off into silence. Nail studied her golden-hued face, lit from the distant bonfires of the Mourning Moon Feast. There was an ivory-peach tint to her skin. Her full lips glistened.

"I've made plans." He thought of his own uncertain future. "Perhaps I can design stained-glass windows for chapels, maybe a cathedral." Though he wondered if he would ever be able to do anything without Shawcroft's permission.

"You are a splendid artist, Nail. The best in the village. Never change. I like you just the way you are." Her statement moved him profoundly. Nobody had ever said such a thing to him, certainly not his master. Her words sharpened his desire for her.

He leaned in and kissed her. Her lips were soft and tasted of cinnamon. She pulled away a little quicker than he would have wanted and rested her hand in his. "You're so nice. So strong. Handsome, too. You will make some lucky girl very happy one day."

Nail didn't know quite what to make of her last comment. But in the moonlight, her soft-glowing eyes sparkled like pools of cool water. There was a scent of flowers about her. He ached to kiss her again.

"That odd woman we saw on the mountain," she continued, looking nervous, "that cloaked woman on the red-eyed horse who spoke to you, did you know her?"

Nail shuddered, imagining the Vallè woman's terrified face as Shawcroft put the knife to her ear, the screams as she'd burned. "She was just a lost traveler or something."

"There's been talk of a Sør Sevier spy in town. Was it her?" There was real worry in Ava's eyes. "Will the White Prince attack here?"

"Why would he attack here? Gallows Haven is so small." His mind was whirling. *You are not of my blood. Still, they will be coming for you,* the Vallè woman had said. Shawcroft had called her a Bloodwood. *Bloodwood assassins have hunted us your entire life, boy!*

Stefan Wayland had drawn his bow on the woman that day. Nail had done nothing. Stood dumbfounded as she'd muttered nonsense at him. Some days he wondered if he truly had anything to offer anyone.

Stefan was the best bowman in Gallows Haven. Earlier tonight, just outside the keep's courtyard, he'd won the Mourning Moon Feast archery competition. His prize: a finely carved, solidly weighted Amadon Silver Guard bow from Baron Bruk. Gisela Barnwell, Maiden Blue of the Mourning Moon Feast, had kissed Stefan right then and there. Even Dokie Liddle had attended the competition, his face showing scarcely any signs of his lightning burns. With an enthusiastic shout, Dokie had assured everyone that Stefan would win the archery competition against Tomkin Sty and Peddlers Point conscripts when they held their annual tournament between towns.

"Do you believe in *The Way and Truth of Laijon*?" Ava asked, resting her head on Nail's shoulder. "Do you believe in Laijon?"

"I reckon I believe," he muttered. Shawcroft certainly took issue with much that was taught within the holy book. And some of those doubts had been instilled in him. But his master rarely explained himself when it came to matters of faith. "It's just sometimes, the writings of *The Way and Truth of Laijon* seem awfully hard to decipher."

Ava giggled. "At least you are honest, Nail. You say what comes to your mind, even if it is nonsense. You just might be the most honest young man in all of Gallows Haven. It is admirable, to be sure. My mother, when she lived, was devoted to Laijon, almost to the point of distraction. She carried the cross about her neck and rubbed the Ember Gathering beads in her hands. When I am given my cross and beads, I will do the same. *The Way and Truth of Laijon* has commanded us to shrug away the cloak of unrighteous doubt. I have prayed often and felt Laijon's Holy Spirit warm within my body, within my own heart. His spirit has frightened away the wraiths that might steal my soul. He answers the prayers of the worthy."

Nail admired her devotion, wishing he could find the warmth of Laijon's spirit within his own heart too. It seemed some were blessed with a gift of faith, a type of faith that he longed for. That he couldn't summon it within himself was frustrating.

Ava lifted her head from his shoulder, took his arm, and pulled him down. They lay in the sand, gazing heavenward. "When you look at the stars, what do you see?"

Nail studied the southern Gul Kana sky. Pinpricks of frosty light twinkled from horizon to horizon. "Seems so big. Makes my life seem so . . . insignificant."

"I wonder what the sky is," Ava spoke softly. "*The Way and Truth of Laijon* speaks of heaven being in the sky. But why can I not see it up there?"

Nobody had talked to him about the sky since he was a child. He recalled the fellow, Culpa Barra, who had lived with him and Shawcroft for a time in Deadwood Gate. Culpa had read to him from old scrolls, taught him secrets of the stars and the lights of the borealis, ideas and concepts he only half remembered.

"There was a man, a friend of Shawcroft's, who once told me of heaven," he said, his voice reverent in tone. "He spoke of Laijon and the other Warrior Angels. He spoke of those fighters who have died in the service of Laijon being raised into heaven to live among the stars—"

"How horrid," Ava said, leaning on one elbow, looking at him now with revulsion. "And did you believe such blasphemous ideas?"

Nail was taken aback. "He spoke of stars without end," he said hastily, thinking if he explained himself further, she would understand. It was one of his fondest memories, Culpa Barra taking him aside and teaching him of the stars. "All created by Laijon, numberless and without end."

Ava sat up, folding her knees against her chest, wrapping her arms around them. "He seems full of Mia-worshipping witchcraft, this man. Heaven is a glorious place of spirits, not Warrior Angels living among the stars. The stars are too small. A warrior would crush a star between the tips of his fingers. I don't recall Bishop Tolbret reading anything like that out of *The Way and Truth of Laijon*. The holy book says the Blessed Mother is to be revered, never worshipped. It is taught that she was a great woman. But we are not to worship her in place of Laijon. Goddess worship is wrong. Ol' Man Leddingham heard tell, long ago, that before Baron Bruk came to Gallows Haven, he burned a raggedy Mia-worshipping witch who preached such wretchedness in Amadon. Leddingham said this woman was unclean before Laijon and deserved to die by Fiery Absolution."

The entire conversation was not at all going the way Nail had hoped. Now it looked as if he had offended the only person he wished not to offend. Both of them being parentless, he'd always felt a shared bond with Ava. But that now seemed to be unraveling. "Perhaps I misheard," he stammered.

Ava was looking south down the beach. Two figures were making their way up the waterline. They veered off and began climbing the grassy knoll toward Gallows Keep. When the firelight from the Mourning Moon Feast struck the two figures, Nail could see it was Jenko and Jubal Bruk.

"We should get back to the feast." Ava stood and hurried up the beach. Nail grabbed his armor and sword and followed.

† † † † †

"There's one too many boys here." The Bishop strolled up from behind, brown cassock brushing the ground beneath him, prayer book in hand. "I've not enough Ember Lighting robes for you all. There's one here who will not be fitted tonight."

Every boy in front of the chapel hung his head, none in the group daring to make eye contact with Nail. Even Stefan, Zane, and Dokie looked away. The silence lasted a while. Nail's eyes crawled up the steep face of the chapel, gazing toward the stained-glass windows high above. Somehow he knew what was coming. The disappointment seemed almost too unfathomable to grasp, especially in the state he was in, slightly drunk. He felt the sword at his hip and looked down at his pile of armor, stacked against the chapel's outer wall with the armor of the other seventeen-year-old boys.

"Nail's been studying for moons." Stefan's face blanched a dark shade of red. "He knows the Ember Lighting Prayers better than all of us."

"I've only so many robes to go around." Tolbret reached out and pulled Nail away from the group as if tearing a thistle from the garden. Nail looked toward the others, pleadingly, yet he knew no help lay there. In fact, at the moment, he just wanted to find a spot in the trees behind the chapel and relieve himself. He had to piss something fierce. *Too much drink at the feast!*

Stefan spoke again. "I will sit out the Ember Lighting this season. I'm not feeling up to the task anyway. There's always next year. I shall allow Nail to administer the fire in my stead, and wear my robes."

"Nail sits out." Bishop Tolbret spoke emphatically.

Stefan shook his head. "I don't mind. Just reserve a robe for me next year—"

"Listen, boy, lest I smack you," the bishop growled. "Nail will not put on an Ember Lighting robe today, nor will he ever, as long as I live."

He riffled through the pages of his holy book, quickly finding what he sought. "*The Way and Truth of Laijon* clearly states, and I quote from the Acts of the Second Warrior Angel, 'A bastard shall not enter into the Smoke and Fire. Even to the tenth generation shall a bastard not enter into any Ember Lighting or Ember Gathering of Laijon.'" Tolbret closed the book.

Nail's heart plunged in humiliation as he looked at the pile of armor through the locks of blond that veiled his face. He felt the lightning burn on the back of his hand flare in pain. It wasn't the words of *The Way and Truth of Laijon* themselves that angered him; it was the venom within Tolbret's voice as he read those words that stung. In that one moment, Nail came to a sudden realization of what Bishop Tolbret truly thought of him. It was sobering. He realized it wasn't just what Tolbret thought of him, but it was what everyone in Gallows Haven had always thought of him. *A bastard shall not enter into the Smoke and Fire.* In this world, a bastard was truly nothing. Even in a world created by the great and merciful Laijon, a bastard was nothing. He kept his gaze trained on the cold ground. *At least Ava Shay sees the good in me.*

He felt Stefan's arm on his. "It's all right, Nail." But Nail knew nothing had ever, nor would ever, be just "all right." This little episode was final proof of his one and only place in this world. No one needed a bastard. Not even Master Shawcroft. *I will run away from this place with Ava! We don't need anyone but each other.*

When Nail looked up and brushed the hair from his face, he saw something. Behind their bashful, solemn eyes, it was written on every boy's face—deep down, Nail could see they were all clearly relieved it wasn't they who would be excluded from the Ember Lighting robe fitting tonight or the Ember Lighting Rites coming up.

And when Bishop Tolbret opened the chapel door and beckoned them in, they leaned their swords against the entryway near their armor and went: Dokie, Zane, all the other seventeen-year-olds in

Gallows Haven, all save Nail. Stefan lingered at the door, sword still at his side. "Just go," Nail said, fighting the pain in his bladder, wanting to just run off into the woods and piss. Stefan drifted soundlessly into the chapel, leaving Nail alone with the bishop, shuffling from foot to foot, the stinging pain in his bladder almost too much to bear. There was no kindness or mercy in Tolbret's stare. "Unless Shawcroft makes your true parentage known, all future Ember Lighting dealings, along with the ceremony itself, will proceed without *you*."

Nail returned the man's gaze, defiant. Here too was Bishop Tolbret—the very man who had taught him, and every other boy in Gallows Haven, reading and writing, along with the importance of the Ember Lighting Rites—betraying him *once again*. He recalled how on the grayken hunt, after their harrowing adventure in the bloody ocean, Tolbret had placed his hands on Zane's head and given a blessing, but when Nail had knelt, the bishop had refused him. *Trust no one.*

"There's one more passage I will read you." Tolbret flipped through the pages of his holy book again, quickly finding what he sought. "And I quote again from the Acts of the Second Warrior Angel, 'A bastard shall not be taken in marriage within the church, nor should a bastard perform any ritual therein. It is written for now and forever that a bastard's place is not within the Church of Laijon, nor will it ever be.'" He slammed the book shut and looked at Nail. "I am here to remind you of your place, boy. How does it feel to know you are naught but a bastard, unwanted, even by Laijon?"

With those words, Nail couldn't fight it anymore. The anger. The bitterness. The searing pain on the back of his hand. But mostly he couldn't fight the need to piss.

He slapped *The Way and Truth of Laijon* from Bishop Tolbret's hand. The book hit the ground with a dull thud. The bishop, face lit with rage, bent to snatch it up. But Nail had already pulled down his leather greaves and the front of his breeches—just low enough—and released a raging, warm stream of piss on the book.

"To the bloody underworld with you," Bishop Tolbret snarled, jerking his hand away. The two stared at each other a moment as Nail finished, then pulled up his greaves.

"I ought to order Baron Bruk to hang you!" The bishop stormed into the chapel, leaving his *Way and Truth of Laijon* reeking and wet on the ground.

Nail stood there stunned at what he'd done. Almost in tears. But he would not cry, not over this. He would never cry. Not over anything.

"Not the wisest thing, pissing on Tolbret's book." Shawcroft came up from behind.

Nail turned, disappointed, ashamed, drunk, surprised to see the man here tonight. He didn't care at all. Music struck up in the center of the keep's courtyard. Leaving his armor, Nail made his way toward the keep, Shawcroft following, Nail scarcely noticing.

Villagers had started dancing under a canopy of evergreen boughs near the keep. A row of boys played bagpipes under the Gallows Haven banner that hung from the wall of the crumbled inner courtyard. Several women shook deer-horn rattles as a row of old sailors banged on drums stretched with elk hide. The clatter of their thin grayken-bone drumsticks striking the taut skins sent up a rhythmic beat. Even the village elders who typically sat about the feast smoking their spirit pipes rose to dance.

Ava Shay was in the middle of it all. She had two white feathers tied in her hair. In the torchlight the feathers glowed like a flicker of flame against her flowing blond locks. She danced with her eyes focused on the ground, swaying, her arms over her head. Her frayed woolen skirt rode low on her hips. Nail noticed a hint of white flesh and the curve of her buttocks peeking above the skirt line when she moved a certain way. As she danced with her arms held aloft, twirling, her faded tan shirt lifted just enough, exposing her belly button and the tantalizing curves of her midriff to the torrid glow of the bonfires.

"We must talk," Shawcroft said, still following him, voice barely above a whisper now. "We must talk of what I have found in the mines." He grabbed Nail, turning him.

Nail only noted what the man was doing and saying with a certain detachment, his eyes on Ava as she twirled slowly, her waist swaying like a slender fall of water.

"You must understand," Shawcroft continued, "I had good reason for killing that Vallè Bloodwood." Nail pulled his gaze from Ava. He had not expected the man to mention the Vallè woman again. He thought he detected a small measure of sadness creeping into the man's eyes. Then he realized it was not necessarily sadness growing there, but fear.

"I wanted you to know that dark creatures such as her can be killed." Shawcroft spoke in a frank tone. "I fear we will run into more of them in the coming days. And I do not want you to be scared. That woman's motivation is destruction and pain. Indeed, the motivation behind all a Bloodwood does is to destroy. War is coming. There are things that the White Prince and his minions may seek to annihilate in every corner of Gul Kana. Secrets are hidden within the very fabric of this land. In the coming days, Nail, remember that. Hatred and vengeance are a dangerous combination."

The man's words only angered him. "Hatred and vengeance are dangerous. That I'm to remember, while my own mother's name remains hidden from me, whilst I am forced into servitude to a man who cares little for my well-being? Baron Bruk offered me employ. Legitimate work. Not gold digging and treasure seeking. Everything you do is pointless. Hatred and vengeance are the worst of things? What of murder?"

Shawcroft's face paled. Nail forced his eyes to remain impassive, determined to show no weakness in front of him, and placed his hand on the pommel of his sword.

"We are nearing the one-thousand-year anniversary of Laijon's great sacrifice," Shawcroft said. "For good or ill, many prophecies are soon to be fulfilled. Our world is changing, Nail. You are now a man, and things will be changing for you, too."

Jenko Bruk caught Nail's attention. The baron's son was heading toward the keep's courtyard, straight for the dancers, straight for Ava Shay. Nail's heart fell into a black, heavy rhythm as Ava welcomed Jenko with open arms, kissing him on the lips.

"Everything I've done has a purpose," Shawcroft said. "Moving us to Gallows Haven. Mining. Killing that Vallè woman. Soon you will learn the why of it all."

But Nail could barely hear the man's words through the jealous rush burning in his head at the sight of Ava and Jenko. The firelight gleamed off Jenko's shined armor and his sword clanked against his greaves as he broke from his kiss with Ava before walking away. Nail's emotions were whirling painfully through his entire body. His previous drinking, along with the parade of conflicting thoughts rampaging through his brain, did not make clear thinking easy.

"Everything you do has a *purpose*?" he sneered at his master. "I don't even know who you are, *Shawcroft*. Or is it Ser Roderic?" From the corner of his eye he never lost awareness of Ava's continued dancing. Jenko was still walking away from her through the crowd. Perhaps the kiss had meant nothing. *Just a friendly kiss.*

"The mines," Shawcroft said. "I'll show you what I've found."

"Leave me alone." Nail stalked away, no longer listening, anger welling in his heart, souring his insides. *Jenko had kissed her! And she him!*

"Come back, Nail," he heard Shawcroft say. But he kept going. Kept walking. He unclenched his jaw and smiled as he approached Ava. The bonfire's light was playing on her skin. Her eyes caught the flickering light too, so that she appeared to have flames growing within her. Nail's heart was like a caged beast in his chest as he held his hand forth. Somehow he knew his heart would stop racing once he felt her delicate touch.

"May I have a dance?" he asked.

"I dare not, knowing Jenko watches." The look in her eye was one of shame.

Nail's hand froze, now poised awkwardly before her.

"I'm with Jenko tonight."

Nail could feel his pulse like a drum in his ears. His lungs began to throb as the breath swelled inside him. He tried to keep the hurt from his face. But seeing the pitying look that came over Ava, he knew he had done a poor job of it.

"You are a good friend, Nail, like a brother to me. I can always count on you. We've shared much. I treasure our time on the mountainside together. Me carving. You drawing. Us talking. You do know that, don't you?"

Nail swallowed hard as he felt the anger slide down his throat, with it traveled a sense of foolishness followed by light-headedness and finally strength. He looked up, flicking the hair from his eyes. "Why Jenko?" he asked, the question coming out rough, accusing.

"Any girl in my situation and so near her Ember Gathering would consider herself lucky to fall under the eye of a man like Jenko." A good deal of the softness in her voice was now missing. "His future and standing in Gallows Haven is assured. A blessing for me and my siblings. Jenko will be captain of a grayken-hunting ship someday, a baron even. I've spent my life praying for such fortune."

So near her Ember Gathering. Nail thought about what the bishop had just said about his own Ember Lighting. Was everything meant to be so unfair? He desired to say something that would confound her, something that would allow himself to walk away with some semblance of dignity. But cutting remarks about Jenko being naught but a braggart and a rich man's son full of nothing but arrogance came and went; most would sound desperate anyway. After all, he was as big and strong and confident as Jenko. He thought of her wood carvings . . . and his drawings. *I'm more talented and creative than Jenko . . . but with no blood kin . . . and not near so rich.*

"How could you be with him?" he asked, knowing he began to blush as the words spilled out. "You've nothing in common."

"You deserve someone better than me." When Ava spoke, a portion of the softness had returned to her voice. But it was obvious by the look in her eyes that she knew she had hurt him on many levels, deceived him, and she was now doing her best to smooth it over. "You will make some lucky girl happy too . . . one day."

And what girl could possibly ever consider herself lucky to be with a slave? A bastard's worth as a person was measured differently from that of a legitimate son. Nail knew his place in this world now. For a surety.

The musicians struck up another lively jig and dancers swirled to life around them. Ava Shay quietly left, not meeting his gaze as she walked away.

Shawcroft awaited him at the edge of the feast grounds. Nail wandered in the opposite direction and continued on toward the ocean. But the beach seemed naught but a dark and lonely place. Baron Bruk's black cauldrons were lined up like dark sentinels, their thick black smoke billowing up into the sky, casting an ominous pall over the stars now. He looked back and could no longer see any sign of Shawcroft.

He'd probably sat there an hour when he heard giggling and turned to see Stefan leading Gisela Barnwell down the grassy slope. As the two drew nearer, their laughter grew more distinct. Gisela was kissing Stefan vigorously. He held his new Amadon bow in one hand whilst his other circled the girl's lithe waist. Stefan's dark hair flopped over his eyes as he and Gisela stumbled down the beach. Stefan's greeting was just a drunken slur as he passed by. Jealousy welled up in Nail at the sight of the happy pair.

Zane and Liz Hen Neville were playing fetch with Zane's dog, Beer Mug, at the edge of the feast grounds. Nail watched the dog bound about with youthful enthusiasm, catching sticks for a delighted Liz

Hen. Pets were full of unconditional love that they never betrayed. He remembered Radish Biter. He had pulled the calf from a muddy bog one day on his way home from the mines. Radish Biter had become a fine milk cow and the closest thing to a pet he ever had. But a pack of silver-wolves had attacked her. A good-sized chunk of her hindquarters had been shredded. The wounds had become infected until the cow could no longer stand on her own. Nail attempted to nurse Radish Biter back to health. But she just wallowed in the center of the corral, wasting away in piles of manure. Eventually Shawcroft ordered Nail to cut the cow's throat to ease her suffering. That was the one and only time Nail could remember crying. Shawcroft had scolded him, saying tears were only for the weak-minded.

Nail noticed two others drifting away from the feast grounds and out into the darkness. Hand in hand, this new couple stole quickly from the keep and down the grassy knoll. It was Jenko Bruk and Ava Shay. They loped down the beach and into the ocean, splashing in the water as they skipped southward along the shoreline, running, laughing. Ava pushed Jenko into the water. He stumbled and laughed and threw her in too, holding her under for a time. When he let her up, she sputtered and beat against his chest with her delicate small fists. Jenko grabbed her wrists and shouted at her. When he released her, Ava clung to him, thin, willowy arms around his neck. Jenko picked her up by the waist and slung her over his shoulder, muscular arms wrapped tight around the back of her thighs. They continued down the beach, Jenko carrying her like a sack of potatoes.

Nail, hidden by the night's cloak of darkness, remained unseen. He didn't know why he did it, but he pulled out his sword and followed.

† † † † †

Baron Jubal Bruk's manor was a dark silhouette against the moonlit sky a mile south of Gallows Haven. A two-story, gray stone affair, complete with an upper floor and a basement and a long wooden wraparound porch, the manor was set against a thicket of tall oak. Many outbuildings, sheds, and barns dotted the land round about. Nail marveled that the baron and his son lived alone in this vast expanse.

The night was alive with ghostly color, everything bathed in a pale silver sheen. He had lost track of Jenko and Ava in the darkness. Sword still drawn, he circled the house, moving with as much stealth as he could muster. He heard a goat scratching at the dirt behind a picket fence, its bell tinkling. That and the drone of the nearby ocean added a sense of dread to his mission.

He detected the sound of voices, and a sparkle of yellow light sprang up between the slats of a barn less than a hundred paces south of the house. Nail headed that way. He could hear talking, male and female—the timbre of Jenko's voice rough in contrast to the soft pleading of Ava. As he approached the barn, Nail imagined the girl struggling to free herself from Jenko's clutches. He felt for the reassurance of his sword.

Torchlight flickered through the wood-plank walls of the barn. Ava giggled. Nail's blood froze as he realized there was no fear in her voice or sounds of a struggle.

Nail drifted closer to the barn and risked a glance through the wooden slats. With his face pressed against the coarse wood, he peered through the crack. The lofty barn was filled with an orange glow of hay and light. A center post in the barn held a lantern hanging at eye level; above that was a hay-filled loft.

In the alcove under the loft stood Ava, naked from the waist up, lamplight flickering along the gentle hollow of her stomach and the quivering swell of her chest. The delicate curve of her hips was mesmerizing. But the real shock was seeing the pale pertness of her exposed breasts, nipples the color of faded roses. Nail's mouth went dry.

Jenko Bruk stood directly behind the girl. He was also shirtless, his dark, tousled hair nearly brushing against the underside of the hayloft above. Ava closed her eyes and leaned back into him, her golden-blond curls nestling softly against his corded, muscular chest. Jenko's bulk swallowed her up as he wrapped her in his arms. The two stood that way for some time, almost seeming to melt into each other. Motes of straw dust floated about them—yellow sprinkles in the torchlight.

Nail's heart thundered and blood rushed to his head. He made a conscious effort to slow his own breathing. His vision wavered. Something beyond jealousy rushed through his stomach and curdled his bowels. And when Jenko's hand slipped down into the folds of Ava's skirt and caressed the spot between her legs, Nail turned and ran.

As he dashed away into the forest, legs pounding, the night around him was naught but a vast realm of anguish and hurt, a floating landscape of suffering that rolled its horizons onward endlessly and forever. Total loss engulfed him with searing pain.

His running dwindled to an aimless walk. He found himself panting, gasping for air. His lungs burned and loneliness sang its unforgiving song. His fingers still clenched the hilt of his sword with a rigid resolve. They ached from the strain. He spied a fallen tree branch on the ground before him and struck at it. The branch snapped in twain as his blade bit into it, both sides popping up onto the air. Lurching forward, he found another fallen twig and busted it also. A lone aspen tree rose up in his path. Screaming aloud in a black and violent need for absolution, he hefted the sword over his head and brought it crashing down against the tree. White bark splintered and snapped. He struck the tree again, then a third time, a fourth. Tightly drawn anger flared bold and brilliant, then narrowed into a grim, icy blade of rage. Then came a sickening twang as his sword snapped just above the hilt and the blade spun away into the forest.

He held the hilt of the shattered sword up, not knowing quite what to think. The broken blade stared right back at him, as if to say,

You pathetic, pathetic fool. Now look what you have done. He stumbled away from the aspen tree in a fog, still gripping the ruined sword. As he drew nearer to town, the sounds of the still lively feast grew in volume, the noise like a beacon in the night. He soon found himself standing in front of the Grayken Spear Inn. He let the broken sword fall from his fingers to the dirt. Alone on the street, he stared at Ol' Man Leddingham's building, the only place in all of Gallows Haven that had ever given him joy.

He moved on, reaching the docks, finding Lord Jubal Bruk's grayken-hunting ship moored there. He gazed heavenward through the spiderweb of her lofty mast and rigging; the stars glittered between crisscrossing ropes and beams. Nail realized that the *Lady Kindly* might be the only mother he'd ever known. Slowly, he climbed onto her. Climbed her rigging as high as he could go. Once atop the crow's nest, alone and filled with sorrow, he curled up in his cold leather greaves, tormented, powerless, and lost.

Folded in exhaustion, swaddled in darkness, Nail remained on his perch all through the night.

Wars raged across the breadth of the Five Isles. Man turned against man,
Vallè against dwarf against oghul. And those who rose to become Demon
Lords railed against all—atop their fiery winged steeds, they ruled.
—The Way and Truth of Laijon

CHAPTER FOURTEEN

TALA BRONACHELL

1ST DAY OF THE MOURNING MOON, 999TH YEAR OF LAIJON

AMADON, GUL KANA

His cell is at the end of a blind turn in the corridor behind an outer door that is shut off from the other prisoners." Roguemoore felt the wall of the passageway with calloused hands. "We will proceed into his cell undetected easy enough."

Jondralyn held the torch to the wall, illuminating it. This task couldn't have been more accommodating to Tala's own needs had she prayed to Laijon asking such favor. Things were falling into place. Tala had twined together a wreath of heather—a crown of flowers wrapped in white thread. The gift was Jondralyn's idea, as were the sack of food and crock of water, all for Squireck Van Hester.

Roguemoore had guided them to the Amadon Castle stables and to a sewer grate hiding under a stack of dung-riddled hay at the rear of the fourth stall of the second row. Under the grate was a circular hole and a ladder, which they climbed down a considerable length. Once at the bottom, a dark path sloped down even farther underground. Tala had noted a number of narrower passages leading off the main pathway. There were many locked iron grates, and the dwarf knew all the secret latches. "Fear not, Tala," the dwarf had said. "A maze of hidden doors and dead ends. But I always find my way out." Tala, too, had a keen sense of direction, and a knack for memorizing passageways. If she'd been to a place once, she could get there again.

The passageway eventually leveled off, and they continued single file through a narrow tunnel, the dwarf leading, Tala in the middle, and Jondralyn, carrying Squireck's food and water, bringing up the rear, all in heavy cloaks with hoods pulled up. Water wept from cracks in the walls, splashing their feet. From the smell, Tala figured they were traipsing through the sewers of Amadon. She'd felt the need to breathe through her mouth to avoid the stench. Her imagination began conjuring up images of a dark-cloaked Bloodwood with poisoned daggers lurking around every turn.

At one juncture, Roguemoore pointed out a stairway that disappeared up into the gloom, telling her that it emptied out of a sewer grate near the docks. If the castle were ever attacked, that would be a good escape route, Tala made note.

After a dozen more turns and dark hanging stairways, they reached the very spot they now stood in, facing a gray stone wall, feet soaking, clothing smelly and cold.

"I may talk with Squireck about things best kept secret," Roguemoore said, locating a hidden latch on the wall, silently working it with his fingers, "things regarding Ser Roderic Raybourne. Whatever you overhear, neither of you repeat to anyone."

The dwarf motioned for Jondralyn to extinguish the torch, and they were plunged into blackness. With a faint creaking, a portion of the corridor's wall swung open a crack, and dim golden light spilled forth from a small room on the other side. The dwarf bade them enter. Jondralyn squeezed through the door first. Tala had to duck as she stepped into this new place. "Stinks in here," she said.

"Quiet," whispered Roguemoore. He removed the mace strapped to his shoulder, wedged it between the door and wall, then stepped over it and into the room behind her.

Tala's eyes quickly adjusted to the dim light. This new room was small and dark save for flickering torchlight drifting in from the iron-barred window set in the door opposite the one they'd entered. The chill air was musty and damp. There was a figure wrapped in a blanket on the floor in the corner of the room and a pile of bright red armor next to a small circular drain in the middle of the room.

With a start, Tala realized they were in Squireck's cell under the arena. Her eyes focused on the pile of armor and the red-spiked helmet and a thought struck her. *Is there no place in Amadon safe from secret tunnels?*

Squireck Van Hester stood. He towered over them, blocking the light, long blond hair glowing, backlit and silhouetted by the golden beam streaming through the barred window.

"Who is here?" He rubbed his eyes. A chain, fastened to another short chain that connected the iron manacles on both wrists, was bolted into the floor near where he'd lain.

This was not the Prince of Saint Only Tala had known as a child. There was a brutishness about this Squireck that marked him as a criminal of the gladiator pit. Tala found she was frightened of him, felt in awe of him, and sensed pity for him all at once.

"Surprised?" A smile tugged at the dwarf's beard as he dropped the hood of his cloak.

"A hidden doorway opens up in a dungeon cell and three cloaked figures emerge from the darkness," Squireck said dryly. "Nothing surprising about that."

"Don't think you can escape just yet. It only opens from the opposite side. My mace holds it open. Had it closed behind us, we'd all have a lot of explaining to do."

A trace of puzzlement hung over Squireck's face. "Why after nearly a year do you visit me now?"

Jondralyn was nothing more than a cloaked shadow moving in the dark. She set the sack of food and crock of water on the floor, then retreated to the back of the cell.

Squireck's eyes lit up. "Jon," he exclaimed, face bright and alive, reaching for her. But the chain that held him to the floor also held him far from her. He tugged on the chains at his wrists in frustration. "I have missed you so. What brings you here?"

"To help you." She motioned to the food and water.

"You came just to give me food?" His sorrow-filled eyes lingered on the sack, while his desire for Jondralyn was evident in his very stance. "Though don't think me ungrateful. I am glad for it. I've been given nothing but a few crusts of bread and a pot or two of water these last seven days."

Roguemoore said, "Jovan decreed that nobody is to give you anything but bread and water without leave from him."

"The guards will find this stuff you've brought. They will take it. And a whole host of questions as to its origins will open up. They might just find you here now."

"I care not if the guards find me," the dwarf said. "But things being as they are, it's best they not see Jon in here and report it to Jovan. So our visit will be brief."

"Who is this with you?" Squireck bent forward and looked at Tala. She removed her hood. "Tala?" The surprise and joy in his voice sounded genuine. "Last I saw you, you were a full year younger. What a difference a year makes. You take after your sister. Beauty beyond reckoning."

Tala felt both flattered and ill at ease under his scrutiny. After all, this was an imposing man before her. A man chained in a cell for murder, a man who had viciously slain other men on the arena floor with ease. Indeed, this hard-muscled stranger looming over her was not the fair-faced, smiling Prince of Saint Only she remembered. The blanket slipped off his shoulder and she could see the swollen square gladiator brand on his chest, red and raw. She grew more nervous under his gaze and looked away, eyes traveling to the red pile of armor and the spiked helm that sat atop it.

"I did not come just to bring you food," Jondralyn blurted. "It would be a lie if I left here with you believing that. I've another purpose."

Squireck stood up, expectant, drinking her in with his eyes.

"What must one do to train for the arena matches?" Jondralyn asked. "In ages past, nobles, even kings, ofttimes fought in the arena to gain favor with the public. I wish to do the same. I feel it's my calling."

"Your calling?" the dwarf said, his face impassive.

An impatient look came over Jondralyn as she met the dwarf's gaze. "Jovan is grossly misled by his councillors, especially Val-Korin, Denarius, and the quorum. My fear is the same as yours, Roguemoore, that my brother will never muster arms against Sør Sevier and defend our shores. Were I king, I would have Gul Kana's forces doubled, tripled, ready to meet the Sør Sevier invasion."

"How does this explain your interest in training for the arena?"

"I'm afraid I may have to supplant my brother as ruler of Gul Kana."

Tala drew a deep breath, feeling it catch in her throat. Her older sister's blunt proclamation smacked of treason. She wished she had not heard such words.

"I dare not kill Jovan myself, nor have him assassinated," Jondralyn said, trepidation in her voice. "The arena is the only way the public will accept my claim to the throne. It has happened once before. Long ago. A woman ruling Gul Kana, a woman gladiator. Adonna Bronachell. She was a sister to the king, betrothed at a young age to an influential lord. She was a princess who triumphed in the arena and usurped a king. She ruled for a generation."

Tala's whole body had grown rigid. She realized with a sinking heart that things in Amadon were growing dire. The bonds of her family were being torn asunder. She feared that she herself was now getting more deeply involved in this grim business that had sprouted up between her older siblings.

"I've been studying some of the hidden histories Hawkwood shared," Jondralyn continued. "In the first centuries after Laijon's death, a son or brother of the king could challenge the crown by declaring his right to do so and then proving Laijon's favor by fighting in the tournament. If victorious, the crown was transferred to him. Why cannot a sister of a king do the same, like Adonna of old?"

"Adonna Bronachell is but a myth," the dwarf said.

"I found her name in the histories. I aim to follow her path."

"You share books with Hawkwood?" The tone of Squireck's question betrayed immense jealousy. He turned toward Roguemoore. "Now she wishes to fight in the arena? Did you know of this folly, dwarf?"

"I am as shocked to hear of it as I'm sure Tala is," Roguemoore said, adopting a stern tone, looking at her, concern etched on his face. "You must never speak of this to anyone, dear Tala. I fear bringing you here may have been a mistake." Roguemoore gave Jondralyn a severe look. "Fighting in the arena? Squireck is right. What folly is this?"

"No more foolish than dueling four Dayknights," Jondralyn said.

"Dueling four Dayknights?" Squireck turned to the dwarf.

"It's Hawkwood's fight," Roguemoore said with a mirthless smile. "Nothing you need worry about." He turned to Jondralyn. "The duel with the Dayknights will teach the king and his advisers a great lesson—"

Squireck interrupted, "You and Hawkwood cannot think to smash sense into Jovan's head by force of arms and duels. It will only make both him and his advisers more militantly opposed to our cause. Let me prove the truth of our cause in the arena. As we agreed. As was planned. As is *prophesied*."

There was silence between the two. Squireck continued, "However"—he looked squarely at Jondralyn—"I do see some wisdom in what Jon says about supplanting Jovan. There is nobility in it."

Jondralyn dipped her head at his praise.

"If you attempt this, Jon, you wll die." The dwarf spoke with distaste. "I think it a foolish quest."

"You would." Jondralyn shot the dwarf a cold look.

Squireck was still looking at Jondralyn. "I would train you. Alas, things being as they are, that is impossible. But rumor is, even deep in the dungeons of the arena, that you and Hawkwood are close." Squireck swallowed hard. "Perhaps he already trains you."

"Hawkwood has trained me some. But I want to know how to fight in the arena. I want to learn to fight like a gladiator. I want the power to *win*."

"Like a gladiator?" Squireck said, his tone questioning.

"Yes." Jondralyn stepped toward him. "Like a gladiator." She stood on her toes and kissed him lightly on the cheek, her hand touching the side of his neck, fingers lingering there a moment before she stepped back.

"As you wish," Squireck said. "Like a gladiator. Visit Anjk Bourbon in Amadon's northern market district. He's a crabby old bloodsucker for sure, a blacksmith who sells weapons. He may be shriveled and leathery and distrustful of humans, but he's one of the best oghul fighters. Pay him well and he will teach you the brute strength and conditioning suitable for heavy swordsmanship, plus a few oghul tricks. Spend six hours a day with him. In Val-Korin's retinue there is a bodyguard named Val-So-Vreign. For a little coin, he will work with you and keep your training discreet. Spend another six hours a day under his tutelage. Val-So-Vreign will train you the Vallè way— speed and accuracy with both sword and knife."

"Twelve hours a day?" Jondralyn asked. "It seems so much."

"If you cannot dedicate yourself to a strict regimen, do not step one foot into the arena. It's a dangerous place to venture untrained. More so for a woman."

"Perhaps I can ask Val-Draekin to help." Jondralyn turned to Roguemoore, her eyes lighting up. "He has already offered."

"Val-Draekin?" Squireck said the name slowly, deliberately, eyes darkening.

Jondralyn went on, "He offered to train me to fight as the Vallè do. He certainly seems competent. And he may prove to be more discreet than Val-So-Vreign even."

"I scarcely see the point," Roguemoore said. "It's a foolish undertaking."

"Who's this Val-Draekin?" Squireck's eyes were boring into those of the dwarf with some expectation.

"A raven-haired Vallè we rescued from a dockside saloon," Roguemoore said. "He claims to be in love with Val-Korin's daughter Breita."

The dwarf pulled a golden coin from his pocket. "He gave me this."

Tala was taken aback by the grin that spread over Squireck's face at this seemingly trivial trinket. "Laijon is truly with us."

"Aye." The dwarf stuffed the coin back into his cloak. "The scrolls were right. Our cause is just. But do not become too overjoyed. Rumor is, Aeros Raijael has reached the Laijon Towers. King Torrence's last stand. If Torrence dies, or if he's already dead, his death will be a blow to the Brethren. It could be weeks before word of his fate reaches us. And the White Prince would then likely be in possession of one of those artifacts we had wished kept secret."

"Ser Roderic is still in Gallows Haven? He still watches over the boy?"

The dwarf nodded.

"*Val-Draekin,*" Squireck said the name again, an undertone of reverence in his voice.

Tala thought of the Vallè—Val-Draekin—how even injured, he could fight better than any in the Silver Guard. *What is so special about his name?* Her eyes traveled to the pile of red armor, her thoughts on

Lawri and the poison that was slowly killing her. She was mesmerized by the lump of spiky leather armor. But she could think of no good excuse to venture forth and lift up the helm and examine it for the assassin's clue. She found herself shivering.

"Don't let it frighten you, child," Squireck said, noticing where her eyes were planted. "The man who wore it is quite dead."

"Are you collecting the stuff?" Jondralyn asked, eyeing the pile of red armor too.

"As of now, they are my only worldly possessions."

"That reminds me," Roguemoore said. "Tala has brought you something."

Squireck looked at Tala, curious. She stared back at him, not sure what Roguemoore was referring to, her mind on so many things: Jondralyn and gladiator training, Lawri and the Bloodwood; she even found herself thinking of Glade Chaparral and what he might think of all this.

Then she remembered the wreath of heather she'd constructed. She pulled it forth from the folds of her cloak and held it out to Squireck.

He took the wreath from her, holding it up into the light. "Where did you get this?" he asked, looking down upon her, eyes intense.

"I made it."

Tala was shocked to see tears now welling in his eyes as he said, "You made this for me?" She nodded. He smiled. "The other gladiators will run scared from a man with naught but leaves on his head." He laughed, admiring her handiwork in the dim light. "I shall wear this crown of flowers during my next match." The emotion in Squireck's voice was so real, so heartfelt and substantive, that she was left speechless.

"I'm sure Tala would be honored," Roguemoore said.

"Such a beautiful gift," Squireck said. "Such a *perfect* gift. It will cause quite a stir among Denarius and the quorum of five when they see this wreath about my head at the next match. Thank you, Tala."

She found herself actually bowing to him. "You're welcome."

"I have nothing of value to give in return, though."

Tala recalled the last two lines of the assassin's note: *Your first clue is this: Retrieve the red helm of the dead demon and read what is inscribed therein.* Without thinking, she took two steps toward the pile of armor and picked up the helm that had dominated her thoughts for so long. It was a heavy hunk of metal and she had to hold it in both hands tightly for fear of letting it clank loudly back to the floor. "Can I have this?"

"What a gruesome thing to ask for," Jondralyn commented.

"Take it," Squireck said. "I've no use for it. As a matter of fact—" He turned to Roguemoore. "Tell Denarius that I shall never don armor in the arena again. I choose to fight without worldly protection. I will forsake even my shoes. Tell him that I train as if everything depends on me, but that I fight as if everything depends upon Laijon."

"You walk a dangerous line," Roguemoore said. "The bouts will only grow in difficulty. You must wear *some* armor. Or you will not survive."

"Exactly," Squireck said with conviction. "No one can survive without armor. That is the point. What better way to prove the truthfulness of our cause? For when I win, people will cry, 'Despite all odds, Laijon hath seen the Prince of Saint Only victorious!' It *will* come to pass. Jovan, Denarius, the quorum of five, they will be forced to acknowledge the truth of *The Moon Scrolls of Mia.*"

Tala had no idea what Squireck and the dwarf were going on about, so consumed was she with the red helmet. She turned it over in her hands, careful, so its spikes did not cut into her flesh. Something was clearly stamped into the metal inside the crown of the helm.

Her heart thumped wildly in her chest. In the darkness she could barely read what was written there. Squinting, she could just make out the words.

Property of the Filthy Horse Saloon

It is true that before the birth of my beloved—the great One and Only,
the King of Slaves, the First Warrior Angel, the man named Laijon—
common images did take root in the Five Isles. But I, your Blessed
Mother Mia, say unto you now, the prophecy of his birth was not only
carved on totem and in stone, but 'twas also written in the stars.
—The Moon Scrolls of Mia

CHAPTER FIFTEEN

JONDRALYN BRONACHELL

2ND DAY OF THE MOURNING MOON, 999TH YEAR OF LAIJON
AMADON CASTLE, GUL KANA

Jondralyn stood with the rest of Jovan's court but felt all alone, damp heavy cloak wrapped tightly around herself. The ground was sodden underfoot. Gray clouds hung low in the noontime sky. It looked as if every single Silver Guard in the city lined the battlements of Black Glass Courtyard. In black surcoats and silver armor they stood vigil. The courtyard itself was jammed with Dayknights. There was an open circle about fifty paces in diameter in the center of the crowd. Within the circle stood Hawkwood and four Dayknights.

Hawkwood, a thin cutlass in each hand, wore naught but a simple shirt and rough-spun woolen breeches, his face peaceful, his movements unhurried as he proceeded through a series of stretches and gracefully fluid exercises. The hilt-guard of each cutlass sprouted a profusion of serrated spikes designed to trap opposing blades and wrench them from the wrists of his foes.

She had not seen Hawkwood in days. He'd been kept under guard in the Hall of the Dayknights and had been allowed only one visitor, Roguemoore, who'd confirmed to Jondralyn the decency of his accommodations.

The four Dayknights he was to fight stood at attention. Each bore the standard black helms, shields, and black-lacquered armor of their station. They all brandished Dayknight blades, thick leather-wrapped hilts, black opals set in their pommels.

At the edge of the circle stood King Jovan, Sterling Prentiss, Grand Vicar Denarius, and the quorum of five: Vandivor, Donalbain, Spencerville, Leaford, and Rhys-Duncan. Roguemoore was also there. He wore leather armor, spiked mace strapped to his back. All of Amadon's other dignitaries were lined up in ranks behind the king.

All save the Val Vallè ambassador, Val-Korin, who was walking into the center of the circle. "A fight to the death!" he announced loudly for all to hear. "Those are the rules!" And when he gave the signal, the fight began.

The four Dayknights advanced guardedly upon Hawkwood, their caution born of experience. As the most highly skilled fighting force in all of Gul Kana, the Dayknights were trained to take no opponent lightly, especially one who had trained them.

The four knights struck, their positioning and sword strikes perfectly timed. Hawkwood moved fast, both weapons whirling, his cutlasses thin and light in comparison to the longswords of the Dayknights. Still, he parried each strike with ease and stepped back, watchful. Then, just as quickly, he leaped, smashing the knight nearest him with the flat of his blade atop the helm. The knight crumpled with a heavy thud. Hawkwood had pulled the blow, sparing the man, leaving him sprawled in the grass.

The three remaining knights advanced, heavy blades raining down on Hawkwood, precise and rapid. He spoiled each sudden thrust and arcing strike almost as soon as it had begun. He ducked a flurry of blows from all three, lashing out at the same time with each cutlass. His attack was fierce, smashing head, thigh, arm, keeping all three knights at bay. He gave ground for but an instant, boldly striking one of the remaining knights over the head, felling him instantly, the blow meant to stun, not kill.

With a second knight fallen, the two remaining Dayknights quickly retreated out of harm's way, nearly tripping over their downed compatriots in the process. Hawkwood set his stance firm. The two knights moved to either side of him and rushed, their black shields at the ready, blades poised to strike. Hawkwood lunged forward, braced himself, then lurched backward instantly. The two Dayknights collided, shields and breastplates clashing, swords still aloft in a useless position. They both tumbled to the ground.

Jondralyn chuckled, as did others. The duel seemed almost a comedy now. Hawkwood fell upon one of the downed knights, bonking him on the head with the hilt of his sword before he could stand. The fellow flopped to the ground, unconscious.

The one Dayknight remaining stood and lumbered toward Hawkwood, sword upraised, swinging hard. Hawkwood avoided the knight's slow charge with a turn and retreated, then circled quickly and reversed with a skill that was beautiful to watch. The confused knight spun and swung wildly. Hawkwood parried and stepped aside and clubbed the man to his knees with a blow to the face from his elbow and backed away. The wearied knight stood, took a labored breath, and then unleashed a plodding attack. Hawkwood ducked away without moving his feet. He struck the knight's helm from his head with a sweeping blow, then knocked the knight out cold with a punch to the face. All four Dayknights now lay on the ground, unconscious and unbloodied.

"I have been trained by the best warriors in Sør Sevier!" Hawkwood's voice boomed through the courtyard, both cutlasses still waving in each hand. "There are tens of thousands like me gathering across the Mourning Sea!" He slid both blades casually into the sheaths on his belt. "This is how the Sør Sevier army will fight you! Some of you even fought at Borden's side! You know Aeros' savagery! I see naught but a quick end for Gul Kana if you do not better prepare! If you do not offer up even a slim resistance, there will be none of you left alive! I know Aeros! He will slaughter all!"

The whole courtyard was still. In the waiting tension, many held their breath, looking at the king. Jondralyn's attention flew toward Denarius and the quorum of five. She felt a hollow prick of excitement. Sweat ran from the vicar's bald forehead, beading down over the plumpness of his face. *Sometimes it is best if you make them believe the trap is theirs,* the dwarf had said last week. The duel was brilliant. In only a few minutes, Hawkwood had demonstrated not only to Jovan, but also to every Dayknight and Silver Guard in Amadon, how deadly their enemy truly was.

Jovan stepped forward, eyes on Hawkwood. "It was to be a fight to the death." His voice was calm, assured. "But every man involved yet lives."

"He spared them, Your Excellency," Roguemoore growled, then coughed, harshly clearing his throat. "Gul Kana cannot afford to lose good fighters."

Jovan thrust his finger toward the four downed knights. "I say turn around and finish those men, Hawkwood!"

"I will not," Hawkwood said without emotion.

"Then you refuse a direct command from your king?" Jovan scowled.

"You are not my king." Hawkwood met Jovan's gaze.

The king spun, looking squarely at Sterling Prentiss. "Bring forward your most trusted man," he ordered.

Sterling removed his helm and tucked it under the crook of his right arm. Turning to the mass of knights behind him, he shouted. "Ser Culpa Barra, step forward!"

Jondralyn instantly recognized the name. There was a jostling from near the back of the courtyard, and a lone Dayknight made his way through the parting throng and stood before his king. He was taller than most. And when he pulled his black helmet off with two black-gauntleted hands, it was him, the man Jondralyn knew, square jawed, with a firm look set in his dark blue eyes. He looked older than Jondralyn remembered, but still familiar, though she hadn't seen him in years.

"Your age, Ser Culpa?" Jovan asked.

"Twenty-eight, if it please Your Excellency," the Dayknight answered, lifting his chin, chunks of his tousled blond hair clinging to his forehead in sweaty ringlets.

"Young for a Dayknight."

"I've earned my place."

"If memory serves, you were a friend to that murderer, Squireck Van Hester."

"I no longer hold friendship with the Prince of Saint Only."

Jovan turned to Prentiss. "Can this man alone kill Hawkwood?"

"He cannot."

"In that case, let us bestow an easier task." Jovan pulled a pearl-handled dagger from his belt and held it out for Culpa. "Cut the throats of your four disgraced fellows."

Jondralyn's heart lurched at the injustice of her brother's command.

Without hesitation, Culpa Barra nodded and placed his helmet on the grass and took the dagger. He set his jaw and walked toward the center of the courtyard and the fallen Dayknights. Hawkwood moved to block the young knight's path, a dangerous look on his face. Culpa stopped, wary. He looked back at his king.

Jovan signaled to the Silver Guards lining the battlements.

Instantly, there were a hundred bows stretched taut and a hundred bristling arrows aimed right at Hawkwood.

Jovan nodded for the young Dayknight to continue. Culpa Barra pushed his way past Hawkwood, kicked the helm from the head of the closest fallen Dayknight, and cut the unconscious man's throat. Blood oozed over the green grass as Culpa moved to the next fallen man and did the same. Anger welled within Jondralyn. After the third Dayknight's throat was cut, the fourth had regained his senses enough to stand and locate his sword. He rushed Culpa, but his charge was aimless and slow. Culpa effortlessly avoided the ponderous swing and thrust Jovan's dagger up under the Dayknight's throat into his brain. The man gasped. Blood sprayed over Culpa's silver surcoat in ropy splatters. The dying knight slid to the ground.

Culpa stood in the center of the four dead Dayknights, face devoid of expression.

"That dagger is yours to keep, Ser Culpa," Jovan said, and turned to Hawkwood. "And you will hang for your disobedience."

"He won the duel!" Jondralyn shouted, wanting to rush forward and put an end to this whole farce. But she didn't know how. There was no answer to this madness.

"Yes, he won the duel," Roguemoore followed.

"He will be held in Purgatory," Jovan continued. "And then—"

"You lack honor?" Roguemoore interrupted.

Jovan yelled, "In the arena, before the final match, Hawkwood will be hung!"

"You lack honor!" the dwarf raged, standing solid, his shouting like claps of thunder. "You! Lack! Honor!"

"Silence!" Jovan's eyes smoldered and fumed. "Hawkwood refused to carry it to its rightful end—death. He won nothing. It is he who is lacking in honor."

Jondralyn stepped forward, her voice a growl. "He's to be hung for sparing the lives of four Dayknights that you in turn killed?"

"He's to be hung for consorting with the thief and murderer and traitor to Gul Kana, Squireck Van Hester, Prince of Saint Only." Jovan stepped toward her. "Odd thing, one moment the guards at the arena claim that Squireck has the red helm of the Wyn Darrè gladiator in his cell, and the next moment it's gone, replaced with a sack of food and a crown of heather and white flowers. Now, I am aware that some of the noblewomen in Amadon like to sneak away from their husbands and fuck the gladiators, but you see, there were no visitors recorded entering the arena dungeons yesterday. Nor do I peg Squireck as the sort to dally with a married noblewoman. Nor do I think he is some form of magician, conjuring up crowns of heather from the air."

Jondralyn's heart thundered. She wondered how much her brother actually knew.

"For conspiring to help the criminal, Squireck Van Hester, against my direct orders, Hawkwood's execution will be in the arena in five days' time!" Jovan shouted, his face ugly with triumph as he motioned for Sterling Prentiss and Culpa Barra to bind Hawkwood's hands. "Take him to Purgatory!"

To Jondralyn's surprise, Hawkwood offered no resistance. *He should be fighting for his life to stay out of Purgatory!* Those cells under the Hall of the Dayknights were the worst, most dank, rat-infested dungeons in all of the Five Isles. Many had gone insane confined within them in less than a moon.

A halfhearted cheer rose up from the Silver Guards and Dayknights in the courtyard as Hawkwood's hands were bound and he was led away. Jondralyn's face was frozen with bitterness. Every cheer from the Dayknights and Silver Guards ate away at her until she could stand it no longer.

Jovan, always Jovan. They fawned over him. No matter what happened or how dishonorable and unfair he was, her older brother garnered more unwarranted praise than any ten men. *Amadon deserves a ruler of dignity and honor. Not a Jovan Bronachell, looking out for nothing more than the glory of himself.*

Jondralyn momentarily thought of talking some sense into her brother. Yet the thought hung there uneasy in her mind. That she might be able to converse with Jovan as equals was a notion long dead. She'd scarcely shared more than a few arguments full of terse words with him since he'd been crowned. And the curtness and distrust between them were all *his* doing. Wrapped in her cloak, she met her brother's eyes through the crowd.

Jovan was standing right next to her now. "You must know that I forgive you," he said softly.

"Forgive me?" Jondralyn feigned surprise.

"You wish to be a man. So I now give you a manly job. The punishment for your part in this crime is to build a pyre and burn the four pathetic fools who died here today. They are an embarrassment. Still, their souls will take flight into heaven. They did only as I bade them do. Hawkwood is right about one thing. The Dayknights have grown soft." Jovan paused, actually looking introspective. "As for you, Jon, don't ever assume that I don't know about everything that is said or done in this city. I will not forgive you or Tala a second time. Her punishment will be soon in coming, I assure you that." Jovan spun and stalked away.

Jondralyn's heart felt as empty and hollow as a Sky Lochs cave. Jovan had just as much as admitted that he knew Hawkwood had nothing to do with her and Roguemoore's jaunt down into the dungeons to visit Squireck. Yet he'd still sentenced Hawkwood to hang for it.

She looked from Jovan's retreating form to the four dead Dayknights, then to the Val Vallè ambassador, Val-Korin, who was whispering something into the ear of the grand vicar. Both men then followed Jovan from the courtyard.

But as the vicar passed by, Jondralyn could clearly see, Denarius had a vicious little smile hiding behind his lips.

† † † † †

Less than one hour after she had burned the four Dayknights, Jondralyn unhooked her sword belt and leaned it against the arm of the settee in her bedchamber and sat—collapsed onto her settee, more like, then slouched, totally exhausted. She took comfort from the simple colors of the walls and columns and arched ceiling that encompassed the room. She even took comfort in the mahogany bookshelves full of the hundreds of books that she had collected over the years. Her pastel settee and couches were pleasing to sink into and let the strains of the day's burdens fade away. The silken bed-spread that folded over the arm of the settee was cool to the touch, and comforting. The stark cleanliness of her room never failed to ease her mind. She rested her eyes on the patterns of the rich maroon rug under her bed. There was a knock at her door. Too lazy to stand, she shouted, *"Come in!"* Roguemoore entered her room.

"I don't know who's the bigger fool, Hawkwood or Jovan," she said. "Jovan's vanity shines through. Am I the only one who notices? The Silver Guard and Dayknights all fall in line for him." She groaned, shoulders slumped, her posture like that of a whipped dog. "And then there's you and Hawkwood. Your plans to weaken my brother only make him stronger."

"Our plan was not to weaken Jovan." Roguemoore sat on the settee by her side. "True, your brother boasts of the prowess of the Day-knights and even the Silver Guard at times, yet he keeps them safe in Amadon. Few of them are battle tested. He can see no further than the petty rules and traditions that Denarius and the quorum have hammered into him. You are different from him, Jon, a freethinker. Jovan fears you. He always has. And since your father died, his para-noia, fueled by the grand vicar and Val-Korin, has become worse."

Jondralyn wasn't really listening. "I know not my purpose any-more. I have no idea what just happened today."

"And I know not who may be hiding in these walls," Roguemoore continued in a quieter tone. "Jovan somehow found out about our foray into Squireck's cell. There could be an army of spies from every clan and kingdom crawling through Amadon Castle, including Jovan's own spies. Even spies from Sør Sevier."

"You admitted that today's duel was a mere setup to some grander scheme. But I cannot see it, Roguemoore. Now Hawkwood is in Purgatory. And whatever your ill-conceived plan was, it seems to have failed miserably."

Roguemoore leaned in, his voice firm. "The duel went exactly as planned."

The conviction in the dwarf's voice unsettled her. But she'd long since run out of patience. She spoke clearly. "Your plan was to get Hawkwood tossed into the dungeons under the Hall of the Day-knights, the worst place in all the Five Isles, and then hung in the arena before thousands of witnesses? What kind of madness is that?"

"He will not be put to death." The words leaked from the dwarf's lips, which barely moved. "The Bloodwood assassin may be hunting Hawkwood." He looked right at her, his face more sunken and strained than she'd ever remembered it being.

As she digested what the dwarf had just said, she felt a strange thrill, a surge of excitement and dread. Roguemoore put his hand on her knee. "For the time being, the deepest dungeons of Amadon may be the safest place for Hawkwood."

But despite what he said, Jondralyn saw the held-in emotion behind Roguemoore's eyes. She felt a hollowness in her stomach and sensed the dwarf was not telling her everything. She studied the spines of the books on the shelf across the room. *The Adventures of Silver Guard Curtis Fiore, The Mouse of Avlonia Castle, Things Hor Hey the Mule Taught Me.* Books her mother, Alana, had read to her when she was a child. The gold-embossed spine of *Fairy Tales of the Val Vallè Princess Arianna* stood out to her. It had always been her favorite. *They replaced Arianna's likeness with mine on the Gul Kana copper coin.*

"I don't know what to believe," she mumbled.

"Yet you wish to train for the arena. What madness has stricken you, Jon?"

"Hawkwood has taught me much. But he's been under guard. Now he's imprisoned. Still, I must train. It is the right thing to do."

"You wish to supplant your brother as ruler of Gul Kana. You cannot beat Jovan in that way. I worry for you. I worry for all of Borden's children."

Hidden behind his concern, Jondralyn thought she sensed something else in the dwarf's voice, something unsaid, some urgency. *Sometimes it's best if you make them believe the trap is theirs.* Those words haunted her now as she wondered if it was *she* who was being played for a fool. True, she'd asked Squireck how to train for the arena matches. *But was that truly my idea?* Racking her brain, she was unable to define precisely where she fit into the dwarf's plans. She couldn't shake the premonition that there were things about the Brethren of Mia that the dwarf was keeping from her.

She had so many questions. Her mind went to Squireck first. She did not know how she felt seeing him shackled in the arena dungeons so. "You showed Squireck the gold coin Val-Draekin gave you. What does it mean? You mentioned that if King Torrence Raybourne dies, it would be a blow to the Brethren, and the White Prince may come into possession of one of those things the Brethren had wished kept secret. Squireck asked if Ser Roderic was still in Gallows Haven. And something about a boy. I didn't inquire whilst we were in the dungeons because Tala was there, but what was that all about?"

"A long list of questions, there—"

A low, grinding noise filled the room. Jondralyn flew to her feet, dagger in hand.

The bookshelf across the room slid aside, revealing Sterling Prentiss and Ser Culpa Barra—the latter fully armed, his armor spattered with blood.

"It's all right, Jon," Roguemoore said. "Put your knife away."

But Jondralyn brushed past the dwarf and set the point of her blade against Sterling's breastplate. "What is the meaning of this?"

The Dayknight captain growled, "I'll bend you over my knee if I have to."

"I am a princess of Amadon." She stood tall and straight, eyes piercing into his.

"A strutting she-wolf you are."

"You dare speak to me so—"

"Stow your dagger, Jon," Roguemoore urged. "They are the truest of friends. They are welcome here."

"Welcome in *my* bedchamber?"

The dwarf leaned into her. "Sterling and Culpa have been working with the Brethren. Hawkwood and Sterling, along with Lord Kelvin Kronnin, have been secretly garrisoning Lord's Point with legions of Dayknights and Silver Guards sympathetic to our cause. Lord Kronnin tripled the size of his own Ocean Guard. Some in Gul Kana are with us. We prepare to defend against the White Prince."

Jondralyn stole a glance at the armed Dayknight, Culpa Barra, beside Sterling Prentiss. His face and curled blond hair were familiar, though he was older now. He bowed to her. "M'lady."

"Jondralyn is right about one thing." The dwarf's voice was brazen as he addressed the Dayknight captain. "You risk your life, and the life of the knight beside you, coming to her chamber. If the two Silver Guards stationed in the corridor hear you, they may come in."

"I do not have to explain myself to any hallway guardsman," Sterling said.

The dwarf was not deterred. "You'd have to explain yourself to Jovan if they report that you'd entered Jondralyn's room through the secret ways."

Jondralyn looked from Sterling to the bookshelf behind the two men, wondering if there were more people wandering through the castle's secret passages at any given moment than used the common corridors.

"My life is my own to risk," Sterling said. "Remember, it was I who orchestrated that duel with Dayknights against my better judgment. Had I known your plan would cost four men their lives, I would never have agreed to it."

"We could not have foreseen that Jovan would have them killed," Roguemoore said.

"Indeed," Sterling snapped, spittle flying from between brown teeth.

He's a rough old cob, Jondralyn thought. Not an ugly man exactly— yet repulsive nonetheless. His breath, for one thing, was already stinking up the room. And for another, his gut didn't quite fit within the confines of his armor. Looking at his pockmarked face was like looking at a pitted piece of granite. Realizing that Sterling also had ties to the Brethren made her feel as lost and powerless as a hunk of driftwood left to the whim of the ocean waves. She thought back on the fracas at the arena a week ago; it was indeed Sterling Prentiss who had kept the argument going between Hawkwood and Jovan. Things were being revealed to her too fast, one on top of the other. She did not trust the Dayknight captain, despite the dwarf's reassurance to the contrary, and despite his loyalty to her father years ago. *Trust no one.*

And the cold-blooded look of Culpa Barra sent a shiver through her body.

Sterling cast a dark eye on the dwarf. "This castle crawls with traitors. But I come bearing ill tidings. Hawkwood has escaped Purgatory."

Jondralyn's eyes flew to Roguemoore. He remained stoic in the face of the news.

"Jovan has declared him a fugitive," Sterling continued, shaking his head as if purging his brain of a terrible nightmare. "This escape does not look good on a man of my position, charged with the law and order of a kingdom and the safekeeping of a king and a king's court. I have been charged with hunting Hawkwood down and killing him. His body is to be brought to Jovan, where the king will have him drawn and quartered and hung from the four gates of the castle. Ser Castlegrail and I have dispatched contingents of Silver Guards and Dayknights throughout Amadon. They will search the breadth of Gul Kana if need be. Though I wish it otherwise, to speak plainly, I had no other choice. If I find him, I will bring him to Jovan to be killed."

"I understand," Roguemoore said.

Sterling grabbed the dwarf by the shoulder and whispered, "So tell me, dwarf." His voice hissed between clenched teeth, barely audible to Jondralyn. "Have we been betrayed by your friend, or is Hawkwood's escape part of some larger plan?"

Sterling let go of Roguemoore's shoulder. "Think on it. I'll need your answer on the morrow. Otherwise, Culpa and I are out of the Brethren. There is much I am not being told. Though I dearly loved Borden Bronachell like a brother, things have become too dangerous for the likes of Culpa and me to remain involved in the schemes our late king set in motion so long ago."

With that both Sterling and Culpa disappeared back through the hidden doorway behind Jondralyn's bookshelf.

'Twas an age when man wandered soulless and lost, until the images of glorious prophecy took root: standing-stones with carved crosses, circles painted green, red, blue, black, white, images of a boy with a spear, a young man in slave chains, a warrior with a sword, an ax, a crossbow, and a helm, killing winged demons; a man nailed to a tree, a man laid out on a cross-shaped altar.
— THE WAY AND TRUTH OF LAIJON

CHAPTER SIXTEEN

NAIL

3RD DAY OF THE MOURNING MOON, 999TH YEAR OF LAIJON
GALLOWS HAVEN, GUL KANA

The chapel bell boomed. Nail shot upright, rubbing the sleep from his eyes. He smelled flowers in the breeze and could hear the breakers crashing against the large rocks just north of Gallows Bay. He noticed the angle of the sun. Midafternoon. His joints groaned as he pulled himself upright. He'd been curled up in his stiff leather greaves atop the crow's nest of the *Lady Kindly* for twelve hours.

The church bell boomed again. He heard frantic shouting below. From his perch, he watched villagers scramble up and down the main thoroughfare in front of the Grayken Spear Inn, their shouts urgent and full of fear. The bell sounded a third time.

The signal for attack! Nail whirled, eyes cast to the sea.

The sun reflected gold and blinding along the vast swell of the ocean. In the far bright distance were dozens of ships. One after the next they crested the horizon, plying the sea, sails seeming to dance on the water. With ever-growing dread, he counted the ships—thirty-five total—all cutting through the ocean from the northwest.

Nail stared, enthralled, for he knew that death rode in them.

† † † † †

It took less than an hour for the ships to anchor within a hundred yards of shore, each ship twice the size of the *Lady Kindly*. By then Nail was making his way to the keep with the rest of the men of the village. From the ships, legions of armed warriors and heavy horse were rowing ashore on smaller vessels. Most had already disembarked and were wading up the beachhead, gathering among Baron Bruk's still smoking black cauldrons, fitting their mounts with armor, testing their weapons. Nail could hear the clanking of their bridle bits and the snorts of their chargers, and here and there shards of sunlight blazed off their silver armor.

Under Baron Bruk's direction, the three hundred or so men and boys of Gallows Haven had arranged themselves into an undisciplined-looking formation along the crown of the low hill just a stone's throw north of the keep. Those few who possessed mail or armor of any kind had put it on. Most wore simple raiment and carried weapons that they had hurriedly assembled—useless things, really: rakes, hoes, shovels, tree branches, rocks.

As Nail waded through the throng, some men were in the midst of sharpening these rudimentary implements on whetstones, whilst others argued about who should be lining up on the right or left. More than a few were vomiting from nerves. There was much anticipation and fear as Nail searched for a friendly face. He located Stefan Wayland and Zane Neville, standing in their armor near the front. He quickly took his place in line between them.

Stefan thrust a familiar breastplate at Nail. "It's yours. Put it on. I snatched it from in front of the chapel. Someone else likely scavenged the rest of your gear, though."

Nail hurriedly fastened the breastplate around his chest. Next to Zane was Dokie Liddle, sword in hand. Nail's scrawny, lightning-struck friend was dressed in full armor, the visor of his helm up, eyes transfixed by the sheer wonder of the ominous-looking warriors gathered across the field from them. "The army of Sør Sevier," he muttered. "The White Prince, finally come to kill us."

It was only then that Nail truly realized what it was they now faced. Arrayed below him along a sloping plain of grass a hundred yards away was a seething, glittering sea of death. Wearing silver armor and white surcoats with a blue cross emblazoned on the chest, the opposing legion stretched from the beach all the way up the slope and over the north road almost to the chapel, and their formation looked equally as deep. Archers made up the front ranks— motionless they stood. Battle knights on huge war chargers were arrayed behind the archers, their half-pikes and halberds jutting skyward like an iron-tipped forest. Plates of armor covered their horses' foreheads, iron-studded bands encircled their legs and flanks, war paint slathered their hides in grisly patterns. It was row upon row of evil warriors that seemed more like demons from the underworld than men of flesh and bone. Buried within the hollow eye slits of their frightful helms were dark chasms that revealed naught but destruction and slaughter. Banners flapped above the army, the colors of Sør Sevier—a blue sword on a white field. This was what death looked like. And Nail wanted to vomit.

Unexpectedly Shawcroft stood before him. The man wore no armor but had a sheathed sword strapped to his broad back, a black opal on the pommel. Shawcroft's features were as pallid as ever, face strained, his words abrupt. "We must leave. Now."

"Leave?" Nail said, incredulous. "None of us can leave."

"This will be a slaughter."

"Bloody rotted angels." Zane looked askance at Nail's master. "You're full of encouragement."

Shawcroft grabbed Nail, pulling him from the line. "This is madness."

"I stay and fight with my friends. I'm no traitorous, *murderous* coward." As the words tumbled from his mouth, he saw the pain in Shawcroft's eyes.

"Your destiny is not here, Nail."

"And what destiny does a bastard have?" Nail shot back.

"Go with Shawcroft," Stefan said, nervously stroking the Amadon Silver Guard bow he had won last night at the Mourning Moon Feast. "You haven't a sword or shield or helm. Some of the women are holed up in the chapel with Bishop Tolbret, some at the Grayken Spear, a few in the keep. Many ran for the mountains. You and Shawcroft know those mountains. You could—"

"I'm no woman who hides with the children," Nail snapped.

"I was gonna say you could help them *hide* in the mountains."

After the things he had seen last night between Ava Shay and Jenko, Nail cared not if he died today. "I aim to fulfill my duty and fight with the rest of you."

"No," Shawcroft growled, grabbing his arm. "We go now."

The Sør Sevier army parted as a group of six horsemen galloped through the throng toward the small Gallows Haven army. Both Shawcroft and Nail turned and looked. Splendorous white hair billowed out behind the lead horseman. The Sør Sevier leader was a wondrous sight atop a gloriously armored white charger. He wore chain mail under a white cloak that rippled in magnificent waves, a bright longsword at his hip.

"The White Prince," Dokie Liddle murmured, "Aeros Raijael."

To the White Prince's left rode two men, one baldheaded, the other a dark-haired, bearded fellow with a black eye patch. To the

White Prince's right galloped a red-haired woman, starkly pretty, with a crossbow and quiver of grim heavy-looking quarrels strapped to her back. Many Gallows Haven men spat curses at the sight of this woman warrior. Nail found her to be astonishingly regal. Next to her rode a bearded behemoth of a man, blue paint crisscrossing his face. This giant carried a huge ball mace wrapped in spikes and barbs in one hand and a gigantic round iron shield in the other. All of them were on tall white stallions with heavy hooves that shook the very ground.

Last was a black-cloaked fellow on a black horse. *A Bloodwood!* Nail's heart was racing now. The Bloodwood's hair was cropped short. He wore dark, boiled-leather armor under an even darker cloak that appeared to soak up the surrounding sunlight. His coal-black stallion had those unmistakable eyes that oozed red light. *Demon-eyed like the horse the Vallè woman rode!*

There was visible fear on Shawcroft's face as Baron Bruk walked out to meet the White Prince, armor clanking. The baron wore some armor and a belt studded with links of chain and thick boots that rode high on his legs. He carried a wooden shield, with a heavy iron boss that was painted black. The baron's huge broadsword with its leather-wrapped hilt and black opal-inlaid pommel swayed at his hip. *A sword identical to the one Shawcroft has strapped to his back!*

Murmurs ran through the crowd. Jubal Bruk stood before Aeros Raijael and his five mounted companions. The baron looked small out there alone. From where he was, Nail couldn't hear anything that was said, but there was a brief discussion, and then the White Prince and his five guards whirled their mounts and galloped back to their forces.

"Prepare yourselves!" the baron hollered when he rejoined the Gallows Haven army. He drew his sword and raised it above his head. "Form a shield wall, boys!"

"Sweet bloody papa." Zane Neville's mouth was agape, eyes wide.

"Bend me over and bugger me senseless. As Laijon is my witness, we're liable to get our heads caved in by these rascally bastards. We'd be absolutely barking mad to try and fight them." Zane tossed down his helm and shield, gaze racing up and down the ragtag line of Gallows Haven men. "I'm going to find my family, find Beer Mug. Flee into the hills. I'm done with this madness." With that, he turned and ran.

"You all swore an oath!" the baron roared, spittle flecking his beard, eyes following Zane. "I will not suffer cowards! You all swore a covenant with church and king to defend your homeland! We'll fight like warriors and carve them up good and proper and send them back to Sør Sevier on the dung-ships they sailed in on!"

Baron Bruk's roaming gaze touched Shawcroft's and locked there a moment. "We all fight! The next who leaves I will chase down and kill myself!"

The back of Nail's hand now stung with a white-hot pain. He looked down at the almost forgotten, but still red and blistered, crosslike burn on his hand—the burn caused by his gauntlet when the lightning had struck Dokie. *But my gauntlets are probably with some old farmer now! So ill-prepared!* Nail now knew he would die here today.

Baron Bruk raised his sword and yelled, "By the word of Laijon, I command you to all form a shield wall—"

There was a hollow, metallic *thunk!* A thick crossbow bolt bounced off the back of the baron's helm and fell to the ground. He dropped unceremoniously to his knees, stunned, helm knocked askew.

Nail's eyes flew to the ranks of the Sør Sevier army. The red-haired woman stood about ten paces in front of the rest of the Sør Sevier army, nocking another quarrel to her crossbow. She looked so regal and skilled and deadly that what little regard the Gallows Haven men had previously had for fighting was rapidly wilting.

Shawcroft's eyes were racked with emotion. "We must go. Now. Much rides upon your surviva—"

Nail heard the snap of the red-haired warrior woman's crossbow and the wind of the quarrel's passage and the *whhppt* of cleaved air.

Shawcroft's knees buckled like broken saplings.

Nail's master crumpled to the ground and rolled onto his side. Blood welled from around the thick shaft sunk deep in his back, bubbled through his fingers as he reached to pull the quarrel free. Nail's breath clamped tight in his chest.

The sight of Shawcroft stuck with a crossbow bolt, wheezing for breath, broke the nerve of some men nearby. They began fleeing one at a time, then in small groups.

Nail felt nothing. He reached down and pulled Shawcroft's long-sword from its sheath. He hefted the weapon, testing its weight in his hand. Heavy. The black opal on the pommel exactly like that on Baron Bruk's sword. *A Dayknight sword?*

Silence had fallen across the field. The terror in the village ranks was palpable. Nail could feel it welling up within him, too. Sweat trickled down the sides of his face. When the soaring wail of the Sør Sevier bagpipes sounded over the landscape, Nail had to swallow his own fear and impulse to flee.

A bloody hand reached up and tried to take the sword from him. Nail moved back from his master and the hand fell away. "Help me up," Shawcroft said. Nail took his master's hand the second time it was offered and, with all he could muster, pulled the man to his feet.

The enemy knights began clanging swords upon shields. It was a fearsome sound and the very ground appeared to shudder. As one, the Sør Sevier archers nocked their arrows and took aim.

"Just run." Shawcroft was now trying to stand on his own, pleading, pushing Nail away. Blood was soaking his clothes fast. "Run. Now. Leave me."

The rising music stopped.

Silence.

And instantly the scene was chaos.

Nearly every Gallows Haven fighter turned and fled. Stefan Wayland with his new Silver Guard bow ran. Dokie Liddle ran. Everyone was running toward town.

But Nail stood rooted in fear. He saw two others nearby: Brutus Grove from the baron's grayken-hunting skiff, and Jenko Bruk, both trying to help the baron stand.

The Sør Sevier archers lowered their bows and stepped aside and the vast army behind them set heels to flanks and charged. As the Sør Sevier army thundered toward him, Nail couldn't believe what was happening. So quickly this horror had come to them. One day they were celebrating at the Mourning Moon Feast, and the next day the armies of Sør Sevier were here to kill them all. He pulled at Shawcroft's arm, tried to get the man to flee with him. But Shawcroft shoved him away roughly. "Go, Nail. Now."

And at the sight of fifteen hundred knights bearing down upon him, something snapped inside of Nail. An instant of self-preservation, a primal instinct, kicked in. He did as Shawcroft bade him do. He ran.

After about thirty frantic paces, he turned and looked back. Watched in terror as the charging cavalry trampled Shawcroft over.

Nail fled toward the keep. It was a frantic sprint. And in only a few short steps, his lungs began to burn. They heaved against his chest armor.

He looked back in fear, watched as a frothing war charger bore down on Brutus Grove and Jenko Bruk. The large bullnecked Sør Sevier man with the red beard and blue tattoos struck first. The fellow's mane of wild red hair flamed and flew in the sunlight as his massive ball mace met armor and bone and Brutus Grove exploded upward in a spray of blood—the heavy mace arcing high, slinging trails of red into the air. Jenko Bruk dodged the flashing blue long-sword of the White Prince but was quickly trampled under the stark white charger of the red-haired warrior woman with the crossbow. Jenko tumbled under the churning hooves, his sword, shield, and helm scattering. Baron Bruk was trampled underneath too. And the enemy cavalry stormed on toward Nail.

He found himself in a whirl of pounding hooves, eyes scarcely registering the turmoil around him except in glimpses: the blur of Sør Sevier armor, the flashing of blades, the prickle of spearheads, the scattering of buffet tables and decorations, remnants of last night's feast. The only solid thing he could focus on was the wide slab of the keep's crumbling wall and the slope of its debris. With his master's heavy sword still in hand, he swung out madly at a passing rider, striking nothing, still running. There was a clamor and roiling around him, a cacophony of sound, and something smashed into his side. He was forced stumbling to the right. A charger crashed into him, knocking him over, Shawcroft's sword spinning from his hand, lost in the confusion.

Nail scrambled to his feet just in time to see another white war-horse bearing down, its corded muscles under spiked armor heaving and strained. The charger's stern-faced rider was completely bald and focused. The man swung low at Nail with a fearsome-looking long-sword. Nail dropped to the ground again, dirt kicked up into his eyes as the blade whistled overhead. The bald rider moved on, swinging again, decapitating an old farmer who held up a rake in defense.

Nail lurched to his feet and headed for the keep, shouts of death and destruction all around. Sør Sevier knights swarmed the keep's entrance. Nail veered to the left, spying a wide crack in the building's crumbling wall. There was a dark opening there, just big enough for a man. Another entrance. And no Sør Sevier fighters.

He sprinted for the wall and dove into the crumbled access, only to slam into a frenzied-eyed fisherman who was attempting to duck into the same opening. The collision sent both sprawling. Nail regained his bearings and hurtled through the craggy slit first. The fisherman followed but ended up lodged between the jagged mortars. Red bubbled from his mouth as he was speared in the back by a menacing-looking Sør Sevier knight. Nail fled from the man's blood-curdling screams, eyes trying to adjust to the darkness. He stumbled over a crate and fell headlong into a moldy stack of cloth. Frantic, he regained his feet, continuing onward toward a dim light at the end of a narrow passageway. He busted through a rickety wooden door and into a large roofless room, squinting against the glare of light pouring in from above. Beams and rafters had caved in ages ago and littered the floor in jagged, twisted piles. He instantly knew he was in the keep's long-unused dining hall. There were women and girls huddled in the room. They screeched in horror as flame-lit arrows began to rain over the walls. In one teeming mass they ran for an open tunnel along the far wall. A flaming arrow struck one girl, who fell scream-ing into a pile of wooden rafters on the floor. Instantly smoke and heat billowed.

Nail lurched after the remaining women, joining them in their dash down the dark opening and farther into the abandoned keep. The tunnel was already filled with smoke and flame. Some women dropped to the ground, crying, their companions dragging them from the spreading fires. Nail helped a village girl pull an old woman over a crumbled cobblestone barrier. Then he noticed the woman he helped was dead, an arrow shaft sprouting from her chest. He let her go and ran.

Dark smoke roiled around him. He saw the fleshy bare legs of another woman in a threadbare skirt race by. He followed her. Orange light flared up and waves of heat bore down. Then the woman in front of him suddenly disappeared. He tumbled down a flight of stone stairs, landing atop her with a thud. As he untangled himself from the woman, he heard horrific pain-filled screams coming from the stairs above.

Then a soft breath of fresh air grazed his face. In the opposite direction of the stairs was a narrow tunnel, a brilliant blue glow at its far end. Nail urged the woman to run toward the light with a swift push. She ran, clogging the passageway before him with a limping, lumbering gait. Her silhouette was dark against the stark blue of the tunnel's exit, her hair bouncing and shimmering in crazy patterns in the light. When she broke free from the tunnel, sunlight engulfed her.

Nail stumbled out of the keep behind her, eyes adjusting to the light, the lady running free along the beach in front of him, her skirt awhirl as her bare feet churned up the sand. She was met by a charging Sør Sevier horseman, who cut her in half with a huge flashing blade. The top of her body, arms flailing, was sent spinning into the surf, a string of guts trailing. Her legs folded and slid in the sand.

Like swarming ants, Sør Sevier fighters were everywhere at once.

Nail stopped. He gazed upon a beach littered with bodies. Villagers were everywhere: farmers, sailors, women, and conscripts still in their armor, they were all of them running and screaming whilst Sør Sevier blades appeared to leap and slash at them from every direction. An older woman fell next to him, silent, her tattered skirt torn, belly ripped open, her slashed and bruise-colored entrails steaming in the sand.

Gulping in the squalid air, Nail tottered forward and dropped to his knees in the sand near a portion of the crumbled keep. He could hear the swish of the receding tide in between the screams of the dying. With scarcely any strength in his legs, he tried standing again. Every muscle in his body twitched in protest.

He knelt there, head down, sifting his fingers through the sand, knowing that his life would soon be over. He found himself cowering, hugging the broken stones of the keep, willing himself to disappear beneath them.

As the chaos swirled around him, he looked toward the sea, its white rolling breakers in the distance, the unfurled sails of the huge warships floating beyond.

It seemed a lifetime ago that he had been sitting on this very beach under the stars with Ava Shay.

A villager in boiled leather armor and a rusted iron helm stumbled toward him, blood vomiting from his mouth, a bloody spear point jutting through his chest. The rest of the spear's haft protruded from the fellow's back. One of the rowers on Jubal Bruk's hunting skiff. Nail could not recall his name. The man dropped his sword and fell forward into the sand in front of Nail, his helmet bouncing from his head, blood pumping from his open, gasping mouth. The sand of the beach greedily absorbed the spilled blood.

Nail knew the sight of the sailor dying would be the last thing he would ever see, that and the Sør Sevier knight walking casually toward him.

What set this knight apart from the hacking and slashing and swirling tumult of the beachhead slaughter was the knight's calmness— and his youth. He wore no helm, yet his silver armor and white surcoat were bloodstained red and he bore a sword nearly as long as his body. Nail took in every detail of the athletic-looking young man. *A fellow not much older than me, a young man who has probably already witnessed a hundred battles and a thousand bloody deaths. A true warrior indeed.* There was a feral, animal-like bearing about this young Sør Sevier knight that transfixed Nail. Perhaps it lay in his squinting eyes—eyes that were dark and fierce and bore what appeared to be thick smears of blue war paint under each. Or perhaps it was the young man's carefully pressed russet braids, which draped down his back like long cornrows of snakes—braids that were now flying out behind him as he picked up speed, for this young knight had noticed Nail kneeling there and had begun to run in loping strides toward him, longsword upraised in both hands.

As death closed in, Nail sat there unmoving. Weariness had drained him.

Onward the young Sør Sevier knight ran, evil grin bearing down, sword poised above like an ax in an axman's hands, preparing to split Nail's head like a melon.

Death comes to claim me.

Nail thought of his twin sister, his only family, a girl he would never now find, a girl he would never now get to know. *Was she out there somewhere in the Five Isles, as lost and alone as he? Did she know that he even existed?* There were too many questions that would forever go unanswered.

But Nail did not want to die just yet.

He scrambled for the dead sailor's rusted iron helmet and sword. Picking up both, he slammed the helmet over his head and rose to meet his foe.

But the Sør Sevier youth was already upon him, longsword swinging in a great huge arc downward.

Only halfway to his feet, Nail's head exploded in a shower of stars and all things instantly went black.

And the shamans and stone carvers did prophesy, "There are gods many and lords many, but soon there will be but one lord greater than the rest. A savior. An ensign unto all kingdoms. A great hero born by the sea. One powerful enough to slay the winged demons and their evil lords. One whose feet shall be washed by queens and kings."
—THE WAY AND TRUTH OF LAIJON

CHAPTER SEVENTEEN

AVA SHAY

3RD DAY OF THE MOURNING MOON, 999TH YEAR OF LAIJON

GALLOWS HAVEN, GUL KANA

Crabs scuttled among the heap of dead bodies as seagulls cried above, their shadows weaving over the rippled, bloodstained sand and waves rolling ashore. White fins of sharks, slithering up from the depths, were coming closer to land. They could taste death in the water. Baron Bruk's cauldrons had been overturned by Sør Sevier warriors to empty them of grayken oil, then, for some reason unkown to Ava or any of the other captives, refilled with boiling tar, the black bubbling broth sending up fumes that scarcely masked the stench of the bloated corpses. North of Gallows Keep rose up another pile of the dead, all afire, burned by the Sør Sevier knights, never to be given religious rites or proper burial.

Ava Shay could feel the flies lighting on her skin now, scurrying, little feet dancing madly across her face. With hands bound behind her back with rope, she could not swat them away. Trying to ignore the tickling of the bugs, she took note of her fellow survivors. There were only a paltry thirty souls left of the five hundred or so who had once populated Gallows Haven. Smoke and grit coated their faces.

The Grayken Spear Inn had been reduced to cinders. When the inn had been set afire, only Ava, along with four other serving girls, Tylda Egbert, Gisela Barnwell, Polly Mott, and Liz Hen Neville, managed to escape. The memory of the Grayken Spear's fiery destruction tumbled mercilessly through her head. She could not dispel the image of her younger brothers and sisters burning as Ol' Man Leddingham tried to save them. Her whole family was now gone. Ol' Man Leddingham, too. She could still hear their inhuman screams, still smell the air bitter with the reek of their charred flesh. Smoke billowed from the keep and chapel too. It appeared everything had been ravaged and burned.

Tears welled in her eyes. This did not feel like a dream. Yet it didn't seem quite real, either. She tried to regain some sense of sanity. Her gaze traveled to Baron Bruk's grayken-hunting ship, cast adrift in the bay. Swirling fire leaped to the sky from its flaming skeleton, and black smoke billowed heavenward.

It would have been better to have just died. The others beside her in line looked as destitute as she felt, their faces shocked with pain, their eyes barren. Ava noticed Stefan Wayland and Dokie Liddle near the end of the line. Stefan wore his armor, though it was dirt-crusted and dented. Dokie was wearing naught but a shirt, torn leather tunic, rough-spun woolen leggings, and a few scraps of dented plate strapped to his chest. Next to them were Gisela and Polly; like Ava, they wore simple woolen shifts tied at the waist. She recalled the joy on Gisela's face last night as she'd danced with Stefan. But it now seemed all such innocent joys had been forever wiped from the world.

Jenko Bruk stood to the right of Tylda, head hung low, hair

covering his bruised face, armor battered. His mere presence was a small but blessed comfort.

The bulk of the Sør Sevier army was setting up camp on the grassy field just north of the keep. She could hear the rattle and clanking of the wagons they had scavenged from the town. A group of knights milled about the beach directly in front of the prisoners. Their fearsome warhorses were painted in the colors of Sør Sevier, blue circles and spirals around their eyes, ears dyed white and rimmed in blue.

At least a third of the Sør Sevier warriors were women, fierce and ugly. Some had removed their armor and were now watering their mounts from buckets of fresh water. Some were knee deep in the ocean, washing their weaponry free of blood. The beach was streaked red with froth. Another group of female knights were sinking hooks into the hacked bodies still on the beach and dragging them behind their mounts up toward the bonfire. These heaps of tortured flesh were villagers Ava had known her entire life. To look upon them now with their hollow eyes and bloated faces was like a nightmare.

It could not, Ava told herself, be happening. Yet it was. The gray-visaged Sør Sevier knights standing on Gul Kana soil before her were a reminder of the lessons of *arduous truths* written in *The Way and Truth of Laijon*, that *the wraiths of death stalk every life, everywhere*. Today was her time to die. The trauma of everything she'd just been through was paralyzing. And the shock of it all played with her thoughts. She could feel the vast persistence of the wraiths planning their attack upon her shivering mind. They would soon come a-creeping into her brain with a trembling certainty. They would destroy her like they had destroyed her mother.

Her mouth was parched, her thirst like a raging saber-toothed mountain lion clawing up her throat. Ava felt she might faint without water. She couldn't think of a suitable Laijon prayer for what was happening to her. So she just uttered his name over and over and awaited her fate.

And fate stalked the line of prisoners now.

Ava braced for death as a pretty, red-haired Sør Sevier warrior woman drew near, flipping a copper coin over and over in her hand. The woman wore leather armor fastened with a gleaming silver breastplate and shoulder plates. Leather greaves and steel armor covered her thighs and shins. She wore thick, dark boots, also studded with steel. The top of a crossbow and quiver of thick, wicked-looking bolts jutted from over her shoulder. A giant tattoo-faced fellow followed her—seven feet tall if an inch, his hair also fire red. The two stopped before the young Gallows Haven boy first in line, asking him his name.

"My ma was shot with arrows," the boy answered. Smears of blood encrusted his face. "She's on the beach." He nodded toward the water. "Can I go tend to her?"

The Sør Sevier woman informed the boy that his mother was dead. Then she and the large tattooed fellow moved to the next in line—a Gallows Haven conscript who swayed almost drunkenly on his feet, dented helmet atop his head. Thick streaks of blood covered the fighter's face. It was dried and crusted on his neck and chest-plate armor too. The red-haired woman ordered the conscript to remove his helm. But the fellow just stood there on wobbly legs.

"Helm's been smashed onto his head." The woman turned to her giant companion. "See if you can't club it off, Hammerfiss."

Hammerfiss. The name terrified Ava. With broad shoulders and muscles like an ox, Hammerfiss looked stouter than a full-grown oak. Bones, fetishes, and bangles were tied into his hair and beard. The blue tattoos covering his face spoke to the evil that Ava felt must surely breed within his soul. He wore a belt lined with a brace of long knives and a leather harness over his silver armor bearing a massive mace that hung at his back.

With one meaty fist, Hammerfiss smacked the underside of the conscript's helmet and it popped free, revealing Nail's face. He stumbled back, landing on his butt in the sand, hands bound behind him. Thick, murky rivulets of dried blood marked Nail's face, mostly obscuring it. With listless eyes, he looked up at the two warriors from Sør Sevier, then rolled onto his side and barfed in the sand.

"This one's useless." The red-haired woman flipped her copper coin. "Kill him."

Ava's heart plunged as Hammerfiss reached down and latched onto the front of Nail's armor and yanked him to his feet. "He'll recover soon, Spades." The tattooed giant gently slapped the boy's blood-encrusted cheek. "He seems a stout enough lad."

The blue tattoos that covered Hammerfiss did not seem as frightening now as they had before, and Ava's heart warmed to the giant. In that one gesture from Hammerfiss, she sensed a morsel of concern in him for the prisoners. The tattooed giant now looked more their savior than their killer. *He'll recover soon, Spades. He seems a stout enough lad*. For in hearing those few words, Ava knew that they might not all be murdered.

The red-haired woman named Spades had moved on to Polly Mott. "Name?" she ordered. Polly muttered her name. Tears were flowing over the brown mole sitting there like a smudge of mud under the corner of Polly's left eye. Polly Mott was known more for the unsightly mole on her face than anything else. She was sixteen and scared.

But Spades had moved on to the next girl in line, Gisela Barnwell, who gave her name, then started crying too. Spades and Hammerfiss moved to Jenko Bruk next. Jenko's bruised face was dark and unsavory behind sweaty locks of matted hair. There was a murderous look and hunger for vengeance about him—it lay in the angle of his chin and shards of hate sparking from his eyes. He did not say his name when asked.

"This one will be trouble," Hammerfiss observed.

"He can be tamed." Spades had to look up to meet Jenko's eyes.

Now that the red-haired warrior woman was closer, Ava could tell, Spades had a lovely porcelain face with a delicate bone structure behind a spray of bright red curls. There was a tint of innocence to her over-all features, but an expression of absolute cunning in her eyes. Indeed, glowing beneath that dainty, freckled skin burned something wicked and furious. Ava hated her more than she had ever hated anything.

"Do you wish to kill me?" Spade asked Jenko, flicking her coin up one last time, then stuffing it into a hidden pocket of her leather greaves. Jenko glared at her.

"I see," Spades said. "You wish to fuck me instead?" The casualness of the statement stunned Ava. For some reason, despite the state-ment's preposterousness, rage and jealousy welled up within her. She fought back the sudden urge to lash out. Her mouth was too dry for such an outburst anyway. Nausea overcame her.

"I recognize the cut and polish of your armor," Spades said to Jenko. "Was you who stayed with Baron Bruk when he fell. I'm sur-prised my quarrel didn't pierce the fool's helm. Never did find his body. No matter. I'm glad to see that you survived, a bit battered and bruised, though. I sense braveness in you. That will bode well for you in Aeros' eyes. Was the one who Hammerfiss crushed with his mace your brother? Your father?"

Then Jenko did what Ava had wanted to. He spat on Spades. But the woman turned her head and what little spray flew from Jenko's mouth sprinkled her hair, missing her face. Her eyes sparkled as she turned back toward him. "Now I always thought I was charming," she said with a bemused smile, "but not that charming. See. I knew you wanted to fuck me." Jenko remained silent, though a danger-ous glare remained in his eyes, and those eyes remained on Spades. But she moved away from him with casual ease and examined Tylda Egbert briefly, before stepping up to Ava.

"Well," Spades said, looking straight at her. "Aren't you just an impossibly pretty little thing?" And that was all.

Spades and Hammerfiss moved past Ava to the very end of the line. Bishop Tolbret was there, hands tied behind him too, stoic in his mud-encrusted cassock, which was torn down the side. The priest-hood robe underneath was stark white and pure in comparison to his dirty cassock. He seemed unaffected under the scrutiny of the enemy.

That is, until Spades drew a dagger and cut the rope that bound his hands, snatched him by the arm, and pulled him from the line. He prayed aloud as he was marched before the other prisoners.

"Silence!" Spades shoved him to the ground. He kept praying. She yanked him up again and violently tore off his long brown cassock. It puddled at his feet as he prayed louder and louder. The silk priest-hood robe he wore underneath covered his torso from neck to knees but was of a flimsy weave, nearly transparent in the sunlight.

"We're the most battle-hardened sons of bitches who've ever stepped foot on these shores!" the red-haired woman yelled as the bishop kept praying. "And lest any of you doubt my words, I mean to behead this blasphemer here and now."

Tolbret shrank away from her. He bowed his head and prayed more fervently, doing the three-fingered sign of the Laijon Cross over his heart.

"Let me tear his scrawny cock off first," Hammerfiss snarled.

Any affinity Ava had previously felt for the bearded giant vanished as the large man pulled a dirk from his belt and moved toward the bishop, a wide smile developing over his tattooed face. Tolbret instantly cupped his groin protectively, his prayers seemingly at an end.

"Why do you bother to protect your balls?" Spades laughed. "As a bishop of Gul Kana, you're not allowed to use them anyway."

"Unless he's twiddling the kids in an Ember Gathering." Hammer-fiss grinned.

"What's your taste, boys or girls?" Spades asked Tolbret.

"More like the goats and chickens, I wager," Hammerfiss said glee-fully.

"Indeed," Spades said. "I've heard that the bishops in this land have a certain affinity for the beasts and the fowl and the fishes. I hear you give Ember Gathering to the ducks and seagulls and preach your *Way and Truth of Laijon* to the saber-toothed lions. Some have said you bishops even flagellate your cocks before the goats and geese."

"It's the worshippers of Raijael who pervert the will of Laijon." Bishop Tolbret's shaky voice rose. "It is you demons from Sør Sevier who blaspheme against Laijon!"

"And what about the hundreds of years of Gul Kana oppression heaped upon Sør Sevier in the name of your church? Was Wyn Darrè not raped and stolen from us? Why are there no women priests in Gul Kana? Why no women warriors?"

Despite his vulnerable position, it appeared as if Tolbret was starting to compose himself. He held his head high and answered. "Women are too emotional to do the will of Laijon. They've little bravery. The Ember Gathering confirms their feeblemindedness."

"Feeblemindedness," Spades repeated flatly, appraising the bishop, touching his silken robe. "Your silly white costume is an affront to Raijael. Will it truly protect you from harm? Is this ridiculous belief in magical robes the kind of nonsense you brave and manly idol worshippers believe?"

"They are sacred!" Dokie Liddle stepped forward, hands tied behind his back. He stood as tall and proud as he could. "They are the robes of Laijon's priesthood!"

Spades appraised the boy with some admiration in her stony countenance. "Sacred?" she asked, eyebrow raised. "Or just plain fucking stupid?"

"You would not understand," Dokie said haughtily. "His robe was blessed and anointed by Grand Vicar Denarius himself—"

"Under whose authority?" Spades cut him off, looking angrily at Tolbret. "Certainly not that of our great Laijon. For the power of Laijon resides in the seed of Raijael."

"Denarius is Laijon's holy prophet." Young Dokie was standing taller now, a proud lift to his chin. "'Twas he who anointed Bishop

Tolbret's robe with holy oils and then placed it over his body in the Royal Cathedral upon his confirmation into the priesthood. It is a protection meant only for Laijon's servants. I will not see you insult it. Or Bishop Tolbret."

"Indeed, you seem quite attached to the bishop . . . and his clothing."

"I have seen Laijon's power manifested in Bishop Tolbret," Dokie said proudly. "You could never understand."

"I pray you, tell me. I'm curious."

Bishop Tolbret interjected, "You needn't speak on my behalf, son."

"The boy will speak if he so pleases," Spades said.

Dokie straightened. "I was struck by lightning. After he healed me, the bishop told me a story of the priesthood robes' strength. In Hopewell, when Bishop Tolbret was but a boy, he witnessed the most astonishing of miracles." Dokie spoke as if giving this foreign warrior woman an Eighth Day sermon of his own. "There was a fire in the chapel's dormitory, and one of the bishops perished in the flame. When they pulled his body from the charred wreckage, his limbs and head were burnt off. Yet under his priesthood robe nary a hair was singed or a scratch found. So Bishop Tolbret told me."

"A miracle then," Spades commented flatly.

Dokie performed the three-fingered sign of the Laijon Cross over his heart. "Under the sacred robe not a burn was found."

"But his head was gone." Spades cocked her brow.

Dokie's eyes were wide. "The story proves the robes offer bodily protection to the worthy by the will of Laijon."

Spades' words were rapid and rich with sarcasm. "So you really believe the priesthood robe will protect your good bishop from physical harm?" A hint of a smile tugged at her lips.

"Indeed," Dokie said without pause. The bishop's countenance, on the other hand, went through a remarkable change. Color drained from his face.

"Let's test your theory, boy." Spades pulled the crossbow from over her shoulder and walked away from Tolbret, nocking a quarrel into the weapon as she went.

Bishop Tolbret's face blanched, but he remained rooted in place. There was a stillness that fell upon the beach for a moment. The prisoners watched him, eyes wide, as if they were about to witness something truly miraculous.

When thirty paces separated Spades from the bishop, she whirled around and aimed the crossbow and its thick bolt straight at him. The girth of the bolt's shaft looked as big and round as a grown man's thumb. "If you're correct, boy, and his holy robe saves him from my quarrel, then I say the armies of Sør Sevier will leave these shores and never return." Then she pulled the trigger.

There was a metallic *snap!* And Tolbret was launched backward through the air, heels skimming the beach as he flew, his back plowing a furrow into the sand where he landed. "No!" Dokie screamed. The bishop expelled a terror-filled cry of his own as he sat up, clutching at the crossbow bolt in his stomach. He doubled over and fell sideways into the sand, blood pooling under him.

Spades returned her crossbow to the harness on her back and walked up to Dokie. "I reckon your bishop's miserable robe proved as useless as a rack of bloody paper shields."

Hammerfiss yanked Tolbret roughly to his feet. Spades stepped forward and gripped the shaft of the quarrel lodged in his stomach. "It looks as if the armies of Aeros Raijael will remain in these lands." And with a yank, she tore the bolt free. The bishop cried out as his gut ruptured. Entrails slithered from his rent robe like snakes from a gunnysack. Hammerfiss stepped back. Tolbret dropped to his knees and wailed. His hands scrabbled among his own spilled guts, trying desperately to hold the glistening slithery coils of his intestines in. But the shimmering purple loops slipped through his fingers to the sand, the tide licking them up.

Horror dropped like a shawl over Ava's shoulders. Tolbret now seemed no longer human, no longer a man of Laijon at all, but a fleshy pink sack of raw guts and blood—just a fellow townsman filled with terror and despair, the thin white robe about his legs dripping brown with feces.

"What we've got here is a rather wretched situation." Spades spoke loudly to the line of prisoners. "It does seem a horrible crime that you have all been saddled with such feeble company as ourselves. I'm sorry to burden you with the formalities of warfare, but we need to discuss some issues without rancor." She paused, pacing before them. "We can either put you to death or—"

"Not." Hammerfiss finished the sentence for her.

"So you feel there must indeed be some divine purpose to this madness?"

"I don't claim any divine purpose, nor do I think their situation is entirely hopeless."

"Indeed, nothing is hopeless." Spades' eyes were on the bishop. Tolbret moaned, crawling through the surf after a clump of his entrails that the incoming tide had taken.

Spades turned from the bishop to Hammerfiss. "Since we've already established that we have no qualms about speaking frankly, what say you of their fate?"

Hammerfiss' mouth spread into a mad grin. "I've always felt that some previously useless lives can be converted to a better purpose. That being said, I say that the children of Gallows Haven are now the property of Sør Sevier! You are to be adopted into the covenant of Raijael and raised up in true righteousness and faith as citizens of Sør Sevier and believers in Aeros Raijael, your true One and Only!"

Though Hammerfiss was shouting now, it was difficult for Ava to hear him. Bishop Tolbret was kneeling in the lapping waves of the beach, crying out in thunderous gasps, his attempts to gather his own guts and stuff them back into his stomach a lost cause as they swam around him in the water like eels.

Hammerfiss continued to shout over the bishop's cries. "And those of you older than twelve are now slaves, under the control and whims of our armies! You will serve as our pack mules, armor polishers, and errand runners as we conquer your lands!"

There was crying from the prisoners, whether they were cries of relief at being spared or cries of despair at becoming slaves, Ava couldn't tell. She remained stoic and unfeeling, stunned, really. And above it all, Tolbret continued to create an awful shrill racket in the water with ear-piercing wails and screeches.

"Holy shit, man!" Hammerfiss bellowed. "I can't hear my own self speak!" Pulling a long knife from his belt, he tromped over to the bishop, who was still lying half in the water. Planting his knee right in the bishop's back, the red-bearded giant sliced Tolbret's throat clear to the spine, then shoved the dying man face-first into the surf. Red water lapped up against the bishop's body as Hammerfiss walked away.

Dokie Liddle ran. In bare feet, he ran, sprinting awkwardly down the beach in the direction of Gallows Haven, hands tied behind him, legs churning, feet kicking up sand.

Spades drew her crossbow, nocked a quarrel, and fired.

The bolt cleaved the air and punched through the back of Dokie's thigh. He went down, tumbling. Undaunted, he did not cry, but kept going, crawling on his stomach, inching forward, plowing through the sand, arrow-pierced leg dragging a bloody trail.

Hammerfiss lumbered down the beach, picked up the struggling boy, and carried him back under the crook of one arm. He set Dokie on the ground before Spades.

Despite the quarrel dangling from his tender leg, Dokie stood defiant before her.

"You really must hate our company, lad," Spades said, admiration for Dokie's strength in her voice. "So I'll make a deal with you." She pointed to the legions of Sør Sevier warships anchored a hundred yards offshore. "If you can swim to the nearest ship and back without getting eaten by a one of the sharks circling about, I'll let you go free."

"You'll let me go free?"

"Aye." Spades untied Dokie's hands. "I swear it."

With his hands free, Dokie threw off his bits of armor and leather tunic and dashed into the ocean. In just his shirt and breeches, he was quickly in water up to his knees, then thighs, then stomach. Soon he was swimming, thick quarrel still lodged in his thigh.

"That little fellow is bloody mad," Hammerfiss said, watching Dokie go.

The fins of the sharks were like tiny white sails slicing through the sea between the distant ships, quietly slipping below the water, then resurfacing. Ava felt her breath catch in her throat when she lost sight of Dokie momentarily among the choppy waves. There was a sudden thrashing of water where he should have been, and her heart sank.

"I see him!" Hammerfiss pointed. "Look!"

Dokie was pounding the palm of his hand against the nearest ship's hull, letting all ashore know that he'd reached it. The dull banging was faint, but Ava heard it.

"He's still got to swim back," Spades said. "He'll be bitten in half soon enough."

As Dokie swam back, one of the swerving fins darted toward him with the speed of an arrow. The distant splash of his paddling arms and feet ceased, and he vanished under a boiling blanket of water. An eerie calmness came over the ocean. A few tense heartbeats passed, then to Ava's relief, Dokie surfaced, swimming vigorously. It wasn't long before he was wading ashore, limping, quarrel still lodged in his thigh. What little was left of his shirt hung in ragged shreds over his chest, and blood oozed from a shallow furrow of teeth marks that cut an arcing swath across both his back and belly. Despite all, Dokie Liddle, breathing heavily, stumbled from the bay and stood before Spades.

Hammerfiss' booming voice was dripping with amusement. "Them shark bites ain't more than a fingernail's breadth deep." His dancing eyes fell on Spades. "I'm relieved you didn't tell the whelp our entire army would leave Gul Kana."

Spades pointed Dokie toward town. "You've earned your freedom. Now git, before I change my mind." And just like that, Dokie limped away from her, crossbow bolt in his leg, shark bites lining his body.

Ava stood a little prouder as she watched Dokie gather his armor and make his way back into Gallows Haven. His small victory over their tormentors had given them all hope. "If I swim out there, may I go free too?" an eager voice sounded from the line of captives.

Spades' eyes were alight with anger as she drew her sword. "You'll find yourselves lucky if I don't just slay you all now!"

† † † † †

Moments later, two Sør Sevier knights, one bald, the other bearded and wearing a black patch over one eye, broke through the line of prisoners, dragging Baron Jubal Bruk between them. The baron's hands were tied behind his back. He was brought directly to Spades. She appraised him with unbridled disgust.

"Found him in a shed near the chapel," the dark-haired knight with the eye patch said. The man carried a deadly-looking sword in one gauntleted hand. Scars ribboned his face. His one good eye cast stony indifference at the prisoners. "The fool who rode out to offer us his surrender. Baron Jubal Bruk."

"I can see that, Stabler," Spades snapped. "I have two eyes."

Stabler backed away, face reddening under his eye patch, a sneer spreading across his scarred face. "Lest you forget, I lost this eye saving your skin in Agonmoore."

Spades' full attention was on Baron Bruk. "My bolt shoulda killed you. Running you down with my horse shoulda killed you. Yet here you are. Still alive."

"Aye. I am lucky in that," the baron said.

"Luck for a coward," Spades sneered. "They found you in a shed. Are all Gul Kana barons such cowards, Jubal? Are all barons trained to hide?"

"I ran to save the women in the chapel from slaughter. My purpose was to lead them into the mountains. Any sane man would've done the same."

"Listen, you overgrown sack of chickenshit," Spades snarled. "Don't insult me or the few survivors standing here who yet live."

"He guarded no women," the one-eyed knight named Stabler said. "And he offered scant resistance when we pulled him from the shed."

"Nobody in this place has yet offered resistance." Spades stepped up to Baron Bruk, appraising him. "An entire town sacked, and Sør Sevier did not lose one fighter. Not one of us even injured. I daresay the codfish and herring offered us more concern when we rowed ashore." A grunt and chuckle from Stabler bespoke similar sentiment.

It was then that the bald knight with Stabler looked at the prisoners, looked right at Ava Shay. At first his eyes were flat and watchful as his gaze traveled over her. Something in his eyes flowed raw and dangerous in his quiet stare. Ava found she could not turn away. She felt an immediate connection. He was handsome—strikingly appealing, but in a brutal way. His bald head and neatly trimmed goatee were a stark contrast to the dark splatters of blood and gore that covered his armor. His shoulders were angular with plate armor and his shortsword hung low on his hip. The longsword strapped in the baldric across his back looked well used and deadly. She wanted to drop her own gaze, look away, but his eyes lingered upon her with such bold curiosity, she wondered what he saw. There was one certainty: lust did not live in his eyes as it had in most men who looked at her. His eyes were filled with something she could not quite define.

He looked away from her and up the grassy knoll. Ava followed his gaze. A weaponless man with short-cropped black hair was riding down the hill on an equally black horse. He was dragging a wooden crate by a length of rope tied to the horse's pommel. Beast and rider seemed bleak and rootless as they galloped by, the crate dragging behind, pushing up sand. The surface of the man's dark cloak and leather armor seemed to be seething with endless death. The glowing red eyes of his mount looked feverish, demonic. Ava was sure that his fiendish-looking steed was a wraith from the underworld, kin to the nameless beasts. Veins followed twisting paths beneath its glistening hide, and its corded muscles appeared taut. Ava's heart hammered. She'd seen a similar horse before; with Stefan Wayland and Nail high on the Roahm Mine Trail.

This evil newcomer heeled the demon-eyed charger in front of Spades and dismounted. He offered Spades and Hammerfiss a curt nod before untying the rope and pooling it in the crate. "The box you requested."

"Baron Jubal Bruk lives," Spades said. "Perhaps you'd like to test your skills against the baron in a duel? After all, it seems neither one of you have used your weapons today."

"Some other time." The black-clad man appraised the baron with flat, vicious eyes. "Despite what you believe, today's battle has taxed my strength."

"I'm simply swooning with sympathy, Ser Spider. But I'm not interested in your pouty complaints. I say you should fight this man."

"Would be a waste of my time." The one Spades had called Ser Spider mounted his demon-eyed charger, set heels to flanks, and galloped away.

"Insolent fool," Spades sneered.

"He does tend to go his own way," Hammerfiss said.

"As do most like him," Stabler chuckled, earning a dark look from Spades. Her hand traveled to the sword at her hip. "Are you still

under the misapprehension that Hawkwood fights for our cause?"
Stabler continued. "His allegiance lies elsewhere now, with his new
lover, Jondralyn Bronachell."

Spades' knuckles were white with strain, hand tightening around
her sword.

"Even the Spider wants him dead," Stabler went on. "Shouldn't
that be answer enough for you?"

"Stop it." The bald knight stepped between the two. "You speak
too boldly in front of the captives." Ava liked the sound of his voice,
the command it held.

Spades moved toward the crate, and with the tip of her sword
pried the lid off. Ava craned her neck. From her angle, the wooden
box appeared empty. It wasn't large by any means, just big enough for
a child to curl up in and hide.

Spades returned to Baron Bruk. "That boy who swam through
the sharks has put me in an unsavory mood." She stepped behind the
baron and cut his bonds with her sword. "I aim to offer you a deal."
The baron's hands swung free and he rubbed his wrists, working the
circulation back into them, the muscles of his jaws bunching.

Spades held forth her sword, hilt out.

Baron Bruk immediately grabbed the weapon. Courage seemed to
wash over his face with a sword in hand. He held it up as if preparing
to strike. But Spades turned her back to him and began unhooking
her crossbow and quiver of quarrels. She tossed them to the sand,
then donned a pair of leather gloves taken from her quiver. Turning
to the baron, she held her arms away from her body, gloved hands
empty, weaponless.

"Here is the deal," she began. "Fight me to the death. If you win, you
get the privilege of delivering a message to the Silver Throne for the
Angel Prince. If you lose, well, you'll still be delivering the message
to Amadon, only"—Spades pointed to the crate lying in the sand—
"you'll make the journey in that."

The baron's face revealed a moment of dismay, his courage ebbing. Ava risked a glance at Jenko. But he was looking straight at the ground, hair covering his face.

Spades cocked her head, hands still held out from her body, palms up as if in supplication. "You can strike at me whenever you chose."

A short, sharp laugh burst from Baron Bruk. "To the underworld with you, bitch!" He swung. Spades grabbed the sword by the blade in midflight and yanked it from his hands. She flipped it in the air, caught it by the hilt, and rammed it through the plate armor covering his thigh. The baron wobbled back, the sword buried in his leg almost to the hilt—half the bloody blade sprouting from the other side. Spades kicked with the flat of her foot, connecting with the baron's chest, sending him sprawling to the ground. She snatched the hilt of the sword and pulled it from his leg. He cried out as the blade screeched free of his armor. Spades stood over him, bloody sword at his throat. "Stand up."

"My leg!" he spouted.

Hammerfiss stalked forward, grabbed the baron by his shoulders, and pulled him to his feet. Baron Bruk listed to the side, favoring his injured leg as blood pumped from it. The red-haired woman ripped off her leather gloves and threw them at Baron Bruk's feet.

"Take off your armor."

"What?" the baron said between pain-clenched teeth.

"Strip!" Spades shouted.

Baron Bruk managed to unbuckle his leg and shoulder armor without falling over. Then he slowly divested himself of his outer plate armor. Tears flowed freely from his eyes in the effort. His leg bled profusely as he stood before Spades in a mixture of sweaty gray shirt and woolen under-leggings, bloody from the thigh down.

"Take it all off," Spades said.

The baron removed his shirt, revealing a broad chest of dark, matted curls of hair.

"All of it." Spades motioned to his leggings.

"I'm liable to bleed to death as it is." Baron Bruk's lips quivered in pain.

Hammerfiss shoved the baron to the ground, then snatched the man's pants by the ankles and yanked them from his legs. The baron hollered in pain, then curled into the fetal position, clutching at the wound in his thigh. From head to toe, Baron Bruk's naked body was a ratted mess of sweaty hair. Dark curls even covered the vast expanse of his bunched and clenching buttocks.

"For fuck's sake." Hammerfiss pulled Jubal to his feet. "Handle it like a man."

The baron could barely stand. He leaned against Hammerfiss for support, blood gushing down the pale skin of his leg. He bore a thick thatch of graying pubic hair, and his scrotum dangled beneath the short stump of his manhood like the wrinkled face of a bearded old man. Spades stood there, eyes traveling over the naked man before her. "Well," she said after a moment of reflection. "I suppose you could call that a cock."

Hammerfiss laughed. So did Stabler. The bald knight remained silent.

"The boiling tar for our ships," Spades said to Stabler. "Fetch me a kettle."

Smiling, Stabler ambled toward the line of Baron Bruk's black cauldrons, a renewed energy in his step. Spades snatched up her bloody sword and spun about, eyes crazed. As she made her way ominously down the line of prisoners, many cowered from her. Even Ava tried not to meet the deranged woman's stare.

Spades stopped in front of Jenko Bruk. "The baron will soon bleed to death," she said. "What say you to that?" Jenko looked beyond her, refusing to meet her gaze.

Spades grabbed his chin in her hands and forced him to look at her. "I confess to having some skill at figuring men, in both body and character. You have a vicious streak, I can tell. Quick to anger. Quick to notice weakness in others and exploit it. Yet, I imagine, you were well liked in town." She jerked Jenko's face down to hers, until their eyes were level. "A real scoundrel, you. And proud of it." Jenko remained silent, nostrils flaring in and out as he breathed.

"The truth is"—Spades released his jaw—"I like what I see in you." She forced Jenko around and cut through his bonds with her sword. His hands were free. She stepped back from him quickly, the tip of her blade poised between them. Instead of attacking her, Jenko hung his head, hair covering his eyes.

"The baron will bleed to death soon," she said. "I wish you to finish him for me."

Jenko looked up, eyes glowering beneath the locks of his hair.

"You will kill Baron Bruk." Spades placed the tip of her sword under his chin.

"I will not." Jenko's voice was low, menacing. Despite all, there was still courage in him. It was clear the woman did not know that Jenko was Jubal's son. Ava could tell that Spades, despite her insanity, did not intimidate Jenko at all. Perhaps it was the inevitability of all their deaths that had caused such callousness within him. Either way, Ava knew that he would never do what Spades asked. He would die first. Not out of loyalty to his father, but out of pride, a need to never do what anyone demanded of him, especially under these circumstances. She was proud of him for his defiance.

Spades removed the sword from under his chin and stepped in front of Tylda Egbert, who stood trembling. "What is your name again?" Spades asked, lifting the girl's face. Tylda seemed devoid of speech as she raised her downcast eyes. In her face welled a depth of hopelessness and despair. A bright tear coursed slowly down her cheek, cutting a wet, cleansing path through the dirt and soot. Spades placed the tip of her sword under Tylda's chin whilst looking at Jenko. "Kill Jubal Bruk for me. Or I kill this girl."

Ava held her breath. She saw a brief moment of indecision cross over Jenko's face. As Ava watched him, her heart breaking, she could see the pain and confusion in his red-rimmed eyes. Then he looked away from Spades, seemingly unconcerned.

"Don't hurt me," Tylda whimpered, her trembling eyes fixed on the red-haired Sør Sevier woman before her. "I beg you." The bleak sadness in Tylda's voice was so raw that Ava had to blink back her own tears.

Spades rammed the sword up under Tylda's chin and into her brain. The girl jerked, head instantly skewered on the end of the weapon. When Spades pulled the blade free, Tylda's body folded to the sand, her woolen shift flying up around her hips, exposing the full length of her legs, which now twitched and spasmed.

Ava felt a flash of rage, a flash that vanished a heartbeat later as she realized Spades had moved to her. The tip of her sword, still fresh with Tylda's blood, was now poised under Ava's own chin. "And your name again, darling?" Spades asked.

Ava's voice cracked as she spoke her own name. Thirst was lodged like a broken bottle in her throat, yet she answered with a voice that was far calmer than she felt.

"Will the lad let you die too, pretty Ava Shay?" Spades pressed the tip of her sword against the flesh of Ava's neck. "Well, girl, will he—"

"I'll do it," Jenko said. Spades turned.

"I said I'll do it!" he repeated, voice laced with venom. "I will kill him."

Spades lowered her blade. "I could see you didn't care much for yourself," she said. "But I figured I could eventually find one you did care for."

Ava felt a measure of relief at not being killed. At the same time, she found herself shivering in fright as Jenko followed Spades toward Baron Bruk.

Hammerfiss shoved the baron to the ground. Jubal Bruk held

his wounded leg gingerly out of the sand in both hands. His cold, dark eyes were trained on his son. But those eyes betrayed nothing. Jenko's eyes were vacant too.

Stabler returned, carrying a black iron kettle of tar in one hand and a horrific-looking longsword in the other, its inner serrated edge honed sharp. He handed the jagged sword to Spades and set the kettle in the sand in front of the baron, steaming tar sloshing over its sides. The baron eyed the boiling broth with a concerned look.

"I don't actually want you to kill the baron." Spades handed Jenko the serrated sword. "He is of more use to us alive. But I did promise Jubal that if he lost the duel, he would be making a trip to Amadon in that box. So cut off his injured leg first. And then I'll decide how many more limbs need to be removed before he'll fit in the crate."

"Laijon have mercy, no!" The baron scooted away. But Hammerfiss was kneeling behind him, blocking his path. One of his massive arms encircled the baron's neck and shoulders, holding him in an iron grip.

"Do it, lad." Hammerfiss growled at Jenko. "And make it quick."

Jenko hefted the blade in both hands, testing its weight. He looked at Spades, uncertainty in his eyes. She nodded toward the baron. Jubal Bruk was unable to keep still, legs kicking out, thrashing madly, head trying to turn this way and that in Hammerfiss' grasp, hands clawing at the red giant's arms. Stabler immediately fell upon the baron's legs, yanking them apart until the man was spread-eagled in the sand. The bald knight stood back, watching the display with flat, hard eyes. To Ava, it seemed the bald one had little use for any of what was happening.

Jenko knelt before his father's injured, quivering leg. "You don't have to do this, Jenko," the baron said, pain quaking in his voice. "Let *them* kill me."

Jenko placed the serrated edge of the blade along his father's thigh above the previously torn flesh. Ava wanted to look away, yet couldn't. Jenko's face was devoid of expression now. And Ava's sorrow-filled heart reached out to him. An anguished cry of horror formed inside of her, a silent, bone-weary howl of inner pain.

"Cut him," Hammerfiss snarled.

Jenko seemed rooted in place. Frozen.

"Damn you, boy, do it already."

Jenko slashed, cutting deep. The baron's leg spasmed.

"You don't have to do this!" Baron Bruk yelled. "Let *them* kill me!"

Jenko lifted the blade, eyes on his father.

"Keep at it, lad," Hammerfiss growled. Jenko sawed back and forth.

Screaming, the baron raised his hands to stop the blade as it ate at his leg, but Jenko sawed until the serrated cleaver scraped against bone. Baron Bruk inhaled deeply, rapidly, through lips that sputtered as the air whooshed by.

"Fuck almighty, lad!" Hammerfiss yelled. "Just get it over with! Chop it off!"

Jenko stood. He raised the blade overhead like an ax. With two quick swings of the sword it was done. Stabler tore the leg free of the torso, severed muscles fluttering. Thick scarlet pumped in great gouts from what little remained of the baron's thigh—the bloody stump freckled with pale sand. Jenko's father was silent, unconscious.

Crying now, Ava stood there alone, motionless, the trauma taking hold of her mind again. She felt the wraiths prowling restlessly, roving within as if eager to wrap around her soul. For her soul was all she had now. Her family was gone. Her home was gone. And the crystal clear innocence of her thoughts was gone too, stained forever by this horror.

Hammerfiss picked Baron Bruk up and carried him toward the kettle of boiling tar. Jenko's father dangled limply in the giant's thick-muscled arms as his seeping stump was dipped into the steaming kettle and held there a moment. Hammerfiss lifted him free and dumped him on the ground in front of Jenko.

"Take his other leg," Spades ordered.

At those words, Ava felt sorely unbalanced. She shuddered and drew a deep, ragged breath, wishing Jenko would just stop this madness somehow. Ava gazed one last time with empty eyes at the large blade as it fell. Then she lowered her head, blond hair falling over her face. She could hear the wet sound of Jenko's sword as it chopped into his father's remaining leg. The wraiths now gnawed at Ava with a keen hunger. She'd seen too much. Horror. Trauma. Stress. All engulfed her.

"He's not so heavy now," she heard Hammerfiss say, his voice distant and wavering. All was quiet as the baron's second stump cooked in the tar. The dreadful silence of the air was heavy with the stench of burnt flesh. It mixed with the cloying smell of hatred and fear. She'd never be rid of this nauseating taste of death. There was a hiss and thrum in her head as she clenched her eyes shut.

"Now his arms," Spades' voice said as if from a great distance.

Time wore on, and the sounds and odors that surrounded Ava grew less and less distinct. It felt as if an eternity passed. And when she looked up, she was surprised at the faint red glow suffusing the hazy scene. The sun was setting, she realized, her mind working slowly now. Multiple suns along the horizon, repeated versions of a fiery globe, some sharper, some brighter, some brilliantly red, others orange. "Isn't the sunset beautiful?" she murmured. But only the rhythmic rushing sound of her own blood in her own head answered. Her parched throat stung with every dry breath.

"The sun has not set," a distant voice sounded from somewhere, a concerned voice, a familiar voice. Perhaps it was Nail. But she didn't understand his words.

Of course the sun is setting. The glare of it burned her eyes. She was angry that someone would question that. Her anger focused her mind, cleared her thoughts . . . almost.

Then she found herself under the scrutiny of the White Prince himself. She hung her head, letting her hair cover her face again like a curtain, now realizing the significance of her situation—this was Aeros Raijael standing before her, the Angel Prince of Sør Sevier.

"Name?" he asked.

And her name spilled forth in a stuttering mumble as if she had scant control over her own mouth. Then, for some reason, she drew sustenance from the sound of her own voice. It took all the courage she could muster, but she lifted her gaze, shook the hair from her eyes, and met those of the White Prince.

His bearing was beautiful, like a marble sculpture, like the statue of Laijon in the chapel. He wore a white cloak open down the center; underneath, his pearl-colored chain-mail armor glistened smooth, as if freshly dipped in natural oils. Blond hair hung unbound to his shoulders in shimmering white waves. His skin looked bloodless, translucent, hollow. Veins pulsed, moving like worms under the paleness of his face, yet despite their grotesqueness, those slithering smears of blue only added to his charisma and allure. But it was his eyes that captured her; they were dark and wild at one moment, empty the next, the whites clear as a snow-driven field, the pupils like twin circles of blackness spiraling into the underworld.

But Aeros Raijael's eyes lingered on her for a brief moment longer than was needed, as if he were reluctant to turn away. And the way he looked at her, no, *leered* after her lustily, was familiar. Most men, it seemed, looked upon her that way.

His look was more than she could bear. She closed her eyes again, tightly, and found herself lost in a hazy pink landscape of unrecognizable sensations she had never experienced before—a pink, weaving haze that left her trembling.

And the wavering pink bliss consumed her until all faded to black.

A man is commanded to memorize his own bloodline, and identify the heritage and bloodline of his fellow man. The grand vicar and Quorum of the Five Archbishops of Amadon have confirmed upon themselves the mantle of Laijon's righteousness. But they are worse than fatherless. For under what birthright do they rule? For it is only in Laijon's son Raijael where the true mantle of divinity is found.
—THE CHIVALRIC ILLUMINATIONS OF RAIJAEL

CHAPTER EIGHTEEN

GAULT AULBREK

3RD DAY OF THE MOURNING MOON, 999TH YEAR OF LAIJON

GALLOWS HAVEN, GUL KANA

It was the beginning of a dark and starless night. In the light of the nearby bonfires, the whites of the prisoner's eyes were stark moons against the black rivulets of blood that matted his blond hair and face and streaked down his battered breastplate and leather greaves. Gault gripped the young man's right arm whilst Spades held the glowing branding iron against the underside of his wrist. There was the hiss of hot iron against flesh. Then smoke.

The blood-covered prisoner didn't even scream as Spades' branding iron sizzled against his skin. When she pulled the iron away, staring back was the raw brand marking him an official Sør Sevier slave—a broken *S*. He was the first captive to be branded tonight. As Gault handed the new slave over to Stabler, he made note that the young man also bore a thin, crosslike scar on the back of the same hand.

"Clean him up before you put him in the tent," Spades instructed Stabler. "See if you can get a name out of him. If he still refuses to talk, we'll beat it out of him later."

"What should we do with his ratty plate armor?" Stabler bound the boy's hands behind his back again.

"The prisoners can keep what clothes or armor they have until we find something more suitable. Until the rest of our supplies arrive from Wyn Darrè, we make do."

Stabler marched the blond fellow up the grassy slope toward the slave tent. To Gault's reckoning, these Gallows Haven folk had certainly been ill-equipped for war, clad in naught save a patchwork of rusty scrap armor, poorly tanned leathers, and the crudest of weapons. Perhaps this crusade against Gul Kana would be easy and over soon. For him, the redundancy of hard steel rasping from a sheath and striking warm flesh had grown old. It had taken five years to reclaim Wyn Darrè. He wasn't sure if he had another five years of war left in him.

Enna Spades, on the other hand, relished the butchery. When the small band that defended Gallows Haven had fled the battlefield, none had been more displeased with the cowardice than she. Gault knew Spades hated lack of courage in a foe more than anything. She gloried in the wildness and excitement of war and admired those who would stand up to her and fight. She craved chaos, thrived on her own pain, and reveled in the pain of others. She was possessed of a pure wanton cruelty. And with today's actions on the beach, she had taken the entire Sør Sevier army and bonded them all together as monsters in the eyes of the survivors of Gallows Haven.

A fortuitous boon if all of Gul Kana proves as ill prepared. The speedy conclusion of this war might finally earn Gault that small measure of peace that had been denied him these last ten years. Though fighting had felt good in the beginning, he hated himself for having *loved* it so much. The truth was, war was naught but marching and boredom.

Yet in those brief moments of true fighting, the savagery was heady. At times it had been his sustenance, the sudden bursts of brutality and terror and blood, enough to keep him awake for days. A soldier's life boiled down to one thing: survival. But over the years, Gault had come to realize that if a man wasn't killed in war, then that man's mind, spirit, and emotions decayed, or, even worse, were willfully buried because of it. War was a swift death for some, a gradual death for others. *And having Enna Spades by your side in battle could age a man fifty years.*

The next prisoner Stabler escorted down the grassy hill was the tall, brooding fellow who had dismembered Baron Jubal Bruk. The young man stood erect before Spades, head held high, pride fixed in his eyes, and despite all, a hint of arrogance in his stance. And like the first captive, this young man also did not squirm when Spades, smiling, pulled the iron poker from the fire and pressed it to his flesh. Perhaps these Gallows Haven folks had more moxie than Gault was giving them credit for.

Spades, ever confident in her charms, flashed the captive her winsome smile, which was as always a trace lopsided, seductive, and deceptively shy. "You'll warm to me soon enough," she said to the fellow. "You'll soon realize I'm not the beast you think I am."

There was a puckish glint in her green eyes as she snatched up a strip of cloth from the satchel under her stool and stood. She walked a few paces down the beach and dipped the strip of cloth into a bucket of water, wringing it out. Her legs were sleek and long in the firelight, clad in tight leathers tanned a dark umber. The young man's eyes followed her every motion as she walked back toward him. The curves of her body were aglow in the torrid light of the various bonfires that lit up the beach. When she knelt in front of the prisoner and began wiping the damp cloth over the still-smoking slave mark on his inner wrist, the neckline of her billowy shirt hung open before him.

"Perhaps I'll make you a slave of a different sort." Again she flaunted that provocative smile under deep, flirtatious eyes and fire-red hair. Something smoldered beneath the prisoner's eyes—not rage, not lust, but perhaps a sickly combination of both. Either way, Gault knew this young fellow wouldn't be the first, nor the last, to fall under her spell. More than one lovesick man had crumbled in the fervent desire to win her love.

But only one man truly held Spades' heart. Spades nursed a hidden simmering anger that commanded every aspect of her being. Hawkwood haunted her. All of her twisted complexities stemmed from that one man's betrayal. Killing, torture, slaughter, this was how she took her revenge upon the world.

"You are hard for me now," Spades said, reaching for young man's crotch, palm against the leather armor covering his groin. He backed away as if scorched by her hand.

And she grinned. At all times, Enna Spades seemed unashamedly pleased with herself. "As I said, you'll soon warm to me, boy." She turned and jammed the branding iron into the glowing coals of the fire.

The next prisoner Stabler brought was the blond girl, Ava Shay—the girl who had fainted in front of Aeros right after Baron Jubal Bruk's dismemberment. Despite the despair plastered on her face, Ava Shay reminded Gault of his stepdaughter, Krista, who now lived under the care of King Aevrett's court in Rokenwalder. Krista had been a mere twelve years old when Gault had last seen her. He recalled their final parting before the invasion of Wyn Darrè five years ago. He could still envision her hair shimmering like white gold in the sunlight as she wished him good-bye, her bright eyes sad at his leaving, yet full of life and youth, her fine face aglow with boundless enthusiasm. Krista would be seventeen now. This Gul Kana girl, Ava Shay, looked no older than that.

In a heartbreaking way, Ava also reminded Gault of his wife, Avril, who had died at the tender age of twenty. Gault was twenty-three at the time; only two years they'd spent together, and after all this time, he missed her still. The smell of her hair and the sound of her laughter, the feel of her skin on his—it was a feeling no other woman had been able to replicate. Avril had come into his life and filled it with joy, only to be claimed suddenly by a fever. Gault had a vivid recollection of the day he had first met her—a lone cloaked figure, shivering and stumbling across the dusky plains of the Sør Sevier Nordland Highlands, a babe in swaddling blankets in her arms. Gault, newly knighted in King Aevrett's army, patrolling the highlands, had ridden up to her on his roan destrier.

"Don't take me back to him, Ser," she had said, the hood of her tattered cloak falling from her face, revealing the eighteen-year-old beauty beneath. "I beg of you, Ser knight, don't take me back to that monster." Gault did not take Avril back to whatever monster had fathered her baby girl. He did not ask for the man's name, either. Instead he had swooped Avril and the babe up onto his roan and carried them to Rokenwalder. In the city of their king they married. Together they had named the baby Krista, and for the next two years Avril and Gault had raised her, Gault treating the babe as his own. Even after Avril had died, Gault looked after the girl as a noble knight should, never telling Krista that she was not the seed of his own loins, never feeling the need to. The war in Adin Wyte had torn him away from Krista when she was but seven. A brief visit with her at twelve, and then off to conquer Wyn Darrè. King Aevrett watched over her now. Gault missed her so. As he missed Avril. He sometimes felt so lonely for his wife he feared the pain of it would someday be the end of him.

The sight of this Gallows Haven girl, Ava Shay, standing there so vulnerable in her simple woolen shift, struck a deep chord of longing within Gault he had not felt in years. Pale and wan and hollow-eyed, Ava appeared even more wraithlike and ashen-skinned now than when she had fainted on the beach. Had she fainted from thirst, hunger, or plain fright at laying eyes on Aeros Raijael? Gault knew not. Still, he had been the first to rush up and kneel at her side when she'd fainted. At the time, her skin seemed naught but a delicate, egg-shell covering over her thin frame in the pink light of the sunset. Aeros had him carry her limp form to the slave tent. And Gault had done as Aeros bade him do, with much worry in his heart for the waif. Now here she was again, about to be branded by Spades.

"Jenko." The girl's voice was soft and low amid the cracking of the surrounding fires, an all-consuming love and concern for the prisoner, Jenko, in her greeting. But the young man she called Jenko did not answer, just hung his head, eyes hidden behind dark locks of thick hair as Stabler led him back up the grassy slope to the slave tent.

"Laijon spare me." The girl cast her eyes toward Gault, pleadingly, as if desiring some measure of sympathy. Gault realized his initial assessment of her pallor had been wrong—there in fact was a tinge of color returned to the tone of her skin, a healthy look in her eyes, vigor in her movements. She was like a shining jewel embedded on this godforsaken beach. Her eyes stayed on him.

"You appear well, m'lady." The words somehow spilled from his mouth.

"M'lady?" Spades looked from Gault to the girl and back. "Seems Gault here would desire his own personal slave."

"Don't be a blathering fool," he said.

"Then quit mooning and hold out her arm."

Gault cursed inwardly, knowing that nothing good could come of any overt display of worry where Ava was concerned. It was best he swallow his emotion and just behave as if this girl was of scant significance. Grasping her roughly by the arm, he forced Ava to kneel before Spades.

As the branding iron seared into Ava's skin, Gault was utterly aware that this girl's once presumably pleasant life had just been reduced to naught but suffering and despair. It would soon be made evident to her; human cruelty was to never be underestimated, always to be believed in, even above and beyond any belief in Laijon. Despite his best efforts to remain unfeeling, Gault felt a pang of sorrow at her suffering. Spades' attempts to ask the girl questions got nowhere. Ava remained as silent as the two young men before her.

Stabler came back with a new prisoner, a pudgy red-haired girl. He yanked Ava to her feet and led her away. Gault watched her go, his heart crumbling for her with each step she took up the hill. "Best not get your hopes set on that one." Spades smiled. "I reckon Aeros will lay claim there."

Gault tore his gaze from the girl and looked up the beach. Hammerfiss was leading a stout draught mare toward them. The dapple-gray horse was pulling a flatbed cart with a crate, propped at an angle, strapped to it with roughened leather straps. Four torches, each attached to a corner of the cart, bobbed and swayed in the darkness as the cart lurched toward them, illuminating the contents of the crate—Baron Jubal Bruk. The once stout baron was nothing more than a naked torso now, the stumps of his arms and legs cauterized with black-hardened tar just above his nonexistent elbows and knees. Without his extremities, what remained of him fit surprisingly well in the box. He was alive, moaning, face pale beneath the matted tangles of his beard. The man's severed arms and legs, now blackened and dead, were stored in the small triangular space under the propped-up box.

"The Spider rubbed pungent salt under his nose," Hammerfiss said on arrival. "It woke him, though I don't know how long he will last."

Spades examined the four stumps of tar that used to be the baron's arms and legs, tapping one gently with her fingertip. "Can he understand me?" she asked Hammerfiss.

"Aye, he's lucid enough."

Spades pulled the Gul Kana coin—the one emblazoned with the face of Jondralyn Bronachell—from her pocket, tossed it once, then made it dance lithely between her fingers as she spoke to the baron in the box. "Normally one who has allowed himself to amass such a vast array of injuries would be dead from the trauma and blood loss. It would take a miracle for you to make the journey to Amadon, even in a box so filled with comforts. But you can thank our Bloodwood for the lesser degree of pain you now feel. He has tended to your wounds with tenvamaru, a rare serum used only by the torturers in the dungeons of Rokenwalder. Its design is to act as a numbing agent and keep prisoners alive for—well, let us say for various purposes. So, fear not, you will arrive in Amadon quite alive, and in surprisingly good comfort, all things considered."

Jubal Bruk's bearded jaw quivered as he said, "You savages hadn't the decency to leave me with one hand to feed myself."

"You won't be able to wipe yer own arse, either," Hammerfiss scoffed. "Or fiddle yer own cock. You should consider yourself lucky we left you with that."

"He won't be much good for fighting anymore either," Stabler said, one eye asquint, head tilted to the side as he looked down into the box at the baron.

The fat, red-haired Gallows haven girl who stood beside Stabler wore a look of horror on her face as she stared at Jubal Bruk. She was dressed in naught but a thin doeskin smock tied at the waist with a thong of leather. "He lives and even talks," she muttered, then purged an endless stream of vomit in the sand at their feet.

Spades stopped fiddling with the coin in her hand, pocketed it, and pulled forth a dagger. She stepped over the puddle of vomit and cut the girl's bonds. "You're a plump one, aren't you?"

The fat girl rubbed the circulation back into her hands, tears welling in her eyes as she wiped the puke from her chin with the sleeve of her smock. "My pardon," she stammered, crying. "I ate a lot last night. It was the Mourning Moon Feast, you know."

"Forgive my manners," Spades said. "I had no desire to make you cry." She held forth the dagger, hilt first, to the girl. "What is your name, sweetheart?"

"Liz Hen Neville." The girl eyed the dagger with apprehension.

"What a beautiful name." Spades forced the hilt of the dagger into the big girl's trembling hands. "You're a natural with a blade, I assume?"

The girl looked frightened beyond measure, staring at the dagger now in hand.

Spades asked, "What do you propose we do about Baron Bruk's sudden lack of fighting abilities?"

The girl shrugged, eyes never leaving the dagger.

Spades took the fat girl by the arm and guided her toward the baron. "Well, Liz Hen, clearly your copious girth strangles your imagination." Spades snatched the torch from one of the corners of the cart and waved it dangerously close to the baron's face. He flinched, trying to move his head away from the heat. But propped up there limbless inside the box, there was not much he could do beyond leaning slightly.

Spades turned to the girl. "Seeing as I am a trifle more intelligent than you, Miss Liz Hen, how about I explain how you yourself can magically restore Baron Jubal Bruk back to the great and deadly fighter he once was."

Liz Hen's eyes traveled over Jubal's illuminated face. The look that came over her round features was one of both horror and pity. She fingered the hilt of the dagger nervously in her hands. "Do you want me to kill him?" she asked, voice hoarse.

Spades grabbed the black-tarred stump of Jubal's left arm, thrusting her torch up under it. "I want you to turn him into a great warrior." Tar bubbled under the torch's flame as the baron tried to squirm away. Soon the once-hardened tar that had earlier cauterized his arm was a black and boiling and dripping mass. Satisfied, Spades pulled the torch away and turned to the plump girl. "Jam the hilt of that dagger into his stump. And make haste, Miss Liz Hen, before the tar hardens."

Without questioning why, the fat girl pushed the hilt of the dagger deep into the softened tar. "Not too far," Spades advised. "Bury just the hilt."

Liz Hen left the dagger's hilt buried in the cooling tar of the baron's stump, only its thin silver blade poking out.

Spades pulled forth another dagger, melted the tar on Baron Bruk's other stump with the torch, and had Liz Hen push the hilt of the second dagger into it as well.

Spades placed the torch on the bracket on the corner of the cart and admired the fat girl's handiwork. "You've turned Jubal Bruk into a warrior again." The baron now had dagger blades protruding from either stump. "Not that the coward will ever use them to fight," Spades said, and looked at Liz Hen with a wry grin. "But at least he's armed."

Jubal Bruk had passed out.

"You deserve a reward, Miss Liz Hen." Spades smoothed the fat girl's skirt with her hand. "For turning the hardy baron into a warrior again, I won't brand you. That will serve as reward, and save you some pain, I suppose." Liz Hen's round, frightened eyes were fixed on Baron Bruk's stumpy arms and the dagger blades sticking out.

Spades was looking down the beachhead toward five advancing horsemen.

Aeros Raijael, atop his white charger, was galloping toward them. He wore his white cloak over chain-mail armor, his blue sword, Sky Reaver, at his side. The Bloodwood, on his gaunt Bloodeye stallion, followed a few paces behind. The horse's ribs gleamed with the oils that had been rubbed into its velvety-black hide, and the beast's eyes glowed red.

Gault knew that Spiderwood, like all Bloodwoods, injected his mount with rauthouin bane serum daily. The injections, over time, turned the horse's eyes, along with its entire disposition, into a fiery torrent. A fully drugged Bloodeye horse was like a rabid dog, ferocious, deranged, and ready to strike at any foe in defense of its master. The beast's sharpened hooves could thrash and claw, whilst its crushing jaws had razorlike teeth. A few lengths behind Aeros and Bloodwood rode three young Rowdies.

Upon Aeros' arrival, Gault, Spades, Hammerfiss, and Stabler bent their knees to their lord.

The Angel Prince dismounted and glided toward the cart holding Jubal Bruk. Spiderwood dismounted and followed Aeros toward the cart. The three Rowdies dismounted too, yet stood a little way off, subdued.

"You assured me this man would be fine." Aeros cast a harsh eye at Spiderwood.

"Last I saw Baron Bruk, he was awake." Spiderwood glared at Spades. "Of course, last I saw the baron he wasn't sporting two blades from the stumps of his arms."

"You dour-faced bastard," Spades growled. "I'm growing weary of your looming over every bit of my happiness like a damp cloud."

"Your idea of fun is another man's box of horrors."

Aeros snapped, "I grow tired of your bickering already."

"Pardon," Spades said, bowing, and motioned to Liz Hen. "But it was the fat girl who stuck those knives in him."

Liz Hen cowered, as if realizing it was she who might be blamed for the disfigurement of Jubal Bruk.

Aeros looked from Spades to the Bloodwood and back. "I'm beginning to think that landing in this forsaken village was a mistake. Rosewood was to meet us here. She has not. The information she obtained about this pathetic place has yet to prove correct. No Roderic. No boy."

"Information gathered by a Bloodwood is always reliable." Spiderwood bowed. "Rosewood will be here soon."

Aeros grunted dismissively, looking down at Jubal Bruk. "Wake him."

Spiderwood pulled a small flask from his cloak and waved it directly under the baron's nose, then slapped the man's face. Jubal Bruk sputtered awake.

"Can you hear me, man?" Aeros asked him.

"Aye," Baron Bruk mumbled, face clouded with confusion. "I can hear you."

"I'm going to ask you about a man, Ser Roderic Raybourne, an ex-Dayknight who goes by the name of Shawcroft. I've news that he was living here in Gallows Haven. Both my father and I are desirous to know the man's whereabouts."

Jubal Bruk remained silent, looking woozy.

"This won't do." Aeros looked at Spades accusingly. "The man is a mess."

Spades grabbed one of the baron's severed arms from behind the triangular alcove under the propped-up crate and used it to slap the baron's face repeatedly. "Wake up!" she yelled. "Ser Roderic, where is he? Answer!"

Jubal Bruk's eyes darted between Spades and Aeros to the two dagger-blades protruding from the tar-covered stumps of his arms. His eyes lit up with terror.

"Answer, else I will cram your own arm down your throat," Spades threatened.

The baron sputtered, "I know n-n-nothing of Roderic's whereabouts."

"There is a boy with him," Aeros said, "About seventeen. Do you know him?"

"Aye. Shawcroft and his ward are likely dead. You didn't leave many alive."

"There are some who enjoy slaughter too much." Aeros' eyes settled on Spades.

"You are all evil."

"Even if Shawcroft were alive, I doubt he'd give me the information I seek. It would bode well if the boy were found alive." Aeros turned to Stabler. "Have we interrogated them all? Do we know the names of our captives?"

"Between Spades and me, yes, we've spoken to all. Aye, Spades?"

But Spades was not listening to Stabler. She was stroking the side of Jubal Bruk's cheek with the stiff fingers of his own detached limb. "When was the last time you were in Amadon?" she asked.

"Eight moons ago," the baron answered, "end of last summer."

"What do you know of a man named Hawkwood?"

"I know that he's from Sør Sevier, a good fighter. He helps Ser Prentiss train the Dayknights. There are some in Jovan's court who don't trust him, I hear."

"What about Hawkwood and Jondralyn?"

"Rumor from Amadon is, the princess grows fond of him."

"Princess," Spades repeated in disgust, and tossed the severed arm in the box with Jubal Bruk. It came to rest half on his chest. A look of utter desperation came over him as his now useless body rocked back and forth in the box, trying to move away from the offending object. It seemed Baron Bruk was just coming to realize that his new body lacked the ability to do much at all.

The Angel Prince motioned to the three Rowdies behind him. "Baron Bruk, may I introduce Ser Marcus Gyll, Ser Patryk Laurents, and Blodeved Wynstone."

The baron's eyes fixed on Blodeved, a tall blond woman in her early twenties who, even in her armor, radiated beauty. Gault himself had taken notice of Blodeved many times.

Aeros continued, "These three will accompany you by ship to Lord's Point. From there, you will travel overland along the King's Highway to Amadon. You were once a Dayknight, Jubal—use what influence you have to speed your journey over the King's Highway and to keep my soldiers safe. Shouldn't take more than seven days. If these three honorable Sør Sevier fighters do not return to me unharmed, things will go poorly when we meet again. Do you understand, Baron?"

Jubal Bruk's face remained still.

"I consider your silence an answer of affirmation," Aeros said. "The news you will deliver to the Silver Throne is simple enough. You tell Jovan Bronachell that our warships are returning to Wyn Darrè now. They will continue to sail back and forth until all of my finest warriors are on Gul Kana soil and ready to march on Lord's Point. Do you understand?"

Baron Bruk nodded.

"Excellent," Aeros continued. "Jovan Bronachell can meet us at Lord's Point to offer up his surrender. You tell all in Amadon—the king, the grand vicar, the quorum of five—tell them that I, Aeros Raijael, am the supreme spirit, the Lord of both heaven and the underworld—of all worlds, the preexistent world, this world, and the next, and the ones beyond that. I am the long-awaited return of the great One and Only, whose arrival was foretold by the Warrior Angels long ago. I am the giver of life and the bringer of death, created before the very foundations of the world. I am known by many names: the Angel Prince, the true and living Heir of Laijon, the great One and Only—and yes, I am even sometimes called the White Prince. And as the prophecies in *The Chivalric Illuminations* have foretold, I, Aeros Raijael, the heir of Laijon, Mia, and their one and only son, Raijael, have returned to reclaim what is rightfully mine and the time is coming when all will call me God. Tell all in Amadon that any who refuse to pray to Raijael will be slaughtered."

Aeros paused, taking a breath. With a hiss of steel, the Angel Prince unsheathed his sword, Sky Reaver, and held it up before Jubal's face. When he spoke again, there was a calm malice in his voice. "And you tell Jovan Bronachell that if he refuses to surrender at the appointed place and at the appointed time, with a certainty, our war to reclaim Gul Kana will be fought with extreme savagery."

Gault's gaze drifted from the baron to the sharp blade in Aeros' hand, a keen blade that shimmered crisp waves of blue in the light of the torches, an ancient and merciless blade responsible for the stark and bitter death of thousands. And every one of those cold deaths was reflected right back into Jubal Bruk's eyes.

All shamans claimed to know the day of the boy's birth. They spoke of him not only as a great hero who would save man from the Fiery Demons, but also as a savior who would purge man of all sin. Such thinking was a common thread, bonding all men together. The prophets foretold that the carvings on the standing-stones would be the same signs found upon his flesh, and such symbols would give him dominion over all.
—THE WAY AND TRUTH OF LAIJON

CHAPTER NINETEEN
TALA BRONACHELL

3RD DAY OF THE MOURNING MOON, 999TH YEAR OF LAIJON

AMADON, GUL KANA

B loody rotted angels," Lindholf Le Graven cursed as his foot skidded through a steaming heap of brown. Tala stifled a laugh, as did Glade Chaparral. The docks of Amadon were proving to be a filthy place indeed.

Glade helped Tala over the offending pile. "Don't want to get your feet wet with horse dung, my sweet Tala." Tala's heart fluttered; hearing her name on his mouth felt like a caress. She wholeheartedly admired Glade for his gallantry. Even concealed behind the bulky armor and helm, Glade looked dashing, his mere bearing vastly more regal in comparison to Lindholf's clanking about.

This was the most daring thing she'd ever done—a quick trip to the stables in the still-dark hours of the morning, an open grate under a stack of hay, and down they went, barely escaping the eye of the stable marshal, Terrell Wickham. Tala led the way, along the same route she and Roguemoore and Jondralyn had used to visit Squireck's cell a week ago. Tala's deft fingers opened all the locked iron grates, and she showed Lindholf and Glade what stones to push on to reveal more secret tunnels, eventually finding the stairway that Roguemoore had claimed led up to the docks. The stairway was a long, sloping affair, but it had led to a heavy sewer grate that had opened up into a dank and narrow dockside ally. Now the three of them—Tala concealed under a coarse woolen cloak and hood, along with Glade and Lindholf, hidden within stolen Silver Guard armor and helms—stood before the Filthy Horse Saloon. The saloon itself festered alongside the cramped road, with its back to the bay and its crude sign hanging on rusty hooks over the door.

The sun had risen about an hour before. The brightening morning revealed a side of Amadon so repugnant it caused Tala's stomach to roil with its unwholesome stink. The mud of the narrow streets had been churned into a putrid broth, and tides of rubbish clogged the alleys and side streets. Beggars loitered in doorways, whilst scabby street urchins with bleating little voices played in piles of garbage. Not far from where she stood was a group of bloodletters, flagons of blood at their feet and purple bruises on their necks. These wretched, degenerate souls would open the veins in their own wrists and necks, drain what blood they could before passing out, and then sell it to hungry oghuls. This dirty, poverty-stricken place made her feel alive yet, at the same time, disgusted her to the core.

Tala clutched the gunnysack that hid the red helmet of the Wyn Darrè gladiator tightly in her hands. She'd hidden it inside the hearth in her room for a week, trying to decide how to proceed, finally coming up with this plan. But the helmet was proving to be one uncomfortably spiky, heavy bulk to lug around.

Glade had advised against their journey, claiming it unwise for a princess to venture uninvited into the seedier parts of the city. But

Tala had assured him that her face would be hidden under her the hood of her cloak. And with him and Lindholf dressed as Amadon Silver Guards, they would be safe. She had also appealed to his adventurous side, claiming she had a secret delivery to the docks on behalf of Hawkwood, knowing both her cousin and Glade would probably do anything to help the man. Despite his recent imprisonment, they were both infatuated with him and his fighting styles. She'd also promised Glade that she'd have them back by morning's end, in time to attend the arena matches.

"You expect us to enter that lord-forsaken tavern?" Glade's voice threw off a hollow twang from under his helm. "We're likely to get skewered and ate alive in such an unholy dive. I hear sailors are grumpier than bloodsucking oghuls early in the morning."

Lindholf removed his helm. His corn-colored hair stuck out in matted, sweaty clumps. He breathed in deeply, as if the helmet had been suffocating him. "I also hear a drunken sailor would just as soon cut your throat as piss on you."

"Put your helm back on," Glade said. "The sailors might rape your skinny arse is what they might do."

Lindholf jammed the helm back over his head. "I can't rightly breathe in this damn thing. Or see, for that matter. Some deranged pirate could come creeping up on me from the side and I'd never know it."

"Even if you could see him creeping up on you, there's not much you could do to stop him, you fumble-footed layabout."

"And I suppose you think you could best a pirate with a sword?" Lindholf said. "You're not the fighter Hawkwood is. Nor could you best Seita, either."

"Aye, Seita," Glade said. "That's some wild cunny there."

Lindholf laughed. "I wager those nimble hands of hers could work miracles under the sheets."

"Can we not talk of such things?" Tala said, irritated. "Let's just go into the tavern and deliver the message." As soon as the words were out of her mouth, a dirt-crusted urchin of about five ran up and stood before her. The stick-thin boy wore naught but a soiled shirt, his tiny privates all a-dangle between his bony thighs. With brown smudges about his mouth, he looked like he'd just been sucking on the teat of a dung-covered swine. "A crust of bread to spare?" He held forth his hand.

"Bloody Mother!" Glade shoved the boy to the ground. "Scat!" He reached for his sword, unsheathing it halfway. The boy scrambled to his feet and scampered off.

"You didn't have to be so rough," Tala said.

"Aye, he was just a child," Lindholf followed. "Granted, a scruffy and rather naked child . . . with his pecker on display . . . and what appeared to be poop smeared about his face . . . but still, you oughtn't have been so mean."

"I understand they are poor," Glade said, ramming the sword home again. "But who gives a spit? Do they have to let their children run around pant-less? Do they have to live in such squalor? Can't they at least clean this place up?" Glade threw out his arms and shouted to the street in general, "Have some dignity! Vermin!"

"Shhhh." Lindholf restrained Glade. "Or you'll be the one buggered."

"Not likely. It's I who does the buggering. Just ask Seita."

"Would you stop talking about her!" Pigeons scattered nervously out of Tala's way as she stomped toward the Filthy Horse Saloon. Lindholf rushed forward, reaching the wooden door before Tala, and knocked loudly with a gauntleted fist.

"You dolt." Glade brushed Lindholf aside. "You let yourself into a tavern. You don't knock." The door swung open with a screech as Glade pushed against it. He stepped through and disappeared inside. Tala followed. The saloon was dark and heavy with the heady reek of mold, ale, stale smoke, and body odor. The place appeared empty.

As her eyes adjusted to the dim light, she noticed a floor full of drunken, snoring sailors. There was a loud *thump thump* behind her, and she turned to see Lindholf picking up an overturned chair. "I'm going to take my helm off," he said. "I can't see a thing."

"Act like a guardsman," Glade hissed. "If you can."

"What'sh going on o'er there?" a gruff voice issued forth. "Thelia! Thelia!" the drunken voice slurred. "What's sha fuck, Thelia!"

"Shush it, Erik!" a female voice yelled. "It's nothing but Guntar's farting." A girl appeared out of the darkness and took Tala by the hand. She wore what appeared to be a crown atop her head. Although in the dark, Tala couldn't make out much.

"Come. Sit. If it pleases m'lady." The girl led Tala deeper into the tavern toward the bar. "I've been expecting you. Although I admit, I figured you and your friends would be in much sooner than this."

"Expecting me?" Tala's blood turned to ice.

The girl walked around the bar and lit a lantern. The light was dim, but was enough to illuminate the immediate area. The wooden bar was chipped and stained and showed signs of hard use. Liquor bottles lined the shelves behind the girl. Tala's flesh prickled at the sight of the crown atop the girl's head. It was a wreath of heather tied with white flowers—just like the one she'd twined for Squireck.

Tala placed the gunnysack with the red helmet down on the floor and sat at one of the many bar stools, but not before looking upon the stool with trepidation, grimacing at the thought of getting anything gross on her. It was one thing to secretly crawl around through the dusty, unused corridors of Amadon Castle, another to infect oneself with the unsavory filth of a dockside tavern. Glade and Lindholf remained standing on either side of her, their armor now agleam with the yellow light flickering from the lantern.

"I'm Delia," the girl said. Tala did not offer her own name, just looked at the girl.

Delia wasn't exactly pretty, but she had dimples and freckles and thrust out her chin and chest proudly. She wore a startlingly low-cut corset. Her eyes were grayish-blue and completely alive and flirtatious as she looked upon Glade and Lindholf standing in polished armor near Tala. The barmaid was just the kind of common trollop Tala disdained, supple and full and all abloom with sexuality. The girl's large breasts nearly jiggled free of her corset as she bent to retrieve three mugs from under the bar. She set the mugs out and began to pour from a large brass pitcher. As Tala watched the brownish-gold-colored liquid flow into the mugs, she immediately felt inadequate near this tavern girl. First Jondralyn and Seita, now Delia—all three, it seemed, trumped Tala in overall womanly appeal. She imagined both Glade's and Lindholf's hungry orbs were planted right in Delia's cleavage.

"You were expecting me?" Tala asked again, apprehensively.

Before Delia could answer, the bulky shadow of a sailor at the far end of the bar stood and moved toward them. "Silver Guards must remove their helmets to drink in the Filthy Horse." The man's voice vibrated through the room as he stepped into the light. He was a wide-faced, tall fellow with a slow, deliberate manner about him. He sported a wild beard and a head of tangled hair that smelled of salmon. And he was definitely sounding more sober than drunk, his voice deep and unhurried, not slurred, but matter-of-fact. "It's an insult to wear a hat of any kind in here." The sailor stepped toward Lindholf. He was so large and burly Lindholf had to step back. "Remove your helmets," the sailor commanded, his coal-black eyes unreadable. "There've been too many come in here with their faces covered."

"We are Silver Guards." Glade shoved his way past Lindholf. "We don't take orders from commoners who dwell in swill-infested shit holes like this."

The sailor raised one eyebrow. Thick silence now infused the tavern and fear twisted gently inside Tala. She felt Glade's presence behind her and let out a breath she had not realized she was holding in.

"Remove your helm if it will ease his mind," she said.

Glade looked from Tala to the barmaid and back. Delia nodded for them to take off their helms. Lindholf took his off first. His eyes were as wide and round as dinner plates on his thin, scarred face, and his matted yellow hair curled into wild clumps and spikes. With his goofy, doe-eyed expression, Lindholf looked all of ten years old. Glade removed his helm, looking far more regal, dark eyes glaring at the sailor.

The man laughed. "You two look to have the makings of very poor soldiers."

"It's a wonder we can even buckle on our armor some days," Lindholf chuckled.

"Fiery dragons," Glade hissed. "Keep your mouth shut."

Tala's eyes widened at Glade's profanity.

"Don't spew such filth around me, young pup," the sailor growled. "The curse of the nameless beasts will not be spoken here. I'll have your tongue for such blasphemy."

"You dare threaten the Silver Guard?" Glade squared his shoulders to the sailor.

"If you're a Silver Guard, boy, then the dough-faced lad standing next to you must be Laijon himself." The man laughed as he appraised Lindholf.

"They removed their helms, Geoff," Delia said. "Now leave them be. They are guests of mine."

"Aye," the sailor grumbled, then threw Tala a dark look. "Show yourself." He motioned for Tala to remove her hood. Delia nodded for her to do so. Reluctantly, Tala pulled her hood back.

"Cute little thing." The sailor appraised her. "But watch yourself, lassie. The men around these parts are always on the prowl for a fresh bit of pussy to squeeze into."

He turned and strolled back to his place at the end of the bar, boots clomping heavily.

By the look in his eye, Glade wanted nothing more than to stab the man.

"I assume that you have something in that bag that belongs to the Filthy Horse?" Delia motioned to the gunnysack on the floor.

Tala's heart pounded. She reached into the bag and handed over the red helmet, glad to be rid of the ungainly thing. Delia held the object up and studied it closely, turning it over and over in her hands, perplexed, as if she'd never seen its like before. Then she saw the wording stamped inside the helm, raised her brow, and set the red spiky bulk on the bar with a heavy thump.

"Leave us," the barmaid said to Glade and Lindholf. "I need to speak to your friend in private. You can stand near the front door if you wish."

A disapproving look had come over Glade's face.

"She'll be within eyesight," the barmaid said. "I won't hurt her."

"I will be okay." Tala nodded to Glade. "I need to speak to her alone."

Reluctantly Glade and Lindholf retreated to the front of the saloon and settled into two chairs near the front door.

Delia's sea-blue eyes focused on Tala. "Near a week ago, a Vallè thief came in here and started a fight. Princess Jondralyn Bronachell and two others from the castle, a dwarf and a handsome dark-haired man, were at a back table. They broke up the fight. Three sailors were killed in the scrum. Then there was a pirates' duel, and the Vallè killed one of my most loyal customers."

Delia paused, staring. Tala fidgeted under the barmaid's scrutiny, mind awhirl, wondering if this wild story was true.

"Anyway," Delia continued, "I was hoping that perhaps you might know what they were all doing here, you know, considering you live in the castle with these people."

"What makes you think I live in the castle?"

Delia did a quick sweep of the tavern with her eyes and leaned forward against the bar. "To my recollection, this pirates' duel seemed more a distraction than anything else. You see, during the duel, while no one was paying attention, I was approached by someone who asked me to hold something for you. In fact, this person paid me rather handsomely to hold something for you."

"Something? What do you mean? And how do you know it was me you were paid to hold this . . . thing for?" Tala asked. Despite the dread in her heart, her curiosity was piqued.

"I know you're the right person because the one who paid me said you would be dark-haired, about sixteen, and bearing a red gladiator helmet with the name of the Filthy Horse stamped on it. I was also told that you would be escorted by two young men posing as Amadon Silver Guards. That you would be none other than Tala Bronachell, princess of Amadon."

Tala's mind reeled. How could the assassin have known a week ago that she would ask both Glade and Lindholf to accompany her and that they would both be wearing stolen guardsman armor? Tala felt her heart squeeze. "Was the note given to you by my sis—by anyone in Jondralyn Bronachell's group?"

"I was also told that you would ask that very question," Delia said, but now there was no kindness in her face, but a hardness, a resolution. "I was also paid *not* to answer it. So I will not. But why do you assume it is a note I have for you?"

Tala's eyes darted about nervously. "What else would it be?"

Delia put both elbows up on the bar and tented her fingers against her lips. "I can only give this thing to you if you promise to do me a favor."

"A favor?" Tala absorbed this and asked, "Is the favor part of what you were paid, or a merely personal request?"

"You must get me into Amadon Castle for the last night of the Mourning Moon Celebration . . . as a cook, or a dancing girl, or a serving wench, whatever, but I must attend."

Again, Tala felt her heart lurch. The last night of the Mourning Moon Celebration was the grandest event in all of Amadon Castle.

Throughout Gul Kana, the Mourning Moon Feast was a one-night affair celebrating the beginning of spring and the upcoming planting season. In Amadon Castle, there was not just the Mourning Moon Feast, which had taken place last night, but two more days of festivities ending in the final night's celebration with the grand vicar and the final four gladiators.

"Why do you wish to attend the final night of Mourning Moon?" she asked.

"Let's just say I have to collect a debt."

"Can you not tell me more than that?"

Delia adjusted her corset and straightened the wreath on her head. "Jondralyn Bronachell has yet to pay her tab." Delia's eyes scanned the saloon as she continued, "The three of them, along with the Vallè, just ran out of here, you know ... after killing my friends. Without paying."

Tala tried to sort out what was being said, but deep down felt that this tavern girl was manipulating her in some way. "So the only reason you need to attend the last night of the Mourning Moon Celebration is to collect a bar tab? I'm sure I can make other arrangements for the debt to be paid."

Delia's nervousness was scarcely visible as she asked firmly, "Can you get me into the celebration?"

Tala sat back, eyes on the red gladiator helm. If this debate with Delia was part of the assassin's game, it certainly had the effect of vexing Tala to the point of utter irritation. "I suppose I could secure a position for you in the kitchen, but not without being subject to a host of questions by the castle staff. I need to know the real reason for your interest in attending the final night of the Mourning Moon Celebration."

Delia cast her eyes to the floor, then looked up, fidgety again. "Maybe it's because I am interested in the princess, your sister."

"Interested in Jondralyn?" Tala was not expecting that. "Interested how?"

It seemed Delia sensed Tala's apprehension. She glanced down and said, "Your sister is most beautiful," then raised her face shyly. "I want to meet her again." She was now looking at Tala unflinchingly. "I want to seduce her."

Shocked, Tala shook her head in distaste.

"I can't stop thinking about her," Delia continued, her voice rising in excitement. "And I'm sure she would be grateful to see me again. She flirted with me when she was here. I'm sure she would be grateful if she were to see me again in the castle—"

"It's out of the question." Nothing about this journey to the Filthy Horse was going at all like Tala had envisioned. She didn't know whether to believe anything the woman had to say. "Jondralyn flirted with you?"

"Yes. Flirted. That's a big deal for someone like me. Please, you must help." Delia looked near tears now, her eyes roaming to the darker corners of the tavern, as if she expected whatever lurked there to leap out and slice her throat. Tala looked about nervously too, almost thinking that there was someone watching them.

Delia, her expression wavering between trepidation and resolve, leaned in and whispered, "You must grant my request."

"No." Tala said, irritated. Confused.

"But I cannot give you what I am supposed to give you unless you agree to get me into the last night of the Mourning Moon Celebration."

Tala stewed, angry, fed up with the entire game. "Fine," she blurted. "I'll get you into the castle for the celebration."

"Excellent." Delia's face lit up.

"I've returned the gladiator helm," Tala spouted with impatience. "Now what do you have for me?"

Delia removed the wreath of heather twined with white flowers from her head.

"I was to give you this."

† † † † †

Shkill Gha effortlessly killed his foe, sucked a mouthful of blood from the dead man's neck, then refused to vacate the field of battle until he'd untied his armored-leather breeches and pissed on the dead man under him. Then with a guttural roar he exited the arena, bloody broadsword awhirl above his head in a showy display. The arena crowd brayed and thundered. Most had heard rumors of the oghul Hragna'Ar raids in the Gul Kana northlands, including Tala. She wasn't sure if there really was such an oghul prophecy as Hragna'Ar, but to imagine a war with such creatures made her shudder. The oghuls weren't at all like the peaceful dwarf farmers of the Iron Hills in Wyn Darrè. The dwarves never caused ill to anyone, traded freely and fairly, had no armies, wanted no fight. In fact, it was rumored, Aeros Raijael's merciless host had skirted around the Iron Hills entirely, not even bothering the dwarves in his riotous crusade.

A cool westerly breeze began blowing, and several drops of rain pattered on the tan awning above Tala. As the second match of the day drew nigh, she sat next to Lawri in the king's suite, preparing to ignore the carnage soon to be raging below. But Tala knew Dame Mairgrid would bark at them to act like royalty and watch .

Ever since she'd collapsed in Greengrass Courtyard, Lawri's face had grown more gaunt and sickly. Tala no longer harbored much hope of gaining the antidote and saving her cousin. Earlier that day, after returning from the docks, she'd examined the wreath the barmaid Delia had given her, looking for a note, a clue, anything. She'd shredded the wreath until every petal was naught but white confetti strewn about her bedchamber. The wreath was worthless. Not a clue at all. As the truth of the situation hit her, Tala knew the Bloodwood was playing her for a fool.

The rain fell heavier now as Obray Titan, Monster of the Lochs, strode into the arena. The man was seven feet tall and weighed over three hundred pounds. The thick ivory tusks of a glacier mammoth sprouted from either side of his helm, a helm that did not quite cover his sunbaked face. He also wore a thick cloak of tangled mammoth fur over scuffed ox-hide-leather armor studded with dull iron spikes. He carried a bulky, wide longsword. Tassels and fetishes hung from his braided beard. After Shkill Gha, he was the tournament's second most feared fighter.

Squireck Van Hester entered the arena to a chorus of boos from the crowd. As he'd promised, he wore no armor, just a leather loincloth. Even his feet were bare. He wore Tala's twined gift atop his head. Seeing the wreath of heather she'd made was but another hard reminder to Tala of how she was failing in her quest to save Lawri.

Rain was now falling in ponderous droplets on the awning above, echoing the droning movements of the orchestra. On the floor of the arena, the combatants slowly circled each other. Squireck, though big and muscular, was dwarfed by the Monster of the Lochs. The bigger man swung first, and the ringing clash of sword upon sword sang throughout the arena. The Prince of Saint Only quickly backed off, then lunged with a thrust. The Monster of the Lochs parried and plunged his own great blade toward Squireck's stomach. But the Prince of Saint Only had already danced away. His initial thrust had been a trick to throw the bigger man off balance. As the Monster of the Lochs stumbled forward, Squireck struck at the man's exposed neck. His blade sank deep.

A scream tore through Obray Titan's throat as Squireck tore his sword free and struck again. His blade sank through the bigger man's woolly cloak and leather armor and deep into his collarbone. Squireck ripped the sword free and swung a third time in one fluid motion. His blade sliced into the unprotected flesh of the bigger man's face, knocking the man's helm askew and slashing open his jaw. The Monster of the Lochs stayed afoot. Squireck spun, his sword whipping down in a great arc, connecting with solid perfection.

Obray Titan was smashed to the ground, his horned helm cleaved in half, skull split in two. A crimson torrent spurted across the floor of the arena as the Monster of the Lochs lay in the dirt, head flayed open. Tala recoiled at the sight.

Squireck stood over his foe and chopped down with his sword. With a meaty crack, what remained of the gladiator's head rolled free. Wordlessly, Squireck snatched up Obray's mangled head by the hair and tossed it twirling into the stands. It split in two midair, one half landing atop the awning just above Tala. It slowly slid downward, leaving a smear of blood and brain on the tan fabric stretched above her head.

A collective gasp rustled through the king's suite as the partial head flopped to the ground at Lawri Le Graven's feet with a wet slap.

Tala regarded the gruesome thing with abhorrence, barely holding back the bile that filled her mouth. It took all the strength she could muster just to tear her gaze from the dead man's empty eye.

Below, Squireck Van Hester shouted, "May the Blessed Mother Mia shine on us all!" He struck a pose with his sword held aloft, blade pointing toward the cloud-covered heavens, raindrops now streaking his bronzed, muscular form. His skin glistened like rain-soaked marble. Statuesque, the Prince of Saint Only stood that way for but a moment; something in the peculiar way he posed tugged at Tala's mind.

Squireck was growing into a murderous beast to her. How could he not? After she'd seen him toss so many heads into the stands, he was becoming more and more a killer in her mind. But he soon broke his pose and took the wreath of heather from his head, bowing low. He stood straight and tall, his eyes boring into Tala's before he saluted the arena, saluted all those who came to see him slaughtered. He walked from the battlefield to a great many calls of "*Boo!*" One of the Dayknights in the king's suite moved to pick up the mangled head.

"Leave it." The grand vicar rose from his chair and made his way toward both Tala and her cousin. He spoke in a deep, honeyed voice. "I can see that the brutality of the Prince of Saint Only is disturbing some of the king's guests." He placed his hands over Lawri's shoulders. "Keep in mind, the vile bloody mess at our feet speaks to Squireck's guilt." He bent over Lawri. "Perhaps I should escort you back to the castle, my dear, so you do not have to be party to such violence."

Lawri jerked to her feet, throwing off the vicar's hands. "Don't touch me," she said, her words weak, but under her lilting voice was anger, her face showing visible strains of illness.

"I only fear for your well-being," Denarius said, placing the palm of his hand over her forehead. "You've been ill as of late. You're as hot as the bottom of a teakettle."

Lawri slapped his hand away. More than one person gasped, including Dame Mairgrid, who let out a sharp squeal and tried to grab Lawri. But Lawri took a quick step away from her. All the Day-knights stood as one.

Sterling Prentiss stepped forward. "Young lady, your crudeness is an affront." But Lawri just glared at Denarius. Sterling bristled, hand on the hilt of his sword. Tala sensed the weight of everyone's eyes on her cousin now.

"Behave yourself, dear." It was Mona Le Graven who spoke. Horror registered on her face, eyes darting from Denarius to Jovan to the Dayknights before drifting back to Lawri. "Our holy vicar has prayed for you nightly. He has blessed your sickbed and sat at your side as you lay in fever. He's watched over you even more so than your sister, Lilith. We owe His Grace a great deal of gratitude. If fortune shines upon our family, it will be Denarius himself who administers your Ember Gathering Rites."

"I don't want him touching me," Lawri snarled, "or touching Tala."

"But he must, if he is to bless you," Mona said. "His Grace has been administering the priesthood oils to you nightly without rest for himself."

Tala knew it was common for the grand vicar to minister to the sick in Amadon Castle—if they were royalty, or of the king's court.

"He shan't bless me again." Lawri's face twisted into ugliness. "Not at my Ember Gathering. Not ever. I won't have it!"

Now realizing that Lawri had strayed onto perilous ground, Tala braced herself for what might come. Denarius was taken aback too. His bulbous face flushed whilst thready veins pulsed atop his fleshy forehead. Still, with a wave of his hand, he ordered the Dayknights near him to stand down. "She is feverish, babbling," he said. "I will minister to her as soon as we reach the castle."

"You will not touch me." Lawri's eyes glazed over, and she began weaving on her feet as if drunk.

"Your daughter insults His Holiness." Jovan was standing now too, eyes boring into Mona's.

"I apologize, Your Excellency." Mona's voice was pleading. "Our holy vicar is correct, she has been sick as of late." She turned to Lawri. "Aren't you, dear, you have been afflicted with much sickness?"

Lawri's eyes looked bleak as she nodded halfheartedly. "I do not feel good."

Mona looked at Tala. "You spend time with her. You, Lindholf, Lorhand, Lilith. All of you tend to her daily. The wraiths have been eating at her mind. Is she not sick?"

Tala stood there, not knowing what to do.

"Well, answer her!" Dame Mairgrid ordered from somewhere behind her.

"She is sick." Tala maintained the facade of politeness and nodded as she spoke, knowing Dame Mairgrid's bulging eyes were probably boring holes into the back of her head. Tala was deathly concerned for Lawri's safety, recalling what had happened to Hawkwood when he had challenged Jovan and Denarius. "She has been sick for a while."

"Keep her from me." Jovan recoiled. "Quarantined. I won't risk the plague."

Tala's heart almost stopped at the mention of the plague. She had not considered such insidiousness possible.

"Her symptoms are not that of the plague," the grand vicar said. "They are more akin to the sweating illness or the fever. But you are right. The arena is not the place for her. She shall remain tucked warmly in a bed near a roaring fire to sweat out the sickness." Denarius fished a small leather-wrapped box from the pocket of his long cassock and opened it. Inside was a Vallè-worked bracelet of intricately carved silver etched with crescent moons and a bright ruby stone set in its center. "For you." He held the bracelet out for Lawri. Tala was not surprised by the gift. The vicar gave the children of royalty presents from time to time. But now seemed an odd time for gift giving.

Tala's older cousin just stared at the trinket. Her eyes, now lazy and roving, gave her face a crazed look. Then Lawri did something terribly unexpected. She stooped and picked up the mangled head of the gladiator that still lay at her feet. Clenching a handful of ratty hair, she thrust the hideous prize aloft.

All in the king's suite gasped as blood and chunks of gray matter dribbled down her arm. Then Lawri unleashed a shriek from her throat that scorched everyone's ears.

Reeling with fear and revulsion, Tala felt faint. It was all coming true: the note from the assassin had warned of just such a thing—the slow dementia of her cousin.

Lawri swung the head at Denarius. With a meaty slap it lit against the front of his cassock and gold chain accoutrements and slid to the stone floor at his feet.

Immediately, every Dayknight converged on Lawri.

Jondralyn was instantly at Lawri's side. "Let me spare you a clumsy fray with a sick court girl," she said. The tips of the Dayknights' swords now balanced a finger's width from her throat. Undaunted, Jondralyn took Lawri under her arm and began to lead her away. But Lawri shrugged off Jondralyn, too. She stepped out of the king's suite under her own power, madness in her eyes as she walked toward the exit with Jondralyn in tow. Tala was lost in a sea of horror at having just witnessed her cousin's deranged actions; she was proud of Jondralyn's bravery, and ashamed of her own fear and revulsion.

Jovan turned to Mona Le Graven. "Cursing the holy vicar of Laijon is treason. Your daughter just ventured within a hairsbreadth of being hung. Now that Hawkwood's escaped, we need someone to hang in his place. Pray it is not your daughter."

"Again, my apologies, Your Excellency." Mona bowed deeply. "It won't happen again. I swear it. As Laijon is my witness, I swear it. I will pray and flagellate myself at Laijon's feet in the temple all day and night to make it right."

Despite the confusion and terror swirling through her head, Tala imagined her aunt prostrate before the great Laijon statue, praying for forgiveness on behalf of Lawri.

The image struck a chord in her mind. *The Laijon statue!*

The peculiar way that Squireck had posed flashed into her mind— sword held aloft, wreath of heather crowning his head . . .

Then she had it—Tala had the answer she'd sought since entering the Filthy Horse Saloon. Blood rushed to her head. Lawri's defiance of Denarius combined with her aunt Mona's words about the statue of Laijon and Squireck Van Hester's pose at the end of the match were the sparks that jogged her memory.

The Temple of the Laijon Statue. That was where the assassin wished her to go! Squireck had posed with his sword aloft, eyes cast heavenward, wearing the wreath of heather about the crown of his head.

It has been spoken in the darkest of corners, that a Vallè maiden of royal blood can
foresee the future. But I say unto you, any such Vallè prophecy is like unto a spring
of poison waters that ought not be swallowed. So beware that Codex of Angels,
hidden deeper than even the stones, hopefully never to claw its way up to the light.
—THE MOON SCROLLS OF MIA

CHAPTER TWENTY

JONDRALYN BRONACHELL

3RD DAY OF THE MOURNING MOON, 999TH YEAR OF LAIJON

AMADON, GUL KANA

With a toss of her head, Jondralyn flicked the hair out of her eyes and refocused on the bear-shouldered oghul before her, Anjk Bourbon. The oghul hefted a giant sword with one brawny arm and flexed. The padded blade quivered in Anjk's grip as corded muscles swelled in ridges along his coarse gray arms. The beast stood a good two hand spans taller than Jondralyn and was thrice as wide.

Jondralyn was poised on the balls of her feet, her own padded sword held out, steady. She wore leather greaves and a jerkin of stiff ox hide across her chest. The studded leather wraps tied around her forearms were cinched tight. Despite the exhaustion that had moments ago coursed through every fiber of her being, the urge to triumph over her torturer was now flowing hot in her veins.

But the oghul's opening charge was fierce. His sword arced out in a series of wide, but surprisingly fast, strokes. Each connected. Jondralyn had scarcely parried the first blow and was knocked flat onto her back in the sawdust at the second. She heard clapping and cheers from those gathered in the little courtyard. She stood slowly, glaring at the curious faces lining the crumbling wall that ringed the small makeshift training yard in the rear alley behind Anjk's smith shop and armory. The audience was naught but dirty street urchins and other scum-covered oghuls in Anjk's employ.

No sooner was Jondralyn back on her feet than the oghul cuffed her brutally across the face with a strong backhand. She was flung to the ground again, her padded sword spinning from her hand. She lurched to her feet, every previously tired muscle in her body now coiled in anger. "How dare you strike me unprovoked," she snarled, gathering her wrapped sword and holding it up. "That's not how to train someone!"

"You weak-spirited," Anjk said, his voice a deep growl. "I train you to fight like warrior. Not princess. Now shut up. Else go home." Unlike most oghuls, Anjk had mastered the human tongue; his speech, though choppy, was mostly unslurred. Jondralyn did not like him one bit, but she needed his expertise.

Through a series of underground couriers from his cell under the arena, Squireck Van Hester had sent word to Anjk that Jondralyn was worthy of being trained. The Prince of Saint Only had gone to great effort on her behalf, and Jondralyn did not want to disappoint him. Feeling the red imprint of the oghul's hand swelling on her cheek, she swiped away the twin ropes of snot hanging from her nose and bowed in apology. But the oghul merely stared back at her, his expression always gray and blank, his gaze unreadable. He reached out and took her chin in his leathery hand and peered at her. "You pay double my fee today. Only 'cause you such awful fighter."

Jondralyn shuddered under the terrifying grip of Anjk's hand.

She looked down at the stout strips of leather wrapped around the oghul's mighty wrist and up the ridged rinds of his arms to the thicker muscles supporting his broad shoulders and neck. Anjk's face, like that of all oghuls, was a fearsome mask, rugged as a storm-battered rock. He was a man, and yet he was not. With bulky ears more pointed and Vallè-like than human, a flat nose, cracked leathery lips, and thick brows that protruded prominently and were pierced through with several clunky iron rings and studs, Anjk was a monster.

His expression could become untamed and formidable without warning. His gusty shouts and growls had injected a hustle into Jondralyn's step all afternoon. He had ripped out sulfurous oaths, cursing Laijon and the Fiery Demons of the underworld in the most heinous ways. His gums were warped, sick-looking things, and made Jondralyn feel green with loathing. Whenever he yelled, his rancid breath burned the flesh of her face.

Right now, as he ordered her to drop and do a hundred push-ups, spittle flew from between the fangs that jutted from both his upper and lower jaws. It stung as it hit her brow. She knew of Anjk's need to drink blood. The entire oghul race had a lust and thirst for its sustenance. She also knew that their lips and gums would become swollen and inflamed if their thirst for blood was not sated weekly.

As she dropped to her hands and knees in the sawdust and began her push-ups, she wondered if this monster that stood over her wished to sink those four long teeth into her neck and drink. *And to think, I left today's gladiator matches early for this.* She could hear the occasional roar of the crowds in the distance. The immensity of their sound carried throughout all of Amadon.

She had left the arena early with Lawri Le Graven. Her crazed cousin had actually thrown a partial severed head at the grand vicar. Jondralyn was missing the final matches of the day but took solace as she did her push-ups. Helping Lawri had been the right thing. Anyway, soon *she* would be a gladiator. Soon *she* would be the show.

Anjk's conditioning regimen alone was enough to crush any man, or woman. It had all started when Jondralyn arrived, black scarf tied about her nose and mouth to avoid recognition as she searched for the oghul's blacksmith shop. It had taken a while to find his shop and convince him that Squireck Van Hester had sent her. But he'd finally agreed to train her—something that probably had more to do with the many silver coins she paid him than anything else. Training began with a series of exercises that had tested Jondralyn's muscles to the point that she nearly fainted from the pain. That was followed by weight training that left her arms and legs quivering. Next Jondralyn had found herself running up and down the two flights of stairs behind Anjk's shop with forty-pound sacks of wheat slung over each shoulder, followed by a never-ending series of push-ups. At one point, she had collapsed in the sawdust, only to have the oghul place his heavy foot against her back and demand she do more, to the very moment of complete exhaustion. The worst had been standing, arms outstretched, with a rock the size of a baby's head in either hand. If she dropped the rocks or lowered her arms, Anjk would punch her in her straining gut and shout, "You welcome pain!" Then came the running—hundreds of circles around the tiny courtyard, lumbering through the sawdust in heavy leather armor. A sluggish wind had dragged over her sweat-drenched leathers like an oily rag.

All this work led up to the finale, a spar with Anjk, a spar that Jondralyn had just lost in a most embarrassing way.

"Tomorrow," Anjk barked. "In the morning. Early. Before sun even up. Same routine." The oghul chuckled, and within the timbre of that guttural laugh lived twice the sarcasm of any man. "Perhaps in five years you ready for arena."

Humiliation burned within Jondralyn. Muscles burned too. Her hollow stomach growled, reminding her that she hadn't eaten much today. She could barely hold herself upright. But she would prove this ugly beast wrong. If it was the only thing she did with her life, it

would be to make amends for this abuse. And once she proved to this oghul that she could fight, she would kill him.

Anjk Bourbon smiled, as if he could read her every thought. "Now git the fuook out of my property," he hissed, and shoved her to the ground.

† † † † †

Jondralyn tossed the lightweight cutlass from hand to hand, eyes glued to the two Vallè before her: Val-Draekin and Val-Korin's body-guard, Val-So-Vreign. The three were in Jondralyn's own courtyard—a hidden, thirty-foot-by-thirty-foot open-air alcove resting just behind her own private rooms. Jondralyn's chambers were located near Tala's room, relatively high up Mount Albion. From her knowledge of the castle's hundreds of buildings, baileys, and spires that engulfed the mountain, this hidden alcove was the rooftop of one of the many cavelike armories carved into the castle. Over the years, Jondralyn had taken this secluded, walled-in courtyard, placed a few benches along its ivy-draped walls, and spread rugs about the floor. It was her sanctuary. The only other balcony that had even a partial view of this hideaway was the one attached to her dear departed parents' room not far above. Jondralyn felt fairly secure that her training with the two Vallè would be hidden from prying eyes.

Overall, in comparison to the training with Anjk Bourbon, the evening spent with these two Vallè was a relief. Jondralyn did little but sit back, practice a few tricks with her cutlass—like tossing it from hand to hand, as she was doing now—and watch the two Vallè spar with each other.

Val-So-Vreign wielded two curved cutlass-type blades; Val-Draekin held one similar blade in his uninjured hand. At times, the three whirling swords were naught but a blur to Jondralyn. The footwork and balance of both Vallè were impeccable. There was a detached yet self-assured beauty in how they fought. It was like watching two highly trained acrobats working in concert. Now and then, rather than parry a blow from his partner, Val-So-Vreign would toss one of his swords spinning high into the air, dodge away, catch the hilt in midair, and strike. Instead of blocking, he would just smoothly move himself and his weapon away from Val-Draekin's blow and retain his rhythm.

Squireck Van Hester had been correct in recommending Anjk Bourbon and the Vallè for training. Jondralyn knew she would soon become strong, clever, and fast of hand and eye once she mastered both the brute force Anjk was teaching and the quickness and sword skill of the Vallè.

Val-So-Vreign walked up to her, his two curved swords now sheathed crossways on his back. Jondralyn knew the Vallè could unsheathe the swords with lethal speed. Like Val-Draekin, Val-Korin's bodyguard was green-eyed with coal-colored, shoulder-length hair. The two Vallè could be brothers, for all she knew. Then again, with their narrow feline features and pointed ears, all Vallè men looked alike to her.

Val-So-Vreign took her sword and held it out, pommel in hand, blade pointing skyward. With a flip of his wrist, he sent it tumbling end over end into the air, catching the hilt again after one rotation. "Now practice that for the next hour," he said, handing the sword back to her. He rejoined Val-Draekin in the center of the courtyard.

Jondralyn did as instructed, held the cutlass point up, and tossed it spinning into the air. She dropped it the first few times, yet quickly got the hang of it. Soon she could catch it in rhythm, sometimes sending it spinning up to a height that it would rotate twice in the air. As she tossed the cutlass, she hearkened back to what Roguemoore had said about Val-Draekin: *We must keep him close.*

At the sound of a cutlass crashing to the ground in the center of the courtyard, her gaze flitted momentarily to the two Vallè.

Val-Draekin was bending down to retrieve his fallen blade. He smiled at her, though the friendly expression didn't quite reach his eyes. They remained frosty and seemed to cleave the air with the power of two barb-tipped arrows. *Keep him close*, she repeated the words of the dwarf in her head. And the look in his eyes changed, almost as if he had read her mind. And those eyes remained on her, big round eyes of a flat, unnerving green.

Shuddering, Jondralyn broke her gaze away from Val-Draekin and went back to tossing and catching her sword.

† † † † †

The young Dayknight, Ser Culpa Barra, guided the small skiff to the rickety old dock at the edge of Rockliegh Isle. A second skiff, empty, trailed behind by a short length of rope. The dreary outcrop called Rockliegh Isle was situated in Memory Bay not half a mile east of Amadon; nine acres of land at the most, sharp, jutting rocks sprinkled on the northern end along with a fifty-foot-high lighthouse, the southern end sporting a dock and a boulder-strewn grassy slope that led to an abandoned stone abbey in the isle's center.

Roguemoore held his hand against the weather-beaten wood of the dock to steady the skiff. Lazy waves lapped against the gravelly shore. Jondralyn gathered her woolen cloak tightly about her neck with one hand as the night pressed in, dark and windless. Culpa Barra stowed the oars in the bottom of their boat near the tarps and began folding the hinged mast and sail. Roguemoore climbed out of the boat and onto the dock first. Jondralyn carefully stepped from the wobbly skiff and onto the dock next, gaze fixed on the old stone abbey. "Why bring me here in the middle of the night?"

"Patience," the dwarf answered.

"Patience," Jondralyn repeated. "Always patience, dwarf."

"Let me ask you, Jon," the dwarf started, "who do you count as your friend? Have you ever noticed how, as Borden's child, you have never had any *real* friends? Royalty has no lack of *courtly* friends. Folks who may seek favor for this or that. Jovan has been close with Leif Chaparral his entire life. And Tala spends plenty of time with Glade and Lawri and Lindholf. But they too are royalty, plus the latter two are your cousins. Is that the only kind of friends a prince and princess should have, other royalty?"

"But for my looks, half the nobility in the king's court cares little for me anyway," she answered, realizing the dwarf's question and her own glib answer stung deeply. She could admit to her own loneliness. Still, he had caught her off guard. "I reckon my only friends are you, Squireck, Hawkwood . . . along with a surly old oghul, I suppose, but I only met him earlier today and wouldn't really call him friend. Seems he hates me, too."

"An old oghul?" Roguemoore looked at her questioningly, then shook his head disapprovingly. "The oghul trainer Squireck told you of?"

She shrugged. Ser Culpa Barra stepped up onto the dock next to the dwarf. His short blond curls were matted against his forehead in the damp air, the black Dayknight armor under his cloak dull and lusterless.

"You will learn things here tonight on this Isle, Jon," Roguemoore said, "things only a select handful know. Only the Brethren of Mia's most trusted are allowed certain knowledge. It's why I brought Culpa Barra with us. He is to be your *friend*. Your teacher. He is the most trustworthy of all the Brethren. In fact, it was Culpa's father, Tatum, the most skilled sword maker in all the Five Isles, who introduced me to the Brethren. Tatum Barra and my brother, Ironcloud, were the truest of friends. Culpa Barra and Squireck Van Hester grew up together in the Brethren. They are the truest of friends. I would see you and Culpa become as such. Truest of friends. It is how the Brethren great each other. How we can know our own."

You cannot just thrust two people into friendship. Jondralyn looked
at the young Dayknight, Culpa Barra. He stood stoic in the darkness,
unresponsive to the praise heaped upon him. She could read nothing in his eyes. Most men grew a bit weak-kneed in her presence.
After all, she was royalty. She was beautiful. Her likeness graced the
coppers in their pockets. But Culpa was a rock. He reminded her of
Hawkwood in a way. Calm silence. Young like her. But a killer. She
recalled how coldly he had slit the throats of the four Dayknights
Hawkwood had refused to kill. She dimly recalled the friendship
Squireck and Culpa had shared as youngsters. But Culpa was a
stranger to her now. And could this stranger really even become her
friend? *Truest of friends.* Or would Culpa assume he could become
her lover? It seemed that was the way most men thought. And when
they found out she wasn't interested, they turned mean, certainly
not *friendly.* Nobody was her lover. Nobody had *ever* been her lover.
Certainly not Squireck. Even Hawkwood—for all his confidence and
charms—remained in compliance with the Silver Throne in matters
of chastity at least when it came to her. A princess of Gul Kana was
to surrender her maidenhood only upon her wedding night. *Indeed,
who are my friends? Squireck? Hawkwood? The dwarf? Now Culpa Barra?
Is that the real reason I desire to belong to the Brethren of Mia? Because
only they have ever shown me true friendship?*

The dwarf added, "Before Aeros' conquest of Adin Wyte,
Squireck's father, King Edmon, was deep set against the Brethren
of Mia. But Squireck's mother and sisters were not. It was they who
raised Squireck in the ways of the Brethren. Squireck's aunt, Princess
Evalyn Van Hester, was given in marriage to Agus Aulbrek, lord of
the Sør Sevier Nordland Highlands. There is a fighter named Gault
Aulbrek, son of their union, cousin to Squireck, who is now a revered
knight high up in Aeros Raijael's army. A Knight Archaic. Remember
that name."

The moon's pale light brushed over a dark silhouette coming

down the grassy slope toward them. Jondralyn's heart soared when she saw it was Hawkwood. He was barefoot and dressed in a simple brown shirt and matching woolen leggings—typical prison garb. He urged them to follow him up the hill lest they be seen by any passing vessels or, worse yet, the lighthouse watchman. The way was dotted with high grass and patches of rock hidden in the reeds. Jondralyn stepped lightly.

When they drew near the abbey, the dwarf handed a small object to Hawkwood. The Sør Sevier man held the object to his lips and blew into it. He then held it out for her and Culpa to examine. "A whistle carved of a Bloodwood tree. Soundless to the human ear. A Bloodwood-trained kestrel can feel the whistle's vibrations for over a hundred miles. Each whistle has its own unique pitch. The Blood-wood hiding in the castle is likely communicating with the White Prince in Wyn Darrè with whistle-guided kestrels. The odds that this whistle will intercept the assassin's birds are slim, but worth a try."

He then led them into the abbey. It was a doorless relic, crumbled down and decrepit, nothing but a moss-encrusted ruin near a stand of crooked trees. Brushes and bramble stems clogged the entrance, tearing at Jondralyn's cloak and leggings as she walked inside. Enough light streamed in from the broken windows to illuminate her surroundings. There was nothing in the entry room save a flat stone bench and an overturned table. Patches of paint clung to the walls but flaked off to her touch.

"Did you find it?" the dwarf asked Hawkwood, expectation in his voice.

In answer, Hawkwood slid aside the stone bench and pulled forth the most startling, exquisite battle shield Jondralyn had ever seen. He held the shield up in the pallid light of the abbey. The shield itself was pure and unadorned, snowy white but for a pearl-colored cross inlay that stretched from side to side, top to bottom. The cross inlay was, if it were possible, even brighter than the shield itself—like undulating waves of wood grain, the peculiar substance that made up the cross inlay was different, unrecognizable. *Like bone.* Jondralyn shuddered. So fine and tightly woven were the grains in the cross, so intricate the workmanship of whoever had inlaid this strange pearl, that the entire surface of the cross rippled and danced with wavering sparkles of light, much like a crisp, rushing brook on a sunlit day. Hawkwood laid the shield flat out on the stone bench. Jondralyn picked it up, hefted it by the white leather strap attached to its back side. It seemed to weigh *nothing.*

"*Ethic Shroud,*" Culpa Barra said reverently, dropping to one knee in front of her and doing the three-fingered sign of the Laijon Cross over his heart.

"And what of the stone?" the dwarf asked.

Hawkwood pulled a swath of black silk from under the bench and carefully unfolded it. Nestled within the black cloth was a small, white, nearly transparent stone. The stone stole Jondralyn's breath, especially when a flickering, glassy gleam of radiance—misty radiance that defied description—moved dreamlike within. It was as if the stone were alive and pulsing with a brilliant crystal heartbeat of its own. Jondralyn laid the shield back on the bench and stared at the white stone.

"A miracle," Culpa Barra murmured, standing. "As beautiful as the red angel stone Ser Roderic and I found at Deadwood Gate, but in a more elegant, exquisite way."

"Safe and sound under our feet all these centuries," the dwarf said. "The scrolls Squireck stole have proven to be more valuable than a million crates of gold." Tears glistened in his eyes. "Do I truly gaze upon an angel stone?"

Jondralyn drew in a deep breath. "An *angel stone,*" she murmured, reaching for it.

"Be wary." Hawkwood drew the stone away. "A curse follows it. As *The Moon Scrolls* warned. It is why I hold it in the silk."

Curse! Jondralyn's mind whirled. Ethic Shroud*! Angel stones!* A thousand thoughts raced through her head. Foremost was the realization that what she'd been taught her entire life had just been proven wrong. *The Way and Truth of Laijon* was clear—the weapons of the Five Warrior Angels and their angel stones had been taken into heaven with the body of Laijon at his death. But here one was. *If I am to believe these men.*

Roguemoore noticed the myriad of questions on her face. "Upon translating a portion of *The Moon Scrolls of Mia* stolen by Squireck, I discovered a curious thing about Amadon. The scrolls spoke of a place under the city called the Rooms of Sorrow, a place sealed away under water that held great treasure. Within the scrolls was a coded map that showed the way. The Rooms of Sorrow and the underground rivers that led to them could only be accessed through Purgatory, the dungeons under the Hall of the Dayknights. A place none of us could just explore without arousing suspicion. Thus a way to get Hawkwood thrown into the dungeons was arranged."

"The duel with the Dayknights," she said flatly, mind reeling, eye on the brilliant angel stone.

"With the map committed to memory"—Hawkwood took over, folding the stone back into the silk, slipping it away into his cloak—"with tricks I learned in Sør Sevier, I was soon out of my cell and on the path to finding the Rooms of Sorrow, by the light of old torches snatched from the walls of the prison corridor. Deeply hidden the path was, sealed for centuries, the way perilous, full of many traps that took me some time to circumvent, or dismantle. The way led to a rushing stream, deep under the city. I followed the swift-moving waters until they disappeared under solid rock."

Hawkwood paused. It was the only time Jondralyn had ever seen fear on his face. But he swallowed and continued, "Here is where I almost faltered. For the map had spoken of this subterranean obstacle. The Rooms of Sorrow and *Ethic Shroud* were but a minute away.

All I had to do was submerge myself in the stream and let the current carry me under the rock and into the Rooms of Sorrow. But that is a long time without air. I must admit, my faith wavered. But I had to trust the *Moon Scrolls*. I had to trust the map. Otherwise Squireck's theft of the *Moon Scrolls* would be for naught."

Hawkwood shuddered, as if the memory frightened him still. "With much trepidation, I lowered myself into the stream and let it suck me down into the cold deep, under stone and earth and into utter blackness. The water rushed and roiled. It seemed a lifetime dragged by as I was swept along, trying desperately to cling to the walls, floor, ceiling, whatever, I did not know; I was just desperate to keep my sense of direction. My lungs were burning by the time this devilish, churning nightmare spit me out into a large cavern and I could finally breathe. The stream still rushed me headlong toward another wall of solid rock, but I caught hold of the jagged bank and pulled myself to safety before I was swept under again."

He took a deep breath, almost as if he was still in the cavern in the midst of his adventure. "Anyway, the scrolls were right. 'Twas an hour or so before I was able to spark my torch to light again. But once I could see, I found a short tunnel branching off from the cavern, which led to a room, a room dug by ancient Vallè, I would assume, as there were intricate scrollwork carvings on the walls and the cross-shaped altar I found. *Ethic Shroud* and the angel stone were there, hidden, inside that altar."

"What of *The Way and Truth of Laijon?*" she asked. "This flies against all of it. The weapons and stones were taken into heaven with Laijon at the time of his death."

"And that myth served the stones well," Culpa Barra said. "For centuries nobody has bothered searching for them. Until now. In our day."

"But why would the holy book lie?"

The dwarf answered, "*The Way and Truth of Laijon* that you have believed your entire life is not to be trusted, Jon. The quorum of five, the grand vicar, and all those vicars before Denarius would have you believe the angel stones and weapons of the Five Warrior Angels were translated into heaven at Laijon's death and the mantle of Laijon passed on to them and the church. They believe that Laijon will bring the stones and weapons back with him at the time of Fiery Absolution and they, the vicars and quorum, will rule by his side for eternity. But they are wrong. Their belief in Fiery Absolution is a lie. The church they've built around the life of Laijon is false. There is only one uncorrupted truth: that penned by the Blessed Mother Mia in the *Moon Scrolls*."

Hawkwood looked at Jondralyn squarely. "You are now privy to the most guarded secret of the Brethren of Mia. For the time to gather the lost weapons of Laijon and the five angel stones has begun. It is the Brethren's task to make sure Fiery Absolution does not happen."

"And the enemies of the Brethren," Roguemoore said, "are any who wish for Absolution. Most in Jovan's court find great glory in their fatalistic acceptance of Fiery Absolution and do all that they can to hasten its coming. Val-Korin and the grand vicar have all but convinced your brother that he is doing Laijon's will by just remaining patient and letting the war come to him. They connive and they convince with verse and script from *The Way and Truth of Laijon*, all to bolster their agenda in the minds of the nobles."

Culpa Barra added, "Had Jovan stayed and fought in Wyn Darrè after your father's death, it would have bought the Brethren more time to find the weapons and stones. But with Jovan's retreat, Aeros' conquest was fast in coming. Borden's main reason for fighting alongside Wyn Darrè was to buy Ser Roderic time to find the lost weapons of Laijon, to give Roguemoore more time to find where the last of Mia's *Moon Scrolls* were hidden. Every move your father made was to buy time so the Brethren could stave off this needless and savage crusade of Aeros Raijael. And now Aeros is at the very brink of conquest. The scrolls of Mia speak of the weapons and stones of Laijon as a way and means to *prevent* Absolution."

Jondralyn felt her brow twist in puzzlement. Some of what the dwarf had said hinted at the things her mother had spoken of when she was pregnant with Ansel before her father had died in war. Alana's fear had been that those councillors left around Jovan would fill his head with lofty ideas about the return of Laijon, and use him and his position as the new king of Gul Kana for their own ends. She'd been especially wary of Val-Korin and the grand vicar. That these things Roguemoore, Culpa, and Hawkwood were speaking of matched her mother's own concerns so closely was vexing.

But there were other things bothering her too. She asked Hawkwood, "How did you get out of the Rooms of Sorrow with the shield and stone?"

"The map I'd committed to memory. It claimed all I need do was crawl back into the stream and let it carry me under the second wall and . . . and out into Memory Bay. But neither Roguemoore nor I could decipher *where* in Memory Bay I would be dumped. On that, the map was silent. Otherwise, trust me: I certainly would have tried that route instead of the harrowing one through Purgatory."

"So where then did the stream take you?"

"Again, with great dread, I forced myself to venture into the water and was immediately swept under the rock, *Ethic Shroud* and the angel stone clenched tight in either hand, neither seeming to weigh an ounce. This time, within seconds, the rush of the stream ceased and I could see daylight twinkling off the surface of Memory Bay about twenty feet above. I kicked my way to the surface and found myself floundering, angry waves dashing me against the jagged cliff side of Mount Albion, Amadon Castle rising high above me. I clung to the rocks for a moment, gathering myself, then pulled my way along the cliff side south until I came to a small inlet with a few out-buildings clinging to the side of the rocks. There was a small dinghy tied to a rickety old dock. I waited hidden in a cleft in the rocks until darkness, stole the boat, and rowed myself out to Rockliegh Isle, the rendezvous point Culpa, Roguemoore, and I had agreed upon. Kicked a hole in the bottom of the boat. Set it adrift. Then waited."

Jondralyn was at a loss for words, her eyes on *Ethic Shroud*, wondering how much of what she had heard was to be believed. *He carried this strange shield the entire way.*

"Ask any question you like," Hawkwood said. "For tonight, here on this isle, will be the only time these things are ever spoken of again. We four are the only ones to gaze upon these treasures in a thousand years. I think the dwarf will agree that *Ethic Shroud* and the angel stone I found should both be returned to where I found them. Now that I know the rear entrance to the Rooms of Sorrow, I want to put them back. I made note of the cliff side. The underground stream spit me out not twenty feet below the surface. I can easily swim back into that place now."

"Returned? Why?"

"Safekeeping," Roguemoore said. "We dare not bring them out into the open yet. We dare not go traipsing around the countryside with these treasures. That mistake was made before. After Roderic found *Lonesome Crown*, he gave it to his brother, Torrence. And that started a war."

"You mean another stone and artifact have been found?"

"They've all been found, Jondralyn. All but one. And Ser Roderic searches for that last one now, in Gallows Haven."

"I've so many questions," she muttered. "But I don't even know where to begin."

"If I may." Culpa Barra bowed to her. "The White Prince's bloody crusade through Adin Wyte and Wyn Darrè: What reason would you give for that?"

"To take back those lands lost to the heirs of Raijael long ago," she answered.

"Partly true," Culpa Barra said. "As you know, King Aevrett and those followers of Raijael in Sør Sevier also believe in Fiery Absolution and desire to hasten its fruition too. They wish for Laijon's prophesied return as much as, or more than, those in Gul Kana do. They seek Laijon's return in their own way, according to their own *Chivalric Illuminations*, through war. They believe that Raijael was the one and only offspring of Laijon and Mia, and the mantle of heaven was passed on to him and his heirs. Aevrett Raijael believes the stones and weapons are bound to come into his son's possession before the return of Laijon. Whether the stones and weapons will be delivered to Aeros from heaven or some other way, the *Illuminations* are not specific. But he believes it will happen. In fact, it probably *has* happened. He had his son invade Wyn Darrè to gain possession of one of these artifacts."

"I always believed Aeros' crusade was to take back lands believed stolen from Sør Sevier," Jondralyn said. "It is what my father told me."

"That is what Borden would have everyone believe," the dwarf said. "But he was one of the Brethren. He knew exactly what Aeros Raijael and his father were after. *Lonesome Crown* and one of the angel stones are in possession of King Torrence Raybourne. Aevrett and Aeros Raijael desire these treasures. With Wyn Darrè almost completely destroyed, rumors now filtering in of King Torrence's death, Aeros may already have *Lonesome Crown*."

Culpa Barra added, "The Brethren of Mia have long believed that the five angel stones and weapons of the Warrior Angels were hidden by the Blessed Mother sometime after Laijon's death. *The Moon Scrolls of Mia* bear this out. Mia left clues within the scrolls as to where she hid the weapons and stones. Each in a different location, each hidden deep. There is one man in the Brethren who has dedicated his life to studying the scrolls and finding the angel stones and weapons. Three of them he's found. One of those, the sword *Afflicted Fire*, I personally helped him find at Deadwood Gate over five years ago. The angel stone I saw then was exactly like the one Hawkwood has just found, but red as flame. Before that, Shawcroft found the crossbow *Blackest Heart* high above the Sky Lochs. The fourth one, the battle-ax *Forgetting Moon*, he searches for now in Gallows Haven. Both *Forgetting Moon* and *Ethic Shroud* have always eluded him. Now, thanks to the *Moon Scrolls* Squireck stole for us, Hawkwood has found the shield here under Amadon Castle."

"Who is this man Shawcroft who spent his entire life looking for the stones?" Jondralyn asked, eyes on the brilliant white shield still on the bench. "You mentioned Ser Roderic before, Culpa. Is it him?"

"Yes. Ser Roderic Raybourne of Wyn Darrè. It is he who found *Lonesome Crown*, *Blackest Heart*, and *Afflicted Fire*. He left *Blackest Heart* in Sky Lochs, *Afflicted Fire* in Deadwood Gate. *Lonesome Crown* he found first, twenty years ago, and gave it to his brother, King Torrence. Though Torrence held this treasure in secret, Sør Sevier spies caught wind of it. And like I said, Aeros Raijael's father was most desirous to possess it."

"Sør Sevier invaded Wyn Darrè for an angel stone and the helmet of Laijon that Ser Roderic found?"

"Partly, yes," Roguemoore answered.

"Ser Roderic was one of Father's Dayknights when I was a little girl. I barely remember him. He just seemed to disappear. Rumor was he was exiled from his brother's court and just vanished."

"Rumor was." The dwarf nodded.

"I ran into him once soon after his exile," Hawkwood said, something approaching admiration in his voice. "About fourteen years ago."

Roguemoore took Jondralyn's hand. His skin was rough against hers as he clenched her fingers tight. There was a penetrating look in his eyes she had never seen before as he said, "There is more you need know about the Brethren of Mia, Jon. In fact, there is more you need to know about yourself. *The Way and Truth of Laijon* speaks of the return of Laijon during the time of Fiery Absolution. But *The Moon*

Scrolls of Mia that our Blessed Mother penned speaks of the return of *all* five Warrior Angels. Not just Laijon."

"How does this affect me? What does it have to do with the Brethren?"

"We have found the five," Roguemoore answered. "They are all alive, now, living among us. The Princess, the Gladiator, the Assassin, the Thief, and most importantly the Slave. Each a descendent of one of the Five Warrior Angels, each tied to one of the Five Isles by blood, each ready to play a part in summoning forth the true heir of Laijon and bringing about his return as the *Moon Scrolls* have foretold."

A shiver ran up her spine. "I don't understand."

A grin grew out of the dwarf's grizzled beard. "You, Jondralyn Bronachell, are one of the Five Warrior Angels reborn. The Princess, wielder of *Afflicted Fire.*"

Jondralyn was trembling, trembling with fear rather than under-standing. Her mind recalled one of the scriptures from *The Way and Truth of Laijon,* a snippet from the Book of the Cross. Something about the Five Warrior Angels gathered in a grove of trees and an abomi-nable magical darkness that had overtaken them. They thought they were dead, prayed for life, and saw a bright light above that defied all description. It was angels descending toward them, bearing five colorful stones and five mighty gifts: a red stone and a sword for the Princess, a white stone and pearl-colored shield for the Thief, a black stone and a black crossbow for the Assassin, a green stone and a war helm for the Gladiator, and lastly, a blue stone and an ax for the King of Slaves. She could not recall the exact words of the scripture but remembered the gist of it.

A sword for the Princess. She had always liked that part of the scripture as a child, imagining a princess wielding a magical sword beside Laijon, fighting for truth and justice. *Afflicted Fire.* If the dwarf thought she was the Princess reborn, then who were the other Warrior Angels?

Hawkwood offered the faintest of smiles. "I know what you are thinking. For I thought the same thing when Roguemoore told me I too was one of the Five Warrior Angels reborn, the Assassin, future wielder of *Blackest Heart*."

"And Squireck Van Hester, the Gladiator," Culpa Barra added. "Wearer of *Lonesome Crown*."

"I can hardly believe any of this," she muttered, heart thumping, hoping what they said might be true, because it was wildly fanciful and exciting. But she was unable to quite grasp it all. She searched the dwarf's eyes, looking for deception, finding conviction. Culpa Barra looked at her expectantly. Hawkwood was unreadable. But clearly he believed. *The Assassin?* It frightened her. *And me the Princess!*

"The King of Slaves?" she asked. "Who? And the Thief?"

Roguemoore answered her. "The one who is to wield *Forgetting Moon*, the King of Slaves reborn, is being watched over now. At your father's behest, he was found as a babe, then hidden. Seventeen years ago it was. He will remain hidden until the time is right to reveal his identity. Royal is his bloodline. More royal and secret than any."

"And *Ethic Shroud* is now found." Hawkwood motioned to the shield resting on the stone bench. "Reserved for the Thief, one whom you know, one whom you've been told to keep close."

"Val-Draekin?" She looked at all three men in turn, then at the shield.

"Yes. Val-Draekin." The dwarf looked at her firmly. "Though I've had my doubts. And I do not fully trust him yet. He's told me that there is division amongst the Vallè. He claims the armies of the Val Vallè will only help Gul Kana fight against the White Prince if Jovan is removed from the Silver Throne. He says Val-Korin is in strong disagreement with his countrymen. Val-Korin supports Jovan. It is a quandary."

Her heart thudded. *This is why Roguemoore wanted me to keep Val-Draekin close. He thinks that the Vallè is a descendent of one of the Five Warrior Angels.*

And I am a descendent too? Then her heart really pounded as she came to the realization that the blood of one of the Five Warrior Angels possibly flowed in her. Everyone knew the stories of the Five Warrior Angels. *The Way and Truth of Laijon* hinted at the five as the Princess, Gladiator, Thief, Assassin, and Slave. But other than Laijon, known as the Slave, or sometimes as the King of Slaves, the scriptures had never mentioned the names of the other four Warrior Angels. Roguemoore had claimed she was a descendent of one of the Warrior Angels. But how could he know?

She realized Roguemoore still held her hand when he squeezed it, saying, "According to *The Moon Scrolls of Mia*, in the last days, the Princess, wielding *Afflicted Fire*, will lead vast armies against those who threaten to destroy Amadon. You, Jon, are that princess. The Princess who will lead all armies. Jovan is right to fear you. Soon Aeros Raijael will fear you too."

Jondralyn slipped her hand from the dwarf's grasp and took a few steps back, looking out the door of the small abbey. "Trust no one" was the Brethren's motto.

"I know this is a lot to take in," Roguemoore said in a tone of finality. "You can ask Culpa any question that may arise. But Hawkwood and I are leaving to meet Ser Roderic and Hugh Godwyn, another of the Brethren of Mia, at the Swithen Wells Trail Abbey on the morrow. We plan on returning to Sky Lochs and Deadwood Gate with Ser Roderic to retrieve the stones and weapons Roderic left there and prepare to battle the White Prince. In his last letter, Roderic claimed he'd finally broken the code to circumventing the traps around the altar that holds the *Forgetting Moon*. He claimed he was close to breaking the seal to the tomb holding that relic. I am as nervous as I am excited. The quest to gather the angel stones and weapons Ser Roderic has found is finally underway."

"It has been years, if not decades in the coming," Culpa Barra said. "We should rejoice that the task has fallen to us, in our time. We should fall to our knees and give thanks to Laijon that a man such as

Ser Roderic Raybourne dedicated so much of his life to finding those things hidden for so long."

"Indeed," the dwarf said gravely. "Many of the Brethren have toiled, suffered, and died to prepare the way. Deadwood Gate. Sky Lochs. Gallows Haven. But it was the final scrolls Squireck stole, combined with the scrolls already found by my brother, Ironcloud, that have proved most valuable to us here and now. They led us to the Rooms of Sorrow in the catacombs under Purgatory."

Hawkwood added, "And now Squireck's efforts in the arena may very well prove to be the Brethren's greatest accomplishment of all."

Jondralyn hung her head whenever anyone made mention of Squireck Van Hester. She found strength and good quality in both Hawkwood and Squireck. But at the same time she wondered if everything they were involved in, all things associated with the Brethren of Mia, wasn't just so much craziness. But what was it Roguemoore had called her? *The Princess who will lead all armies.* She did like the sound of that. She could see the world around her made right with a title like that!

"Your clothes and a fresh cloak lie under the tarp in the second boat," Culpa Barra said to Hawkwood. "Your cutlasses and harnesses along with your brace of knives and shortsword are there too." He turned to the dwarf. "Plus, there are enough dried oatcakes and cheese to last your journey. Remember, all roads are being watched. Sterling will focus most of his search efforts for Hawkwood along the main routes in the north. He's only set a few to search for Hawkwood by water. Traveling to Lord's Point along the King's Highway is out of the question. The tolls are garrisoned with Silver Guards, Dayknights, even Wolf Guards from Rivermeade at times. They are all on the lookout for Hawkwood. Sterling's made arrangements for the horses, palfreys for hard traveling, but you'll have to sail to Eskander to get them. I suggest you two leave with utmost haste, especially if you plan on taking our treasures back to the Rooms of Sorrow. After that, six days afloat at most. I've brought you a fast vessel. From Eskander, head south to Swithen Wells and the Swithen Wells Pass into the Autumn Range. You won't miss the abbey as long as you keep to the trail. The entire journey shouldn't take you more than fourteen or fifteen days. I traveled the route with my father once to visit Godwyn and Ser Roderic. It is not a bad trail, weather permitting. From there continue to Lord's Point. If you become separated, I've arranged with Ironcloud for the rendezvous point to be the Turn Key Saloon in Lord's Point. From there you can sail north to Stanclyffe and head east to the Sky Lochs."

"A saloon?" the dwarf asked flatly.

"Ironcloud sent word that is where he would await you."

"My brother has a knack for choosing the worst of inns," Roguemoore grunted, stroking the wiry, grizzled hair of his beard. "The Turn Key Saloon. I can picture it now. A place most assuredly to be run by the dregs of society."

Hawkwood's eyes narrowed fiercely. He was quickly at the abbey's open door, eyes peering into the darkness. "Something moves against the rocks under the lighthouse," he hissed. "We're about to be compromised." He turned back to Culpa Barra. "Were you followed?"

"Let's hope it's just a stray goat." Culpa hustled to the door. With his back to the wall, he craned his neck around the opening for a look himself. "Or perhaps just the lighthouse keeper. There are no other boats ashore that I can see."

"Someone from the tunnels?" Hawkwood cast a concerned look at the dwarf.

Jondralyn moved silently up behind the dwarf and peered over his shoulder. A low fog hung about the base of the lighthouse. Moonlight bathed the isle in a wan gray light, dimly illuminating the mass of jagged rock formations that jutted up around the narrow building. There were a thousand shapes and shadows amongst those pale rocks, some just indistinct forms bulging out of the moonlit vapors. High above, the lighthouse flame did little to light the island, but at ground level it did create tendrils of mist the color of bone. She thought she heard the rustling of the sea grass, but there was no breeze. Nothing at all moved among the lichen-covered rocks but the listless swirls of fog. Her heart raced just the same.

"I see him," Hawkwood said. There was a rare tension in his stance. "Look, dwarf, there under the T-shaped crag in the boulder just left of the lighthouse."

"Aye," Roguemoore offered up slowly. "The bloody bastard. Just standing there in plain view. Lookin' right at us. Our Bloodwood assassin. Up from the tunnels."

Jondralyn searched the bleak darkness, yet she saw nothing. Her eyes roamed the jumble of rock and shadow, traveling up the spire of the lighthouse itself and even beyond that to the looming bulk of Amadon Castle itself. Points of fiery light stood out from torches lining its many battlements and towering spires. Even from where she stood in this small abbey a mile away, the castle towered over the bay and blocked out the stars. Amadon Castle originally started as a fort thousands of years before the birth of Laijon, built atop Mount Albion against Vallè invasions and raids of the savage oghul tribes of the north. It had grown upon itself exponentially over the centuries, spreading down all sides of the mount to become the colossus it was now.

And in that time was a thousand years' worth of different folks digging around for different purposes under the castle, mount, and city, all the tunnels and carvers and hidey-holes creating an interconnected labyrinth of passages that led everywhere. That underground streams and rooms of treasure and tunnels stretched even under Memory Bay as far as this lighthouse boggled her mind. *Who would think to dig under the sea?*

She finally spied what she thought was a hooded shadow under the lighthouse, darker than the rest. It was an unholy blackness awash in evil, and with it came a feeling of danger. She shuddered, her eyes riveted to the cloaked form that seemed to swallow the moonlight.

This thing, this Bloodwood assassin, leaned languidly against the rock. It moved then, seeming to fade in and out of existence.

"He approaches," Roguemoore said.

"He wants to be seen," Hawkwood said. "He wants us to think that he has heard all we've said."

"Do you recognize who it is?" the dwarf asked.

"If it were my brother, we'd all be fighting for our lives right now," Hawkwood said. "I fear this Bloodwood is one I do not know. One who joined Black Dugal's Caste after I fled Sør Sevier, someone with movements I am unfamiliar with."

"What is Dugal's game?" Roguemoore growled.

"I know not," Hawkwood said. "Lucky I spotted the Bloodwood quick. He never came close enough to hear us. I am sure of that. Still, we must remain wary. And if he came up from a tunnel, that means he has no boat, which means we should be safe. We can get back to the Rooms of Sorrow without him knowing. He will figure we are sailing into the darkness to escape him. But we must leave in haste."

The cloaked figure slunk back into the shadows, and just like that there was nothing. "Gone," Roguemoore said.

"Aye," Hawkwood agreed. "Perhaps." Then Jondralyn felt Hawkwood's hand unexpectedly in hers. Their fingers entwined. Her heart pounded. Then, like a whisper, his hand was gone. But a slip of parchment was left behind. She quickly slipped the note into the folds of her cloak. Neither Culpa nor the dwarf had seen.

Hawkwood snatched up *Ethic Shroud* from the bench and led them all silently from the abbey and to the two boats awaiting them. All of them were on guard.

† † † † †

Jondralyn sat on a bench in the privacy of her courtyard, tired, yet unable to sleep.

It had been a full day. By the time she was back to her room, it was nearly dawn. There were no further sightings of the Bloodwood on her and Culpa Barra's journey back to the castle via the extra boat they had brought. Her eyes were heavy-lidded as she gazed up at the faint light emanating from the many torch-lit towers of the castle above.

She took from her cloak the parchment Hawkwood had earlier slipped into her hand and unfolded it. She could tell right away it was a crudely drawn map from the dungeons under Purgatory to the Rooms of Sorrow, where he had found *Ethic Shroud* and the angel stone. The map did not show the back entrance to the Rooms of Sorrow that Hawkwood would presumably be using tonight to return the shield and stone. But it did show the way from Purgatory. She knew immediately why he had given it to her—in case something were to happen to him, she would still have access to *Ethic Shroud*.

And then the ink, exposed to light, slowly faded away and the page was blank. To read it again, she would need Roguemoore's lavender deje powder. She folded the map and entered her room and headed straight for her bookshelf. On the top shelf, behind the third book from the left, was a small panel. She hid the parchment there, eyes roaming the walls round about, wondering if the Bloodwood watched her now. *Am I to be this paranoid the rest of my life? Is this what being privy to the Brethren's secrets means?*

Wearily, she took off her black riding boots and slipped on her leather training boots, then stood. Her leather armor hung on a hook on a post behind her bench. She quietly slipped out of her cloak and into the leathers.

Resolute, she marched from her room. Her destination: Anjk Bourbon's smith shop in the market district, and another day of training. As she left her room, she had but one lingering question on her mind.

Am I truly the Princess who will lead armies?

And it came to pass that in the place of Only was born a boy, the firstborn son
of a fisherman, a humble child who followed in the footsteps of his goodly father,
living and fishing and growing strong by the sea, killing merfolk and shark and
grayken alike with the strength of his own hands. And his name was Laijon.
—THE WAY AND TRUTH OF LAIJON

CHAPTER TWENTY-ONE
TALA BRONACHELL

4TH DAY OF THE MOURNING MOON, 999TH YEAR OF LAIJON

AMADON, GUL KANA

It takes my breath away," Lindholf Le Graven said, gazing at the four-story edifice that was the Grand Vicar's Palace. Sheathed in white marble gilded in gold, it rose up between the gray, brick, mortar, and timber buildings of the surrounding city like a bright shard of heaven, serene and refined. "But it seems so gaudy."

"Denarius and the quorum of five live well," Glade Chaparral said as if lecturing Tala's cousin. "As is their right." As their horse-drawn carriage rumbled over the cobblestones, the streets of Amadon were teeming with people. A Silver Guard led the team of horses, Glade Chaparral at his side. Tala and Lindholf sat directly behind them in the open carriage. Tala was swathed in a heavy cloak of brown wool. A detachment of a dozen spear-wielding Silver Guards escorted their carriage on horseback. Glade continued, "When one is called as grand vicar, he takes upon himself the mantle of Laijon. His word is law. When Denarius speaks, it is as if Laijon has spoken. One such as that *should* live in a palace."

Tala wasn't sure about all that. Yet Glade seemed so sure of his viewpoint all the time. Sometimes he could wear his opinions, as well as his looks, with unbearable conceit. Yet that, in a strange way, was one of the things that drew Tala to him. One thing was for sure: these quests the Bloodwood had set her upon were also affording her an opportunity to be near Glade.

As they continued down the thoroughfare, Tala cast one last glance at the opulent building, home to the most powerful religious figure in the Five Isles, and its glittering, gold-trimmed, ornamented facade. She wished she could see Grand Vicar Denarius as the perfect man Glade thought him to be. But she had spent too much time in Denarius' company for that—she'd witnessed his gluttony firsthand. Not that overeating was a direct pathway to the underworld. The sight of the gladiator's mangled head sliding down the front of his cassock still brought a shudder to her. *My poor Lawri.*

As their carriage bounced along, they passed under a section of the city's aqueducts, and Tala now remembered why the place stank so. They were nearing the River Vallè. Aqueducts from as far away as the Autumn Range and the northern Sky Lochs brought cool mountain water into the city. The River Vallè itself was mostly for sewage. Human waste and other sloshing refuse would be wheeled in barrels and dumped into it. It was widely known that the riverside district was the haunt of the bloodletters and covens of witches. That the Grand Vicar's Palace, and both the Royal Cathedral and Temple of the Laijon Statue, were near such dreadful places made Tala shudder.

Still, this new quest to save Lawri was a diversion that held some measure of excitement. Without it, Tala felt she would be driven mad with the unmerciful sameness of life in the castle. This assassin's puzzle, this game, now that she was sure she had figured out the clue of the wreath, was putting Tala in better spirits. Lindholf also appeared to be in good spirits. There was a spring in his step today, and he'd been full of more chatter than normal, spontaneously singing wonderfully absurd songs on their journey from the castle and recounting several maddeningly intricate tales of his hunting exploits in Eskander, each story ending with a belly laugh for Tala. She had delighted in his antics. At the same time, she knew she should feel guilty for enjoying her adventures with him, adventures that she had been set upon at Lawri's expense.

The carriage rounded a corner, and the Royal Cathedral and the Temple of the Laijon Statue stood before them. Both edifices soared at least three hundred feet above the cobbled pavement and were constructed of brilliant ivory-color Riven Rock–quarried marble. Knights with pikes lined the entrances of both the temple and chapel, all wearing the black-and-silver livery that marked them as Amadon Silver Guards. They kept a trained eye on the comings and goings of all.

When the carriage clattered to a stop, Tala, Glade, and Lindholf hopped from it and marched up to the fountain in the center of the temple's outer courtyard, accompanied by six of their Silver Guard escort. The fountain was surrounded by marble pillars carved with crescent moon charms, crosses, black Laijon trees, and other sacred symbols. Water splashed about the base of the fountain, yet was calmer along the outer edges and afloat with flowers. A crowd swirled around the temple's arched entrance. A host of pilgrims and worshippers bringing their tithes clogged the stairs leading up to the great opening. A group of flagellants were clustered there too, all whipping their own naked backs for forgiveness and penance for sins of the flesh.

As her group hustled up the stairs and through the archway and into the cooler shade of the building, the crowds stepped aside. Once they were inside the foyer, the noise of the city was reduced to a faint, subdued thrum. Tala immediately sought the holy Ember Stone, a round dais at the center of the lobby. She knew from her Eighth Day lessons that the temple's Ember Stone had been laid in the second century after Laijon's death. It was hard to fathom such a breadth of time.

She dabbed some ash from the stone basin set upon the dais, touched her forehead with the ash, and made the three-fingered sign of the Laijon Cross over her heart. She allowed Lindholf and Glade the same privilege. A bell sounded and the small choir in the balcony above began to sing. A pair of bishops walked by, swinging copper jars of smoky incense before them. Tala drank in the sounds of the choir and fragrance of the moment, then proceeded toward the huge polished doors to the temple's inner dome.

Two Silver Guards snapped to attention, and one pulled on a braided rope. The door swung open without a sound and Tala, Glade, Lindholf and their six Silver Guard escort were let inside. A handful of other worshippers scuttled in behind them, and the guards closed the doors.

Tala was always struck by the majesty of the place and the vast chamber's impossible height. She couldn't help but stare straight up, her eyes drawn to the domed ceiling three hundred feet above. She turned her gaze from the perfectly circular ceiling and looked upon the inner temple itself, eyes roaming, searching. The coils of smoke from a thousand candles sailed heavenward. The place was silent save for the occasional creak of shoe leather on the marble tile floor and the faint whispers of the temple's occupants. Silver Guard spearmen stood like statues along the curved walls, their armor and spearheads gleaming, their shields black and painted with the silver symbol of the Laijon tree. There were discreet crossbowmen along the second-story gallery as well. Hidden in the shadows, their ring mail glimmered faintly. Above the gallery, stained-glass windows sparkled jewel-like, resplendent with graceful reflections of sunlight. It was a holy place, and the Quorum of Five Archbishops of Amadon insisted it always be heavily protected from criminal activity. Several dozen citizens were milling about the chamber, admiring the statue.

In the center of the vast room, upon a ten-foot-high raised dais of splendorous gray-veined pale stone, stood the great Laijon statue itself, over five stories tall from head to feet. The likeness of Laijon was carved of pure Riven Rock marble, one muscular arm held aloft and a great silvery sword in that hand pointing heavenward. A wreath of heather crowned the statue's head, and Laijon's gaze was fixed heavenward. The statue's intricately carved chain-mail armor sparkled in the light. Booted feet were planted firmly upon the dais. The tiered stone dais was ringed by five massive black-and-silver iron cauldrons from which incense smoke swirled. Each cauldron was set firmly upon the back of a life-size marble-carved ox. The creatures' heads and great horns faced outward as if guarding both the statue of Laijon and the cauldrons upon their backs. Each cauldron's surface was carved with divine symbols inlaid in white, black, green, blue, and red, each a representation of the magical stones and weapons of the Five Warrior Angels: *Blackest Heart*, *Ethic Shroud*, *Forgetting Moon*, *Lonesome Crown*, and *Afflicted Fire*—the Five Pillars of Laijon.

This was the great statue of Laijon—the reason for the construction of such a massive temple. It was a place of worship and pilgrimage, the focal point of both faith and art in all the Five Isles. Some would come from the far reaches of Gul Kana to stare at it for days, to cleanse the spirit, or just be near the likeness of their great One and Only.

"I haven't seen anything so awe-inspiring and brilliant since I slithered free of Mother's womb into the sun-drenched snowfields of Eskander," Lindholf murmured from behind her. "I'm apt to burst into a greater torrent of tears now as I gaze upon the blinding brightness of the great One and Only than I did as babe entering a new world."

"Mother Mia," Glade snapped. "Your babbling is inappropriate, and liable to split my head in half. The more you blather on today, the more I wish I'd stayed at the castle."

"Pardon me," Lindholf said, eyes still fixed upon the statue above. "I suppose I can see your point. I *can* wear on some folks."

Tala had coerced both Glade and Lindholf into accompanying her on this new adventure by claiming Hawkwood had specifically asked them to retrieve a note left at the temple and deliver it to Jondralyn. She believed both of them still held the man in high regard. They had talked of little else but Hawkwood's duel with the Dayknights. As predicted, they'd jumped at the chance to help her.

The three slowly circled the great work of art, the Silver Guard escorting them on all sides. The statue itself was roped off—none were allowed to get within ten paces of it. As she walked, hand brushing along the rope that encircled the statue, Tala cocked her head like a wary sparrow, gazing nervously up at the wreath that crowned Laijon's head, her eyes traveling down the length of his body. But there was nothing there. No clue.

Disheartened with each step, Tala began to wonder if this was truly where she was supposed to have come. Amadon Castle itself was filled with thousands of likenesses of Laijon: statues, bronzes, paintings, and tapestries. But searching all of those would take years, if not a lifetime. She continued to circle the statue, eyes even more focused, hoping that something would suggest itself.

A Silver Guard not in her personal entourage moved briskly toward her and held out a gauntleted hand, stopping them. He removed his helm, revealing a head of thinning gray hair, and bent his knee before her. "I was not informed that one of the royal family would be coming to the temple today." He placed his helm under the crook of his arm.

"I've come to pray at the feet of Laijon," Tala said.

The gray-haired guard turned and gave a quick hand signal to the guardsmen above. Soon, all of the Silver Guards, including the six who had accompanied Tala's small group from the castle, were ushering the common citizens from the inner dome.

A bishop rushed forth and hurriedly anointed Glade, Lindholf, and Tala's foreheads with consecrated oil from a bull-horn flask, then blessed them with a brief prayer and scuttled away behind the last of the guardsmen to exit the inner temple.

"We should have been notified of this through the proper chain of command, through our captain, Ser Castlegrail," the guardsman said, bowing. "It is customary that the temple be emptied for the arrival of any member of the king's court."

"My comings and goings need not be announced to you," Tala said. "I am here now and wish to pray."

The gray-haired guard's face hardened at the abruptness of her words. Still, he bowed before her a second time. "As you wish, m'lady."

Tala injected an insolent tone into her voice. "I've come to pray on behalf of my dearly departed father and mother. I pray that that gruesome Prince of Saint Only will soon be vanquished in the arena and the traitor Hawkwood caught and hung. They are an affront to justice, an affront to the Silver Throne, and an affront to Laijon and our most holy vicar and quorum of five." She knew that would be something the Silver Guard would want to hear.

"An affront to the grand vicar and quorum indeed." The guard bowed again, doing the three-fingered sign of the Laijon Cross over his heart.

Tala looked up at the majestic marble face of Laijon—so stern it was, so perfect in its symmetry and allure. Even from her angle looking almost straight up, it was perfection. If there was a heaven, it was Laijon who ruled it. She recalled an Eighth Day sermon in which the grand vicar had read from the Ember Lighting Song of the Third Warrior Angel near the end of *The Way and Truth of Laijon*— the climactic part of the scriptures. The verse recounted the final day of the Vicious War of the Demons—the final day of the Blessed Mother's pregnancy. Laijon, bleeding from the wound in his neck, had just been nailed, still alive, to the Atonement Tree by the Last Demon Lord, who then also lay down wounded and dying in the dirt at Laijon's feet. The final battle between the Last Warrior Angels and the beasts of the underworld had come down to combat between the two men. Both had suffered mortal wounds. It was Mia herself who, after the Demon Lord had died and after Laijon had spent nine days nailed to the tree, thrust the fateful sword, *Afflicted Fire*, into the chest of her husband, easing the suffering of her beloved, sacrificing his life for the sins of all humankind, fulfilling the prophecies of the ancients that the last of the demons would only be vanquished when the sins of all men were atoned for. Then, as sacrament, she drank of his blood. The next day, Mia gave birth to the baby Raijael.

For the nine days Laijon's body had hung on the Atonement Tree, the Demon Lord rotting at his feet, thousands had flocked to see their fallen king before Mia and the remaining Warrior Angels had cut his body down. Laijon's body was dressed in his finest chain mail and horned helm, then placed upon a cross-shaped altar along with all the weapons of the Five Warrior Angels. Mia inserted the angel stones that had once belonged to the Five Warrior Angels into the wound in Laijon's chest. The shield, *Ethic Shroud*, was laid atop him, covering the wounds. Then his body was taken up into heaven. And it was prophesied he would one day be reborn and return on the day of Fiery Absolution, along with the other Warrior Angels, to rule forever.

As Tala stepped back from her spot directly under the statue, she began to wonder how anyone could stand guard under such grandeur of the statue of Laijon and not be profoundly moved by its glorious spirit. It surely cast a spell over all. The curve and cut of each muscle rippled under chain-mail armor, arms and legs even stronger than the marble of which they were hewn. This aesthetic perfection in marble was, Tala believed, why men followed Laijon;

why knights and gladiators over the centuries were desirous to forge their own flesh in his image. This massive sculpture of Laijon was perfect, supreme and ideal, from his squared chin to the smooth lines of his exquisitely carved mouth and nose and stoic jawline, to his eyes, which—although they gazed toward the dome of the ceiling— seemed to emanate a bravery and caring that no human could possess yet remained set upon heaven forever, and to the polished sweep of his brow leading to the wreath—

—and then as she stepped farther back, she saw it. The flaw in the statue.

It was scarcely discernable, perhaps a trick of light. One petal of the carved marble wreath was a different shade of white than the hundreds of others that encircled Laijon's brow. "I wish to be alone now," she blurted. "All must leave save my two friends here." She nodded toward Lindholf and Glade.

"Of course." The guard bowed again. "If it please m'lady." He turned and snapped his fingers. What few guardsmen remained filed out of the inner temple through the polished cedar doors, the spurs of their boots clicking against the marble tile floor. Even the crossbowmen in the gallery above fell back into the shadows. It was customary for the Silver Guards to remain unseen whilst royalty worshipped at the feet of Laijon.

Once the two massive doors were closed and no Silver Guards were left in the temple, Tala's gaze flew to the top of the statue's head and the discolored patch on the wreath above. She couldn't figure how someone could have changed the coloration of that leaf so high up. How could one remain unseen by those who came to worship at the feet of the statue every day all hours of the day? Yet someone had. *The Bloodwood*. There it was. The object she sought, yet impossible to get.

"What are you staring at?" Lindholf asked, eyes trained upward, voice echoing through the dome.

"The note." Tala pointed, voice hushed. "Hawkwood left it there. On the wreath. Step back here with me, and you can see it."

"I see it." Glade pointed once he stood beside her. "One of the petals is duller than the rest. What of it?" he chuckled. "You think that's your message from Hawkwood?" He began spinning the chain-mace toy Seita had given him deftly with his wrists, the two small balls just a blur to Tala as they whirled around on the chain, making a low humming noise. She had seen Glade do some interesting tricks with the toy lately, but to Tala, now, here next to the Laijon statue, was neither the time nor the place.

"Put that away," she said.

"It relaxes me."

"It makes too much noise. You'll bring the Silver Guard back."

"Why leave the note up so high?" Lindholf asked in a whisper. "It's impossible to get at now."

"You can climb for it." Glade laughed.

Lindholf stepped back toward the statue and hopped over the rope barrier.

"Cool your coals." Glade stopped spinning his ball mace. "I was only joking. The crossbowmen may still be on the balcony."

"The guards dare not look," Lindholf said. "They fear getting caught watching those of royal blood pray at the feet of Laijon. It will be quite safe to scale the statue unseen." He was literally beaming at the idea of climbing the statue.

"I don't know," Tala said. "Do you think you can?"

"Indeed."

"Far be it for me to object to the desires of the king's sister," Glade said, looking at her. "But I think you're going a bit too far this time."

"Bullocks," Lindholf said. "I thought you were one for adventure, Glade." He turned to Tala and bowed. "I insist on retrieving Hawkwood's note for you, m'lady."

"The consequences be upon you, Lindholf," Glade ceded with a grunt. "But I'll take no part in desecrating Laijon's likeness."

Tala was stung by Glade's refusal to help. She nodded at Lindholf to proceed. He had been doing everything she'd asked almost to the point of doting. Not that she minded all that much. If only some of his enthusiasm could rub off on Glade. She felt a trifle guilty, realizing she had conned the two into this adventure by telling them it was a note from Hawkwood they sought. She had even convinced the Silver Guard into escorting her to the temple to pray. Escorting a group of royals into the city was no small undertaking.

And how would she explain to Lindholf what he might truly find up there? *Oh, it's nothing, Lindholf, just a note from an assassin who has poisoned your sister.*

Lindholf scooted around the ox and cauldron and climbed the ten-foot-high tiered dais. Once on the dais, he scrambled atop the statue's foot and jumped. He grabbed one of the bottom links of carved chain mail that hung below the statue's knees and nimbly pulled himself up. Soon he was scaling the links of Laijon's armor as easily as one would climb a ladder. Candlelight played eerily through the empty dome now, and the flicker of red and gold light danced over the chain-mail links that her cousin scaled.

Tala looked back at Glade. He was no longer by her side but now leaning against a carved stone arch supporting the gallery some distance away. He'd put away his chain-mace toy and nonchalantly straightened his mussed-up hair as he watched Lindholf.

Tala tried to concentrate on the progress of her cousin, yet in reality, she couldn't. Her thoughts were fixed on Glade now. How could he be so infuriating sometimes and other times so charming? Though her eyes were trained upward at Lindholf, her every sense was tuned to the dashing lordling behind her. Having him there was almost like standing with her back to a burning hearth. Every slight movement he made prickled her ears and sent goose bumps racing over her arms. *Why am I so obsessed?* It seemed awfully court-girlish for sure. She was practically betrothed to the boy. She needn't act so flustered around him. As a princess of Amadon, it was she who held the upper hand in the relationship. Still, she found herself most nights lying in bed, thinking about those fierce dark eyes of his. But just what sort of young man there might be behind those eyes remained a puzzle. At times Glade could be so happy-go-lucky and full of enormous bouts of joy—especially when they'd been kids. Other times, especially as they'd grown older, he appeared too determined, conceited, and not in the least friendly.

She glanced back at him and his dark eyes met hers. She turned, blushing.

A yelp came from Lindholf. Her eyes darted upward. Her cousin had slipped, but caught himself, dangling by one hand from Laijon's shoulder, clinging to a carved link of chain mail. But he gathered himself and was climbing again. If he were to fall, Tala would never forgive herself. She felt as if her heart was squeezing itself through her lungs. Soon Lindholf was perched fifty feet up, atop the left shoulder of Laijon. There was hardly room for him as he clung to the side of the great One and Only's head, which from neck to crown was taller than him.

Lindholf stretched for the discolored petal on the wreath above Laijon's forehead. But it was just out of reach. Tala's heart snuck up her throat as her cousin gained a foothold in Laijon's ear hole. Still, he had to cling to the top of the statue's ear as he reached around the forehead of Laijon. Lindholf stretched and strained, fingers coming ever closer to the prize. Glade was standing beside Tala now—she noticed his eyes were now glued to Lindholf as her cousin inched his outstretched fingers farther and farther. . . .

"He got it," Glade said, a smile playing about the corner of his mouth. Tala looked from Glade back up at Lindholf. Her cousin had the petal in hand. He began climbing down, his descent a bit slower than his climb. Pride swelled within Tala. Lindholf had made a good account of himself today. Soon he was scuttling down the raised dais and walking toward her.

The strain of climbing had left him a tad purple-faced as he stood there flushed and disheveled, his hair all a-tangle, scarred forehead and cheeks a red rash. He also looked a bit disappointed as he held the cream-colored parchment out for her to take. "There's nothing on it," he announced.

Tala turned the slip of parchment over and over in her hands. It was blank.

"Naught but some bit of garbage blown in by the breeze." Glade's eyes blazed like black jewels in the candlelight. "You've put us at risk for nothing, Tala. No more of your wild-goose chases. No more of these silly girlish games."

Glade's words caused her a momentary pang of heartache.

And something had also set Lindholf into a spell of blackness. For some reason the abrupt turn in Lindholf's demeanor concerned Tala more than the blankness of the parchment. His eyes kept returning to the crown of heather atop Laijon's head. In fact, something dark was growing behind Lindholf's eyes as he spoke. "Glade is right. It's not exactly part of the Dayknight training, strictly speaking, to climb the Laijon statue."

"The entire thing is loopy," Glade said, disgust underlying his words. "Bloody Mother Mia. Let's just get out of here." And he marched for the doors.

The clacking of his boots against the tile floor pounded through Tala's head. She wanted to crumple the offending slip of paper into a wad and throw it away or rush over to one of the many rows of candles and just burn it, let the flame devour the useless thing.

Then she remembered something. *It's so obvious!* The note the Bloodwood had left pinned to her bedroom stool the night Lawri was stabbed was written in an ink that, in time, would slowly fade.

She studied the blank paper in her hand. *Yes!* Her heart soared. There was something written there all right. She just couldn't see it yet.

† † † † †

Tala was in the secret ways again. She held the candle out before her, hands quivering. Despite the flickering flame that lit her way, the corridor shrouded her in its dark embrace. The words of the assassin's note were burned into her brain.

> *Your next task is to get both Glade Chaparral and Lindholf*
> *Le Graven to kiss you at the final night of the Mourning*
> *Moon Celebration. No peck on the cheek. But a real kiss.*
> *Do this and your next clue to finding Lawri's antidote*
> *will be revealed.*

The request seemed so childish. Sure, she would love to kiss Glade—that is, if he were to kiss her first. Yet to act the aggressor, that was a different pill to swallow indeed. But Lindholf, her own blood relative—it was disgraceful.

After returning from the temple, Tala had bid good-bye to Glade and Lindholf and made her way through the secret passages to Roguemoore's private chambers, hoping he wasn't there. It was a familiar route she'd traveled often. Her excitement at possibly deciphering the note had her stalking the secret ways again like a hungry cat. Once at her destination, she'd pushed her way through a square block in the wall near the dwarf's writing desk, then searched his belongings, which were scattered about the room—a room that appeared to have been ransacked recently, by either the Silver Guard, the Dayknights, or Jovan himself; she didn't want to hazard a guess. But she certainly didn't want the dwarf to blame her for it, wherever he was. She wanted to find what she came for quickly.

She'd found the small round tin she was looking for concealed in a hidden pocket of a leather pouch tossed carelessly into the corner of the room. Tala had seen the dwarf digging through the hidden pocket before. She prided herself on being observant like that. *Like when I found the secret panel in Jondralyn's bookshelf years ago and read all the little love notes Squireck Van Hester had given her over the years.* After opening the tin, she'd dipped her fingers into the black powder and then rubbed her fingers over the piece of paper. *Ink from the squid of the Sør Sevier Straits,* the dwarf had said. *Rare and expensive. The ink fades quickly but the writing remains intact.* Soon, through the smeared black powder, the assassin's words were legible again, though barely.

After slipping it into her pocket, she had left the dwarf's room the same way she'd entered, sick at the thought of having to kiss Lindholf. But she needed to put all thoughts of kissing anyone out of her mind and concentrate on getting back to her room. There was still an assassin lurking about the castle—a Bloodwood assassin from Sør Sevier, a Bloodwood who had chosen to play a dangerous game with her. So she focused on her path, guiding herself almost by sheer instinct through every twist and turn and secret doorway along her dark route. Perhaps she was being followed to her room right now, perhaps not. Of course, the assassin already knew where her room was. The assassin was one step ahead of her at all times. In fact, the entire affair was approaching the point of being ridiculous. *Kiss Glade and Lindholf? Of all the stupid things!* Yet here she was, playing this silly game with one of the trickiest and deadliest creatures alive. It excited her. And it made her feel guilty, too. Lawri was sick and it was all her fault. But it was Lawri's illness and dementia that convinced her that the game was real.

As if touched by a breath of cold air, the tiny flame of her candle flickered and went out. Cursing, Tala snatched the flint from her purse and relit the wick. It danced about in the soft breeze and she shielded it, walking slowly toward the iron door in front of her. She twisted the door's handle, only to find it stuck. She tugged at the handle again, harder this time, but no luck. Some doors had the habit of locking into place. She knew another route, a branching corridor about thirty paces back that would take her to the long hallway that would empty her out into the castle's armory. From the armory there were several other passages that would lead back to her chambers. It would take longer to get to her room that way, but she had no other choice.

Keeping the flickering light of her candle under the palm of her hand, she retraced her steps. It wasn't long before she found the inter-section she wanted. There was a crumbling, white-plastered wall to her right and a vast dark hollow of wood beams and pillars to her left that stretched into the unknown. The velvet shadows lurking about the dark forest of wood stretching away into the blackness gave her a fright. She hustled her step. A musty smell of mice droppings and moldering wood flooded the air. She came to an area where scattered rays of light rose from cracks in the floor. At one point she thought she might have heard the grand vicar's voice coming from below. Curious, she slowed her pace, ears trained for any sound. And there it was, a muffled voice from below. The excitement she felt at listening in on a secret conversations grew within her. She continued on, wary, ears alert, stepping lightly, the cracks in the floor growing bigger and the light beaming up brighter.

Her candle flickered out. Suddenly there was a hollowness in the pit of her stomach. She could feel a prickling danger in the air. There was a faint *clink, clink, clink* just at the edge of her hearing. She stopped, concentrated her gaze, looking for a reflection, a glint of movement, a hooded figure, trying to let no black niche or shadowy alcove escape her scrutiny. There were over a dozen tiny shards of light shooting up from the floor around her, but none bright enough to illuminate her surroundings.

She felt the icy tip of the blade at her throat. A voice spoke in a soft rasp. "I warned you to stay out of the secret ways."

Tala dropped the candle. Before her was a shadow that devoured what little light there was. There was an unsettling quiver in her voice as she spoke. "You knew I'd use the passages to get to Roguemoore's rooms unseen. You knew I had to find his black powder to decipher your note."

"Heed my words." The voice was now tinged with malice. "Do not venture here again, unless I specifically tell you to do so."

"And how will you tell me?"

"By the notes I leave you, girl." The voice carried a hiss of anger, the blade at her throat pressing in.

"Have you infected Lawri with the plague?" Tala asked.

"No." There was soft amusement in the voice. "Not the plague. But like the plague, through affliction comes transformation."

"What have you poisoned her with? Why?"

"You are both being prepared, Lawri for her task, you for yours. Everything has a purpose, my dear princess. Every task you complete serves a purpose in a much bigger plan—a plan that's been in the works for centuries."

"Prepared? Tasks?" Tala was even more confused, but felt some courage build within her. "What if I don't want to be a part of this plan? What if I decide not to play your game?"

"But you *want* to play my game," the voice said matter-of-factly, the icy blade at her throat now easing away slightly. "You *want* to complete the next task. I know you."

"You know nothing of me."

"I know that Borden's brood is a fickle lot, spoiled to the last." There was a mocking, almost lilting tone to those words. "And both of his daughters willing to fall for any reckless rogue or harebrained scheme—"

In one rapid motion, Tala took a step back and clapped. She felt the palm of her right hand connect with the back of the Bloodwood's gloved hand and the palm of her left connect with the boiled-leather wrapping of the inner wrist. The move was executed exactly as Seita had taught her, and the dagger spun free. Tala heard it clatter to the wood floor ten paces away.

"You fool," the assassin said, but the voice came as if from a great distance.

There was nobody in front of Tala now. Somehow, she knew that she was alone again—the Bloodwood was gone. Her heart thundered as she dropped to her hands and knees, trying to catch her breath. She crawled to where she thought the Bloodwood's knife had landed, hands groping at the floor, searching, her palms now a filthy mix of sweat and dust. She found the blade and clutched it to her chest with both hands as if having just discovered a great treasure. *A Bloodwood dagger!* her mind screamed. She could feel her heart pounding against her own clenched hands.

"You are being prepared, young one." It was the grand vicar's voice. She heard it clearly. Her heart, once thundering in her chest, now stopped cold. "Being prepared to stand in glory at the side of the most holy of Laijon's servants."

The vicar's voice was coming from somewhere below. Tala leaned toward the few thin slivers of light sifting up through spaces between the wood planks and beams under her knees. She put her eye to each shard of light, searching for a knothole or crack, searching for one just big enough to get a clear view. The grand vicar spoke in hushed tones. "Everything I do for you is in preparation for Laijon's return."

Tala found a wide enough crack—the burrowing and nibbling of mice had created an uneven crevasse between the beam and joist, forming a hole just big enough. She pressed her face to the dusty floor.

What she saw froze her blood.

She was looking straight down upon her cousin Lawri's bed-chamber, a small room with a high ceiling. Tala's perch was perhaps twenty or more feet above the room.

Thick woolen rugs covered the stone floor of her cousin's room.

There was an armoire against one wall, several stools and a velvet-cushioned chair in one shadowy corner, and a table and bench in the other; a fire crackled in the hearth. Lawri's bed, draped in a wine-red velvet quilt and satin pillows, was directly under Tala. The four ornately carved bedposts of gold-inlaid wood stared straight up at her.

And Lawri was lying on her back in the center of the bed.

Her eyes were closed . . .

. . . and she was naked.

Grand Vicar Denarius knelt on the floor at the side of Lawri's bed. He was now muttering incantations, the words of which were indiscernible. He held a bull-horn flask of consecrated oil at an angle over the girl's still form as he prayed, the amber-colored liquid slowly dribbling from the flask over Lawri's pale skin. Tala wanted to look away, for many reasons, but mostly because she knew that what she was doing was wrong—sinful. She had crossed a line here. Spying in the secret ways seemed like harmless fun. But this was different. This was spying on the private ministrations of the grand vicar—spying on Laijon's holy prophet. If she were caught, it could mean her death. Then there was Lawri—she looked so helpless, so vulnerable, so sick and alone and naked. . . .

Tala kept her eye to the hole. Denarius corked the bull-horn flask, set it aside, and with one puffy hand, rubbed the oil over Lawri's flesh, touching legs, stomach, forehead, her breasts—

—Tala jerked away from the scene, eyes blurred, tears flowing.

I don't want him touching me! Lawri had shouted earlier that day at the arena.

In the fog that clouded Tala's mind, one thing now glowed with certainty—the assassin had planned it all. The Bloodwood had planned that she would be at this spot at this time and witness this very scene.

We can say, "O cursed the day when Laijon was falsely enslaved." Yet we must not. For his slavery had been foretold on totem and standing-stone alike. For it was within the filth of enslavement that Laijon met his four companions, villainous rogues each—Princess, Gladiator, Assassin, and Thief. And together they became as one. Together they became the Five Warrior Angels.
—THE WAY AND TRUTH OF LAIJON

CHAPTER TWENTY-TWO

NAIL

4TH DAY OF THE MOURNING MOON, 999TH YEAR OF LAIJON

GALLOWS HAVEN, GUL KANA

I t was near dawn. A few birds were beginning to make noise outside the tent. But Nail could scarcely hear them. Not far from where he sat, hunched over, head hanging, clumps of blond hair partly veiling his eyes, there was an erratic yet constant crying. Each harsh wail and muffled sniffle sent a peal of agony through his brain. He shut his eyes, but that brought only a small measure of relief so he opened them again.

"Bloody Mother Mia," Jenko Bruk snarled from somewhere in the darkness. "Cork it already, you whiny bitch."

"She's only frightened." The sound of Stefan's voice was weak and didn't carry far. "You must be quiet, Gisela, lest the guards come back in here. The worst is over."

Gisela Barnwell continued sobbing. She put her face into the

crook of Stefan's chest and arm, melting into him. That stifled her sobs some. Stefan laid a soft kiss on top of her head. Still she cried.

"Bloody rotted angels almighty, I can still hear the bitch," Jenko hissed.

"Leave her be," Stefan snapped. "Her family is dead. She saw them killed."

"We all saw death today," Jenko's voice rasped. "But none of you had to do what I did. I had it the worst." The baron's son was silent for a time. Then he angrily snarled, "None of us have slept 'cause of her damn blathering."

Nail closed his eyes again and forced them to stay that way. He also wished Gisela would quiet down. But he wasn't sure if he could voice his opinion without slurring his speech or fumbling the words or just plain fainting. His memories were slowly returning, but they were unreal and difficult to sort through. In those few bleary instants of coherency were fleeting memories of the siege of Gallows Haven and its aftermath: Bishop Tolbret's guts in the sea, Tylda Egbert stabbed in the throat, Baron Bruk screaming. He recalled the tattooed face of the red-haired giant who had slapped the helm from his head. And even worse, he remembered the face of the young Sør Sevier knight with the braided hair and dark war paint under his eyes, the one who had struck him down on the beach. He feared the inescapable images were forever seared into his brain.

His hair was still caked with dried blood. His head ached with a dull throb. The wound on his scalp, he imagined, was raw. He had to fight back the urge to reach up and feel it. Even if he tried, he wouldn't be able to. His hands were secured tightly behind his back with coarse rope, as were everyone's. The ropes were tearing tracks of stinging flesh around his wrists. His feet were bound equally as tight. They ached. He could feel the scorching pain of his newly branded wrist. And his vision wavered in and out. The lucid moments were growing fewer and further apart. He could no longer count on his instincts and senses to steer his mind right. Any movement sent a lance of pain clean through him. *And the thirst!* His mouth was so dry it burned with each breath. With his throat in such torment, just a swallow of water would work wonders.

"Hands tied or not, I'm just about to strangle you myself, Gisela." Jenko's rough voice filled the tent again. It was clear that the baron's son was not inclined to make anyone's experience in captivity pleasant. "Shut up. Just shut your screeching hole now before I come over there and smash your whiny little face."

Nail opened his eyes and stared into the gloom. Only the faintest of pale moonlight rained in from the small hole in the roof of the tent. The peat fire in the center had died to embers. The tent was scarcely large enough to hold them all. A couple of dozen drab villagers were hunched along the grassy floor, all squashed together like sheep in a pen, all bound hand and foot. The ripe odor of their warm, sweaty bodies was inescapable. Some had soiled themselves. Those who slept were the blessed few, for they could rest despite Gisela's crying. Nail could scarcely make out their faces—some of those nearest him were familiar. But their skin appeared dull and lusterless. Only a few of the faces were touched by the glow of the embers. An old farmer snored softly next to Nail. Thick swaths of dark blood covered the left side of the fellow's rough-spun tunic and breeches. Nail still wore his own pathetic breastplate. Jenko and Stefan were still in their armor too—armor that in comparison to the armor of the Sør Sevier warriors was, to Nail's estimation, complete and absolute shit.

In fact, life was shit. He did not want the morning to come. Baron Bruk had offered him a spot aboard the *Lady Kindly*. And now all of Gallows Haven was gone, dead, the baron's vessel naught but charred wood at the bottom of Gallows Bay. Shawcroft was likely dead. Shot with a crossbow bolt. Trampled by heavy horses.

Gisela Barnwell, former Maiden Blue of the Mourning Moon

Feast, continued to cry on Stefan's shoulder. *Was it just last night that I watched her walk arm in arm from the feast with Stefan, both admiring his new Silver Guard bow? Where was that bow now? Destroyed. Just like everything else good and wholesome.*

The farmer's snoring was taking on a trancelike rhythm, breaking Nail's line of thought. He fixed his eyes on the dampened fire pit and tried to regain focus. He let his awareness of the uncomfortable ground beneath him fall away. "Will they feed us?" he heard Liz Hen Neville ask. His own stomach growled.

"You best pray for your food, you fat pig," Jenko said. "Or better yet, have that fool of a bishop pray for your food."

"How 'bout I shove my fist up your arse," Liz Hen said.

"Fiery dragons take you, bitch."

"No blaspheming," Polly Mott spoke, a feigned strength in her voice. "I won't hear that kind of talk."

"Fiery dragons take you, too, you mole-faced cunt," Jenko said.

"Leave everyone be, Jenko," Stefan said.

"It was you who always talked of leaving for Bainbridge, Stefan. With such talk, you're no better than a deserter. And in the end you ran with the rest."

"I stayed and fought. We all fought. Eventually."

"You ran!"

"Stop bickering." Ava Shay spoke so softly it was barely audible. Her voice sounded like a light fluttering thing in her throat. The sound of it tugged at Nail's heart.

"Stefan fought in the village," Polly Mott said. "May the wraiths take you, Jenko, I saw him. He did not abandon us."

"No. It was Bishop Tolbret who abandoned us," Jenko said, the bitterness in his voice cutting through the darkness like a knife. "This shit-smelling tent is grim testament to our bishop's holy powers." He snorted out a sharp laugh. "It's all empty and false. *The Way and Truth of Laijon.* The Ember Lighting. And that robe Dokie Liddle believed would protect the bishop. He was a fool. Dokie's only usefulness now is to pray Laijon may smite the enemy for us! He made a fool out of the lot of us with his going on about the bishop's priesthood robe. Bloody shit! Got the bishop killed is all he did!"

"The bishop was unworthy in the eyes of Laijon, you clodpole," Liz Hen countered. "Otherwise his silk robe would've protected him. Tolbret should have taken it off and flagellated himself before Laijon, you know, before he was crossbow shot."

"It seems it's the White Prince we ought to worship now, you stupid sow."

"I ought to smother the life out of you, Jenko, for saying such." Liz Hen's voice simmered. "Such foul thinking is wrong in the eyes of Laijon."

"Fuck you, you fat whore," Jenko spat. "And fuck Laijon, too!" The tent was quiet for a moment. Nail took a deep breath, trying to stifle the pain still thrumming through his head. In most ways he agreed with Jenko Bruk. To believe in Laijon was a fool's hope. The entire church could rot for all he cared.

"Laijon struck Dokie Liddle with lightning." Liz Hen's voice cracked the silence. "But it was Bishop Tolbret's blessings that brought him back from near death. But for what? To make us all look like fools? I don't think so. There must be some divine plan in all of this we don't understand yet."

"It was that Sør Sevier woman who made us all look like fools," Jenko said. "Not Dokie Liddle."

"Dokie was unworthy too." Liz Hen's voice was grim. "Full of sin. Otherwise, Laijon would have spared the bishop. They were both sinners, Dokie and Tolbret."

"Dokie swam with sharks and lived. Escaped. You're a fat fool with no logic."

"We are all unworthy," Liz Hen said. "We must come to Laijon with broken hearts and humbled spirits if we wish to be saved." She paused, face gently twisting in concentration as she said, "They sent your father away in a box." Jenko's gaze sharpened at the news. Liz Hen continued, "I saw it with my own eyes. They sent him to Amadon with a message for the Silver Throne. The White Prince said he was going to conquer all of Gul Kana. Said he would kill all who refuse to pray to Raijael."

"See," Jenko muttered. "Who's the true God now?"

"You just bragged of escape not a minute ago," Liz Hen said. "Have you so soon converted to Raijael? You, who chopped off your own father's limbs? Who does such a thing? Who but a traitor?"

"I'm no traitor."

Liz Hen grunted. "The White Prince is capable of marching straight to Amadon and destroying all in his path, Jenko. And it now seems you'll likely be his lackey and errand boy along the way, chopping the limbs from us all. Unless you repent."

Jenko's silence was sobering, but Liz Hen wasn't done. "Make up your mind, Jenko. You're a tough one, right. Which is it? Escape? Or do you wish to become a slave to these scum? It seems you're the only one doing the whining now."

Despite his bonds, the baron's son lunged over the fire pit straight at the red-haired girl. But Liz Hen rolled aside and Jenko landed on nothing. The big girl, now on her back, ankles still tied, kicked Jenko in the ribs as he tried to right himself. Her stout feet and legs were thudding heavily into the armor about his midsection, denting it, punching away his breath. Soon Liz Hen was sitting atop Jenko, his bound wrists caught under his own awkwardly twisted body. The boy was soon struggling for breath under the bulk of the much thicker girl.

"Let him up." Ava Shay was scooting across the tent toward the two. "He can't breathe. You're too fat for him! Let him up!"

Liz Hen eventually let Jenko go. "I told you I could smother you," she said.

Jenko rolled over, coughing and spitting in the dirt. The few who had been asleep were now awake and voicing their complaints about the commotion.

"The White Prince was asking the baron about Shawcroft," Liz Hen said over Jenko's gagging coughs. Her eyes fell on Nail, and they glowed a darkening orange hue from the embers of the fire pit. "He was asking about a boy who lived with Shawcroft."

Jenko grunted, "If they attacked us because of that bastard—"

But Jenko was interrupted by a sound from just outside, and the tent flap sprang open, a swath of moonlight burst in. "Quiet down!" a Sør Sevier guardsman yelled, then punctuated his warning by flashing the cold steel of his sword for all to see before stepping back out. The tent flap closed behind him, blanketing them in darkness. They all listened intently as the guard's heavy boots clomped away, followed by a long moment of silence. With dread, he thought of what Liz Hen had said. *Aeros asked about me!* A lump was growing in his gut, clawing its way up his throat. *Was the death of everyone in Gallows Haven my fault?*

"You're so tough," Liz Hen finally said. "You should have fought that guard, Jenko."

"Shut up and leave me alone."

There was a sudden rustling of canvas opposite the tent's main opening. Then, as if the tent were being torn open from the bottom up, a sliver of moonlight shone in from where the canvas had parted in a pale shard of light. Someone from outside spread the canvas open, and the space was filled with a hulking form. The opening closed, leaving a darkness more powerful than before. Nail felt a sudden rush of fear and dared not shift or stir. No one moved. All was silent.

Nail watched as the shape of a man formed itself out of nothing directly in front of him. It took a moment for him to realize, but it was Shawcroft. *He's alive!*

The man had his thin boning knife in hand, a glinting orange shard in the dying embers of the fire. He crawled behind Nail and began cutting the rope around his wrists. He showed little outward signs of having been shot with a crossbow bolt earlier that day. But Nail could tell his master's face was sickly pale, and he winced in pain when he spoke.

"I had thought you dead," Shawcroft whispered as Nail's hands were freed. "But Dokie Liddle informed me otherwise, bless his soul." He sliced through the rope binding Nail's ankles and handed him the knife. "Take this. You may need it."

With the feel of the knife against his flesh, the last frail threads of Nail's mind caught up with the reality of what was happening—his master was rescuing him.

"Make haste," Shawcroft whispered. "Crawl through the hole in the tent."

Nail's head was pounding with pain, his vision unstable. But what faint light remained in the tent was enough: he could see that there were lines of both pain and worry in his master's ashen face that had not been there the last time he had seen him. He noticed a longbow and quiver of arrows were strapped to Shawcroft's back. Plus, the man again wore at his belt the heavy longsword Nail had taken from him on the battlefield. *He must have found the sword . . . wherever I dropped it.*

"We must go. Now," Shawcroft said.

There came the sound of stifled sobs from somewhere in the tent. It was Gisela again. Knife in hand, Nail scrambled toward her. "No." Shawcroft reached out.

Nail shrugged off his master's grabbing hand. "I must free the others," he hissed, reaching Stefan and Gisela, slicing through their bonds. Shawcroft crawled forward and took both Stefan and Gisela by the hands and stood them up. He guided the two toward the opening in the back of the tent. Nail hacked through Polly Mott's and Liz Hen Neville's bonds next. They scurried away, crawling through the opening too.

Other prisoners were standing now, all aware of the sliced-open part of the tent and the bulky form of Liz Hen shoving her way through it. Everyone hobbled toward the hole, clogging it, making far too much noise.

Nail moved toward Ava Shay. She twisted around, craning her neck, looking back at him. The luminescence of her face in the dim light stole his breath. Her eyes glowed, and he soaked in the sight.

"Hurry," Jenko said, urgency in his voice. "Us next."

There was a flicker of hope in Ava's eyes as she repositioned herself for Nail to cut her bonds, a faint trembling in her straining arms and outstretched hands as they touched his, the feel of her bound hands on his cold flesh like a caress.

"Hurry." The sound of Jenko's voice assaulted him. "What's wrong with you? Hurry. Cut us loose."

Nail looked at the dark form of Jenko hovering just beyond Ava. There were both cold anger and impatience in the older boy's look. Nail's gaze fell upon Ava again, and the look in her eyes betrayed her impatience too. He backed away, Ava's soft hands falling from his. She reached for him. But he scooted farther away. Her eyes locked onto his, questioning, pleading. And by the look that fell over her face, Nail could tell that the girl knew his intent.

Nail slipped the knife into his belt and hurled himself toward the back of the tent, shoving his way through the huddle of villagers there, pulling at them, dragging them out of his way. And when the opening was clear, he scrambled through it toward the gray light of dawn and freedom.

† † † † †

A grim quiet resided outside the tent. The moist, warm air was muted and lifeless. Yet the watery silence didn't last long. The pain in Nail's head thrummed to the rhythm of his now rapidly beating heart, his vision fogging in and out.

Shawcroft pulled him to his feet, pointing him at once toward the dark bulk of the chapel in the distance, shoving him roughly in that direction. Nail almost tripped over a villager who had escaped the tent. The fellow was still bound hand and foot, crawling along the ground. Nail followed the dark forms of Liz Hen, Stefan, Gisela, and Polly Mott in a mad dash toward the chapel. His legs were stiff and he had to force them into action, somehow managing to gather speed.

The ground was littered with bodies in lumps and heaps, all of them Sør Sevier knights. Nail's heart quailed at the sight. At least two dozen dead. It was clear that Shawcroft alone had killed them. Even sorely injured, he had killed all these men. And he'd done it in obvious silence and in a systematic way so as not to strike up a clamor.

The thing was, now Shawcroft scared Nail—scared him deep. *Who was this man? A murderer! A cold killer! His rescuer?*

A man back from the dead . . .

"Escape!" the alarmed voice of a Sør Sevier guard yelled. "Escape!" There was a burst of more frantic shouting, and Nail risked a glance back. Warriors bearing torches spilled around the tent. They muttered curses when they saw their fellow knights on the ground. The villagers, still bound hand and foot outside the tent, were soon stabbed and hacked by swords that flashed in the moonlight.

Shawcroft was running just behind Nail, urging him on. The man hunched in pain as he ran. Then came the sound of barking dogs. It now sounded as if the entire enemy encampment was roused. As his legs churned, Nail sensed they had a decent enough head start on the enemy, though the pain in his head was still a sharp reminder that he too was injured and everything was a half-muddy haze in his mind. The sound of pursuit grew louder, the feet hammering behind closer. His throat pained him with every raw breath. He imagined the entire

Sør Sevier army was swarming behind him like a dark flock of crows. He felt the slender knife slip from his belt and fall to the ground, lost.

Ahead, Liz Hen Neville, despite her bulk, ran as if the wind pushed her. Stefan and Gisela ran beside her. Reaching the cracked-open double doors of the church first, the three of them slipped through. Polly Mott tripped over the wattle-and-daub fence that lined the hardened dirt roadway in front of the chapel. Nail jumped over the fence with ease, Shawcroft right behind him. They both lifted Polly to her feet, Shawcroft pushing her forward. But Polly shoved Shawcroft away with a deranged shout. Soon dogs swarmed around them, barking wildly, feinting and snarling, snapping at their legs. One dog bit the inner flesh of Shawcroft's thigh, tearing a large chunk from it. With a startled shout, the man pulled his black sword and swung at the dog, who danced away.

Nail sprinted the remaining yards to the church. He slipped through the doors. Shawcroft followed, hunching, limping, sword now sheathed. His leggings were bloody and shredded. He slipped inside the building behind Nail.

They turned to help Polly through the doorway. But the mole-faced girl lingered near the fence, disoriented, dogs tearing at her clothes. A Sør Sevier knight closed in on her fast, his long halberd striking with speed and deadly precision. Polly was speared in the back and she fell, dragging the halberd from the knight's hand as she went face-first onto the road and rolled over. Her mouth stretched open in silent agony, and her dirt-smeared face twisted back to look at Nail, one hand reaching out for someone to save her, the other swiping the dirt from her own face, revealing her one legacy, the one thing Nail would forever remember her by, the unsightly mole under her left eye.

Shawcroft put his shoulder to the heavy door and pushed. An arrow thudded into the door just as it closed with a slow grind. Shawcroft reached up and threw down the iron bar, locking it. "We haven't much time before they find another way in." He led the huddled escapees deeper into the dismal church. As they scurried over the tile floor, a crunch and clatter of shattered glass sounded underfoot.

Shawcroft's limp had worsened. Blood poured from the fresh wound in his leg as he walked. He was simultaneously tugging at his ripped pants near the injury. "Where's my knife?" he asked, hand out.

"I lost it when I ran."

Shawcroft nodded and kept moving. As Nail picked his way through the darkness, the charred smell of burnt wood was overwhelming, nauseating. The stench added to the difficulty he was having just remaining upright and coherent. He felt the need to puke. But he was not the only one in dire straits. Gisela Barnwell clung to Stefan, both of them panting. Liz Hen's chest heaved from the exertion of their sprint. Her wide shoulders slumped in resignation, curls of red hair stuck to her damp cheeks. She was sucking in hoarse lungfuls of air in a way that suggested she was near done in. It was Liz Hen who made the first comment on the state of the church. "It's completely ruined," she cried as her eyes cast about the gloom. "Where will the boys ever do their Ember Lighting Rites now?"

Nail had always marveled at the village's great chapel and the muscular carving of Laijon that was hung on the even larger black-painted wooden replica of the Atonement Tree in its center. The craftsmen who'd sculpted the statue had been masters. Once, Nail had harbored dreams of being as good an artisan someday. But now those dreams seemed so far away. The statue of Laijon had been toppled. It rested facedown, smashed on the tile floor, arms broken, torso cracked open. The chains used to pull the statue down were still wrapped about its neck. The thick clumps of horse manure that surrounded the statue were evidence of the foul beasts that had done the work of toppling it. The blackened timbers of the great Laijon tree that had once stood so tall and glorious behind the statue of Laijon littered the floor in smashed, jagged splinters.

A faint light fell from the shattered windows above and illuminated their dismal surroundings, illuminated the violence and desecration visited upon the holy building. The benches of the church, which had been piled against the walls of the chapel and set afire, were now mere jagged remains in a pool of black ash. Some patches of wood still smoldered. Smoke rose here and there in spiraling tendrils. The entire chapel was naught but a tangled mass of burnt and broken destruction. All things the villagers had once considered holy were covered in a layer of soot and foul, burning stench. Nail was most heartsick at the sight of the millions of exposed, glittering shards of stained glass littering the ash-covered floor like colorful jewels.

There were desperate and bewildered looks among Nail's companions as Shawcroft hobbled toward the bishop's altar in the center of the chapel. Blood oozed black and thick from the wound in the burly man's upper thigh.

The altar stone had been removed, something Nail had never considered possible. It lay flat on the floor in front of the altar. What looked like a ladder descended into the altar. "I opened the altar earlier," Shawcroft said. "I feared we might have need of it."

Nail heard a flurry of shouts from outside. Heavy banging began on the barred front doors. Gisela spit out a shriek. Her ever-widening eyes darted about frantically. From the rising clamor, it sounded as if the Sør Sevier army would soon burst through the doors. Nail imagined a horde of hundreds was out there, circling, trampling poor Polly Mott's body underfoot. The image of Polly being speared in the back was a fresh wound in Nail's mind. But he was too drained to feel much sorrow.

"Down the ladder." Shawcroft was helping Stefan climb down into the altar.

Nail stepped forward and leaned over. Concealed within the altar stone were a dark opening and indeed a thin wooden ladder descending straight down into it. A strange orange glow was coming from somewhere below. "The ladder will empty us into a tunnel," Shaw-croft instructed. "There are torches already alight at the bottom. Wait for me. There are many tunnels leading to many unsavory places."

Stefan's face disappeared into the pit as he scurried down the rungs. Shawcroft helped Gisela into the altar next. She descended a tad slower, less steady and sure of herself, eyes glazed with tears.

A flaming arrow sailed through one of the broken windows high above. As it arced into the church, Nail lurched back to avoid being hit. The arrow lit hard on the floor at his feet, its flame dashed in the soot. A second arrow flew in through the dark opening, landing in the shadows of the nave. Nail kept his eyes trained on the black opening above, where the colorful stained glass used to live. He recalled the intricate designs of the windows that had once graced those now vacant holes, angelic images that had once cast graceful shadows of red and blue and green over the congregation. But it was all naught but sprinkled glass under Nail's feet now, the destruction a grim reminder of the evil residing within the heart of the enemy.

Liz Hen descended the ladder next, head disappearing down the hole. Nail lifted his leg over the lip of the altar, finding the top rung with his foot. He heaved his other leg up and over and began his descent. The last image he had of the Gallows Haven chapel was of another flaming arrow arcing through the window, dropping through the smoky haze, smacking into the forehead of the downed statue of Laijon with a flurry of sparks, arrow skittering off into the darkness.

Some claimed Laijon was born of goodly parents and raised in righteousness
from a humble birth by the sea, that he had the powers of heaven bestowed
upon him by angels. Whilst others claimed Laijon could divine where gold
lay hidden in any streambed or cave. Truth is, he led many astray who paid
him for such false divinations. He was deemed a fraud, and for his crimes
was sold him into slavery to rot in the pits of Riven Rock.
—THE CHIVALRIC ILLUMINATIONS OF RAIJAEL

CHAPTER TWENTY-THREE
GAULT AULBREK

4TH DAY OF THE MOURNING MOON, 999TH YEAR OF LAIJON

GALLOWS HAVEN, GUL KANA

W hy were the iron shackles and neck collars not used?"
Aeros asked.

"Some supplies were left on the ships returning to
Wyn Darrè, my lord," captain of the Hound Guard, Rufuc Bradulf,
answered, his pinprick eyes shifty in the half-light of dawn. He stood
over the body of a dead girl in front of the Gallows Haven chapel.
"It's naught but a few escaped peasants," he continued, thin mouth
grinning, bits of food stuck in his rotting teeth. "Plenty such folk
escaped in Wyn Darrè. We paid them no mind."

Aeros Raijael cocked his head, as if in deep contemplation, nodded
once, pulled a thin ivory-handled dirk from the folds of his white
cloak, and handed it to Gault.

Gault took the blade, carefully planted his torch into the ground, then rammed the dirk up under Rufuc's chin and into his brain. Rufuc's body spasmed once, eyes bulging in surprise. He slumped lifeless to the roadway, his mouth still stuck in a dirty grin.

As Gault retrieved his torch, he watched the light die in Rufuc's eyes, then looked away. He just didn't care anymore. It was these ever more frequent passionless moments of coldness that were bothering him. He had grown too familiar with the *Illuminations* ritual of "cleansing of emotions." These past five years of war and death, he had been keeping his heart utterly empty.

He handed the knife back to Aeros. The Angel Prince's enraged eyes roamed over the crowd of Rowdies and Hound Guards and their squires gathered before the chapel. "Has the ease of our first battle in Gul Kana made us lax in our duties, forgetful of our discipline?" His question shot forth angrily. "Why were the prisoners kept so near the edge of camp? Why not closer to the middle?" Nobody answered. "We cannot take our enemy lightly, no matter how crude their weaponry and how inept they seem. Even a mangy dog can kill a knight if it gets lucky." Aeros looked at the corpse lying in a spreading pool of blood at his feet. "The next Hound Guard captain better not prove as sloppy as you, Rufuc."

As far as the Hound Guard went, Aeros usually paid them no more than passing attention. Yet lately he appeared especially bent on berating them as lazy vermin, lower than the squires, naught but a nuisance set to infect the entire might of his army.

Aeros pointed to the dead girl lying in the road by Rufuc. "I want her head on a pike planted at the entrance to the prisoner tent as a warning. Send Rufuc's body home. No pyre will be built for him. We will not honor him with the purging flame of redemption."

Sending Rufuc's body home was a grave insult to his legacy as a warrior. But there was nothing to be done for it; Rufuc had gotten what he deserved. Gault tried to dig any sort of emotion out of himself, but he could not. He held his torch low, examining the dead girl lying beside Rufuc. Even an hour after her death, she was still pretty, one might say, pretty but for the strange mole under one eye. The unfortunately large blemish, Gault surmised, no doubt caused the girl much torment in life. How could it not? Any boy worth his salt would be hard-pressed to overlook such an unsightly splotch on a woman.

Gault followed Aeros through the open doors of the Gallows Haven chapel, stepping into a stench-filled gloom. Aeros' white cloak skimmed across the floor as he walked, stirring the soot, setting it awhirl in smoky spirals behind him. The Angel Prince wore Sky Reaver this morning. Gault examined the black-scorched walls of the church. Everything within the chapel had been eaten by flame. Small fires still licked at the blackened bits of scattered benches and rugs. Acrid smoke lingered, hanging in oily clouds above.

In Sør Sevier, the closest thing one could find to a structure devoted to Laijon were tiny prayer lodges, but those were mere wattle-and-daub, thatch-roofed affairs found only in remote wilderness areas. In Sør Sevier, it was taught, buildings such as this Gallows Haven chapel were for idol worshippers.

Every abbey, chapel, and cathedral in Adin Wyte and Wyn Darrè had been destroyed by Aeros' armies. Gault had taken part in their destruction. But such pointless pillaging left him feeling hollow over time. Aeros promised he would desecrate each place of idol worship in Gul Kana, too. He preached to his armies that the followers of the grand vicar in Amadon were superstitious fools in need of purging. And he would begin by destroying their majestic places of worship and blasphemous statues. He railed against the stupidity of the holy white robes of their bishops and their insane flagellation ceremonies. He claimed their works and flagellations would not save them. Only the grace of Laijon could save one's soul. The followers of Raijael need only study *The Chivalric Illuminations* and believe in Laijon and swear fealty to his rightful heir, Raijael. One was saved by the

Atonement Tree of Laijon, not by Ember Gatherings and works of goodness and flagellation ceremonies and idol worship inside opulent cathedrals.

For Gault's part, he'd seen too much blood and death in the name of both Laijon and Raijael to care much about the intricacies of belief. He still held to what his mother, Princess Evalyn Van Hester of Saint Only, had taught him of religion. No one belief system should be trusted. Her faith had been simple. The weapons and stones of the Five Warrior Angels would one day return to the Five Isles and rid the world of war and sin. And that was what Gault fought for. To see his mother's dream fulfilled. That Aeros might have found one of those stones on the battlefield in Wyn Darrè only added to his inner conflict. Though he admired his lord, he did not believe Aeros Raijael, under any circumstance, could possibly be the one to rid the world of suffering and war. King Aevrett had bred nothing but bloodthirstiness and savagery into his only son.

Enna Spades, Beau Stabler, Hammerfiss, and the Bloodwood were standing near the fallen Laijon statue. Several other Knights of the Blue Sword were milling about the periphery, but the chapel's gloom seemed to swallow them up.

"I take it you were none too impressed with Ser Rufuc's handling of the prisoners," Stabler said, bowing before Aeros.

Aeros' eyes strayed to the rectangular altar in the center of the church. The altar stone had been removed, revealing a hole and ladder.

Spades bowed too. "Poor Rufuc." Her voice drooled false sentiment. "But he was an idiot, a foulmouthed ass-licker. He deserved a knife in the neck. Wish I could have done it myself." To Spades, those of Gul Kana needed to suffer agony at the hands of the brave and righteous warriors of Raijael. And if anyone in the Sør Sevier army didn't see it that way too, well, then, they could be excused from the fighting as politely as Aeros had just excused Rufuc.

"Rufuc was near to earning holdings near Morgandy." Stabler, on the other hand, acted appalled at war's brutality from time to time. "His family will be disappointed to learn of their loss."

"And what of our loss?" Aeros demanded. "This army grows lazy. What news of those who've escaped?"

"Your best trackers already search the corridors under the chapel," Stabler said. "We will soon find where they've gone."

Aeros' eyes narrowed as two armed men entered the church. Gault could tell his lord was in a black mood and would not go gentle with anyone. A deep-rooted tension was in the air. Aeros' eyes cut through the gloom toward the entrance of the chapel.

"Hound Guard from the watch," Stabler said.

The two Hound Guards approached Aeros. They both dropped to one knee before him and, without so much as an ounce of enthusiasm, introduced themselves as Karlos and Alvin. The torchlight was a ruddy glow in the eyes of the two newcomers.

Karlos, the bigger of the two, stood spoke first. "We've news, my lord," he said, eyes nervously traveling back toward the broken doors of the chapel, past the barely visible lump of Rufuc Bradulf outside on the roadway and beyond. The wet sounds of two knights sawing the head from the mole-faced girl's body could be heard. Karlos' heavy-jowled face took on a sunken look. He nervously folded his arms over his protruding belly. The man's bulk accentuated his overly shined armor, which shimmered in the light of Gault's torch.

Aeros looked expectantly at Karlos. The younger one, Alvin, stood and shuffled nervously. He sported a frightened smile of grimy-looking teeth. "They're all dead," he muttered.

"Who's all dead?" Aeros' gaze turned to Alvin.

"The rest of our regiment. The two dozen with us patrolling the town for stragglers and hiding villagers—all killed."

"Killed how?"

"A man," Alvin blurted, "a dangerous man, dangerous like we ain't never seen before. He had a big black sword. Then there was blood all over. Everywhere. Now, I seen plenty of folk die on the battlefield, mind you; I'm used to the blood and whatnot. But there was something brutal in this man's killings. More deadly and evil than even a Bloodwood, I reckon."

"Killed as silent as a Bloodwood too," Karlos added with a worried smile. "I didn't even know what was happenin' till most of our contingent were dead and bleedin' in the dirt."

"It was most certainly Ser Roderic Raybourne they saw." The Bloodwood turned to Aeros. "King Torrence's brother, Shawcroft. I have dealt with him before. Trained as a Dayknight, he is a deadly foe, even for a Bloodwood."

"He looked right at me." Alvin's voice dwindled to a whisper. "He was injured. Arrow shot maybe . . . yet still deadly, like the Spider says. But he vanished, the man did, quick as he come."

"And why did you not rouse the camp immediately," Aeros said, "before he could steal away with my prisoners?"

"We stayed hid in a root cellar." Alvin looked embarrassed.

"Idiots," Hammerfiss piped up. "You should've spoken to this man. You likely coulda knocked him dead with your bloody rotten breath, Karlos. Your information is practically useless."

Both Alvin and Karlos hung their heads, Karlos' sunken eyes traveling to the lump of Rufuc Bradulf still lying in the roadway outside.

Hammerfiss continued. "Your armor is obnoxiously bright, Karlos. Is it your ability to find root cellars to hide in that keeps it so shiny?"

"A tin of pig fat," Karlos said. "I polish my breastplate with it daily."

"Utterly astonishing," Hammerfiss laughed. "Ser Roderic could not have helped but notice that massive hunk of brilliance strapped about your belly. Like the Eastern Star, it illuminates your comings and goings. You'd be less visible if you set your hair afire. Had Ser Roderic killed you and then left your fat body shining away on the road, it would have surely given his location away. I imagine he was happy that you found that root cellar."

"Indeed, as you say, Ser." Karlos bowed.

"Remove that glare from our eyes," Hammerfiss continued. "Never let me see you wearing it again. And furthermore, use that tin of pig fat to grease down your anus. Now that, I'm sure, Alvin will appreciate."

Humiliation scrawled on his mug, Karlos shuffled off. Alvin bowed to Aeros before following on the heels of his shiny companion.

"How is it such daft fools made it into this army?" Spades muttered. "For it seems they cannot even manage the very simplest parts of soldiering."

Aeros Raijael had remained silent throughout the exchange, sheer unbridled annoyance alive in his eyes.

Mancellor Allen brushed by Karlos and Alvin on his way into the chapel. He was a tall fellow not much older than twenty, with braided rows of dirt-colored hair and Wyn Darrè fighting tattoos under his eyes. He had been captured during the initial siege of Ikaboa, but during the course of his captivity he had seen the light of righteousness and was now a true believer in Raijael and a warrior fighting on the side of Sør Sevier. He walked up with confidence, armor clanking, boots clicking, helm lodged in the crook of his arm. He was a newly made Knight of the Blue Sword.

Mancellor acknowledged the presence of the Angel Prince with a formal bow. "I have news for Stabler, if it pleases my lord." Aeros nodded and Mancellor directed his comment to Stabler. "The main tunnel leads to a pond not half a mile away in the foothills of the mountains. The escapees have headed into the hills. They will likely seek shelter in the mountains higher up. I didn't have many men with me, but I did send two Rowdies to follow them. The escapees have left a well-marked trail."

"Good." Stabler turned to Aeros. "They will be tracked down soon, my lord."

"It is not good enough." Aeros aimed his gaze at Spades. "That Ser Roderic risked so much to rescue these few *children* tells me that the boy I seek is with them. I requested each prisoner be accounted for by name."

"That task was fulfilled," Spades said, familiar copper coin dancing between her fingers in her hand held by her side.

Gault could tell she was lying. The *Illuminations* said, *Through the light of the eyes, one can glimpse the soul.* Spades' eyes now sparked nervously, coin moving more rapidly between her fingers.

"Not fulfilled to my satisfaction, it seems." Aeros' ice-colored eyes, as always, remained void of light and feeling.

"There was one who did not name himself." Worry was etched on Spades' face, but also satisfaction. "An injured fellow who seemed delirious. I gave charge to Stabler to interrogate him further." She looked at Stabler coldly.

It was clear from the glint in Stabler's iron-gray eye that he resented Spades' accusation. He smiled, but there was a hard animosity in it.

"You've always boasted of being Sør Sevier's best tracker." Aeros' eyes were fixed on Stabler too. "Take fifty knights and the Bloodwood, join up with the two Rowdies. Follow the escapees for a time. See where they go. See what they carry. But bring them back alive."

Stabler bent his knee to his lord and bowed low. "I will bring them back alive."

"Do so. You know the price for failure."

† † † † †

Standing outside the chapel, Gault breathed in the welcome fresh air. The remaining Hound Guards had stuck the mole-faced girl's head on a stake, then planted the stake into the soft peat just off the hard-packed dirt roadway. A handful of squires were now strapping Rufuc Bradulf's body to a litter bound for whatever pitiful gravesite they could find.

Again, Gault found himself drawn to the girl's face and the blemish there. He resisted the urge to turn away. He felt he was an interloper witnessing her sweetly silent and detached reverie. Her sightless eyes were glued upon the burnt hulk of the church. She had no choice. She could not avert her eyes from the disgrace that had once been her place of sanctuary. A head without a body was always disconcerting to Gault. The drying orb with the dripping neck had once been a talking, breathing, eating entity. Now it just floated in the darkness, silhouetted against pale light of the dawn.

The gray chill of the morning coiled chainlike around Gault.

What if it were the blond girl, Ava Shay's, head on the pike? How would I feel then? He felt the sting of bile working its way up his throat. *It would remind me of my own daughter back home is what it would do.* Sudden sweat was beading on his bald head, and the first hint of a fever sent a shudder through him. His breath came in jerks and his pulse raced. But he refused to be sick. *Of all the horrors I've seen through the years, why is this one severed head on a pole affecting me like this?* His heart ached for the mole-faced girl. *What was her story? Had she a boyfriend? Did he die during the siege? Was she heartbroken at his death? What about her family? Were they dead too?*

He closed his eyes and gained control of his breathing. Over the years he had spent too much time protecting himself from his own compassion—he had to. Warriors were trained not to feel. Sympathy in battle made one hesitate. Hesitation made one die. *Never wish ill on your enemies,* the *Illuminations* read. *Reap it.*

In the end, Gault knew, it was better to see a mole-faced girl's head on a stick than your own.

*On the eventide of their escape from the slave pits, the Five Warrior Angels
gathered in a grove, their hearts open to glory. Angels descended in their
midst, bearing five stones and five mighty gifts: a red stone and a sword for the
Princess, a white stone and a pearl-colored shield for the Thief, a black stone
and a black crossbow for the Assassin, a green stone and a war helm for the
Gladiator, and lastly, a blue stone and a battle-ax for the King of Slaves.*
—THE WAY AND TRUTH OF LAIJON

CHAPTER TWENTY-FOUR

NAIL

4TH DAY OF THE MOURNING MOON, 999TH YEAR OF LAIJON
GALLOWS HAVEN, GUL KANA

The Dead Goat Trail rose up the mountain in a steep twining
path just beyond two towering boulders. Above the two boulders, the tops of the trees were cast in a golden sheen. The sky
was mottled with fire-rimmed clouds. Still, the air was chilled, and
morning dew lay heavy on the ground.

Nail, Stefan, Gisela, and Liz Hen stood between the boulders,
looking down at Shawcroft. The pale-faced man lay against the
stone with a blood-soaked shirt wrapped around his upper leg. Blood
flowed freely from the dog bite. His leather breeches were sopping
red. For the group of escapees, it had been a panicked flight from the
tunnels under the chapel to this point at the foot of the Dead Goat
Trail. Enemy knights had been swarming the landscape, searching.

It wasn't until now that Nail really took notice of the black longsword on Shawcroft's lap and the bow and quiver full of arrows there too. It was similar to Baron Bruk's sword. There was that same black opal on the sword's pommel. Its naked blade ran thick with congealed blood. Shawcroft also carried his leather satchel, its strap thrown over his shoulder. He winced visibly as he unslung the bag. "Of all things, do not lose this satchel, Nail. You must make sure it reaches the Swithen Wells Trail Abbey and Bishop Godwyn."

Shawcroft stood slowly, struggling mightily to do so, sword and bow sliding from his lap to the ground. He draped the satchel's leather strap over Nail's head and tugged on it, making sure it was secure, its flap buckled securely on the side. The Vallè-designed scrollwork inlays stamped into the leather had always fascinated Nail.

Shawcroft picked up his sword. Nail found he could not look away from the blood along its blade. "Aye," Shawcroft said, following Nail's eyes. "Been a long time since I've felt Dayknight steel in my hands. My old sword. I kept it hidden in the eaves of the cabin all these years. A fine-made blade. I thought I'd lost it when you took it from me on that battlefield. I'd thought I'd lost you. But a Dayknight will always be able to find those things most important to him."

Gingerly, Shawcroft picked up the longbow and quiver of arrows, holding them out to Stefan. "Also from the eaves of the cabin. Now yours, Stefan, to make up for the lost Amadon Silver Guard bow. It's a shame you won such a fine weapon at the Mourning Moon Feast, only to lose it in your first battle."

Stefan took the bow. It was elegantly made.

"A Dayknight bow," Shawcroft said. "Made of ash and witch hazel. The most accurate bow ever crafted by the hand of man. Mighty powerful, too."

Stefan strapped the quiver of arrows over his shoulder and tested the bow's grip and tightness. "It's a good bow."

Shawcroft's eyes roamed the forest around them. "I've done a poor job covering our path. I've lost much blood. I won't be able to make it up that trail with this leg. I'm but a liability now. Dog bit. Arrow shot. Dying."

Nail's mind grew numb. But the truth was evident. Blood pooled under his master. Baron Bruk had taught his conscripts that an edged weapon thrust into to a man's throat or heart was a rapid death, and a strike to an armpit or inner thigh would bleed a man out quickly. And judging from Shawcroft's pallid face, Nail could now see that the bite of a dog could accomplish the same thing as a well-honed blade. The dog bite had accomplished more than the crossbow bolt from the red-haired witch woman who plied the slaver's brand. His heart grew faint.

"It was good I found Dokie Liddle and Zane Neville wandering the hillside near the cabin after the Sør Sevier invasion," Shawcroft said, eyes still on Nail. "Even as injured as they are, they helped load food and supplies onto Bedford Boy and Lilly. I sent them up the trail in the middle of the night with the ponies. I bade them wait for us at the top of the trail in the meadow near the old ruins. I hope they listened and did not become spooked. Sometimes one must place trust in others, as I did in them. Both are brave boys, I suspect. Though Zane is grievous injured—"

"What's happened to my brother?" Liz Hen blurted. "Aeros asked about you and Nail," she continued rapidly. "Why? What's going on?"

"Never mind that." Shawcroft cocked his head to the side as if listening to the wind. Nail's eyes darted into the forest. The leaves of the trees were thick with dew. He could feel the blood rush to his head. His vision wavered and something black swooped past his eyes. He tried focusing on the two boulders flanking the path beyond Shawcroft. He'd heard tell a man could be touched by the wraiths after a serious head injury. And he had taken a wicked blow during the battle, which had addled him to the point where he now imagined his skull was cracked. *Could the wraiths squeeze in?*

He found Liz Hen was glaring at him. He turned to Shawcroft and asked, "Did they really sack Gallows Haven because of me, because of us?"

"Shhhh." Shawcroft waved the question away. "From the sound of heavy hooves, I figure the knights bearing down on us number around fifty, all on horseback, palfreys from the sound of it, lightly armored for fast travel. Dogs travel with them. We may have but ten minutes before they get here." He pointed to the east, up the steep trail. Almost a hundred feet above, clinging to the craggy slope, was a tall, swooping pine. Shawcroft turned his hardened gaze to Stefan. "By the time you reach that tree, the knights should be upon me. Use the bow; kill as many as you can."

"I can't," Stefan mumbled, eyes darting between Gisela and Shawcroft.

"You have the skill," Shawcroft said.

"It's not my skill with a bow that worries me." A fearful look fell over Stefan like a shroud. "It's just"—he paused—"I've never killed a man before."

Shawcroft, his face a chunk of stone, pulled Stefan close and looked him square in the eye. "The power to kill is the only power that matters now, boy." He poked a thick finger roughly at the rusty iron armor over Stefan's stomach. "Despite what armor a man wears, always aim for his belly. His gut is vulnerable, naught but skin and water and precious little else. One arrow to the stomach and a man's done. Got it? I heard tell you were good at killing merfolk. This is no different."

Stefan gulped and nodded at the same time, his eyes roaming back up toward the pine clinging to the ragged slope.

"That trail is steep, narrow, difficult for horse and rider," Shawcroft said. "They may have to dismount and guide their horses if they wish to follow you. I can only hold them at bay so long. Once they are past me, they will most assuredly follow you."

Shawcroft's piercing gaze was now focused on Nail. "You know these mountains. You know each vale and standing-stone. You've panned every stream and hiked every trail, ofttimes alone. You can see the others to safety. They are each one your friends."

Nail was at once bolstered and confused by his master's praise. Shawcroft looked at him squarely, unwaveringly. "You are harder, tougher, smarter than most men. It is how I raised you. You saved Zane from the sharks. There is nothing more brave than to save a life." Then his face dropped. "But you can also take life, son. And there can be bravery found in that, too. If any lag behind, you'll have to leave them in the mountains. Remember Radish Biter. Though they hide it, Dokie and Zane are sorely wounded. I'm afraid Zane won't make it far. You must reach Bishop Godwyn above all else."

"What do you mean?" Liz Hen asked. "What's happened to my brother?"

Shawcroft slumped to the ground, his face drooping even more.

The man had called him *son.* It was the first and only time Nail had ever heard that word directed at him. He reached down to lift his master up.

But Shawcroft brushed his hands away. "Follow the Dead Goat Trail. Do not dawdle. Do not leave the main road. Go to the small cabin by the Written Wall. I've stashed torches and two more quivers of arrows for you there. Take the Hot Springs Notch behind the cabin to the Roahm Mines. Don't forget the scarves. They are in Lilly's pack. You know how skittish the ponies can be in the mines if their eyes are not covered. Once in the mines, make your way to the bridge. You remember the bridge, don't you?"

Nail nodded in answer. Yes, he knew the way to the bridge over the chasm—the dark hole deep in the mountain that had no bottom.

"I once told you that bridge was too dangerous to cross," Shawcroft said. "But heed me now. It is quite safe. And today you must cross it. Beyond the bridge is an underground pool. The Place of the Skulls— you will know it when you see it. Beyond the pool is a wide hall- way. You will find a set of stairs carved into the right-hand wall of the hallway. They lead up to an empty tomb. The way is mostly clear. "If you see silver fluid dripping from the walls, do not touch it." I've already dismantled most of whatever traps were set around the place. But first—the third step up, far left stone, push it in but an inch, and the rest of the stairway above will be free of traps. Once at the top, remove the altar stone in the center of the tomb. There you will find two items. I dared not take them from their resting place myself. I fear that task has now fallen to you. Once you have the items, descend the stairway from the tomb and continue down the wide hallway. It leads upward. Avoid all other staircases and ladders. Stick to the hallway. You will eventually come out on the northeastern range just below the Swithen Wells Trail. You know the trail. Follow it to the abbey. You remember Bishop Godwyn from the abbey, don't you?"

Nail nodded somberly. Bishop Hugh Godwyn was the old hermit who lived alone in the Swithen Wells Trail Abbey. Shawcroft and Nail had visited the man a few times.

Shawcroft said, "Godwyn will lead you to Lord's Point and then—"

"Lord's Point," Liz Hen blurted. "Why Lord's Point?"

"What will we find in the altar stone?" Nail asked.

Shawcroft's brow furrowed. "Best you not know until you reach the altar, lest you are captured. Many things are found hidden beneath the ground. Men and kings and ancient warriors and the weapons they forged. All are eventually buried. Ages pass and important truths are hidden, forgotten. Yet most men never look beyond the surface of their farms and forests and within their own castle walls for knowledge. But those who search the deep . . . find salvation."

There was now the clear rumble of hooves pounding and dogs barking in the distance. "Remember your stances, Nail," Shawcroft added. "Remember your footwork, the way you swing a pick. And don't forget the backswing. Rake with both hands tight. The precision of all I taught—it is now a part of you. It all matters." Shawcroft pointed up the Dead Goat Trail. "Now go."

✝   ✝   ✝   ✝   ✝

They were all four winded when they reached the pine tree. Liz Hen and Gisela slumped in exhaustion. Nail leaned against the tree to catch his breath. The pine was skirted with damp green moss about its northern base, but firmly planted into the steep slope. Stefan peered over the edge of a lichen-covered boulder near the tree.

From where they stood, almost two hundred feet above the sea, a clear view of the town below was revealed. Wispy threads of smoke were rising from the vast Sør Sevier encampment north of town. Parts of Gallows Haven still smoldered. The Grayken Spear was a husk of burnt rubble. The *Lady Kindly* was sunk in the bay, naught but a dark skeleton of char and ash just visible under the water. Piles of bodies burned on the beach. The village dead would never receive proper funeral rites, Nail realized, never be committed to the ground to be buried with respect, their heads propped up in their graves with dignity, their eyes facing east as was custom. It saddened him.

But there was a more immediate threat just below. The mounted Sør Sevier knights had reached the two boulders that marked the Dead Goat trailhead. The barking of many dogs and the clatter and thunder of the horses' steel-shod hooves echoed up the craggy slope. Shawcroft had been right: Nail counted around fifty mounted knights, all of them wearing light leather armor, some clad in simple breastplates; very few wore helmets. Their palfreys were unarmored too, smaller than the gruesome chargers they'd ridden yesterday. Still, these men and the beasts they rode were built for killing and death. *How could the villagers not have seen that yestermorn? Why didn't they all just run for the hills at the first sighting of the warships?*

Sunlight bled through the trees and pooled on the Dead Goat Trail around Shawcroft. A lump found its way into Nail's throat; it grew as he watched his master awaiting death. The approaching knights were formed in several columns. At the head of the middle column rode a dark-haired, bearded man in a mail shirt with a patch over his right eye, the only knight on a tall white charger. He reined his steed sharply as he reached the two boulders, as did the knights behind him. With a shout, the one-eyed knight silenced the dogs. The notch between the boulders was not wide, perhaps enough for a wagon to pass through, but that was all. The knights waited before it.

From so high up, the words exchanged between Shawcroft and the knight with the eye patch were indistinguishable, but Nail got the gist of the conversation when Shawcroft braced his stance and brandished his sword. One of the knights lowered his spear and set heels to flanks and plunged his steed through the notch at a breakneck pace.

Shawcroft easily dodged the low-hung spear. He stabbed his sword into the chest of the speeding palfrey, pulled his weapon free, and swung high, decapitating the falling rider as the horse folded to the ground, dead.

Shawcroft's rapid dispatch of the first knight sent a ripple through the other Sør Sevier men. Their eye-patched leader sent another knight through the notch. Shawcroft killed that man and horse too. Again Nail was taken aback with both shock and, dare he admit, pride at how good his master was with a sword. Even sorely injured, Shawcroft was a deadly fighter. And there was something indefinably familiar in the way his master was fighting.

Nail glanced at Stefan. His friend placed the quiver of arrows on the rock before him, then unstrapped his armor. Stefan wore a threadbare, sleeveless tunic underneath. He picked up the Dayknight bow and flexed it once, twice, testing its tightness, fear in his eyes.

Below, the leader of the Sør Sevier knights made a sweeping motion with his arm, and twenty of his fellow fighters dismounted. They drew their swords and rushed through the notch at Shawcroft. He fought off the initial surge, killing some, knocking others to the ground, his sword a whirling steel curtain before him. More knights poured through the gap, barking dogs on their heels.

Stefan nocked an arrow. His muscles strained as he pulled back on the bow, the knuckles on his fingers whitening as he held the arrow in place. Jubal Bruk had once taught the boys the exact drop of an arrow in fifty-foot increments. But from so high up, it was the distance that was uncertain; that and the steep angle rendered the arrow's drop and all of Jubal's lessons moot. The updraft rising from the trail might give the arrow lift. Stefan appeared to be calculating such things in his mind as he sighted down the shaft.

Moments passed. Nail willed his friend to fire. Shawcroft was fighting for their lives down below. Still, Stefan hesitated. Nail needed only look at the throbbing veins on Stefan's neck and the sweat forming on his forehead to know that his friend was scared.

"Shoot the bastards already," Liz Hen urged through clenched teeth.

Stefan let the arrow fly. It zoomed away, plummeting over a hundred feet in the blink of an eye. The arrow caromed off one of the tall boulders below and caught one knight in the hind part of his leg, dropping him. Stefan nocked another arrow, sighted down the shaft, and fired again. His second arrow sailed true, hitting the knight nearest Shawcroft. The force of the impact plunged the arrow into the fighter's breastplate, hurling him to the ground. Liz Hen yelped in triumph. After that second shot flew true, Stefan leaned and spat, nocked another arrow, and fired again, striking another knight in the stomach. He plucked the next arrow from his quiver with more confidence and let it fly. It struck a knight about to stab at Shawcroft. The knight released his hold on the sword, clawing at the arrow now buried in his arm.

More than a handful of Sør Sevier knights now littered the ground at Shawcroft's feet. And Nail could tell that his master now fought with more vigor. Shawcroft's initial surge of energy seemed bolstered further by the sight of the many dead around him.

Stefan continued to launch shaft after shaft down into the fray. Several knights were now pointing with their swords up toward the source of the arrows. Soon the knights began loosing arrows of their own. But their arrows lost speed and fell against the mountain far short of Nail's perch.

A big gray dog, much bigger than the rest, darted through the notch far below and tore into the face of a knight at Shawcroft's flank. "It's Beer Mug!" Liz Hen yelled. "Zane's dog's down there!" The dog leaped from knight to knight in a snarling streak, ripping at throats, hamstringing legs. The dogs belonging to the knights leaped and bounded at Beer Mug, trying to bring the larger dog down. Yet Beer Mug was a brute, big and fast, shrugging off the smaller dogs as if they were of no account. Soon the knights and dogs backed off, leaving Nail's master and Beer Mug standing alone among the dead.

The fighting stopped, and Nail wondered if his master might indeed prevail.

That was when the man in black leather arrived and slid from his ink-black stallion. *A Bloodwood!* Nail's mind reeled. The man sauntered confidently through the milling knights and straight between the cleft of the boulders. His red-eyed steed, like a sinister statue, remained rooted in place. The man walked right up before Shawcroft and Beer Mug and stood there. Confident. Cool.

A few muffled words were exchanged between Shawcroft and the newcomer.

There was a brief moment of stillness . . . and then the lithe darkness struck. Like black lightning, blades with the glimmer of midnight. So fast was the man, Beer Mug had no chance to react to the whirl of movement and flickering daggers.

Nail didn't fully see it, but Shawcroft fell to his knees, arms and torso crisscrossed with many red, welling wounds. Beer Mug darted backward with a sharp bark that echoed up the cliff. The fiend in black backed away from the dog.

Stefan fired his last arrow. It smacked into the leather-armored shoulder of the black-clad Bloodwood and glanced away harmlessly. The man looked up the cliff face once, nodded toward Nail, Stefan, Gisela, and Liz Hen, then stepped forward and plunged his final dagger deep into Shawcroft's chest. The blade tore a bloody path downward through Shawcroft's stomach, ripping him open.

Nail's master folded sideways to the ground, coming to rest on his back. Beer Mug sniffed at Shawcroft whilst the dark killer turned and walked toward his demon steed without a backward glance and rode casually back toward Gallows Haven.

Nail could no longer watch as the remaining knights galloped their mounts through the notch over Shawcroft's body.

"Well, that was something," Stefan said, tears in his eyes. "But your master was right. They'll have a bloody hard time following us up here." A hollow look was on Stefan's face as he gathered his armor. He sprinted up the Dead Goat Trail, Dayknight bow in hand, Liz Hen and Gisela on his heels.

† † † † †

They found Zane and Dokie waiting in a meadow at the top of the trail. With them were Shawcroft's two chestnut ponies, Lilly and Bedford Boy, both munching grass. Next to the meadow were the ruins of an old fort. Its walls were crumbled in spots and covered in growths of ivy. The terrain was sprinkled with large rocks and pines and a layer of moss and fern and dewy undergrowth.

"Look at you," Liz Hen said to her brother. "You *are* hurt."

Zane's eyes, usually laughing, were tightly closed, his face a grimace of pain as he tenderly favored his left side. From mid-chest down, the left side of his armor was coated in a sheet of dried blood. There was a gash in his armor and an open, seeping wound underneath. "I tried to help Ma and Pa flee into the mountains," he said.

"But some of them knights caught up to us before we even reached Puddleman Pond. I didn't fare well in the fight . . . neither did Ma. Pa fought like a bear. But he was kilt. After I got struck, I played dead. Not that heroic, really. But I'm alive, I reckon."

"Ma and Pa." Liz Hen looked resigned to the news. "At least they're with Laijon now, together with the great One and Only."

"What about my folks?" Gisela asked, eyes wide and worried. "Did anyone see them? What about my little brother?"

"We should go back," Dokie said, scratching his own rear end vigorously. "See if anyone is looking for us." He favored his leg, wincing as he limped around Bedford Boy. Dokie had been hit with the arrow on the beach. But the thin boy seemed in much better shape than Zane, even with the row of teeth marks crossing his chest and back, the wounds barely visible under his ramshackle armor and torn tunic. Any evidence of the lightning strike was long gone.

"We should see who's left alive down there," Gisela said.

Nail's mind flew immediately to Ava Shay. *Is she still alive?* Or was she now as dead as Polly Mott, a spear in her back? *I could have saved her. . . .*

"Everyone is dead or captured," Liz Hen snapped. "We should flee as Shawcroft wanted. Those knights still chase us."

"Shawcroft killed fifteen of those knights himself," Stefan said.

"You probably killed ten too," Nail added, and then wished he hadn't, for his words brought immediate tears to Stefan's eyes. Nail felt a lump well in his own throat now, thinking of his master. A shudder rippled through him as a vision of the Bloodwood sprang forth. He shook it off, looked at Zane. "Your dog was down there."

"Beer Mug?" Zane asked with hope-filled eyes.

"He fought alongside Shawcroft," Nail said, his voice cracking.

"What a good boy, that dog." Zane smiled, but that smile only slightly covered the pained look in his face. "I hope he wasn't hurt. I'd sure love to see him again."

"Shawcroft won't be coming with us," Stefan cried. "He's dead."

Stefan's words were met with a grim silence. Nail fought back the tears. He didn't want the others to see him cry. His master had taught him that crying was for fools and the feebleminded. "We must keep going," he said.

But Stefan folded to the ground at Gisela's feet and wept. "Why should so many men have died just for us to escape?" he asked, his face a mask of grief. "I killed so many. How can I ever live with that? And Shawcroft dead too. For *us*. Why?"

"You did what you could to save him," Nail offered, knowing they should flee this open meadow. "He wanted as few men hunting us as possible."

"Why would they want to hunt us?" Dokie asked. "What have we ever done to them? What do we mean to them?"

"Was Laijon who allowed our escape," Liz Hen said, staring right at Nail, as if she truly believed all of this was his fault. "Our Lord is great and he is merciful. He will not allow those men to find us. Jenko doubted Laijon. And now look where he is, still enslaved."

"My sister has the right of it," Zane said. "Laijon will see us to safety, or Laijon will see us dead. His will guides us now."

Stefan stood and wiped the tears from his eyes. "Those knights still follow us. We've wasted much time gabbing."

"We'll need weapons." Liz Hen began rummaging through the bags strapped to the ponies. Soon she was chirping instructions to everyone, ordering them to help her search. Gisela immediately joined in. Nail silently urged the girls to speed their inventory of the supplies. But curiosity and hunger got the better of him, and he soon found himself rummaging through the bags. Bedford Boy carried sacks of flour, dried beans, and smoked elk jerky along with a handful of empty rawhide water skins. He handed out strips of jerky to everyone. They all began gnawing on it with great relish. On Lilly's back was a parcel of bedrolls and wolf-hide blankets, a cooking kettle, flint and matches, four daggers, and a hatchet. Stefan took one of the daggers and buckled it to his belt and handed another to Dokie. Zane took a dagger too, as did Nail.

"I should have a weapon." Liz Hen snatched the dagger from Dokie and slipped it into the twine belt circling her shift. Gisela, not to be left out, untied the hatchet from Lilly's back and slipped it through her thin belt.

Then they were off, moving as quickly as they could. Nail led the group, Liz Hen right behind him, guiding Bedford Boy. Dokie, limping a little and using Lilly for support, followed next. Stefan and Gisela walked hand in hand. Zane brought up the rear, lumbering along slower than the rest. The Dead Goat Trail bore them through the meadow toward the higher ridges of the Autumn Range in the distance.

Nail looked back. Their tracks were just the palest of disturbances on the trail. Still, easy enough to follow, even for the most inexperienced of trackers. And Nail was sure that the Sør Sevier knights crawling up the trail behind them were far from inexperienced. The very thought that he was possibly responsible for the deaths of so many was almost too much to bear. *Why would they want to hunt us?* Dokie's question plagued his mind. *What have we ever done to them?*

† † † † †

Around midafternoon they reached Sabor Creek, not having seen any sign of the knights or their dogs. The creek was swollen from the spring thaws, churning and roiling. It was the first fresh water they had come upon. All of them took long drinks. Stefan filled the rawhide water skins.

Dokie stripped off his armor and shark-torn tunic and dropped his britches. "I messed myself when swimming with them sharks. My arse is chafed something fierce." Bare-bottomed, he submerged himself in a shallow bend in the creek, lifted his torn shirt, and washed the row of shark bites. He dipped his pants into the water, wringing those clean too, all this to the consternation of Liz Hen, who berated him for holding them up.

"I itch," Dokie said. "I can't go on with soiled skivvies. Mamma said a bum-crack left begrimed is liable to offer up constant arse pain."

"Arse pain," Liz Hen said, disgusted. "On top of all the injuries you and the rest of us have suffered, you're worried about your stupid soily bunghole."

"I can't help that my arse started hurting."

"Hurting? I should cram a knotty tree branch up your rosy-red spinkter, you stupid." Liz Hen kicked dirt and pebbles Dokie's way.

"I ain't stupid." Dokie ducked. The rocks lit in the creek behind him. "What's a spinkter?"

"Don't ask stupid questions." Liz Hen picked up a rock to throw at him.

"I think she means sphincter," Zane said. "You know, your rectum."

"What's that?" Dokie asked, then dodged the rock aimed at his head.

"Fancy there's a chamber pot in one of them sacks for our stinky companion?" Zane asked of no one in particular. "I'm with my sister on this. Lightning-struck. Shot by an arrow. Nearly ate by a shark. And his only concern is the putrid offense in his britches. As Laijon is my witness, now we all have to suffer hearing about it. Stupid shark-bit fool."

"That shark took me down gentle as you please," Dokie said, running shivering wet fingers over the wounds along his chest before pulling up his pants. "But I reckon I wasn't to his taste. He let me go as swift as he took me."

Nail shuddered, recalling his own experience in bloody waters surrounded by sharks. And the mermaid, cold scales wrapping around his legs, pulling him down. He took Shawcroft's satchel off his shoulder, unbuckled the flap, and opened it, his master's words rolling in his head. *Of all things, do not lose this satchel, Nail. You must make sure it reaches the Swithen Wells Trail Abbey and Bishop Godwyn.* Inside were a handful of rolled-up scrolls and a complete copy of *The Way and Truth of Laijon* bound in leather-covered boards and tied together with a slim leather lace. He thumbed through the pages. It was full of many splendid interior drawings. The print was small. Nail hadn't seen a complete compilation of *The Way and Truth of Laijon* but for the massive bound volume that Bishop Tolbret had kept in the chapel. Nobody but bishops and barons ever got to read the holy book, and now here was one right in his hands. But such a thing would do them no good here. Disappointed with the satchel's contents, Nail put the items back. He mourned the loss of his own satchel of drawings, left in Shawcroft's cabin, lost forever.

When Dokie was once again clothed, the group clattered through the creek and continued on, a hustle in their step. Hiking in battle armor was not easy. The skin under Nail's breastplate was being rubbed raw in places. Each hurried step was a slow torture. He thought of removing the unwieldy bulk, but he had no other clothing or protection.

Signs of Dokie's limp had all but disappeared since his wash in the creek, though he still scratched at his bum from time to time. Zane, holding his side gingerly, continued to lag behind, only to catch up after stern words from his sister spurred him on. There was no sign of pursuit. Nail counted them fortunate for that one bit of luck. As the trail rose higher and grew steeper, snow still lay in patches and melting drifts along the way. The Sabor Creek became a silver ribbon winding through the yawning gorge far below.

Near late afternoon, they reached the valley of the Roahm Mines, with still no sign of the Sør Sevier knights. They picked their way through the broken-down wooden hovels of the long-dead ghost town. The steep mountains were honeycombed with mines on either side. Many were collapsed, some closed off by stretched elk hides, the majority just open dark holes. Pine and birch grew tall and lush along the ridges. A crown of rocky peaks surrounded the valley, their jagged tops covered in brilliant sheets of snow and ice.

Nail guided them through the valley. The Written Wall soon towered over their trail on the right, like a massive watchtower. A gentle slope of fern, aspen, and lichen-covered rock rose to the left, creating a jagged ravine for about a hundred paces. The trail under the cliff was rough and studded with large boulders. The two ponies navigated the obstacles with ease. Sunlight twinkled through the aspen leaves above and rained down upon them in a golden shower, littering the path with drops of sunshine. But once under the cliff and out of the sun, Nail noticed it was bitter cold next to the stone wall.

The others stopped and gazed up the sheer rock face, which vaulted two hundred feet straight over their heads. "Wow," Gisela said, her thin voice creating a small echo against the cliff. Hundreds of drawings and carvings lined the wall—the crude communications and artwork of the long-dead inhabitants of Roahm. The drawings were mostly of animals, and even though they were simple, Nail had always been able to distinguish what each drawing was: bighorn sheep, birds, snakes, stick men with bows and spears, and with just a few skillful strokes, the artists had captured the subtle differences between deer, elk, and moose. One drawing even depicted what appeared to be a crude scene of a man wearing a crown washing the feet of another man wearing a wreath of flowers.

There were symbols: squares, circles, crosses, broken S's, what looked like jagged rows of teeth or mountains. Nail shuddered. Many of the carvings were similar to the marks he had on his own body. *Many similar to the red-glowing symbols I saw in the bloody water with the mermaid.* Frightened by the coincidence, Nail urged the others on.

There was a squalid little cabin ahead, its roof mostly fallen in, spots of dirty old snow at its base. So lonely and forlorn-looking, it hunkered under the massive Written Wall like a whipped cur. A cleft in the cliff lay just beyond the cabin—the Hot Springs Notch. It was the notch that would lead them to the main entrance of the Roahm Mines. Nail stepped inside the cabin and found the torches and two quivers of arrows left by Shawcroft. He handed the arrows to Stefan, then tied the torches to Lilly's back.

Liz Hen was outside near a corner of the cabin, looking down into the large elk trap Nail and Shawcroft had dug into the hard ground years ago. "Looks just like the horse the dark guy who killed Shawcroft rode."

Nail walked toward her. The pit was about ten feet square and ten feet deep. At the bottom, impaled by many long wooden stakes, was a black horse. A mare. Dead. Guts ruptured, ripe and rank, its once-red glowing eyes now a foggy burnt umber. *The Vallè woman's steed!* Nail didn't remember ever placing huge wooden spikes at the bottom of the trap. He took a step back, picturing Shawcroft shooting the Vallè woman with a blue-feathered arrow through the top of the shoulder as she looked up at him from the pit.

"What a gruesome foul beast." Liz Hen made the three-fingered sign of the Laijon Cross over her heart. "And what a gruesome foul smell."

"The lady on the trail rode a similar black mare," Stefan said. "Remember, Nail? Do you think this horse is hers? Do you think she's okay? That man who killed Shawcroft reminded me of her. Do you think they are in league together?"

Nail was not going to venture any information on the Vallè woman Shawcroft had killed. Nearby, willows lashed in the breeze. A brisk wind set the leaves in motion and tree limbs to gnashing. Nail thought he heard the clanking of armor behind him and whirled, pulling the dagger from his belt. He wasn't alone in his fear. Stefan also had his bow drawn. In the far distance came the barking of many dogs.

The Sør Sevier knights had found them.

A gray form streaked from the underbrush straight at Zane. But rather than cower, Zane yipped for joy as Beer Mug barreled into him. The two tumbled to the ground, Zane crying out first in pain and then joy as he hugged his dog. Beer Mug lapped at Zane's face, and then whimpered as Zane climbed to his feet, tenderly holding his arm to the wound at his side. "I knew I'd see him again," Zane said, ruffling the short fur on his dog's head. "As Laijon is my witness, I just knew he'd find me. What a good boy he is."

He then looked at his sister gravely. "I don't know how much farther I can go. Now that Beer Mug is here, perhaps I should stay behind. We'll be safe."

"Nonsense," Liz Hen said. "You're coming with us. The knights draw near."

"We should go," Nail urged as more dogs could be heard in the distance.

He led them away from the elk trap with the dead horse, past the cabin, and into the Hot Springs Notch. The notch was narrow at first but then opened up, lined with gnarled birch and aspen clinging to the rock rising above. A bleak fog sifted up through the cracks in the ground, gases seeping from the hot springs deep below the mountain. The mist wreathed the narrows in an ethereal gloom that only grew thicker the farther they traveled, draping the forest in a cloak of sickly green. The scuffs of their footfalls were swallowed up by their surroundings. Still, the sounds of the knights and dogs following them grew in volume. They stuck close together on the trail. No one spoke. Only Beer Mug seemed lively, ears pricked, always looking back in the direction they'd come, toward the sounds of the other dogs.

When the trail leveled out, the opening to the Roahm Mines was before them. In front of the mine's entrance lay the still waters of a small mossy pond. Massive pale support timbers framed the dark opening of the mine like the columns of a cathedral. The beams bowed inward and appeared strained under the jagged rock. Hundreds of initials were carved into the wood, the antique workings of long-lost miners.

They all stared at the dark opening before them—all but Beer Mug, who stood silent vigil at the rear, ears alert to the coming dogs and their armed masters.

Fear gripped Nail as he stared at the ominous black shaft sunk into the mountain. It was a type of fear he had never felt before. He had been in these mines time and again. But tonight, Nail questioned his master's wisdom that they should venture into their dank depths. Nail knew these mountains. There was a high trailhead not far away that would lead them over these peaks and see them safely to the Swithen Wells Trail Abbey.

There was the sound of a horse whinnying. The *chink* and *clink* of armor followed. Gisela squealed in fright. The barking of the dogs grew more frenzied with the cracking and snapping of branches and grown men's voices. Gisela clung to Stefan, eyes wide, pupils darting here and there. Beer Mug growled low and deep. Liz Hen grabbed him by the scruff of the neck in time to stop him from lunging into the trees.

As the sound of pounding hooves grew louder and the voices of the knights grew more distinct, Nail's survival instinct screamed for him to turn and run into the hills and leave his friends to fend for themselves. *Laijon will see us to safety, or Laijon will see us dead,* Zane had said earlier. Nail didn't know the truth of such a platitude. But he now realized the mines were their only escape route.

In the echoing canyon, obscured in dense fog, there was no telling how close the advancing knights were. Nail hastily dug through Lilly's pack and found the scarves. He tied them around both ponies' eyes. Stefan found flint and matches and lit two torches. He handed one to Nail. Torch in one hand, Lilly's reins in the other, Nail moved quickly. Wading through the brackish pond before the tunnel's entrance was a cold shock. And he had to duck as he entered the deep darkness.

"Must we enter this dungeon?" he heard Liz Hen whisper to Dokie. "I have a feeling some of us won't make it out of here alive."

"I do hope you're wrong," Dokie said softly, scratching at his rear. "I do hope you're wrong."

† † † † †

The passageway sloped down and to the north. It was cold, musty, and bitter. Within just a few short steps, the tunnel became so dark it ate the torchlight. Large chunks of rock and wood littered their path. Chisel marks peppered the cavern walls on either side. The tunnel continued down. It grew colder. Nobody spoke. But the sounds of their travel never quite disappeared. The click of the ponies' hooves, their snorts, Liz Hen's heavy breathing, all just bounced from wall to wall and back again, circling about, growing louder, deeper, softer, splitting behind them, returning ahead. Creating such a ruckus was unavoidable. *The Sør Sevier knights will have no trouble finding us in here,* Nail thought. These caves were a death trap.

They followed this singular dark corridor for what felt like hours before it split. Water dripped endlessly from a gnarled rock that hung low over the intersection. The tunnel forked in a perfect Y; the right path led up, the left down. Nail did not hesitate. He knew these tunnels well and chose the path leading up. They followed it for some time.

Hours passed as they walked. Beyond the torchlight lived a deep blackness. In some places, the ceiling was low and they had to duck and push the ponies through, sometimes removing the sack strapped to Bedford Boy's back. Nail was expecting the toilsome work, having experienced the like with Shawcroft and Bedford Boy before. But

Liz Hen grumbled that the ponies were holding them back. "When will we be out of this damnable place?" she kept asking.

During the quiet moments, Nail listened for the sounds of pursuit. He could hear nothing. Onward they went. The narrow mineshaft had soon become a twisting and turning maze of passageways. Numerous tunnels branched off at all angles. At times their path would open up into cavernous rooms. Some caverns had steps carved into the stone, rising straight up, others had stairs spiraling down into the dark. There were ladders disappearing into dark pits in the floor and ladders climbing up into holes and cracks in the ceiling. But Nail avoided those, never hesitating in his course, the others shuffling along behind. Nail had swung a pickax in most of these rooms and tunnels. Always with his master over his shoulder, holding a torch aloft, barking orders, making sure he swung the ax just right. Rake the stone away from the wall with the horns of the pick. Never dig at the rock with your hands. Let the tools do the work. With Shawcroft it was patience and perfection in everything. To Nail it had all been so pointless.

After a while, Nail stopped and untied a water skin from Lilly's back and let the others drink. The glow of the torchlight created a pocket of light around the group, burnishing their faces in a sullen amber glow. Zane's freckled face was pale and more pouchy-looking than ever. Everyone's faces were lined with worry and fatigue.

"Are you doing okay?" Stefan asked Gisela as she drank from the water skin.

She took several gulping swigs, then handed the skin to Zane. "I'm scared," she said, wiping water from her face with the sleeve of her shirt.

"Me too." Stefan kissed her gently on the forehead. Gisela clung to him as if longing for some reassurance that she was not alone in this dark place. Stefan's armor gleamed in the torchlight. Nail examined his own rust-splotched breastplate. It was splattered with blood.

The skin on his face was tight and numb—and then he remembered he was still covered in blood from the battle. He felt the gash on his head through his matted hair. He must look a bloody sight in the torchlight. *And to think, the battle was only yestermorn.* It seemed a lifetime ago.

A whisper of breath touched the back of his neck and he shuddered, thinking he heard the metallic clinking of armor in the tunnels behind them. It was time to move on.

Another hour dragged by as they walked. The mine was cold and lonely, and they rarely spoke. Each fork in the road led them ever upward. Beyond the torchlight, everything was submerged in a swamplike blackness. They stumbled over piles of broken rock where large stretches of ceiling had fallen. They skirted dripping stalactites that brushed the floor. They stepped over cracks that could snap an ankle. Some cracks in the floor were so wide they had to lengthen their stride just to clear them, then gently coax the blind ponies leg by leg, for fear their sticklike limbs might get caught.

Nail was sure of their path and told the others that the bridge Shawcroft had told him to aim for was just around the next corner. Zane vomited up a bloody stream against the wall; the sound of his retching was thunderous. When the sounds of Zane's vomiting died, they heard the distant barks of the dogs float out of the darkness behind them.

Heart pounding, Nail ushered the group quickly around the bend and into a large cavern, the walls barely discernable fifty feet around them in every direction. In the torchlight, the dark slash of the open pit before them extended from one wall of the cave to the other, completely cutting off their path. The chasm was black and bottomless. Nail had thrown a rock into it once and never heard it strike bottom. Above, the ceiling was also nonexistent. The opposite rim of the chasm was over twenty paces away; shovels, picks, buckets, and other mining tools lined that edge like a row of pale teeth in the torchlight. Across the chasm, on the far side of the wall, was the dark oval opening of a tunnel Nail had never explored before.

To their right was a narrow stone-and-mortar bridge that spanned the chasm, about three paces wide and a foot thick. *The bridge Shaw-croft warned me never to cross.* The thought of crossing it now sent a ripple of fear through him. His master had earlier said it was indeed safe. But it didn't look safe, bowed in the middle and drooping. Most of the mortar holding it together looked to have crumbled and fallen into the pit.

The voices of the knights behind them were growing louder.

"I can't cross that," Gisela said.

"We've no choice." Nail's heart fluttered anxiously as he led Lilly toward the narrow causeway. He placed one foot tentatively on the crumbling stone, leg shaking as he did. Lilly sensed his nervousness and stepped back, pulling on the reins. "Come," he said in a voice that cracked with fear. The pony followed him, her eyes covered still.

Nail, torch in one hand, the rope leading Lilly in the other, traversed the chasm as fast as he dared. He thought he heard the stone bridge cracking under Lilly's weight, gray mortar sloughing off into the pit. But they both reached the other side.

Nail turned back to assure the others the way was safe. Zane, wasting little time, was already on his way over the narrow bridge, Beer Mug right behind him.

"I'm too heavy." Liz Hen handed Bedford Boy's reins to Dokie. "Lead the pony."

"But my arse feels itchy," Dokie exclaimed.

"I don't care what your arse feels." Liz Hen waddled her way over the bridge, holding her chubby arms out for balance. Once she'd cleared the chasm, Dokie, scratching at his rear with one hand, began pulling Bedford Boy slowly toward the bridge, reins in the other. Nail risked a glance behind Stefan and Gisela. The dark opening they had just come through was now aglow with torchlight and loud voices. *The knights!*

There was a scrape and a muffled noise, and both Liz Hen and Gisela screamed.

Nail turned just in time to see Bedford Boy tumble from the bridge. The pony's scarved, chestnut-colored face turned up to his briefly as it dropped and disappeared into the darkness and was gone—vanishing like a vapor of smoke into the blackness.

Dokie Liddle stood in the center of the bridge, eyes wide, urine staining his britches and running down his legs. He stood that way, frozen; then with two quick strides he was across the span to safety. "You stupid!" Liz Hen smacked him across the face, crying aloud, "That pony carried all our food, you stupid!" She hugged him to her thick body, sobbing. "All our food," she muttered between sobs.

The sight of Bedford Boy plummeting into the ghastly chasm was fixed in Nail's mind. It was a soundless fall. He stared at Liz Hen and Dokie. They clung to each other in an embrace of both horror and relief—horror that the pony was gone, relief that Dokie was alive. "He just stepped right off," Dokie kept muttering, "just stepped right off."

Flickering torchlight advanced up the tunnel behind Stefan and Gisela as a host of knights bearing torches boiled toward them from the opening, a handful of barking dogs behind them. Stefan immediately swept Gisela up into his arms and, in four loping strides, carried her over the bridge. He ran by Nail and disappeared down the passageway in the far wall. Zane retreated down the tunnel too, Beer Mug on his heels.

Nail felt an arrow zing past his head. He whirled in time to see several knights drawing their bows, while at the same time a line of five other knights and three dogs were running over the stone bridge toward him. A second arrow pierced one of the canvas sacks Lilly carried. The pony bounded away from Nail, knocking Liz Hen and Dokie aside as it raced away down the tunnel. But Liz Hen and Dokie were quick to pick themselves up and follow the pony in its mad escape.

Then, with a deafening crack, the stone bridge gave way.

Rock and mortar and four of the Sør Sevier knights and all three dogs plummeted down into the black nothingness. The fifth knight lunged forward with a clamor, landing halfway on the lip of the chasm, his lower body hanging over. The man clung to the edge of the pit just a few paces from Nail, arms scrambling to find purchase on the stone, hands grasping at the pebbles and buckets and bits of wood scattered there. But his efforts were to no avail. He slipped and disappeared from view, screaming as he fell.

Nail, torch in hand, was alone now, facing the remaining Sør Sevier knights and dogs. They stared at him from across the open chasm, all of them appearing as shocked as he, having just witnessed their five companions tumble away into the darkness.

They gathered their wits quickly, though, and in an instant, the knights' bows were again drawn. Nail whirled and sprinted into the tunnel, arrows whizzing by, clattering off the stone wall behind him, one striking the torch from his hand. "Aeros wants them alive, fools!" a gruff voice shouted. Nail ran on, gladly leaving his torch and the Sør Sevier knights and the gaping black pit behind.

† † † † †

The passageway leading from the bridge was long and narrow and dumped them into a second cavern about the same size as the one they had just fled.

There they stopped to catch their breath.

"They won't soon cross that chasm," Stefan said, handing a newly lit torch to Nail. "With the bridge gone, no man can jump that distance."

"I wouldn't be so sure of that," Zane said. "Remember Cotton Stansfield at the Mourning Moon Feast two years ago? I daresay he ran and jumped near twenty feet to win the athletic competition."

"I don't think they will follow us," Nail said. "And if they do, it will take them a while to figure out a way across that pit." But one thing was certain in Nail's mind: if there was another way across that chasm, those men would soon find it. There wasn't much time to linger.

Nail led them onward. Their path clung to the far left of the chamber. To the right of the path lay a sheet of ghostly water, an underground pond fed by melting snow seeping through cracks from above. It lay flat and still, and scarcely stirred when Nail's boot kicked in a pebble. The stillness of the pool was disconcerting. Cobwebs of mist rose from the water in places. The bitter air about this new cave was damp and harsh to breathe.

They skirted the pool along the narrow path, all eyes on the black water, all of them drawn to it as if transfixed. Beer Mug lapped at the water. Zane bent to take a drink too, but his sister stopped him with a firm hand and admonished him not to.

A cool drink sounded good to Nail. But Bedford Boy, along with their water skins, was gone. And from the looks of it, Zane needed fresh water in a bad way. But this pool appeared less than fresh. It looked dead. Nail, unable to keep his eyes off the water, stopped and knelt, holding his torch out, studying the eerie black pool, shuddering as he did so. Something was in the water.

He jumped back, startled at what he saw. Like ivory ghosts, the floor of the pool was lined with human skulls. But upon closer inspection, Nail wondered if the skulls were human at all. The dark water distorted what he saw, or what he thought he saw. Be they human or monster, either way there were skulls down there, hundreds of them, all bone-white and awful. Although the pool frightened Nail, it also reassured him; it proved that they were still on the right path. Shawcroft had called it the Place of the Skulls.

Nail led them away from the pool. Nobody but he, it seemed, had noticed the skulls in the water, or if so, they kept the awful sight to themselves. The path they followed led to another tunnel. It eventually widened out and continued on straight and slightly upward, though it seemed that this passageway was newer, with freshly chiseled walls. To their right was a wide set of stairs leading up into the darkness— the staircase so wide a group of twenty horsemen could have climbed it abreast. *The stairway Shawcroft asked me to climb!* Nail wondered what was up there. To his thinking, it was best they just continue on and leave these mines as soon as possible. Still, the stairs pulled at him.

"Should we go up the stairs?" he asked Stefan.

"We haven't the time. We dare not tarry. And Shawcroft mentioned traps."

"He said he dismantled them."

"Traps?" Zane uttered. "I don't know what you boys are carrying on about, but I don't think those knights can get across that chasm." He sat down, easing his back gingerly against the tunnel's wall. "I'm taking a load off. I need a rest, perhaps a little nap." Zane nodded his head toward the wide staircase. "That'll give you two plenty of time to find out what's up them stairs."

Beer Mug lay down next to Zane, placing his head on the boy's lap.

Nail looked at Stefan. "Come with me."

"You mustn't leave me, Stefan," Gisela pleaded.

"You can come, Gisela." Stefan handed his torch to Dokie. "Don't let it go out. These two torches are all we've got left."

Third step up, far left stone against the wall—Nail bent and pushed on it as Shawcroft had instructed. With just a touch, the stone seemed to move of its own volition, but just barely. There was a howl of wind from the darkness above, then a faint metallic *clink, clink.* Then silence.

Nail marched up the stairs, holding his torch aloft, hearing Stefan's and Gisela's rustling steps not far behind. He grasped the hilt of the dagger at his belt, more for comfort than out of a belief that the short blade would be of any use on this dreadful stairway.

The stairs emptied them out onto a square room with a high ceiling. The carved columns that supported the roof were draped in spiderwebs. Wooden coffins lined the wall. Some had crumbled and fallen open, revealing bits of cloth and bone. Some skeletons were embedded in the walls, their bones rotting away in the sullen air. It was a dire place. *A tomb.* The mournful darkness of the grim room seemed to press in on the torchlight. Tiny streams of silver liquid seemed to bleed from random cracks in the walls, slowly pooling on the floor.

Nail entered the coldness of the room, Stefan and Gisela right behind him, the girl's eyes glued to the skeletons in the walls. Nail handed the torch to her. Its light lay softly upon an altar that dominated the center of the vaulted room. It was cross-shaped, about waist high, and capped with an altar stone similar to the one in the Gallows Haven chapel. Beautifully worked carvings encircled the base, eerily similar to those stitched onto Shawcroft's satchel.

With Stefan's help, Nail slid the slab of stone aside, revealing what was hidden inside the altar. He wasn't really sure what he had expected to find, but sealed within the silence of the stone box was a gigantic double-bladed battle-ax. Its curved, gleaming edges and pointed horns looked as sharp as a slice of grass. The weapon had a thick haft of steel wrapped in black leather interwoven with Vallè runes and silver thread. It was the most magnificent thing Nail had ever laid eyes on. He glanced up at Stefan. The boy's eyes were wide with wonder, Gisela's even more so. Nail's mind reeled. *Is this what Shawcroft was digging for? Here? At Sky Lochs? With that fellow, Culpa Barra, at Deadwood Gate? Sparkling weapons?* The questions flittered away as he looked back into the altar.

Nail reached down and picked up the ax. It was twice as heavy as it looked and took some effort to lift, the finely honed blade scraping against the stone of the altar as he dragged it up and out. A curious feeling stole over him. It suddenly felt as if he *knew* this weapon, as if he had held it before, and holding it now was in some way the right thing.

He thought he saw tendrils of blue smoke misting up from between his fingers wrapped around the iron hilt. But then the vision was gone.

Still, he felt a strange sense of connection to the thing, of completion. His own blood-streaked face reflected back at him in the ax's gleaming surface. His image was twisted, distorted. With matted blond hair coated in dried blood, he looked like a demon child of the underworld. His eyes, now peering from under the strands of his bloody hair, were feverishly aglow in the image that danced back at him from the wondrous ax blade.

"What's this?" Gisela said, thrusting the torch over the open altar.

Nail looked from the ax to the girl. She was reaching her free hand into the altar toward a bright blue stone that sat atop a black swatch of silk. She snatched up the sparkling azure gem and held it in her trembling fingers. "It's so pretty," she said. "It glows like the stained glass in the chapel when the sun shines."

Nail was disappointed that he was not the first to find the marvelous stone. It shimmered blue shards of brilliance in the torchlight and set Nail's heart to racing.

Nail scowled at Gisela and set the ax down against the altar.

"Give it to me," Stefan demanded with a stern voice. He reached onto the altar himself, taking up the black silk, then held the silk out to Gisela. "Give it."

A guarded look was on her face as she placed the blue gem carefully within the silk. Stefan hastily wrapped the stone in the cloth and handed it to Nail. "Shawcroft wanted you to have it. This place frightens me like nothing else. Let's go."

Tucking the silk-wrapped stone into Shawcroft's satchel next to *The Way and Truth of Laijon*, Nail hefted the huge battle-ax, once again admiring its quality.

Is this my destiny? It was as if he had seen it all before, hovering at the edges of his dreams. *A blue stone? An ax?*

Stefan and Gisela were already heading back down the stairs. Nail took a step to follow, but then noticed that on the first step down, the stone against the far left wall was moving. Then came the low, moaning rumbling of rock grinding against rock from the room behind him. He turned and looked one last time at the cross-shaped altar, which now seemed to be sinking into the floor.

It wasn't the sight of the altar slowly disappearing that froze his blood. It was something far worse. *They shouldn't be there!* his mind raged. To draw them was strictly forbidden on pain of death. And to carve them . . . no, his mind couldn't grasp what he saw.

They were only small carvings. But it seemed they numbered in the hundreds, all of them, one after the next, receding into the floor as the altar sluggishly sank downward.

Carved at the base of the vanishing altar were burning eyes, flashing teeth, leathery clawed wings, serpentine tails—nameless beasts of the underworld.

Dragons!

† † † † †

When they reached the bottom of the stairs, they found Dokie and Liz Hen tending Zane's wound. Beer Mug, sad eyes fixed on Zane, whimpered.

"Have a gawk at this, boys." Zane said, trying to keep an unconcerned look on his face, but there remained a strange, sickly glaze over his eyes. His armor was off, strewn about the wide corridor at the base of the stairs, all of it coated in congealed blood. The wound in his side was shocking to behold. Broken shards of rib were visible there beside his inner organs, the skin around the wound just mangled, clotted, torn meat. The stench of it engulfed Nail, nearly causing him to retch. He had not realized how injured Zane was. It was obvious to them all now: Zane was dying.

"What in all of creation is that?" Zane asked, pain-filled eyes on the heavy battle-ax cradled in Nail's arms.

"What a thing to have to lug around now," Liz Hen snorted, squinting at both Nail and the ax with disapproval. "As if we didn't already have enough to worry about. Now we have to haul that thing about too? What use could that thing ever be to anyone, Nail? You stupid, stupid bastard."

After clawing their way free of slavery, the Five Warrior Angels arose
again, each with an angel stone, each bearing a divine weapon. Thus
they began their War of Cleansing. The demons of the sky, once fearsome
with fire and might, shook and trembled before them. All came together
under the Warrior Angels' Banner of Cleansing, dwarf and Vallè and
oghul alike. And the Fiery Demons and their dark lords fled before them.
—THE WAY AND TRUTH OF LAIJON

CHAPTER TWENTY-FIVE
TALA BRONACHELL

4TH DAY OF THE MOURNING MOON, 999TH YEAR OF LAIJON

AMADON, GUL KANA

The flutist, a woman with deft fingers and delicate windpipes, blew an upbeat tune whilst dancing a jig to the tempo of the kettle drummer behind her. Half the revelers in Sunbird Hall danced; the other half dined on all manner of food. Servants, wild-eyed and flushed with heat, rushed from hall to kitchen and back again at the beck and call of the celebrants. Serving girls carried silver trays laden with pewter goblets of ruby-colored wine. Dishes of roast duck, ham, and Autumn Range elk, along with large bowls filled with grapes, apples, carrots, figs, and nuts of every hue covered the tables. All celebrants were dressed in their finest attire, many women with garlands of beads wrapped around their heads. The Mourning Moon Celebration was full of pomp and frivolity. The steward, Ser Tomas Vorkink, had overdone himself in preparing

Sunbird Hall this year. The entirety of the king's court was full of joy and laughter.

All save Tala and Lawri. They were sitting alone at the end of a long table. Lawri was listless, sickly, her once beautiful face sunken and sad. And Tala's mind couldn't rid itself of the image of Denarius blessing her cousin. . . .

Tala clenched her eyes shut. *Do not think of it.* Would she never be able to wash away the fog of numbness and disbelief that clouded her mind over the event?

She knew that the spirit of Laijon worked in mysterious ways. Not all prayers and priesthood anointings were meant to be understood by the layperson. But the more rational side of her mind wished to claw the man's eyes out. In the depths of both her mind and heart, what she'd seen was wrong.

Lawri, seemingly unaware of her surroundings, looked sicker by the day. She folded her arms on the table and rested her head on her hands, feigning sleep. Tala's heart ached for Lawri in so many ways. She felt for the black dagger strapped to her thigh under her dress. Only after clutching the dagger's hilt could she relax. Having the Bloodwood blade at her side was reassuring. She had been carrying it ever since she'd knocked it from the assassin's hands.

The music of the celebration had softly worked its way down to naught but a solo bagpipe, its flowing notes seeming to contain ages of sorrow. It put Tala in a mood now more befitting the ill look of Lawri.

"Wine, if it pleases m'lady?" The barmaid from the Filthy Horse Saloon, Delia, held a silver tray with five goblets. Tala graciously took one, sipped of the fruity wine, then nodded nervous thanks to the dimple-faced girl. The fact that she herself had introduced Delia to the castle's kitchen matron, Vilamina, earlier that day worried Tala. The assassin's game had taken on many angles, and Tala was not yet sure what part Delia had to play. But here the lowly barmaid was, serving drinks to the royalty of Gul Kana.

As with all of the serving wenches, Delia wore a short plaid skirt and a billowy white shirt cut low about the neckline, with a tightly cinched corset that accentuated her already large breasts. As she made her way through Sunbird Hall with the tray of wine, the barmaid drew the admiring eyes of many a soldier. To Tala, the girl was a bit rough around the edges and looked terribly out of place surrounded by so much finery.

At times, so much finery made Tala sick to her stomach. The mass of painted royalty and strutting soldiers filled Sunbird Hall with their myriad of voices, all but drowning out the delicately played notes of the harp and bagpipes. Many sat at the long tables, while others lounged on soft-cushioned furniture, long benches, and stumpy divans covered in velvet and expensive bearskins. Black pillars lined the chamber. The walls between the pillars were strung with tapestries that portrayed Laijon's journey from young fisherman to great grayken hunter, to slave, to demon slayer. Large candelabra lined the walls too. And there were hundreds more candles atop the rows of polished wooden tables set throughout the room. The overabundance of torchlight and candlelight threw an almost blinding warm glow over the room. The rows of wide double doors to the Sunbird Hall balcony high along the easternmost end of the room were thrown open, allowing for a breeze to cool the red-faced crowd.

Tala knew she fit in well here, to a point. She was wearing a richly embroidered velvet night-cloak over a maroon dress laced up the front. She thought the ensemble worked well with the darkness of her curled hair. But there were so many pretty noblewomen and court girls in the hall tonight, all of them showing more flesh than she. Each painted girl who walked by was revealing a bit more cleavage than Tala was comfortable with. As she looked around at all the merriment and frolicking, she realized that as the youngest female member of the royal family, the more interesting parts of life were passing her by. That was really what sickened her most about the whole celebration: the unfairness of it.

She missed her mother and father. Each of their deaths had come so suddenly. Each death had been a hard blow to Tala, scarcely eleven years old at the time. She could still remember her mother, Alana, dying painfully in bed whilst giving birth to Ansel. Then came the news of her father a few moons later, killed in battle while fighting in Wyn Darrè against the White Prince. Tala had realized at too young an age that there was nobody left to properly raise her with love and tender care, nobody save her older brother, Jovan, and what few Silver Guards he posted outside her room each night. Tala wished Jondralyn would pay her more attention. Tala's joys in life were few. Lawri and Lindholf's visits from Eskander were the only highlights in her otherwise drab existence. But even that had turned out poorly this time. This plight with Lawri and the Bloodwood was taking its toll on Tala's sanity. She felt so lost and alone.

She spotted Seita, Glade, and Lindholf sitting together at a table not too far away. The fragile lines of the Vallè princess's tight dress were lecherous. Val-Draekin was mingling with Val-Korin and some other ambassadors behind Seita. Glade was dressed in dark leather pants that clung tight to his legs, a billowy white shirt tied at the waist with a thick black leather belt, and a black cape that was slung carelessly over his left shoulder. There was something a tad brooding about the way he sat there with Lindholf and the Vallè princess. He was keeping his eyes to himself, mostly. Lindholf, on the other hand, was wearing such a clash of colors it would be hard for anyone not to notice him. He'd donned a maroon-colored doublet and tight blue pants the color of the sky, along with a bright green cloak that hurt her eyes. The scarf draped about his neck was as red as an Avlonia strawberry

His movements were jerky as he began recounting some wild story for Seita and Glade. Tala strained to hear him. "At any rate," he said. "I spilt the jug on my breeches in a most disadvantageous way. Looked as if I'd just pissed myself. Now, I couldn't go back looking like a bed-wetting fool. But I hadn't much time to think things through properly. So I figured if I just got the rest of myself all wet, it would all blend in, you know. So I took the remainder of the wine jugs in the pantry and doused myself with them and then proceeded back into her bedchamber, sopping wet from head to foot." The sound of Seita's laugh, more gentle than the harpist's melody, made Tala groan inwardly.

"Nonsense," Glade said. He sounded drunk. "You ain't never been inside no girl's bedchamber."

Lindholf ignored him and continued. "As I stood there all a-drip in wine, I told the girl she could lick me from head to foot. But she'd have to catch me first." Lindholf stood and began to caper to the music, long arms swinging disjointedly. "She chased me about her chamber, bare-arse naked, tongue wagging like a dog. She wanted me all right. Wanted to lick me clean." Seita laughed at the story.

Glade put his mug down, stood, and wandered toward Tala. "That cousin of yours is as crazy as a bug in a mug." He sat, snatched up a handful of nuts from the bowl in front of Tala, and started munching them.

Delia, at Tala's table again, placed a small mug of mead in front of him. "A beer for my young master?"

Glade eyed the girl curiously. "Fancy seeing you here." Then he burped.

"Fancy indeed," Delia responded with a smile. Tala thought she sensed a veiled watchfulness in Glade as his eyes roamed over the barmaid, who walked away.

Tala's gaze traveled to the raised dais in the center of the southern wall, where Jondralyn sat in a richly brocaded blue gown and even darker blue cape fastened with a delicate silver brooch. She looked positively radiant. The stone dais under Jondralyn was strewn with soft white rugs. Across the table from her was Jovan. A row of Day-knights stood behind the king, their backs against the velvet-draped wall, arms folded over heavy black breastplates and mail, longswords hanging under their silver surcoats, their countenances glowering.

Tala needed some air. Glade was clearly drunk and the room was growing crowded. She felt so lost and alone in the middle of it all. Lawri's sickness and the assassin's game vexed her mind. She asked Glade to remain with Lawri and stood, straightening her dress. She then made her way toward one of the two staircases to the balcony that branched off to either side at the eastern end of Sunbird Hall, pushing through the crowd. She climbed quickly, buoyancy in her step. The rows of ivory-paneled doors were open tonight, revealing the outside balcony beyond. Once atop the stairs, she could breathe easier. Tala caught a sideways glimpse of herself in the strip of polished glass scrollwork embedded in one of the doors. She turned and stood there for a moment, appraising the image staring back at her. She concluded that she didn't look half-bad; more cute than most, all things considered.

Head held high, she strode boldly through the doorway and onto the balcony outside. The lulling scent of flowers was pleasant in comparison to the heavy woodsmoke of the hall. Ivy festooned the carved stone balustrade, trailed over the balcony, and climbed the castle walls. Crimson petals and twining vines draped the weblike trellis that arched over the row of doors behind her. A wistful tune drifted in from Sunbird Hall, which was a haze of yellow light in her periphery as she soaked in the cool night air.

Alone now, Tala rested her hands on the stone railing. She cast her gaze down to Memory Bay below. The moonlit view fell dizzying into space. In the restless harbor, ships of every size bobbed with the curling waves. Far below, the tide crashed, spewing foamy water high against the rocks at the base of Mount Albion and the castle. Scores of stone structures huddled down there, clinging to the vast structure's base. Crisp winds blew in from the bay, moaning over the battlements and spires above. Those same towers blotted out the stars behind her. The Mourning Moon hung low on the horizon.

Tala wanted to think of anything other than assassins, black daggers, poisons, Lawri, or the grand vicar. She stared at the moon hanging above Amadon. For many in Gul Kana, much happiness and joy hinged on this, the first moon of spring: farmers began to till their soil, trappers and game hunters ventured into the Autumn Range again, grayken-hunting ships set sail, and feasts were held the breadth of the land. But in Amadon, the final night of the Mourning Moon Celebration was a waste of time to Tala—a yearly tradition that stretched back thousands of years, so ancient that probably no one even remembered what its original purpose was. Tala's older sister would know. Jondralyn knew everything about Laijon and the holy book and the convoluted, bloody histories of Gul Kana. The Mourning Moon was mentioned briefly in *The Way and Truth of Laijon,* as were all of the fifteen moons and seasons. Despite how hard Dame Mairgrid tried with her, Tala was not the type to study books. But she knew the moons. In the dead of winter fell the first moon—the Afflicted Moon, followed by the Blackest Moon and the Shrouded Moon. On the first day of spring was the Mourning Moon, then Ethic Moon, Angel Moon, Fire Moon, and next, in the middle of the summer, came her favorite moon—the Blood Moon. Summer faded and turned to fall with the Heart Moon, followed by the Crown Moon, Thunder Moon, Archaic Moon, and Lonesome Moon. Snow season began again with the Forgetting Moon and really got frigid with the Winter Moon—fifteen moons in all, twenty-four days each, three hundred sixty days total, one year, and then it all started over again.

"Why did you leave me?" She heard Glade's voice from behind. She tore her gaze from the dark skies to find him unexpectedly at the balcony next to her. He slid one of his hands over hers. Stunned at his unexpected touch, she jerked away.

"I only wish to share the view, if it pleases m'lady." Glade flashed a cunning smile. He looked less inebriated than Tala had initially thought. "Why did you leave when I sat with you?" he asked again.

"You're drunk and you seem far too besotted with Seita?" she answered, knowing as soon as the words spilled from her mouth that they rang with pettiness and jealousy.

"Lindholf is monopolizing her with silly stories. I only played drunk and excused myself to be with you."

Tala was hurt by his answer. It appeared Glade would have been more than willing to spend his entire evening at Seita's table. But since Lindholf was annoying him, retreating to her and Lawri's table was his only option. She furrowed her brow and glowered at him. But a lock of his hair had strayed over his face, making her fingers itch to brush it back so she could clearly see his dark and beautiful eyes.

"Seita wishes you two could become friends," he said. "You can be so cold and aloof, Tala. Around Seita, that is."

Me, cold? That Seita wanted to be friends was news to her. *Aloof?* She didn't know how to respond, so she was silent, letting Glade's statement sink in.

"You seem upset," he said.

"It's nothing," she responded, confused.

"Your hair looks divine. The way it falls and frames your face, curled so."

Tala gazed at the ocean. Her heart beat like a kettledrum. She fought off a smile, but lost, and ended up grinning madly.

"Your smile is a treasure," he said. "We would indeed match up well." He reached for a few stray tendrils of her hair, brushing her cheek with the back of his fingers. She felt her face flush. He had a beguiling way about him that made everything he did, every small gesture—like touching her hair—seem intriguingly dangerous.

"The famous raven Bronachell hair," he said, dark eyes boring into hers. "We would make such beautiful children."

"Truly?" Tala asked, heart light in her chest.

Glade let the wisps of her hair fall from his fingers. "But you do such unladylike things." He gave her his characteristically apathetic shrug. "For such a pretty girl, you're weird. I don't know how I can even contemplate—"

"Unladylike?" Tala raised her chin and looked him full in the face, her smile now gone. Everything he did caught her off guard. "What is so unladylike about me?" she challenged.

"Secret treks to dockside taverns. Having Lindholf climb the statue of Laijon. And that barmaid from the Filthy Horse. Here? Tonight? What are you up to, Tala?"

What do I dare tell him? Tala's mind spun. *Who may be watch*ing? She felt she was going insane. She took a deep breath and took Glade's hands in her own, facing him. "Perhaps I'll tell you what I'm up to . . . for a kiss." Tala couldn't believe her own brashness. She knew this was a dangerous precipice she now teetered on. She tried hiding her embarrassment behind a fluttery giggle.

"Don't be daft," he said with laughing eyes, moving back a step, letting go of her hands. She felt a surge of disappointment. It was all going so embarrassingly wrong now. But with a roguish grin, Glade spoke again. "You'll tell me what I wish to know whether I kiss you or not." He took up her hands again, pulling her close. A cool breeze plucked at her cloak and dress. But the sensation of Glade's body against hers was like a hearth fire on her flesh. Now, instead of feeling lost and alone, Tala felt a wild sense of completeness with Glade, of being made whole. She tried to suppress her desire as he wrapped her in his arms.

Tala closed her eyes. Then his lips were on hers, moist and soft and perfect. She drank in the taste of him. The wine still on his breath was sweet, intoxicating. His hands roamed as he kissed her, caressing her shoulders, drifting down her back. . . .

Eyes opening wide in shock, she found herself facing the crowd over Glade's shoulder—she could see the entire room below. The Bloodwood could be any one of the two hundred or so revelers crowding Sunbird Hall. People danced, drank, ate, but nobody appeared to take note of her and Glade's embrace. Nobody but Dame Mairgrid, that is. Tala spied her tutor down below, glowering up at the balcony—the woman's fat gut was half stuffed under a table and half resting atop it. Tala knew she would catch a scolding from the woman for sure. *Perhaps the Bloodwood hides in the walls.* At that thought, her eyes shot upward. The lofty ceiling was crisscrossed with arched buttresses and heavy rafters. Woodsmoke curled there, thick and dense.

Glade kissed her with fervency now. He thrust his tongue into her mouth. It was a sudden and alarming thing, thrilling and disgusting and intimate all at once.

He pulled his lips away from hers then, looking satisfied, arms still encircling her waist. "Has kissing me got you all moist and slippery inside?"

She shoved him away.

"But you must remain a virgin until we marry," he continued, a mocking hunger in his eyes. "So I'll be finding some other lass tonight."

Tala wanted to jab the Bloodwood's dagger into his eye. Jab it in and twist. Fighting back a growing tide of anger, she tried to formulate a respectable response. But Glade snatched her around the waist and pulled her tight against him again, stroking her hair. "I must go," he whispered gently. "But fear not, our wedding night will be a special time for you." He turned and glided down the stairs, his black cape a-swirl, billowing at her in defiance with each retreating step.

Tala wanted to vomit her churning insides out all over the pretty flowers lining the balcony. Was that all young men ever thought of? She was so disgusted by Glade that she wished he'd just drop dead. How could he be so charming and repulsive at the same time? There was not an ounce of niceness or humility in him. She'd seen the same impertinence fester in her older brother—Jovan had used and then tossed aside every girl who crossed his path.

"Has Glade upset you?" Lindholf's white leather boots clicked on the stairs as he made his way toward her. The hues and brightness of Lindholf's garb nearly blinded her. Tala swore her cousin's cheeks and forehead were rouged, perhaps to cover the burns and scars of his childhood accident, or more likely, to cover the legion of pimples gathered on the other parts of his face. Everything about her cousin clashed horribly.

"He has an angering effect on the ladies, you know." Lindholf bowed before her, sweat gleaming on his forehead. "And the more oafish he is, the more the girls fawn over him." Tala wrinkled her nose at the smell of his breath.

"Were you talking about Seita?" he asked. "I think Glade is in love with her."

"You don't say," Tala groaned, wondering why every conversation she had with Glade or Lindholf revolve around the Vallè princess.

"Glade would jam his pecker into anything, even a Vallè," Lindholf said. "But Seita toys with him. It can only end poorly for him."

"What do you mean?"

"I mean Seita would chew Glade up and spit him out. Then Val-Draekin would cut his throat. Glade ought not mess with the likes of them. The Vallè, that is."

"What have you got against the Vallè?"

"It's the tone Seita uses when speaking of you, Tala. I care not for it."

Tala's brow furrowed. "What do you mean?"

"She made mention that you're none too bright when it comes to certain things."

"None too bright," Tala repeated, stung. Her eyes roamed Sunbird Hall for any sign of the Vallè princess. "What did she mean by that?"

"She didn't specify. You know how girls talk."

"Why would you tell me such a thing?" Tala said, upset. "As if I don't have enough to worry about."

But as Lindholf rattled away his answer, Tala was already lost in thought. After all, Glade had just informed her, Seita wanted to be friends. *Now Lindholf comes with his bad breath bearing the exact opposite news.* Tala searched the crowded room below, a knot building in her throat. She located the Vallè princess standing near a table with her father, Val-Korin. Dame Mairgrid was tending to Ansel, both of them near the main hearth at the far end of the room. Tala's eyes scanned the tables for Lawri, but she could not find her cousin. "Where's your sister?" Tala asked.

"Not feeling well," Lindholf answered. "Mother took her to her chambers."

"Why would you tell me Seita cast insults my way?"

"As cousins we should stick together," he said. "Our realm has grown full of peril. You must have allies, Tala. You must have one person you can trust above all others. For my part, I think you are the fairest and smartest girl in all of Gul Kana."

For some reason the sincerity in Lindholf's words touched her deeply. Within her cousin, she knew there lived no guile, no bravado or pretense. At all times he meant what he said. Then an image of Lawri's sickly face flashed into her mind. Guilt flooded her. She straightened her back and told herself to get a grip on her emotions.

"You're right, Lindholf," she said. "We should stick together. I value your friendship more than you know. You've such a sense of humor. You can make me laugh with but a look. You're so funny, and truth be told, much more interesting than Glade. I've always felt close to you." She grabbed his hands in hers, looked into his trusting eyes. "We have a connection that most people will never have."

"You truly think so?"

"Aye."

"I've always loved you, Tala." The words spilled from Lindholf's mouth as if he could not stop them, and he bashfully looked away.

Tala's heart skipped a beat at his tender admission. With her hand, she caressed his burn-scarred cheek, pulled it around so he was facing her again. "And I love you, cousin," she said, looking into his emotion-filled eyes, wondering what it was her cousin was really confessing to here.

He has such dark pupils. Just like his fair-haired sister, Lindholf's eyes were strangely black and, at the moment, full of hunger. But there was a gentleness behind that hunger too, a tenderness that touched her heart. "Are you okay, Lindholf?" she asked, her hand still caressing the burns on his face, seeing the tears springing from his eyes.

"I would not trust Glade." Lindholf leaned into her, his face melting into her hand still on his cheek. "Though he has been my best friend since childhood, I see now his only concern is for himself. I do not want to see you hurt. Our family visits to Amadon are too few." His body leaned into her, face bowing down to hers. "If I could live here with you, I would."

A small, sane part of her mind wanted to pull away from him. The other part of her mind, the part stricken with desperation to save Lawri, was glad, though.

"Protect you I would," he said, and quickly gave her a bashful little peck on the cheek, then pulled away as if stung by a bee. "M-my apologies, m'lady," he stammered in a nasally voice, his breath still reeking of drink.

"Don't be silly," Tala said, realizing they were not quite in full view of Sunbird Hall. She fought off her better judgment, now determined to do something she knew might be painful but necessary. Her knees were weak as she took him by one of the knobby wrists and pulled him toward the stairs and into full view of the hall. She clung to him now, her eyes cast up into his. "Kiss me again."

Lindholf's eyes were wide, as if he'd finally realized what she'd said. Lust was buried there just beneath the surface of his every glance. Tala could see it there and felt shame for what she was doing. Her heart throbbed heavily as he took her in his arms and kissed her with a fervency she did not know could exist in any one person.

She returned his kiss with a certain detachment, though, eyes open, ignoring his bitter breath, scanning Sunbird Hall over his shoulder. From what she could see, there was not one person in the room below looking up at them; even Dame Mairgrid had moved from her normal spot. The whole exercise seemed futile—even cruel.

Then she saw Glade Chaparral.

Glade stood down there in the center of the milling crowd, still as stone, dark locks of hair slung over his forehead, even darker eyes boring into hers as she clung to Lindholf. There was a challenge in those eyes. Tala sensed it. Glade turned and stalked away, lost in the swirl of the crowd.

Lindholf pulled away from her, his expression lofty with joy as he took her by the arm and led her farther back out onto the balcony. "I never knew you felt as I did. I admit to being a bit confused."

"I too am confused," she said, stunned at what she had done.

"Tala, know that I would defile a thousand Laijon statues at your whim."

Lindholf's impulsive burst of candor made Tala feel all the more guilty. And his mouth was on hers again, wet and slippery and unwanted. "Enough." Tala pulled back from him a little more abruptly than she'd have liked.

Lindholf's expression grew sulky. From the look he gave her, it was clear that he was just now realizing that there was something going on here beyond his understanding. The silence between them grew thick.

"I will not let you make a fool of me," he said, backing away from her. "I will not let you use me like the other girls, only to find out it is Glade you really want." His voice was pleading, and yet the guilty look on his face was telling. Tala could see that her cousin was truly embarrassed by what had just happened between them and probably considered the entire mess his fault. Deep down, she knew that Lindholf was so inexperienced with females he probably affixed a romantic significance to every innocent touch, word, or sigh. Certain besotted young men could misread the most casual of gestures as a promise of devotion.

"Pastry, m'lady?" Delia was walking up the stairs toward them, a silver tray in hand, only one pastry left on the tray. But Lindholf ignored the serving wench, fleeing down the stairs and into the crowd without a word.

"It wasn't for him anyway," the busty barmaid said, watching Lindholf go. She turned back to Tala. "They're so good. The best the kitchen is serving tonight. I saved this last one just for you, m'lady. That Vallè fellow, Val-Draekin, was scarfing them down faster than I could bring them out. They say the holy vicar will be here soon. And the last four gladiators, too. Tonight has been like a dream."

Delia held the tray out for Tala. The pastry was the size and shape of a small seashell, delicate, flaky, and covered in a thin white glaze with a dab of cherry-red frosting on top. "Cream-filled. Take it, I beg you," Delia implored. "A gift from me. For all you've done. It couldn't have been easy to get me this job."

Tala snatched up the pastry, eyes following Lindholf's retreating form as he pushed his way through the crowd. Her heart thumped in her chest, for many reasons.

"We play a cruel game, you and I," Delia said bluntly.

The barmaid's statement caught Tala off guard. "I don't know what you're talking about," she declared, mind frantic.

"I think you do."

Tala stepped away, her back stiff, her face set. But Delia kept talking. "I've seen tavern wenches play this very game. Nothing good can come of it, playing one lad off the other, the flirting, the kisses, pretending interest in both, never committing to either, always hinting of something more, dangling sex in front of them—"

"Such a thing has never crossed my mind." Tala flushed.

"Feigning interest in many men. It's just something we silly girls do."

"This hasn't anything to do with you," Tala said.

"You were correct the other day," Delia said. "I had no idea I would be subject to so many questions by the kitchen workers. Who am I? Where was I born? Do you know Princess Tala? Are you friends with her? They've certainly noticed me. I've even seen your sister glancing my way from time to time. I'll get the courage to talk to her later, I'm sure. Or perhaps, if I'm lucky, perhaps Jondralyn will approach me."

Tala was now disgusted and ashamed of herself for allowing this uncouth creature into the castle. The girl's breasts were about to puff up out of her top and spill all over everything. Tala actually caught herself scowling.

"I can see that I bother you." Delia bowed sharply. "I did not mean to interrupt you and your, uh, friend's kiss. Enjoy the pastry." The barmaid turned and beat a hasty retreat down the stairs toward the kitchen, empty tray in hand.

A simple thank-you for the pastry would have been a more appropriate response than a dirty scowl. Irritated with herself, Tala put the pastry to her mouth. With one bite, her blood turned cold. She gagged on something that seemed to grab onto her tongue and stick to the roof of her mouth like rough parchment. Instinct took over and she spit the offending object out. Fearing she'd just been poisoned, Tala frantically spit and spewed until she was sure her mouth had been completely purged.

Scattered over the balcony before her were the offending chunks of half-bitten food. And in the center of the mess was a small slip of coiled paper—the thing that had grabbed the top of her mouth and startled her.

Heart pounding, she picked the paper up and wiped it clean with her fingers.

It was a note. She read.

> *Shame. Shame. Two lads. The kissing. Oh, the juicy trouble that shall cause.*
>
> *It is time to open your eyes, girl. Jovan should have married Karowyn Raybourne as was arranged. He should have sent troops to the aid of Wyn Darrè years ago. Yet Denarius advised against it on both accounts. Find out what keeps your brother, the king of Gul Kana, so beholden to the grand vicar. You've already been shown one clue.*
>
> *Leave your answer for me in this same spot on this very balcony.*
>
> *Only then will you get your next clue.*

Next clue! Tala's mind raged with frustration—finding the cure for Lawri's affliction was yet again put off. The game continued. A thrill shot up her spine. Tala stuffed the paper into her dress and raced to the edge of the stairs, her eyes scanning the crowd, looking for the barmaid. But the girl was nowhere to be found.

More startling, a line of Silver Guards, all fully armored with thick crossbows in hand, were now marching up both sets of balcony stairs toward her. Tala's heart leaped into her throat at the sight of the gruff-faced fighters advancing on her.

"M'lady." One of the guards bowed to her. "None are now allowed on the balcony for the arrival of the last four gladiators, not even royalty. You must go down and prepare yourself for their grand entrance. Grand Vicar Denarius arrives with them soon."

*The Last Warrior Angels would have you believe my beloved was a man
unblemished and without fault, innocently enslaved. While those who enslaved
Laijon would tell you he was a charlatan and a thief. Either way, the fact
remains, Laijon was the King of Slaves, bathed in scarlet, bathed in blood. And
he carried an angel stone in hand and bore the Mark of the Slave upon his flesh.*
—The Moon Scrolls of Mia

CHAPTER TWENTY-SIX
JONDRALYN BRONACHELL

4TH DAY OF THE MOURNING MOON, 999TH YEAR OF LAIJON

AMADON, GUL KANA

The gladiators' entrance into Sunbird Hall began with the low groan of bagpipes. Drums beat dully and deep. Then the swelling rise of a dozen flutes soared above it all, a tide of joyous sound punctuated by the thunderous gongs of a large iron bell. Every royal, soldier, and servant now faced the closed double doors at the western end of the hall, ecstasy in their eyes. The Silver Guards were in place, lining every wall and alcove, including the two sweeping staircases at the eastern end of the hall leading up to the balcony, spears and crossbows at the ready. The crowd hushed in awe.

The drums and gong erupted into a fury of whirling and pounding, building to a crescendo, then falling silent. Only the fluttering of the flutes and the low moan and sigh of the bagpipes hung in the air, and then they, too, faded.

Three hundred or more pairs of eyes stared eagerly, almost hungrily at the wide double doors that now swung open to twelve swarthy-looking Dayknights, who pushed their way into Sunbird Hall, Grand Vicar Denarius in full regalia not ten steps behind. The five archbishops of Amadon followed him. The Dayknight captain, Ser Sterling Prentiss, black-lacquered armor buffed and shined, followed the five archbishops. Behind Sterling, in silver armor, was Ser Lars Castlegrail, commander of the Silver Guard. And behind Ser Lars, the last four gladiators were introduced by the arena herald one by one: Squireck Van Hester, the oghul Shkill Gha, and two dark-haired Vallè pirates named Val-Ce-Laveroc and Val-Rievaux. The two Vallè walked straight into the center of Sunbird Hall with confidence. They stood together, dark and brooding. But it was the anvil-jawed oghul, towering over everyone, who garnered the most attention. In his bull hide, spiked armor, and steel-toed leather boots, Shkill Gha stood more than seven feet tall as he shoved his way between Val-Ce-Laveroc and Val-Rievaux and roared, to the shock and delight of all those present.

The Prince of Saint Only stood behind the other three, dressed in a simple white robe, the wreath of heather Tala had made for him about his head. Jondralyn could see the venom in his eyes as he stared at the vicar. Six of the Dayknights now flanked Squireck, three on either side. The Prince of Saint Only was also the only one of the four gladiators shackled at the ankles, wrists bound behind his back. The other three fighters were able to move about freely, chains around their waists and wrists, but long enough that they could hold plates and feed themselves—the two Vallè pirates were sipping from goblets of wine already, and the oghul had a hunk of cooked meat in hand.

Indeed, the entrance of the four gladiators had certainly gotten everyone's attention, none more so than Jondralyn. The arena was her *destiny*. She was weary, her muscles sore from today's training, scarcely able to move at all, it seemed. But seeing the four warriors birthed a renewed energy into her exhausted body and soul.

In her uncomfortable, suffocating gown, she walked stiffly toward the gladiators, every muscle protesting. Anjk Bourbon had certainly set her onto a rigorous path. It had been nearly two days since she'd slept. She ambled across the room, trying to look as lucid and regal as possible, trying to make sense of the swirl of thoughts spinning in her head; thoughts of angel stones and the bloodline of Laijon. She was still trying to wrap her head around what Roguemoore, Hawkwood, and Culpa Barra had revealed to her about the Brethren of Mia. She wondered if she had dreamed the entire evening on Rockliegh Isle. Hawkwood had given her the map. That was real. It was still safe in its hiding spot in her room. *But whom do I trust?* Squireck was here. *Can I trust him?* He was a member of the Brethren. She'd almost reached him when she was diverted by the Val Vallè ambassador. "I must take up an issue with Sterling Prentiss," Val-Korin said. "And your gracious presence could help, if it is not too much to ask?" Val-Korin bowed deeply. "It would take but a moment, and I would be forever grateful, m'lady."

She agreed, a bit reluctantly, though, allowing Val-Korin to take her arm and lead her in the direction of the Dayknight captain, who was helping himself to a pastry.

"May I speak freely?" Val-Korin bowed to Sterling upon arrival.

"Of course." The Dayknight captain dipped his head in return. "I consider us friends." But to Jondralyn the look in his eyes bespoke different sentiments indeed.

Val-Korin talked in a less than cordial manner too. "The Silver Guard is not clearing the temple in a timely manner. Seita and I wish to worship at the feet of Laijon unmolested. Breita was due to arrive last week. She has not. Our hearts are filled with worry. We pray for her safety. To pray at the feet of Laijon offers comfort and solace."

"The Silver Guard does the best it can, I am sure," Sterling apologized. "And I am sorry to hear of Breita's absence. I do hope she is well and arrives at court soon."

"With the money the Vallè give to the church, you'd think the Val Vallè ambassador could pray at the feet of Laijon without a mangy crowd wailing and flagellating themselves directly behind him." Val-Korin looked at Jondralyn for affirmation. "Or should I take up my concern with Denarius himself?"

"No need for that," Sterling said without a trace of emotion. He was not easily ruffled. "Vallè money has indeed purchased much influence in Gul Kana, this I know."

Jondralyn couldn't fathom why the Val Vallè ambassador was bringing up such a petty problem now, or why he needed her at his side to do so. Still, Val-Korin held her eyes a moment before turning to Sterling and continuing, "The common street rabble should never be allowed in the temple. It is a holy shrine. A grand work of art sculpted by Vallè hands. It should be a sanctuary for royalty only. I should not fear being accosted by the degenerate when taking my daughter there to pray."

"It is indeed a holy shrine created by the great Vallè artisans of old," Sterling conceded. "But you forget its purpose. Faithful followers of Laijon travel for hundreds of miles to pray at the feet of Laijon. For some the journey is the culmination of their life's desires. We cannot close off the statue to these pilgrimages."

"The place smells of urine." Val-Korin gave the captain a flat, unfriendly stare.

Sterling was quick to answer. "That a foul odor dwells in the Temple of the Laijon Statue is a gross dereliction of duty. I will give Ser Castlegrail explicit orders to more hastily clear the temple even when Vallè royalty choose to visit, and to have the floors scrubbed thrice daily."

"It's more than likely the Silver Guards who are pissing in the corners."

"I assure you, each of your concerns will be taken care of." Sterling bowed low and just a tad curtly to Val-Korin.

"I certainly hope so." The hint of coldness living in Val-Korin's eyes now carried with it a hint of impatience too—almost a look of having been slighted by this oversight. To Jondralyn, it seemed scarcely a concern at all. She knew that the Vallè kingdom had supported the Church of Laijon financially in its fledgling years, providing most, if not all, of the artisans who had done its great paintings and sculpted its great statues and built its chapels and towering cathedrals and temples. But that was ancient history. True, the church owed the Vallè much. In fact, the Vallè were still the largest contributors to its coffers, donating far more gold than could ever be spent. Jondralyn knew that the bishopric was beholden to the Vallè, but only to a point.

Still, by the way King Jovan groveled at the grand vicar's feet and in turn how the vicar's Dayknight captain had just groveled to Val-Korin, one could deduce that it was the Vallè who truly ran things in Gul Kana.

With another bow, Sterling parted company with Jondralyn and the Val Vallè ambassador. Val-Korin thanked her for her help and moved on too, leaving her to wonder what she had been needed for, if anything.

A busty serving girl sauntered by and gave her an impish little grin, then turned and moved through the crowd toward the stairs leading up to the balcony. Jondralyn couldn't quite place where she knew the serving girl from, but she'd seen her before. She tipped her head at Squireck, who bowed in return—the Prince of Saint Only stood a few steps behind the other gladiators and assumed the bearing of the Laijon statue itself in his plain white robe and wreath of heather. Sunbird Hall, she realized, was not the place she could have a frank conversation with him about Brethren of Mia matters.

Directly in front of the Prince of Saint Only, Val-Ce-Laveroc and

Val-Rievaux looked to be sharing a joke. The two Vallè gladiators were athletic and deadly. She had seen them kill in the arena with as much precision and skill as either Squireck or the oghul. Both Vallè warriors wore simple black leather pants over shirts of overlapping, scaled leaf mail. It was customary that the gladiators attend the celebration in full battle gear. The royals reveled in seeing their fighters all dressed up in their gladiator regalia—minus the weapons, of course.

Shkill Gha was stuffing his mouth with meat and pastries. As he chewed, his ponderous lips peeled back, revealing a gaping maw crowded with rows of fanglike yellow teeth. His hideous face wore an expression of contempt for any who approached him asking of the tournament. He snarled at all comers, a deep rumble setting many to scatter. The three other gladiators appeared to be the only ones in the room unaffected by his grandiose presence. To be honest, this particular oghul was profoundly more ugly than Jondralyn's trainer Anjk Bourbon. Shkill Gha's arms were as corded and rough as old stumps and hung lumbering and low beneath his shoulders. His beady eyes drank in the sight of the Vallè princess, Seita, standing a few paces away. She was talking to Claybor Chaparral. The oghul shambled forward and stood over her, smiling wide, globs of food in his teeth. Lord Claybor looked at the beast in utter revulsion. Yet Seita bowed graciously to Shkill Gha and handed him a pastry from her own hand; he gobbled it immediately. Jondralyn had heard stories of this oghul's crimes. He was a brutal killer of hundreds. Humans were his prey. To kill so habitually was a sickness, many said, a sickness caused by the wraiths that could never be reined in. It was clear that the wraiths afflicted oghul-kind, too. Shkill Gha noticed her staring, curled his lip, and growled.

Jondralyn blanched and made her way back to her brother's table on the raised dais at the eastern end of the room. Shkill Gha was a fright. Unlike Jovan, she believed the rumors of oghul Hragna'Ar raids in the far northlands of Gul Kana. Oghuls had their own prophets and shamans, shamans who spoke of the end of times as the great Hragna'Ar, which included raiding and pillaging, and, it was also rumored, human sacrifice.

Jovan was alone at the end of the long table, the remains of his dinner spread before him. A row of six Dayknights, ever watchful of the crowd, lined the velvet-draped wall behind the king. To the far left of the six knights was the tall Silver Throne itself, always covered in white sheets, scarcely used or even seen since Borden Bronachell's death. Jovan wore a black cloak trimmed with silver at the wrists and neckline with a black leather belt embellished with shiny brass looplets. Diamond and ruby rings adorned his fingers, jeweled bracelets circled each wrist, and gold chains, each hung with glistening gems, were draped about his neck. The only simple thing about Jovan was the royal crown upon his head—a silver band nearly a thousand years old.

Unlike her brother, Jondralyn wore no finery with her already richly brocaded gown. Just a simple silver brooch. No gold chains. No rings. She didn't want people to begin thinking of her as overly extravagant in anything. She desired the populace to see her as different from Jovan in every way.

She sat at the opposite end of the table from him. She dipped her hand into the bowl on the table, snatched up a handful of nuts, and popped them into her mouth one at a time. Her gaze was fixed on a bracelet Jovan had removed from his wrists. He began shining it with a white silk handkerchief. The sight of her brother so engrossed in polishing such a useless trinket sickened her. She wanted to take the bracelet and cram it down his throat. There'd been a time when she felt her brother was not so unreachable; but of course they had been young children then. It was highly doubtful they would ever reclaim that closeness they'd once shared. And after the duel in the courtyard, where Jovan had so soundly thumped her in front of everyone, she knew there was little love left in him for any of his siblings.

She took solace in the fact that she was privy to information that even her brother was not. Jovan was unaware of the Rooms of Sorrow buried under the city. He did not know of the white angel stone or Laijon's shield, *Ethic Shroud*. Jovan was not part of the Brethren of Mia as she was—as their father mother and father had been.

"Ale to wash down your nuts, m'lady?" The serving girl who had earlier caught Jondralyn's eye curtsied before her. The girl held forth a silver goblet. With her ordinary looks, this girl was just another servant in the crowd, simple, bland, and unassuming. It was her breasts that set her apart—puffing from the top of her corset in a most obnoxious, attention-grabbing way. Jondralyn took the offered goblet, trying to place the face of the girl.

"Do I dare ask to sit with you a moment, m'lady?" The girl threw her a shy look.

"You can sit where you like," Jondralyn said.

"Not on your lap, I assume," the girl said, giggling. Jondralyn shot the serving girl a dark look as the girl straddled the bench in front of her. "If Dame Vilamina sees me here, I would get a scolding for sure. She brooks no slouching from her staff."

The girl certainly had a flirty, confident way about her that Jondrayn imagined enthralled most men. From the way the girl brazenly sat, facing her, Jondralyn could see up her skirt almost to the top of her inner thigh. The girl placed both hands on the bench before her and pressed her breasts together with her arms, leaning in. She had a way of ducking her chin and making her eyes look big and round and, well, rather beautiful. Those eyes also twinkled with mischief.

"You look familiar," Jondralyn said. "I've seen you at court before? Yet I cannot recall your name."

"You don't recall my name?" The girl's eyes grew a tad cold as she pulled back. "I must say, I'm hurt." She flashed a nasty, flirtatious little grin.

Jondralyn felt herself blushing and, casting her eyes about, noticed Tala standing at the edge of the crowd, scowling like a thundercloud. Jondralyn frowned at her younger sister and turned back to the serving girl. "What is your name?"

"Delia," the girl said, her voice dark and creamy, almost husky with lust.

Then it dawned on her. "You work at the Filthy Horse Saloon. What are you doing in the castle?"

"Who's this?" Jovan's voice rumbled down the length of the table. "Who's that girl with you?" Jovan was pointing at Delia, his voice slurred. Jondralyn could tell her brother was not quite fully drunk yet, but getting there. "Introduce me," he said.

Delia shot to her feet, then immediately dropped to one knee before her king, bowing low.

"What is your name, girl?" Jovan stood.

"Delia," she said, straightening. "If it please Your Excellency."

Jovan staggered the length of the table toward the girl, his ceremonial sword clanking at his side. "You're not considering sneaking away with my sister tonight, are you? The way she dresses some days, one *might* think it was indeed women she fancied." There was a hard tightening around Jovan's eyes. Jondralyn was learning to notice these small warning signs. Jovan was spoiling for an argument. He hovered drunkenly over Delia now. "I'm afraid that Jondralyn does not care for men, if you take my meaning."

"I'm sorry, Your Excellency." Delia bowed again, still on one knee. "Perhaps I should go."

"Don't let me scare you off, sweetheart," Jovan said, holding forth a hand and helping Delia to her feet. She stood graciously and bowed to him again. But Jovan was looking at Jondralyn. "How does oghul cock taste?" He spat the question angrily at her. "I hear their peckers are over a foot long and covered in boils."

Jondralyn snatched the goblet from the table and took a long drink from it.

"Don't think I don't know about your gladiator training," Jovan said, hostility now carved on his face. "I hear Anjk Bourbon would only train a human if that human suckled his cock as payment. So tell me, how does it taste?"

Jondralyn settled into a seething silence, now sipping from her goblet of ale. She did not want to get into a fight with her brother now. But Jovan pulled his black sword. It rang from its sheath with a hiss, earning a frightened squeal from Delia.

Jondralyn flew to her feet. "What's the meaning of this?"

Tala was between them, begging. "Please, Jovan, no." The look on her face was one of such worry and fright.

Jovan brandished the weapon, eyes glinting like steel. "I can only imagine what foul oath that—that—dwarf made you take to join his brotherhood."

"I—I know not of what you speak," Jondralyn stammered, eyes bouncing between Tala and Jovan. She had never been asked to swear an oath of any kind by Roguemoore or Hawkwood or Squireck when she was introduced to the Brethren of Mia. But for some reason, she now wished she had swore an oath of some kind, if for no other reason than to spite Jovan.

"That dwarf's witch-worshipping cult is an affront to Laijon," Jovan snarled. "I should have you flogged for your insolence, now that the dwarf has disappeared. And if I find out that you had anything to do with Hawkwood's escape from Purgatory, I *will* have you flogged. Perhaps worse."

"Please, Jovan, come sit with me." Tala took Jovan by the arm, trying to lead him away, trembling as she did so.

But Jovan shrugged Tala off, his jaw twitching with anger as he turned on Jondralyn. "Beware, sister, someday someone may hold you to account for this un-un-unfathomable treachery you are involved in."

"Please, Jovan, you're drunk," Tala pleaded again. "Come sit with me and Ansel."

"He's bloody well lost his mind." Jondralyn sat again, taking another swig of ale.

With a forceful motion that made her flinch, Jovan sheathed his sword and said, "You know I suffer from a rabid intolerance of idealism and . . . and . . . folly, both of which abound in you. The arena is no place for a woman. It will gain you nothing but your own bloody death, Jon."

Jondralyn was gulping at her mead now, both hands clenched tight around the goblet. She eyed Jovan with what she hoped was unmistakable belligerence, but Jovan's attention was now elsewhere—he was apologizing to Tala. "True, I am drunk." Jovan's voice was slurred. He scratched at his head wildly. "I am behaving poorly before guests and serving girls and even my dearest sister. Please forgive my brash behavior, Tala."

But Tala was looking straight at Delia, who appeared to avoid her stare.

Jovan's glassy gaze also shifted to the serving girl. "You also must accept my apologies," he said, holding his hands out to her. "I insist."

But Delia was frozen in place, staring at the king with wide, terrified eyes.

"Poor thing, I've frightened you." Jovan bowed to the Filthy Horse barmaid. The silver crown slid from his head this time. It landed gently on the thick white rug under Jondralyn.

"Do you mind?" Jovan motioned to the crown at Jondralyn's feet. "I dare not reach down for fear of toppling over drunk. And I apologize to you, too, Jon. Much weighs heavy on my mind of late."

Jondralyn picked up the crown and handed it to him. Jovan placed it firmly back atop his head, then slapped her, a backhanded blow across the cheek that knocked her reeling against the table and sent her goblet of ale splashing over the rug.

"Only the king is allowed to touch the royal crown!" he spat. "Mind your place!"

A bone-deep weariness washed over Jondralyn. She felt the sting on her cheek. This was a battle she would not win now. She knew it.

This abuse at the hands of her brother would not be over until she had proven her quality in the arena. She would usurp him. Then she would have to kill him.

He was staring directly at Delia, his head leaning closer and closer down toward her, so close Jondralyn feared Jovan might very well topple drunkenly into her, face-planting himself right in her pale cleavage.

"Like a little kitten, you charm without knowing it," Jovan said to the girl. "Have you ever fucked a king?"

"No, Your Excellency," she answered.

"Neither have I." Jovan took her by the hand, pulling her toward him. "Perhaps you can tell me what it feels like." With a snap of his fingers, the six Dayknights standing against the wall stepped forward and escorted Jovan and Delia out of Sunbird Hall.

Oh, that chaotic War of Cleansing! How it raged! Demons great and small
fled before the might of the armies of the Five Isles, the Five Warrior
Angels leading the way, reaping destruction. It mattered not where the foul
demons slunk off to, be it mountain, sea, or cave, for they were found and
they were slain. To the very last they died, to the last day of the Vicious
War of the Demons, that final cleansing under the great Atonement Tree.
—THE MOON SCROLLS OF MIA

CHAPTER TWENTY-SEVEN
STERLING PRENTISS

4TH DAY OF THE MOURNING MOON, 999TH YEAR OF LAIJON
AMADON, GUL KANA

Sterling felt cursed as he opened the door to the entry hall of the king's chamber. Beyond that he made his way through a small foyer and cordoned-off library and then into Jovan's bedroom. Culpa Barra followed.

Sconces lined the walls, illuminating the scene. Jovan's bloody clothes and bedsheets were strewn about the floor. The Val Vallè ambassador, Val-Korin, was examining the king's four-post mahogany bed and blood-soaked sheets. His daughter, Seita, stood on the thick bearskin rug at the foot of the bed; another Vallè, the dark-haired fellow who'd been accompanying the ambassador's daughter as of late, by her side—Val-Draekin his name. Sterling didn't like the looks of him.

The gray stone walls of the room were draped with velvet tapestries and hung with an astonishing number of decorative swords, all opulent with intricate jeweled hilts and delicately sculpted crosspieces. Every surface of Jovan's scrollworked armoires and cabinets was covered with golden trinkets, glittery goblets, and jeweled Laijon statuettes.

A kitchen girl, the front of her corset covered in blood, slumped against the wall near the cold stone hearth. Blood splatters adorned the priceless horsehair divan near her. Six Silver Guards flanked the girl, spears held at the ready. She wasn't going anywhere with that much steel pointed in her face.

"I've already had Jovan carried to the infirmary," Val-Korin said, and bowed to Sterling. The Val Vallè ambassador wore a long black robe; the red brass pendant of his rank hung about his neck from a slender, bejeweled chain. "He was escorted by Ser Landon Galloway himself. Val-Gianni, my own physician, accompanied him."

"How grievous were his injuries?"

"With a bit of Vallè luck, he may pull through."

Sterling studied the crimson-coated bedsheets with ever-growing dread. Jovan had lost a lot of blood in the attack. Though the captain held scant love for Jovan, the fact that an assassination attempt had happened so easily within the castle was a failure of staggering magnitude. It could cost Sterling his life. It was his solemn duty as Dayknight captain to protect both the Silver Throne and the grand vicar. As things stood, with the king near death, the vicar would be hard-pressed not to have Sterling hung.

"We held her for you to question." Val-Korin motioned to the distraught girl under guard. "A serving wench from the kitchen staff. Or so she claims."

"How could one such as she cause such chaos and havoc?" Sterling asked Culpa.

It had been a long night for the two of them. The grand vicar's anointing of the last four gladiators had already put Sterling in a state of prickly agitation that had lasted all evening. Every year it was the same, and in Sterling's estimation, it was an uncouth tradition. Dousing criminals with consecrated oils, and then uttering the Angel Warrior's Prayer over each, was an affront to human decency. Yet the priesthood blessing administered over the four gladiators was specific in its intent—the winner of the tournament was deemed holy and therefore ultimately innocent in the eyes of Laijon. Sterling doubted the validity of any of it. Agitated, he scowled at Val-Korin, Seita and Val-Draekin. "What are your daughter and this other *person* doing here?"

"They were both with me when the guards raised the alarm," Val-Korin answered cordially. "Naturally, they followed me here."

The Val Vallè princess nodded to Sterling, as did Val-Draekin.

"Odd to bring a lady of the king's court into such a bloody mess."

"My daughter's here to learn an important lesson on abstaining from rash action, using caution in one's life. You know, that life is not always a vase of fragrant flowers."

"Whatever." Sterling looked from father to daughter. "This is a Dayknight investigation now. Archbishops will be involved too. You all must leave."

He moved toward the serving girl, who still cowered against the wall. Tears streaked her cheeks Sterling admired the cut and fit of the girl's outfit. Even covered in blood, the garment suited her well. "Name?" he asked.

"Delia." Even scared and shaking, the girl possessed a rich, throaty voice. Her eyes darted about the room and rested on Culpa, who'd stepped up behind Sterling.

"What have you to say for yourself?" Sterling continued.

"He desired to sleep with me," the girl blurted. "But then he got suddenly angry with me. I tried to soothe him. But then he would not have me."

"So you stabbed him?"

"No, Ser. He fell asleep. Then I fell asleep. When I woke, he was already stabbed." Four Silver Guard spears immediately threatened her throat. Fear flashed in her wide, round eyes. "It was I who shouted for the guards," she said, voice shaking.

Sterling looked askance at Culpa, who shrugged. Jovan was not one to dally with the kitchen help. The captain appraised the girl with a cold eye. She had a wild, untamed look underneath her fear. But he was certain that this girl had *not* stabbed Jovan.

"I fell asleep," Delia said. "On the floor. When I woke, he was already bloody."

Sterling's eyes roamed the room, looking for any sign of a hidden passageway. Nothing was apparent, but his look was cursory. He made a mental note to come back later with Culpa Barra and search the chamber more thoroughly. Perhaps there were passages here that Jovan had not told him of, or that he himself did not know about because they were so ancient. The hidden tunnels in the castle were countless. But he did not want to discuss the secret ways with Culpa whilst the other guards and the three Vallè were still present. To his consternation, the latter hadn't left yet.

"Your story makes little sense," he said to the serving girl.

"If I'd done the killing, why then would I yell for help?" she asked pleadingly.

Val-Korin spoke. "I must say, minus her unimaginably noticeable bosom, this girl's ordinary appearance is the perfect disguise for an assassin."

Sterling's brow furrowed with annoyance. Still, the Vallè had a point.

"Everyone can imagine a slim girl being an assassin," Seita added. "But bosoms like hers are the perfect disguise. They sort of cancel any attempt at going unnoticed. I ask you, Father, who would ever think a girl sporting breasts of such magnificence would be apt to knife the king?"

"Yes," Val-Korin said. "And again, any girl endowed with such delights would surely gain the attention of the king. Then, once alone in a room like this, with a knife . . ."

"The perfect crime," Seita said.

It was an asinine theory. This girl hadn't knifed the king.

Truth was, Sterling could scarcely tolerate the Vallè. They had a knack for locating the absurd in everything and prattling on about it until any sane person wanted to tear out their own hair. No matter what, life was just one big game to them. As an entire species, the Vallè's propensity to conjure havoc for havoc's sake knew no bounds. They were always running some scheme or con purely for their own amusement. Sterling wouldn't put it past either Val-Korin or his daughter to have staged this entire assassination attempt just to garner a few Vallè giggles at his expense—merely looking at their delicate, smug faces made him want to punch someone, or something. He'd sooner trust a bloodsucking oghul than a Vallè.

"It would be a nuisance to keep her around," Seita said. "I foresee only trouble if she lives, Father. We should behead her now."

"I agree," Val-Korin said.

"Please, no," Delia said frantically. "I had nothing to do with this."

Val-Korin pulled a slim dagger from the pocket of his tunic under his black robe. His thin lips turned up at the corners in a faint grin.

"You dare draw a weapon in my presence?" Sterling queried, annoyed. "Put it away!"

"As you wish," Val-Korin said, a trace of amusement dancing behind his maddening little smile. "I'm only trying to be of assistance."

"Frightening the girl does little to assist me."

It was Culpa Barra who advocated the wisest course of action. "Best we lock her in the dungeons under the Hall of the Dayknights until we've investigated this further."

The serving girl hung her head, hair covering her face. In a way, Sterling actually kind of agreed with Seita—behead the serving wench now and be done with it. But what the Vallè princess didn't realize was that killing the girl now would not solve the more obvious problem: the real assassin. That dark shadow, whoever it was, still stalked the halls of the castle. And if Sterling did not find the assassin soon, it might be he who suffered a swift beheading.

"The king didn't want to bed me," the serving girl muttered. "He got mad at me."

Sterling stepped in front of the girl and lifted her chin in his hand, studying her face. He could spot a lie in anyone. And this serving girl was easy to read. She was not lying. Her eyes bored into his, pleading. "I shouldn't even be here," she said. "Don't you understand? This is not what I was asked to do. He got *mad* at me."

If what she said was true, and Jovan had not bedded her, it was a shame.

"I was supposed to be with Jondralyn," the girl said softly, more to herself now than to anyone in the room, eyes cast to the ground. "Doesn't anyone understand?"

"Perhaps you meant to steal from His Excellency the king?" Val-Korin said.

Sterling's brow again furrowed with annoyance. "Gather a contingent of Silver Guards and escort her to Purgatory," he ordered Culpa Barra. "I will interrogate her there later."

As he watched Culpa tie the girl's hands and march her from the chamber, Sterling's mind churned. Someone, quite possibly in Jovan's own council, was behind the assassination attempt. Val-Korin came to mind first. The archbishops next. He distrusted all of them. *But if this is the Vallè's—or even the vicar's—doing, why?* Jovan was their puppet.

Perhaps it was Edmon Guy Van Hester. After all, the Lord of Saint Only had ample reason to hate Jovan. But killing the king would not free Squireck. So Edmon seemed an unlikely culprit too; he was a conquered lord living in a conquered castle. He had no power anywhere.

If it was a Sør Sevier assassin—again, why? If it had been a trained assassin, Jovan would certainly be dead. And from the evidence, whoever attacked him also had plenty of time to slay Delia as she slept. But, again, why? *A Bloodwood would be better off assassinating Jondralyn. Or even me, for that matter.* After all, Jovan had offered no resistance to their recent conquest of Wyn Darrè. Even now, the king offered scant resistance to their inevitable invasion of Gul Kana. It was as if the new king, in his apathy, was speeding Absolution along at a breakneck pace. At the very thought, Sterling fumed. Not everyone in Gul Kana harbored such a death wish—certainly not Jondralyn, nor Roguemoore. And perhaps that was why Sterling had taken sides with the Brethren of Mia.

King Borden Bronachell and Sterling had been like brothers. The king had tried to get Sterling to join the Brethren before his death in Wyn Darrè. He had confided in Sterling many of the secrets of Mia, which Sterling had, at first, found alarming. Not until after Borden's death and Jovan's taking of the Silver Throne had Sterling finally realized the ever-growing ineptitude and futility of Jovan's reign and joined Roguemoore's secret organization in hopes of forging a better Gul Kana—a Gul Kana of which Borden would have been proud—a Gul Kana that would fight against the White Prince. But to this point, Sterling had done little as a member of the Brethren of Mia except help Roguemoore in seemingly petty schemes: arranging horses for Hawkwood and the dwarf in Eskander, the harebrained plan of picking a fight with Roguemoore just so Hawkwood could challenge the Dayknights to a duel and get tossed into Purgatory. That fiasco had cost four good Dayknights their lives. Clearly, the Vallè were not the only ones in Amadon concocting wild schemes and cons. He was not privy to all the inner workings and secrets of the Brethren. But in truth, Sterling enjoyed helping them. It was with the dwarf that he, with the help of Kelvin Kronnin, had begun organizing legions at Lord's Point and Lokkenfell, preparing behind Jovan's back for the

Sør Sevier invasion. Plus, there was something insidious in the way Jovan was being manipulated by Denarius and the quorum of five, but Sterling could not put a finger on exactly what. It was with the Brethren that he could do his part behind the scenes to counteract all the political machinations of Val-Korin and the grand vicar when it came to Jovan and the young king's rule. And that was a worthy cause in and of itself.

Now that Jondralyn was part of the Brethren, all the better. He saw Borden's strength in her. It was clear that Hawkwood saw that strength in her too. Jondralyn, at least, desired to stand up and fight. She had honor. The very last prophecy in the Revelations of the Fourth Warrior Angel in *The Way and Truth of Laijon* warned that the wrath of Laijon would be great if those able to bear arms in Gul Kana did not fight the righteous war. Even in the face of Absolution, they were still to defend themselves. *For Laijon would only arise again for those who would defend themselves.* When he was younger, Sterling had wondered if the prophecies in *The Way and Truth of Laijon* weren't all just nonsense. But things seemed to be coming to pass rapidly now. Fiery Absolution might be inevitable, he surmised. But Gul Kana need not go down without a fight, as it appeared Jovan was leading them to do. He hated Borden's son. Jovan was a miserable, overly pious, fickle boy who distrusted those he should trust and trusted those—like Val-Korin—who ought to be slapped in irons and thrown into Purgatory.

Perhaps this assassination attempt *was* the work of Roguemoore, or Hawkwood, or even Jondralyn. Whatever the reason, someone had tried to kill Gul Kana's king tonight. And to Sterling's way of thinking, it was a shame Jovan had not died in the attempt. He recalled the first verses from the Book of the Slave in *The Way and Truth of Laijon*: *For if it needs be that one man die so an entire kingdom falls not into destruction, then so be it done in the name of Laijon.* Still, Sterling did not want to be hung for negligence in the death of his king. So the task was upon him to hunt down an assassin in a castle full of more nooks and crannies and hidey-holes than there were fish in the sea. He could already feel the anger and frustration rise within him.

"I offer my help and the help of my retainers in tracking down this killer," Val-Korin said. "Val-So-Vreign, one of my best guardsmen. Even Val-Draekin can help. He is more skilled than any of your Day-knights, an expert tracker—"

"Enough." Sterling glared at the Val Vallè ambassador. "The only help I'll need from the likes of you, or any of your kind, for that matter, is to lick my arse clean after a ripe shit." The insult shot through the air like an arrow. And in the immediate wake of his out-burst, Sterling desired to take the words back. But it was as if those words had been trussed up inside, waiting for their chance to escape, ever since the Vallè ambassador had accosted him earlier that evening about Silver Guards not clearing the Temple of the Laijon Statue fast enough. "I ordered you leave this chamber long ago."

Val-Korin took a step back from Sterling, astonishment on his face, a delicate hand rising to his chest. His voice now simmered. "Well, I must say, I've never been treated so vile. The holy vicar will hear of this. Come, Seita. Come, Val-Draekin. Let us relieve Ser Sterling of our presence."

As he watched the insufferable Val Vallè ambassador strut out the door, his daughter and Val-Draekin following, Sterling fumed—fumed at himself for not controlling his own anger.

And once he let that anger get to him, Sterling knew, there was no telling what he might do.

† † † † †

He found it hard to believe that his short investigation led him to the bedchamber of Jovan's youngest sister, Tala. The slim, dark-haired princess sat on the edge of her bed, looking up at him with a blank, sleepy stare.

"Why would you have your brother killed?" He leaned over her menacingly.

She answered with silence. Yet he was struck by the sudden intensity in her eyes. This surprised him. For he figured the news of her brother's injuries would set off a great flood of royal whining and histrionics in the girl. Yet here she sat, calm, the look on her face one of deep, dare he say, reflection. It was as if this girl too was trying to mull over in her mind the whys and wherefores of the attack on Jovan. But one telling thing about her reaction—she wasn't shocked at the news. Though she did ask how her brother was.

"Jovan lies in the infirmary," was all he gave her. The old Vallè sawbones, Val-Gianni, who had cleaned and stitched Jovan's wounds, claimed the king had been stabbed five times, yet somehow the blade had missed every vital organ and artery.

Sterling had learned from the head kitchen matron, Dame Vilamina—an aged windbag who knew each and every morsel of gossip in Amadon Castle and could prattle on about it for hours— that Delia was put on the serving staff at the request of the king's sister Tala. Several things had started falling into place in Sterling's mind. Also, more questions arose. Especially when Dame Vilamina claimed that both Glade Chaparral and Lindholf Le Graven had been spotted with Tala near the docks in stolen Silver Guard armor. Sterling had Vilamina escorted to Purgatory under the Hall of the Dayknights and placed in a cell near Delia. He ordered the guards to stay within hearing distance and see if they discussed anything of note. If they were part of a plot, or just unwitting players, Sterling would soon find out.

Sterling studied young Tala Bronachell as her dark eyes stared into space. She was transforming into a young woman of graceful, almost spiritual beauty. In a few years, she would surpass even Jondralyn as the jewel of Amadon.

"Even a sister to the king can be hung for treason," he said. "Tell me what you know and your brother might be lenient with you . . . if he survives."

Still she stared, eyes boring into the cold stone hearth behind him. Sterling leaned toward her, taking the young girl's chin in his hand, forcing her head up so she could look him in the eye. "Vilamina will surely hang. Is that what you want? If this was your doing, or if someone put you up to this, best spill it now. It would be a shame if the poor kitchen matron was executed because of you . . . and the serving girl hung too."

"I do not know what you are talking about," Tala spoke. Her usual affable and charming voice was buried somewhere deep within herself.

"Things do not look good for you, young lady. Tell me what you know."

There was a flicker of emotion in her eyes now—and hatred, too. "If my brother is injured, I demand that you take me to the infirmary." Her words were a challenge and defiance, a command really. Insolence now emanated from her in waves.

"That is out of the question." Sterling wondered if the hatred he detected within Tala was directed at him. It wouldn't be a surprise. With the exception of Jondralyn, he'd never found favor with the Bronachell children ever since Borden had been killed in Wyn Darrè. He knew that Jovan hated him and considered him of little importance, preferring to keep council with Denarius and Val-Korin. And he sometimes felt that Jondralyn only tolerated him because of his deep affection for her father and now because of his links to the Brethren of Mia. For as much as Sterling had admired Borden whilst he was alive, and for as much as he was grateful to the king for making him Dayknight captain sixteen years ago, deep down Sterling knew that Borden's son was different from his father—weaker, more afraid. Jondralyn had more spirit than a dozen men. She was the future of Gul Kana. And Tala? Tala showed potential; she was gathering some strength now.

She brooded darkly in front of him. "I order you to take me to my brother."

"You've heard of Purgatory? Perhaps I shall escort you there, personally."

"You haven't the authority," she said calmly.

She was correct, and he was actually starting to admire her for standing up to him. Any incident involving the royal family brought into play many meetings and much discussion among the nobles and king's council and even the grand vicar. One could not just march the king's sister off to the dungeons under the Hall of the Dayknights without serious repercussions. Tala was certainly more stoic and far smarter than he had originally thought. Interrogating her like this was going to get him nowhere. Still, he was convinced she was hiding something. He backed away from her. She relaxed visibly. Her posture now carried with it a smidgen of victory.

"That serving girl who tried to bed the king is a killer," Sterling said. "Keep in mind, Tala, when anybody from the streets of Amadon is given entry into the castle, the possibilities for calamity are infinite."

The girl blanched at his words.

"But I see now, perhaps Vilamina is lying and you had nothing to do with this." He would let Tala think she was off the hook for a while. "You've never seemed overly burdened with an abundance of ambition," he continued. "To plot an assassination is most likely beyond your limited wits."

He glanced at her one last time before leaving her chamber. Real anger burned in her eyes. *Yes. This girl is hiding something.* He grinned at her, admiring her audacity. He knew he would find out what she was hiding. He would pull the information from her. It might not be today, but he would succeed. His life depended on it.

*I, Raijael, begin this Illumination in hopes that all will learn how my
mother stripped me of my birthright. Laijon died, nailed upon a tree,* Mia
piercing him with Afflicted Fire. *Upon a cross-shaped altar she did lay
him, weapons at his side, five angel stones thrust into his wounds,* Ethic
Shroud *atop his chest. I was born at his side. Heir of Laijon. Dragon
Claw. As for my birthright . . . you will see what Lady Death hath stolen.*
—THE CHIVALRIC ILLUMINATIONS OF RAIJAEL

CHAPTER TWENTY-EIGHT
GAULT AULBREK

5TH DAY OF THE MOURNING MOON, 999TH YEAR OF LAIJON
GALLOWS HAVEN, GUL KANA

Crabs and seagulls had picked the beach clean. Crows pecked
at the still-smoldering pile of corpses behind Gault as he
walked along a grassy knoll toward the prisoner tent. All
morning his thoughts had been on the small green stone Aeros had
taken from King Torrence Raybourne. *If only my lord would show it to
me one more time.*

It was a pleasant morning, and though he'd been awake since
yestermorn, it had been a pleasant night as well. He'd made love to
Spades just before dawn. It had been over six moons since the two
of them had shared a bed. As a man who prided himself on his lev-
elheadedness, Gault didn't personally care for the unsteady nature
and evil temperament of the red-haired beauty. And he'd promised
himself he wouldn't get involved with her again. But Spades had long

legs, a smoky stare in bed, and a beguiling nature when it came to the arts of seduction.

The mole-faced girl's head was still on a stake near the entrance of the prisoner tent. There were also four dead bodies under the stake, hands still tied with rope behind their backs—the captives who had died yestermorn in the escape attempt. The line of prisoners standing in front of Spades could not tear their eyes from the dead. Some looked sick, as if their will to live had transformed into poison and was eating them from the inside out.

Gault counted the fetching blond girl, Ava Shay, still amongst the prisoners. He felt a strange relief seeing that she was still here. The thought that she might have been killed had made his blood run cold. He averted his gaze, for he found that she watched his approach with uneasy anticipation. Spades turned, eyebrows raised in question. He gave her a brief nod, acknowledging that Aeros was on the way.

With the familiar copper coin—the one emblazoned with the likeness of Jondralyn Bronachell—twining through her fingers, Spades strode toward the prisoners.

"Well," she said, stopping before Ava Shay, running the fingers of her free hand through a lock of the girl's blond hair as if inspecting a fine silk scarf. "Aeros will be pleased you are not among those who escaped." Spades tugged at the girl's hair and stroked the girl's face, ending her caress with a sharp, friendly slap to the girl's cheek.

Ava Shay looked right at him. Caught in her gaze, Gault found only further undoing of his thoughts. She was so frail, so deeply wounded. Looking at the girl made him sad. And he hadn't felt sadness like this since leaving his stepdaughter Krista in Rokenwalder.

Spades marched down the line of prisoners, smiling broadly at the sight of Jenko. He slouched in his bloodied armor and matted hair, a sulking look on his face.

"And here I'd had you pegged as the brave one," Spades said. "Yet somehow you're still tied up. My, my, I reckon you're stupider than I thought. How humiliated you must be. Your countrymen manage to escape, and here you remain, the trussed-up fool."

Her words were finding a sore spot as Jenko's posture was stiffening, and he no longer sulked. His eyes now smoldered.

"Have you no tongue, boy?" Spades flipped her coin up once and caught it casually. "Or was it removed by the one in your group brave enough to organize an escape?"

"Piss off," Jenko fired.

"You do have a tongue." Spades stepped back. "That's what a girl wants to hear. A fellow without a tongue is of little use to a lady, if you take my meaning."

"Piss off!"

"Keep spewing that kind of sweet talk, my love. I just may show you a tongue-lashing you won't soon forget."

Gault stole a glance at Ava Shay. The girl's frightened eyes bounced between Spades and Jenko. From the look on her face, it was clear that it was not death this girl feared, but something worse. Gault figured Ava had every right to harbor that fear. Spades was never satisfied unless everyone around her was miserable. As if these few survivors of Gallows Haven didn't have enough to contend with: the destruction of their town, the slaughter of their loved ones, slavery—and now Enna Spades.

Every prisoner recoiled in fear as the Angel Prince crested the grassy knoll. He was flanked by Hammerfiss and Spiderwood. Aeros' spectral presence had a way of striking despair into even the most seasoned of warriors, and those less hardened stood no chance— especially with Hammerfiss and Spiderwood looming at his side. The feeling of utter dread was palpable among the prisoners as the Angel Prince, stark-white hair billowing out behind him in the breeze, stalked down the knoll toward them. He was wearing his customary white cloak, open in the front, revealing his blue sword, Sky Reaver, knee-high black boots with iron-studded toes, and tan woolen leggings over which lay the pearl-colored chain-mail tunic and black belt. When he came to a stop near Gault, his milky eyes bore down on the prisoners, black pupils narrow and focused.

"Bring that one to me," Aeros said, pointing at Jenko.

Hammerfiss grabbed Jenko and yanked him from the line.

"Give me your name," Aeros ordered.

Jenko remained silent, defiance in his eyes.

Hammerfiss slapped his face. "Name!"

"Jenko."

Hammerfiss slapped the boy's face again. "Do it proper," he said coldly.

Jenko's eyes now burned as hotly as the red mark on his cheek. Spades stepped up next to Hammerfiss. "What he means is you must bow before your lord when speaking to him. Now say your name again. Bow and say, 'My name is Jenko, my lord.' And give us your last name too while you're at it."

Jenko spat at the feet of Hammerfiss. With a meaty fist, the red-haired giant punched Jenko in the breastplate so hard it left a dent and knocked the young man to the ground. Hammerfiss kicked sand into his face before hauling him to his feet again.

"There, there." Spades pocketed her copper coin, brushing the sand from Jenko's shoulders and hair. "Things will only go bad for you until you do it our way. It's not so hard. Now, go on, show the others how it's done proper."

Jenko looked at the ground, humiliation and anger in his very posture.

"We haven't all day," Spades added.

Jenko bowed, wincing as he did so, and said, "My name is Jenko Bruk, my lord."

"Excellent," Aeros said. "Son of Baron Bruk, I presume?"

Spades smiled wickedly. "A man who would slice up his own father to save a girl. I like it. Very delicious."

Aeros said, "You will have the pleasure of accompanying me on a short journey, Jenko Bruk. But first, I insist that you tell me the names and ages of every person who escaped two nights ago. Start with the four dead on the ground, then name the girl up there." Aeros' long finger pointed languidly up to the mole-faced girl's head.

Jenko's gaze went from the dead townsfolk to the head on the stake. "Why should I answer to you?"

Hammerfiss slapped him across the face again. Aeros said coldly, "I will have Hammerfiss kill you if you do not answer me."

"I'm already dead." Jenko's dark eyes traveled from Hammerfiss out to the bay, where the masts of a grayken-hunting ship stuck up out of the dark water of the sea like skeletal fingers clawing from a grave.

"I too feel remorse." The Angel Prince followed his gaze. "Truly, that ship could have been put to a much better use. Some soldiers don't think before they act. Battle lust hits them and they just pillage and burn. I could have used that ship to ferry more Sør Sevier soldiers onto Gul Kana soil. Many thousands more of us still wait in Wyn Darrè."

Aeros studied the masts of the sunken ship. "To take back the lands of Adin Wyte and Wyn Darrè that were stolen from us ages ago is one thing, but to bring about the utter ruin of the nation of Gul Kana and the Church of Laijon, who orchestrated the stealing, is quite another. At the same time, to destroy such a fine ship is a waste." He then nodded to the Bloodwood.

Spiderwood stalked forward and snatched the girl Ava Shay from the line and marched her toward Aeros, a black dagger at her throat.

A hollow feeling crept into Gault's gut.

The Angel Prince's gaze sharpened as he leaned closer to Jenko, voice now laced with menace. "Answer my question. Who are they?"

Jenko remained silent. Hammerfiss slapped him again, saying, "Torching the chapel after taking a shit on your bishop's holy book gave me great pleasure." He looked at Ava Shay. "As will watching ten of my lord's largest warriors rape your pretty little girlfriend right here, right now, right in front of you. And afterward I will order Bloodwood to split her open."

At Hammerfiss' words, the hollow feeling in Gault's gut grew. He realized that he did not want to see the girl hurt any more than Jenko did.

"We already know you love the girl. We know you would maim and torture your own kin for her. So do as my lord has asked," Hammerfiss continued in a tone low and deadly. "Now, who are they?"

Jenko looked to the bodies on the ground, swallowed hard, and quickly rattled off the names of the dead. "Simon Maclean. Livingstone Parry. Gabby Wiffel. And the last one is some old mud farmer from around Bedford, and I don't know his name."

Aeros pointed up to the head on the stake.

"Polly Mott."

"And who escaped and how did they escape?"

Jenko swallowed again, brow furrowed. "Stefan Wayland escaped," he said, eyes on Ava Shay. She trembled as the Bloodwood's dagger tightened against her throat. "And Gisela," Jenko said. "But I don't recall her last name. Beyond that . . ." He stopped, frustration on his face.

"You must remember all," Aeros said. "There are two others unaccounted for."

"Liz Hen Neville," Ava Shay blurted. "Plus Nail. That's all of them. Now I beg you, leave him alone." Spiderwood tightened his grip on her.

Aeros' eyebrows rose, his gaze traveling up and down the length of the girl. "You must really love Jenko Bruk to speak without my leave," he said.

Ava's simple woolen shift clung damply to the front of her body. Gault found it hard not to look at her.

"How did they escape?" Aeros drew close to Ava. "Who was it that killed my guards behind the tent? Was it the man Shawcroft as the Bloodwood claims? Who is Nail?"

Ava's nervous eyes found Jenko. Her mouth moved, yet no words issued forth.

Aeros reached out, the backs of his pale fingers touching her cheek. "It seems you know more about this town than Jenko." His fingers then gently pushed Spiderwood's black blade into her flesh, breaking the skin; blood trickled.

"Nail is just a bastard," Jenko said with a sudden, strained eagerness in his voice. "His master cut the tent open. It was he who killed the guards. His name is Shawcroft."

"Thank you." Aeros' eyes were now darting between Ava and Jenko. "Now if you will both kindly come with me?"

† † † † †

As if guarding the dead, the two lichen-covered boulders rose over the path like unmovable sentinels. The trail beyond the two rocks was littered with about twenty-five dead Knights of the Blue Sword, one horse, and a lone Gallows Haven man—a stout fellow with short-cropped dark hair. He lay in the center of the carnage. A longsword bearing a black opal hilt was in the dirt at his side. A Dayknight blade. Gault had seen their like before—King Borden Bronachell had borne one similar. So had Jubal Bruk.

Many of the Sør Sevier dead were familiar to Gault. Some had arrows protruding in sharp angles from their breastplates and the tops of their shoulders, others with deep, bloody gashes from a powerful edged weapon of some kind. Gault gazed up at the steep, winding trail ahead, locating an overhanging pine some distance above. Whoever had fired the arrows had fired them from up there. It would take skill to shoot so many from so high. Beyond the pine, storm clouds gathered at the mountain peaks higher above. At the sight of the boiling gray clouds, Gault was glad it was Stabler searching for the escaped prisoners and not he.

"Recognize him?" Aeros kicked the corpse of the Gallows Haven man. He looked at Jenko and Ava, both of whom Hammerfiss now untied. Ava held her hand over her mouth as her gaze ranged over the bloody scene. By the frenetic movements of her eyes, Gault figured she was searching for someone familiar among the dead. But it seemed the stout fellow with the Dayknight sword was the only Gallows Haven casualty here.

"Well?" Aeros continued, eyes on Jenko. "What do you make of this?"

Jenko knelt, examining the corpse. "This is Shawcroft. He was the one who slit open the tent and rescued the others."

"As I said." Spiderwood seemed to be looking straight through Aeros. "I've met the man before. It was Ser Roderic. I killed him. A death long overdue. A death your father has long sought, a man your father ordered me to kill."

"I would have preferred him taken alive," Aeros said.

"Taking Ser Roderic alive was never an option."

"Who do you wager fired these arrows into my men?" Aeros asked Jenko, turning form the Bloodwood.

Jenko stood, eyes on the arrows bristling from the dead Sør Sevier knights. "Stefan Wayland was good with a bow. He bested me in the archery competition. Stefan could've easily shot these men."

"What a load of hog shit!" Spades grunted. "There is no way one village boy shot down nearly ten of *our* knights."

"He could if he were perched somewhere up on that trail." Beneath Hammerfiss' beard was a wide, mocking smile. "I doubt even a Bloodwood could cause so much havoc with just one bow."

Spiderwood, still near Aeros, pretended not to hear, though Gault detected a further tightening around his eyes. "There were four people up there, actually," the Bloodwood remarked to no one in particular. "A young bowman was with them. He nicked my armor with one of these scattered arrows. A good shot, to that I can attest."

Aeros pointed up the trail. "Where does it lead?"

"Most trails around here lead to the Roahm Mines," Jenko answered.

Aeros squinted. "None of my archers or soldiers or even their squires were killed during the siege of this town. Now this one man, Shawcroft, has killed near a dozen guardsmen near the tent, twenty more in town before that, and with the help of a lone bowman, these twenty-five at our feet. That's a lot. Killed as silent as you please— that's before my Bloodwood finally took him out. What say you to that, Jenko Bruk?"

Gault noticed a small transformation on the young man's face. Gone was the boorish defiance. Grit and moxie and pride now showed in him. He was a stout lad; dangerous, too. After all, here was a fellow who had dismembered his own father.

There was something new and calculating lurking behind Jenko's eyes now, and the words came spitting from his mouth in a rush. "I say it's a fucking wondrous thing that Stefan Wayland and Shaw-croft killed so many of you bloodsucking oghuls."

Aeros did not react to the outburst. Instead he looked up at the steep winding trail and the billowing clouds casting dark shadows over the rugged terrain higher up.

"Well," he said, eyes falling again on Jenko. "Shawcroft rots at your feet. And Stabler will have Stefan Wayland back here soon. Or he'll have him dead. Either way, I care not. It is Shawcroft's young ward, Nail, that I want brought back alive."

And it came to pass that at the time of final Dissolution, he died upon the tree, nailed
thusly, purging all man's Abomination, the sword of Affliction piercing his side.
Thus all was sanctified. Upon the altar they laid his body in the shape of the Cross
Archaic. And as prophesied in all Doctrine, Mia took up the angel stones. And it
came to pass, the five stones of Final Atonement she placed into the wound manifest.
—THE WAY AND TRUTH OF LAIJON

CHAPTER TWENTY-NINE

NAIL

5TH DAY OF THE MOURNING MOON, 999TH YEAR OF LAIJON

AUTUMN RANGE, GUL KANA

They'd spent most of the night in the mines with no sleep. Nobody complained, though, so scared of the pursuing knights, they just kept plodding along. Now they were out and still hiking. Morning had come. The bowels of the mountain had been chilly, but this stream-carved gorge was a dauntingly frigid place. Its rock walls were sheer in spots, jagged in others, but constantly looming black and oppressive. Roiling crisp waters crashed and thundered over stone and boulder beside their path. Soot-gray clouds were billowing in overhead.

Once out of the mines, Nail had removed the scarf from Lilly's eyes. This led to a renewed vigor in the pony's step. The click and clack of Lilly's hooves now echoed behind him, Liz Hen leading her, Zane and Gisela following. The huge battle-ax was strapped to the pony's back along with what little remained of their gear.

Ever since Nail had first touched the ax, it seemed almost a breathing, living thing. He could not stop thinking of it, or the stone.

He held no illusions that they had lost the Sør Sevier knights in the mines. He knew men as determined as those would find a way over the chasm. He just hoped they had put enough space between them and the knights to reach the abbey safely.

"This old armor has rubbed me raw in more places than I can count," Stefan said from the back of the line.

"See," Dokie muttered, elbowing Liz Hen. "Exactly how my bum feels too."

"Shut your yapper." Liz Hen shoved the smaller boy up the trail.

Nail also felt his chest plate rubbing him raw, though he scarcely noticed anymore unless he specifically dwelled on it. And even though the air around him was colder than a witch's knucklebone, the bulky armor was making him sweat. But there was naught he could do. It was the only thing keeping him somewhat warm.

They traveled in silence, traipsing up the trail, following the roiling stream to the top of the gorge and out onto a flat bit of terrain that led them into a thick forest. Up so high, the air held a trace of pale crispness, but the fast-rolling clouds above would soon make things colder come nightfall. Shawcroft had warned of being caught high in the mountains at night. The spring temperatures in Gallows Haven far below might be comfortable, while the high places of the mountains could freeze a man dead in hours.

Aspens flanked their path. In some stretches, the trail was lined with columns of cone-shaped pine with low-swooping boughs. Through breaks in the trees, Nail saw the vaulting terrain high above. They were probably no more than halfway up the Autumn Range, perhaps five thousand feet above sea level. On all sides reared steep mountains, and at over ten thousand feet, their snow-crusted peaks were cloaked in shades of deep purple and blue.

They broke from the forest into a clearing pocked with standing-stones. Their meandering path, bounded by reeds and thickets of undergrowth, led them around a deep mountain lake that Nail knew was teeming with fish. But without a way to catch them, or to cook them properly, there was little reason to stop. That savage black bears and saber-toothed mountain lions haunted the Autumn Range was not lost on Nail's imagination. He missed Shawcroft's calm, steady presence in the mountains. He had never worried when traveling these paths with his master.

Zane's breathing had been fading in and out ever since exiting the mines, eventually settling into a long, rattling wheeze. The boy soon toppled over on the trail, landing flat on his face, moaning in pain. Beer Mug barked, scampering in circles around Zane, then stopped and howled mournfully. Liz Hen dragged her injured brother to his feet. Zane's freckled face was gray and drooping in pain.

"Let's divide the gear. Zane can ride on Lilly," Nail suggested, though he knew the pony was too small an animal to sustain Zane's weight for long. Still, he untied the ax and sackcloth packs. They slid from the pony's drooping back to the ground.

"I'll never again be full of the gumption and pluck I used to have," Zane said as Stefan and Nail struggled to help him climb atop Lilly, the strain of the effort breaking beads of sweat on Zane's brow. "Everything on me hurts, Nail. My guts. My legs. My brain."

Whilst helping Zane crawl safely onto the pony, Nail saw the raw slave brand on his own inner wrist, the shape of a broken *S*, red and welling. It soon would blister.

"That red-haired lady who branded us was a witch if I ever saw one," Stefan said, eyeing the fresh slave mark on the underside of his own wrist too. "Pure evil in her."

"Bless Shawcroft for savin' us." Gisela made the three-fingered sign of the Laijon Cross over her heart. "And bless you, too, Nail, for leading us through them mines."

Feeling nothing like a savior, Nail began divvying up the gear from Lilly's various packs, keeping Shawcroft's pouch and the ax for himself. The mere presence of the ax set his nerves on edge. It seemed the weapon had some kind of hold on him, making him feel invincible one moment, vulnerable the next. He knew he was no hero. He'd left Ava Shay to whatever fate awaited her at the hands of the enemy—if she were still alive. No, Gisela shouldn't be thanking him.

"Everything hurts so much," Zane said. "I'm goin' to die, ain't I, Liz Hen?"

"You're goin' to be fine," she answered.

"I wager if I ate anything, it would just spill from the hole in my side."

"We ain't got no food anyway," Liz Hen said.

"It's my fault there ain't no food," Dokie said. "What a miserable couple of days."

Losing the pony and food had essentially rendered all Shawcroft's preparations for naught. It wasn't Dokie's fault the food was gone. Nail knew it was his own. He should have guided Bedford Boy over that bridge himself.

"I'm hungry too," Liz Hen said. "I reckon I'm the most hungry of us."

"Can't we eat something?" Gisela asked.

Nail's stomach ached too. He hadn't eaten but a few strips of elk jerky since the Mourning Moon Feast three days before. But there was nothing to be done about it. Not unless Stefan could shoot a rabbit or a deer with his bow. Shawcroft had taught Nail how to identify over twenty different kinds of animals by track alone. But they had yet to come across any signs of wildlife. They hadn't seen any game since exiting the mines.

"Without food, we'll be reduced to stumbling skeletons in days," Liz Hen said. "We'll get starvation sickness. The black gums. Swollen tongues. Bleeding eyes and teeth dropping out of our heads. Lockjaw. Maybe even the staggers."

Gisela's eyes were wide with fear. "I don't want the staggers."

"You'll only get everybody scared with that kind of talk, Liz Hen," Stefan said. "I'm sure we'll get enough food when we reach the abbey."

"And when will that be?" Liz Hen demanded.

"By the end of the day," Nail said.

"A person will wilt away after only a few days without food."

Dokie said, "My pa had a goat from Adin Wyte he kept chained behind our house. Nobody never fed it, leastwise not that I ever seen. It lived for years."

"It likely nibbled the grass," Liz Hen said.

"Weren't no grass out back."

"'Cause the goat ate it, you stupid." Liz Hen smacked Dokie on the forehead with the back of her hand.

"I ain't stupid."

"Well, I ain't goin' years without food," she announced. "I'll find some grass and nibble like a goat if I have to. I'll eat anything. Leaves. Pinecones. Tree bark."

"I've heard that a man can survive on moss and lichen scraped from the eastern face of a standing-stone," Dokie offered.

"Not the western face, or northern?" Liz Hen asked. "Or what if the stones are set at an angle?"

"Standing-stones are never set at an angle," Dokie said proudly. "The stones of the ancients always face north and south."

"What if they're round?"

Dokie's face twisted in puzzlement. "I'm just saying one can survive on moss and lichen if need be."

"Rubbish," Liz Hen snorted. "No gibbering craven goat, even if it was from the arse end of Adin Wyte, would nibble lichen from a rock."

Dokie's eyes lit up again. "I also heard you can suck milk from the stock of a green willow reed."

"Suck milk from a willow reed," Liz Hen scoffed. "That sounds about as useless as sucking on a fat man's nipple. The only green living willow reeds I know of are down by the sea. Ain't gonna do us much good up here."

"Best not to speak of food we don't have," Nail said, putting an end to their talk. Leaving only a few minor implements tied to Lilly, he loaded a bundle of furs onto Stefan's back and spread the lighter stuff out between the others. Stefan helped him strap the huge battle-ax onto his back. Nail thought his legs might buckle under the weight.

Onward they went, up the trail worn into the bitter, loamy soil of the mountain forest. Dokie's limp was near gone. He wasn't poking at his rear as much as before. And they traveled faster now that Zane was riding on Lilly. Beer Mug brought up the rear.

As he struggled to find a comfortable pace, Nail could hear the others shuffling along behind. The battle-ax was not the only burden Nail carried. As he trudged up the path, he began to feel the sorrow as the realization of the loss of his master began to claw at his heart. The man was the closest thing to a family he had ever had. *And a Bloodwood killed him.* Shawcroft had called him *son* before the end. That thought warmed him some. But briefly. *Did he ever give two hoots about my art, my drawings?* Nail figured it didn't matter now. With the armies of the White Prince destroying everything of worth, there wasn't much use aspiring for a better life. His dream of pursuing art was at an end.

As he walked, Nail would quickly suppress his emotion one minute, only to have it rise up in him again. There were moments he could not breathe for the sorrow that cleaved his heart. He thought of talking to the others about it. *But what could any of them do?* The others had lost more than he. It was best he keep his feelings hidden. *Besides, who am I to mourn for anything? Especially after what I did to Ava Shay.*

The first storm arrived with sickening speed. Rain drove horizontally straight into their faces, half blinding Nail. The others wrapped themselves in the hides and furs Shawcroft had provided. But there weren't enough, so Nail went without. It wasn't long before he grew so tired he felt like folding into exhaustion with each step. The ax along with his waterlogged clothing and chest-plate armor grew heavier and heavier until he figured he might as well be carrying Zane.

Drooped over Lilly's back, Zane looked the most comfortable of them all. Stefan dragged Gisela along, her small hand engulfed in his, the other hand clutching her hatchet—she hadn't let go of the thing since taking it from the pony's pack yestermorn.

For a time, the trail took them up a steep mountain studded with boulders, treacherously slick with mud, the occasional gnarled tree root jutting up into their path. The rain turned to hail that pelted their faces. Their path grew increasingly rough, some of the mud underfoot stiffening, turning to ice. Every step was a slippery one.

Beer Mug growled. Nail looked into the trees. Two cold, pale orbs caught his attention—a silver-wolf. Its piercing, predatory eyes watched them. Nail knew that a lone silver-wolf would rarely attack a man, and would never approach a group. But a pack of wolves could be trouble. And they were in the heart of silver-wolf country now. With such beasts lurking amid the woods, Nail knew that Sør Sevier knights and freezing to death were not the only things they need worry about. What he feared most was being spotted by a saber-toothed mountain lion. A saber-tooth would stalk a group of men for hours and rush straight at them, singling out the weakest.

With that thought in mind, wet, cold, and miserable, Nail continued on. The silver-wolf watched them pass by.

† † † † †

Near nightfall they were still a day away from reaching the abbey, and a second storm arrived. It sapped their strength and stopped them cold. The place they chose for shelter was a lonely wooded glade where a half-frozen stream meandered through a copse of pine dusted in light snow. The grove was studded with boulders the color of bone in the dwindling light.

Stefan and Gisela, the latter with hatchet still in hand, immediately went in search of kindling to start a fire. It was growing viciously cold, and Nail warned her not to touch the hatchet's iron blade lest her hand freeze to it.

Liz Hen cleared a flat spot of ground for Zane, threw a blanket down, then helped her brother from Lilly's back. Beer Mug curled up on the ground next to Zane immediately. Liz Hen covered them both with one of Shawcroft's furs and started scratching away the snow and half-frozen moss on the ground with a stick, digging a fire pit. Dokie helped her.

It was a struggle, but Nail removed the battle-ax from his back by himself. He set it on the ground near Lilly. When he stood up and stretched, it was as though Laijon had blessed him with winged feet. He thought he might float away in the icy breeze.

It was bitterly cold as the mournful wind picked up. He could feel the insides of his nostrils freezing together. That dampened his spirits. Under Shawcroft's care he had never been caught this high up in the mountains when it was this soul-jarringly cold. He couldn't even hear the sound of Gisela's hatchet cracking wood anymore above the wail of the wind.

He looked at the tall, leaning boulders nearest him, hoping to take shelter from the wind behind one. They were arranged in a crude circle of sorts. He found himself drifting curiously closer to them. There were markings carved into the rock at eye level, barely visible, blanketed in layers of lichen, moss, and snowflakes. A sinking feeling began to grow in his gut as he noticed that these markings were similar to the marks he had on his own body, similar to the red-glowing symbols he'd seen under the sea whilst in the clutches of the dread mermaid. His heart was thumping in his chest now, heavy and hard. He could taste his own fear in the back of his throat as he ran a hand over the nearest carving. Indeed, it was in the shape of a cross. Next to that was the Sør Sevier slave mark—the broken *S*—just like the one on the underside of his wrist. And under those two carvings was what looked like a row of shark's teeth, exactly like the tattoo on his bicep. Nail felt light-headed. There had been similar such markings near the entrance to the Roahm Mines on the Written Wall. He thought of the battle-ax, the blue stone, and Shawcroft's last words: *Many things are found hidden beneath the ground. Men and kings and ancient warriors and the weapons they forged. All are eventually buried. Ages pass and important truths are hidden, forgotten. Yet most men never look beyond the surface of their farms and forests and within their own castle walls for knowledge. But those who search the deep . . . find salvation.*

"What are they for?" Nail turned at the sound of Dokie's voice. "There have been standing-stones like this all along the trail. Why so many? And those markings carved there. After the lightning strike, crosses just like that were burned all over my skin, from my armor. And the shark bites too. Do you know I have dreams of such markings, Nail? What are they for, the markings, my dreams?"

Nail remained silent, shaken by Dokie's confession of dreams and the coincidence of similar markings on his own flesh.

Dokie continued, "Some say demon lords crafted stones like these in a bygone age. Others claim it was oghuls cast down from the stars who left them thousands of years before men arrived on the Five Isles. Some say it was fey creatures, ancestors of the Vallè, who placed them here."

Liz Hen came up behind them. "I heard they were put here by the druid Mia worshippers." Her eyes were dark and her brow furrowed. "They used to practice their goddess worship and witchcraft in the hidden places of the high country."

"Goddess worship." Dokie made the three-fingered sign of the

Laijon Cross over his heart. He looked haunted. "These stones frighten me something awful. They frighten me almost as much as being hit by lightning, or swimming in an ocean full of sharks."

"We made a grave error coming here." Liz Hen backed away from the circle of stones. "One shouldn't venture into these mountains without a necklace of bear claws, mermaid teeth, rat tails, or some other amulet to ward off the hexes these foul druid stones are liable to cast our way."

"There must be a better place to camp," Dokie said, scratching at his rear again.

"We dare not search for another spot so late." Nail walked back to the pony, leaving Liz Hen and Dokie with the standing-stones. He took up the ax, somewhat glad to feel it in his grasp again, if but briefly. He tied it to Lilly's back, then tucked one hand beneath the saddlebags to keep it warm against the chestnut pony's steaming flesh.

"It's all right, girl." He patted the pony's muzzle with his other hand. "You can take a breather now." Lilly nickered, pushing her head against his chest. Her breath steamed high into the darkening forest. She was one of the few things Shawcroft had left him. Nail realized he was now alone in an unforgiving world. The freedom he had longed for was laid out before him, and it was terrifying.

Stefan and Gisela returned bearing armfuls of dead pine needles and brush. They placed them in the clearing Liz Hen had created, then left for the trees again, returning with smaller branches and stacking them at the edge of camp. Liz Hen piled the wood and brush over the pine needles. Dokie lit a torch and jammed it into the pile. The brush hissed and smoldered, and small wisps of smoke wafted this way and that. But soon the torch flame took hold and the damp wood sputtered and sparked. They all gathered around and stared into the crackling glow.

It was Gisela who broke her gaze from the fire first and noticed the snow-covered mushrooms growing at the base of the standing-stones. She went to them immediately and attempted to pull them up, unsuccessfully. She set to chopping at them with her hatchet and brought back a handful, asking if they should be cooked first. Beer Mug took one sniff of them and curled back up with Zane.

"I wouldn't eat them," Nail advised.

"He's right," Stefan added. "Some mushrooms are known to make folks ill."

"But I can't go another day without food." Gisela's voice rose in pitch.

"I'm with you, sweet pea," Liz Hen said. "I'm for eating them."

"I hear poison mushrooms can rot your face off," Dokie piped up.

"Well, I'm already ugly." Liz Hen snatched a mushroom from Gisela's hand. "So if they're goin' to turn one of us into a blood-sucking oghul, it best be me." She shot Nail a satisfied look whilst biting down on the cold mushroom. It crunched in her teeth, and her face twisted in disgust. But she plowed on.

Wide-eyed, Gisela watched Liz Hen chomp away as if the big girl might actually turn into an oghul. But Liz Hen eventually spit the chewed-up bits of mushroom into the fire. "They're disgusting," she said. "And I'm the type who'll down anything."

Gisela put a mushroom to her lips and nibbled, swallowing the morsel and nibbling some more. "Not too bad if you take them in slowly." It wasn't long before she'd nibbled the entire collection of mushrooms in her hands and went back to the standing-stones for more.

"Do you think the knights still follow us?" Dokie asked. "Their dogs terrify me."

Nobody answered him. A creeping darkness fell over their camp like a mantle, the only sounds the crackling fire and Gisela's chewing.

"I want to see it again." Gisela swallowed her last mushroom. "Will you show it to us, Nail?"

"Show you what?"

"The shiny blue stone. The one I found in the altar. The one in your satchel."

Shawcroft's leather satchel was still hanging around his shoulder. He had become so used to it dangling there against his armor that he had nearly forgotten about it. He opened the leather flap and searched inside, finding the silk cloth with the stone buried under the scrolls and prayer book. He pulled it out, unfolded the silk, and gazed at the stone—shards of brilliant blue sparkled from its polished surface in the firelight.

"Do you think it's valuable?" Liz Hen asked.

"It must be," Stefan said. "Shawcroft asked Nail to get it, along with that ax."

"Can I hold it?" Dokie asked. Nail offered it to him. But as the stone slipped from the silk into Dokie's outstretched hand, Nail felt a pang of worry. That someone else was handling it didn't seem quite right. Dokie studied the oval gem, his eyes seeming to gaze into its blue depths. "It reminds me of the angel stones in the stained-glass windows of the chapel. One of those is blue. Do you think it is one of the angel stones?"

"May the wraiths take you, Dokie." Liz Hen grunted. "Don't be a damn fool. The stones are in heaven with Laijon. Have you not read *The Way and Truth of Laijon*?"

Gisela barfed into the fire, dampening the blaze and sending a shower of sparks heavenward. The cold quickly dropped around them like a shroud.

"I told you not to eat those," Stefan said. Gisela buckled in pain, crying.

Nail took the stone from Dokie, wrapped it in the silk, and placed it gently back into Shawcroft's satchel. He felt more at ease now that the stone was under his protection.

With the fire now mostly doused by vomit, it was growing cold.

He gathered an armful of wood and put it over the dying flames. Soon the fire was crackling at full strength again.

"Falling asleep in this cold will kill us for sure," Dokie said. "We should stay awake. If we huddle together under the furs, we will be warm enough. Especially if we keep the fire stoked."

Nail figured they should sleep in shifts, with one person staying awake and keeping the fire going. He told the others the plan, then volunteered for the first watch. He was exhausted, but not sleepy.

"You boys will need to remove your armor," Liz Hen said as they all began to gather under the furs. "You all smell like dirty iron pots."

Nail and Stefan removed their cumbersome breastplates but kept their leather leggings on. Zane, already asleep, stayed in his armor, closest to the fire, curled up with Beer Mug. Liz Hen lay next to her brother, Dokie enveloped in her bulky arms. Gisela fit snugly next to Stefan, but she still moaned in pain. Shoving his legs under the furs next to Stefan, Nail positioned himself farthest away from the fire, sitting, readying himself for first watch. Clumped together, they all shivered on a great nest of dark roots and frozen ground, the furs and hides provided by Shawcroft piled over them. It wasn't long before Nail could hear Liz Hen's loud snores.

As he sat there, he pulled the makeshift blanket up around his shoulders, staring at the sky, Nail knew he would not be able to sleep. The still night sky now quaked with cold. The clouds had parted and the starry sky shimmered with a wan glow. Tendrils of shivering light began to form into crooked streaks of white flame that spread over the horizon. Though Shawcroft never talked much, he'd once explained that an aurora was just the moonlight dancing off the ice crystals floating in the sky, the way candlelight would through a clear jewel.

Shawcroft claimed that an aurora on a cold night spoke of Laijon and his Warrior Angels. He would say things like this from time to time, genuine awe in his voice whenever he spoke of the misty lights of the heavens above. The only thing comparable that Nail had ever looked upon with anything approaching awe was how, with utmost grace, the tawny curls of Ava Shay's hair would dance and glow in the candlelight of the Grayken Spear Inn. He could feel the necklace she'd made him still around his neck, the wooden turtle pressing into the flesh between his armor and chest. That it was still there with him was both reassuring and confusing. It angered him too. And filled him with guilt. He didn't want to think of Ava Shay.

A light wind kicked up again, freezing against Nail's face. He lay back, resting his head against the pile of his armor. The clouds snuffed out the stars and borealis overhead. Soon the wind pounded through the trees and standing-stones, accompanied by the deep baying of silver-wolves somewhere in the dark.

† † † † †

Nail emerged from sleep well after sunup. Light flakes of snow were lazily drifting down. The chestnut pony, Lilly, snorting pale puffs of vapor into the air, was standing in the dead coals of the fire pit for warmth. Nobody had stoked the fire during the night. Nail crawled from under the furs into a brittle, bone-chilling cold. His toes were numb and he could scarcely stand. His fingers were so cold they were nearly useless. He could scarcely grip a thing as he struggled into his breastplate and armor.

Gently pushing Lilly aside, Nail began tossing wood onto the fire pit. He struck flint to steel, then lit a torch and jammed it into the pile of wood. Soon smoke rose up and the fire started anew. Zane crawled from the pile of bodies next, upper lip crusted with frozen breath and snot. He looked near dead and scooted even closer to the fire as if in a daze, glassy-eyed. Even Beer Mug looked uncomfortably cold. Soon Dokie joined them, wanting breakfast, complaining of hunger. When Liz Hen arose, she stood, wrapped herself in one of the furs, then grabbed another, revealing Stefan underneath, lying on the ground alone. "Where's Gisela?" she asked.

Stefan sat up, groggy-eyed, and stretched. Then he lurched to his feet and looked around frantically. "Where is she?" His voice quaked in the cold. "Where'd she go?"

All eyes now roamed the campsite, searching for any sign of the girl. Stefan ran into the woods, shouting her name, then quickly returned, shivering. Flakes of snow hit his heated skin and melted off. He hastily fastened together his leather armor and breastplate, snatched the fur from Liz Hen, and ran off into the woods again.

Nail, Dokie, and Liz Hen joined the search, leaving Zane and Beer Mug at the fire. They covered the perimeter of the camp, circling outward in a disorganized but ever-widening pattern.

It was Nail who found her.

Not far back along the trail that had brought them to the campsite, Gisela lay, stretched on her back, looking as fragile as a frosted figurine made of hollow glass. She was dead. Frozen. The icy air around her looked uncannily pure. The hatchet she always carried was on her chest, handle clutched tightly in one frost-covered hand. The other hand was clenched in a fist at her side. The fingertips of both her hands were black. Frostbitten. The rest of her exposed skin had taken on a sallow color in the cold. Her eyelashes were rimmed with ice. And vomit from both corners of her mouth was frozen down the sides of her cheeks. Here she was, Maiden Blue of the Mourning Moon Feast. Gone.

Nail called out for the others. One by one they came shuffling toward him through the light drifts of snow, even Zane and his dog. Stefan dropped to his knees and sobbed at the sight of Gisela's delicate, stiff body lying on the hard ground. Beer Mug whimpered. Dokie cried, face nestled in Liz Hen's bosom. The big girl held tightly to him, tears streaming down her face. They all just stood there in grief, hovering over Gisela as feathery snowflakes lazily brushed her skin.

"I should have held on to her tighter." Stefan reached for the hatchet in her blackened hand. "She was so sick." His fingers and palm instantly froze to the metal. He jerked away, ripping the flesh from his fingertips. With that, he ran back to camp, murmuring wordlessly.

Liz Hen wiped her tears away, then walked up and punched Nail hard in the shoulder. "You didn't wake us up in time for our turns at watch! I told you we shouldn't camp so near those standing-stones, stupid bastard." Then she and the other two boys and the dog followed Stefan, leaving Nail alone with the frosty, pale corpse.

Nail tried to rub the pain in his arm away. He knew that the others depended on him to get them to the abbey safely. Yet he had failed them again. Nail also knew that he had to do something for Gisela—he just didn't know what. The hatchet was attached to the girl for good, or at least until she thawed—unless they chiseled it from her hand, and Nail figured nobody would be up for that.

Then he saw *it* from the corner of his eye, just a flicker of blue, but enough to draw his attention to Gisela's other black-fingered hand, the one clenched in a fist at her side. He could see that her frozen digits were not clenched in a fist at all but rather wrapped around something—something that now shone like a dazzling sapphire gem between her fingers. Nail knelt, and with some effort, pried her blackened fingers back enough to let the blue stone slip from their frozen grip.

The stone lay in the snow for a moment until Nail gathered enough courage to pick it up. It was surprisingly warm to the touch. He examined the stone closely. It was faint, but something like light glowed deep within it. He felt a spike of fear and stood quickly, slipping the stone into the pocket of his rough-spun breeches under his armor, wishing to gaze upon it no more. *The thing is a curse.*

He shivered as he recalled the unholy carvings of the beasts of the underworld he'd seen at the base of the cross-shaped altar where he had found the ax and stone. *It killed Gisela.*

He had the sudden urge to take the stone from his pocket and hurl it into the trees. But for some reason, he knew he could not.

The girl needed to be buried, needed to be given proper priesthood rites to rid her soul of the evil that had taken her life, and to be laid to final rest with her head toward the east. But he hadn't any priesthood power to cleanse her soul. Nor was a bastard even worthy of it, according to Bishop Tolbret. Besides, as Jenko Bruk said, Laijon's powers were probably empty and false. Still, he made the three-fingered sign of the Laijon Cross over his heart and dropped to his knees. He began shoveling snow over the dead girl with his cold bare hands. But it was no use. The snow was too crisp and light and fine and did naught but sift fruitlessly through his fingers. In actuality, most of what he had tossed upon Gisela was brown twigs and dead leaves.

Can I do nothing right? I make a mess of everything. All my artistic talents, all my dreams, and yet here I am, cold and alone and a failure. Letting what few companions I have die, alone, in the snow.

He stumbled away from Gisela, the girl now half-covered in snow and twigs.

A bastard truly has no place in this world!

It is prophesied that in the last of days, pride and sin will bring about our destruction at the hand of Raijael, yea, even a Fiery Absolution. Only then will Laijon come again with his Warrior Angel companions. Thus, we have devised Ceremonies of Ember, Smoke, and Flame to honor Laijon, and taken to the building of great cathedrals that you may pay homage to the great One and Only as you await the day of his return.
—THE WAY AND TRUTH OF LAIJON

CHAPTER THIRTY

AVA SHAY

6TH DAY OF THE MOURNING MOON, 999TH YEAR OF LAIJON

GALLOWS HAVEN, GUL KANA

Swathed in a hooded cloak, the man Hammerfiss called the Spider came for Ava Shay. Fear gripped her when she saw him. It wasn't his black cloak or black boots or all-black boiled-leather armor that disturbed her. It was his eyes. Of all those in the Angel Prince's horrendous army, it was this silent, raven-haired man who frightened Ava the most. There was nothing of value living behind his steely eyes—eyes that were streaked with red veins, almost glowing in color. It was as if he and his eyes had been bred for the specific purpose of creating terror in her soul.

As he wordlessly untied her bonds and led her from the tent, Ava caught a scent of him. It was the second time. The first was when he'd held the knife to her throat the day before.

He smelled of cloves and newly polished leather. This man was no dirty soldier, rather something vastly different. As he led her past Polly Mott's rotting head, Ava tried not to look up, knowing that looking would merely add more trauma to her soul. Only the wraiths lived for such ghastliness. But she could not help herself and risked a glance. The crows had picked clean Polly's eye sockets. Ava quickly looked away.

The Spider guided her toward his oily-looking horse, which had eyes of molten fire. His steed was eerily similar to the horse she'd seen on the Roahm Mine Trail with Stefan Wayland and Nail. He effortlessly lifted her onto the back of the dreadful beast, then smoothly mounted the horse himself, sitting behind her. His leather-covered arms enveloped her, pulling her close. At any moment she expected that cold blade at her throat. The sweet and pleasantly revolting scent of him struck her like a fist. She tried to lean forward and away from him as he took the reins and clicked his tongue. She felt the rippling and bunching muscles of the powerful red-eyed beast under her as they galloped away from the prisoner tent. As Ava steadied herself with her hands, she noticed that the demon's hide was not oily but rather as clean and polished as its master.

As they wended their way through the vast Sør Sevier encampment, which reeked of death and was plagued with bugs, Ava kept her eyes on the sky and the noisy seagulls wheeling overhead, trying her best to ignore her own dark thoughts. She silently prayed to Laijon. The wraiths, if you allowed them, were capable of taking a person to many evil places, some places lacking even the substance of light, devoid of hope. In this profound gloom, one could become subject to the lord of the underworld himself, and, as *The Way and Truth of Laijon* said, *Empty was his domain and nameless were his beasts.* Ava had seen her own mother overtaken by the wraiths. She had watched the white foam frothing from her mother's mouth as the wraiths possessed her convulsing body. As a young girl, Ava had vowed never to become like that, never to allow the wraiths a foothold into her head. The wraiths had taken her mother shortly after Ava's father had been killed in a logging accident high in the Autumn Range. Ava knew there was a correlation between the wraiths, trauma, death, and slaughter. Her whole family was dead now. All her siblings burned. It just didn't seem real.

The encampment they traveled through was massive—more people and horses and flying gnats gathered in one place than Ava had ever seen. Their numbers dwarfed those of the entire town of Gallows Haven. And hundreds and thousands more were arriving by ship daily. Tents, campfires, wagons, mules, more tents, stacks of weaponry, and moldering piles of horse dung stretched as far to the north of Gallows Haven as she could see. And the warriors: grim, brutal-looking folk. Not a kind face among them. Killers all. Their painted war chargers too. Beasts. Even the women. It was all immensely ugly and murderous and wrong.

As the demonic steed carried her onward, Ava closed her eyes to the hordes that surrounded her and prayed more fervently to Laijon. But thoughts of Jenko filled her mind. It had been only yesterday the White Prince had taken her and Jenko to see Shawcroft's dead body. Ava was proud of Stefan Wayland and the others for managing to escape and to kill so many of the enemy. She also felt bitter. She had seen the cold hurt in Nail's eyes. He could have cut her and Jenko loose, yet had not. Her anger at Nail would come and go. But she wanted to be like Laijon. *Forgive all, The Way and Truth of Laijon* taught. *For the wraiths thrive in hateful souls.* Jenko Bruk would not abandon her as Nail so cruelly had.

With another click from the Spider's tongue, the horse slowed its pace and stopped. Ava opened her eyes and fear rippled through her heart. A white tent almost as large as the Grayken Spear Inn dominated the center of the Sør Sevier camp, and the White Prince stood before it. Aeros Raijael was dressed in leather breeches and a white shirt laced at the front. A slim dagger was tied to his dark leather belt. He was blowing into a thin whistle but making no noise.

A black kestrel came zooming in from the east and landed on his outstretched arm. He untied a silver tube attached to the small bird and opened it, pulling forth a scrap of parchment, reading. Done. He crumpled the paper and motioned for the Bloodwood.

The Spider dismounted behind Ava. Aeros handed the kestrel to the black-clad man, then glided toward Ava and helped her from the horse. His hands were gentle but cold. Ava felt only faint relief as she slid from the back of the fire-eyed horse and into the arms of what she considered the most evil being that had ever walked the Five Isles—the White Prince, Aeros Raijael.

The knight named Gault stood guard at the entry of the tent. He watched, eyes aimed at her, as Aeros led her by the hand. She was careful not to stare at Gault too obviously. She'd first learned his name when that horror, Spades, had teased him about her. Of all those in the White Prince's gruesome army, it was only this knight Gault whose aura exuded a small measure of kindness. It was in his eyes—cool blue eyes flecked with silver-gray. His lean, muscular stature and clean-shaven head gave him an almost predatory look, but it was those eyes that softened his overall demeanor. As she followed the White Prince into the tent, she felt Gault's hand on her shoulder. She turned and looked up at him. He gave her a nod of reassurance. But there was a hint of sadness in his look too. Even so, the bald knight's small gesture touched her anguished heart.

The tent was warm. In the entry was a round wooden table, circled by high-backed chairs with dark velvet upholstery; a ceramic bowl of fruit was at its center. Candelabra were positioned everywhere, lit and glowing. Aeros led her through several hanging partitions that created numerous rooms. Many of the colorful partitions were heavy woven tapestries depicting battle. Thick bearskin rugs adorned the floor, yet these were pure and white as new-spun wool. She'd heard stories of the large white bears of the Sør Sevier Nordland Highlands and figured the rugs under her feet were made from such beasts.

Elaborately carved furniture was set about in nooks and alcoves, numerous painted vases rested atop stools. Several iron braziers and an ornate thronelike chair on a stone dais were in the central room of the tent. Everything was spotless and clean. Ava realized with sadness that this tent was the most opulent thing she had ever seen—ten times bigger and nicer even than her own home. The Angel Prince led her into the largest of the partitioned rooms. This area was lit with numerous candles and had a massive bed in the center. Near the bed was a large wardrobe of dark lustrous wood. He motioned for her to sit on the cushioned bench at the foot of the bed. She remained standing.

"Please relax," he said. "I mean you no harm."

Ava had resolved not to speak to this pale-faced demon. Nor would she follow any of his commands. Yet she could not take her eyes off him—so near he was to her now. At first glance, his bearing was beautiful, like white marble. Even his eyelashes were pale. His lank blond hair, white as the bearskin rug he stood upon, shimmered in the candlelight. It was the blue veins pulsing under his translucent skin that changed his overall manner from appealing to grotesque. His eyes held her captive, though. Dark and wild and empty they were.

"You will soon change your mind about me." He picked up a ceramic cup and poured water from a sparkling pewter goblet into it. He held the ornate cup out for her. Ava's mouth was dry. Yet she would not take what he offered.

The White Prince gulped the cup of water down, then asked, "Tell me what you know of Shawcroft." Ava looked away, gritting her teeth.

"This boy that Shawcroft kept, what was he like?"

Her gut churned. She wanted to remain silent, but couldn't. "Is it truly Nail you are after?"

"Well." He paused, reflective. "Yes. In a way. The one named Nail is but a diversion to the greater prize." He moved closer. "And it looks as if I have found that prize." His fingers gently brushed her hair, her cheek. She recoiled. He tilted his head, dark, piercing eyes now softening some. "Tell me of Shawcroft and Nail."

She decided then and there she would not speak to him. Ever.

Aeros poured himself another drink. "Let me tell you of a young Wyn Darrè man, Mancellor Allen. He was about the same age as your friend Jenko when we took him captive in Ikaboa. Mancellor was stubborn like you. But he eventually came to the realization that the light of Raijael is right and true. And once he came to that realization, he rose from the ranks of slave quite rapidly. Now he's spent almost four years fighting at my side, having risen in the ranks: squire, Hound Guard, Rowdie, Knight of the Blue Sword. He's become such a prize. I'm considering making him one of my personal guards, even. There is growing discord among my Knights Archaic. Sure, they bandy about harmless insults at times. As do all soldiers who wage battle for as long as we have. They try not to do it around me, though. But I hear them. And I fear there is genuine hatred growing between them. Oh—I don't know why I share this with you now. I suppose I feel some sort of kinship with you. And I see us becoming friends in the days to come. I don't come upon friendship easily, or often. But I do desire it. Do you?"

She hung her head, wondering why he was talking to her—wondering what he was talking about. But the tone of his voice was less raw and commanding than it had been yesterday. There was a warmth to his manner that Ava found even more disturbing.

"Perhaps you too will become one of my elite soldiers," he said.

Ava looked up at that.

"Indeed, it is possible," he continued. "I can have the Bloodwood teach you sword fighting. Spades can train you with the crossbow—"

"It's her who causes it all." The words spilled from her mouth of their own accord. She cursed herself inwardly for engaging this white devil in conversation. There was a sinking, hollow feeling in her gut now. A boiling rage.

The White Prince was staring at her, his face contemplative. "Spades." He nodded. "Yes. You're right. The others are none too fond of her. She tends to behave poorly when I am not around. She causes deep divisions wherever she goes." He smiled at her, a widening of his perfect, unblemished lips, revealing teeth brilliantly white and pure. "Smart you are. I can see we will get along as friends. I am unashamedly pleased you have finally spoken. Your voice is like the sound of a harp strung with silken—"

She slapped him. She didn't just slap him, but clawed his face with her nails, catching his lower lip in her fingers, screaming as she did so. It happened so fast. It was a flurry. A quick burst of anger. Just one short, sharp slap and scream.

As he slowly turned his face back to hers, there was genuine surprise and hurt in his eyes. She glared at him, defiant, half-stunned at what she had done. He would surely kill her now. Blood trickled from a split in his lip.

With extreme delicacy, the White Prince lifted his hand to his reddened cheek, feeling it, working his jaw up and down as if her slap had truly caused him injury. As he moved his jaw, one thin, pale finger caught a bit of the blood from his split lip. He jerked his hand away from his face as if his own fingers had just stung him. His eyes widened at the smear of red on his hand. The transformation that came over his face was unexpected.

"My blood," he whispered, then whirled, and ran out of the room.

And just like that, Ava was left alone—and utterly confused. She sank down on the bench at the end of Aeros' bed, heart thumping. She thought of fleeing. But she was certain her head would be on a stake in front of the prisoner tent if she did. Still, her instinct to escape was strong. She began formulating a plan but realized that the Bloodwood was more than likely still outside. Gault was outside the tent too. Perhaps she could tell the bald knight with the kind blue eyes what had happened and he would . . . *No, he would do nothing for me.* She was trapped here. And death was closing in.

Staying rooted to the bench, she scanned the room for a weapon, eyes coming to rest on the bed behind her. The mattress was thick, with four intricately carved posts rising from floor to ceiling. A white silken canopy was stretched over the entire affair. It was grand. A family of ten could stretch out on it comfortably.

There were sounds coming from the room next to her—water sloshing in a stone basin. That the White Prince had shown such an aversion to his own blood was disconcerting on many levels. She smiled inwardly, knowing she had at least caused him some discomfort. If she were to die, at least she had drawn blood from the enemy.

When Aeros returned, he came bearing a goblet of wine. "I only meant to bring you into my tent and allow you a little respite from your recent travails," he said, holding forth the goblet. "I insist you drink this."

Ava decided that nothing he could do or say would scare her. Her eyes traveled from the goblet to his face. The split on his lip was scarcely noticeable, just a trifle swollen was all. There was an odd, yet familiar, look in Aeros' dark eyes now. And she was startled to realize that she had seen this very same look before. It was this longing, wanton look in men that sickened her. But in that look was revealed many other things as well. The White Prince wished her no harm. He wasn't going to kill her. At least not yet.

Tentatively, she reached out and took the goblet of wine from him. The wine's flavor was glorious to her dry tongue. She drank it down slowly, savoring each drop. Her eyes remained on Aeros, standing above her, pale and silent. Then his milky-white visage grew ever so blurry, and she felt the cup drop from her limp hand.

Ava knew she'd been wrong. He had just poisoned her.

† † † † †

"You don't snore." Aeros was sitting on the bed next to her. "It's as if by merely watching your face I can see your dreams. As if I can hear the longings of your heart just from its soft beating. I could watch you lie there for days."

"How long was I asleep?" she asked groggily, unsure of where she was.

"It was Royal Bedlam I put in your wine. A sleeping draught. It lasts but a while. Wyn Darrè nobles are notorious for slipping it into the court girls' drinks and then having their way with them once they pass out. Of course, I've killed most of the Wyn Darrè nobles. So you needn't worry about them. But it will loosen one's tongue. You will now answer my questions freely."

The White Prince moved closer, lying down. He leaned his head on one elbow and brushed back a lock of her hair that had become stuck to her lips whilst sleeping. "You took my breath away the first time I laid eyes on you," he said, brushing the hair from her eyes. "Had I known what a beautiful creature you truly were, I would've raced into Gul Kana. I would conquer all humankind without a slip of remorse just to gaze upon your face but once. You are like a precious gem, a delicate flower."

How could he have such a sweet, honeyed tongue yet look on her with such harsh, black, metallic pupils? His nearness was unsettling. She inched away from him.

"I know you fear me," he said. "That thought pains me. But soon I will make the world look very different for you, and for your lover, Jenko. He is your lover, no?"

Despite the Royal Bedlam drug, whatever its properties might or might not be, at the mention of Jenko, Ava did not feel like talking. This was surely a nightmare.

The White Prince continued, "I'm sure Jenko possesses an animalistic desire to rut with you all the time."

Ava drew farther away, hoping she might just fall out of the bed altogether. But it was so vast she found herself still stuck in the middle.

"Jenko, though full of pride, seems possessed of no great wit," Aeros went on. "Now that Spades has set her wiles on him, I wager he will have little interest in you. What I mean by that is—I can see you lack experience, if you take my meaning."

He sat up on the bed, looking down on her. "Everyone here, soldier or slave, lives or dies upon my sufferance. If we're to be friends, you'll soon have to renounce your church and your vicar and sing praises to a new Laijon. You shall be born again under heavenly sessions and enter the covenant of Raijael."

Ava's blood froze. *Renounce the grand vicar and the church?* The very notion of abandoning her beliefs had never crossed her mind. Belief in Laijon's promises was all that had sustained her since her parents had died.

Then she remembered Bishop Tolbret's fate at the hands of Hammerfiss. The impossibility of his death staggered her. *They shot an arrow clean through his holy priesthood robe!* With that thought, her faith wavered. She tried to cling to it, reel it back in. All her life she had dreamed of a wedding in the chapel. All her life she had dreamed of a happy life with a man of the community such as Jenko and children of her own. She felt the darkest fears of her heart rise up—and foremost of those fears was that she would now never know love.

"Just lying there in that simple woolen dress, you look like a goddess," Aeros said. "Do you not see what a treasure you are? You make every other woman in the Five Isles look unutterably plain. Gault is simply smitten with you. He grows gawky and flummoxed at your very nearness. I see the way he looks upon you. And Spades is treacherously jealous. This is why she's set her sights on your boyfriend. You seem to have upended my entire contingency of Knights Archaic with naught but your beauty."

Ava barely heard what he said as tears welled in her eyes. Through the fog of her dreams and half-rememberings, she recalled her former life just days before: working in the Grayken Spear, cooking salmon over the hearth, tending to her siblings, carving a turtle for Nail, longing for love and marriage with Jenko Bruk. But most importantly she recalled her faith in Laijon—only moments before it had sustained her. She closed her eyes and prayed for its return. *They shot an arrow through Tolbret's priesthood robe!*

"They all think I am a god," Aeros said, his tone soft, but far from comforting. "My father, Aevrett Raijael, has raised me as such. But I must confess—and you, of all people, must allow me this one weakness—that I suspect, some days, that I am no god. But they all believe that I am, that I have powers beyond those of a mere mortal. And I fight at their side in every battle to prove my worth. I never lose. And they look to my victories as proof of our cause. Still, ofttimes I fear I am naught but a fraud, that my father's trust in my divine future is misplaced. It's hard when everyone's expectations are so high. I am purposefully willful, headstrong, and ofttimes cruel. Could I be a god? Sometimes I believe there is greatness in me. Somewhere. You will come to see that. My greatness. Come to worship it as the others do. Our heavenly sessions shall be divine."

Worship him? Ava wished for his death. Right here. Right now. She would kill him. She had bloodied him once. Though when she looked at his lip, there was no scar where she had raked him—no trace of injury whatsoever. Who was he? That the White Prince had healed himself so rapidly was disheartening, and confusing. *How can it be?*

"What type of man are you?" Her voice was but a whisper.

"I am the type of man who would concern himself about the secret desires of a simple slave girl. I know what is in your heart. For that same desire lives in me, too."

"You know nothing of me." Pure darkness filled her. She wanted him dead. This man before her had done such awful things.

"How old are you?" he asked.

"Seventeen," she answered, unthinking, her mind in turmoil.

"I'm twenty-eight," he said. "Not that much older than you." The flat black pupils of his eyes now possessed a hungry look.

She recoiled from him. The darkness was creeping in. Some claimed that Laijon talked to them—the bishops swore to it. They said the grand vicar spoke to the spirit of Laijon face-to-face in the temple in Amadon. But it was said that others, the ones full of sin, heard the wraiths whispering in their head. Ava could hear them now. They were sounding deep booming drums to the beat of her heart. She clenched her eyes shut and uttered a prayer to dispel them. She prayed and prayed until the wraiths were little more than a silent breath and a whisper sounding in her head. But even that was not enough, for she knew that these shades could slink and sneak—like cats—evil they were.

The White Prince was now kneeling on the bed over her. Like a hawk perched in a tree branch, he loomed above—dark eyes a glare, piercing like a raptor. He pulled a thin-bladed knife from his belt. "Your beauty has overwhelmed me," he said, running the cool steel blade along the length of her arm and up her shoulder. "As a prince, one grows used to stripping the finery off the noble women. Not much excitement in that after a while. What I desire most is to rip the simple, coarse, filthy raiment off the peasantry, particularly the fetching young peasantry."

With one hand, he held the knife. With the other, he began to untie the dark leather belt from around his breeches.

Ava could see the wraiths now, their shape watery, their substance naught but shadow, their movements soundless—their goal to lure her into a realm of eternal darkness and despair and death.

O that King of Slaves, that great One and Only! O that day of his fall!
O that we could go back to that day when Mia placed the five stones of
Final Atonement into the flesh of his wound. O that we could accompany
his body as it was born into the tomb. For when we ventured into that
veiled place days later, that great Cross Archaic we found empty. For
Laijon had been translated into heaven, the weapons and stones with him.
—The Way and Truth of Laijon

CHAPTER THIRTY-ONE

NAIL

7TH DAY OF THE MOURNING MOON, 999TH YEAR OF LAIJON

AUTUMN RANGE, GUL KANA

As Nail heaved one weary foot in front of the next, the taunting sun did nothing to lessen the cold. As they'd hiked, the clouds had parted and daylight began to filter through the pine and aspen, revealing a wispy ground mist. They'd spent the entire previous day trudging through low-hanging clouds and snowstorms making scant headway, eventually losing the trail altogether. Now he felt like they were completely lost.

Nail's mind bounced from one thing to the other, wrestling with problems and emotions he could not fully understand. A lifetime of Shawcroft's bullying. Shawcroft saving him in the end. Confusion. Death. War. The most traumatic thing his mind was trying to deal with was Gisela. Her death had shaken them all, most especially Stefan. "I should have held her tighter," he kept saying. "She slipped away as I slept. I should have kept watch. Had I only held her tighter, she'd still be with us."

"There was nothing you could do," Dokie tried to reassure Stefan.

But Nail knew that Gisela's death had been his fault. He had fallen asleep and had failed do wake Stefan for the second watch. He had not told the others that he'd found the blue stone in Gisela's fingers. The stone rode comfortably in his satchel now. Nail was beginning to hate it. And the cumbersome ax—it, too, got a free ride, strapped to his back like the weight of the world. He felt that the ax and the stone were somehow aware of him, knew him, stalked his mind even.

With each step, the endless hard ground underfoot sent pain through Nail's legs. He and the others crossed an ice-encrusted stream and encountered another ghost town of sorts—a place unfamiliar to Nail, a dozen small cottages hacked out of the forest, relics of a long-dead mining operation, the small string of stone huts reclaimed by twisting vines and underbrush. Stefan searched each broken-down building for food Nail knew would probably not be found.

A few miles later, they encountered two other travelers—a leather-clad trapper with a grizzled, dirty look to him, along with his young son, wrapped in a heavy cloak. The trapper guided a sway-backed pony laden with muskrat pelts toward them. These were the first people they had seen since the Sør Sevier knights in the mines. But when the two drew close, they all realized with a shock that the trapper was an oghul and the son a big-nosed, bearded dwarf. Dokie let out a tiny gasp. The oghul was wearing a red quilted cap and a fur cape with a hood over his leathers, his coarse face barely visible under the collection of rough vestments. The dwarf's bearded face was just barely visible under the hood of his heavy vestment. Dwarves stayed mostly to themselves in the Iron Hills in Wyn Darrè. Nail had seen plenty of oghuls years ago with Shawcroft in the far north near Deadwood Gate. It was rumored there were many oghul communities in the bigger cities like Amadon. And now and then an oghul trading ship would land in Gallows Haven. But to spot an oghul and a dwarf this far south into the Autumn Range was rare indeed.

Nothing was said between the two trappers and Nail's group as they passed one another. Beer Mug barked at them. But the squint-eyed oghul just scrutinized their ripped and ragged clothing and dented armor with a gray stone face. The sight of Zane slumped over the neck of Lilly, his armor blackened with blood, did not seem to faze either fellow. But the oghul's leathery-lidded eyes did widen when he spied the gleaming ax strapped to Nail's back. He began to hustle his pace away from them when Liz Hen begged him for a bite to eat. The dwarf scurried along behind him.

"Crookbacked horse turds!" Liz Hen shouted at them before the two trappers entered a patch of pine trees and disappeared. "May the wraiths take 'em both to the underworld," she moaned. "Witless dribbling oghul arse couldn't even spare us a scrap. Not even one scrap."

So they continued on, miserable, cold, and hungry.

† † † † †

Thick snow was falling now. They still hadn't reached the abbey. And Nail was still lost.

As the afternoon wore on, Nail began to suspect they were being hunted. Beer Mug sensed it too. The dog trotted alongside Lilly, hackles raised at half-mast, ears pricked up, staring off into the trees. Nail thought that even he himself heard things moving around out there. But unlike Beer Mug, Nail knew that the wind and snow distorted sounds, made them more sharp and ominous. As of yet, there had been no sign of the Sør Sevier knights. But Nail knew the men had not given up the chase.

Soon, the big gray dog was barking up a racket. Lilly snorted and shuffled, causing Zane to cry out as he tried to stay atop her. Nail's eyes scanned the trees. Thick flakes of snow piled up around them. Everything was awash in white.

He saw the slinking shape as it emerged silent as a tan-colored ghost from the blinding whiteness—a saber-toothed mountain lion. It came stalking toward them over the top of a pile of snow-covered deadfall, pacing back and forth, its head hung low. The devilish rumble emanating from deep within its throat sent shivers rippling through him.

Beer Mug growled. The lion roared back in answer. Like the stark rasp of a dull saw blade, the beast's roar emerged so rough and ferocious that Nail's heart froze at the sound. But it did not frighten him into complete immobility. He still had wits enough to unsling the ax from his back. It was a struggle, and though the weapon was heavy, it still felt strangely at home in his hands, as if it *wanted* him to wield it. Nail noticed that Stefan had nocked an arrow to his bow and was taking aim. The lion was loping back and forth now, looking ever more eager to get at them. *It's sure to devour us!* The ax quickly grew heavy in his arms. The lion roared again; the enormity of the sound took his breath.

Beer Mug let loose a sharp, venom-laced snarl, raised his hackles to full mast, and shot over the snow toward the beast, white powder kicking up in his wake. The lion leaped away amid a flurry of snow, darting behind a birch in an instant. The dog lunged, glancing off the tree gracefully and landing on all fours. Beer Mug rushed the beast again, tearing the cat's side with his teeth. Blood welled from the wound. But the saber-toothed cat struck back just as quickly, its murderous large teeth snapping a hairsbreadth from Beer Mug's muzzle as he danced away. Beer Mug spit and growled, slowly backing the big cat down. The dog's bloody lips curled back, flashing scarlet gums and razor-sharp whites that glistened and gleamed, and the fur along his back and haunches rippled. The dog snapped at the saber-toothed lion again. But the big cat leaped over the fallen trees, scrambled away through the snow-covered bracken, and vanished.

"Fuck you and the fucking feline demon who spawned you!" Liz Hen shouted, throwing her dagger at the spot of whiteness where the lion had disappeared. She then snatched the one from Nail's belt and threw it too.

"What'd you do that for?" Nail found that he was breathing through his mouth. His throat and tongue were dry and raw. He didn't know if his heart would ever stop its pounding. *And that lion's roar—it had split the air and shook the very ground itself.*

He still couldn't believe Liz Hen and thrown the daggers into the woods. "Two of our only weapons and now they're lost. I should send you after them."

"Not with that thing out there, you won't." Liz Hen's brow furrowed.

Atop Lilly's back, Zane grimaced. "As Laijon is my witness, I didn't think a dog could run off a saber-tooth."

Nail had the urge to laugh but didn't do so out of fear he might weep at the same time. That Beer Mug had chased off the lion was, at the very least, extraordinary. The daggers were of little use anyway.

"Why did you not let your arrow fly?" Liz Hen asked Stefan accusingly.

"I may have to kill men and merfolk." Stefan slung the bow over his shoulder. "But I refuse to kill an innocent creature again, even if it is a saber-tooth bent on eating us. It was just doing what mountain lions do. It was no demon. It was only hungry."

"What sort of bloody awful logic is that?" The red-haired girl looked at Stefan with pure disdain. "I'm the innocent beast! Me! Liz Hen Neville! I'm the one who's most hungry! Did you ever think had you kilt that damn cat maybe I coulda ate it?"

† † † † †

It was late afternoon, and the snow was so thick it was clear to them all that they would not find the trail any time soon. Reaching the abbey before nightfall was out of the question. He had failed his friends again. They barely plodded along through a grove of tall pine and pale birch. Lilly could scarcely move, Zane still atop her. Soon the pony just stopped altogether, breathing hard, legs quivering. A rancid odor was coming from Zane as he slid from the pony to the frozen ground. Nail could smell his injured friend from ten feet away. As he lay on the ground, Zane began mumbling that he wanted to die, that he just wanted the pain to end. Liz Hen, Stefan, and Dokie began clearing a spot on the snow under him.

Nail unslung the ax from his back, used to the weight and bulk of it now. He made sure Shawcroft's leather satchel was still snug about his shoulder, and headed into the trees to gather firewood. He found a host of fallen saplings covered in snow and began chopping at them with the ax, the heavy blade slicing through the wood as if it were naught but crumbled parchment. A stiff wind set the forest to creaking, branches clashing above in a slow dance.

Weary, Nail sat on a rock and stared into the blowing trees, body and mind numb from the cold. He didn't think of anything, mind blank, muscles sore. He didn't know how long he sat there, but when he was finished gathering firewood, the sun was going down.

When he returned to the others, he found Liz Hen kneeling over Zane, praying. The boy lay on his back atop one of the wolf-hide blankets, all of his armor removed, in naught but his stiff woolen underclothes. Liz Hen's arms were extended, palms up, eyes closed, head thrown back like Bishop Tolbret reciting Eighth Day prayers. At first Nail thought Zane was dead. Then the boy coughed. Blood bubbled up from his lips.

Nail dropped the wood in the snow near Lilly and stepped closer to Zane. He really just wanted to retreat back into the gray gloom of the trees and be alone. Only the ceremonial weight of the moment being played out here in the midst of their encampment kept him rooted to the ground.

He listened to the words of Liz Hen's prayer. "We give thee hearty thanks for delivering us so far from our enemies, dear Laijon," she said, head raised to the heavens in supplication. "Keep us all from the miseries of this sinful world. And we beseech your gracious goodness to deliver Zane from the burden of his flesh. Hasten thy kingdom come, so that he may depart this existence to join you in the true faith of thy holy name. May you consummate our prayer with bliss, both body and soul in eternal everlasting glory through you, Laijon, forever and ever, amen."

"Amen," Stefan and Dokie repeated. Even Beer Mug, who appeared to be sitting in reverence next to Zane, lifted his head and let out a dismal howl.

"He's too sick." Liz Hen looked up at Nail. "The pain of his injury is too great. He can't even breathe without crying out in agony."

Dokie wept. Beer Mug lay at Zane's side. There was sadness in the dog's eyes. Liz Hen peeled back the fabric of Zane's woolen underclothes. A great stench hit them all at the same time. The swollen flesh around the deep gash in Zane's side was dull and waxen, the wound itself livid and angry, oozing blood and yellow pus. Zane's entire midsection was naught but a bulbous, purple sheen.

"My pa said a wound goes rotten in a week," Stefan said. "You can survive longer than a week sometimes, if your wound is on an arm or leg, that is. But one so near the heart will claim a man in just days."

"What a glum thing to say." Liz Hen glared at Stefan as she stroked her brother's matted hair.

"Pa also said infection slows in such cold," Stefan muttered, hanging his head. Then he looked up, tears streaming down his cheeks.

Zane tried to sit up, watery blood seeping from the corners of his mouth. Liz Hen gently held her brother's head in her lap. Zane's placid gaze found Nail as he spoke, his voice shallow. "It's time to pay the butcher's bill, my friend."

"What does he mean?" Nail looked up at Liz Hen.

"You must rescue him from the suffering," Liz Hen said, lips quivering, tears freezing on her face. "He's in dreadful agony."

"The lions are attracted to my smell." Zane's voice was naught but a gurgle as more blood dribbled from his mouth and over his bluish lips. "You must send me away, Nail. If I stay, the saber-tooth will keep after you. And Lilly can't carry me another step." He reached up and squeezed Nail's hand, and then his hand slipped away to fall limply at his side. "You have to release me unto heaven."

"I can get you to the abbey," Nail said. "Beer Mug can take care of the lions."

"The abbey could be weeks away, for all we know," Liz Hen said. "We're lost. Even if we can find the abbey, he'll still die. His injury's too infected."

"We're not lost," Nail lied. "The abbey is near."

"You must end his agony."

"You want me to kill him?" Nail backed away from Liz Hen.

"One of us has to," Liz Hen said. "And . . . and . . . I can't."

"Nor I," Dokie said. Stefan did not look up, just stared at the ground.

"I can get him to the abbey," Nail said, voice resolute. "If I have to carry him myself, I can get him there."

"He won't last," Liz Hen cried.

Nail looked at his friend on the snow. With each labored breath, the boy gasped in pain. "Please, Nail." Zane's voice was but a whisper. "Do it for me. I'm so sick."

Nail felt great floods of emotion swell within him, but he held back his tears. His own voice cracked. "I don't want to."

"We don't give a gob fart what you want." Liz Hen loosened the dagger at Zane's belt, stood, and held it out for Nail, hilt first. "Take it!" she roared. "You're nothing but a bastard boy anyway. Everyone in Gallows Haven is dead because of you. What's one more? Grab the knife! May the wraiths take you, but you'll do as I say."

Nail recoiled. Liz Hen was looking at him not only in anger, but with that same impatient glint in her eyes that Ava and Jenko had shown him in the prisoner tent. He knew at that moment that something terrible and hard was growing within him. He felt the first stirrings of anger. *What do I owe any of them?* He wanted to defy Liz Hen and carry Zane to the abbey himself. He would show them it wasn't impossible. Show them he was strong enough. He was better than them all, more determined. He bent down and tried to scoop Zane up in his arms, but couldn't lift the boy even an inch. Zane cried out in pain. Even without armor, Zane was big and Zane was heavy. Nail refused to give up. "Help lift him onto my back," he urged the others.

Liz Hen huffed. "My brother's nearly three hundred pounds, you clodpole."

"But if you help put him on my back, we can keep going. I will alternate carrying him with Lilly. The pony can rest some."

"You don't understand," Liz Hen said. "It's over."

Then Nail recalled Shawcroft's words: *You can also take life, son. . . . If any lag behind, you'll have to leave them in the mountains. Remember Radish Biter. . . . I'm afraid Zane won't make it far. You must reach Bishop Godwyn above all else.* Shawcroft had foreseen this.

Zane *would* have to be put out of his misery. And the task had fallen to him. At that moment Nail wanted to run. Run so far away from this place it would be forever lost to him. He closed his eyes and took three deep breaths. The bitter air froze the insides of his nostrils, but at the same time awakened his mind. He recalled the unbearable pain Radish Biter had been in before Shawcroft ordered him to put the cow to sleep. It had been the right thing to do then. And it seemed the right thing to do now. But Zane was a person, not a cow. *Zane is my friend!*

It was that last thought that settled Nail's mind. When he reopened his eyes, Liz Hen was already placing the hilt of the dagger into his hand, and his cold fingers were already curling around it. And Stefan and Dokie were already leading Lilly away into the woods. Liz Hen knelt and kissed her brother one last time and stood, crying. "Make it quick," she said to Nail. "I don't want him to suffer." Then she too withdrew, following Stefan and Dokie into the snow-covered trees.

Only Beer Mug remained. Zane lay still as a stone on the wolf-hide blanket. The big gray dog growled deep and low as Nail approached. It took some effort, but Zane put one weary hand on Beer Mug, calming him. The dog's tail wagged at Zane's touch.

Dagger in hand, Nail knelt by his friend. He knew he must have had the most dreadful look on his face. Zane spoke to him calmly. "Don't be sad, Nail, you'll only make me cry. I don't wanna go out of this world crying, you know."

Nail knew his own eyes were wide with pain, but there were no tears. Zane looked up at the sky. A faint yellow glow illuminated his ashen features. Nail looked up too. The clouds had parted, letting the last rays of sunshine through, revealing the peaks of the mountains around them. Still, there was little warmth from the sun. And the soft wind whispered through the treetops above.

Nail took up a corner of the wolf-hide blanket to cover his friend's face.

"No." Zane's pallid lips trembled. "I wanna see the sun as you do it, Nail. Watch it go down. Can you see it glistening off the mountains? So far up we are. Near where Laijon dwells. His kingdom on high, they say. Let me look at the sun for a moment. . . ."

So Nail sat by Zane and the two of them watched the sunlight gleam off the mountains. The peaks were broken by many jagged canyons. The sun danced off the snow and sliced into the shadows, creating a dazzling scene of brilliant reds and deep purples. It was beautiful. The howling wind and immense cold slithered around them, freezing Nail's face stiff.

"I never properly thanked you for saving me from the sharks," Zane said.

Nail shuddered, recalling his plunge into the bloody ocean and the cold grip of the mermaid. He *had* saved his friend's life. Now he was to take it. Everything about the situation seemed cold, unfair. Nail wondered if anything he'd ever done in his life had truly even mattered. His friend was dying again, right in front of him. *Who but me could save a life, only to see it wither away with infection and excruciating pain weeks later?*

Zane took Nail's hand in his own—the hand that held the dagger. Zane placed the tip of the blade under his own ribs at an angle and said, "Put the knife in under the bone and push up a little and to the left. That will do it clean. No worries. Little pain. At least I hope." With his other hand, Zane pulled Beer Mug's face close to his own and kissed the dog. "Do it now, Nail." Zane looked up as the last sliver of sun vanished behind the mountain peaks. "Do it now."

But Nail, feeling sorry for himself, for Zane, for Gisela, for everybody, couldn't do it. He was frozen. Immobile. He could only stare at his friend's pain-racked face. He looked at the dagger in his own hand, a hand that was poised to take a life. *This can't be happening. How can it be happening? We went on the grayken hunt together. I saved him from the sharks! Everyone was proud of me. Even Shawcroft.*

Beer Mug was nuzzling Zane's neck. The dog's sad brown eyes gazed questioningly up at Nail, as if asking why he hesitated. And so, with every ounce of determination he could muster, Nail did it. He angled the dagger under Zane's ribs, up a little and to the left. And pushed. One motion. Quick. Right in the heart.

Zane gasped, eyes widening. Beer Mug squealed a sad note.

Nail knew if he lived a thousand years, he would never forget that final look on Zane's dying face. For there was one thing beyond all else still alive in his friend's eyes: faith. Faith in Laijon. And in that last moment, Nail saw it.

Zane truly believed that Laijon was awaiting him in the hereafter.

Livid red blood drained from the wound when Nail withdrew the blade. But Zane's countenance now glowed with a serenity not present moments before.

Nail knew he had done the right thing. Still kneeling, he cleaned the dagger in the snow, Beer Mug remained planted at Zane's side, a low whimper in his throat.

Nail stood. "Come," he said to the dog. But Beer Mug stayed put. The terror and love in the dog's eyes hit Nail with such force he had to look away. Like Gisela, Zane would never be properly buried. Instead he would be left alone, Beer Mug at his side. But in Nail's estimation, there was no more fitting monument than that.

Following Lilly's tracks in the snow, he left his friend with the dog. Zane's still-steaming chest bled a river of scarlet heat over the wolf-hide blanket and onto the frozen ground.

*We, the last Warrior Angels, bear witness to the covenants between Laijon
and mankind. For the wrath of our sin was taken out on the Atonement Tree.
'Twas the blood of Laijon that paid for all sin and banished all darkness to the
underworld. It is by his grace that we are saved from the wraiths. Only continued
sinfulness and sloth will bring back the Fiery Demons and their dread lords.*
—THE WAY AND TRUTH OF LAIJON

CHAPTER THIRTY-TWO

TALA BRONACHELL

7TH DAY OF THE MOURNING MOON, 999TH YEAR OF LAIJON
AMADON, GUL KANA

Sterling says the bitch skewered me good." As Jovan sat up in
the bed, wincing, and motioned for Tala to enter, the covers
fell from his chest. His torso was bandaged from stomach to
neck. He wore a thin white robe.

Tala bid good day to Dame Mairgrid and the king's chamberlain,
Ser Landon Galloway, and made her way through the entry hall and
of her brother's chamber. The small foyer beyond was complete with
plush settees and a small cordoned-off library. Jovan's room itself
was spacious. She heard Ser Landon close the door behind her, leaving her alone with her brother. The bedroom portion of the chamber was divided into several sections by partitions, in effect creating
many smaller rooms out of the one big space. Jovan's living quarters
were filled with all manner of fine sculptures and ornately carved

furnishings. His bed was in the farthest right-hand corner, near an open window overlooking the city. A cool morning breeze blew in, a bit chilly for Tala's taste.

Jovan's legs lay under a thick pile of blankets. "I don't feel much pain."

"That's nice." It was the only reply she could think of as she sat beside him on the bed.

"Sterling seems bent on pinning this on you. But rest easy, Tala. Pay him no mind. He will not question you again, lest he suffer my wrath. He's all but worn out his usefulness anyway. If he so much as looks at you askance, tell me. I will deal with him. You're but a pawn, I'm afraid. Insignificant. A piece in a bigger game my enemies play."

"How are you feeling?" she asked, throat dry.

"My only disappointment is that the doctors won't let me leave this bed. You'll have to bring back a detailed accounting of this afternoon's fights for me."

"I hate the gladiator matches."

"You hope that Squireck wins."

"I just don't want him to die. He was once my friend. Jondralyn's betrothed."

Jovan took her hand in his. "He will die today. Of that I am certain."

"Can we not speak of such things?"

"Times are dangerous, Tala. You must harden yourself. This attempt on my life has awakened me to the truth. Be prepared. The time is soon upon us when I will have your sister brought before the king's court and quorum of five on charges of treason against the Silver Throne. Not all in this family wish me well. Though I can't prove it yet, I see Jondralyn's hand in this. After all, that serving wench was with her. She wishes me ill. Denarius says it is so."

Tala winced at the name of the grand vicar. "Jondralyn had nothing to do with this." She stood, her mind spinning. This beastly game the Bloodwood was playing had far-reaching tentacles. She had come to Jovan's chambers today for one purpose, her mind on the note from the Bloodwood: *Find out what keeps your brother, the king of Gul Kana, so beholden to the grand vicar.* But this conversation had taken a turn that she hadn't expected.

Jovan continued, "Watching Squireck die today will be good for you, Tala. It will steel your heart for the much more difficult things to come."

"Jon only dislikes you because you treat her so poorly," Tala said, her mind a jumble. "If you were nicer to her, perhaps—what I mean to say is that you wouldn't harbor such suspicion if you only tried to get along with her. She loves you . . . though she may not show it. But in truth, you don't show it either. If you two would be nicer to each other, then we could all live happily as a family—"

"Such girlish optimism." Jovan caressed her hand in his. But there was a wintry smile on his lips. "The world isn't a frilly present wrapped up in a bow for us to look upon gleefully. Our parents are dead. Our family is fractured. And others such as Roguemoore and Hawkwood have since weaseled their way into our home and infected those that I love with treasonous thoughts."

"But you've belittled Jon and treated her with nothing but scorn since childhood," Tala said heatedly. "She means you no ill will."

"I like seeing that fire in you. It is a good thing that you defend your kin. I would expect no less of you. You have always been pure of heart. I wish there was a way for us all to be happy. And I confess I have knowingly treated Jondralyn badly. I don't know why it happens, yet it does. But here we are. I must trust Denarius. He sees things that mere mortals cannot. He is Laijon's prophet—"

"He is fat and lecherous!"

"Do not speak of the holy vicar in such ways," Jovan snapped.

"I saw him praying over Lawri." Her voice trembled.

Something like hurt crawled into Jovan's eyes. It reminded her of the look on Lindholf's face after she had kissed him on the balcony. It was a pleading look. That such a look could be found in Jovan's normally cold eyes confused her.

"Proper steps must be strictly adhered to for the healing blessings of Laijon to work." Impatience was growing in his voice. "The consecrated oils are to be administered in certain steps. It is the way some holy things are done. The complexities of the priesthood will be made clear to you as you grow older. Not everything written in *The Way and Truth of Laijon* is to be understood by silly court girls who have not yet seen their Ember Gathering."

"Silly court girls. Is that what you think of me?"

"Hardly," he sneered. "As of late, you have taken to dressing like your sister. Shirt. Pants. Do you carry a dagger, too? A sword? Do you, too, wish to be a warrior?" Something like fear crept into his eyes. "I have seen war. No kin of mine should have to witness the horrors I have. You should attend court like the other girls your age."

"A court girl, is that all you want for me?"

Jovan slumped in the bed, holding his chest. Agony was stitched in every line of his face. Tala wanted to reach out and comfort him. He rolled onto his side, long hair hanging over his feverish eyes, now peering through those dark locks at her sideways. "The grand vicar is the holiest of men. He communes with the spirit of Laijon daily in the temple. He is Laijon's one and only prophet. Denarius is Laijon's mouthpiece. His actions are Laijon's actions—in whatever he says or does. And Laijon, in all his righteousness, will never allow the grand vicar to lead us astray. There is no disputing that. *The Way and Truth of Laijon* cannot be more clear—the Acts of the Second Warrior Angel read, and I quote, 'Having the grand vicar in your midst is as having Laijon in your midst.' Do you not recall your studies of the holy book, Tala? Do you not have a belief in the truthfulness of *The Way and Truth of Laijon*? Are you falling away from the truth as Jondralyn has done?"

"This has nothing to do with my belief in Laijon."

"It has everything to do with it." Jovan's voice was warm now—reverent yet impatient still, and laced with authority. "To bring into question any act of Denarius is to bring into question the very existence of Laijon."

Everything Jovan said was true, of course, strictly speaking. At least it was true according to what was written in *The Way and Truth of Laijon*. But Tala harbored no illusions that Denarius was infallible and not in some way capable of falling into sin, as all men were. The holy book did claim that any man called to be grand vicar was rendered perfect in the eyes of Laijon. But could *The Way and Truth of Laijon* be taken literally concerning human flesh and frailty? That question had weighed heavy on her heart since she had witnessed Denarius with Lawri. Tala had learned in her short life that the idealized things written in *The Way and Truth of Laijon* so long ago were not often compatible with the realities of life here and now.

The fact was, her brother's rigid words were sowing fresh terror into her already pounding heart. It seemed more than ever, in all matters, Jovan deferred to what the holy book said. It was true. The Bloodwood was right. Jovan was beholden to Denarius, more so than her mother and father had been. *And it's my task to find out why.* Or Lawri would continue to slowly die. Tala knew that there was no priesthood prayer or healing oil of the grand vicar that could save her. *Only I can save Lawri.* But after listening to Jovan, it was now dawning on her that, like Lawri, the kingdom of Gul Kana itself might be endangered by this game the Bloodwood played.

"Let me tell you of when I first met Denarius." Jovan's eyes were boring into hers. "It is deeply personal to me, something I have not related to anyone. Before you were born, Father took the family to Rivermeade to stay a few summer moons with the Chaparrals. Leif Chaparral and I, both eight years old at the time, became fast friends. There is a bond between us, Tala, a brotherhood, even. Leif was with me on the battlefield when Sør Sevier first attacked Wyn Darrè. He was with me when Father was killed at the Battle of Oksana. Nothing brings men together more than battle, except for maybe things that bond them together in youth. You see, toward the end of our family trip to Rivermeade, there was a boar hunt. All the young boys were invited to participate. Our first hunt. It was quite a thing. And Leif and I anticipated this event, practiced for it, trained with spear and sword. Even at eight years old, we had already fancied ourselves brothers in arms. We were brimming with excitement over this hunt. But guess what happened?"

Leif Chaparral had had a noticeable limp since Tala could remember. Glade had once hinted that his older brother's leg injury had happened on a hunt of some sort when Leif was younger. That Jovan had also been there when the injury occurred was news to her. Still, Tala wondered at the point of this story. "Leif was hurt," she answered.

"Yes, Leif was hurt." Jovan shifted his weight in the bed. "But I was hurt too. Near to death, in fact. You see, armed with naught but small spears meant for eight-year-olds to use as play toys, Leif and I foolishly set out on our own, and we became separated from the rest of the hunting party. We had it in our minds that we were chasing piglets about, I suppose. But the boar we had the misfortune of finding was no piglet. Seven hundred pounds if it was ten, the size of a full-grown cow, tusks as long as a grown man's arm jutting from its snout. When it charged, Leif jumped into the beast's path in an attempt to save me, taking the point of one of those tusks in his thigh. The boar, with a flick of its head, flung him into the brush and aimed itself at me next. Its heavy, gore-covered tusks crushed into my chest and forced me to the ground. The beast trampled me then, goring me over and over as I tried to squirm. I squealed like a small girl and then blacked out. I found out later that Leif, a ragged hole in his leg, had crawled near two miles, yelling for help all the way, nearly dying of blood loss. When he led our father and the other men to me, the boar stood on top of my body still, upon my head and neck. When they attempted to kill it, it trampled me more in its death throes, its body dropping on me as it died from a dozen spears. They say it took ten grown men to push the beast away.

"When I finally awoke, weeks later, the first image I saw was that of Bishop Denarius. He was kneeling over my bed, blessing my body with healing oils, praying for my recovery. Leif, also recovering from his wounds, lay in a separate bed at my side. Denarius was just the humble bishop of Rivermeade back then. He had not yet been called to be grand vicar in Amadon. But Father told me that he had fasted and prayed at our bedsides, forgoing food and drink and sleep for two weeks straight. By the grace of Laijon and the faith within that great man, I, to this day, suffer no ill effects of that boar attack. None. But as you know, Leif was not so fortunate. He suffers from a limp to this day. Yet he will always be a hero and a brother to me. As will Denarius."

Jovan paused, his lips quivering of their own accord. Tala could see her brother desperately trying to hold back the emotion as he continued, "The injuries and ailments of the flesh must be exposed to Laijon's healing powers. There is no other way."

"Why does he not pray at your side now?" The question spilled from Tala before she could rein it in. "Why is Denarius not here healing your injuries and ailments of the flesh?"

Jovan's emotion-racked face hardened. His eyes locked onto hers. "Have you not listened to a thing I've said?"

"Lawri threw the gladiator's head at Denarius," Tala said. "Don't you see?"

Jovan pushed her aside and climbed out of bed. It took him a great deal of effort; his face was a mask of pain. Tala rose and backed away from him, worried. They stood there, brother and sister, face-to-face, Jovan in naught but a robe and bandages, his dark eyes piercing her. "That you accuse the grand vicar of foul deeds bothers me greatly.

Perhaps it is our cousin, Lawri, who tries to seduce the holy vicar?"

Tala was so flabbergasted by the statement, it rendered her speechless. At first, she had been warmed by his sharing of the boar story. It had seemed so heartfelt. But now she was angry. Anytime she tried to get close to Jovan, she was always met by not only rejection but cold, brutal indifference—and now ignorance to the point of mockery.

Yet she found that she longed for his love and acceptance even more because of it. Perhaps that was what also attracted her to Glade. Much of what was in Jovan could be found in Glade. This thought made her angrier still, and she cursed herself. *Why do I continually grope for the attention and understanding of males who are clearly uninterested in anything I have to say?* "I love you, brother. I love you so much. And ever since Father died, I have prayed for our family daily."

"I believe you have. You are so idealistic."

"And you are so blind." Her tongue, before she could rein it back into her mouth and lock it up, spewed forth more. "But how can anyone so blind rule a kingdom?"

His face was nothing but a cold mask now, and his hard finger was now pointing in the center of her chest. "Do not make it a habit of asking such treasonous questions of your king." His index finger was hitting her with enough force on her breastbone that she stumbled back a few steps. "Pray that I do not change my mind about your involvement in the attempt on my life. Sterling Prentiss mocks my leniency concerning you. If it were up to him, you would all hang— you, Glade, Lindholf. What you may not know is that our dull-faced cousin, Lindholf, confessed much to Sterling. He admitted to climbing the Laijon statue to retrieve notes you exchange with that Sør Sevier traitor, Hawkwood. He admitted to helping you sneak through the secret parts of the castle and escorting you to dockside saloons on errands for Hawkwood."

Tala's heart was racing now. *And I thought I was so clever. Was everything out in the open?* She should never have involved Lindholf. He was so soft and pliable. It was no surprise that Sterling had worked the information out of him. It was all a ruin! For a moment, she thought of telling Jovan the real reason why Lindholf had climbed the Laijon statue. She thought of telling him everything about the Bloodwood dagger and Lawri's poisoning, too. But she did not.

There was sadness creeping into Jovan's eyes. "Because of Lindholf's confession, Sterling believes it was Hawkwood who tried to kill me. And I am not so sure I disagree. I know that Roguemoore and Jon wish me gone. The dwarf most of all. But he hasn't the balls to kill me with his own hands. He would send Hawkwood, though."

Tala's mind was a flurry of anxiety, anger, and dread.

Gingerly, her brother sat back down on the bed, eyes downcast. "Does everyone in my family hate me so much? Am I so bad a brother? Am I so poor a king? I wish Father were here. It is so hard without him." He lay back on the bed now, his head settling into the pillow. His eyes found Tala again. "Do you hate me, Tala?"

Tala didn't answer. She trembled. Her mind spun wildly. *Why is Jovan so beholden to the grand vicar?* The Bloodwood's question had been at the forefront of her mind ever since entering Jovan's chambers. She now knew the answer.

"Well," Jovan said, closing his eyes. "Do you hate me?"

"I cannot remember the last time I saw you laugh, or the last time I saw joy in your eyes," she said. "I do not hate you. But you make me sad."

But Jovan did not hear her answer. He was asleep.

† † † † †

Tala's note to the Bloodwood read,

> *Jovan nearly died during a boar-hunting accident when he*
> *was a child. Denarius fasted and prayed over his injuries*

for two weeks. Jovan believes the grand vicar saved his life.
That is why my brother is so beholden to Denarius.

Tala folded the parchment carefully, slipping it under a thick vine
that draped over the stone balustrade. She rearranged some leaves
of ivy over the note, obscuring it, then wrapped her shawl about her
shoulders. The morning air was cold. The view of Memory Bay below
was crystal clear—both sea and sky a brilliant blue. But Tala hated all
things pretty at the moment. The beauty of the bay was an insult to
the dreariness in her soul. She had no worries that the Bloodwood
would find her note. After all, this was where she'd been instructed
to leave it. She was only doing as she was told. But it infuriated her
that this game was dragging on whilst her cousin's illness worsened.

She turned from the view, gaze traveling down the stairway into
Sunbird Hall. Glade and Lindholf sat at the end of one of the long
tables. She stepped down the stairs toward them, dreading the conversation she knew was to come.

"Jovan told me that you confessed everything to Sterling Prentiss,"
she said to Lindholf as she sat at their table. Lindholf looked stunned.

"You scuttle-brained corncob," Glade said, his gaze slicing into
Lindholf's. "What did you go and do such a thing for? You've implicated us all."

"It's not as bad as it seems, Glade," Tala said.

"It's a wonder Prentiss hasn't come to collect our necks yet."

"He hasn't come for us because Jovan ordered him not to." She
turned to Lindholf. "What you told Sterling did more harm to
Hawkwood than us. Jovan now thinks Hawkwood, Roguemoore,
and my sister are behind the assassination attempt. He thinks I'm
too naive to conjure up an assassination plot against him. He thinks
I'm merely a pawn in some grander scheme cooked up by Hawkwood
and Roguemoore."

"Are you?" Glade asked. "After all, you've been less than forthright with us. Having Lindholf climb the Laijon statue? Who's to say it wasn't you who invited that barmaid to the party? Or Hawkwood? Or Roguemoore? I fear we made a great mistake, Lindholf, worshipping Hawkwood so."

Tala wanted so desperately to tell them both everything. But she could not bear it. She feared that if she did, the Bloodwood would follow through with the promise to hasten Lawri's death.

"Well." Glade stood up, clearly irritated. "I must excuse myself, Tala. I'm done following you around. It has only managed to put me plumb in the middle of an assassination attempt on my king. I can only imagine what my father will think. I can only imagine what Leif will think. He loves Jovan like a brother."

Glade turned a condescending eye on Lindholf. "And Sterling Prentiss, how could you cave to that fat fool?"

"I can see what you all think of me." Lindholf's face was mottled red with a combination of embarrassment and anger. "I was only trying to help Tala." Tears glistened in his eyes as he stood and fled the hall.

"Lindholf!" Tala called after him, her mind in torment. "Don't go," she whispered with panic, but he was gone. The entire situation was unraveling. "Don't treat him like that." She turned to Glade, angry. "Don't you ever treat my cousin so poorly in front of me again."

Glade stood across from her, leaning over the table now, brow furrowed. "I probably should not have been so harsh with Lindholf. He's been a friend to us both."

Moments like these, when Glade showed genuine contrition and concern for those around him, melted Tala's heart. It was this side of him she wanted to see more of.

"I feel badly for my treatment of your cousin." Glade sat back heavily in his chair.

She looked down at the table, unable to meet his eyes. She didn't really harbor any ill will toward him for putting down Lindholf so. After all, she was guilty of the same.

"You do owe me an explanation," he continued. "I have a feeling the note Lindholf pulled from the Laijon statue had nothing to do with Hawkwood. May the wraiths take you, Tala, but was it from Roguemoore? Or was the note from a lover? You seem awfully close to Lindholf lately."

Tala's eyes shot to his. Was there jealousy in those dark orbs? Could this be what truly bothered him? It made sense, in a way. Glade *had* seen her kiss Lindholf. If their roles were reversed, might she conclude the same?

"The tavern girl who stabbed Jovan, is she your lover?" he asked. "Do you fancy other women?"

"Don't be horrid." Tala stood. He stood too and made his way around the table toward her. She backed away from him. But he closed the gap quickly.

Taking her hands in his, he looked deeply into her eyes. "I know which cell they keep the girl in. I would surely love to watch you with her."

She tried to pull away. But his grip was strong, and he held her hands fast.

"I saw you kiss Lindholf." An edge of coldness showed in his voice. "Incest with your own cousin? Is that how Jovan wants you to act? Perhaps it is Lindholf with whom you share your secrets."

"Why are you so mean all the time?" Her question came out as more of a pleading whine than she would have liked. "I won't have you treat me like you treat Lindholf. Let me go!"

He withdrew his hands from hers and looked away. "I think you are very beautiful," he said. "Ofttimes that makes a man act in ways less than appropriate."

"I do not care if you think me pretty," she said. "A woman wants to know what a man thinks of her heart and her soul. I want a man to like me for what is in my head. I want a man to value my opinions."

His eyes roamed the room, looking at everything else but her.

He leaned in and kissed her then—a gentle and tender kiss that lasted a short and sweet eternity. And during the kiss, his hand touched her cheek softly. And when he pulled away from her, his eyes met hers again. "That's what's in my heart," he said.

At this moment, she could almost melt into his arms and weep. Tears welled in her eyes now. A kiss wasn't necessarily what she'd wanted from him. But the fact that someone was showing her any affection at all meant a great deal. Nobody had held her since her mother had died. Nobody. She wrapped her arms around him and clutched him close, her head resting on his shoulder. And before she knew it, she was whispering in his ear.

The story that she'd been hiding from everyone these past few days spilled forth in fragments and bursts, interrupted only by more unwanted crying on her part. But she told him most everything from the start: the Bloodwood, the stabbing of Lawri, the poison, the notes, the clues—though she did not tell him about the note she had just left for the Bloodwood on the balcony this morning, nor the fact that the Bloodwood had given her the task of kissing both him and Lindholf on the final night of the Mourning Moon Celebration. The disgusting thing she'd seen between the grand vicar and Lawri she pinned on Sterling Prentiss. She didn't know why she did it, but she did. She accused the captain of the Dayknights of molesting her cousin. It was her one outright lie. Yet in telling Glade as much as she had, a weight was lifted from her shoulders. She felt as light as a feather now, almost airy. A flood of relief spilled from her and she found herself clinging to his broad shoulders as she wept, glad that he was there as the waves of sorrow spilled out. Finally, she might have someone to discuss her problems with—a confidant.

But when she pulled back and looked into his eyes, she knew she had once again misjudged him. He broke away from her embrace.

That hard cockiness had gathered in his eyes again. He gripped her shoulders. There was a certain cunning in his voice now. "An odd story you tell. Assassins. Poison. Clues. What's the point of it? A fanciful bard's tale or something. Nonsensical. And Prentiss touching Lawri like that?" Abhorrence was on his face. "For my part, I think you've made the whole thing up." He released his hold on her.

Tala's heart was slaughtered. She couldn't even breathe.

"Well," he said, grinning. "Now that you know how I feel, I shouldn't tarry. Things being as they are, it's best none of us show up late for the gladiator match this afternoon. We might be implicated in some outlandish crime—that's if we don't have an alibi for our whereabouts at all times."

As he pulled his chain-mace toy from the folds of his jerkin and walked out of Sunbird Hall, spinning the fist-sized balls in a blur as he went, the hurt and rage boiled up so quickly within her she could scarcely see. Gasping, she dashed up the stairs onto the balcony, taking in long breaths of the crisp morning air. Her insides burned with fury, and her tears blurred the bright sky overhead. So she rubbed the tears away, closed her eyes, clenched them tight, and pounded the railing in front of her with her fists, contemplating just throwing herself over it. When she opened her eyes, she saw the note she had left under the vine.

She snatched the slip of paper up in her trembling hands, meaning to rip it to shreds and toss it over the balcony to scatter to the sea. But it was folded so crisply, so cleanly. The thought of the care and precision she'd taken whilst writing it made her want to vomit. She unfolded it roughly—roughly on purpose, hoping to destroy it before she was forced to read her own stupid, insipid, carefully thought out words.

But it wasn't *her* words she found staring back at her. This wasn't the note she had left at all! Her note was gone. This was the Bloodwood's response.

You are on the right path. But you must search deeper. Only when you discover the truth about Jovan and Denarius shall you risk leaving another note. Be careful who you confide in lest they betray you to Lawri's ruin.

I warn you but once: trust no one unless I instruct you otherwise.

Though many will be blamed for the death of my beloved, I say unto you,
the fall of Laijon was the work of one person and one person alone. Laijon
was betrayed by the Fifth Warrior Angel. Some called her Assassin; I call
her Betrayer, but history knows her better as the Last Demon Lord.
—THE MOON SCROLLS OF MIA

CHAPTER THIRTY-THREE
JONDRALYN BRONACHELL

7TH DAY OF THE MOURNING MOON, 999TH YEAR OF LAIJON
AMADON, GUL KANA

Val-Draekin's thin rapier was aimed straight for Jondralyn's chest, coming swiftly. She drew her arm up to parry with her own thicker sword, blocking the Vallè's stab. The hum of the blades vibrated the air as Val-Draekin's strike was turned aside.

"Very good," the Vallè said, and backed away. But his retreat was brief. He lunged forward again, swinging from above. Jondralyn watched the blade come down and withdrew her own blade, concentrating on her form and footwork. Val-Draekin's blade came sweeping past her face, making the air cry.

"Are you mad?" she exclaimed, stabbing her own blade toward the Vallè's feet.

"Quite mad," Val-Draekin responded, leaping, kicking the sword from her hand.

Jondralyn stood there, angry with herself. "I'll never get it. With one arm injured, you can still best me in less than two moves."

"No matter," the Vallè said, picking up her sword and handing it over. "You'll get it soon enough."

"You can teach me foot movements and stances and pirouettes all day, but I'll never get it."

"It comes easily to few, if any. Most moves can't be perfected for years."

Jondralyn sheathed her sword, mad at the clunky thing for betraying her time and again—the Vallè's wispy rapier seemed far more useful in a fight. She just wanted to plop down on the nearby bench and rest.

"I reckon I've stabbed the straw man a thousand times," she said. "And the stuffed bastard has wrenched the blade from my hand more times than I can count." Her eyes traveled up the jumble of dark stone walls around her. There was naught save the hollow windows and arches and spires of Amadon Castle leering down upon her pathetic courtyard. "I can't even best an inanimate object."

Val-Draekin leaned against one of the wooden pillars that lined the yard near the bench. "Most humans wield a sword about as gracefully as a potbellied hay farmer swings a pitchfork. You must come to worship your blade as you worship Laijon. The Vallè believe that their souls live in their weapons. You must think of your blade as your lover. Become like the Vallè and find a weapon that steals your very soul."

Val-Draekin lifted his blade and sighted down its length. "You've got the talent to grow beyond what most humans can do, Jondralyn. You're tall and athletic. With the right weapon in your hand, you could be formidable indeed."

She perked up at the praise. "The Vallè are blessed with speed. Like your two countrymen who will fight in the arena this afternoon against Squireck and Shkill Gha. Val-Ce-Laveroc and Val-Rievaux. They are not strong. The swords they use are crafted of the flimsiest of steel. And yet they kill with such swiftness and skill."

"Speed is good." Val-Draekin still examined his sword, running lithe fingers down its sharp steel edge. His shoulder was no longer wrapped in a sling, yet he still favored his injured arm some. "But there is advantage in brute strength, too. I daresay Squireck is the best fighter Amadon has ever known, a combination of both power and speed. He is like no gladiator I've seen. I doubt my Vallè countrymen can kill him."

She sat on the cold stone bench near Val-Draekin and thought of her once betrothed. "Could I be as good as Squireck someday?"

"The secret to winning a sword fight is to keep moving." Val-Draekin sheathed his own blade. "Dance, even. Make your foe respond with awkward moves, keep him off balance. Do the expected as much as the unexpected. All fighters have mannerisms that give them away to one with an earnest eye. Some men will furrow their brows before they strike, or widen their eyes; some will take a step back, some forward, or drop their shoulders, twitch their fingers, or lick their lips, any number of things. In time, I believe you will come to pick up on these cues as the Prince of Saint Only has. The bad habits of others will give you that precious heartbeat's advantage. Squireck does all these as naturally as a ballet dancer. There are few in this world who could best him, and certainly none left in the arena bouts. Neither one of the two Vallè nor the oghul will beat the Prince of Saint Only. His victory is assured. I daresay only one who was trained as a Bloodwood could kill Squireck."

"What do you know of the Bloodwood?" she asked.

"That they are unequaled in the art of death."

It was subtle, but Jondralyn detected that the Vallè's eyes scanned the surrounding castle and its hundreds of turrets and battlements above as he'd spoken. There was now a hint of nervousness in Val-Draekin that she had never seen before. It roused her suspicions—suspicions that had never really left her since meeting the Vallè in the Filthy Horse Saloon. "Who are you?" she asked.

Val-Draekin tipped his head to the side, green eyes gazing down at her curiously. The gesture reminded her of a cat she'd once had as a youngster—a very curious cat who would hunker down and cock his head and stare with two big glowing orbs before pouncing on a toy she'd tossed on the cobbles. The dwarf had told her that Val-Draekin might be one of the Five Warrior Angels returned, along with her. But was he? And did he know?

"Who are you?" she repeated, undaunted.

There was amusement in Val-Draekin's eyes. "Roguemoore and I share similar scholarly interests."

"That doesn't answer my question."

"I think it does." There was an openness in his voice as he continued, "If you think on it for but a moment, the answer you want shall come. If you desire to become one of the Brethren, you must learn how to decipher deep mysteries on your own."

Jondralyn did not like that answer. "I know enough. Tell me, why did you make such an entrance into the Filthy Horse Saloon two weeks ago?"

"I was testing someone."

"So your grand entry into the saloon was all a ruse." Irritation was growing inside of her. She remembered with great clarity how much of a fool she had made of herself that night in defense of the Vallè. "The whole thing was all just some game between you and the dwarf? Or a game with someone else? Me?"

"I wouldn't call it a game." It was quick, but before he spoke, the Vallè's eyes did another tour of the surrounding castle, drinking it all in. "Rest assured, Jondralyn. I am quite harmless." Then his eyes returned to their dark and impenetrable normality.

"Harmless?" She stood. "I've seen you with a blade. Why barge into the Filthy Horse and start such a row?"

"Like I said, it was a test." Val-Draekin drew his sword again, holding it out in his slender, unsettlingly graceful hand, sighting down it again with one cold, keen eye. "A test to see if certain people were worthy of my attention, a test to see how serious they were."

"Roguemoore does not fully trust you, you know."

Val-Draekin gave her a blank stare over the gleaming steel of his rapier. He looked dangerous with the cold blade up to his eye like that.

"Are you one of the Brethren of Mia?" Jondralyn placed her hand on his knee. She wondered how far she dared tread with her questioning and comments. "Was it the barmaid, Delia, you were testing? Did you have anything to do with the assassination attempt on Jovan?"

Val-Draekin lowered his blade quietly and slowly shook his head. He sat on the bench beside her.

"And I'm to believe you?" she asked.

"You must follow your heart in all things. That is the way of the Brethren. Trust no one. Right?"

It seemed the Vallè was set on merely bandying words back and forth. Jondralyn had harbored no suspicion that Val-Draekin was responsible for the assassination attempt. But now, everything seemed a secret with him. *The secret to winning a sword fight is to keep moving. Dance, even,* the Vallè had said earlier. *Make your foe respond with awkward moves, keep him off balance. Do the expected as much as the unexpected.* And it appeared this was also true of the way the Val-Draekin chose to conduct what should be a simple conversation. Well, Jondralyn decided, she could play that game too. She kept her hand where it was on his leg. "You gave Roguemoore a coin. What was that?"

"Has he shown it to anyone else that you know of?"

She didn't like her questions followed with another question of his own. "Why does the dwarf not completely trust you?"

"Some may think of me as naught but a thief and the son of a hog farmer," Val-Draekin said with a rueful smile. "But the dwarf is one of the few in the Five Isles who knows my true nature." Shifting his position on the bench so that her hand slid off his leg, he pulled out a whetstone from the folds of his tunic and began honing his blade with it. "Everything is set to fall into place at the end. The dwarf has seen to it. Trust that. But if Roguemoore has not yet chosen to tell you who I am, then far be it from me to step in and reveal things that I should not."

"Well, the dwarf is not here." Jondralyn was annoyed that the Vallè had again dodged her so effortlessly. "Why don't you just tell me, since Roguemoore cannot?"

The Vallè's alert eyes, under piercing brows, were as sharp as daggers now as he calmly honed his blade with the whetstone. Jondralyn drew back from him, wary. *The Way and Truth of Laijon* hinted at the Vallè's facility to discern one's thoughts. She had always felt safe within her own head, within her own mind. But it now seemed this Vallè was working some form of witchery on her—trying to read her, as if the very power of his wintry eyes could crack open her skull and leach her thoughts right out of it. She could feel him pulling at her now. It was as if she stood at the edge of an abyss, losing all sense of balance.

"Why cannot Roguemoore answer your question?" Val-Draekin asked, the whetstone sliding up the blade with a faint, keening wail.

Jondralyn, confused even more, answered the obvious. "Because he is not here."

"And where is he?" the Vallè asked, unblinking eyes fixed on her.

And she nearly answered, *After finding* Ethic Shroud *and one of the lost angel stones in the Rooms of Sorrow under the city, the dwarf and Hawkwood boarded a sailboat bound for Eskander. They are on their way to an abbey in the Autumn Range*—but then caught her tongue. *So this is why Roguemoore wanted me to keep Val-Draekin close. To see if I can figure out what information the Vallè knows and what he does not.*

The dwarf claimed that the Vallè was a descendent of one of the Five Warrior Angels. *And I'm a descendent too?* Everyone knew the stories of the Five Warrior Angels. *The Way and Truth of Laijon* spoke of the five as the Princess, Gladiator, Thief, Assassin, and Slave. But other than Laijon, known as the Slave, or sometimes as the King of Slaves, the scriptures had never mentioned the names of the other four Warrior Angels. *But I am the Princess. He is the Thief.* A chill crawled up her spine as Val-Draekin's eyes continued to bore into hers. She'd just assumed that this dark-haired Vallè knew where Roguemoore and Hawkwood were. But it was now apparent that he didn't.

"Well," Jondralyn said flatly, breaking her gaze from that of the Vallè, "if Roguemoore has not yet chosen to tell you where he went, then far be it for me to reveal things that I should not." She stood from the bench and stalked away, leaving Val-Draekin sitting alone in the courtyard, still honing his blade with the whetstone.

† † † † †

Sweat rolled down Jondralyn's face and under her sodden shirt as Anjk Bourbon swung the iron-studded maul up and around and straight back down. She ducked away, sending the hunk of iron pounding into the ground in a cloud of dust. It was an agile, Vallè-like move, and Jondralyn was proud of herself for managing it.

She could hear the distant roar of the frenzied crowd as she swung her sword at the oghul. But the beast jumped away, tossing the maul—his only weapon—aside. It was a foolish move to be sure, and Jondralyn grinned in triumph. But she realized a moment too late that the move was meant to distract. Anjk struck her, open-handed, in the face. She was sent sprawling sideways to the ground, her sword spinning away.

With a feverish roar, the arena crowd across town groaned and then booed.

For an instant, Jondralyn lay there, face in the dirt, paralyzed with shock. The entire left side of her head throbbed in pain. Fury swept through her system. She hurled herself from the ground straight up at Anjk, who sidestepped, tripping her to the ground again. Another thunder of boos cascaded over them.

As the oghul dropped on top of her with a force so heavy it crushed the wind from her lungs, Jondralyn knew she had lost again. She felt as weak and useless as a newborn foal under the weight of a giant bear. Anjk quickly put her in a headlock between his gnarled legs. The foul stench of the oghul's groin, covered by naught but a ragged gray loincloth, hit her with a force far greater than had the open-handed slap from his meaty paw. The oghul flipped over in the dirt, twisting her awkwardly between his coarse legs so that she was looking straight up at the sky, unable to move.

The arena was silent for a time, then roared back to life with another wild storm of boos, the sound carrying over the city of Amadon, filling Anjk Bourbon's small courtyard. As she lay there, pinned between the oghul's heavy legs, she looked at the blue sky above and listened to the crowd. It was the end of the second match of the final four. And from the gusto exhibited in the baying and booing of the crowd, Jondralyn knew that Squireck Van Hester had just won. Had he vanquished Val-Ce-Laveroc or Val-Rievaux? There was little chance the crowd would react with boos unless it was for the Prince of Saint Only. Only the championship bout remained.

The jubilation emanating from the arena during the first match of the day between the oghul, Shkill Gha, and the first Vallè had been far more riotous. She did not know who had won, though. Jondralyn wished she were there. If she closed her eyes, she could almost believe she was in the arena now. She wondered why she had chosen to forego the final fights. Why did she have to so rigidly adhere to this training routine? Why was she trying so desperately to find discipline in her life? Things were much easier without the burden.

The oghul released his hold and her neck was free.

"You defend against my club like the gnarled hairs that guard an oghul whooman's poosy!" Anjk stood and grinned a wicked grin. "You just scratch and prick and do nothing but irritate! Then I clobber!" The street folk—mostly urchins, dwarves, and other oghuls—gathered along the stumpy, crumbled stone wall around Anjk's courtyard laughed uproariously at his wit. Anjk continued, "You pay me much. That is only reason I train you. You have no hopes of being good fighter."

Jondralyn stood slowly, rubbing her shoulder. The more time she spent with this brutish oghul, the less she could figure out what she was to learn from him. It seemed the blood-thirst was on Anjk badly today, evidenced by his overly raw and swollen gums and his ornerier-than-normal demeanor. Jondralyn just wanted to leave before the foul fellow sank his teeth into her neck and tore off a chunk of her flesh.

A slim-faced oghul in filthy clothes—one whom Jondralyn had not noticed there before—jumped the crumbled stone wall at the southern end of the small courtyard and sauntered toward Anjk. Seeing this new gray-faced fellow approach, Anjk turned to her. "Training over today. You go now." He pointed toward the smithy.

Glad that the day's training was done, Jondralyn picked up her sword and left the courtyard to the jeers of the dwarves and gap-toothed urchins and other less-than-savory-looking oghuls gathered on the wall. Once inside the oghul's smithy, she looked for a pan of water to wash the stink from her neck. Benches and tables were lined with clubs and mauls and maces and a few short, thick-shafted spears. As she waded through the spiked gauntlet toward the door in the opposite wall, a hanging forest of curved scythes and heavy oghul sabers nearly sheared her hair. It was an unkempt obstacle course strewn with anvils, cauldrons, tools, and weaponry of all kind and make—none worthy of a princess. The sword that would—as Val-Draekin said—steal Jondralyn's soul was not amongst the battered and crude implements Anjk had either found or forged with his foul oghul iron-craft. She spied what looked like a horse trough amongst the junk against the wall. *Surely Anjk doesn't sup from a trough like a common mule?* That was probably exactly how oghul-kind preferred to take their drink—hunched over and lapping at it like dogs.

The trough was full of naught but an oily-looking sludge, plus it smelled like oghul arse. A spout was mounted on the wall and a rusted handle to a pump was nearby. She leaned her sword against a bench and yanked up and down on the pump until a stream of what looked like clean water trickled from the spout into the sludgy trough. Looking about for a bowl or cup to hold under the spout, she found the next best thing—a shelf full of pewter wine goblets. She filled one with water and drank greedily.

In her haste, the goblet slipped from her hand and clattered to the floor with a splash. Her muscles were sore and her balance seemed off. Cursing, she picked up the goblet, filled it again, and drank deeply, more carefully this time. Fatigue washed over her as the cool water quenched her parched throat. She filled the goblet again, pouring the liquid over her head, scrubbing down her neck. The overspill of her washing was adding to the spreading wetness on the stone floor.

She heard the two oghuls just beyond the door to the smithy. Anjk's deep voice was the loudest. "The prince will surely die with what I just give you."

Jondralyn froze, wine goblet still in hand, eyes on the rectangle of yellow light bleeding into the room from the door still open to Anjk's training yard. She tore her gaze away, searching for an escape. But the door to the street was farther away, closed. She could never make it through all the junk without knocking into something and causing a terrible commotion. She thought about tying a black scarf about her face—the one she kept in her pocket to avoid recognition as she traveled to and from the oghul's smithy. But that seemed pointless now. She remained motionless, hardly daring to breathe, eyes back to the open door. "Is a rare oghul mixture I sell Arkbishop

Spenkcerville," Anjk Bourbon continued. "The rarest. Much expensive. The Arkbishop has money. No?"

The other oghul spoke, his voice mousy. "Shkill Gha was wounded in his fight with the Vallè swordsman, Val-*See*-Layvearok." He couldn't quite pronounce the gladiator's foreign name. "Nasty, filthy creature, that Vallè. Took it to our oghul kinfolk. Odds are, the Prince of Only will win the tournament. This will help greatly to kill him."

"Spread on Shkill Gha's blade," Anjk said. "One scratch and the Prince of Only die. One pinch cost more than all I own. When can I expect payment, G'Mellki?"

"You get pay when the poison does its job," the one named G'Mellki answered. "No sooner. The final fight starts soon. I must get this poison to Shkill Gha or neither G'Mellki or Anjk get paid."

"If Arkbishop Spenkcerville does not pay," Anjk roared, "I find G'Mellki, and I kill him!" Anjk's great bulk blocked out the light of the doorway as he stepped from the courtyard right into the smithy, not ten paces from Jondralyn. He once more carried the deadly-looking iron-studded maul. Her wine goblet slipped and hit the floor with a clang.

At the noise, Anjk Bourbon spotted her. His liquid brown eyes sparkled with malice as he growled, "You hear things you shouldn't." He brandished his maul, hunched shoulders bunching, slabs of muscle flexing beneath the taut gray skin. His leathery lips curled back, exposing rows of jagged teeth behind slavering jaws. The oghul had a look of determination on his rough-hewn face. But as much as panic wanted to send Jondralyn running, she gathered herself and snatched up her sword.

With a roar that shook the smithy, Anjk hurled himself at Jondralyn, his maul upraised, swinging for her face. She lunged at the oghul, sword now firmly in hand, point aimed at the oghul's heart. She knew her attack was nothing if not suicidal as Anjk's heavy maul arced toward her head.

But the oghul slipped and fell in an ungainly sprawl, his maul swinging wildly over Jondralyn's right shoulder whilst her own sword found its mark. It plunged deep into the oghul's rough chest. Anjk slumped against the trough as the maul fell from his grubby paw, his body finally sliding down to rest in the pool of water.

Jondralyn held tight to the sword as the oghul hissed one last curse through his yellow teeth and blood dribbled from his slackening jaw. She yanked on the sword. But the weapon protruding from the dead oghul's thick chest remained stuck as if fixed in stone. Her hands shook uncontrollably as she tried to wrench it free.

She saw the other oghul in the doorway—the one named G'Mellki. The smallish oghul, hearing the commotion, had stepped back into the room. Their eyes met. Whereas Anjk's face was flat as an oar blade, this oghul's was as thin and narrow as a hatchet, but no less greenish-gray and repulsive. Jondralyn, hand still fastened to the hilt of the sword in Anjk's chest, watched the slow, animal-like blinking of the smallish oghul's heavy gray lids. The ugly fellow quickly sized up the scene, turned, and fled.

Jondralyn gave one final tug on the sword lodged in Anjk's chest and pulled it free. She took a deep breath, fatigue forgotten, and darted to the chase. If what she'd heard was true, one of the five archbishops, Spencerville, had paid for the poison the oghul was going to spread on Shkill Gha's blade. She had to stop the oghul from reaching the arena.

She tore from the smithy and into Anjk's small courtyard just in time to see G'Mellki shove his way through a group of dirt-covered dwarves, leap the far wall, and dash off down the alley. Jondralyn's legs churned under her, the soft sand of the training yard kicking up behind. The dwarves scattered as she passed by, her sword still in one hand. With her free hand on the wall, she leaped up and propelled herself over in one bound, landing cleanly, scarcely breaking stride. G'Mellki was a good fifty paces ahead, his gait more ambling than running. Still, the narrow-faced fellow was fast for an oghul.

As her quarry rounded a sharp corner and disappeared, Jondralyn uttered a vulgar oath. She had gained some ground, but the fellow probably knew these streets and alleys like the back of his own cracked and leathery hand. She flung herself around the corner just in time to see him disappear down another side alley.

After racing through a few more twists and turns, Jondralyn had again gained on him considerably. She soon found herself chasing the oghul down a more open thoroughfare, sparsely populated. What few people there were quickly scurried out of their way. With more room to run, she picked up her pace but kept her sword out in front of her, ready in case the oghul were to whirl about with an outstretched blade of his own.

Jondralyn closed in and nearly seized the fellow, but the oghul took a sharp turn and dashed into another side street. She turned and ripped down the new street too, now lagging over ten paces behind, two pigs rooting in the center of the lane setting her farther off course. A score of religious beggars were in the mud and dung beyond the pigs, and weaving through them bogged her down further. G'Mellki was small for an oghul—and agile, too. In this narrow and crowded alleyway, Jondralyn felt ungainly as she ran. A few toothless women in rags shuffled aside as she shoved by. She had fallen more than twenty paces behind the oghul now. He was passing under a vine-covered archway and into a crowded marketplace. People shouted as the oghul pushed his way through. Jondralyn followed, holding her blade high. She and the oghul broke from the crowd and into the open at about the same time, the oghul taking an abrupt right, leaping a waist-high brick fence. Jondralyn jumped the fence only to find herself face-to-face with a dusty yellow dog, barking up a storm. The deranged beast was wearing a spiked iron collar and trailing a length of heavy chain. It charged. She flung herself away. The dog hit the end of its rusted leash, whipping the snarling monster around by the neck.

At a full run, she chased the oghul around another corner. Jondra-lyn instinctively threw her left leg wide, narrowly avoiding smacking her knee on a water trough. But she slipped and fell, tumbling into the legs of a crowd of people. When she stood, she realized she was face-to-face with a gaggle of the worst scum Amadon had to offer—bloodletters. Filthier than dockside whores, these grotesques would stand about shady corners, waiting for swollen-gummed oghuls, then open the veins in their necks and wrists and fill flagons with their own steaming blood and sell it, slaking the thirst of their oghul customers.

Jondralyn's eyes darted beyond the bloodletters to see that G'Mellki had run into a dead end not fifty paces away. A stone wall, twelve feet high, now blocked his path. Until now, G'Mellki had managed to avoid all such blind alleys.

The bloodletters stared at her, recognition dawning on some of their faces. Jondralyn knew that some streets in Amadon, without warning, could turn from familiar to sinister. She was lucky that this alley held only the few bruise-necked bloodletters and was empty of any brigands or outlaws. She realized she'd best cover her face soon.

As G'Mellki dragged a wooden barrel toward the wall, Jondralyn shoved her way through the bloodletters and sprinted toward him. G'Mellki climbed atop the barrel, grabbed the lip of the wall, paused to kick the barrel aside, and pulled himself over just as Jondralyn lunged for his grubby boots. She cursed as the oghul escaped her grasp, his footsteps slapping on the cobblestones beyond.

Jondralyn righted the barrel and threw herself over the wall, only to see the small oghul now moving through a wrought-iron gate and out of sight around a bend that sloped down toward the docks. Jondralyn reached the gate quickly and flung herself around the bend just in time to see the oghul, down a steep narrow alley, slip by a wagon laden with lodgepole pine logs, dip into a doorway, and disap-pear. Jondralyn darted down the uneven stones of the alley. She was breathing hard now. She sidled past the wagon of sharp, tar-smeared poles, and continued down the cobbled slope, checking what few doors there were. They all looked the same, and all were locked.

The alley came to a dead end at the bottom—another stone wall, this one about ten feet high. She looked back up the cobbled slope. The hatchet-faced oghul was removing the last of the wooden blocks from under the wagon's wheels, releasing the wagon to lurch and rumble down the steep alleyway—its heavy logs now a rumbling, roaring forest of spears aimed right at her. Jondralyn's heart thundered. The alley was narrow. There was nowhere to go. Her eyes darted about frantically. There was no escape.

At the last moment, she turned her back to the careening wagon, dropped her sword, and jumped for all she was worth, her fingertips barely grabbing the lip of the ten-foot-high stone wall above. With all her remaining strength—propelled by pure terror—Jondralyn threw her legs up and swung her body to the side as high as she could. Her momentum carried her completely over the stone wall just as the wagon full of logs smashed into it with the sound of thunder and a billow of dust and mortar.

Weaponless, she dropped to the other side . . . and found herself in a dirty little courtyard, smack in the center of five dour-looking men—one elderly, fat and bloated, the other four younger, all looking like ruffians in their patched shirts and ripped rough-spun breeches. The fat one pulled a thick-bladed shortsword.

Immediately, she turned and leaped again, grasped the lip of the same stone wall, scrambled back over, and landed atop the wrecked wagon and scattered logs that had nearly killed her moments before. Dust still billowed. She could hear the curses of the five men coming from the other side as they tried to climb over the wall after her.

She coughed. Her eyes quickly scanned the narrow alley, but G'Mellki had already slipped out of sight. She shuddered when she saw what the impact of the wagon against the wall had done to the logs under her feet. They were shattered and splintered and tossed about in every direction. The wall had buckled from the power of the crash. Had it struck her, the wagon's load would have pulverized her to mush against the wall.

Weariness settled upon her as never before. G'Mellki was lost to her now. There was no use searching this bewildering maze of ruined stone houses and alleys rife with twists and turns. She coughed again and quickly pulled the scarf from her pocket, tied it over her nose and mouth. Now she could breathe again and, more importantly, travel back to the arena unrecognized. She gingerly climbed from the wagon of ruined poles and searched for her fallen sword. It lay atop the weed-encrusted cobbles under the wagon, undamaged. She could reach it if she crawled on her belly—but decided to abandon it where it lay when the head of one of the five ruffians appeared over the wall. "I see her, lads," the dirty fellow said. "A pretty thing! Push me up."

Jondralyn wasn't about to wait for the other four. She turned and bolted up the alley as fast as her tired legs would carry her.

She ran in hopes that she could still reach the arena in time and warn Squireck.

The Last Warrior Angels chose to embellish, ignoring truth. In their account, Laijon was stabbed in the neck by the Last Demon Lord and then nailed to the Atonement Tree. But I, his wife, was there as Laijon drank in those last breaths. I saw the wound in his neck. It was no treacherous stabbing. What I beheld was far more inglorious—it was as if the neck of my beloved had been shredded by the claws of a beast.
—THE MOON SCROLLS OF MIA

CHAPTER THIRTY-FOUR
STERLING PRENTISS

7TH DAY OF THE MOURNING MOON, 999TH YEAR OF LAIJON
AMADON, GUL KANA

The flesh under Sterling's black-lacquered Dayknight armor itched—it itched something fierce and he could do nothing about it. He hated the damnable stuff. He would give all that he owned for the chance to remove the cumbersome scrap and relax as he awaited the final match. Sitting just below him in the king's suite was Grand Vicar Denarius, resplendent in his clean cassock and priestly silk robe—and probably comfortable, too. The Quorum of Five Archbishops sat behind him as usual, Vandivor, Donalbain, Spencerville, Leaford, and Rhys-Duncan. Dayknights guarded them.

The king was not present. Nor was Jondralyn. Or Tala. In the absence of the royal siblings, the mood in the king's suite was far less tense. Glade Chaparral and Lindholf Le Graven were two rows below Sterling. All afternoon they'd been fawning over Seita. It disturbed

Sterling to see any human male, be they a lord's son or not, make such an overt display over such a skinny piece of Vallè scum. The Vallè sickened Sterling on every level—especially the females, too hard and sinuous.

With a metallic groan, the large wrought-iron gates on either end of the arena opened, chains rattling. There had been a low, anxious murmur in the crowd for the last hour or so, but now the fifteen thousand were utterly quiet as the final two combatants stepped into the arena. It was tradition that the final matches take place on the same day—the first bout at noon to determine the championship fight, and the final bout an hour later. Fighting one bout so soon after the next, the last two combatants' strength would be sorely tested. The victor of such a taxing ordeal was surely the chosen of Laijon. But Sterling thought the rule and tradition was a waste. By this time most gladiators were so beaten down and beset with injury that the final match was ofttimes a bore.

The oghul, Shkill Gha, was one such wearied fighter. Out of the northern gate, he hobbled into the arena, plate armor strapped over heavily bandaged arms, many of the wounds still bleeding through, coating the armor black. Only the shards of his jagged yellow teeth and prickling eyes were visible between the bars of his horned iron helm. He carried a massive serrated longsword in one limp hand. Though he had emerged victorious, Shkill Gha's earlier battle with the Vallè pirate, Val-Ce-Laveroc, had not gone well. There was an eagerness in the way the young Vallè swordsman had fought—he'd had a quickness of reaction and footwork that grabbed one's attention, held one's eye, his sword work dazzling, riddling the oghul with jab and cut and counter. But it had taken just one forceful, if not lucky, blow from Shkill Gha's mighty sword to squash the head of the lithe Vallè. The toll the earlier fight had exacted on the oghul's body was apparent to all. More than likely, by order of the arena judges, the oghul had been pumped full of numbing agents just to make his entrance.

Squireck, on the other hand, strolled through the southern gate and into the arena unbloodied, wearing naught save a leather loin-cloth for armor and a wreath of white heather crowning his head. He gripped a sword in one hand and two silver daggers in the other. The Prince of Saint Only had proven to be the most cunning gladiator Sterling had ever seen. The Vallè pirate Squireck had been earlier matched against was a quick one with about a half-dozen small daggers hidden in his scaled leaf-mail armor. He whipped them out early and fast, zinging them one after the next at Squireck—his wrist a flicker of movement. But Squireck danced away each time. His own long silver dagger tumbled through the air with a snap of his hand, punching into his foe's stomach, staggering him. Squireck rushed in and jammed his sword into the Vallè's chest—twist and then out again, quick as you please—and the Vallè pirate, Val-Rievaux, dropped to his knees. Squireck plunged his sword straight down through the fellow's neck and into his heart, ending it.

At Squireck's victory, a roar of boos had washed over the arena as the Prince of Saint Only held his sword aloft in mock salute to the crowd, then struck the head from his dead opponent and tossed it into the stands in the direction of the grand vicar.

There came a low hum from the orchestra as the names of the final two were announced: a roar of cheers for Shkill Gha, a thunder of boos for the Prince of Saint Only. Then the orchestra bells gonged a deep *Boom! Boom! Boom!* and the crowd began to chant, "*Shkill Gha! Shkill Gha! Shkill Gha!*"

Sterling thought of Edmon Guy Van Hester, King of Adin Wyte, the conquered and fallen Lord of Saint Only, father of Squireck. Word of the gladiator matches had surely reached the impoverished Isle of Adin Wyte by now. What must the disgraced father think of the disgraced son? The once-golden Prince of Saint Only had certainly fallen from favor: betrothed to the sister of the king of Gul Kana as a child, the most beautiful woman in the realm, prince of a fallen kingdom as an adult, imprisoned for murder, a gladiator after that. The murder of Archbishop Lucas was the most infamous crime of an age. Much rumor had swirled around the fallen king of Adin Wyte in the aftermath. Some said that King Edmon Guy Van Hester initially denied his son's sins. Others claimed that Edmon had promptly disowned his son, leaving it to the graces of the grand vicar to decide Squireck's fate. A few asserted that King Edmon had bribed Denarius with what few riches were left in Adin Wyte in an effort to stay the immediate execution of his boy. And still others believed that it was Edmon who had forced his son into the gladiator arena to prove his innocence and to fight for the honor of the entirety of Adin Wyte. But Sterling had his own theories. In truth, great shame had driven the once-proud King Edmon into the highest towers of the Fortress of Saint Only. It was there that he remained most days, in a self-imposed exile, supping with the dogs he kept company with, his conquered kingdom fallen into ruin, living purely by the sufferance of Aeros Raijael.

As the two gladiators prepared for battle below, Sterling glanced at the grand vicar, expecting to see Denarius' face stamped with worry. Squireck was fresh, the oghul not. But as the vicar looked back at him, his eyes sparkled with confidence. Sterling's own eyes traveled back to the arena floor when the signal to begin the fight was given.

To Sterling's surprise, the oghul, with renewed vigor, swung his sword over his head and roared, his massive, serrated-steel blade gleaming in the afternoon sun as he charged. Squireck jammed the point of his own sword into the sand, pulled back his arm, aimed one of his daggers at the oghul lumbering toward him, and threw.

The first dagger, like silver lightning, spun end over end straight and true. It punched through Shkill Gha's breastplate but did not slow him. The oghul picked up speed. Squireck's second dagger sank into the oghul just under his thick neck. But again, Shkill Gha did not break stride; instead he raised his weapon, closing fast. The Prince of

Saint Only yanked his own sword from the sand. He lunged toward Shkill Gha with springing steps, almost skipping as he swung.

There was a brutal, deafening clamor. The sound of the two great swords clashing sent a tremor through the air, the concussion nearly wrenching the weapons from both gladiators' hands. *Magnificent!* Sterling thought as the huge blades hit. *All power and raw fury!*

Squireck stumbled away, legs churning in the sand, searching for balance. Shkill Gha stood his ground, swinging again in a burst of speed never before seen in the beast. The prince ducked the blow. The oghul's serrated steel snagged a stray lock of hair and sliced it clean off. Squireck rolled in the sand as the oghul swung again, blade a humming blur, striking the ground where Squireck had just been. But the Prince of Saint Only was on his feet in a flash, backing away from Shkill Gha.

Sterling soon realized that someone had drugged the oghul not only with pain-numbing agents, but with rauthouin bane as well, a drug known for injecting the user with sudden, unnatural bursts of strength. Some in Sør Sevier—Bloodwood assassins to be exact—gave the drug to their horses to make them feisty and rabid in battle. A red-eyed stallion or mare infected with rauthouin bane was considered more dangerous than the assassin atop it. The oghul's previous injuries would not be a factor in this bout.

Excitement rippled through the crowd as Shkill Gha again charged Squireck, roaring, thick legs a storm of motion. Squireck backed away, shifting the weight of his own blade, stumbling again as the oghul's next swing almost took him in the face. Squireck did not try meeting the much more powerful oghul blade-for-blade again, except for the occasional glancing block. Instead he used quick, flawless foot-work to gain back his advantage and methodically wear down the oghul. The magnificent muscles of his arms and shoulders swelled and rippled with every smooth slash and counter.

In the end, Shkill Gha was fighting against his own impatience, his mistakes becoming clear and frequent. Disappointment was again infecting the crowd. The oghul's attacks grew more ponderous and slow as the rauthouin bane wore off. It wasn't long before the oghul stopped attacking altogether and just leaned there on his sword in the center of the arena, breathing heavily.

Squireck did not end it there, though. Sword in hand, he paced before the oghul, back and forth, back and forth, almost taunting the beast. The orchestra bell gonged a deep *Boom! Boom!* Squireck began circling his opponent. The orchestra bell gonged another deep *Boom!* And Squireck circled. *Boom!*

Chants of *"Shkill Gha! Shkill Gha! Shkill Gha!"* sounded through the arena. But oghul just leaned on his sword, legs wobbly, heavy horned helm drooping further with each passing moment.

Then it happened. With blistering speed and power, Squireck Van Hester struck the oghul with the greatest burst of rage yet seen. Still planted in the sand, the oghul's own sword buckled and gave way under the power of Squireck's blow, the prince's sword sweeping through the beast's midsection and out the other side. A shower of blood bloomed outward from Shkill Gha's chest as Squireck's sword cleaved through plate armor and all. The oghul threw back his head, gurgled a barrage of guttural sounds, and then fell heavily to the ground, horned helm tumbling from his head, body splayed on its back, blood spraying from his wound. Not a drop fell upon the Prince of Saint Only.

The crowd was silent as Squireck placed one bare foot on the oghul's sword, pinning the serrated weapon to the ground, and with the tip of his blade touched the base of his opponent's leathery throat. Squireck leaned on his sword, pushing it clear through Shkill Gha's throat and up into the oghul's brain case, killing him.

Squireck Van Hester, Prince of Saint Only, removed his bare foot from the dead oghul's blade and stepped away, triumphant eyes finding the king's suite above.

A sudden commotion under one of the wrought-iron gates drew everyone's attention. Princess Jondralyn Bronachell came striding from under the gate and out onto the floor of the arena. She carried a clay jug that sloshed clear liquid onto the sand. She headed straight for Squireck, with several Silver Guards as escort. When she reached him, she dropped to her knees and took up one of the champion's bare feet. Pouring the liquid from the jug over it, she washed it and then the other foot, scrubbing vigorously and with purpose. This seemingly humble act by Jondralyn Bronachell set the crowd to clapping and cheering with wild applause that grew more robust as she continued to scrub.

Many eyes in the king's suite were on Denarius, including Sterling's. The portly man was trying to put on a smile, but what he managed looked more like a leering grimace. He seemed to be glaring daggers at one of the archbishops—Spencerville. And when he looked away from his fellow churchman, Denarius seemed a bit older than just moments before, fleshier even, with new lines under his eyes.

Sterling found that somehow pleased him.

There was a tug on his cloak, and he turned to find a fellow Dayknight standing behind him, a grim look on his mustached face. "I've bad news to relay, Ser." The dour-faced knight leaned over and whispered in Sterling's ear. "The kitchen matron, Dame Vilamina, was found dead in her cell under the Hall of the Dayknights. And the serving wench, Delia, the one who knifed King Jovan, has escaped Purgatory."

† † † † †

Sterling awaited the arrival of the grand vicar. He took the time to make sure that everything in this hallway hadn't also gone to shit in the short time that he'd been gone. But everything seemed in order. So he dismissed the two Silver Guards and opened the door behind them to check on the sick girl. Lawri Le Graven lay on her bed, snug asleep under the covers, pale face poking out, alone in the room. He shut the door and stood guard. He would watch over the girl before the vicar arrived, while the vicar ministered to her, and after. Grand Vicar Denarius had ordered the Dayknights to keep her safe. And at the moment, the only person Sterling trusted with the post was himself.

As things were, there was no place now safe in Amadon, no dungeon impervious to escape. First it had been Hawkwood who'd escaped Purgatory. And now, the serving wench, Delia, apparently having killed the nosy old kitchen matron in her escape.

Perhaps the slave quarry of Riven Rock out near the Hallowed Grove was a more secure place to keep captives. He would advise Jovan to use it in the future.

Sterling had been certain the serving wench had *not* been the assassin. Now he wasn't so sure. His investigation had turned up little. Delia's cell was empty. Vilamina was dead in the cell across the hall. Both cell doors were locked when Vilamina's body had been discovered. The two Silver Guards posted at the top of the stairs above the cells had not seen or heard a thing. Sterling had them stripped of their rank and then sent out to Riven Rock to pound stone themselves. He wasn't naive enough to believe that the Hall of the Dayknights was immune from secret passageways that even he did not know of. He had once prided himself on knowing almost every nook and cranny of the city, along with every secret passageway in Amadon Castle, the Grand Vicar's Palace, the Temple of the Laijon Statue, and the Hall of the Dayknights combined. But over time, he realized there was much he did not know. Now he was a mere hairsbreadth away from being stripped of his rank and tossed into the dungeons himself.

He stood straighter at his post as his attention was drawn to the sound of voices at the far end of the corridor. He straightened his chain-mail cuirass and leather greaves. Tonight he wore the more casual attire of the Dayknights, more comfortable than the formal black armor he was forced to wear at the arena and other such events—at least this light chain mail did not itch like the black-lacquered armor.

Tala Bronachell rounded the corner of the passageway. She came with Glade Chaparral and Lindholf Le Graven. As the three approached, Sterling felt a cold whisper of dread. Protocol demanded that each member of the royal family be accompanied through the castle by at least two Silver Guards at all times until they turned eighteen. That Tala was unescorted was troubling, especially in light of the assassination attempt on Jovan.

"What brings you here, m'lady?" he asked, injecting a hefty ration of authority into his voice. "What Silver Guards were assigned to you today? I will have their necks. And where is Dame Mairgrid?"

"We've come to visit my sister," Lindholf Le Graven said.

"I was not speaking to you, whelp," Sterling snapped. "Nobody is allowed into Lawri's chamber but for the holy vicar himself."

Tala fired, "And what right do you have—"

"The right granted by the grand vicar." Sterling cut the princess off brusquely, eyes still fixed on Lindholf. "Do not presume to test my patience." Though he held the lord of Eskander in high regard, he had never cared for Lord Lott's son. It wasn't necessarily the clumping of unsightly scars and burns and deformed ears on Lindholf's face that disturbed Sterling, but more the young man's narrow eyes. Lindholf's eyes were hard and black, an off-putting contrast to his pale skin and unkempt hair.

Glade, loitering a few paces behind Lindholf, was spinning a small Vallè-made ball-and-chain mace around his arms in a whirl. It made a humming noise that echoed down the passageway and set Sterling's nerves atingle. "Put that away," he growled. Glade kept the thing spinning as if he hadn't heard.

"As the king's sister, I order you to let us pass," Tala said.

"I take my orders from the grand vicar," Sterling said evenly, his hand now lingering on the black opal in the pommel of his Dayknight sword. "And with all due respect, m'lady, the vicar outranks even you."

Sterling had known Tala her whole life. Normally a submissive, shy girl, it was only recently that she had shown signs of that Bronachell stubbornness so prevalent in her father and her mother . . . and her older sister. It was to be admired. But not today. In most situations, Sterling tried to make his face as expressionless as he could. His intent was to show nothing. Not even a raised eyebrow. But this time, he gave the princess his most scathing look, hoping to frighten her off.

Yet the determined expression on her intelligent face didn't change. Nor did the Chaparral lordling's face. Chain-mace toy still spinning in one hand, Glade was studying him through dark, flinty eyes. Sterling did not like what he saw there. Lindholf, on the other hand, had already backed down the hall. That was no surprise. There was always something slouched and drooping about Lindholf Le Graven—the boy was one dopey hunk of sod.

"Off with you now," he said, seeing that none of them had much more prepared beyond staring. They had probably gathered together just moments ago and hatched their plan: *Let's throw our royal names about and frighten the doddering old Dayknight captain into letting us into Lawri's room.* They must have thought it would be that easy.

"Go on, git," he said.

Tala's dark brown eyes glared at him with open malevolence.

"Please don't pout and cry," he said. "Heaven forbid I get accused of setting off a great flood of royal whining. You must learn to deal with things as they are. Make the best of things. Soldier up, as we say in the Dayknights."

"I'm afraid you are mistaken," Tala said, the anger growing behind her eyes. "We will not whine or cry. We will see our friend Lawri."

"Git, I say. Now!"

The girl glowered, her dark eyes boring into his, face expressionless. *She's good, this one.* Sterling's eyes traveled over her, scrutinizing her garb. *Indeed, she's taking after her older sister.* Today she was even dressed like Jondralyn was sometimes lately apt to: shirt, tunic, leather belt, and black-handled dagger at her hip, unladylike leather boots and pants. He saw a lot of Jondralyn's fire in young Tala.

"Lawri is to remain alone by order of the vicar," he said, softening his tone. "He will be arriving soon." Clearly his hardened approach was not working. Most everyone confronted with his harsh orders adopted a servile tone and immediately obeyed. But the children of royalty were not like the common soldier who'd grown up in the smith shop or on the sheep farm. It was hard for the spoiled youth of the court to take orders.

"Lawri's illness could be catching," he continued, thinking how full of life the girl had been before this illness had struck. Truth be told, it bothered him that Lawri was suffering from such a debilitating sickness.

He stood straighter. "My order is to bar entry to all but the grand vicar. I am to stand guard while he ministers to her. Do you wish me to fall derelict in my duty, what with the events surrounding the attempt on our king's life?"

"If guarding Lawri is so important," Glade said, "why are there no other Silver Guards with you?"

Tala added, "You keep the Silver Guards away so you can be alone with Lawri, spy on her. Spy on the vicar." Her tone was light and casual.

"Preposterous." Sterling tried to stem the embarrassing gout of laughter that burst forth uncontrollably. "Why would I wish to be alone with Lawri?"

Tala's mouth crinkled with distaste. "Why indeed?"

Panic began to stir gently within Sterling's gut.

"There's been talk of Jovan replacing you," Glade said. "You've let slip your duties, Captain. Hawkwood's escape. The serving wench Delia, too. Word is Jovan is sorely displeased. You may soon find yourself relieved of duty."

Sterling blanched in anger. Glade was coming close to outright taunting him now, almost throwing a challenge. The boy hadn't even stopped whirling his ball-mace about.

"Stop playing with that *toy*." The tension in the air was as thick as smoke. Sterling set the palm of his hand back over the pommel of his sword. "I will never be replaced."

"Can you be sure?" Glade's dark eyes were glinting with pleasure.

He's actually enjoying this, Sterling realized, taking a step toward the young man. Glade backed away, a sliver of fear creeping into his eyes. He stopped twirling the mace.

"There are certain laws and protocols," Sterling said, barely managing to quell his anger enough to speak. "And just so you are not mistaken, Glade Chaparral, let me remind you, it would take a consensus of both the grand vicar and the king along with all five in the quorum to relieve a Dayknight captain of his duty. And though what you say about Jovan's displeasure might be true, Denarius would never give that consent. I am valuable to him in ways that you will never know."

Glade's eyes were now downcast. And that seemed to be the end of it, until the young man looked up again. The glint of insufferable royal arrogance returned. "The post may not be stripped from you. But make no mistake, Captain, you *can* be removed."

The slow building of dread in Sterling's gut was now a palpable, physical thing.

"It would have been better had you just let us into Lawri's chamber." Glade strapped his chain-mace toy to his belt. "But you'll soon be one less fool we need suffer."

"And what is meant by that?"

"I only pass along a bit of gossip," Glade said casually and confidently—too confidently for one his age. "You make of it what you will."

How Sterling wished to slap that smug look from Glade's face. "And who might Jovan be grooming to take my place?"

"My brother, Leif," Glade shot back quickly.

"That fop." Sterling laughed aloud, then coughed nervously, the truth hitting him like a hammer blow to the gut. The lord of River-meade's son and Jovan had been best friends since childhood. The bond between them was deep. But Leif Chaparral was no swordsman worthy of captain. He was middling at best. He was but a princely ornament to trot out occasionally to make the women swoon. Sterling composed himself, adding a gruff tone to his voice. "I hear your brother lazes around Lord's Point like a dandy in heat. Truth is, he ain't worth a silver-wolf's ripe fart in a fight."

"He could take you," Glade said, then laughed. "I could take you."

"You insolent child." Sterling's sword rang from its scabbard. "You dare speak to the Dayknight captain so? You risk being flogged." He stepped forward, sword point now under Glade's chin. "Or how about I just cleave your skull in twain right here and now?"

"I am not worried about you," Glade said, hands held forth, palms open in supplication. "Do to me what you must, Ser Prentiss. But before you do, know that I think of you as nothing but an incompetent fat fraud."

"You're coming close to calling me out, boy," Sterling said slowly. "Is that truly what you want? The sister of the king is witness to your insults. Perhaps Jovan would grant me favor to battle it out with you in Black Glass Courtyard on the morrow."

"What battle have you ever been in, Prentiss?" Glade shoved Sterling's blade aside, turned on his heels, and walked away down the hall. He stopped at the end of the corridor near Lindholf, turned, and bade Tala follow him. But the girl just stood there, looking from Glade to Sterling in slack-jawed astonishment.

Sterling resheathed his blade. The insolent chap had certainly unhinged his mind. He turned to the princess. "It's best you follow Glade and get yourselves out of here."

Tala made her way down the corridor toward Glade and Lindholf. Sterling expected to see them disappear around the corner and out of sight, but instead they huddled together in discussion. Sterling groaned.

It was Glade who returned alone, chain-mace twisting slowly at his side again. The two balls, each about the size of a child's fist, spun up and around in a strange dance. It was a Vallè construct, of little use in real battle. Sterling had only ever seen such weapons used by Val-Auh'Sua, the Vallè acrobat troupe.

"They're not good for much." Glade lifted the small chain, his wrist working it back and forth, and the speed at which the balls spun around in front of him increased. "They seem to be the only thing that can relax my nerves lately. A gift from Seita." He flicked his wrist a couple of more times and the balls did a quick reversal and really got to whipping about, almost in a blur, humming. "I've taught myself a lot of tricks."

"That's nice." Sterling shrugged. "Now git."

"Well, I won't *git*, because I aim to visit Lawri in her room."

Sterling took a step back, hand on his sword again.

As the young man whirled his small chain-mace about, there was a peacefulness and certainty of purpose about him that was nearly unsettling. "Tala and Lindholf insist on seeing Lawri. I don't know why, but they are my friends—"

There was a slight flicker in Glade's wrist movement followed by a thin, keening wail. Then a sudden explosion of pain erupted in Sterling's groin.

His legs gave way and he dropped to the floor like a felled oak as the wind was sucked from his lungs. It was paralyzing. The deep-rooted pain that flared within him was so excruciating he forgot to breathe. This blaze of unrelenting agony clawed its way from his balls clear out to the tip of each and every one of his extremities. His mind swam with nausea and dizziness.

"Do you dare have *me* flogged?" Glade looked down upon him and smiled a sweet, strangely innocent smile; and with his weapon, he whacked Sterling again right in the throat. Sterling's head snapped back from the blow he didn't even see coming.

Wondering if his larynx had just been crushed, Sterling felt tears seeping from his bulging eyes, blurring his vision. He saw the wavering silhouettes of Tala and Lindholf running up the hall toward him. Sterling screamed, but no sound save a strained gurgle issued from his throat, which flamed in pain.

Glade spit on him. "You foul scrap of stoat-shit," he said as Lindholf and Tala pushed their way into Lawri's chamber. Glade stepped over him last, saying, "What Tala told me about you sickens me, Prentiss. Your days are soon at an end."

As he reached for Glade Chaparral, confusion clouded his mind. He felt his grip on reality slipping away. The young man squirted from his grasp easily enough and darted into the room, slamming the door shut behind him. Sterling thought he heard the door's locking mechanism click in place.

A blessed darkness was creeping up on him, overtaking the agony. He thought of trying to stand. But he could barely muster a breath. So he just lay there on the cold stone floor, curled up, praying that the pain would go away. He stayed that way until the dizziness swamped him and he slumped back against the wall, unconscious.

After Laijon's death, 'twas the wraiths that would eat at a man's soul, devour him from inside. The wraiths would launch their escape, stabbing at a man from within until he was naught but a slobbering fool. To stave off the wraiths, some become worshippers of the sun, moon, or stone. The abhorrent worshipped trees that could bleed, whilst the truly disgraced sniffed white chalks of the Vallè, chalks that would alter the mind and burn like flame.
—THE WAY AND TRUTH OF LAIJON

CHAPTER THIRTY-FIVE

NAIL

8TH DAY OF THE MOURNING MOON, 999TH YEAR OF LAIJON

AUTUMN RANGE, GUL KANA

Dawn declared itself with a soft brightening of the icy air. It wasn't long before Nail had to squint against the glare of the sun as it danced off the sparkling snow. It was a relief to travel again under skies not constantly smothered in clouds. Still, no amount of sunshine could lighten his mood. His heart was laden with sorrow over the death of Zane—along with abandoning Ava Shay and the death of Gisela, another failure to add to a long list of failures.

But his one solace was, he finally knew where they were.

The towering stones that marked the beginning of the Swithen Wells Trail were outlined against the cold morning sky. Nail could see the scarcely defined trail of steep switchbacks, which led fifty-odd feet up toward a saddle between two snow-covered peaks. Near a half-dozen streams of water fell over the lip of the saddleback and tumbled down the winding switchbacks—runoff from the melting snow. These twining branches of water cascaded over the steep path like skeletal white fingers.

"Only a few miles more." His voice cracked. "Then we reach the abbey." He hitched Shawcroft's satchel a bit tighter to his shoulder and led the march toward the saddleback ridge.

"Laijon save us," Liz Hen mumbled, clicking her tongue, tugging on Lilly's reins, helping the pony along. With Zane no longer with them, Lilly carried all their gear and the heavy battle-ax, too.

They had spent the night wide awake, plodding through the snow and clouds and dark. Nail had grown worried that he was leading them farther astray or into a snow-covered bog or over a cliff. The surface of the snow was hard, icy, having frozen overnight, yet it was soft underneath. Lilly kept breaking through. Soon her legs had begun to bleed, rubbed raw by the crusty shards of solid snow, and her progress was painful and slow.

There was scant mention of Zane. They were all somber with weariness, weaving on their feet as they went. Cracked lips and parched stomachs. They all knew the ache of hunger and the heaviness of a night without sleep. Just before dawn, they had spotted a rabbit. Stefan refused to shoot at it. So Nail had spent a good portion of Stefan's arrows trying to kill it himself. But his cold fingers could scarcely pull the bowstring taut. The arrows he launched were lost in the snow. It was then that Nail came to realize that the higher reaches of the Autumn Range were not a gift from Laijon to be enjoyed. They were an enemy to be battled, grimly, miserably, unremittingly. These mountains sought to crush his spirit and resolve. Still, he knew, the others would plod along behind him until the last scraps of stamina that were holding them upright gave out and they just collapsed. Now they'd finally reached the switchbacks leading to the Swithen Wells Trail. Nail led them up. Liz Hen held Dokie's hand as together they hiked up the trail behind him, Lilly with them.

Stefan brought up the rear. The normally sure-footed pony stumbled as she climbed the first few doglegs of the steep path. Nail knew the chestnut was nearing the end of her strength. She plodded up the path on weary legs. The water cascading over the switchbacks, combined with patches of melting snow, were making this last leg of their journey difficult.

They were about three-quarters of the way up the trail when Nail first glimpsed the six Sør Sevier knights. He sensed them before he saw them. And when he turned and looked down into the small valley below, there they were. When the knights came out of the pine-filled draw one by one, his heart skipped a beat. Holding his breath, he looked away, careful not to gaze directly at them in fear he might spark their attention.

Of course, Liz Hen saw the men at the same time and gave a quick shout. She slapped Lilly on the rump, causing the pony to whinny and bolt up the switchback.

The six men filed out of the forest and into the light of day, all afoot. There were no dogs with them now. But Nail's group had left a clear trail in the snow below for the men to follow.

The knights quickly spotted Nail and the others near the top of the switchbacks and were now running toward them. "Why do they still chase us?" Dokie asked, eyes round as dinner plates. watching the men advance.

Is it me they want? Nail wondered. *If I just surrender, will the others be spared?*

Looming dread now hovered over them all like a cloud. "Hurry it up!" Liz Hen shoved Dokie up the trail. "They're liable to kill us if they catch us!"

"We cannot outrun them this time." There was a grim look on Stefan's countenance as he pulled his bow over his shoulder and an arrow from his quiver. "They'll scurry up the trail much quicker than we."

The knights looked warm and well fed and strong. And the switchbacks, though steep, would give the Sør Sevier knights scant challenge. They came in chain mail and leather—cloaked and armed, longbows strapped to their backs, the naked steel of their drawn blades sparkling bright with danger in the sun. Nail had seen these men slaughter an entire village. It was clear to him: their flight to the abbey was at an end.

Stefan, tears forming in his eyes, began nocking the first arrow to his bow. He took careful aim as the knights neared the bottom of the switchbacks and sent a shaft slashing down through the air. The bolt caught the first knight at the top of the shoulder in the neck, staggering him. Then he fell dead. Liz Hen gave a triumphant shout as Stefan nocked his second arrow. The men, wary that one of their own had been killed so swiftly, began to draw their longbows and take aim. Stefan's second shot missed the lead knight by a hairs-breadth. Soon there was a volley of arrows soaring up toward their perch on the trail. Nail dropped facedown onto the path, as did the others, as arrows clattered against the hillside above.

"Come down from there and we will spare you!" the lead knight shouted up to them. He was the same bearded man with the menacing black eye patch they had seen before at the bottom of the Dead Goat trailhead. The man who had ordered the knights to attack Shawcroft. "We don't wish to kill you, just take you back to the White Prince! You will not be harmed!"

"Fuck you and the butt-fucked whores who spawned you!" Liz Hen shouted, and picked up a nearby rock the size of a baby's head and hurled it down into the midst of the five knights. The rock shattered on the trail between two of the men, nearly knocking one from his feet. Unfazed, the knights started up the trail. Liz Hen picked up a second rock and flung it. It was a lucky shot. It crushed the head of the second knight in line, sending him stumbling into the legs of the man with the eye patch, dropping both face-first onto the muddy trail. As the man with the eye patch climbed from under his dead friend, he shouted. "We will not be so merciful now, you fat bitch!"

The four remaining knights dashed up the trail.

Liz Hen roared at her own success and hefted a third rock, launching it over the side. Dokie began throwing rocks too. Stefan was firing arrows at the remaining knights. But his arrows flew wide and he quickly ran out. Nail cursed, realizing he had wasted far too many precious arrows trying to kill the rabbit last night. Stefan dropped his bow and began searching the trail for rocks to throw.

Nail whirled and untied the battle-ax from Lilly's back, its cumbersome weight now welcome. It felt right in his hands—hands that now grew tingly and cold. His red scars flared in pain: the cross, the slave mark, scars from the mermaid's claws, even the tattoo on his bicep. It seemed wisps of smoky blue light played over the battle-ax's silvery, smooth shine.

The four knights were advancing rapidly up the switchbacks, to the dogleg only twenty feet straight below them now. Nail could see their faces, gruff men all—the first in line, the one with the black eye patch, had a grim determination in his eye. A boulder, pulled from the mud by Stefan, rolled down the hill and crashed among the knights, doing little harm but forcing them to clump together on the trail.

With a bellowing shout, Liz Hen took a running start and launched the full weight of her portly body into the side of Lilly, sending the pony over the edge. Lilly, still laden with heavy saddlebags, wolf-hide blankets, and torches, dropped straight down atop the Sør Sevier men. One of the pony's hooves cracked the man with the eye patch square in the head, knocking him flat, whilst the weight of Lilly's body swept two of the other knights over the edge with her. With a clatter, the two men and the pony tumbled forty feet down the steep and rugged switchbacks like rag dolls, sending swords, armor, and all the gear strapped to Lilly scattering.

Only one knight remained standing. He shouted a bloody curse and sprinted up the trail, taking the sharp turn in the switchback in two strides, sword poised to strike.

Liz Hen screeched like a wild boar. She flew by Nail and down the trail to meet the charging knight bare-handed. Bloodlust was in her now.

The knight, having the disadvantage of coming at them from below, took a wild swing with his blade at the girl, barely missing her legs as she launched herself through the air. The great bulk of Liz Hen's body enveloped the knight about the chest and head, sending the two of them rolling and sliding down the slick and muddy trail. The knight lost his sword.

Dokie, quick on Liz Hen's heels, grabbed up the man's fallen blade and began awkwardly hacking at the knight as he wrestled with the girl. The much stronger knight heaved her off. Liz Hen tumbled away, but bounded to her feet. Not finished with her attack, she scrambled back toward the knight, who was now trying in vain to stand in the slick mud. Liz Hen beat on the fellow with her fists, whilst Dokie pricked at him with the heavy sword. For a moment the knight fought back furiously, until he slipped to his knees in a patch of melting snow. Then Dokie plunged the tip of the large sword into the man's throat and shoved. The Sør Sevier knight fell back, blood oozing from the wound in his neck. And when Dokie withdrew the sword, it was over. The knight toppled over, dead.

Liz Hen was pounding Dokie on the back. "You slit that bastard like a wet herring, Dokie," she said, half shouting. "You sliced the fucker up good and right."

"I sure did," Dokie responded, in a tone suggesting he thought the girl was mad. The heavy sword fell from his shaking grip, and he dropped to his knees and cried. Liz Hen grabbed the smaller boy in a great smothering hug and the two of them wept together, both kneeling over the dead knight they had just killed.

Numb, Nail looked down at the carnage. The switchbacks below were a-litter with broken knights, scattered gear, swords, broken bows, shattered arrows, saddlebags, and a dead pony. At the bottom of the trail, poor Lilly lay sprawled in the snow, all four legs bent at awkward angles, a gash in her stomach gushing great gouts of blood. Nail was relieved, however, to see that she was completely and unquestionably dead. He'd dreaded having to hear some pitiful cries of agony come from her. Still, his heart went to her—she'd proven a stout traveling companion in the end, and a hardy warrior of sorts.

Shawcroft's satchel! Relief tugged at him when he found it still strapped to his shoulder. At least the blue stone was safe. And the ax still in his hands, its previous blue sheen now gone. *The ax didn't help at all! The others did the killing!*

"Some of those knights might yet be alive." Despite the tears, bloodlust was still in Liz Hen's eyes. "Let's make sure they're dead." She pulled Dokie to his feet.

Nail looked back down the switchbacks. The knight with the eye patch—the one who'd been kicked in the head by Lilly's hoof as the pony had flown past—had a large gash above his one good eye. The wound was seeping a sheet of scarlet over his face and down into his matted brown hair and beard, which ruffled slightly in the breeze.

"I think we should just go," Stefan said. "We dare not fight them twice. That one there *could* still be alive." He pointed to the same knight Nail was looking at.

"Yeah," Dokie agreed. "We dare not press our luck." He began searching the dead knight at his feet. Liz Hen huffed and snatched up the sword belonging to the knight and dragged it up the trail behind her, its tip trailing in the mud. Stefan followed her. Dokie tied a dagger belonging to the knight around his waist, using a strap of leather gathered off the dead fellow. He then dumped the contents of the knight's rough-spun belt-pouch onto the ground. "No food." Dokie looked up at Nail, almost crying. "There weren't nothin' in it."

"We should keep moving," Nail said, hefting the huge battle-ax onto his shoulder. He followed Liz Hen and Stefan up the trail, ax heavy on his back. It no longer felt a part of him, but bulky and awkward. Dokie scurried up behind him.

When they reached the boulder-strewn summit, they paused to catch their breath, all of them drained from the ordeal. The saddleback was windswept and barren. A line of ancient, brooding standing-stones cast gaunt shadows along the ridge. Weather-bleached elk horns were lying in the grass around the stones. The Swithen Wells Trail stretched away in the distance, meandering through a sparsely wooded valley in the far distance. Beyond the valley rose dramatic peaks and canyons cloaked in snow, the highest pinnacles lost in billowing clouds.

The abbey was only a few miles more. Nail bade Stefan help him tie the battle-ax to his back. Once secured, it weighed even heavier on his already weary torso and legs. He felt ashamed. He was bigger, stronger, and more trained than any of his friends. Yet it had been they who'd killed every one of the six knights. He had done nothing.

He looked into the eyes of his companions. A definite change had come over them. Stern they were. He saw relief there too—relief in certain death miraculously averted. But there was also a bold maturity about them now too. Nail saw in his friends' eyes some of the steel the Sør Sevier knights had in theirs.

† † † † †

Several hours later and they had still not reached the abbey. Fortunately, their path was perceptibly downhill. Nail caught the distant scent of spring weather upon the wind, the warm fragrance a rarity in this clime. They marched along a rather rutted road, through a forest of stone, stunted trees, and bramble thickets, between frozen bogs and ponds and snow-covered meadows full of towering aspens that nodded in the breeze. Ironically, this part of their trek was teeming with wildlife. Tawny deer and large, shaggy musk oxen with sloping ebony horns watched Nail's group pass by. Stefan had his Dayknight bow, but no arrows. Hunting was now out of the question.

"I should have killed that pony and cut a shank of meat off it a long time ago." Liz Hen said as she eyed another plump stag atop a snowy outcropping. "We could have made ourselves a nice meal of that useless beast."

"She was not a useless beast," Nail shot back.

"Useless to me." There was anger in the big girl's voice. "Stupid worthless thing couldn't even carry my brother the entire way here. I am glad I pushed it down the mountain."

Nail forgave the girl her bitter words. They had all been through much. They all had reason to be angry at something. Ever since Shawcroft had rescued them from the tent, so much had gone wrong. *So much of it my fault.* Their journey had claimed too many lives: Shawcroft, Gisela, Zane, Bedford Boy, and Lilly. And abandoning Ava Shay, Nail felt, was his greatest sin. When he had seen the impatience in her eyes, he had let his own selfishness and hurt betray him. He knew he had no honor. And if it took his life entire, he would do whatever he could to regain it, to redeem himself for that one betrayal.

Liz Hen made haste down the trail as the first tolling of the abbey's bell drifted up the valley toward them. Just beyond a stand of trees a narrow drift of gray smoke dirtied the clear mountain sky. They all picked up their step. When they broke from the cover of the last forest thicket and saw the stone structures of the abbey yard for the first time, Liz Hen, Stefan, and Dokie wept openly. Nail did not cry; instead, he felt a frank swelling of pride in having finally reached their destination. At least he had done this one small thing right. He'd helped his remaining friends to safety. Shawcroft would have been proud.

The abbey nestled in a snowy clearing of gray boulders alongside a frozen brook with a stone-slab bridge. There were only a handful of outbuildings, several made entirely of stacked rock. There was a small brick chapel, and what Nail knew to be a cozy dormitory adjacent to it. A garden covered in powdery snow, fenced by a high stone wall, lay between the chapel and dormitory. The rest of the scattered buildings were composed of wood or wattle and daub, except for the stable, which was made of stone slabs piled atop one another and roofed with flat timber planks. The place had a clean, well-kept look.

As they drew nearer the abbey, Hugh Godwyn emerged from the chapel. The tall and lanky bishop walked with a bit of a stoop toward the stone bridge that spanned the frozen brook. A thin rim of clear ice skirted the banks of the brook, crystal water gurgled glittery and cold in the middle. The stone bridge was stout, and they all crossed over it eagerly. Godwyn awaited them on the other side. He flaunted a gray curling mustache that spread across his face with a flourish as he smiled. Flowing down his back was a mane of graying hair. He had thick, angular brows that also curled up at the tips. Like most bishops, he wore no finery and carried no weapons, his only adornment a fine brown cassock and a wide black belt. To Nail, Hugh Godwyn, gangly and sticklike, always looked more like an eccentric old vagabond than a bishop.

"Well met, Nail." The bishop spoke in a raspy voice, holding out a hand, eyes lingering on the massive ax strapped to Nail's back. Godwyn's hand was as rough and dry as a cobblestone when Nail shook it. The bishop held out his bony hand for the others in turn, introducing himself, asking them their names. He then inquired of Shawcroft.

"Dead" was all the answer Nail gave.

Godwyn's face grew grave, moisture welling in his eyes. "I'll get the details later. Shawcroft was my dearest friend. This news is most troubling." He wiped at the tears running down his cheeks. "But listen to me go on. You all must have had a harrowing journey. A spring freeze like no other has hit these mountains, and you sad lumps look to have had the misfortune of traveling right in the middle of it." He motioned for them to follow, then led them through the snow and opened the chapel door.

"I hope you've a warm bath ready for my chaffed arse," Dokie said with enthusiasm as he scurried inside. Liz Hen and Stefan eagerly followed Dokie into the inviting warmth of the stone chapel.

But the bishop held Nail outside with a stiff hand. "The ax is quite magnificent," he said. "But I am most curious about what is in your satchel."

Nail scarcely knew what to do. Shawcroft had been insistent that the satchel reach the bishop, but that was before Nail had placed the blue stone into it. For some reason, his instincts were telling him that it was imperative he protect the stone's secrecy.

"I sense your distrust," Godwyn said. "I promise I won't quiz you on the death of your master until you've rested. And you need only speak of it if you wish. But I am eager to see that satchel."

The roasting warm glow of the chapel's open door strongly beckoned, and Nail suddenly didn't care about the ax or the stone. If Shawcroft's satchel was what the bishop wanted, then the satchel he could have. He quickly shrugged it from his shoulder and handed it over. Godwyn opened the leather flap and pulled forth Shawcroft's copy of *The Way and Truth of Laijon*. After a quick scrutiny, he placed it back into the satchel and briefly examined the scrolls next. Then he pulled forth the swath of black silk containing the blue stone. Nail's heart skipped a beat. The bishop carefully, almost reverently, unwrapped the silk and examined the treasure inside, eyes aglow.

"The stone is enough to steal my breath and praise the greatness of Laijon and the Blessed Mother Mia," Godwyn said.

All Nail could do was stare in fear as the man held the silk with the stone nestled within. It was something he couldn't explain, but he desperately wanted the bishop to put the cursed thing away.

Godwyn wrapped the stone in the silk and put it back into the satchel.

Then the bishop did a curious thing. He began to unravel the leather stitching along the side of the satchel. Once he had pulled the long strand of stitching free, a secret compartment in the satchel was revealed. He dipped his hand into this newly revealed pocket and pulled forth a small, thin parchment.

Godwyn read what was written on the paper, placed the paper parchment back into the secret compartment. "Bless Ser Roderic," he mumbled. "The finding of Laijon made so easy." He looked squarely into Nail's eyes and leaned in, planting both hands firmly upon his shoulders, gripping his plate armor, holding him fast.

"And bless you, boy." Tears were now streaming from the bishop's eyes. "Bless you for making it this far." The bishop released his hold. "Now let's get that useless hunk of shiny metal from off your back and some food into your belly."

I beseech thee, my fellow brethren in Laijon. Do not let your castles and keeps fall into disrepair as you await his return. Do not believe that your forts and fortresses will no longer be needed. Lest ye be lax in your stewardship, be ever mindful. The abominable power within the followers of Raijael is both grievous and great. So keep thy blades honed sharp.
—THE WAY AND TRUTH OF LAIJON

CHAPTER THIRTY-SIX
TALA BRONACHELL

10TH DAY OF THE MOURNING MOON, 999TH YEAR OF LAIJON
AMADON, GUL KANA

If Jondralyn didn't have to wear a gown, then neither did she. Tala was wearing a white blouse and a knee-length brown tunic over tan pants and black boots. She watched with a heavy heart as the Prince of Saint Only entered Sunbird Hall through the western doors. He was surrounded by Dayknights. It had been three days since his triumph in the arena, and still he was kept prisoner. The rusted chain around his neck was thick and heavy. As he shuffled toward the king, his leg irons clattered and clanked along the cobbled floor. Other than his gray irons, Squireck Van Hester wore naught but his loincloth and Tala's wreath of heather on his head.

The final gladiator was customarily released at the moment of his triumph. But Squireck had been kept in prison. Over the past few days much chatter in the castle had been devoted to the likelihood that the Prince of Saint Only would never be freed. Rumor was, his continued imprisonment was Jovan's doing—or Jovan's doing at the behest of Denarius and the quorum of five. Some deemed the king's actions a misguided betrayal of a thousand years' worth of tradition. There had been a dark mood within the hallways of the castle as Jovan continued to delay Squireck's release. There was even growing dissension among some Dayknights and Silver Guards over the matter—dissension that Sterling Prentiss had quashed, claiming that the grand vicar would not formally release Squireck until Jovan was healed sufficiently from the attempt on his life to participate in the ceremony, as tradition warranted.

The king stood before his throne at the northern head of Sunbird Hall with the grand vicar and quorum of five, a goblet of wine in hand. Tala knew that Jovan had been numbing himself with spirits these last few days. And today was the first he had risen from bed. He did not look well. Bandaged still. He did not look like one who should be on his feet at all. Jondralyn stood to the side of the throne directly behind him, as if she too expected the king to collapse at any moment. Tala stood on the other side of Jondralyn, worried for her older brother.

She was worried for herself, too, and more for Lawri. Tala still did not know why Jovan was so beholden to the vicar, and the failure to figure it out weighed her down daily. The Bloodwood's game had taken on a depth of deceit that Tala thought unfathomable. Lawri now lay in a hidden room accessed only through Lindholf's bedchamber. Despite the warnings of the Bloodwood to stay out of the secret ways, Tala, Lindholf, and Glade had carried Lawri through the castles hidden passages, anyway, and hidden her there. Nobody knew the girl's resting place but the three of them along with Jondralyn. Tala and her older sister had been tending the sick girl, bathing her fevered body with warm water, changing her soiled bed linens, holding her, talking to her. Lawri's illness was growing increasingly dire, evidenced by her gaunt cheekbones and the hollowed fever in her eyes, the whites of which had turned the color of leather. The entire time in Tala's care, the sick girl hadn't ingested anything save a few sips of water.

As Sterling Prentiss unlocked the iron bands around Squireck's wrists and ankles, Tala felt a pang of guilt. She had lied to Lindholf and Glade. She had laid the blame for Lawri's molestation on the Dayknight captain rather than the grand vicar. Blaming Sterling was easier, and more believable. Tala had feared what the eternal consequences to her soul would have been had she implicated Denarius, Laijon's holy prophet.

But her lie about Sterling had set in motion a succession of events so uncontrollable that Tala could not even begin to grasp their dreadful implications. At the time it had seemed a good thing that Glade had so gallantly confronted the captain, even to the point of threatening him and eventually physically injuring him. But now Tala worried that her lie might indeed lead to Sterling's death. After their Ember Lighting Rites two days ago, Glade and Lindholf had not remained silent on the matter. They had spread her lie. Soon the entire court was aware of Tala's accusations. Sterling was under mounting suspicion. Now Lawri's disappearance could have significant political consequences beyond what Tala could even imagine. Lord Lott Le Graven wanted the Dayknight captain's head on a pike. His twelve-year-old twins, Lorhand and Lilith, were practically in seclusion. But the Dayknight captain fell under the protection of the grand vicar and the quorum of five. Jovan could not act further without the consent of Denarius. And it seemed Denarius was intent on shielding Sterling from further investigations, because, as Tala was aware, who knew where further investigations might lead?

When Sterling Prentiss had been found unconscious in the corridor in front of Lawri's bedchamber by two of the Silver Guard, he'd admitted, much to his embarrassment, that it had been Tala, Lindholf, and Glade who had accosted him, then kidnapped Lawri from her room and from the care of the vicar.

But few believed Sterling Prentiss. Again, because of Tala's lies.

"You must deny whatever Sterling says, Tala," Jondralyn had instructed her two nights ago as they'd tended to Lawri. "Though it pains me to lay such at the feet of the Dayknight captain, an honorable man who has helped our father greatly over the years, you must deny all he says. It also pains me to think that Sterling has been taking liberties with Lawri. But if you claim it is so, then it is so. That our dear cousin lies before me is evidence that what Sterling says about you attacking him and kidnapping her is also true. And it is *that* which you must deny. And if Lindholf and Glade are indeed a part of this, you must convince them to deny it too. The three of you can never admit to Jovan or anyone else what you have done. I do not know whose foolhardy idea it was to attack Ser Sterling and take Lawri from her chamber, nor do I want to know, but what's done is done. Yet that rash action has put the very kingship of Gul Kana and my rulership in Amadon in jeopardy. Not to mention the lordships of Rivermeade, and Eskander Suspicion cannot fall upon any of you in this matter. It must remain on Sterling Prentiss. You must make Jovan believe that it is Sterling who has the girl. The testimony of you three against Sterling may not sway Denarius, but it should be enough to sway our brother and save you all from being locked up, or worse yet, hung."

Glade had agreed with Jondralyn when Tala told the two boys of the plan later that day. "Yet again you've involved me in treasonous acts for which I am not proud," he'd said. "I daresay, Lindholf will spill his guts under the slightest scrutiny, and it will all be for naught anyway. We will all of us hang."

But Lindholf's eyes had grown hard at Glade's words. "You willingly assaulted Prentiss. And don't tell me you didn't enjoy it, Glade. We did the right thing. I already live with the shame of betraying Tala once when I told Prentiss about our trip to the dockside tavern and climbing the Laijon statue to retrieve notes from Hawkwood. I felt your disappointment in me then, Glade. You too, Tala. And I vow neither of you will ever feel such disappointment in me again."

"See that we don't," Glade said.

Jondralyn's plan had been sound. Jovan grilled each of them, ordering each of them to divulge Lawri's location. But the three had remained true to their vow. Lawri was safe from the grand vicar for now. And that was the most important thing. Jovan did not know what to believe, though he nearly had Tala and the two boys flogged for what Sterling accused them of—attacking him and kidnapping Lawri.

Still, as Tala now watched Sterling remove the chain from around Squireck's neck, she was racked with guilt. Lawri was still sick, alone, in a dark room in naught but a damp, sweat-coated smock whilst Tala stood comfortably in Sunbird Hall. She looked at Lindholf and Glade, who stood near. They were both of them in their new ceremonial battle armor, Glade strikingly handsome, and Lindholf, too. Armor did that to even the frailest and homeliest of seventeen-year-olds, turned them into men, that is.

"Is Laijon's will to be served this day?" Squireck asked once Sterling had finished removing the rusted chain from around his neck. His voice was deep and commanded the attention of all in Sunbird Hall. "Am I now to be pardoned as is my Laijon-earned right?"

The grand vicar, his face emotionless, bade Squireck step forward.

By virtue of his height and muscular bearing, all now stood aside for the Prince of Saint Only as he strode, unfettered, toward Denarius. None wanted to hinder the arena champion now. Despite what abhorrence they'd once held for him and the crimes of which he was accused, Squireck Van Hester was the victor, blessed and innocent before Laijon, according to scripture and tradition.

There was silence as Squireck stood before the vicar. Everyone waited.

Jovan belched, eliciting a few snickers. The king appeared quite drunk, yet still calculating as his watchful gaze strayed over the crowd. He stepped toward Squireck, wine goblet in hand. "By the power invested in me as king of all Gul Kana, I release you, Squireck Van Hester, Prince of Saint Only." Jovan held the goblet up in a toasting motion, looking at Squireck above the goblet's rim like a lion would look upon a lamb. "As far as the Silver Crown is concerned, you are free to go." Jovan lowered the goblet, and his raptorlike gaze turned to Denarius.

The vicar, removing a bull-horn flask of oil from under his cloak, spoke loudly. "That you have triumphed in the arena is a great thing." Denarius motioned for Squireck to kneel before him. Squireck knelt on one knee, looking up toward the vicar.

Denarius poured a droplet of oil from the bull-horn flask onto the tip of his own finger. He took his fingertip, placed it gently on Squireck's forehead just below the hairline, and slowly drew a line with the oil to the tip of Squireck's nose whilst beginning his prayer. "In the name of Laijon, and by the powers of his holy priesthoods, I, Denarius, Bishop of Rivermeade, Grand Vicar of Amadon, do anoint your head with this oil that has been consecrated for the purpose of washing away sin unto righteousness."

Denarius drew another line with the oil across Squireck's forehead. "I hereby bless you with renewed stamina in the sinews and strength in the bones that your knees and shoulders may not be ever weakened. I also bless your mind, that your intellect will reign sharp and keen over the wraiths that haunt the soul."

Denarius poured a dollop of oil atop the crown of Squireck's head. "Now I, Denarius, declare before all men gathered: our great Laijon finds you, Squireck Van Hester, innocent of all things accused. May you now walk free and without stain before our Lord and all men. Amen." He stepped back, slipped the bull-horn flask into the folds of his heavy cassock, and looked away, not meeting the Prince of Saint Only's gaze.

Squireck stood. Tala breathed a sigh of relief. If not exactly gracious, the deed was done, and the final gesture of Laijon's forgiveness—the holy vicar anointing Squireck's head with oil and reciting the Arena Incantations—had now been proffered, albeit most grudgingly.

Jovan weaved on his feet, holding his goblet aloft. "And what have you to say of your release?" he asked. "What does the victorious Prince of Saint Only have to say?"

"I have something of great import I wish to say!" Squireck's voice was a deep shout, thick with emotion. He raised his corded arms, palms up, and turned in a full circle for all to see. "That I passed through the gauntlet unscathed, nary a drop of blood spilled, speaks of Laijon's great love for what I have done on his behalf!"

Squireck lowered his arms, his eyes steely. "For the truth is"—he lowered his voice to a menacing growl as his eyes found Denarius—"I *am* guilty of the crimes I was charged with." There was a collective gasp from those gathered in Sunbird Hall as Squireck continued, undaunted by the wave of murmurs traveling through the crowd, his deep-throated voice carrying over all. "I did steal portions of *The Moon Scrolls of Mia* from the archives of the quorum of five. I did slay Archbishop Lucas when he tried to stop me!" The gasps and murmurs now turned to shouts of outrage from the quorum of five, Archbishop Spencerville's voice the loudest, drowning out the others, shouting sharply that the king should execute Squireck now. Many swords were drawn, including that of Sterling Prentiss.

Jovan hurled his wine cup at Squireck. "You dare insult the Silver Throne!" The goblet struck, splashing red wine over Squireck's flesh before clanging to the floor.

The Prince of Saint Only ignored the king and glared at the grand vicar, wine now running in rivulets down his taut skin. "I follow the will of Laijon!" Squireck's booming voice echoed in the hall. "For the voice of Laijon came to me as I debated what to do with the archbishop who found me with the scrolls and then barred my exit from the crypt! With Laijon as my witness, I slew Lucas, for I knew it to be better that one man die than an entire kingdom continue under the deceit of false doctrine, that in ages past the time was not right for the secrets of *The Moon Scrolls of Mia* to be revealed! But that time is now! Archbishop Lucas' soul now sits beside Laijon for his sacrifice! My victory in the arena is Laijon's proof that the Brethren of Mia are to be trifled with no more!"

Never before had the Prince of Saint Only's large, imposing frame been more evident. All present, even the hardened Dayknights like Sterling Prentiss, appeared to recoil from him. For they had seen the carnage Squireck had wrought in the gladiator pit; they had all watched him demolish his opponents with gruesome ease. Terror was in their eyes. He stood before the entire court of Amadon in nothing save a loincloth, large and brutish, intimidating a room full of men, many of them armored knights, with naught but the command of his voice and his startlingly grandiose presence.

He commanded all but one, that is.

"I'll have you put back in chains," Jovan hissed. The predatory glint had returned to his eyes.

"You shall do no such thing." Squireck towered over him. "Lest I have you stripped of your crown as a false king and denier of Laijon's will! You disgrace your father!"

Jondralyn stepped between Jovan and the gladiator, taking the Prince of Saint Only by the arm. "Perhaps its best we get you away from here, Squireck," she said. "Before they heap new accusations upon you."

"Yes, sister, do that," Jovan laughed drunkenly. "I heard that you washed the feet of Squireck as if he were Laijon himself and you one of his Warrior Angels. Now you leap to the rescue of this coward just as his own treasonous words put him exactly where he was before."

But Jondralyn ignored her brother, and with Squireck, strode toward the huge double doors at the western end of Sunbird Hall.

Many trembled and parted before Squireck. When they reached the twin doors, the Prince of Saint Only turned and roared, "Absolution is upon us!"

And the two doors swung open, seemingly at his command.

Two surprised knights, dressed in the maroon-and-gray livery of Rivermeade's Wolf Guard, stood there in the darkness beyond, a wooden crate held between them. Many more knights in maroon and gray were coming up behind the two, soon filling the doorway. Squireck's deep voice sounded through the hall again, and the timbre of it now shook Tala to the core. "War is upon us!"

Squireck and Jondralyn stepped back, and everyone stared at the open double doors and the knights pouring into Sunbird Hall; behind the two carrying the wooden crate, Glade's older brother, Leif Chaparral, was the last knight to enter the hall. His black-rimmed eyes cut through the crowd. He wore the black-lacquered armor and silver surcoat of the Dayknights. The silver-wolf on a maroon-field crest marked him as of Rivermeade nobility. The sword of his rank, with the black opal–inlaid pommel, hung at his side. He held a chain in one hand, the length of which drooped to the floor and back up again to connect to the shackled wrists of a blond-haired warrior woman. This grim-faced yet pretty woman wore silver battle armor of a curious make, over which was a white surcoat emblazoned with a blue cross.

Squireck and Jondralyn slipped out the double doors, disappearing from Sunbird Hall and into the darkness of the corridor. Tala watched their exit. But few others, if any, had seen them leave. All eyes were on Leif Chaparral, who, limping from his childhood boar injury, guided the warrior woman toward Jovan.

"Leif!" the king yelled in drunken greeting as he wobbled toward his friend. "Well met indeed, but what brings you from Lord's Point to Amadon?"

Leif's piercing eyes were as deep blue and fathomless as the ocean, and both his black armor and silver cloak were dust-stained from the road. It looked as if he'd been traveling hard. His face was weary, yet brimming with excitement as he turned and motioned for the knights behind him to pick up the crate and carry it forward.

Leif forced the warrior woman to kneel before Jovan. "I bring you a gift, my lord." Leif snatched a handful of the woman's blond hair and jerked her face up so she was looking squarely at the king. "Blodeved Wynstone," he announced, "a soldier of the White Prince's army."

There was a collective gasp from the room. Whether the gasp was in reaction to the news that the woman was from Sør Sevier or that she was a soldier—a *woman* soldier—Tala couldn't tell. But the sight of this warrior woman sparked something within Tala. It was clear: things were different in Sør Sevier. In that kingdom, the women clearly fought alongside the men.

Blodeved's eyes were dark and fierce as they bored into Jovan's. Even though she was captive and kneeling in a roomful of enemies, she seemed unafraid. "You'll all be dead within the year," she said calmly, with a confidence bred of certain knowledge. Tala admired her for her poise. Few females in Amadon—save perhaps Seita, or maybe her sister, Jon—would dare to remain as brave as they knelt in the court of the enemy.

"Like a feral cat she is," Leif said. "Never to be tamed. And trust me, I tried. I'm sure she's wet for another go." There was a smattering of laughter from the Wolf Guard of Rivermeade behind Leif, though Tala thought she saw Jovan flinch at the quip.

Leif's eyes lit up when he saw Glade there in the crowd. "My brother," he said. "What has it been, a year?"

Glade stepped through the crowd and bent his knee before Leif, took his brother's free hand in both of his, and held it to his lips, kissing it. "Indeed, more than a year, brother."

"Ah, you look a sight," Leif said. "Twice as grown as before. Thrice even. Am I right, Jovan?"

Glade blushed as he stood. It was clear; the boy was in awe of his older brother. Leif was by far the prettiest, most well-proportioned man Tala had ever seen. His dark hair hung straight and perfect down over his shoulders and back, framing a squared jaw under high cheekbones. His blue eyes were captivating—though a few years ago, Leif had black ink tattooed around the rims of his eyes, as was fashionable among some of the young Silver Guards at the time. They claimed that it made them look more fearsome. However, Tala thought the tattoos just made them look slightly girlish, almost as pretty as his sisters, Jaclyn and Sharla Chaparral. Either way, there wasn't one single woman in Sunbird Hall who wasn't drawn to him. The slight limp from his childhood injury only added to his allure.

As for Glade, Tala was still conflicted. He had his uses. Especially with Sterling Prentiss. But he made her angry in so many ways. She felt little affection for him now, where he'd once held her in thrall at all times. She could barely stand the sight of him.

"What do you think of the she-demon I've captured, brother?" Leif asked Glade, a sly grin forming on his face. "Perhaps I'll let you have a go at her," he laughed, rattling the chain in his hand. "Would you like that, Glade? To share in your brother's spoils? To bugger the foul enemy whore?" Glade's eyes lit up briefly and he laughed a sickening, spoiled little laugh that made Tala's stomach curdle.

"It was Patryk and Marcus you buggered as we traveled here," the Sør Sevier woman snarled, looking up at Leif. "You never laid a hand on me." She turned to Jovan. "He took to fucking my two male companions. Warriors each. And he killed them while using them in his twisted pleasures—"

"I do not suffer lies," Leif hissed, his demeanor like ice, his words a spear tip. He ripped a dagger from his belt, grabbed Blodeved by the hair, and roughly tilted her head back, exposing her neck. He then slit her throat with a quick slice and pull.

There was a gasp from many a lady in Sunbird Hall. Tala heard a stifled, guttural choke and saw blood pour out dark red over the Sør Sevier woman's armor. Leif released his hold on Blodeved, who slumped back from her knees to her buttocks, clutching her neck with her shackled hands, trying to breathe. The woman sat that way for a moment as her blood flow became weaker. Tala watched her struggle to rise again. But Blodeved fell sideways to the floor, her cheek thudding wetly in a pool of her own blood.

Glade's self-satisfied laugh filled the hall again as his eyes darted with an almost-baffled pride from his brother to the Sør Sevier woman and to the crowd.

A coldness gripped Tala's heart at having just witnessed the proud and brave Sør Sevier woman, who was probably not much older than she, die like that. Though he was handsome, Tala had always suspected Leif to be a bad-intentioned person. The cold-blooded murder of Blodeved did nothing to change her opinion. And Glade's smug glee in the murderous act only solidified her downward-spiraling opinion of him.

"If the enemy warrior was my gift"—Jovan broke the silence— "I would have preferred to question her before you knifed her."

"She was of no account." Leif bade the Wolf Guard behind him to remove the lid from the wooden crate. "The true gift is in the box. Though be warned, to be sure, it is a grim gift indeed." Two of Leif's Wolf Guard knights pried the lid off the crate, then stood it up on end so all could see what lay within.

Tala's initial thought was that it was a short, bearded man—a dwarf perhaps. *Roguemoore.* The small fellow was totally naked but for a strip of cloth over his groin. Soon the blood began to curdle in her veins at the true horror her eyes beheld.

It was a delayed reaction all around. It seemed that the others in the room were realizing just what it was that they looked upon as gasp after gasp began to echo through Sunbird Hall. It was a bearded man to be sure—and he looked familiar to Tala—yet his arms and legs had been shorn above the elbows and knees, thick black tar smothered the stumps, and two silver daggers protruded from the arms. The sight of the Sør Sevier woman lying in her own pooling blood now paled in comparison to this man in the box.

"Baron Jubal Bruk," someone muttered from behind Tala, and she instantly recognized the man's face. She recalled the old Dayknight fondly; he'd been one of her favorite knights in her father's retinue. She remembered his handsome son, Jenko. She remembered the ash-wood bow Jubal Bruk had given to Lindholf one summer.

Jubal Bruk blinked rapidly, his eyes adjusting to the hall's dancing torch flame. His arms moved as he adjusted himself in the box; then he overbalanced and tottered forward, landing face-first onto the cobbled floor. Two of Leif's knights picked him up and set him back upright in the box.

Leif spoke loudly for all to hear. "It was the woman who lies dead on the floor, along with her two companions, who delivered Jubal Bruk to me at Lord's Point. They arrived by Sør Sevier war galleon bearing the news of the sacking of Gallows Haven—a small coastal fishing village on the southwestern fringe of Gul Kana."

The room now buzzed. Many noblewomen near fainted at the news, whilst more than a few noblemen and all the knights brandished their swords. Heated exclamations and words of distress began building to a slow roar.

"Enough!" Jovan shouted, and the room came together in silence.

Leif addressed Jovan. "Lord Kronnin desires to march his Ocean Guard south and engage the enemy at once. I advised him to hold off until I had word from you. I thought it of more urgency that I bring Jubal directly here myself. We made use of the king's tolls. I wished to reach you with utmost haste, Jovan."

Tala had once traveled the King's Highway with her father using the tolls. The tolls were a series of outposts along the highway provisioned with fresh palfreys and draught horses along with wagons and carts of every size. There was ample food stored at the tolls too. One could travel nonstop the two hundred miles' distance between Amadon and Lord's Point in only four or five days using the king's tolls—it was an express system of travel, meant only for royalty or the wealthy.

"Jubal Bruk bears news from the White Prince." Leif looked at the legless man as he spoke. "Don't you, Ser?"

Jubal's eyes were wandering and unsure, his wiry hair and beard all gone awry from his time in the box.

"Well, out with it," Jovan demanded. "Or did they shear your tongue, too?"

"The White Prince is on Sør Sevier soil." Jubal Bruk's voice was a hard-to-comprehend raspy gurgle at first, but as he talked, the scratchiness in it wore off. "It is true, Aeros has taken Gallows Haven. Slaughtered all but a few who dwelled there. Aeros did this to me, hacked off my limbs."

Gasps of despair again rang through the hall. Jovan silenced them with a look.

Jubal continued, "The White Prince claimed that Sør Sevier warships are returning to Wyn Darrè now. They will continue to sail back and forth until all of Sør Sevier's finest warriors are on Gul Kana soil. And then, from the south, the armies of Aeros Raijael will march on Lord's Point." Jubal Bruk's eyes traveled up to Jovan, who now swayed more drunkenly on his feet above him. He continued, "The White Prince said you can meet him there to offer up your surrender. He said that as the prophecies in *The Chivalric Illuminations* have foretold, Aeros Raijael, the heir of Laijon, Mia, and their one and only son, Raijael, has returned to reclaim what is rightfully his. He said to tell you that if you refuse to surrender at the appointed place, with a certainty, his war to reclaim Gul Kana will be fought with extreme savagery—"

"Enough." Jovan waved the man to silence with a brisk motion of his arm, nearly toppling over drunk as he did so. "I have heard quite enough." His hazed-over eyes now roamed Sunbird Hall, looking for what, Tala could not tell.

"Where is Squireck Van Hester?" Jovan asked. "Where is that traitor?" His eyes traveled the breadth of the room. But as Tala knew, in the commotion of Leif and the box, the Prince of Saint Only and Jondralyn had slipped silently and unseen through the doors and down the corridor. "And where is my sister, Jondralyn?" Jovan weaved forward, half squatting and then half falling to his knees.

Tala rushed to his aid first. She took him in her arms as he collapsed to the floor. His body was heavy and she fell under him, her forearms wrapped around his head so it would not crack against the stone floor.

Then her brother's eyes rolled up and he lost consciousness.

✝ ✝ ✝ ✝ ✝

"That I fainted bothers me," Jovan said. He was lying in his bed again, Tala on the bed at his side. Leif Chaparral had stepped out of Jovan's bedchamber for a moment, leaving them alone. Tala and Leif together had helped the king back to his room along with a few of the Silver Guard. A contingent of Dayknights stood guard outside Jovan's bedchamber. The room itself was rich with the mossy scent of pine incense and witch hazel, the aromatic combination well known to relieve nausea. "It will be looked upon as weakness," Jovan continued. "Fainting is for maidens. It is not kingly. It disgraces the Silver Throne. Father would not have fainted."

"Everyone knows what you have been through," Tala reassured him. "They know of the assassination attempt. They know how sorely wounded you are. Instead they will look upon your attending Squireck's pardoning as a great feat of strength."

"Perhaps." Jovan placed the palm of his hand atop her wrist. He looked contemplative. And for a moment Tala almost thought he was glad for her company until he said, "You must not think to act like your sister. You must not think to dress like her. I've seen war. I see what horrors happen to men in battle. Those horrors haunt my every waking moment. I must keep you safe. You are a lady. Not a man. I grow weary of the way you have been conducting yourself, Tala. So near to your Ember Gathering and you still behave so. Dame Mairgrid becomes lax in her duties. You dismiss her too easily. She must keep a short leash on you. I know you distrust Denarius. I know you think ill of him. But you are misled. What you and Glade and Lindholf have done is an affront to Laijon. You must return Lawri to her bedchamber. You must let Denarius continue his ministrations."

"We have been through this already," Tala blurted, more than a little angry that her brother could be so callous in his accusation, even after she had leaped to his side when he collapsed. Didn't that earn her some measure of love and respect? Even in the face of a Sør Sevier invasion, his mind was still on placating the vicar. "I do not know where Sterling has hidden Lawri. It is he with whom you should be upset. I have done nothing."

"I know not what to believe anymore," Jovan said. "Sterling denies having the girl. And the holy vicar stands behind him. For my part, both your story and Sterling's make little sense. Yet I must do something, and soon. I can ill afford any mistakes with the nobles now that war is upon us. Lord Lott Le Graven will demand Sterling's head. Lott believes his son's story. He insists I place guards around Lorhand and Lilith at all times. As if I didn't have enough to deal with. Oh, Lindholf, that sod. It is he who is most convincing in his tall tale. By rights, I should send both Lindholf and Glade back to their homelands until this mess with Lawri is resolved. Seeing those two gone from your life would be like lancing two troublesome boils from the face of the castle. And to think I've paired you with Glade Chaparral. The two of you are naught but trouble together."

Tala hated this surrounding feeling of helplessness. Her days and nights would be fraught with anxiety until she solved the Bloodwood's puzzle. And the fact that her brother still considered her betrothal to Glade a viable proposition made her heart lurch.

After a few breaths, Jovan launched into his lecture anew. "I cannot banish Glade and Lindholf from Amadon without causing great insult to both Claybor Chaparral and Lott Le Graven. After the Ember Lighting Rites, they will want their sons to remain in Amadon to train as Silver Guards, as is customary. And heaven forbid we break custom. Do you not understand, Tala? Lott asked the grand vicar himself to watch over his sick daughter specifically. Now Lawri is vanished, if not dead. How do I even begin to explain this mess to Lord Lott?"

It seemed Jovan was talking to himself, for his eyes roamed the room, not once looking at Tala. "Squireck, vanished. Laijon knows what he'll be plotting. Roguemoore gone. Sterling has been a disaster. Letting Hawkwood escape. Letting that wench who stabbed me escape. Should I feel bad for him? The poor sap slinking about the castle like a whipped cur, under a cloud of suspicion. I hear that his own men whisper behind his back. I should have him thrown into hard labor at the slave quarry at Riven Rock or, better yet, just have him killed. But I've Denarius to consider. He still speaks in Sterling's defense. I need the counsel of the vicar and the quorum of five the most. We are on the brink of war, Tala, and not just with the White Prince, but now possibly with my own lords and liegemen. I will need Lord Lott's and Lord Claybor's armies the most."

Jovan's hand gripped her arm, and his eyes now bored into hers. "This situation with Lawri could be the unraveling of us all. To get the truth out, I should have you all tortured, you, Lindholf, Glade"—he paused—"Sterling, too."

Tala didn't think Jovan would actually send her to the torturer, but that he made mention of it was beyond worrisome.

She was relieved when Leif Chaparral entered the bedchamber. There was haste in his step as he limped toward Jovan's bed. The scent of cloves followed him. His dark-rimmed eyes glanced at Tala dismissively. Leif's voice was as smooth as his looks. "I've news, though I cannot prove it. Sterling Prentiss has been secretly garrisoning Lord's Point with Dayknights from Amadon behind your back. Kelvin Kronnin and the Ocean Guard of Lord's Point have been helping him. I've the gut feeling Sterling has been taking his orders from your dwarf ambassador, Roguemoore, or perhaps—forgive me for saying—your sister, Jondralyn."

A pang of fear flamed up Tala's spine.

"Denarius was right." Jovan's voice was full of grief. "They all work in concert against me. Of that, I am certain. It's that damnable Brethren of Mia that's at the root of everything. And Squireck Van Hester is in the thick of it. He's made a mockery of the Silver Throne. Disgraced the traditions of the arena. Any word on his whereabouts? Or Jondralyn's?"

"Neither has been seen since they made off from Sunbird Hall."

"It seems both my sisters seek to thwart me." Jovan threw a sharp look at Tala. She returned his gaze defiantly, awaiting an eruption of righteous anger. But there was no outburst. Instead he spoke in a more pleasant voice this time.

"Young Ansel is the only one left to mold in the fashion I wish. The rest are an uncontrollable lot." As Jovan said those words, Tala could hear the warmth returning to his voice, and with it, she realized that her brother loved his family. At that moment, she felt great sorrow for Jovan, realizing that after their father's death, her eldest brother had been thrust into his position on the Silver Throne and was merely trying to do the best he could. That Jondralyn, and now even she herself, had done so much damage to his reign and that he wasn't the angrier for it was miraculous. The history of Gul Kana, and that of the Bronachell line, was rife with tales of kings and princes and princesses slaying their kin over the most inane of slights. The truth was, Jovan exhibited great patience with each of them. Tala felt herself on the verge of tears. Lawri was dying. And she still had zero idea what bonded her brother to Denarius. Her earlier guess had been wrong. Her disposition turned from sad to sour. It seemed any fleeting thought of Denarius did that to her.

"I must go," she said. "That is, if it pleases my king?"

"Aye, you may go, Tala. And you needn't be so formal with me. We are kin, not king and vassal. One day, I will show you, our family will join together again and all will be at peace. It will be as if Mother and Father were still alive. I promise, dear sister."

Tala, now having come to a certain realization about her brother, found there was great strength in him. Tears were in her eyes, and she kissed him gently on the cheek.

"And I would do anything to help you achieve that," she said, knowing how foolish and hollow her promise sounded in her own ears—she would do anything for her brother, anything but tell him the truth about Lawri.

Jovan narrowed his eyes at her. "All we do must glorify Laijon. As long as we keep our eyes focused on that, Tala, our family will not fail."

Tala kissed him again and withdrew from his bedside, warmed by his parting words. The heels of her shoes clicked on the stone floor as she made her way through the partitions of his bedchamber, her mind on Lawri, nerves shredded. It just seemed there was nothing she could do anymore. *Perhaps I should just tell Jovan everything and have done with it.* Perhaps the secret ways could be searched by the Silver Guard and this assassin could be found and tortured.

With that thought, Tala made her way through foyer and hall, out of view of her brother's bed. She reached for the chamber door and the large brass handle that ran the length of it. As she pulled the heavy door open, its hinges squealed faintly. The brass handle was polished and slick. Her hand slipped, sending the door slamming shut with a heavy *clunk*. Then she heard Leif's voice from beyond the partitions. "The brat is gone now."

It wasn't what he said but how he said it that gave Tala pause, his already smooth voice now soft and conspiratorial in tone. Leif's words angered her. *I'm no brat.*

"Glade, Sharla, and Jaclyn tax my sanity some days," Leif continued. "As the firstborn, we can only suffer our younger siblings in patience. Do we not, my king?"

"Aye, truer words were never spoken, my friend. Lie with me awhile."

Tala's interest was further piqued. She remained rooted in place, anger at Leif's insult simmering. She moved with care, drifting back through the foyer, peering around the partition. Leif was climbing into the bed with her brother. He lay on his side, elbow on the bed, head propped in his hand, his back to Tala. She watched as he stroked her brother's hair with his free hand. Then Jovan reached up and ran his fingers through Leif's straight, dark locks. Heart in her throat, Tala felt her anger at Leif's insulting words fade as quickly as it had flared.

Jovan's voice was barely above a whisper now. "Lest you get your hopes up, Leif, I tell you now that I will not accompany you on your return trip to Lord's Point. I must stay here and tend to my wounds."

"Has the assassin been rooted out yet?" Leif asked softly.

"As of yet, no, but the noose Jondralyn has put around her own neck continues to tighten. Did you hear that she washed the Prince of Saint Only's feet?"

"I will go to the ends of the Five Isles to avenge you if I must, my dear king."

"I know you would. Wyn Darrè is conquered as was prophesied. Now that the armies of Raijael have reached Gul Kana's shores, we will soon bear witness to that great and glorious day of Absolution, when I will reign at Laijon's side, you standing with me in glory. The vicar has foreseen it."

"My anticipation knows no patience."

Leif leaned in and shared a long kiss with Jovan. Tala's heart began beating so fast she thought it might flop right out of her chest onto the rug-covered floor. Her body had become so tense she could scarcely move, not wanting to make a sound, at the same time not wanting to witness any more of the forbidden moment between her brother and Leif.

"I will send Jondralyn in my stead to go with you to Lord's Point." Jovan said as she placed her hand back upon the brass door handle and gently pulled.

"Jondralyn?" Leif sounded irritated.

"Yes, Jondralyn. Denarius thinks it wise we send her. You and my sister will hear the White Prince's demands. Jondralyn will inform Aeros that Gul Kana intends to fight as Laijon would have us do. That Gul Kana intends to throw the Sør Sevier armies from our shores."

"Less of an honor to accompany Jondralyn than you, but I will gladly do it."

"As you must know, I bear my sister little, if any, love. Jondralyn, more even than the Brethren of Mia, is our greatest threat. If she were to somehow die in the hands of the enemy, I would be most pleased, and your reward and standing in the eyes of the quorum of five would be great. Now that the armies of Sør Sevier have reached our shores, the death of Princess Jondralyn Bronachell at the hands of Aeros Raijael would give me even more reason to rally our kingdom to war at the proper time to usher in Absolution. It has all been laid out in *The Way and Truth of Laijon*. Denarius read me a passage from the holy book, a prophecy. 'The fall of Amadon will be as the death of one most beautiful.' See? One *most* beautiful. It is her. My sister. She is one most beautiful. It is how the vicar has always spoken of her."

He plans to kill Jondralyn! Tala's heart thundered. Forcing herself to move, she took tentative steps through the foyer and entry hall toward the door again, grasping the brass handle. She opened the door at a snail's pace to prevent any screech of the hinges. The last thing she wanted was for Jovan to know that she had heard his treachery against Jondralyn and seen his forbidden kiss with Leif. She could still hear her brother's voice as she pushed her way through the door. "As much as it pains me to cut your visit short, Leif, you and Jondralyn will leave for Lord's Point on the morrow. My final plans are in motion. You will soon be made captain of the Dayknights. The time of Laijon's return draws near. And we together will hasten the Fiery Absolution and both reign together in glory. . . ."

In the lingering resonance of her brother's words, Tala slipped the rest of the way from his chamber. As she eased the door shut behind her, she realized that this was the biggest secret she had ever stumbled upon, and she hadn't even been sneaking about in the secret ways to discover it.

The answer to the puzzle came to her in a flash. She now knew what to put in her next note to the Bloodwood.

With her heart pounding, she headed straight back to Sunbird Hall.

✝ ✝ ✝ ✝ ✝

This time her note read,

> *In secret, Jovan and Leif are lovers. The grand vicar*
> *knows of the relationship and holds it over them. If this*
> *information were to be made public, both Jovan and Leif*
> *would possibly be killed by the Dayknights. Some knights*
> *believe that it is forbidden for a man to lie with a man,*
> *that a king must wed and produce a male heir else he will*
> *grow ever more weak in their eyes. This is why the king is*
> *beholden to Denarius.*

*I have answered your question correctly. You must end
this game now. I have done all that I was asked. Lawri is
dying and I have told horrible and hurtful lies to keep her
safe from those who wish her further pain. I beg of you,
give me the poison's cure.*

Tala folded the note and slipped it under the vine atop the balcony's
railing and covered it with leaves. As she descended the stairs into
Sunbird Hall, niggling doubts continued to gnaw at her. The hall was
still teeming with people left over from the victory ceremony and
banquet for Squireck: nobles, Silver Guards, the king's own steward,
Ser Tomas Vorkink, barking orders at the servants who were cleaning
the walls and scrubbing the floors. That she had just put such a damning note under a vine and leaves for anyone to stumble upon chilled
her. The thought that she had just made a hideous error entered her
mind and would not let go.

The realization of what she had seen between Jovan and Leif had
stunned her at first, then grieved her. But her heart had immediately
gone out to her brother. His relationship with Leif did not make
her want to recoil from him in disgust, but rather made her want to
comfort and protect him. Wishing to keep her brother's secret, she
very nearly bolted back up the stairs to destroy the note, but forced
herself not to and continued her hesitant march down into Sunbird
Hall. *He plans on killing Jondralyn!* She did not feel so sympathetic to
her brother with that thought. *I must find her and warn her!*

Seita and Val-Draekin were at the bottom of the stairs. Val-
Draekin had Glade's ball-and-chain mace in hand and was teaching
both Glade and Lindholf some new tricks with it. Glade Chaparral
was becoming skilled with the toy, but the Vallè spun it about with
both grace and deadly precision. As they whirled through the air, the
twin balls sang a mournful melody. Seita was clad in black leather
breeches and a slim white shirt, accentuating her lithe, athletic body.

As Tala passed by, Seita offered pleasantries. But Tala ignored her, ignored the way the Vallè princess was dressed, passing no judgment, her mind spinning with confusion. She knew so many secrets and had told so many lies.

She spotted Jondralyn, slouched on a bench in the far corner of the room, talking quietly to Ansel. Squireck Van Hester was not with her. But the young Dayknight, Culpa Barra, was. *Doesn't she know Jovan is searching for her, for Squireck?*

Horror gripped Tala as she realized Jondralyn and Culpa were not only talking with Ansel, but also with Baron Jubal Bruk. He was still in the box, but propped up on a cushion. The box was standing on end so the man could see out. Tala drifted that way, wary. The old Dayknight had wide, thick brows and deep eyes fixed in a pained squint. He had a pocked face lined with age and a bushy beard hanging over his chest. "I know not the fate of Ser Roderic," he was saying to Jondralyn. "He goes by Shawcroft now. Roderic's ward was captured by the White Prince. I do recall seeing the boy in the line of prisoners with my son, Jenko."

Ansel was reaching out his hand, small fingers uncurling to grab one of the daggers sticking out from the stumps of Jubal's arms. Jubal Bruk leaned away as best he could in an attempt to avoid the boy's reaching fingers, his movements slow and unnatural.

Tala recalled that Jubal Bruk had once carried the mantle of a fearsome knight—now he was no taller than Ansel, who could not stop staring at the limbless man and the daggers. Tala tried to steer Ansel away. They were all protective of him, Tala and Jondralyn especially, for Ansel was their last link to their mother. It seemed Ansel remained the last drop of innocence left in the fractured family. They all doted on him in their own way, even Jovan.

"Your arms and legs are black," Ansel stated to Jubal. "Does it hurt?"

"Take him to play with Lindholf," Jondralyn bade Tala. "Culpa and I have much to discuss with Baron Bruk."

"But I've something you need to hear," Tala said.

"Later. Just watch Ansel for me, okay?"

"No. Now," Tala insisted. "In secret."

Jondralyn took her by the arm and pulled her into a secluded corner of the hall. "I haven't time for idle girlishness. What is it?"

Tala was hurt by her sister's inference. In fact, Jondralyn's curtness stung deeply. *I have more of a relationship with Jovan than with my older sister.* That realization almost brought her to tears.

"I just . . . ," she trailed off, trying to collect herself, not knowing how she would broach the subject of Jovan's treachery to her sister anyway. "I just heard something you should know about."

A moment passed. "Well, spit it out," Jondralyn said, impatience etched on her face. The unwanted tears welled up in Tala's eyes. She couldn't stop them. It was everything combined. Glade. The Bloodwood. Lawri. Denarius. Jovan. All of it. Boiling to the surface, flowing out in tears she just couldn't rein in.

Her sister's face softened. "What is it, Tala? Please. Ignore my edginess. I've a lot on my mind. It's not you. What's so important?"

And it spilled out in a gale of hushed words, not that she had seen Jovan and Leif kiss, but that she had heard the two speak of Jondralyn's death at the hand of Aeros Raijael. About the prophecy Jovan had quoted to Leif. That Jovan was going to ask her to go with Leif and parley with the White Prince . . . and that they expected her to die in the process. And when she was done, the look on Jondralyn's face was one of both concern and wonderment. Her sister's reaction confused Tala.

"Let me think on this a while," Jondralyn said. "For now . . . help me with Ansel. Watch him for me. Please." She gave Tala a hug and then left Sunbird Hall.

It was only a short hug, but the feeling of her sister's arms around her lingered long after. Tala grabbed Ansel away from Jubal and Culpa and walked away. Glade and Lindholf were now discussing the White Prince's invasion with Seita, Val-Draekin, and Ser Landon Galloway. Glade's ball-mace was stowed away. A fire was blazing in the hearth near their table. Tala could smell the spices in their mulled wine. She sat with Ansel on her lap and listened to their discussion. Judging from what they were saying, both boys seemed eager to go off to fight in defense of their kingdom.

"We will never be allowed into the ranks," Lindholf said. "Not even as squires."

"You assume Jovan will send an army to meet Aeros in battle." Glade's words rang with bitterness and scorn. "He'll more than likely just let the White Prince trod upon the entire western coast of Gul Kana unhindered."

"He'll be sending Leif to parley with Aeros, I wager," Seita said.

Tala, surprised that the Vallè princess had guessed at part of Jovan's intentions, added, "I wouldn't be shocked if he sent Jondralyn and Leif together. I'm sure he'd go himself if he wasn't so grievously wounded."

"Jondralyn go? Not likely," Glade observed with his usual simplicity. "Jovan would never send a woman. But I am sure you are right about my brother. Perhaps he will take me."

"I think Jovan would be smart to remain in Amadon," Lindholf spoke up. "If he sends Leif and Glade in his stead, should the White Prince use the meeting as an ambush, then the kingship remains intact in Amadon."

"Well, war is never a good thing," Seita added as she and Val-Draekin walked away. Ser Landon Galloway stayed.

"All I know is that if we don't fight, we will surely be conquered," Glade said.

"Purple flowers." Ansel pointed at a bouquet on the next table, now squirming free of Tala's lap. "I want to look."

"Stay where I can see you." Tala let her younger brother slide off her lap.

"Absolution may be inevitable," Lindholf said, ruffling Ansel's hair as the boy scooted by.

"*The Way and Truth of Laijon* speaks of all the armies of the Five Isles on the outskirts of Amadon arrayed at the foot of the Atonement Tree at the hour of Laijon's return. It seems the will of Laijon that all this happen. The Revelations of the Fourth Warrior Angel is clear on the end of days, right, Glade?"

But Glade's attention was elsewhere. He, too, excused himself from the table and snatched a flower from a nearby vase along with a goblet of red wine, then made his way across Sunbird Hall and handed the flower to a blond, freckle-faced noble girl whose parents were visiting the castle from Rosiland. Tala's heart sank.

"War. Girls." Ser Galloway watched Glade. "I fear that boy will excel at both." Then Galloway slapped the table and got up and wandered off too.

"It would break my heart to see you settle for one such as Glade," Lindholf said.

Tala narrowed her eyes at her cousin. "I realize he can be crass," she said, not knowing why she was suddenly defending Glade. "All boys grow out of it in time. He has the potential to change."

"People don't change, Tala," Lindholf continued. "And maturity won't change Glade. And what does potential mean anyway? Potential just means that he hasn't done anything yet. I fall under Glade's spell myself. He is my best friend, capable of making me feel important one moment, and low the next. Over the years, I have come to see into his dark heart. True, he is reckless and charming and daring and complicated. Yes. He is all the things that make the court girls swoon. But in the end, those things are all false. His charisma only makes him more apt to treat people with little or no respect. And his arrogance worsens with each passing day. I implore you to watch yourself."

"I can take care of myself," Tala said.

"Of that I am sure." Lindholf's eyes studied her wistfully. "I believe there is great strength in you, Tala. I see it every day. After all, it was you who saved my sister from Sterling Prentiss, at great risk to yourself. The man disgusts me."

"Shhh. Not so loud." Guilt flooded her. There were so many lies she had told. And her lie about Sterling Prentiss was perhaps the biggest. And to compound the guilt, she had asked Lindholf to lie for her too.

Though he did not realize it, Lindholf's next words were almost mocking to Tala. "There is so much good in you," he said, his eyes now soaking her in. "I hate to see it spoiled by Glade. I would hate to see you become jaded like most of these simpleminded court girls who are tricked over and over again by—"

"You used to be much more lighthearted, Lindholf," Tala cut him off, not wanting to hear an accounting of her noble traits when she knew she was a fraud. He was right about Glade but thought she was just like all the other court girls, infatuated with the young Prince of Rivermeade. "Tell me a funny story," she pleaded. "Tell me how you used to tease Lorhand and Lilith. You could be so clever with your antics. I need a laugh."

"Am I naught but a court jester to you?" While moments ago Lindholf had been absorbing every feature of her face, now he looked away. As she watched the hope die in his eyes, a bleakness as sharp as a dagger hit Tala's heart. It seemed he forced himself to regain a pose of feigned bravery, followed by a slow flush of his cheeks.

"What is it?" she asked.

"Never mind," he said, dejected, the despair in his tone so raw that Tala had to look away. A pained, uncomfortable silence passed between them.

"I should go now," she said, standing, wanting to sprint from the room. Of all those she had hurt over the last few weeks, that she had hurt Lindholf was a thorn that pricked at her soul the most. She walked away from him.

Tala had nearly made it to the double doors of Sunbird Hall when she remembered Ansel. Her frantic eyes ranged over the hall, searching. She found him. He stood alone near Baron Jubal Bruk, who was now asleep in his box. Even from halfway across the Sunbird Hall, Tala could hear him snoring. That Ansel was alone with the man was alarming. Jondralyn and Culpa Barra were gone. Her little brother was tugging at a slip of white cloth impaled on the dagger attached to the man's left arm.

Tala hurried toward him. "Stuck," Ansel said, looking up at Tala as she arrived, breathless. He continued to tug at the slip of fabric stuck on the blade. Tala soon realized it wasn't white fabric at all, but rather a small section of torn parchment.

Curious, she reached out and gave it a swift tug herself. For her, it slipped from the thin blade with ease. When she saw the writing, her blood froze.

> *You are correct about Jovan and Leif. Well done, girl.*
> *Now study the Ember Lighting Song of the Third*
> *Warrior Angel found in* The Way and Truth of Laijon.
> *Pay particular attention to chapter twenty, verse thirty-one.*
> *Study it. Memorize it. And then I will give you your final*
> *clue.*

Final clue! Tala's mind raged. *The game should be over! Lawri can't possibly survive much longer.* And all the lies she had told. Any delay could be ruinous not only to her and her friends but also to Jovan and the entire kingdom of Gul Kana.

Tala raised her eyes from the parchment in her hand. She looked at the daggers stuck to Jubal Bruk's arm stumps, her brow furrowed in anger.

"Who put this here?" She held the parchment out to Ansel. "Did you see?"

"Black," he answered, fingers reaching for the parchment. Tala did not let him grab it, thinking of the clue. She knew the verse well. It was perhaps the most studied and revered set of words ever written.

Chapter twenty of the Ember Lighting Song of the Third Warrior Angel in *The Way and Truth of Laijon* was a record of the deeds of Mia right after the death of her beloved Laijon. In the scripture, it was the final day of the Blessed Mother's pregnancy. Her husband had been nailed to the Atonement Tree for over nine days now, and she had just thrust the fateful sword, *Afflicted Fire*, into his chest, sacrificing his life for the sins of all mankind. She had him removed from the Atonement Tree. And once Laijon was laid upon the cross-shaped altar and the sword removed from his flesh, the Blessed Mother drank of his blood. He was then dressed in his finest chain mail and horned helm and buried with the weapons of the Five Warrior Angels in the sacred tomb, the five angel stones inserted into the wounds in his chest, *Ethic Shroud* covering the wounds.

Like most believers in Laijon, Tala had read the Ember Lighting verses so many times she had relegated the verses to memory. She could recall the words at will.

And it came to pass that at the time of final Dissolution, he died upon the tree, nailed thusly, purging all man's Abomination, the sword of Affliction piercing his side. Thus all was sanctified. Upon the altar they laid his body in the shape of the Cross Archaic. And as prophesied in all Doctrine, Mia took up the angel stones. And it came to pass, the five stones of Final Atonement she placed into the wound manifest.

Angry that the game with the Bloodwood was not yet over, Tala found herself staring at Jubal Bruk asleep in the box. The cushion someone had given the man had tumbled out. That made her even angrier.

"Can someone get this man a couch?" she yelled.

Ansel, startled by her shout, began to cry, big calf eyes gawking up at her. Jubal Bruk was wide-eyed and awake now. He, too, was staring at her.

"Get him a chair!" She whirled and yelled again. In fact, every eye in Sunbird Hall was on her now. "How can you selfish, callous fools leave him in a pine box! A couch! A chair! Clothes! Now!"

Many men of the court began to scurry, all of them rushing to pick up the nearest cushioned couch for Baron Jubal Bruk.

*The Last Warrior Angels believed Laijon had been taken into heaven. But
I knew the Last Warrior Angels desired the stones and weapons for their
own dread purpose and unholy ritual. So I did hide them in deep places.
I did set deadly traps of every make round about lest the unworthy defile
them. Only my most Righteous of Brethren will discover lost things. And
may Dragon Claw forever watch over the bones of my beloved.*
— THE MOON SCROLLS OF MIA

CHAPTER THIRTY-SEVEN
JONDRALYN BRONACHELL

10TH DAY OF THE MOURNING MOON, 999TH YEAR OF LAIJON

AMADON, GUL KANA

Squireck Van Hester stepped heavily from the small boat onto
the shores of Rockliegh Isle. Culpa Barra followed, Jondralyn
just behind. A flash of movement caught her eye. A silvery mermaid slipped from a nearby rock straight into the bay. Always a shock,
seeing one of the merfolk—and the female of the species was always
the worst, glistening and naked. This one hissed low and bared thin,
bloody teeth before retreating under the water, large eyes blinking.
A half-eaten salmon carcass lay on the rocks where the mermaid had
perched. Merfolk frightened her—especially the adults, especially if
they were on dry land. Full-grown merfolk could last an hour or so
out of water, whereas baby merfolk would last no more than a few
seconds.

It seemed neither Culpa Barra nor Squireck had seen the creature.

Squireck's thick boots clomped up the rickety dock, his own dark cloak swirling behind him. He wore the cloak over leather-armored leggings and an Amadon Silver Guard plate cuirass that Culpa Barra had found for him. He also carried a sword at his belt. The wreath of heather he'd worn to the victory ceremony was locked safe in Jondralyn's room—his sparse gladiator accoutrement was no longer needed. Squireck was a free man now—free to live in seclusion on Rockliegh Isle lest he be captured and thrown back into prison by Jovan. It was Culpa Barra who, days ago, had come up with the plan for hiding Squireck here. He'd realized, even before Squireck's foolish confession earlier today, that the Prince of Saint Only would be a marked man upon his release. Jovan would not see him live long. The king's thirst for victory over the prince would not go unslaked. Jondralyn was sure Jovan would set the Dayknights upon Squireck with orders to kill. There was nowhere for him to go. His homeland was a ruin. Everyone knew of King Edmon's shame, living alone in an abandoned fortress in a destroyed city in a conquered kingdom. The man had gone mad. There was no telling what his reaction to his son's newest confession of murder might be. For now, the Prince of Saint Only, like Hawkwood before him, would call the old abandoned abbey on Rockliegh Isle his home.

After tying the boat to the dock, Jondralyn trudged up the path behind the two boyhood friends. The isle looked the same today as it had when she had last been here—sprinkled on the northern end with sharp, jutting rocks and a lighthouse that towered over fifty feet high, and to the south a dock and a boulder-strewn slope of grass that led up to a small stone abbey.

Squireck, eyes on the forlorn abbey, did not look pleased. Jondralyn had been inside it only once before, and it had been dark. But in the fading light of day, the abbey looked even more crumbled-down and decrepit, nothing but a moss-encrusted ruin near a cluster of spindly trees. Brush and bramble stems still clogged the doorway.

"It will offer some shelter of a sort," Culpa Barra said. "Hawkwood made it his home for a time."

"Hawkwood." Squireck said the name as if it were poison on his tongue. "Did you stay here with him, Jon?"

"Don't say such things," she said. "You know me better than that." She hugged her former betrothed, but with reservation.

"Why did you not come to me sooner?" he said, rapt eyes drinking her in. "When you and Tala and Roguemoore visited me in the arena dungeons, it bolstered me. I owe every victory to you. You were my inspiration." He picked her up, thick hands encircling her waist as he spun in the grass, holding her high. He let her slide down his arms into his strong embrace again.

Jondralyn pulled away from him. Her eyes were not kind as she said, "I know not what to think of your confession after the vicar's reciting of the Arena Incantations."

"I merely told the truth," he answered, his eyes barely able to meet hers. Earlier that evening in Sunbird Hall, Squireck had radiated a physical power that was almost supernatural. But he was looking visibly nervous now under her scornful gaze. "It's true. I did kill Archbishop Lucas. No sacrifice too great for the Brethren of Mia. It was only what the dwarf and your father would have me do."

"I don't know how to feel. Murdering one of the quorum of five, Squireck?"

"Rest assured, our cause is just before Laijon," Culpa Barra said. "Squireck's triumph in the arena proves that Laijon is with us. And you washing his feet was a symbol that will not soon be forgotten; 'for kings and queens and rulers will wash the feet of Laijon,' is that not what the Revelations of the Fourth Warrior Angel in our *Way and Truth of Laijon* says? You fulfilled a prophecy with that one act, Jondralyn."

"I washed his feet because Anjk Bourbon conspired to have Shkill Gha's blade poisoned," she said. "A blade that Squireck stood upon with bare feet. A blade poisoned by another oghul at the behest of Archbishop Spencerville on the orders of Denarius. I saw Anjk give the soiled blade to this other oghul, a sneak-thief with orders to deliver it to Shkill Gha."

"Why did you not speak of this sooner?" Culpa Barra looked at her accusingly.

"I did what I could." She lifted her chin. "I killed Anjk for his crime."

"You killed Anjk Bourbon?" Squireck squinted at her.

She nodded, proud. At that moment, she felt some measure of understanding for Squireck's murder of Archbishop Lucas. It just dawned on her. They were all of them killers: Culpa Barra, Squireck, even she. She shivered as the wind shifted and pulled the hood of her cloak up.

Culpa Barra said, "Fact is, the vicar will stop at nothing until you are dead, Squireck. Here you are safe from any of Jovan's Dayknights."

"No matter." Squireck stared at Jondralyn, expressionless. "None can kill me. Laijon guides our fates now. Prophecy is being fulfilled before our eyes."

"I do not doubt that you have a well of courage that is bottomless," Culpa said. "You delved deep into your heart to summon the strength and fortitude to triumph in the arena. But we must all remain wary of the Bloodwood still in our midst."

"You mean Hawkwood?"

Jondralyn's face darkened. "That is not what Culpa meant."

Squireck's face darkened with jealousy. "Is that why he has joined the Brethren, Jon, to infiltrate us, to pretend he is one of the five and then betray us?"

"You know his heritage as well as I," Culpa Barra answered. "You have read the writings of Mia. Hawkwood is as important to our cause as are you, as is Jondralyn."

"I do not trust him." Squireck's eyes were inflamed with passion as he spoke. "We must not slacken our efforts—"

"Hawkwood is with us," Culpa Barra cut him short. "He rounds out the five: you, Jondralyn, Hawkwood, Val-Draekin, the boy—the five together are the Gladiator, the Princess, Assassin, Thief, and the Slave, each of you a blood descendent of one of the Five Warrior Angels, each of you hailing from one of the Five Isles. One of you is marked to become Laijon at the time of Absolution, as the *Moon Scrolls* foretold."

Jubal Bruk wasn't even sure if the boy in Gallows Haven was still alive.

"Hawkwood is with us," Culpa continued. "He found *Ethic Shroud* and one of the angel stones under Amadon. In the Rooms of Sorrow. Using information from the scrolls you stole for us."

Rooms of Sorrow. Jondralyn's mind flew to the map hidden in her room.

Squireck's face was both eager and cautious. "But can we really trust Hawkwood?"

"I saw the angel stone with mine own eyes. Roguemoore saw. Jondralyn too."

Squireck's eyes flew to hers. "Where is the stone? Where is *Ethic Shroud* now?"

Should I tell him of the map? Should I tell Culpa? Trust no one.

"Hawkwood returned them to the place he found them," Culpa answered. "Under Amadon. The safest place for them."

"So only *he* can find them again! And what if something happens to him? How will we be able to find them again? And what of the other four stones?"

"Roguemoore and Hawkwood go to claim them," Culpa answered. "And I've received word from one of Ser Roderic's carrier falcons. He has found *Forgetting Moon*."

"Then we must go and help them retrieve the two stones that Ser Roderic found previously," Squireck said. "The ones still hidden in the north. In Sky Lochs. Deadwood Gate. You helped him find the one in Deadwood Gate?"

"Aye, I helped him in Deadwood Gate." Culpa Barra said. "We must trust that Roguemoore and Hawkwood will get them. And maybe we can help them later."

Squireck winced at every mention of Hawkwood. "I must sit idle and wait while our feebleminded *king* hastens Fiery Absolution." He snarled, his face now wearing a scowl. "While others go and get the remaining angel stones. We must launch an attack against the Sør Sevier army immediately. I shall gather the armies of Gul Kana together. I will lead the charge. We must delay the White Prince's march on Amadon. I must avenge my homeland. My father would not let me fight with my countrymen. But now I am a fighter. A fighter beyond all his expectations for me. We must attack. Now."

"No, Squireck." Culpa Barra's carved face and hardened, alert eyes had carried a generally tense aura during the entire conversation. But his face was softening now. "Leave the war to others. Our job is the stones, the weapons. Gathering together the five before Fiery Absolution destroys all. We must have patience, friend. You will stay here. On this isle."

"Doing nothing."

"Remaining safe. Until you are needed once again. Patience."

"Whilst Hawkwood gets to go off adventuring, I sit idle!"

"It won't be for long, I promise."

"I am needed in my homeland. My father has need of me. I can muster what men are left in Adin Wyte who wish to fight. My homeland is naught but a shell of its former glory. I must redeem it. I am needed to lead the armies. I am needed in the search for the lost angel stones. I am needed everywhere and in so many ways. On this island is where I am needed least."

"You leave this isle, you will be hunted by Jovan, by the grand vicar," Culpa said. "Then all our plans will be for naught. Do you not understand? You cannot die, Squireck. When I first heard you were to fight in the arena, friend, I was sure you would be killed. Had you been slain, all would have come to ruin. Do you not understand how important it is you stay alive? You, Jondralyn, Hawkwood, Val-Draekin, the boy—you must all stay alive for Laijon's return. Your triumph in the arena proves that you are one of the Five Warrior Angels reborn. Your safety now trumps all."

"Forgive me," Squireck said, tears rimming his eyes. "Forgive me, my friend. You're right. I will do as you ask. I will stay here, though it pains my heart to do so."

Jondralyn, touched by the closeness Squireck and Culpa shared, stared up at the hulking bulk of Amadon Castle that rose above the bay. It was nearly dark now, and yellow lights twinkled in the castle's hundreds of windows like tiny stars. It wasn't until Culpa Barra had reiterated that Squireck was one of the Five Warrior Angels reborn that she truly felt the importance of what the Brethren of Mia were doing. *Am I myself one of the Five Warrior Angels as the Brethren of Mia believe?*

And then she thought of Tala's warning earlier, that Jovan planned to send her with Leif to parley with the White Prince, and that her brother planned on her dying in the process. *Parley with Aeros Raijael?* She just couldn't imagine her brother bestowing such an honor on a woman, especially in light of Denarius' thoughts on the matter of women. It was the one detail of Tala's story that made her question the entire thing.

"Are we being watched?" Squireck followed her gaze, looking up at the castle. "I've heard the Vallè have glass lenses they can peer through to enhance their vision, make far things appear close. I sense Roguemoore did not quite trust Val-Draekin."

"Nor do I," Jondralyn added.

"Stay in the abbey," Culpa Barra said. "Do not wander about. You will only draw the attention of the lighthouse keeper. We will visit in the dark of night. We will keep you provisioned. I promise, you won't be here forever."

"I'd be more comfortable in my dungeon cell than exiled to this island."

"You mustn't say such things," Jondralyn said.

"Stay with me, then."

"I must get back to the castle. Jovan is suspicious of me at every turn."

She hugged him good-bye. Squireck's broad back slumped in defeat as she made her way back toward the dock with Culpa Barra.

† † † † †

"Squireck is a free man." Jondralyn faced Jovan from the foot of his bed, challenge in her eyes. Her brother lay under white blankets, back propped up with pillows. "He was pardoned by Denarius. He should be allowed his freedoms. But you have been nothing but unfair, thwarting the rights of the arena, denying him his Laijon-earned due. And now he's fled the city. Perhaps back to his homeland. I know not where. He would not say."

Standing at the side of Jovan's bed, Leif Chaparral smiled, as if he knew she lied. It had only been an hour since she had returned from Rockliegh Isle with Culpa Barra.

"Squireck is of no concern," Jovan said. "I summoned you here for a different purpose, sister. I have decided it is high time you prove yourself as a *man*. That's what you want, is it not, to be a man, to fight for a cause, any cause?"

Jondralyn felt a lump of fear gather in her gut and wondered if her brother was about to challenge her to another duel, or make her fight four Dayknights to the death.

But then it all fell into place when he said, "You will accompany Leif to Lord's Point, Jon. When the White Prince's armies arrive there, you will offer terms, as my emissary, as my sister, as a full-fledged member of my Silver Guard."

Tala was right! At Jovan's words, her heart began to thud wildly. And then it struck her. *Did he just willingly offer to knight me one of the Silver Guard?* It was unprecedented. A woman warrior hadn't been heard of in Amadon or Gul Kana for near a thousand years.

"I've never even been a squire," she muttered. Then another thought struck her. *I am the Princess who will lead armies! A Warrior Angel reborn!* Despite Tala's previous warning, the fact that it was her brother who was entrusting her with so prominent a task was unexpected. *Laijon guides our fates now. Prophecy is being fulfilled before our eyes,* Squireck had said. Whether her brother wished her to fail at this task—as Tala had claimed—mattered not. She knew she would succeed at this proffered commission.

She bent her knee to her king, wondering if she had truly misjudged her brother all this time. "I graciously accept this charge, Your Excellency." She bowed low too.

"Why do you think I tested you all these years?" Jovan asked. "I was unforgiving with you for a purpose. I had to see if you were truly worthy of the tasks and positions I had planned. And you could not know that you were being tested."

Unforgiving. Tested. "You've treated me with brutality, brother. How am I to believe that all these years you've—"

"Stop." He held up a hand. "You've accepted my charge, have you not?"

"I have." A foreboding thought entered her mind as she stood again. "What terms am I to offer the White Prince? Not surrender, surely?"

"We offer no surrender." It was Leif who answered. "We are to relay to Aeros Raijael that Gul Kana will fight. We are to tell him that we will send his armies back to Sør Sevier and him to the underworld."

"Fight?" Jondralyn questioned, her eyes landing on her brother in his bed. *Trust no one.*

Jovan's face was lined with worry. "The challenge to the White Prince must come from you, Jondralyn. You are Borden's blood. I am injured, else I would go. So the duty falls to you. That is why I've decided to knight you one of the Silver Guard. I want this to be the beginning of a new relationship of trust between us, sister, a relationship of pure honesty. You've acted the warrior in the safe confines of our home. But now I ask that you prove your bravery. You will face the White Prince and offer terms. You will tell Aeros Raijael that Gul Kana will stand and fight. You will stand eye to eye with the White Prince and assure him that the Silver Throne will crush his armies. As Borden Bronachell's daughter, it is your duty."

"When do we leave?" The question shot from her mouth, her eagerness unhidden.

"On the morrow. First light. You and Leif along with a small group of Leif's Wolf Guard will take the tolls over the King's Highway to Lord's Point. Leif will be charged with the preparation of Lord's Point and Lokkenfell and the King's Gap for war, along with Lord Kelvin Kronnin. Though rumor has it Lord Kronnin has already began preparations. I will order Lars Castlegrail to send dispatches to every city and town in Gul Kana with orders that all able-bodied men are to gather at Lord's Point. Lord Le Graven will need convincing. As will Lord Chaparral. They will fall in line as soon as this folly involving Lawri and Sterling Prentiss is resolved."

Jovan was right. This problem involving the accusations Tala had leveled against Sterling Prentiss could throw a wrench in his plans if something was not done about the Dayknight captain and the missing princess soon. Jondralyn knew that Lawri was safe. But Lord Lott Le Graven believed her to be kidnapped and held by Sterling Prentiss. Lott would not let his twelve-year-old twins, Lorhand and Lilith, leave his side. He wanted Sterling's head. And the grand vicar stood in the way of Jovan fully stripping Sterling of his post. She would not betray Tala's trust, though. She would not tell Jovan what she knew of Lawri's whereabouts. She leveled her gaze at her king. *Does he really wish me to die in this journey?*

"Denarius will not like this," Jondralyn said to Jovan. "Does he wish to fight Aeros Raijael, then? I'd always assumed he was against war."

"Many are mistaken about the holy vicar's motives," Jovan said. "Roguemoore has polluted your mind against our great prophet. Yes, the grand vicar has always wanted war, but only at the appointed time and place, and only in accordance with scripture and revelation. That time is now, here on Gul Kana soil, as *The Way and Truth of Laijon* has foretold. The White Prince's landing on Gul Kana soil is the dawning of Fiery Absolution. The prophecies of Laijon's return are soon to be fulfilled. And you, Jondralyn, the first woman of the Silver Guard, will usher in Absolution. It is why I did not demand that you give up your training with Hawkwood fully, or your quest to become a gladiator. I could have put a stop to those endeavors long ago. I supported you in my own way. It was *I* who made you into who you are today."

It was all falling into place. Everything Roguemoore had told her. *I will be at the forefront of the gathering of all armies that will hasten forth Laijon.* Her heart thudded even harder. "Everything serves a purpose" was one of the Brethren's mottoes. *Does my brother unwittingly play his own part in the* Moon Scroll *prophecies of Mia?*

Another thought entered her mind. She now knew exactly what she would do when she reached Lord's Point. And it wouldn't be to wait around for the arrival of the White Prince. No, she knew she would not await her destiny at Lord's Point but would grab destiny by the reins and ride it into history. She would attack the White Prince wherever she found him. It was the right thing to do. It was what her mother, Alana Bronachell, would have done had she had the opportunity. *Aeros Raijael's bloody crusade will finally be put to an end.*

It would be written by the scribes, *'Twas Jondralyn Bronachell who rode toward the armies of the White Prince and threw the gauntlet of war in the face of Aeros Raijael.* Even Roguemoore could not have foreseen this. *I am the Princess who will lead armies.*

Jovan rose from his bed, took up his Dayknight blade with the black opal–inlaid pommel, and knighted her one of the Amadon Silver Guard.

He then handed her the Silver Guard sword. She had never before felt so confident, lofty, and proud.

This is how my destiny will play out. I will be the harbinger of Absolution.

If you are destined to perish in war, you force your enemy to break their swords and axes when they battle you. You make them know they have been in a battle! You give them scars and lost limbs and dead families to remember you by. You die with a grin that will haunt their dreams.
—The Chivalric Illuminations of Raijael

CHAPTER THIRTY-EIGHT
Gault Aulbrek

12TH DAY OF THE MOURNING MOON, 999TH YEAR OF LAIJON

GALLOWS HAVEN, GUL KANA

A cloudless sky enwrapped the Sør Sevier encampment. Only a cool breeze from the sea kept the Knights of the Blue Sword who'd gathered in front of Aeros' tent from standing in complete comfort. Aeros was there watching the spar with them, Sky Reaver at his hip. He stood about thirty paces away from the tent with Hammerfiss, Spades, and the ever-brooding Spiderwood.

"You mustn't worry about Jenko," Gault said to Ava Shay next to him. "From what I can see, he can hold his own against any Hound Guard or Rowdie, and probably even most of Aeros' Knights of the Blue Sword." The quick glance the girl gave him was flatly dismissive. Her eyes went back to the two fellows banging swords in front of Aeros' tent; one was Jenko Bruk, the other Mancellor Allen, the young Wyn Darrè fighter with the braided locks of dirty-blond hair and the black tattoos under his eyes. The two battled on a section of sparse grass rife with divots from their boots. Jenko Bruk had initially refused to engage in any such spar with Mancellor, until Hammerfiss had threatened to lop off his cock and rape his arse with it if he did not.

Gault had been paying scant attention to the fight, distracted by the Gallows Haven girl next to him. A roguish wind caressed the freshly combed locks of her hair, giving her a windblown, innocent look. But he sensed that whatever light and goodness had once dwelled within the girl had been forever banished behind her sad, numb eyes. There was something unsettling about her lately. But the very sight of the girl affected the tempo of his heartbeat. For his own well-being, he knew he needed to suppress that knotty lurch in his stomach whenever he found himself in her company.

The Sør Sevier army had been camped in Gallows Haven for more than a week now. This seemingly once proud, productive town with the vast sea at its front and jagged mountains at its back was a ghost of its former self. The massive camp of Aeros' army now dwarfed the town. Tents spread out as far to the north as the eye could see. The few survivors of the siege were slowly becoming acclimated to their new position as slaves in Aeros' army. A few years of servitude in the army of the Angel Prince was not at all a bad thing, especially for those who converted to Raijael.

The obstinate Jenko Bruk was handling his role as slave with less relish than the others. But Enna Spades had slowly taken Jenko under her wing—the young man had spent time, only somewhat reluctantly, under her tutelage. She was bent on teaching him how to fight the Sør Sevier way. As Gault watched Jenko spar with Mancellor Allen, he was impressed with the young man's skill. Spades had a knack for taking the most stubborn and brutish of captives and eventually turning them into Aeros' greatest of assets. Gault chalked her success up to her beauty and the slow seduction of her prey. Because of her, Mancellor Allen was now one of the Angel Prince's most skilled and hardened warriors, and above all, one of his most loyal followers. Indeed, the way Spades worked her wiles, Jenko too would one day more than likely accept the light of Raijael.

The Gallows Haven fellow, in a sleeveless tunic, fought well without a shield. He deftly blocked each of Mancellor's strikes with his two-handed broadsword. He was quick with the heavy blade, yet there was ever-increasing power behind each swing of the sword. Jenko's arms were stout and strong, muscles bunching as he launched an attack of his own. Mancellor danced away, dirty-blond braids swinging free. The Wyn Darrè bore a much lighter sword in one hand whilst wielding a thick wooden shield to block Jenko's heavy-landing blows in the other. Just when Gault thought the Gallows Haven fellow was going to get the best of Mancellor, the Wyn Darrè struck Jenko with a solid blow to the shoulder, knocking him sprawling to the ground. Ava Shay gasped and looked away.

"He'll be okay," Gault said. "Mancellor has control over his weapon. He hit him with the flat of the blade. No harm was done." He looked to the girl at his side. Where Jenko Bruk was a tough nut, this one, on the other hand, was a lost soul. The slave mark on the underside of Ava's wrist was still red and raw and half scabbed over. That Aeros had already bedded her tore at Gault's heart. Not that bedding the Angel Prince was such a horrendous thing. Most would consider it an honor to sleep with their lord. But most girls Ava's age knew nothing of such things; most girls so tender of youth only ended up in a man's bed as one unwilling. Gault could see the torment and confusion on the girl's face as she watched Jenko interact with Mancellor. It was clear this girl loved Jenko. But Jenko had not spoken to her since the Angel Prince had taken her into his tent. Aeros would not allow them near each other. The conflict and hurt in her eyes were infinite.

Ava's eyes followed each of Jenko's moves with an aching stare. Gault knew that this poor girl needed her mind to focus on something else, if only for a moment. So he tried engaging her once again. "I have a daughter," he said. "She's your age."

"That's nice," Ava said, eyes staring ahead, voice laced with strain.

"You remind me of her. Her name is Krista."

"Krista." Ava looked at him in a manner completely void of life. "A pretty name."

"Her mother and I chose the name together," Gault said, thinking of Avril. In Krista's eyes he could always see her mother. After his wife had died, and before the siege of Wyn Darrè, all he could do was cling to Avril's presence, which he saw inside her daughter. His wife's personality revealed itself more in Krista as the girl grew. Like Avril, Krista would whisper to the trees, play with any animal she found, and drink in every moment of life she could, and also like Avril, Krista had a brooding side to her. But Gault's love and longing for his wife and stepdaughter were betraying him in the presence of this girl, Ava Shay. Thinking back to the death of Avril, and how it still clawed at his heart, he began to realize that what feelings he had for Ava Shay were becoming too entwined with that loss. But Gault knew he needed to purge all needless thoughts and longing for the past from his head, lest he succumb to unending weakness. Still, he ached to talk to this girl next to him.

"My wife's name was Avril," he said, finding her name light on his tongue. "She was my first love, my only love."

"And what of Spades?" the girl asked.

Ava's question took Gault aback. "How do you mean?"

"Aeros made mention yestermorn that you were in love with Spades."

Gault's eyes shifted from the girl to Spades, who was now teaching Jenko and Mancellor how to catch a sword blade with bare hands and wrench the weapon from the hand of one's foe without risk of having one's hands shredded.

Ava continued, "Aeros said that Spades was now rutting with

Jenko and that you would become jealous and perhaps kill him. You won't kill him, will you?"

Gault could see the despair in her eyes. This was probably the closest Ava would ever come to giving voice to her sorrow. "I've no desire to kill Jenko."

"Is she rutting with him?" the girl asked, eyes downcast.

"You needn't worry about Spades," he said, instantly cursing himself for caring about this blond waif, cursing too that Aeros had accused him of jealousy concerning Spades. A real warrior was trained to resist such compassion. What was it the *Illuminations* claimed? *The closer intimacy tries to approach, the farther the warrior must draw back. For a warrior of Raijael must act like a unfettered storm cloud, constantly adrift, always creating distance from invading softness of thought, no matter how determined it is in claiming him.* Or some such—ofttimes the exact words of the *Illuminations* escaped him.

The fact was, Gault knew that he wouldn't care at all about this slave girl if she wasn't so beautiful—the same could be said for Spades. But wasn't that the way of it? The *Illuminations* said, *The weak-minded soldier will behave with spineless indignity around a fetching lass.* If Ava Shay were fat and homely, Gault knew that he wouldn't give two cartloads of donkey shit about her. And if Spades were ugly, he would've killed her years ago. *The warrior must rid himself of what tenderness may creep in.*

Gault straightened his back and resumed the proper posture of a Knight Archaic.

It was then that he saw the Bloodwood guiding a familiar figure toward them from the north.

Stabler.

He was weaponless and walked as one injured. As Stabler ambled forward, he held one hand up to his battered face. His one good eye was swollen shut, and he was forced to pry it open with his fingers to see.

"Our tracker returns." The Angel Prince's mocking voice sliced out into the air as he made straight for Stabler. Reaching him, he yanked the man's hand away from the purple-swollen eye. "As I understand it, he arrives alone, minus the fifty I sent with him."

"With regrets, my lord." Stabler dropped to one knee and bowed low, then stood again. The black bulbous injuries done to the side of Stabler's face had so completely shut his eye that he was clearly unable to see.

"You may open your eye," Aeros said.

"As it pleases my lord." Stabler pried the swollen flesh apart with his thumb and forefinger again.

Aeros motioned to Stabler's injuries. "Dare I even ask what happened?"

Stabler bowed again. "Got knocked in the head by a flying pony," he said.

Some of the knights standing around Aeros chuckled at that. Stabler smiled, but it was clear that even smiling took the man some effort.

"A flying pony." Aeros seemed less than amused. "If you're not going to take this seriously, then why should any of us?"

"Sorry, my lord." Stabler bowed again. "But that is the truth. Even knowing the fate that would await me, I still returned, my lord. I will always choose honor."

"Honor." Spades snorted, now standing beside Aeros, the Gul Kana copper with Jondralyn Bronachell's face on it flitting between her fingers. "It's a bloody fuckin' travesty is what it is. The man can't even see out of his own remaining eyeball. Imagine that, my lord. He comes back completely blinded and swordless. What shame. What shame indeed. There is no honor in this."

Ignoring Spades, Aeros asked Stabler, "Where are the escaped captives?"

"I know not," Stabler replied, his tone now grim.

"We found twenty-five of the knights I placed under your care not one mile out of town, slaughtered by a lone man with a sword and possibly a boy with a bow."

"Aye, that would be where we first caught up to them and gave chase."

"Where are the other knights and dogs I sent with you?"

"I thought they would have made it back here by now."

"Only two came back. With all the horses. Your charger, Shine, was with them. But that was all. They say you went into some mines. You must answer for the others. Where are they? Lost?"

"I can only account for the five who went with me to the end. And they are dead. And another five fell into a chasm in the mines. The others I last saw in the mines, I gave them orders to make their way from the mines and report to you, my lord."

"They never returned."

"Lost, then. In the mines still. I will explain as best I can, if it pleases my lord?"

"Continue."

"As you probably well know, the first man we came across held us at bay between the boulders under the switchbacks. He was sore injured already. He had help from big gray shepherd dog and a bowman on the trail above. After your Bloodwood stepped forth and killed the man, it took us almost half a day to work our mounts up the trail. Once we broke free of the switchbacks, we tracked our quarry to the abandoned mining town. I left my steed and the other horses outside the mine with two knights to watch over them." Stabler turned to Spiderwood. "There was a dead Bloodeye horse. A mare. In a pit. A game trap of some kind. By a cabin. Impaled. Wooden stakes. We covered it with bramble sticks and burnt it."

"Rosewood's Bloodeye?" Aeros asked the Bloodwood.

"Doesn't mean she is dead," Spiderwood said.

"Doesn't bode well for her either."

The Bloodwood remained stone-faced.

"Carry on," Aeros ordered Stabler.

"Once in the mines, there were few torches between us. Our going was rough. But our quarry left ample evidence of their passage. We came upon a vast cavern with a narrow stone bridge over a chasm. The first five who crossed the bridge were lost when it collapsed. A few of the dogs, too. Some of us lay on the lip of the abyss, examining the drop as far as our torchlight shone. It was a sheer drop, vanishing into unknown depths. Finding no way to cross, we strode to either end of the cavernous room. The great crack disappeared into the stone mountain on one side of the cavern, yet on the other side, the fissure ended in a solid but sheer wall. It took us the better part of a day to search the passages behind us, but we eventually found some tools, mauls, metal spikes, rods and irons, and old rope and the like, even ladders long enough to span the chasm. But the ladders were old, rotten, and weak and would not hold the weight of a man. We managed to chisel footholds along the sheer wall, hammering and wedging the irons and spikes into what small crevasses we could find. We rigged a rope line of sorts along the wall and inched our way around the chasm. Only five followed me across. The rest I instructed to find their way back and report to you. They had a torch, with flame enough to see them back out."

"Doubtless they are still lost in those mines," Aeros said. "A waste for sure."

"I tracked the escapees the rest of the way through the mines. At one point, they diverted from their route and climbed some stairs. I too climbed those stairs and found an altar, its lid removed—"

"What was the shape of this altar?" Aeros asked.

"The shape of a cross."

Aeros glanced at the Bloodwood, then back to Stabler. "Was there anything of note inside this altar?"

"I regret to say that the contents of the altar were gone. But it was clear the escapees had removed something from it. The dust was stirred round about."

"Do go on."

"Once we were outside the mines, their trail was again clearly marked. We tracked them easily enough. But then the hail started up something fierce. We had nothing for shelter and huddled together and waited out the storms as best we could. We found one of the escapees dead on the trail the next morning. A girl, young, small, a pretty thing, dark of hair, maybe shoulder length. She was frozen on the trail faceup. She held a hatchet."

"Do you recognize the girl's description?" Aeros asked Jenko.

The boy shook his head. Aeros asked Ava Shay. The girl trembled, but in a cracked voice, she told him the girl's name: Gisela Barnwell. Aeros turned back to Stabler and bade him continue.

"The girl wasn't the only dead one we found. The next day there was also a fat boy with red hair lying farther up the tracks we followed. It looked like he'd taken an ax to the ribs. The wound was old, rotten. He'd also taken a knife in the heart. That wound more recent. He too was frozen solid atop a wolf-hide blanket. There were many lion tracks around about the woods, in the brush, the trees. But the body had not been disturbed. A brute of a dog guarded it. We did not bother the dog. I doubt we coulda handled it anyway. It was the same shepherd dog that helped the dead man you found at the trailhead."

"Do you know the dead boy with the ax wound?" Aeros asked Jenko.

"Zane Neville," Jenko offered. "He owned a big gray shepherd dog."

"That's the dog," Stabler confirmed. "Like I said, same dog that helped the man at the trailhead."

"Continue," Aeros ordered him.

"It was cold. Those peaks must be over ten thousand feet high. Hard to breathe the very air. But we finally came upon our quarry midway up a steep switchback. The young bowman was still with them. A good shot, that one. The others threw rocks down upon us. They even launched a pony over the ledge. That is how I got this." Stabler leaned his head in toward Aeros, emphasizing that his hand was holding open a severely swollen eye. "I saw the pony sailing toward me. That is the last I remember. I woke alone in the darkness, blind, or so I thought. The escapees were gone, my men dead, my sword at the bottom of the hill. At that point, I gathered my blade and began my long hike down the mountain, following a winding stream until it dumped me north of town. Holding my eye open all the way, of course. Thank Raijael the stream flowed far north of those mines. I was loathe to travel back through there. Anyway. Here I am."

At the end of the tale, Aeros bowed to Stabler. It was a deep and graceful bow.

When he arose from it, the Angel Prince spoke in an even tone. "Over the years you have been a stalwart and brave companion. I have watched your rise from Hound Guard to Rowdie to Knight of the Blue Sword and now Knight Archaic."

Gault felt the apprehension coiling within him as Aeros continued, "But you have failed me, Stabler. And you know the price of failure."

"I do, my lord. And in so knowing, I came back to you still. I felt it of utmost importance that you hear my tale of failure. I hope what information you glean from my disastrous journey proves useful in furthering the kingdom of Raijael."

"Your words are well chosen. I have indeed learned much from your tale."

"Then I am pleased, my lord."

"I allow you to invoke the Chivalric Rule of Blood Penance. If you so desire."

"I do, my lord. For I wish to redeem myself in your eyes. For I desire to be worthy to sit at your side in heaven, if but for a moment."

The Angel Prince stepped back from Stabler, speaking for all to hear. "Our brave Stabler wishes to invoke his right to atone for his failure! He can be flogged and then rejoin the Hound Guard as a squire, or he may duel to the death with a warrior of my choosing!" Aeros turned back to Stabler. "If you are victorious in the duel, you may resume your position as one of my Knights Archaic and all will be forgotten. Die and I deem your shed blood sufficient reparation. Your body will be burned on the pyre and your soul allowed to take wing into heaven, befitting an honorable death."

"I choose the duel." Stabler let his hand drop to his side, and he drew his sword. "Even blind, I will kill whomever you put in front of me. I swear it."

"Excellent," the Angel Prince said. "A flogging and back to a squire earns one scant respect." His eyes lanced through the crowd; they lingered on Mancellor Allen, then passed over Jenko to Spades to Hammerfiss, landing on Ava Shay. She shrank away from his gaze. Gault's instinct was to say something to reassure her she was in no real danger. Aeros was not about to make her fight Stabler.

"Ser Gault," Aeros said. "I bestow upon you the honor of fighting your fellow Knight Archaic."

Though the request stunned him, years of warfare had taught Gault presence of mind. He remained stoic. "An honor, my lord." Without hesitation he bowed, figuring he knew the words to forestall the duel for a few days at least. "But I will not fight Stabler blinded as he is," he said in a dry, brisk voice. "We wait until he is healed."

"You will fight him here and now," Aeros said forcefully. "Hammerfiss will find something to bind open Stabler's eye."

"Some twine and a darning needle ought to do the trick." Hammerfiss' voice was laced with pleasure as he trotted off in the direction of his own squat tent.

Gault had little desire to duel Stabler, not now, not under these circumstances, and certainly not to the death. He held no more affection for Stabler than he did anyone else in Aeros' select group of

Knights Archaic. But the man was good with a blade. It seemed a waste just to kill him. And kill him he would. Even a healthy Stabler with his own sword would be no match for him. Everyone knew this. Though Aeros' five Knights Archaic were the best fighters in the Five Isles, they each of them knew where their skills ranked within the group; they each of them knew who was best—and that was the Bloodwood. But following the Bloodwood was Gault. Stabler, the newest of the five Knights Archaic, was good with a sword, but he was in no shape to fight. He was worn down by days spent in the mountains. And his one good eye was useless.

When Hammerfiss returned he began poking holes into the purple flesh above Stabler's swollen eye with a thick needle. He threaded twine of grayken baleen up and in and out of the various holes, then tied the baleen into the man's hair, lifting the swollen eyelid up as he did so and cinching the twine tight until Stabler could see. Blood oozed over the man's face from the stitching. But Hammerfiss wrapped a scarf around Stabler's head to stanch the flow. The man looked a sight, black eye patch on one eye, the other sewn open with thread crafted of grayken baleen. Hammerfiss handed him a sword. Stabler readied his new weapon as Spades handed him a shield.

Gault drew his own sword and motioned for Mancellor Allen's shield. The Wyn Darrè youth held the shield out grudgingly. So Gault made a point of snatching it roughly from the long-haired boy's hand, nearly jerking him to the ground.

Most sword fights ended after only a few swings. And Gault was one to end a fight quick. He wasted no time in attacking Stabler. The one-eyed man was skilled enough to block the first couple of blows. But Gault pressed on, backing Stabler down easily. There were no cheers among the onlookers as Gault lunged, and with a swift blow struck Stabler's sword from his hand. The man did not flinch. Even when Gault raised his sword for the final blow, Stabler stood motionless. In a way, Gault wanted to spare his friend this death. But the

years of growing well-honed in battle carried his blade downward in a sweeping arc—there was nothing that could stop Gault's instincts to kill in battle, nothing he could summon up within himself to stop it.

And so, as if of its own accord, his sword came flashing down into Stabler's neck, digging a trench through his leather shoulder-armor and burying itself deep into his chest.

Stabler crumpled silently to the ground as Gault pulled his sword free. Short, shallow breaths hissed from Stabler's lips, but nothing would stem the gushing blood that now pumped over the grass.

Gault looked at Ava Shay and felt nothing. The spell she'd held over him was broken. There was nothing like the intoxicating taste of battle and the killing of a friend to rid oneself of any soft spots left in one's heart. It was like taking a breath of fresh air.

"Well done." Aeros took the shield from Gault's hand and returned it back to Mancellor Allen. "I've always been curious about those tattoos under your eyes," Aeros said to the Wyn Darrè fellow. "I insist you tell me of them."

"If it pleases my lord." Mancellor touched the tattoo under his left eye with long, rough fingers. "In Wyn Darrè it is common that a warrior tattoos dark swaths under his eyes. Squid ink is the best, the blackest. It diverts the sunlight and cuts back on the blinding glare of armor and sword into our eyes. It is a great honor when the baron you've trained under finally offers you the ink."

"Oh yes," Hammerfiss laughed. "Wyn Darrè proved to be just teeming with honorable and tattooed soldiers running about with the sun *not* in their eyes."

Aeros spoke again. "Let me ask you, Mancellor, whom do you worship now?"

"I still worship Laijon as I did before," Mancellor said, standing straighter. "But I no longer pay homage to the grand vicar in Amadon. I no longer pray to stone idols and partake in rituals of Ember Lighting as I used to. I now worship Laijon through the grace of his true and living heir, Aeros Raijael. You are my lord. I will follow you to my very death to prove it. I so swear."

The way he said it, Gault actually believed him.

"You have proven your valor and more." The eyes of the Angel Prince drifted from Mancellor to Jenko Bruk. "Listen well, young Jenko. Not less than five years ago, Mancellor Allen's regiment was destroyed by my armies in Ikaboa. He was naught but a conquered Wyn Darrè captive, a lowly servant as you are now. But over time, and after throwing off the shackles of the Church of Laijon and ridding himself of the rule of the grand vicar and quorum of five, Mancellor found the truth. He is now joined to us heart and soul and has become a part of the covenant of Raijael."

Jenko Bruk seemed less than impressed.

Aeros picked up Stabler's sword from the grass and handed it to the young Wyn Darrè. "This, my servant, is now yours." Aeros bent his knee before Mancellor and bowed low. "And I thus name you, Mancellor Allen, Knight Archaic. Stabler's mount, Shine, is now yours."

Aeros' bow and pronouncement were met with silence. Spades, copper coin unmoving in her hand, raised her eyebrows. Hammer-fiss furrowed his. Spiderwood stared at nothing. Aeros stood back up and clasped Mancellor about the shoulder with a sly grin.

Gault bent and cleaned the blood from his sword on Stabler's pant leg. And once his sword was wiped clean, he rammed the blade home in the scabbard and resumed his spot next to the girl Ava Shay, who now looked upon him with fright-filled eyes.

We have given unto you a Quorum of Five Archbishops to govern
the Church of Laijon in Amadon. And only through the quorum
of five will the name of Laijon's holy prophet be revealed. For the
grand vicar of the Church of Laijon will never be self-sent.
—THE WAY AND TRUTH OF LAIJON

CHAPTER THIRTY-NINE

NAIL

15TH DAY OF THE MOURNING MOON, 999TH YEAR OF LAIJON
SWITHEN WELLS TRAIL ABBEY, AUTUMN RANGE, GUL KANA

Stefan Wayland instructed Nail to hold the bow gently in his hands. "You don't have to crush it with your fingers," he said. "When you draw back, hold your hand at the corner of your mouth and sight down the shaft. Let the string just slide from your fingers. Don't let it snap. Relaxing is the key."

Nail flicked the hair from his eyes, aimed, and fired. The arrow skittered through the grass and kicked up a puff of dirt a good ten paces in front of the target—a large sack of grain with a red circle painted in the center a hundred paces away. He handed the bow back to Stefan, who picked an arrow, aimed, and fired. The arrow whistled through the air and struck the sack of grain a foot above the circle, punching deep, quivering.

Dokie, standing near a crackling fire in Godwyn's firepit by the fence, clapped in approval. He then hopped on the stone fence with Liz Hen, who was knitting a wool shirt. "Just you try and better that shot," he said to Bishop Godwyn. "Stefan is the best bowman in all Gul Kana."

The bishop nocked an arrow into his own bow, sighted down the shaft, then let it fly. With a musical twang, his arrow sang through the air and struck just under Stefan's in the center of the grain sack. Godwyn turned and winked. "Lucky shot, that."

Most days, the bishop would forsake his priestly cassock and white robe for knee-high boots, leather breeches, and a green woolen shirt edged at the elbows with elk hide. His hair, a listless shade of watery gray, was a scraggly mess no matter the clothes he wore. With his garb, amiable mug, and unkempt hair, Hugh Godwyn looked more the part of a rootless bard or vagabond than a bishop.

Godwyn's bow was similar to Stefan's. Dayknight made, constructed of witch hazel and ash wood. The bishop claimed to have been a Dayknight when he was younger. At night he would recount many of his adventures, stories colorful and bawdy. Baron Bruk had been in some of those tales. But whenever the baron's name was mentioned, a pall fell over Dokie, Stefan, and Liz Hen. None of them liked to be reminded of their life before in Gallows Haven. None of them wanted to recall what had happened to the baron.

For Nail, the past seven days at the abbey with Bishop Godwyn had been some of the most contented of his life. Their first feast upon arriving had been wonderful: salted trout, peas, beans, cheese, bread, turnips, and birch wine. The abbey was a cozy place in the middle of a sun-dappled glade, and Nail liked it greatly. After all, it possessed the grand virtue of keeping out the hail and wind. After their harrowing journey through the icy mountains, Nail would never take simple shelter for granted again. The abbey itself consisted of a tiny chapel, scarcely large enough to seat ten or twelve worshippers. Next to the chapel was a dormitory with a small kitchen and several rows of bunk beds. On the far side of the chapel was a library stacked with books. Between the abbey and dormitory was a small walled-in garden, and beyond that the stable. Inside the stable were ten large pigs, six small piebald ponies, and one dun-colored draught mare.

Hugh Godwyn tended to the Swithen Wells Trail chapel and grounds by himself. Nowadays, the remote abbey was merely used as a way station for those traveling between Swithen Wells and Tomkin Sty, or for those taking the north fork road toward Ravenker. But in days long past, the abbey had been the main place of worship for the miners who used to call these mountain peaks their home, or so Godwyn had claimed.

Nail was drawn to the walled-off garden. As the weather had warmed over the past few days, it was becoming bright with clover. The small garden was a peaceful place to huddle under a cloak and read one of the bishop's books or draw on clean parchment with Godwyn's quills and ink. The pictures Nail drew were of fields of flowers or groves of aspen, a blonde-haired girl the focal point of every composition. He'd thought his life as an artist was over. But the abbey had rekindled his dreams.

The abbey was remote and relatively safe. Still, the bishop had advised Nail and Stefan to keep their armor close at hand. He had fitted both boys with shirts and leggings of good wool. Liz Hen still wore what she came with, as did Dokie. But they were all four of them given warm fleece-lined cloaks. Liz Hen would not part with the sword she had taken from the knight she and Dokie had killed. She toted the thing about everywhere, chopping twigs with it, swinging it about in great arcs, slaying invisible foes. It was a magnificent blade. Bishop Godwyn had taken to teaching both Liz Hen and Dokie a few simple block-and-parry moves that they both repeated for hours on end. Dokie showed no lingering ill effects from the lightning strike, the crossbow bolt to his leg, or the shark bites. He was almost completely healed. Nail wondered what twist of fate was keeping Dokie alive, free of infection, whilst Zane Neville, hit once with an ax, had succumbed to his wounds. Gisela had died from cold, or who knew what. Yet Dokie roamed the abbey grounds as healthy as the day he was born. *Lady Death is a fickle mistress,* Shawcroft was fond of saying. And he'd been shot with a crossbow bolt too, then nearly died of a dog bite, before the Bloodwood finished him. It all seemed so random.

Godwyn and Stefan continued their archery practice. Keeping Stefan focused on archery was the only thing that kept him from plummeting into bouts of deep depression. Since arriving at the abbey, Stefan had been a mournful mope. Not even the bishop could console the boy. One night Stefan took a knife and carved Gisela's name into the stock of his Dayknight bow. This act boosted his spirits some. He named the weapon Gisela and from then on, like the sword that Liz Hen carried, the bow never left his side. Sometimes, at night, Nail could hear Liz Hen praying with Dokie. The big girl's prayers were all tears for Zane and despair over the loss of Gallows Haven and wishing death to the white devil from Sør Sevier. Dokie scarcely uttered a word, unless it was in his sleep, and those naught but horror-laced mumblings about lightning, sharks, and soiled skivvies. Liz Hen and Dokie were constantly together, frequently holding hands. These last few days at the abbey had seen the two grow close. "I daresay they are in love," Stefan once mumbled. "It's nice they have each other." Then he would caress the spot where he had carved Gisela's name into the stock of his bow.

Liz Hen was always in a chatty mood with Dokie and Stefan. She was even opening up to the bishop some. But everything she tended to say to Nail was crisp and cold and more than just a trifle unkind. A simmering rage was boiling up within her day by day. *She blames me for everything.* Right now she was sitting atop the stone fence, knitting, but her eyes were not on her work; instead they were glaring at him. There was no reason for it. Tonight the early evening air was moving cool and fragrant around him. The fire was a soothing warmth on his skin. He tried to ignore Liz Hen's gaze, but it kept burrowing into him until he found he couldn't look away from her at all.

"Why do you stare at me?" he asked.

"Because you disgust me, Nail." She plopped down from the fence and waddled toward the fire pit, knitting needles and wool shirt in hand. "You've done naught but lay about this abbey, content and comfortable, since we arrived. You act as if nothing awful has happened to us at all."

"How would you have me behave?" Nail asked defensively.

"I would have you behave like you cared."

"Cared about what?"

Liz Hen grunted. "I was a fool to think it was within you to save Zane, even for a moment. You couldn't have carried him even two steps. Bastard."

Nail didn't know what to say. Liz Hen had placed both fists on her thick hips and was staring down her bulbous nose at him. "What have you to say for yourself? You've yet to shed a single tear for any of us. Not me. Not Dokie. Not Gisela. Not Zane. Not the dead left in Gallows Haven. Not even your master, Shawcroft. May the wraiths take you. Do bastards truly have no soul?"

He wished she would stop calling him that. "I only did what you bade me do. I *could* have carried Zane had you only helped, only given me a chance."

"Don't you be blamin' me for my own brother's death."

"It was Laijon's will that Zane perished." Dokie slid from the fence. "And that is the only comfort I take. Laijon's will."

"You're wrong, Dokie," Liz Hen said. "It was Nail who killed him."

"Only because that is what *you* wanted." The words tumbled from Nail's mouth before he could rein them in. But for as much as his words might've hurt Liz Hen, they were like a cold spear plunging into his own heart. He would never forget the look on Zane's face as he had slipped the dagger up and in. He would never forget the feel of his friend's warm blood pumping over his hands, or forget the mournful sound of Beer Mug. He'd saved his friend's life during the grayken hunt, only to have to take that same life in the cold of the mountains. Nothing about it seemed right or fair. He blinked back the tears he now felt welling in his own eyes. *They all think it's because of me that Gallows Haven was destroyed.* He did not want them to see him cry, especially the bishop, who, along with Stefan, was looking at him now, bows forgotten in their hands.

"You're heartless." Liz Hen clutched her knitting to her chest. "Like I said, you have no soul. Shawcroft died for us and you don't even care. You've not said a good word about him. The man raised you and yet still you remain quiet. Not one good word. How is his soul to rise up and live with Laijon if nobody speaks for him?"

"What would you have me say?" Nail felt the anger broiling within him. Tears were long gone now. It was true. He had detached himself emotionally from Shawcroft. But the man's death had hurt. In some ways, it didn't really seem like his master was dead. He expected Shawcroft to come walking up at any moment and angrily order him to pan the stream near the abbey for gold. But Liz Hen was correct about one thing: Nail *had* enjoyed his time at the abbey. It was relaxing. Nobody was giving him orders. Nobody was watching how he held a pickax, or criticizing how he set his feet as he swung at a solid wall of stone in some dark cave. Nobody was treating him cruelly—until now. Thinking back on the days upon days of working the dark mines with Shawcroft, or panning for gold in the mountains, was now almost too much for his mind to bear. He felt nauseated and slumped down on a nearby stump. He sensed everyone's eyes on him, their faces blurry. "Don't any of you understand how much I hated working those mines and streams for naught but a few nuggets and a handful of dust? Do none of you know how frightened and alone I was my whole life?"

"You were never alone," the bishop said. Nail looked up and tried to focus on the man before him through the strands of blond hair that hung over his face. Godwyn's eyes, under his sharp brow line, were like a silver-wolf peering from a dark cave. "Your master knew what kind of boy you were: hardworking, determined, crafty in the wild. The type of son who would make any man proud." It looked like the bishop wanted to reach out to comfort him but restrained himself. "He was proud of you. Put your mind at ease."

"How would you know?" Nail flicked hair from his eyes and studied Godwyn, trying to decide whether he liked this odd man with the curling, gray mustache or not. "How would you know what Shawcroft thought of me, how he treated me?"

Bishop Godwyn set his bow aside, picked up a long stick, and stirred the fire. He gave Nail a frank yet soft look and said, "Shawcroft was a man who could go about his business with a harsh efficiency that was both admirable and disappointing at the same time. His bluntness carried over into his care of you. I once questioned his hard way of raising you. But he wanted you to be a strong, independent-minded young man."

"But what does it matter?" Nail mumbled, his halfhearted, wounded reaction impossible to mask. "Most days it seemed he didn't care for me much at all."

Godwyn lifted his eyes from the fire and spoke forcefully this time. "Shawcroft gave up all that he wanted to strive for a better future for you. Assassins hunted him the last seventeen years because of his devotion to you. Assassins took his wife because of his devotion to you. He was a tormented soul."

Shawcroft had a wife?

Godwyn continued, "Shawcroft gave up every single thing in his life that was important to him: his chance to rule a kingdom, his chance to have a family of his own. He sacrificed all for you."

"Why?" Nail said through gritted teeth. "That is all I ever wanted to know from him. Why? Why was he watching over me? Who was he? Who am I? He would never tell me any of it. Not about my sister, my mother, my father. None of it."

"Well, there are worse things than *not* knowing who you are, or where you came from, or what your purpose is. There are much worse things than *not* knowing."

"Like what?"

"Like knowing." The bishop's eyes bored into his. "You think your life with Shawcroft was unfair? Sure, he was stern with you. Perhaps even cruel at times. Well, let me ask, were you ever beaten? Were you ill fed? Most orphans live a life of squalor in the lice-infested slums of Amadon. You had it rather easy, I say. Have you ever had bugs crawl in your ears as you slept? Because that is what most fatherless bastards have to deal with. A filthy bed full of bugs. Crawling up into your nose. Your anus."

Dokie squirmed at the word *anus*.

Nail hung his head. He cared not how other unwanted children lived. He only knew of his own life—full of hard work and toil and never an encouraging word. It also pained him to know that the bishop not only thought him a bastard, but an ungrateful bastard at that. He wanted this man to think highly of him. But it seemed that even this well-meaning bishop was more apt to tear Nail down than build him up.

Trust no one. That would be his new rule. *Trust no one. Only believe in yourself.* Shawcroft was gone. *He was a mean old cob.* Nail had watched the man murder a Vallè woman. Bloodwood or not, it was a cruel, evil thing. Even though Shawcroft had saved him from capture, and died helping him escape, Nail still found it difficult to believe any good of the man. He was truly conflicted.

Only one man had ever been nice to him. Baron Bruk. But he was gone too, as was his grayken-hunting ship. *It seems there is no place in the Five Isles for me now.* In a way, during their frozen journey to reach this place, Nail had just assumed that the abbey would become his new home, and Hugh Godwyn his new master. And perhaps that was why he'd felt so comfortable here. But, alas, that dream seemed foolish too.

"Why were those men from Sør Sevier hunting us?" he asked, looking at the bishop, challenge in his eyes. "Why did Shawcroft want me to bring you his satchel? What of the ax? The stone? Why were we to go to Lord's Point? And when? Won't you tell us about any of it? You must know something. You must know of my family, my sister, my parents. You must know who Shawcroft really was. Baron Bruk called him Ser Roderic. Does that name mean anything to you?"

"Well, that is quite a list of questions," the bishop said. "Perhaps you should be asking them one at a time. And I will do the best I can."

"Who were my parents?"

"Shawcroft never told me who your parents were. He only told me that you were important to the Brethren of Mia."

"Brethren of Mia," Nail repeated. "What is that?"

"A brotherhood of scholars and warriors dedicated to ancient secrets."

"Was Shawcroft part of this Brethren of Mia?"

"He was. As am I. As are many."

"Was Shawcroft named Roderic? Baron Bruk also said that Shawcroft had a brother, King Torrence. Is that true? Who are my parents? Was Shawcroft my father?"

"Slow down, now. Did you never ask Shawcroft any of these questions?"

"About my parents, I would ask all the time. But he would say nothing. So what was the point of asking him his true name? He would have likely ignored me."

The bishop's brow furrowed as if deep in thought. "Shawcroft was not your master's real name. His real name and title were Ser Roderic Raybourne, Prince of Wyn Darrè, younger brother to the king of Wyn Darrè, Lord Torrence Raybourne. Both Raybourne brothers were closely aligned with King Borden Bronachell and other members of the Brethren of Mia. Shawcroft—or rather, Ser Roderic Raybourne—was made a Dayknight captain by King Borden. That was long before you were born, Nail."

"Brother to the king of Wyn Darrè," Nail said, wonder, apprehension, distrust, all of them burrowing inside of him at once. "I scarce know what to believe. Why would a man of such station want to live in Gallows Haven, mine for gold and other such nonsense, or become guardian to a bastard like me? I can hardly believe he knew King Borden Bronachell, or that he was a Dayknight."

Stefan piped in. "Shawcroft had a Dayknight sword. We saw it. He said he'd hid it in the eaves all these years. Remember, Nail? He said it had been many years since he had held Dayknight steel. Said it before he gave me the Dayknight bow. Remember?"

Nail recalled the black sword. He'd even held it in his own hands. Ran with it. Lost it on the beach. And Shawcroft had found it again somehow. *A Dayknight will always be able to find those things most important to him.* But a secret sword hidden in the eaves did not make Shawcroft a Dayknight. *Or could it?* Could that be why he'd been so mean all the time? Were Dayknights trained in cruelty? It was clear the bishop's answers were only going to fill his head with more questions.

"Why was Shawcroft watching over me? What am I to a prince of Wyn Darrè?"

Godwyn settled back on a stump of aspen in front of the fire and said, "I only know that Shawcroft was watching over you at the behest of Borden Bronachell."

"Ha, that's unlikely." Liz Hen held her knitting out with a squint, examining the wool shirt she was working on. She looked at the bishop. "Our late king would not give a raccoon's silent fart for one such as Nail. That I guarantee."

"And why do you say that?" Godwyn asked.

"Well, look at him," she sneered. "He's the least important of us all."

"And you're the most important of us?"

"More important than Nail."

"Well, one never knows." Godwyn looked contemplative. "Perhaps you are, Liz Hen, perhaps you are."

"Perhaps has nothing to do with it. I'm better than Nail. And that's that."

Nail kicked at the dirt with his booted foot as if contemplating how best to respond to Liz Hen's derision. *She's quick enough to blame me for the death of everyone in Gallows Haven.* He looked beyond the red-haired girl's sour face to the landscape beyond. Shadows crept out from the forest and the fire crackled. The sun was at an angle, vanishing over the horizon, and the air was crisp but not overwhelmingly cold yet. Still, he shivered as he tried to give Liz Hen his most hardened glare. But she stared back at him with even more venom. Before long, he realized nobody had spoken for a while and he was sulking. So he asked the question that needled at him. "You say that Shawcroft watched over me at the command of Borden Bronachell?"

The bishop stroked his curling mustache. "That is what Shawcroft claimed. Beyond that, I know as much as you. But as for why Shawcroft was in Gallows Haven, well, you need only look to the ax and stone you found in the mines to answer that question. Finding them was his life's work. The work of the Brethren of Mia."

Nail kicked an errant log back into the fire pit, wincing at the pain in his wrist. If he moved just the wrong way, the scab forming over the slave brand on his inner wrist would crack and sting. Nail looked at Godwyn, trying to hide the pain, his eyes casting what he hoped was stony indifference. He did not want to seem overanxious, but he desperately wanted the man to continue. "Can you tell me more of the Brethren of Mia?"

The bishop looked up, the firelight gleaming yellow shards in his eyes. "The Brethren of Mia hold to the truths written in *The Moon Scrolls of Mia*—the lost writings of the Blessed Mother Mia. We believe that secret truths of all things are hidden within the scrolls of Mia. For nothing is as false as the history we have all been taught, especially concerning Laijon and the holy book penned by the Last Warrior Angels. I say it to you now, and for the good of your own souls: the Quorum of Five Archbishops in Amadon, the grand vicar, *The Way and Truth of Laijon*—it is all a lie."

At those words, Liz Hen uncurled one of her hands from her knitting and performed the three-fingered sign of the Laijon Cross over her heart. "You blaspheme," she said, her face reddened with anger. "How do you claim to be a bishop of the church and yet say such evil things? It is goddess worship spewing from your mouth. The holy book says that Mia is to be revered but never worshipped. I testify to you that there is only one true church, and Grand Vicar Denarius is Laijon's holy prophet, and there is only one holy book, and that is *The Way and Truth of Laijon*. I believe with all my heart."

"That you have such faith is admirable, Liz Hen," the bishop said flatly. "But your faith is misplaced. No fault of your own, mind you, but you have been misled. We all of us have been misled. Even the holy vicar in Amadon is misled. He too falls under the illusion of truth created by those who penned *The Way and Truth of Laijon*."

"I won't listen to this." Liz Hen's fleshy face scrunched up in disgust.

"She's right," Dokie added. "Bishop Tolbret blessed me after I was struck by lightning. His priesthood healed me. Laijon continues to watch over me now. I've been through much tribulation and survived unscathed because of Tolbret's blessing."

"Amen," Liz Hen said. "Bishop Tolbret healed you."

"But we all watched Tolbret killed," Stefan said. "What of his sacred robe? I don't believe any of what we were taught."

"Tolbret must've been unworthy then, prideful," Liz Hen grunted.

"That's why Laijon allowed him to die. That's why his priesthood robe did him no good."

"That makes no sense." Stefan looked worried now. "If Tolbret was worthy enough to heal Dokie, then why claim him unworthy of priesthood protections, Liz Hen?"

"Don't be daft," Liz Hen huffed. "You're overthinking it. He was worthy when he blessed Dokie, unworthy when he died. You all saw his pride. It's a sin. Pride."

This coming from the person who thinks she's better than me. Liz Hen's scattered logic made little sense to Nail. He wasn't going to offer his opinion, though. Liz Hen already hated him enough.

The girl continued, "All we need concern ourselves with now is that Godwyn is a heretic and we needn't listen to him anymore."

"Perhaps so," Godwyn said, "heretical to your line of thinking anyway. But the truth is, the answers to the many questions Nail has been asking about the stone and ax can only be found in *The Moon Scrolls of Mia* and the knowledge the Brethren of Mia have gleaned from reading them. And it is not witchcraft. It is not goddess worship. The Mia scrolls have been with us always, hidden, of course, until recently. A portion of them are in the satchel that Nail carried. It was the information in those scrolls that led Shawcroft to Gallows Haven, led him to the mines, and led him to the ax and stone you found there."

Godwyn tipped another log into the hungry fire pit. Nail watched the sparks leap and twirl into the growing darkness, wondering what all this meant. His face was now overly warm from the fire, whilst the cool evening air plucked at the back of his neck. He rubbed his hands over the back of his head, trying to warm it. He felt at the still-raw scab in the roots of his hair—the wound from the helmet that had been jammed onto his head. But he soon forgot about his scabs and pains when the bishop resumed speaking. "As for the reason why the White Prince sent his men to track you through the mountains—well, it is simple: he knew what Shawcroft had found. The battle-ax you carried from the mines is *Forgetting Moon*, one of the fabled weapons of Laijon, and the blue stone is one of the lost angel stones of the Five Warrior Angels."

Godwyn went silent, letting his last remarks sink in. Nail noticed all eyes were on him, glittering with reflected flame. He knew why they looked at him so. *They truly think I brought all this danger and death down upon them.* For his part, he didn't know whether to believe the bishop or not. It was all too much to take in. The cross-shaped mark on his wrist flared in pain. He could hardly move his hand or arm from the unexpected sting. It took some effort, but he squelched an impulse to just stand up and retreat into the abbey alone.

Then came a sudden wild screech from Liz Hen and the girl shot to her feet, her knitting landing in the fire with a hiss, the woolen shirt curling in flame.

The girl stared wide-eyed over Nail's shoulder toward the abbey and beyond. She was gazing out toward the Swithen Wells Trail, both hands clapped over her mouth.

Nail whirled, heart pounding, fearing that more Sør Sevier knights were descending upon them. But it was only Beer Mug he saw. Through the fading light of late evening, the large gray shepherd dog came padding up the trail, tail wagging.

Liz Hen screeched again, then beamed, her face alight with joy. "He must be starving," she squealed. "I must fetch him a bit of meat from the larder."

With that, the plump girl trundled off toward the abbey, giggling with glee and delight, the dog bounding along behind her.

Those who read my writings will be privy to the greatest mysteries of an age. Other than Laijon, what were the names of the other four Warrior Angels? The Way and Truth of Laijon *never mentions them, calling them simply Gladiator, Princess, Assassin, and Thief, Laijon being the King of Slaves. But in due time I will reveal all things, even the names of the Five Warrior Angels, for I knew them well.*
—THE MOON SCROLLS OF MIA

CHAPTER FORTY

JONDRALYN BRONACHELL

16TH DAY OF THE MOURNING MOON, 999TH YEAR OF LAIJON

OUTSKIRTS OF LOKKENFELL, GUL KANA

It's Kelvin Kronnin's Ocean Guard that draws near," Culpa Barra said as several hundred blue-liveried knights crested the far ridgeline, seeming to thunder and flow over the grassy slope like waves. Another hundred or so mounted squires followed. Jondralyn's bay palfrey, sensing her nervousness, whinnied and shuffled back. The horse was unfamiliar to her. She took the beast hard by the bit and pulled it in line with the others—all palfrey travel horses taken from the King's Highway stable in Lokkenfell.

Astride their lightly armored horses, Leif Chaparral, Culpa Barra, and five of Leif's maroon-and-gray clad Wolf Guard from Rivermeade waited atop the ridge with her. Leif wore the black-lacquered armor and silver surcoat of the Dayknights. The silver-wolf on a maroon-field crest marked him as one from Rivermeade, the sword of his rank with the black opal–inlaid pommel at his side. Culpa Barra also wore the armor of the Dayknights and black-opal sword. Jondralyn wore the silver and black of the Amadon Silver Guard.

The mist hung motionless on the valley floor below them. Lokken-fell was a mile to the north, Lord's Point some forty odd miles to the west. A stretch of swampy farmlands and canals lay between the two cities. Stone pathways and gray stone walls crisscrossed the farm-lands, most overgrown with grass and weeds. Livestock gathered in green pastures to the north and east. Squat farmhouses, their chim-neys streaming smoke into the morning haze, dotted the landscape too. The towers of the Lord's Point castle and cathedral were barely visible in the far distance, and beyond that, the sea rolled away to the end of the horizon. Jondralyn thought she could just make out the tip of the Fortress of Saint Only floating just above the ocean crest five miles beyond Lord's Point.

"They should have arrived with more haste," Leif Chaparral said. "Kronnin will soon know that I am most displeased."

"We've only just arrived ourselves," Jondralyn said, a dull and faint feeling of unease settling in her stomach. "I will do the talking." Initially she had found Leif's lurking intensity rather tiresome on their four-day journey from Amadon along the king's tolls. Leif had remained mostly silent during the first few days. And if he did speak to her, it was in a condescending manner. "Someone wielding a Silver Guard sword, afraid of a rodent," he'd jibed when she was startled by a mouse that had darted from underneath one of the toll wagon's bedrolls. "This task scarcely suits you, Jondralyn. Makes me question the wisdom of your brother, the king."

If not for the presence of Culpa Barra, that portion of the journey would have been torment for her. Sterling Prentiss, at the behest of Grand Vicar Denarius, had deemed Ser Culpa Barra standard-bearer of the Dayknights. Both Prentiss and Denarius had insisted that the church be represented along with the king in the negotiations with

Aeros Raijael. And Jondralyn was glad for the young Dayknight's company. She recalled the efficiency with which Culpa had dispatched the four injured Dayknights on Jovan's orders after their duel with Hawkwood. She'd become fast friends with him on their journey from Amadon. Culpa was without guile. He talked to her with an ease most men could not. There was no want or desire or lust in his eyes when it came to her—at least none that she could detect. She was glad for this new friendship. He was her lone connection to the Brethren of Mia.

But the second half of the journey had been different between her and Leif. The Prince of Rivermeade had started noticing her in the all ways Culpa Barra had not, and his lust for the company of a beautiful woman had softened his treatment of her. He'd reverted back to how he'd been as a teen, his manner flirtatious and playful. She could see through his change in character, though. She'd heard that after she'd escorted Squireck from Sunbird Hall, Leif had brought in a Sør Sevier captive and executed her right there in front of everyone. It was this coldness that she believed was his true nature. But she was happy for his reversal in personality. Dealing with a flirt was something she could handle—and more pleasant. She just needed to be on guard and discern the flirting from conniving and play it to her advantage. It would be a fine line to walk.

She could sense that Leif was going to be brusque with Lord Kronnin and wanted to head that off. Kronnin's Ocean Guard reined up before her. The several hundred or so horsemen formed ranks behind Kronnin, their destriers sweaty and damp from the hard ride, their manes braided with ribbons of Lord's Point ocean blue. Outside of special ceremonies and celebrations in Amadon, Jondralyn had never seen so many mounted soldiers and squires before. As they had pounded up the ridgeline toward her, she'd tried to remain stoic, unimpressed. But now her heart was thumping; her own mount's hooves padded apprehensively under her. She tightened her grip on the reins and tried to calm the horse as it jostled into Leif's mount, earning her a scowl from the prince of Rivermeade. Her own armor was startlingly uncomfortable, especially atop her unfamiliar steed.

Kelvin Kronnin, in the silver armor and blue livery of Lord's Point, removed his helm and held it in the crook of his right arm. The blue flag of Lord's Point hung limp from the wooden pole of the standard-bearer behind him. Lord Kronnin was bareheaded with a shaved face. His angular, hard-lined features were accented by an old scar that ran along the bridge of his nose and down his jaw line. From atop his war charger, he bowed to Jondralyn. "It is not often we are privileged with one of the royal family. On word of your arrival, we hastened from Lord's Point to Lokkenfell."

"Hastened?" Leif scoffed, earning a momentary, ill-favored look from Kronnin.

But Lord Kronnin's eyes quickly fell on Jondralyn. "There are some who think highly of themselves because they fought alongside your father when he fell in Oksana."

"And rightly so, old man," Leif said. "Truth is, I've seen more battles than you."

"Must you argue with everyone, Leif?" Jondralyn snapped. Her bay palfrey jittered again and she fought to bring it under control. *Fool horse.* She feared that learning to ride a mount in battle was going to take more practice than becoming a gladiator.

"Pardon, m'lady." Leif dipped his head toward her.

"How is your newborn daughter?" she asked Kronnin once her horse had settled.

"She is fine, m'lady, and healthy. We named her Raye."

"I am sure she will grow to be as radiant as her name suggests, as stunning as her mother, the unbearably beautiful Emogen."

Kronnin's face glowed. "She will." He paused, clearing his throat as he looked from her to Leif and back. "Word is, Jovan was nearly killed. What news have you?"

"No news on the assassin or where he was from." Leif bowed to Kronnin too as he spoke.

The horse under Jondralyn stepped back again and neighed. She was growing frustrated with it. Leif reached out and with a gentle touch calmed her mount. She smiled and bowed her thanks to him, grateful for his gesture, knowing what lustful yearnings were behind his efforts.

She had never hated Leif Chaparral. She had also never been too fond of him either. He'd flirted with her nonstop when she was a young teen. But once she was betrothed to Squireck Van Hester, the flirting had ended. Jovan and Leif had been raised together. But in a way, Jovan's relationship with Leif was a trifle bewildering. The two had a private way of interacting; they seemed to know each other's thoughts. Around them, Jondralyn always felt awkward and excluded. That was the way she felt now. Even though Leif and Kelvin Kronnin clearly disliked each other, she wondered if either one of them had an ounce of respect for her. *They soon will.*

For a time, Jondralyn had believed she was going to be just another pretty, frilly ribbon woven into the tangled historical tapestry of the Five Isles—a broodmare to some lordling. But once her mother had died, she'd known she was destined to be a bright focal point in the history of her kingdom, a soldier, a warrior, noticeable and remembered. And not just for her image on a coin.

"What news of the White Prince's advance up the coast?" she asked Kronnin.

"Word is Aeros has sacked Gallows Haven and Tomkin Sty, and now closes in on Ravenker. He destroys all in his way: burning, killing women and children. What few he leaves alive he enslaves. It is mass slaughter. The question is, can Jovan get the armies of Gul Kana gathered before Aeros can bring the entirety of his armies from Wyn Darrè by ship? The lords and barons of Gul Kana have never united their lands to make war since the crusades to take Wyn Darrè from the worshippers of Raijael over seven hundred years ago. But if they did, if Jovan can muster them, the warriors would number over two hundred thousand. They could all arrive here within two moons, if Jovan acts soon."

"You needn't question the king," Leif fired. "Jovan has sent heralds to marshal armies from every corner of Gul Kana. He even summons aid from Val Vallè."

"The Vallè," Kronnin snorted. "Those prancing fools will be of scant use."

Jondralyn waved the comment aside. "The question for us is what do we do about Ravenker, Bedford, Bainbridge, and the other farms and villages in the path of Aeros?"

"There is naught that we can do." Kronnin took a deep breath. "Unfortunately, they'll be sacrificed while we await more reinforcements from the breadth of Gul Kana."

"Perhaps you will wait, Lord Kronnin." Jondralyn's heart was beating hard inside her chest now. "But I shall ride south and look upon the armies of the White Prince with my own eyes. I wish to know what it is we are up against."

"And risk confrontation or capture." Leif looked at her, bafflement and real concern on his face.

"Leif is right," Kronnin added. "There will no doubt be battles aplenty in the coming moons. No use in rushing to our doom. Aeros exists to wage this war. His knights are vile creatures, ruthless, deadly, and brutal beyond measure. It would be too dangerous to venture south with but a few hundred Ocean Guards."

"Then Ser Culpa Barra and I shall go alone," she stated.

Leif's eyes, again filled with a brief moment of insolence, cut into hers, then softened. "Not without me, you won't. You should come too, Lord Kronnin."

Kronnin's eyes bored into Leif. "You figure we'll just stroll down the coastline, have a gawk at Aeros' armies, and then what?"

Jondralyn's heart had not slowed its pounding. "Are you not the least bit curious, Lord Kronnin?"

"Curious, yes, but not suicidal."

"The time has come to gauge our worth." She faced Kronnin, her eyes unflinching, confidence growing. "These Sør Sevier bastards are whetting their swords with Gul Kana blood, and most in Gul Kana wish to wait and do nothing until they arrive at Lord's Point. Well, I wish to see these invaders with my own eyes."

Kronnin looked off into the distance, his gauntleted hands clutching at the reins of his horse like the hands of a drowning man clutching at a rope. He turned back to her. "It would be unwise to march this many Ocean Guards south. We should send but a few scouts if you insist on this course. I can see some wisdom in doing that."

"And I shall lead these scouts," she said.

"It is madness," Kronnin said.

Do we all possess a wish to remain important to our fellow man? Or is it just me? Jondralyn did not understand the man's apprehension. *Do we all not desire our great actions to be witnessed and sung about by the minstrels and bards? Or am I, a woman, now the only one who aspires to greatness? Can't he see that this is our chance for greatness and bravery?* "You may not wish to go with me, Kronnin," she said. "But I beg of you, please do not thwart me."

"Seems Laijon and I together could not dislodge you from this course," Kronnin said. "But you will not go without at least sixty knights," he continued, bowing in his saddle. "Sixty of my best along with a dozen or so squires shall accompany you, if it pleases m'lady?"

"Very well," she said.

"Then I shall take my leave." Kronnin bowed again to her. "Ser Revalard Avocet will lead my men." He indicated the tall knight to his left. Jondralyn watched as Lord Kronnin whirled his destrier, motioning for sixty of his men to separate from the group and stay behind with Ser Avocet.

She'd won. She couldn't trust her own voice not to sound excited. So she merely nodded her approval to both Leif and Lord Kronnin.

"Let us be off," she finally said, and reined her mount around abruptly, facing south.

They will call me the Harbinger. She watched Lord Kronnin and his Ocean Guard ride away. *The scribes will call me the Summoner of All Armies. Yes, the scribes will write of Princess Jondralyn Bronachell, one of the Five Warrior Angels returned. For I have been preordained to carve my name into history.*

Beware alchemy. Beware evil combinations, lest some things hidden be discovered anew. Potions and poisons can turn one against one's will. Certain poisons can set the wraiths against you, erode one's life unto death. Yet other potions can bring one back to life. Taken in evil combination, poisons and potions can leave one changed beyond all measure. Alchemy is altogether wicked. For it is the work of the Vallè.
—The Way and Truth of Laijon

CHAPTER FORTY-ONE
TALA BRONACHELL

16TH DAY OF THE MOURNING MOON, 999TH YEAR OF LAIJON
AMADON, GUL KANA

Lies. *So many lies I have told.* Tala wanted to shout to all of Amadon that it was the grand vicar who was guilty, and not Sterling Prentiss. *But who would believe that?*

Tala feared the chaotic, swirling thoughts of her feverish and damnable games with the Bloodwood might overwhelm her. She had failed Jondralyn. Despite telling her sister of Jovan's plot, Jondralyn had still left for Lord's Point. *And she'll be killed! And it's my fault. All of it.*

She sat in the sparsely lit room adjacent to Lindholf's bedchamber where she and Lindholf and Glade had hidden Lawri. The room was small, no more than a closet, and Lawri lay on a cot in the center of it. A few candles flickered on a table near her bed. Two of the room's walls were made of solid stone. The other walls were in rougher shape, crumbling brick and mortar with wooden slats showing through, some parts lined with thicker wooden planks to hold up the flaking stone. There were chains and irons along with hefty leather straps fastened high on all but one of the walls. Tala had no idea what those had once been used for. It seemed every corner of the castle held ancient secrets of some kind. She allowed her eyes to stray toward Lawri. Once stunning and beautiful, now her cousin looked a hundred years old, so shrunken and frail a strong breeze could carry her away. Her chest scarcely rose with each strained breath. Her sweat-damp face was pale gray, the flesh stretched tight around her skull and jawline. But it was Lawri's eyes that disturbed Tala the most; they were closed, sunken pits. She took Lawri's hand in her own, startled at how dry her cousin's fingers were, coarse and rough as an old strap of rawhide. *She's almost dead. She'll die before her Ember Gathering.* With her cousin's hand in her own, Tala felt a rush of emotion so strong it frightened her.

Lawri's eyes opened slowly. Bloodshot and dark-hollowed. As her gaze met Tala's, Lawri's dry fingers clutched hers tightly. Tala broke down in tears when she saw the love emanating from her cousin. Those two dark pupils, dry and so near to death, still conveyed the spirit that was Lawri.

Tears accompanied Tala's words, which spilled out beyond her control. "I forbid you to die. I forbid it. Soon we will be exploring again. You'll see. We will be sneaking away from the Silver Guard and crawling through the castle as if we own it. You will soon be running in Greengrass Courtyard, the cool grass under your toes. You will hold your arm out for Ser Castlegrail's hawks. You remember how you liked the hawks? I will have the kitchen bake those sweet wheat rolls that you like."

Tala could barely speak, the tears flowed so freely now. Her mouth quivered. "You—you can feed bits of the bread to the hawks. They will swoop in . . . swoop in and perch on your arm and—and you can feed them. I promise. You will not die, do you hear me?" Then Tala could not speak anymore, and Lawri's eyes drifted shut again.

† † † † †

As she walked, two Silver Guards trailing a few paces behind her, Tala was lost in a bottomless pit of endless grief and torment. She had been wandering the halls of Amadon Castle for hours now. There was little else to do. She could sit in her room, alone, and worry about Lawri—and Jondralyn. But that would only compound her misery. She was well aware of how the howling presence of the wraiths could blight the soul when one was left alone. And as much as she loathed it, walking with an armed escort was more favorable than that. Still, a life spent boxed in by Dame Mairgrid and soldiers paid to protect her was really no way to live either. *Where else but in a prison would one be forced to her room most days and only escorted out by the guards?*

The thought sparked an ire within her that she had scant resolve to rein in. She quickened her pace, and the Silver Guards trailing behind hastened to match it. She knew she could not lose them. They would follow her like bloodhounds until she returned to her chambers. But she knew it irritated them when she varied her gait so. And that pleased her, because her royal imprisonment would never end, and so why not derive pleasure where she could?

She slowed as she turned from the corridor and entered one of her favorite places in the castle, Swensong Courtyard. The yard was bright in comparison to the grim interior of the castle, and full of people. Tala strolled over the many crisscrossing cobblestone paths and through flower beds aglow with blossoming flowers of bright purple and white. The many mingling fragrances of the flowers, which normally filled her with hope and joy, now just added to her despair.

A smattering of statues, some of Laijon, most of long-dead grand vicars, and a few of heralded Dayknights, accentuated the flower gardens and ivy. The statues were old and cracked and weather-stained. The tops of the trees that lined the ivy-covered walls of the courtyard bowed and swayed in a moaning breeze that lazed its way over the crenulated battlements. The grand and narrow Swensong Spire at the far southern end of the yard rose up into the sky like a needle. Of the many spires of Amadon Castle, Swensong—though elegant—was not the greatest or the tallest. That honor belonged to Cember Tower in the center of the castle, atop the pinnacle of Mount Albion.

As she strolled through the gardens, assorted nobility and other castle folk paused to bow to her. She nodded in greeting to those she recognized, but most she ignored. They made her feel lonely; all of them dressed in their colorful waistcoats and dresses, strolling hand in hand, enjoying companionships they made in the yards whilst she sought only solace and reprieve. She thought of Glade. How disgusted she was with him. So gleeful and giddy when his brother had slain that warrior woman in Sunbird Hall.

She recalled Lindholf and Glade's Ember Lighting Rites last week in the Royal Cathedral with the other seventeen-year-old sons of Gul Kana royalty. For his part, Glade had chosen to administer the flame to her—a great honor, and a great ceremony. *But it was all tainted now with his evilness. And all of it administered by the worst of all people. Denarius.*

The grand vicar had anointed Glade's head with holy oil, then performed the Ember Lighting Confirmation. Denarius had pulled down on a thick rope, opening the flue centered in the cathedral ceiling high above and letting in a shaft of light that spilled down upon the main altar. Glade had then offered his Ember Lighting Prayer, confessing his love of Laijon, the church, and Laijon's holy prophet, Grand Vicar Denarius. He then took up a goblet of oil and proceeded to Tala. She, in front of the altar, had held forth a pestle of crushed cloves in her cupped hands. Glade tipped the goblet, dripping the oil into her thin ceramic pestle whilst he lit the flame under it, setting the herbs alight with help of the oil. She freed one of her hands, passing it over the pestle, letting the flame caress her flesh briefly, knowing she was worthy of none of it. The Ember Lighting flame was meant to grant both participants courage, faith, strength, and protection from the wraiths. She then bowed her face to the pestle, drawing in a deep breath, smoke filling her lungs: the smoke was meant to bring them both healing and sustenance. She blew the vapors back out slowly, her essence supposedly mingling with the smoke. Up through the cathedral her essence had floated and twirled, up toward the flue high above, eventually to reach the air and take flight into heaven and dwell with Laijon. *A realm I will never deserve to live in. All my lies and deceptions. My hatred of Glade!*

It should have been Lindholf who offered me the flame. But her cousin had performed the same ritual as Glade, choosing his mother, Mona Le Graven, to administer his flame to first, and next his younger twin siblings, Lorhand and Lilith. Then both Glade and Lindholf and the other seventeen-year-olds had stood before the grand vicar as he draped a string of Ember Lighting beads around each of their necks.

Something about the Ember Lighting Rites made her think of the assassin's last note. *Study the Ember Lighting Song of the Third Warrior Angel found in* The Way and Truth of Laijon. *Pay particular attention to chapter twenty, verse thirty-one. Study it. Memorize it.* During Glade's and Lindholf's Ember Lighting, Denarius had read from *The Way and Truth of Laijon,* read the very verse Tala was to memorize. *And it came to pass that at the time of final Dissolution, he died upon the tree, nailed thusly, purging all man's Abomination, the sword of Affliction piercing his side. Thus all was sanctified. Upon the altar they laid his body in the shape of the Cross Archaic. And as prophesied in all Doctrine, Mia took up the angel stones. And it came to pass, the five stones of Final Atonement she placed into the wound manifest.*

Tala continued through the courtyard, angry at herself, feeling sorry for herself, contemplating the meaning of the Bloodwood's note, the scripture, the Ember Lighting Rites, trying to figure how it all tied in, if at all. As she walked, in some corners children screeched and giggled in play. Benches of ornately carved stonework dotted the gardens. Tala considered sitting but heard the faint chords of a familiar song strike up in the distance. She blinked, her gaze sweeping the gardens. The music was coming from near the spire. So she proceeded that way, the heels of the two Silver Guards clacking on the cobblestones behind her.

The Val Vallè princess, Seita, in leather breeches and billowy white shirt, sat on one of the garden's carved stone benches at the base of the tower. She was playing a mandolin, her fingers skipping lightly over the strings, the sound of her playing blending perfectly with the pale-lavender wonders of the garden. Seita's deft fingers were plucking mellow sounds, which was surprising to Tala, considering she knew not that Seita could play at all. What was stranger still was seeing her cousin Lindholf Le Graven and Val-Draekin dancing to the music not far from where Seita was sitting. Tala quickly realized that the two were not dancing at all but were rather randomly, and quite clumsily, walking toward each other, bumping shoulders, turning and repeating the process.

When she had first met him, Val-Draekin's shoulder had been in a sling. Yet it looked fine now. Tala knew that the Vallè healed quicker than humankind, but the repeated collisions with Lindholf seemed ill-advised. Plus, the warm beauty of the soothing chords emanating from Seita's mandolin seemed at complete odds to the awkward goings-on between Lindholf and Val-Draekin.

Tala observed the interplay for a moment. "Whatever are you doing, Lindholf?"

At the sound of her voice, Lindholf stiffened with a gasp. His dark eyes swung from Val-Draekin to her. Blond curls flopped across his forehead, hiding some of the burns from his childhood. The two Vallè turned and looked at Tala too, the last notes of Seita's song drifting away in the breeze. The Vallè princess stood and bowed, her green eyes like gemstones. The rich wood of her mandolin was polished, accentuating its delicate grain. Tala's eyes were transfixed by the exquisite beauty of the instrument.

"I'm teaching your cousin to be a thief." Val-Draekin bowed to Tala. "He'll soon be the best pickpocket in all of Amadon." He turned to Lindholf. "Won't you?"

"W-well—um." Lindholf's scarred face slackened even further as he stammered. "What he means to say is that—"

"I will show you." Val-Draekin handed a small leather purse to Tala. It was weighed down with coins. "Take these, too." He handed her a gold ring with strange Vallè runes etched into its surface, a string of black and green beads, and a small carved statue of Laijon that fit snugly in the palm of her hand. The tiny statue looked to be carved of walrus tusk and was bleached white as a sun-touched cloud. "Put the ring on," he said. "Tie the pouch to your belt. And hide the other items in the pockets of your doublet."

Tala did as instructed, tying the purse to her hip opposite the pouch that held the Bloodwood dagger that she always kept with her. She slipped the ring onto her finger and put the beads and statue in the pockets of her doublet.

Val-Draekin placed Lindholf's hand in hers. "Walk toward me as if you are out on a lovers' stroll." He turned and marched about twenty paces away and faced them.

Tala felt a moment of discomfort as Lindholf's clammy fingers entwined with hers. His restless dark eyes flickered from her to the battlements above. Tala's gaze also strayed to the walls of the courtyard, draped thick with green ivy. As she and Lindholf began walking toward Val-Draekin hand in hand, she wondered what her two Silver Guard escorts must think of all this.

The Vallè walked briskly toward them. His shoulder knocked into hers much harder than she was expecting. She lost hold of Lindholf's hand and stumbled, falling, until Val-Draekin reached out and caught her by the hand and upper arm. "Oh, I'm so sorry, m'lady," he stammered with embarrassment as he helped to steady her. "My most gracious apologies," he said, and released her when she had regained her feet. "I've been so clumsy today." He bowed. "Have a good day." He turned and kept walking.

"Look at your hand," Lindholf said eagerly.

Tala looked at both hands: the ring she had put on her finger was gone. Val-Draekin turned and held up the string of beads and tiny Laijon statue.

"He's been teaching me for a while now," Lindholf said, grinning from ear to ear. "He and Seita. They know many elf tricks. I can teach you someday, if it pleases you."

"When you get good enough at thievery," Val-Draekin said, "you scarcely need the accidental bumping and jostling, just deft hands. See?" He held the purse of coins he had given her and also her own pouch that held the Bloodwood dagger.

Icy fear slammed into Tala with such intensity she felt momentarily suffocated. She stared at the leather purse holding the dagger, feeling herself quake for breath. But anger overcame her panic. "Give back my *pouch*," she demanded, holding out her hand.

"As you wish." The sharp-eyed Vallè tossed the purse to her. Tala snatched it from the air, examining the cut thongs that once held the leather pouch to her belt. *He sliced right though them. He could have sliced my neck just as quickly!*

"I meant no harm," Val-Draekin said, and bowed.

"He meant no harm." Lindholf tried gallantly to respond in kind. "They can teach you the same tricks, like they taught us about defending against knives, remember?"

Of course, she remembered the lessons well. But learning thievery was different from self-defense. "Why would you want to learn such things?" She glared at her cousin.

"They are skills all should know," Seita answered. "Skills royalty such as we should learn, for there will soon come a day when murder, kidnapping, pickpocketing, blackmail, and even rape will be common currency in Amadon. The White Prince has attacked Gul Kana. It won't be long before he will be at the gates of this city. And then this castle may not be a safe place for even a princess and her two Silver Guards."

"What a grim thing to say," Tala fired back. "I won't hear it. Jovan will fight the White Prince at Lord's Point. Jondralyn travels there now to offer terms of war. You are wrong. Amadon will not be like that . . . ever."

"Then you have not read your own scriptures," came Seita's silken response. "Does not *The Way and Truth of Laijon* speak of Amadon's Fiery Absolution?"

"It doesn't mean we need learn the ways of a cutthroat."

"Well, I'm for learning it," Lindholf said as he straightened his posture. "I enjoy acquiring new skills. It keeps one busy."

"You are wise to learn all you can." Val-Draekin patted Lindholf on the back. "You are important, you and your sister. We should teach Lawri these things too."

"You can't teach Lawri," the words came tumbling forth before Tala could think to stop them. "She's sick and in Lind—" Tala snapped her lips shut at the last moment, realizing that she had almost given away Lawri's location.

Val-Draekin stared at her, as if waiting for her to finish, his piercing green eyes seeming to bore into her. Tala noticed that Lindholf's eyes never remained still but nervously flitted between them all. The intense look on Seita's face sent chills prickling up her back. It instantly felt as if something were crawling through her brain, pulling her thoughts out of it. Tala could feel herself losing all sense of balance.

"I'm sure Lawri will recover soon and be like a new person," Val-Draekin eventually said. "Wherever she is."

"And Sterling Prentiss will get what he deserves," Seita said casually. "I hear this castle is riddled with tunnels. You ought to get to know the secret tunnels if you wish to survive Absolution, Tala. Familiarize yourself with thievery and all the secret places of the city."

Even the Vallè know of the secret ways! Tala's vision blurred and her lungs cried for air. It felt as if a legion of dung beetles were digging into her mind, searching. Her mind spun with the implications.

"I don't wish to speak of Lawri or Fiery Absolution," she mumbled, her hand inside her pouch, feeling the comforting edges of the Blood-wood dagger in her hand.

"You're right," Seita said, and plucked at her mandolin. "Enough of this gloomy talk. How about another song?" Again, pure tones sang from the mandolin, a graceful song that hung over the breadth of the courtyard, brightening the air. Whether Seita played but a moment or all day, Tala knew not; she was so swept up in the music.

"You play beautifully," she said when the Vallè princess stopped.

"You did not know I played the mandolin?" Seita asked.

Tala pulled her hand from the pouch. "I regret to say I did not."

"No matter, there is much you don't know about me." Seita stood, holding the instrument out in both hands. "The mandolin, the lute, and the harp, three of the grandest instruments in the Five Isles. This one is constructed of rare Val Vallè olive wood—the only trees on the Five Isles that live for over ten thousand years, harder to find and far more scarce than even Sør Sevier Bloodwood trees."

Tala's heat pounded at the mention of Bloodwoods. Their very name sent shivers of dread through her. Still, the mandolin in Seita's hands was indeed one of the most amazing things she'd ever seen. Its beauty was transfixing; the dark grain of its wood was polished to a brilliant sheen and glowed with astonishing bright highlights of ochre in the sun.

"Do you know what the great Vallè minstrels do after a grand per-formance?" Seita asked. Tala shrugged, looking from the mandolin to Seita.

"They celebrate their performance by doing this." The Vallè prin-cess took the mandolin by the neck, brought it over her head rapidly, and in one unexpected motion swung it downward, dashing it against the stone bench. With a loud, slinging crack and twang, the precious wooden instrument shattered into a hundred pieces. Wooden shards exploded around the bench and clattered to the cobbles and turf. Stunned, Tala watched as Seita picked up a handful of wood splinters and tossed them out into the garden, saying, "And then they scatter the pieces among the audience to keep as mementos."

Tala and Lindholf shared concerned looks.

"Oh, it's not so awful." Seita picked up two of the bigger shards and held them out for both Tala and Lindholf. Lindholf took the offered piece of mandolin, eyeing it strangely. The shattered hunk of wood Seita handed Tala was about the length of a shoe and felt as light as a down feather in her hand. "They could be very valuable someday . . . very valuable indeed."

Val-Draekin's right hand was buried in the folds of his cloak. With his free hand he gestured for Tala to hold forth the shard of wood. She did, and the Vallè pulled his hand from his cloak, fingers covered in a curious white powder. He snapped his fingers, and a cone of bright fire appeared in the palm of his cupped hand.

Sorcery! Tala's mind screamed, her body frozen in place.

Val-Draekin ran the orange flame back and forth under the shard of wood in Tala's hand, warming her fingers in the process, then blew the fire out with a quick burst of air from his lips. He then casually wiped his once-flaming hand on his cloak.

"Indeed," Val-Draekin said. "That piece of wood is very valuable now."

† † † † †

Terror lashed through Tala's veins when she returned to her room. The great stone fireplace that dominated her bedchamber beckoned like a hollow cave. The secret ways lay beyond, calling her. *I should run, escape this stifling, wicked place and run far away and become another person.* But she knew not where she would go.

She grabbed her wooden stool and placed it before the cold stone hearth. Standing atop the stool, she put the shard of mandolin Seita had given her on the mantel's shelf. She placed it carefully, leaning it against the rough stone so that the polished grain faced into her room, taking the time to make sure that it was centered on the mantel just so.

Once done, she sat back on her bed and folded her hands on her lap. She looked up at what was left of the destroyed mandolin.

It's a cursed thing, she thought, shuddering, *hexed by Vallè magic and most definitely cursed.*

*Nary a drop of blood shall Laijon shed, nor a drop from another fall upon
him. Not until he swimmeth through the Gauntlet of Beasts. Not until he
receiveth his Baptism of Blood. When Laijon returns, you will know the
marks upon him. In that last day before Fiery Absolution, like a spark and
wave of flame, Laijon will reveal himself in the Hallowed Grove. And the
great Atonement Tree will become like a pillar of fire over him.*
—THE WAY AND TRUTH OF LAIJON

CHAPTER FORTY-TWO

AVA SHAY

17TH DAY OF THE MOURNING MOON, 999TH YEAR OF LAIJON
TOMKIN STY, GUL KANA

A mountain of burning Tomkin Sty carcasses marked the end of another Gul Kana village. Like the dead in Gallows Haven, Ava knew that this jumble of dead folk would not be given religious rites or properly buried. Their souls would never reach Laijon. She stood in front of Aeros' tent in a light cotton shift, trying to remain detached from the scene. After all, she knew none of them. The bloated, misshapen faces on top of swollen bodies meant nothing to her. The twisted hands reaching from the pile with grotesque fingers curled and crooked were not beckoning to her. And if they were, she cared not. *What can I do anyway?* The melting flesh dripping from their eye sockets and sagging jowls was a gruesome sight indeed, but a sight she'd grown inured to these past few weeks. The smell of burning flesh was thick, but again, nothing new to her.

They should have fled, fled like all the other farmers in all the hamlets between here and Gallows Haven. Everyone should just flee!

The shoreline north of Tomkin Sty lay silent save the sigh of the wind and the rolling of the waves, silent but for the cries of the crows as they pranced about, feasting on the scattered limbs of the dead. Gulls circled above aimlessly.

A child wandered untended, trailed by a mangy brown hound. The child wailed for a mother it would not find. The few other survivors of Tomkin Sty were granted no sympathy. Ten of them were chained together on the beach just a stone's throw below the White Prince's tent, where Ava now stood. Spades strutted back and forth in front of these trembling prisoners, shouting obscenities, blaspheming the Church of Laijon, and generally scaring the piss out of them all. One prisoner began singing a desolate lament. A portly woman with a pretty face and long dark hair, she belted out the tune from a throat worn raw from crying. That was until Spades ran a dirk up through her chest, ending it.

The cloudless sky above was smothered with a haze of smoke. The Tomkin Sty chapel was naught but a charred ruin. Most of the stone-and-timber buildings that once housed the weavers, potters, smiths, grayken hunters, and other assorted citizens of Tomkin Sty smoldered behind Aeros' tent. The Sør Sevier army had remained in Gallows Haven for nearly nine days before pulling up stakes and marching north, burning every farm and tiny hamlet on their riotous journey between Gallows Haven and Tomkin Sty. The army now reached almost ten thousand strong.

Aeros was intent on destroying Gul Kana entirely. Capturing the kingdom and creating havoc and destruction were not enough for him as it had been in Adin Wyte and Wyn Darrè. The Angel Prince wanted Gul Kana completely razed to the ground. He wanted few if any Laijon worshippers left strong enough to wield a sword against him. He'd as much as admitted that to Ava. His goal was Amadon. He not only wanted to destroy the great castle there but also burn and defile the Temple of the Laijon Statue, the Royal Cathedral, the Hall of the Dayknights, and the Grand Vicar's Palace, and then end the crusade by beheading Denarius at the foot of the Atonement Tree. *Such reckless hate and destruction, for what?*

Hunger ate at Ava daily. Any food Aeros offered, she refused. She drank a lot. The White Prince's tent was well stocked with spirits. That was her one solace—that and her few conversations with Gault. She was only granted leave to venture outside on certain days, and then allowed to stand just outside the open flaps of the tent—always under guard. Usually it was Gault. The bald knight was the only one who ever showed her kindness. For some reason, she found his presence reassuring. The man unhinged her senses. Sometimes he looked upon her with caring eyes; other times his eyes were as grim as a hailstorm. Still, she felt the tension and fear in her soul vanish whenever she found herself near him. He stood near her now.

With the sight of so much death and slaughter, she felt the wraiths roving restlessly through her. *I am impure. Useless and used and shriveled and old.* Her mind had been clothed in blackness of late. *Aeros has stolen the most precious part of me, those parts I'd saved just for Jenko.* Each time she lay with the White Prince was another wound upon her soul. *What must Jenko think of me now?* She hadn't seen much of him lately. Visions of her own bloody death clouded her every waking thought, her mind growing ever more pensive. She missed her wood carvings, missed the joy and comfort of creating, and she was beginning to conclude that life was no longer worth living. *Do I have it in me to just kill myself?* If Aeros or the Bloodwood were to offer to slit her throat, she might just nod in affirmation and be done with it. *But to take my own life?*

After each coupling with the Angel Prince, she roused all the energy within herself and called upon Laijon to strengthen and lift her up—lift her up into the lightness of his being and forgive her sinful state. Aeros termed it his "heavenly sessions." Ava just called it rape. She sought comfort in her prayers. It seemed that after prayer, clear thoughts followed, good thoughts and visions that held promise, promise that perhaps, beyond the next path, or over the next hedge-row, or down the next rutted road, could be found healing and light. Her belief in that future salvation was her only sustenance. *None can save me but for Laijon.*

Then she saw Jenko Bruk.

Ava was startled to see not only Jenko coming toward her but also Hammerfiss and the Wyn Darrè fellow, Mancellor Allen. The three marched up the grassy slope toward Aeros' tent. Upon their arrival, Hammerfiss addressed Gault. "I'm to train the Wyn Darrè boy in the fine art of how to stand post in front of our lord's tent."

Gault stepped aside and motioned for Mancellor to take his spot beside Ava. The Wyn Darrè with the black tattoos under his eyes did as ordered and stood still and stiff next to Ava, eliciting a chuckle from Hammerfiss.

"He seems to have the basics down," the red-haired giant grunted.

Ava's eyes were fixed on Jenko, hoping to pry some reassuring look or gesture out of him. But he kept his head down and would not meet her gaze. Dark locks of hair covered his eyes. She found herself looking to Gault for that reassurance she hungered for, and was swiftly caught up in the embrace of his eyes. Her heart warmed. But he dismissed himself and walked away. *He knows my shame.* She thought of her sordid nights with Aeros and guilt flooded her. She was not worthy of such reverence and kindness from Gault. She was not worthy of Jenko Bruk, either. That was why he would not meet her eyes. *He knows my shame too. I am used. I am useless to him now. Useless to any man.*

Hammerfiss' eyes had followed hers. He'd seen the looks she'd given Gault. The red-haired giant winked at her, then addressed Mancellor. "Stand here. Don't let anybody in that tent who ain't invited by Aeros himself. And don't go lettin' yourself in if you ain't invited, either. And don't touch the girl." He took one thick finger and tapped Mancellor on the forehead hard. "What I'm sayin' is, just use your own fuckin' common sense or Aeros will have your nuts for shark bait. Your training is at an end."

Hammerfiss left. Mancellor was now her guard. Jenko Bruk also stayed. His eyes finally met hers, and she felt her soul instantly shrivel. She could tell by the look on his face that he'd done *nothing* to stop the slaughter of Tomkin Sty, had maybe even participated in it. Cold dread crawled over her flesh. He was not like her anymore. Her eyes traveled the length of him; the slave mark on the underside of his wrist was nearly healed and barely visible. Hers was still raw and red.

"Soon you will wear their colors," she accused. But her voice sounded meek. Hunger clawed at her stomach again. She hoped Jenko would offer her something: food, a reassuring word . . . his love. *I would accept food from him, just not the White Prince.* Despite the weakness she felt in her bones, she stood taller and said again, "Yes, soon you will wear their colors like this traitor, Mancellor."

"What am I to do?" he answered, glancing at Mancellor. "What *am* I to do?"

"Fight back. Resist them."

"As you resist Aeros?"

Ava recoiled as if struck in the face. An unholy din rolled through her head—the black song of the wraiths now awakening, their evil tune prowling through her mind. "You should have saved me from *him*," she spat. But if the venom of her words had any effect on him, he gave no outward sign.

"I have witnessed the power of the Laijon we worshipped, of the bishop we followed, and it wasn't much." He looked fiercely proud of himself as he motioned with a nod to the Wyn Darrè now standing guard next to her. "You may think him a traitor, but Mancellor was once like us—a captive of Aeros Raijael. Look at him now, Ava. The Angel Prince only wishes for us to come unto him and prosper.

These worshippers of Raijael are not the demons we believed them to be as children."

At the sound of his blasphemous words, Ava thought she might faint. "Not the demons we believed them to be? They killed my younger brothers and sisters. Burned them as Ol' Man Leddingham tried to save them. Made you cut up your own father. If that's not what demons do, then what are they?"

"They are just like us."

"They've bewitched you. *The Way and Truth of Laijon* speaks of the followers of Raijael and their sorcerous powers, powers that can poison and turn the hearts of men. What you believe about them is naught but the conjuring of your fevered mind."

"What am I to do?" Jenko asked. "What must my father think? What must he think of what I did to him? If he even still lives. Aeros' victory over all of Adin Wyte and Wyn Darrè, and now his ease in destroying this part of Gul Kana, my own village, speaks for itself."

His words bore the stench of garbage, the stench of evil. The hunger and nausea festered within Ava anew, making her drowsy. A renewed hatred for Aeros enveloped her, cold and unrelenting. She tried to suppress the rage so she could speak with a clear head. *The Way and Truth of Laijon* claimed that hatred was the poisoned soil in which dark thoughts could take root. "You should have saved me from *him*," she muttered. "How can you stand before me and say what you've said?"

"A greater mercy had we all died, Ava," Jenko said, eyes now brimming with concern, confusion. "What am I to do but perhaps join them and live? What should each of us to do but try seeing things as our enemies do?"

She looked at him in astonishment, the wraiths now worming their way back through the crust of her brain like leeches, sucking at her will.

"I will never," she came to her answer in a weary, soul-sick breath, "see things as *they* do." Despair claimed her as she turned and entered the tent of her torturer.

† † † † †

The sounds of footfalls awakened her, along with murmuring voices. Ava opened her eyes to the grainy light of a few flickering candles. Even immersed in the luxury of Aeros' large, soft bed, she could not find comfort. Her loins ached, but not with the sweet, hungry ache she had felt after her first night with Jenko. This slow, throbbing pain was one dedicated to reminding her of the misery of her new life. She could smell the reek of her own sin and knew that no amount of scented oils or perfumes that Aeros gave her could defeat the stench of wickedness that had seeped into her every pore.

As the voices grew in strength, she began to make out individual words. Wearing naught but a short shift, she climbed from the bed and padded softly toward the flap of canvas that separated Aeros' bedchamber from the bulk of the tent. She set her eye to the narrow slits between the canvas drapes. The room adjacent to Aeros' bedchamber was rimmed with candlelight as two shadowy figures stood there. The first was the Angel Prince. But what really got her gut jumping was the sight of the other man swathed in the black leather armor—the Spider, or as she'd recently learned, Spiderwood, sometimes also called the Bloodwood. The sight of him always sent shivers through her. It seemed this dark-haired man could read her mind with but a glance. Ava contemplated retreating back into the softness of Aeros' bed before they caught her spying.

But Aeros spotted her and bade her enter. Slowly, reluctantly, scared of the Bloodwood, she slipped between the flaps of the tent and into the room with the two men.

"What do you think of her?" Aeros asked the dark-haired man. "A treasure."

"Seems she'd be lively enough. Though that young man she fancies appears destitute of genius. I don't know what potential you see in Jenko Bruk."

"You did not know Mancellor when we first took him," Aeros said, his face so white it appeared pale blue next to the darkness emanating from the Bloodwood. "The Wyn Darrè boy was also full of bitterness and hate. There is no triumph more satisfying than turning your worst enemy into one of your greatest allies. Mancellor is as one of us now. He has earned his place at my side."

"And you plan on grooming the Gallows Haven fellow as well?"

"Jenko Bruk is destined to bring great treasure unto me. I have foreseen it. He will prove the most loyal yet. Spades will make sure of that."

"Spades," the Bloodwood said with distaste. "You place far too much faith in one so unbalanced."

"She's a crazed, malignant one, to be sure." Aeros smiled wickedly, winking at Ava. "But that unhinged ferocity of hers gets a deadly point across to those we capture. I like that. I need that. Someone like Spades must do the things that need doing. Violent things that I wish to avoid doing myself. It is how my father uses Black Dugal. For the dirty tasks.

"Or does Dugal use my father for his dirty tasks?" Aeros stepped lightly across the expanse of rugs on the floor and knelt before a gold-filigreed chest set in the corner of the room. At his touch, it opened soundlessly. With great care, he lifted its intricately scrollworked lid. Reaching into it, he pulled forth an ox-horned helm that sparkled shards of dancing yellow candlelight and dazzled Ava's eyes. Aeros handed the helm to the Bloodwood, who held the relic up to the light, examining its burnished surface and intricate gold and silver inlays with a careful eye.

"What do you think?" Aeros asked.

"An old war helm of curious make," the Bloodwood said.

Curious make. Something about the shiny helm struck Ava as frighteningly odd. It was the two horns sprouting from the helm that seized her eyes. They were not oxen at all, but something else entirely, something foreign and unrecognizable.

"Of all my Knights Archaic," Aeros said, "I knew only you would be the least impressed. The Bloodwoods hold no craven yearnings for ancient relics or sacred things."

The Spider ran nimble fingers over one of the helm's strange horns. "You believe this to be the *Lonesome Crown* of Laijon."

"Gault *pretended* to be less than awed when I took it from King Torrence on the Aelathia Plains. But he noticed it, all right. How could he not? He desires much of what I possess." Aeros' eyes wandered to Ava. "Gault knows the importance of these things I collect." He looked at Spiderwood. "Do you?"

"Black Dugal educates all in his care about the mythology of the stones, and of those most closely associated with them. But we Bloodwoods give scant credence to such fables. I've read portions of *The Moon Scrolls of Mia* . . . among other such writings."

"So too has your brother, it would seem."

"Hawkwood will soon be dead." The Spider offered the helm back to Aeros.

"Stabler's report of a Bloodeye mare at the bottom of a pit full of spikes concerns me greatly." The White Prince took the helm and placed it back into the chest. "I fear Rosewood is dead."

"Do not underestimate Rosewood."

"We've heard no word from her. Sending her so near Shawcroft alone could have been a grave mistake."

"That was more your father's decision than Dugal's."

Aeros pulled from the chest a small black swatch of silk and handed it to the Bloodwood.

Spiderwood unwrapped the cloth and his eyes widened. Cradled within was a green stone, flat and oval with polished round edges.

"An angel stone," Aeros said reverently. Smoky waves of green color passed over the stone's smooth surface, and its translucent innards seemed to dance and glow.

Witchcraft! Ava's mind screamed. *Sorcery!* The sight of the glowing stone wrapped icy chains around her heart, constricting it. She found it hard to catch her breath. Had Aeros called it an angel stone? *The Way and Truth of Laijon* held that the stones of the Five Warrior Angels were taken into heaven with Laijon.

Anything the vile White Prince said is surely not to be believed!

The Spider held the stone up to his eyes—bloodshot eyes.

"There is only one thing a cross-shaped altar can mean," Aeros went on. "If we're to believe what Stabler said about those mines above Gallows Haven, it would seem another one of the weapons of Laijon has been discovered."

"If so, Shawcroft's ward now has it."

"Even more reason to find the boy. All the stones and weapons of our Lord Laijon are fated to find their way to me. It is written in the stars."

"You seem sure of yourself." The red streaks in the Bloodwood's eyes almost glowed in the light of the stone as he scrutinized it.

"I am as confident that all the stones will come to me as you are that Rosewood is alive and that your brother will find his way to you."

The Bloodwood peeled his eyes away from the stone. "Jubal Bruk has surely reached Amadon with news of our attack by now. Hawkwood will seek me out. He wishes me dead. He knows what is hidden within the writings my father keeps. Hawkwood knows many truths the Brethren of Mia dare not admit to themselves."

"Well then, let us hope he brings us another one of the five pillars of Laijon when he comes to kill you."

"It will be Hawkwood who dies."

"A confrontation I would pay to see."

Spiderwood gave back the stone, eyes lingering on its translucent surface. "I hold no fealty to whatever legends you ascribe to, my lord. Still, I can see how such a splendid little gem could pull at a man's mind and twist it."

Aeros wrapped it in the silk and placed it back in the chest. "That is why none alive should know of it but the *three* of us." He stood, looking at Ava. She remained motionless, resolved to not even blink. Her determination was, for a moment, absolute.

The Bloodwood said, "Gault was there with you on the Aelathia Plains when you found the stone."

"Aye."

"He will try and take it."

"Unfortunately . . . yes."

"So you will agree to my plan?" the Spider asked. "You know what must be done?"

Aeros gave a slight nod. "Word of what we've done to Krista will reach Gault eventually. Perhaps Black Dugal has already enlightened the girl to the fact that Gault is not her father. If he gets wind that she is part of Dugal's Caste—well, Gault is not quick to anger, he's calm as a pond, but when he does become angry, his rage knows no bounds."

"Aside from creating one's own Bloodwood daggers from the souls of the condemned," Spiderwood said, "part of the Sacrament of Souls is to forsake all one's kin. A Bloodwood is to become fatherless and motherless in the eyes of Black Dugal. If he has not already enlightened Krista as to her true parentage, he soon will. Or he may have some other do the telling for him. Dugal can be devious in his purpose."

"Would Gault know of this Sacrament of Souls and what it entails?"

"The man is an astute observer of all things. I am sure he's heard rumors of the Sacrament of Souls. He will rush to her rescue for sure."

"I cannot have that," Aeros said. "He cannot ruin our plans for her. Much rides on Krista and the tasks Dugal will set her to."

"Dugal also knows this."

"So it must be done, then?" There was hesitation in Aeros' question.

"Dugal has sanctioned our actions."

"Gault is not even a full-blooded man of Sør Sevier." Aeros' face twisted in loathing. "Dugal is right. He *should* die. Most of his own kin are naught but goddess-worshipping witches who King Edmon either killed or had married off to noblemen like Agus Aulbrek. The match of Agus and Evalyn Van Hester was deemed unholy even by the Laijon worshippers in Amadon. Gault is less than a bastard. As the *Illuminations* say, 'Tainted blood is ever treacherous.' He is, by nature, unholy, susceptible to betrayal. There is growing proof of his treachery. He has seen the stone. He *desires* it. And he has, of late, exhibited naught but rough lust for *other* things closest to me."

Aeros' gaze sliced into Ava, the danger in his look real and palpable. His piercing eyes now had her in their binding, unwavering grasp. Hazy candlelight played off Aeros' silky hair in yellow waves as he continued, "Gault thinks me blind to his subtlety. But I see how he appraises my Ava. I have foreseen his betrayal."

Ava swayed on her feet. Nausea now enveloped her and she felt faint. *I am so hungry.* But she did not want to collapse again. She had already done so once earlier that day, in front of Jenko and Mancellor. *I am dying.* Over the last two weeks, she had become willow thin from lack of food. She feared she would wither away, both body and soul. *But wouldn't it just be better to wither and float away into death's embrace?* Over the days, she had stayed steadily drunk on a mixture of red wine and other such drink.

What the Bloodwood said next turned Ava's veins to ice.

"Gault will no longer be a problem for us. I'll see it done in Ravenker. Suspicion will not fall upon you, my lord Aeros. I assure you."

The brave and pure of heart are recorded in scripture, to be sure, but so are the craven, the venal, and the foolhardy. No man is perfect. Remember, even the Warrior Angels were once brawlers, rogues, and thieves. One single man, even be he the reincarnation of one of the Five Warrior Angels, cannot be totally without blemish. Only the reincarnation of Laijon himself is to remain spotless of all stain.
—The Way and Truth of Laijon

CHAPTER FORTY-THREE

NAIL

19TH DAY OF THE MOURNING MOON, 999TH YEAR OF LAIJON
SWITHEN WELLS TRAIL ABBEY, GUL KANA

The dark-haired man came walking out of the fog. Face of a raptor and eyes black as death, he drifted toward Nail like a wraith through the mist, moving with a fluid gait. The stranger's every step across the loamy soil was a haunting reminder of the black-cloaked shade who had killed Shawcroft.

Clouds had drifted in over the mountains earlier that morning and settled over the abbey. Nail had been lounging on a rock, enjoying the solitude, with Zane's dog, parchment, charcoal, and the beginnings of a new drawing in hand—a blond girl sitting at the base of a tall standing-stone, flowers in her hair.

But upon seeing this new stranger, he leaped from his perch. The man's dark hair was shoulder-length. He wore a leather harness bearing two cutlasslike swords crossed over his back, their grips and pommels jutting above his shoulders. These hilts, sprouting a profusion of serrated spikes, looked like antlers above his head. He also wore a brace of long knives at his hip. Slung over his shoulder was a black cloak stained with dirt.

Beer Mug eyed the newcomer with concern, ears pricked. That the dog had not even been alerted to the man's approach was in itself alarming. Nail's hand was trembling as it latched onto the hilt of his sword and pulled it free. He brandished it before the man menacingly. That the stranger held out his hands in peace scarcely eased Nail's mind.

A stumpy, bearded fellow came waddling out of the mist next, leading two roan palfrey horses, a quizzical look on his rough-hewn face. "Put away that blade, boy," he said. "You're liable to slice yourself to ribbons."

"I've been in many battles," Nail said, then immediately felt stupid for saying such a thing as he noticed the pocked and well-used look of the short fellow's iron half-helm, leather armor, and the heavy spiked mace strapped to his back. Nail realized that the squat and grizzled man was in fact a dwarf. He'd seen a few dwarves in his lifetime, but only from afar—ofttimes dwarf trading ships from the west coast of Wyn Darrè would make port in Gallows Haven for a night. Nail and the other boys in town would run to the shoreline to see if they could spy a dwarf sailor or two.

Stout and short, runty and ugly, this dwarf before him had a round, surly face hidden behind a tangled and wiry beard. The dwarf smiled, and that, too, did little to ease Nail's mind. His guard was up.

It was the tall, dark-haired stranger who made the first introduction. "Hawkwood," he said, holding forth his hand. Nail backed away, sword up, ready.

"Roguemoore." The dwarf bowed. "Who might you be?"

"I don't see why you need to know my name." His eyes bounced between the two.

The two strangers exchanged a glance. One of the roans behind them whinnied. Beer Mug approached the dwarf, a low growl in his throat, then sniffed around the stubby fellow. After a moment's investigation, he began to wag his tail.

"We're looking for Hugh Godwyn." The dwarf's tone was affable. He petted Beer Mug on the head. "The abbey we seek should not be far. The fog has turned us around some. I doubt we're too extremely lost, but if you know of the abbey, please tell us. We've journeyed far."

After his initial fright at seeing the two materialize out of the clouds, there was something about the smaller of the two travelers that Nail liked.

"Is the abbey near?" the dwarf asked again. "Do you know Godwyn?"

Bishop Godwyn had told Nail and the others that the abbey was a way station for weary travelers along the Swithen Wells Trail. "The abbey's not more than a hundred paces behind me in the fog," he said, hardly worried about divulging the abbey's location now, figuring the two would stumble onto it anyway. "I'll take you to Godwyn."

"Splendid," the dwarf said, removing his iron half-helm and bowing to Nail again.

"So you've been in many battles?" Hawkwood asked him.

Nail nodded as matter-of-factly as he could.

The man's eyes were sharp and keen. "Then I would be honored if you were to show me your skill with a blade."

† † † † †

The clouds had lifted, revealing the mountains around the abbey. Still, the air was heavy and damp, the ground mossy and wet as Hawkwood's cutlass bit halfway into the pig's corpse before he yanked the blade free. Blood oozed from the slippery sack of flesh. The beast hung from a rope, spinning slowly, a barbed hook through its mouth, its curly tail dangling just above the grass. He reached out and stopped the corpse from spinning. It was suspended from a bowed timber, the length of which was wedged between two crumbled stone walls just south of the abbey, remnants of an old horse stable.

Hawkwood thrust his cutlass straight into the pig's belly, then pulled it free just as swiftly. "Striking flesh is different from clacking gunnysack swords against each other," he said. Nail, Stefan, Dokie, Liz Hen, and Beer Mug gathered around him. "Flesh is soft. It gives. Muscle and bone often catch the blade, jerking it free from your grasp when your foe falls back. It takes more effort, strength, and speed to remove a blade from a combatant's body than to strike into it. Nothing worse than finding your own sword stuck in someone's rib cage whilst someone else cleaves your head from your neck."

He motioned for Stefan to step forward and handed him the blade. "Thrust deep. Hanging as it is, the pig's vitals and ribs are in much the same position as a human."

Stefan jabbed straight into the pig's midsection but was thrown off balance when the pig spun. He struggled to regain his footing, both hands tugging at the hilt, wary of the serrated spikes along the sword's hilt-guard. When the cutlass yanked free, he tumbled backward into the sand as the pig, triumphant, twisted on the rope above.

"Tossed on his butt by a dead swine." Nail laughed and took the cutlass from Stefan. It was a magnificent sword with a long, curved blade, sleek and, but for the thin film of pig's blood and guts, without blemish. The hilt, wrapped in black leather and sporting a profusion of the serrated black spikes along the hilt-guard, was troublesome to hold. Still, he gave it a go. He thrust the cutlass into the pig, keeping his footing while ripping the blade free, the same as Shawcroft had taught him to rake a loosened chunk of stone away from a rock wall with his pickax. The pig swung, a deep hole in its side.

"Good," Hawkwood said. "Now hold the sword with both hands and swing at it with might and power, as if you want to slice the beast right in half."

Wary of the spikes, Nail positioned both hands tightly around the hilt and found himself naturally placing his feet in one of the exact same stances Shawcroft always insisted on. He chose the stance he was most familiar with—his favorite one, the easiest one. He whipped the blade back behind his head, front knee up, foot off the ground, full weight on his back foot. Torso and shoulders bursting with speed and fury, he swung. His full body weight was behind the blade as he brought it flashing around. The curved blade bit deep, and his follow-through sent pig guts and blood spraying off into the trees, the beast swinging upward wildly on the rope.

When the pig ceased twisting and twirling on the rope, they could all see Nail had nearly cut the thing in half. Only its spine held it together.

"Nicely done." Hawkwood nodded to him, admiration on his face. "That was power unlike any I've ever seen. What was that footwork before you swung? I haven't seen its like in ages."

"Just something I learned once." Nail was taken aback by the compliment.

"Well, you're a natural. Keep it up. It will serve you well."

Nail swelled with pride until Liz Hen snatched the cutlass from his hand and jabbed it with a shout into what remained of the mutilated pig. She jerked the weapon out easily. The pig remained still. Nail found himself scowling. Beer Mug barked happily. "The girl's a natural too," Hawkwood said, taking the blade from her.

"I killed a Sør Sevier knight," she boasted, puffing up her chest. "And I got the sword to prove it."

"I helped with that," Dokie piped in.

"Good for you two." Hawkwood sounded genuinely impressed.

"Well, anyway." Liz Hen nodded to the dangling pig. "I'll be cooking that swine for you later, Ser Hawkwood the Handsome," she said with a curtsy and a smile. "I'm just cutting it up now." Since the man had arrived, Liz Hen literally glowed in his presence.

Hawkwood smiled at her graciously and handed Nail the cutlass along with a makeshift wooden shield. "Let's test your skills as a fighter." He pulled his other cutlass from his shoulder harness and sighted down the blade.

Nail swung the shield to the ready position, dropping his left leg back a pace and raising the cutlass Hawkwood had given him. He wondered if his stance looked sloppy to the man. Nail noted that there was always a cool intelligence pouring out of the stranger's burning black eyes. He stepped back, crouching with the rim of his shield just under his eyes, the tip of the cutlass wavering uncertainly.

Hawkwood danced to the side and struck with a swiftness Nail had never seen before, his blade naught but a thin blur. Both sword and shield went spinning from Nail's hands. Liz Hen clapped. She and Dokie had perched themselves on the stone fence not far away. Dokie's legs swung, booted heels thumping rhythmically against the rocks. Liz Hen stopped her clapping and smiled sarcastically at Nail. Glowering at the girl, Nail picked up the cutlass and shield, wiping the dew from the blade. His previous confidence was now gone.

"Use only the sword this time," Hawkwood said. "I can tell the shield hampers you. It may be of use to lumbering knights laden down with battle armor, but I aim to teach you speed and quickness to go with your innate strength. Truth is, most sword fights are over in a couple of swings. Any man can heave a sword about, but it's the footwork that separates the common fighter from the master. And that is clearly what you have a natural aptitude for." Nail dropped the shield. Hawkwood tossed him his other cutlass. Nail caught it by the hilt with his free hand, still cautious of the serrated spikes along the sword's hilt-guard.

"And all warriors should learn to fight with two blades in hand," the man continued. "Swords are attacking weapons, whereas a shield is for naught but defense and a waste of precious speed and energy. Why fight with one sword when you can fight with two?"

Hawkwood picked up a dead aspen branch from the ground. He snapped it in half over his knee and wielded both broken pieces like two swords. "Learn how two swords feel in your hands, learn their weight, their reach. Discover how hard you can swing them before they throw you off balance. Swing until your arms grow so weary you cannot continue. We can incorporate the footwork you already know later. Try and hit me. I will block and parry with the sticks if and when I feel the need."

Footwork I already know? With two swords in hand, Nail had zero idea how to begin. So he just stepped forward and swung one blade after the next. Hawkwood blocked every blow with ease.

"Look at that," Liz Hen jeered. "Even with two swords, Nail can't hit him."

Nail advanced on Hawkwood, cutlasses swinging wildly now. The man backed away, thwarting Nail's arcing attacks. He could tell that even wielding naught but tree branches, this dark-haired fellow before him had soldiering skills beyond what Jubal Bruk had ever taught the conscripts of Gallows Haven.

Though he had just met the man less than an hour ago, Nail wanted to prove to Hawkwood that he could truly fight, that he wasn't just flailing away. And the more he swung, the more he wanted to land a blow. He did not want to draw blood, but just land one solid strike. For some reason, he wanted this man's approval again.

To Nail's great alarm, one of the first things Bishop Godwyn had done upon Hawkwood and Roguemoore's arrival was to take them directly into the chapel's library and show them the battle-ax and the blue stone. "I can finally sing praise to *The Moon Scrolls of Mia,*" the dwarf had said. "That the years of toil and sacrifice of so many have finally borne such joyous fruit is a confirmation of my faith in Mia." The dwarf hefted the ax in his own rough hands and gazed with great wonder upon the shiny blue stone, tears forming in his eyes. Though Hawkwood did not touch either the ax or the stone, he did look upon each with reverence. Nail's stomach had been in knots as the dwarf handled the stone. It had been clear from the start that the bishop and the dwarf shared a history—theirs was a natural comradeship. Nail figured it would have been nice had Godwyn alerted them that he was expecting the dwarf and his friend—though Liz Hen certainly didn't mind the arrival of Hawkwood. She fawned and doted from the start. She was especially thrilled when Hawkwood challenged Nail to a duel.

And now here they were, Nail wildly swinging two cutlasses in seemingly useless gestures at a man who backed away effortlessly and parried with ease. After a time, Nail grew accustomed to the weight and balance of the swords and they became more comfortable in his hands. He gained strength in the realization and became more calculating in his swings, speeding up, pressing the attack.

But soon his arms grew weary, leaden. Sweat plastered errant strands of hair to his face. Panting and tired, arms sore, he was determined to keep going. He swung and swung until he was breathing so hard he thought he might pass out.

"Enough," Hawkwood said, dropping the aspen branches. He cast a direct and steady gaze at Nail. "I only wanted to get a sense of you. I can gauge a man's character by watching him swing a sword. And I can pretty much glean everything I need to know about a man by watching him swing two swords. You have a natural ability, Nail. You exhibit a grace and ease when using them. But your mind is distracted. You wandered off for a moment there. What were you thinking of?"

"I was thinking about you and the dwarf and the bishop." Nail handed the two cutlasses back. "I was thinking about the ax and the stone that Godwyn showed you."

"Ah, yes, the ax and the stone. When Roguemoore and I were looking at them, I sensed that they weighed heavy on your mind. But in battle, your enemy will care not about you or your problems, for he will have issues of his own. And the man who buries his worries away before battle is the man who will return alive to dig them back up. You have the makings of a good swordsman. The problem will not be in teaching you skill with the blade. You've enough confidence in yourself. That is clear. But more importantly, what you need learn is concentration. You must not let your mind wander. I believe if you conquer your own mind, you could be good with a blade, very good, one of the best. And I could teach you." Hawkwood bowed. "That is, if it pleases you."

The thought of this man teaching him sword craft pleased Nail greatly.

† † † † †

"If what Liz Hen saw is true," the dwarf said, "then Jubal Bruk probably reached Amadon some time ago. Jovan now knows of the sacking of Gallows Haven and has, more than likely, come to Lord's Point via the king's tolls to meet with the White Prince and negotiate a surrender."

"How could Jubal have possibly reached Amadon in such a state?" Godwyn asked. "The girl said that he was without arms, without legs, just tar-covered stumps." The bishop sat across the narrow table from Roguemoore and Hawkwood. Zane's dog was under the table, nuzzling against Godwyn's rough boots contentedly. The table was near the back of the chapel. Two tall candles sat atop its burnished surface.

The three men along with Nail were drinking ale and nibbling on the sourdough bread that Liz Hen had baked earlier that day. Up late and unable to sleep, Nail had slipped from his bunk and through the kitchen toward the chapel, his goal the library beyond, and then to the battle-ax, and more importantly, Shawcroft's satchel, if it was not locked away in the bishop's private chamber as it had been since they'd arrived. The note in the secret compartment plagued his mind.

It was such a small thing, that note, and yet it contained a mystery. And he meant to read it. But at the door of the kitchen, he'd heard the men talking and entered. They bade him sit with them. So he had.

"Armless and legless and stuffed into a wooden box," Godwyn added. "Any man would die from wounds so grievous."

"Not if my brother plied him with tenvamaru serum," Hawkwood answered. "He would survive with relative ease. Jubal Bruk would reach Amadon well rested."

"Pointless brutality," Godwyn murmured.

"Enna Spades is full of cruelty," Hawkwood said flatly.

The dwarf looked at his partner, hard eyes unflinching. "The country you hail from is the very definition of cruelty."

"I cannot argue."

"Jovan mightn't even bother meeting with Aeros," the dwarf said. "My feeling is he will send Leif Chaparral or perhaps even Sterling Prentiss to offer up the white flag."

"What then should we do?" Godwyn asked, taking up a crust of bread, ripping it in two, and stuffing it into his mouth. "Do you think he really will surrender?"

"What we must do is concentrate on retrieving *Afflicted Fire* and *Blackest Heart* and the two remaining angel stones that Ser Roderic left in the north. That is where Ser Roderic would have us go, were he here."

Hawkwood said, "I suggest we head north to Ravenker, gather what word we can of the White Prince's advancement up the coast, and carry on to Lord's Point." He turned to the dwarf. "Meet up with your brother at the Turn Key Saloon as planned."

"And take these kids from Gallows Haven with us?" Godwyn asked.

"Aye."

"They've seen enough grief to last a lifetime. They are not like the Bronachells, inured to gruesome gladiator matches at ten years old.

They hail from simple farm folk and fishermen; hardy, yes, less pampered than royalty, true, but when Gallows Haven was sacked, the brutality was a traumatic shock they will suffer the ill effects of the rest of their lives. To march them back into the thick of more such trauma is reckless. Even if we make it beyond Lord's Point without running into Aeros' army, rumor grows that oghul raiders are becoming more brazen in the north near Sky Lochs and Deadwood Gate. The young people needn't be a part of this anymore."

"Every young person in this land best get used to such trauma," the dwarf said bluntly, his deep-set eyes on Nail. "This young man and his friends are bound to the Five Pillars of Laijon, their fates tied to the stones. They have each of them held the angel stone, and that is a bond not easily broken. That the boy, Dokie, has survived a lightning strike, sharks, and arrows is no small thing. They are as the Brethren of Mia now, privy to information few know. Aeros may still have his Knights of the Blue Sword hunting them. They will come with us. The time for coddling the youth of Gul Kana is at an end."

Nail bristled at the notion of someone thinking him naught but a coddled youth. Hadn't he proved his mettle? Was surviving the siege of Gallows Haven and leading his friends through the mines and icy mountains and finding them safety worth nothing? The anger simmered as he felt the blood rising up through his face and cheeks.

"I have no fear of going to Ravenker with you," he said, staring unflinchingly back at the dwarf. "I will fight against the White Prince again if I must. I am not afraid."

"It is good that you volunteer," the dwarf said. Godwyn and Hawkwood appraised him flatly. But nobody spoke beyond that, and the silence was unnerving as they ate.

Nail sat there, uncertainty clouding his thoughts. Many of the things the men talked about were now needling at his mind. There had been more talk of Shawcroft and angel stones. *But will these men answer my questions?*

He broke the silence. "There is much I wish to know about a great many things. But I fear you will keep things from me, as Shawcroft did."

"We did not stop you from hearing our discussion," Roguemoore said, "and invited you to sit, even. We've nothing to hide from you."

"Nothing to hide?" His eyes were trained on the dwarf. "That does not seem possible. Few men speak the truth, especially to me." His eyes moved smoothly to Godwyn before returning to Roguemoore.

"What is it you wish to know?" the dwarf asked.

"You promise the truth?"

The dwarf appraised him with a raised brow. "I give you my word."

"You were a friend of my master?"

The dwarf nodded. "I knew him well."

From his periphery, Nail noticed a sharp frown creasing the bishop's brow. Still, he asked, "Was Shawcroft really Ser Roderic Raybourne, prince of Wyn Darrè?"

"Aye, he was."

"Then where is my twin sister? Who was my mother? Who was my father?"

His questions elicited a sigh from Godwyn, who sat back on his chair and looked straight at the dwarf. Hawkwood looked up too, fixing Nail with a stony gaze.

Roguemoore remained still for a moment before saying, "Shawcroft told me nothing of your sister or mother or father. I only know that he watched over you as a favor to King Borden Bronachell." The dwarf looked down into his mug of ale. "That is the truth." He took a huge swig of his cup.

Nail swallowed hard. A deep silence filled the chapel. He wished to push the dwarf further. But he'd learned the hard way with Shawcroft—pushing too much only made other answers more difficult in the coming. He would drop that subject of his parentage and take a different route. "You claim Ser Roderic found two angel stones hidden in the north? I was with him then, in Sky Lochs. I was still a small boy when we left there. I don't remember any of it. He never showed me any angel stones, leastways. I was a little older when we mined near Deadwood Gate. But again, I remember no angel stones." He paused, his mind on the cross-shaped altar in the Roahm Mines, the stone Gisela had found, and the ax. He thought of the Vallè woman Shawcroft had burned and her dead, red-eyed mare in the pit—wondered if the Vallè Bloodwood had any bearing on what they were talking about now. "Godwyn said Shawcroft has been searching for lost angel stones all his life. Is this why Shawcroft claimed men in black cloaks with demon-eyed horses had hunted us? Is this why Shawcroft was killed? For these angel stones?"

"Yes." The dwarf's answer was quick and left Nail in deep thought. It was obvious that the men at the table with him believed that the blue stone he'd taken from the mines was one of the angel stones, and that the ax was the *Forgetting Moon*. And that Shawcroft had found other stones and weapons of Laijon.

There was much that still didn't make sense to him. "If the ax is really of Laijon, and the stone is really an angel stone, then what are you going to do with them? What use are they to anyone? Why was my master set upon finding them? Did he find them? Did he give them away? Who has them? Or did he keep them in Gallows Haven and I never saw?"

"He found them and then left them where he found them," the dwarf answered, "to be retrieved when the time is right. Traps of every make were set about those mines in ancient times. Shawcroft was adept at sniffing out traps like that, circumventing them, or rendering them useless. But once the angel stones and weapons were found, what traps your master dismantled, he restored, then sealed the stones and weapons back up safe."

"But why would he do that?"

"He made a mistake with the first stone he found," Hawkwood

answered. "Gave it to his brother, a green stone, along with *Lonesome Crown*."

"And that started a war," Godwyn added. "A war that has so far . . . gone badly. Aeros would have those around him believe his crusade is to reclaim lands stolen from Sør Sevier long ago. But it is the stones and weapons he most desires."

The dwarf went on. "And now the time is right to gather the stones your master once found. The return of the Five Warrior Angels and Laijon is at hand. *The Moon Scrolls of Mia* say that for Laijon's return to come to pass, the weapons of the Five Warrior Angels and the five lost angel stones must be gathered. Not only that, but the stones and weapons can only be used by the rightful heirs of the Five Warrior Angels. Only then can Fiery Absolution be averted."

The dwarf looked at him expectantly. Nail looked back at him blankly.

"At the time of Fiery Absolution," Hawkwood continued, "it will be one of those five heirs who will step forward and claim his place as Laijon reborn and destroy the armies arrayed against Amadon. Laijon returned will use the weapons and stones to do this. That is the Brethren of Mia's cause: locating all five weapons, all five angel stones, and then giving them to the heirs of the Five Warrior Angels."

Godwyn added, "It is Laijon's will that we do this, or all of Gul Kana will fall under the yoke of Raijael and the beasts of the underworld will return. It is the sole task of the Brethren of Mia to bring about the return of Laijon. And Ser Roderic Raybourne, the man you knew as Shawcroft, has done more than most to hasten Laijon's return."

Nail's head was full of even more questions. He looked squarely at the bishop, cleared his throat, and began. "If Laijon needs us to have the stones and weapons, then why doesn't he just provide them for us? Why did Shawcroft have to search for them? Why all the mysteries hidden in scrolls and hidden treasures in altars? Why did Shawcroft go to the trouble of searching for the ax from under the mountains? And why must you now risk journeying back to Deadwood Gate and the Sky Lochs to retrieve the ones he left there? Why would Laijon make it so hard? For my part, I do not believe any of it."

Godwyn frowned. Hawkwood leaned back in his chair. The dwarf looked at him straight and answered, "You have seen the ax, *Forgetting Moon*, with your own eyes. You have held an angel stone."

"Laijon is real, Nail," Godwyn said. "It's just that the version of Laijon's history and gospel that you have been taught by the likes of Tolbret is apostate. *The Way and Truth of Laijon* is a false record. It has left the likes of Liz Hen and Dokie, and even you to a certain extent, hollow and confused."

"I am aware that Shawcroft believed little in the Church of Laijon," Nail said. "Yet he always gave me leave to attend Eighth Day service in Gallows Haven when I desired. But as far as the angel stones and weapons go, why would an all-powerful Laijon hide them? Why create all this work to find them. It's a ridiculous god that would behave thus."

The bishop stared at Nail with rigid, cold eyes. "Skepticism. Sarcasm. Cynicism. These are all traits of the weak-minded, Nail. Sometimes Laijon requires great sacrifice. We must humble ourselves before our Lord and prove our worthiness, and only then will Laijon see fit to save us from Absolution. Mia says that nothing in life that is great and worthwhile comes easily. Otherwise, how can we appreciate it? The hardest days of your life are before you, Nail. But you cannot face such tribulation alone. You must learn to let your guard down, if but a little, and you must learn to place your trust in others, even Laijon. Only then will you achieve your potential and do what must be done."

"You speak as if all this angel stone business has something to do with me."

"It does, in a way," Roguemoore said. "You have touched the angel stone, and that is no small thing. Dormant for so long, each stone has the potential to claim the first who lays hand on it. That person will forever be drawn to the stone and the stone to them, be they an heir to one of the Five Warrior Angels or not. Let me ask of you, Nail—does the thought of someone holding the stone cause cold despair to grip at your heart?"

Nail felt a chill fold around him like a blanket. He remained nearly motionless, only reaching forth to grab a chunk of Liz Hen's sourdough bread from the bowl on the table. Nervously he chewed, elbows on the table, thinking of Gisela lying in the snow, angel stone clutched in her frostbitten hand. She'd been the first to touch the stone. "It just seems things should be less complicated," he mumbled, tongue thick in his mouth.

"So you wish things to always be made easy for you?" Roguemoore asked.

Sounds like something Shawcroft would've said. "Nothing has ever been easy for me." Nail scowled again, trying to ignore the dwarf's frigid glare. He'd not meant to sound cynical. He did not want this dwarf, whom he somewhat liked, to think ill of him. He wanted to be a part of something. Wanted to belong. Wanted to believe in something. *But do I want to become like Shawcroft, a cold murderer?* Bloodwoods like the Vallè woman had been hunting Nail his entire life, or so Shawcroft had claimed. And these men had as much as confirmed it. Did he want to become one of the Brethren of Mia, gathering lost angel stones and weapons of Laijon? The notion held some excitement. And he generally did like the men sitting at the table.

He raised his head and looked straight at the dwarf, finding resolve. "It is true, nothing worthwhile comes easy. I have learned that lesson. All of us have, Stefan, Dokie, Liz Hen, me. We all of us have had it hard. But we all of us survived. I cannot speak for them, but even despite my skepticism, I would desire to help you retrieve the stones of Laijon that my master once found in Sky Lochs and Deadwood

Gate." He looked at Godwyn. "For a number of reasons, really. To discover if they really do exist as you claim. And more importantly, to go to those places where I once lived with Shawcroft. To retrace my heritage. Perhaps I can learn the answers to my questions there."

The three men exchanged glances, none of them saying a thing.

"If you'll have me," Nail went on, "I will pledge you my honor, Ser Roguemoore. I am in need of a new master, someone to look after me, anyway. I would desire to finish what Shawcroft started. I pledge to work on behalf of the Brethren of Mia in his stead."

The dwarf slid from his chair and bowed low to Nail. "I accept your pledge. But I will ask much of you. For the journey I take will be toilsome and full of much peril. The burdens I will place upon you may be too difficult to bear. For I fear, eventually you may discover the answers to those questions you seek. If so, do not lose heart, but take faith in the knowledge you gain. Because as you serve me, know this: I truly believe that to some are given the gift of faith. Yet for others, faith must be earned. And it is clear to me, Nail, that part of your journey in life is to acquire faith—faith in yourself, faith in others, and mostly, faith in Laijon's plan for you."

*With much cleverness, the Last Warrior Angels have written destructive words
into their* Way and Truth of Laijon, *that it is better one man be slain than an
entire kingdom fall into destruction and unbelief. Thus, Avard Sansom Bronachell,
first Lord of Amadon and first king of all Gul Kana, began his society of
Dayknights, purging the "rotten stink" of Mia goddess worship from the Five Isles.*
—THE MOON SCROLLS OF MIA

CHAPTER FORTY-FOUR

STERLING PRENTISS

19TH DAY OF THE MOURNING MOON, 999TH YEAR OF LAIJON

AMADON, GUL KANA

Sterling put his eye to the thread of light emanating from the crack in the wall. He had finally found the girl. Backing away from the light, he pushed his fingers into the small fissure, prying at the brick. He heard the small chunks of dried mortar rain to the floor on the other side as he widened the unstable crack and put his eye back to it.

Lawri Le Graven was not more than four paces from him, her lips blue, eyes closed. She lay on a cot in the center of the next room. Candles flickered on the table at the foot of her bed. And from what little Sterling could see of the poor girl, she was reduced to naught but skin and bones, her chest barely rising and then falling with breath.

The dank and dim closet was adjacent to her brother's bedchamber.

Two of the walls were made of fairly solid-looking stone. But with the other two walls, there were places where the brick had crumbled until just slats and mortar remained, and one of those walls was no more than a wedged mass of broken stone. Sterling could see that someone had lined the two crumbling walls with thick cedar planks to hold up the disintegrating stone. There were chains and irons along with leather leg harnesses fastened high on the walls. At some point, the room had been used as a prison cell.

Sterling stood on his tiptoes for a better view and pain shot through him—the lingering effects of his injury when Glade Chaparral had cracked him with the Vallè chain-mace. He wasn't fully healed; the wrong kind of movement hurt beyond imagination. He shifted the weight of his legs, giving his still-sore groin room to breathe in his leather armor.

With the discovery of Lawri, Sterling would soon get his revenge. Of that there was no question. The lies Tala had spread about him would soon be at an end and his honor would be restored. With that thought, Sterling closed his eyes and took three deep breaths. His heart felt heavy with weariness from battling back the wraiths that had plagued him ever since suspicion for the girl's disappearance had fallen upon him. He knew that Jovan would have had him hung days ago if not for the holy vicar's intervention. Sterling knew that he owed Denarius and the Church of Laijon his life. He was now questioning some of his own choices. He'd loved Borden as a brother, but his own recent involvement with the Brethren of Mia had thus far netted him nothing but trouble.

But that was over now. He would soon return Lawri to the care of the vicar and regain the trust of the king. He had resolved within himself that if he found Lawri, his days of helping Roguemoore and his schemes were at an end.

Sterling again focused his eye on the crack in the wall and Lawri Le Graven. Before the sickness had shriveled the skin up around her bones, she had been such a beautiful young woman—seventeen and ripe with beauty. Such perfection could only be found in youth, Sterling believed.

So how can her brother be so ugly? Lindholf Le Graven, with his dark beady eyes, crooked grin, and bread-dough face covered in scars. That sad sack of rotten cabbage didn't seem to be the most lively candle in the sconce, either. Once Sterling regained favor with Jovan, he would see to it that both Glade Chaparral and Lindholf never advanced in the Silver Guard. And they would never become Dayknights so long as Sterling lived. With that thought, he took one last gander at Lawri through the crack in the wall and backed away, satisfied.

† † † † †

Sterling hadn't gone far before realizing he was lost. He knew the secret ways of Amadon Castle could be tricky. That was why he always marked his trail. A scratch from the tip of his sword marked the floor before him, yet he would swear on the grave of the Blessed Mother Mia that he had never been in this particular corridor before. It was fragrant with dust and rat droppings, old stone and rotting wood, and completely unfamiliar. Not a few paces from his mark was a stairway that led up to a crooked, narrow doorway at the corridor's far end. A spray of red light shone from a crack under its ill-fitting door, as if there were a large hearth fire in the room beyond.

He drew his sword and scratched an X over his previous mark, and the faint whisper of metal on wood drifted up around him, sending a shiver up his spine. He cast a wary eye in each direction. But there was nothing. Blade in hand, he advanced up the stairs toward the narrow door and the faint red light, his senses now attuned to any danger.

At the top of the stairs, he pressed his ear to the wooden door. There was no sound. He set his shoulder to the door and pushed.

With a creak, it moved inward and red light rained over him. The room was warm and as he stepped in, sweat immediately sheathed his forehead. High on the far wall was a large stained-glass window, the noonday sun blazing through. Each pane was such a deep shade of red, a scarlet radiance showered down upon everything in the high-ceilinged room. The place was lined with dusty wooden benches. Its white-plastered walls were so discolored and streaked by smoke as to be almost black. Along the near wall hung a tall tapestry, a beautifully stitched likeness of the Blessed Mother Mia gracing its center. This scarlet-hazed room looked spacious enough to hold twenty people. A stone altar in the shape of a cross sat in the center of the room.

Anger flared within Sterling. It was forbidden to construct an altar in the shape of a cross. He shuddered at the thought of what fell rituals may have been played out in this unholy place. There were ashes and fragments of bone strewn about the floor, and the altar's cross-shaped stone top was stained with a dark substance. Dried rivulets of blackness ran down the sides of the evil construct like tar. His eyes followed those twisting, weeping trails of blood down to the floor.

Then he saw the carvings. At the base of the altar, they stared back at him in all their unadulterated blasphemy: jagged teeth, scaly flesh, burning eyes, hooked wings, and snakelike tails. *Beasts of the under-world!* It felt as if his heart had stopped beating. He could not tear his eyes from the hundreds of tiny foul images.

Dragons!

Something stirred above. A sound no more than a lonely breath, the swirling of the stale, dust-filled air. He whirled, sword at the ready. There was nobody. He lowered his blade, feeling foolish that the carvings had spooked him so.

Yet he heard it again, like a hollow whisper. Frantic, his eyes roamed the room, sword held high, ready. But there was nothing. He relaxed the blade a second time and wondered about his own sanity.

"Where did Hawkwood and the dwarf go?" an indistinct voice said from all around him, the sound of it mellow and easy.

Sterling jumped back, eyes swiftly scanning the room. "Show yourself," he commanded, bluster in his voice, sword firm in hand. "Show yourself now."

Nothing. A moment passed. Then, as rich as fine wine, the voice moved over him a second time. "Hawkwood. Roguemoore. They set off from Rockliegh Isle on a boat. I know you arranged horse and transport. Have they made you a full-fledged member of the Brethren of Mia? You and Culpa Barra? I can see glimpses of the future. Some call it fey witchcraft. Some call it the workings of the wraiths. But I saw your death. In this very spot. Saw it many moons ago."

He was slowly circling now, eyes on everything at once. "Show yourself, I say!"

"What did Hawkwood find under the city?" the voice asked. Sterling faced the door he had just come through. *Was I followed?* But now the voice came at him from behind. "I will pull the information out of you. Then I will have one of my pets kill you . . . though I doubt she will enjoy the task."

He caught a flicker of movement in the red light above. Turning slowly, sword ready, he looked up. A dark silhouette clung to the stained-glass window there. It took a moment for his eyes to adjust to the brightness of the light filtering around the figure, but once they did, Sterling could see there was somebody perched on the wide window seat, leaning casually against the stone window frame, faceless, dressed in a black hood and black leather armor, a glinting black knife in one hand.

"The grand vicar rapes the girl," the dark figure continued, voice now sensuous, deep and liquid. "But of course you know all about Denarius' dark lusts, don't you? You stand guard at the doors and let him have his way."

His spine tingled as if chill fingers crawled the length of it. "That the holy vicar chooses to bless the sick in private is none of my concern," he answered.

"It is not just prayers and washings and anointings the vicar performs."

"You falsely accuse the holy vicar. You are misled."

"You *like* to watch him with Lawri. But she is meant for another, one more important than even your vicar."

"Are you the assassin who attacked Jovan?"

"Aren't you the clever one. I was given the name Silkwood by my master, Black Dugal. I am Bloodwood."

Bloodwood! Shards of ice lanced through Sterling's veins, slicing nerves with each beat of his heart. "Come down from there and I will show you the grand vicar's true wrath. Or do you dare not?"

"Oh, I dare." The assassin silently dropped from his perch, almost seeming to float as he landed silently, knife still in hand, glinting.

"It is my sworn duty to protect the honor of the grand vicar," Sterling said rapidly, formulating a plan of attack. The cross-shaped altar still separated him from the dark stranger. He measured himself against the size of his foe. Sterling was no slouch when it came to swordplay, and the Bloodwood was not that big. If it came to a fight, he figured he could win it quickly. But for him to launch a strike now he would have to navigate around the altar, which could prove tricky. He figured it best to keep chatting whilst he strategized. "All of the vicar's actions are sanctioned of Laijon."

"You have the brains of a shit bucket," the assassin said. "But I forget. You are all the same. Inadequate. You damn sick people, so beholden to your false Laijon and your power-hungry quorum. You will all soon be exterminated."

"You dare blaspheme the vicar and quorum of five before one of the Dayknights?" Sterling's voice rose in anger as he stepped to the side, getting set to spring. The black-clad figure mimicked his step—they were now circling the altar like two gladiators, sizing each other up.

"Who is worse, the one who rapes, or the one who enables the rapist?" the Bloodwood asked. "Or do you secretly wish to fondle the young woman yourself? I can see your sins, Captain. That you've raped both women and boys and even children is written on your face."

"I'll have your tongue for that." Sterling's mind was in turmoil. This Silkwood was accusing him of things that no man should. Tala's allegations were far-reaching indeed.

"Oh yes, I can see your sins." The dark figure leaped onto the altar. "For your soul has been laid bare before me." Those previously hidden eyes under the hood now glinted with evil, piercing through the scarlet haze, aimed right at him. What he saw in those two black orbs, both pulsing with utter wickedness, drained him of all bluster. Sterling took one faltering step back. The room now took on a more reddish hue, which spread in crimson waves of light over the cross-shaped altar and the figure now poised atop it.

He came to realize that this wasn't a confrontation he was likely to win. It now seemed this Bloodwood could read his mind, control it even. He *did* feel inadequate. He knew his lack, but that in itself wasn't the problem. It wasn't his present state of cowering before battle that hurt his pride either. It was the fact that he hadn't served the holy vicar the way he should have. His sins were laid before him now. And the most grievous sin: he'd gone against Denarius, he'd gone behind the vicar's back and worked in consort with Jondralyn and Culpa Barra to help Hawkwood and Roguemoore escape. *And this assassin knows! Perhaps Denarius knows too.* Sterling cursed his own weakness.

On the cross-shaped altar, the dark figure loomed over him like Laijon's wrath, ready to strike him down. Sterling took another faltering step back, stumbling into the rough stone wall behind him. He noticed his sword hand trembled, and for a moment he felt it wasn't attached to his arm at all but was instead a foreign, beastly claw belonging to someone else entirely, some dolt who scarcely knew how to wield a weapon of any kind.

Then the assassin pulled back his hood and a face was revealed.

"You," Sterling muttered.

And the now familiar apparition struck—struck like a serpent, like venom flowing. The black blade had scarcely come into view and it was buried in Sterling's chest just over his heart and then pulled free, red and wet. Sterling whimpered.

All feeling left his limbs; stumbling, he felt his face smack against the wall and slide down, the cold, coarse stone eating at his flesh. The last thing he saw was crimson waves of scalding brightness. And the fading memory of a familiar face as it hovered over him before all dissolved into total blackness.

The face of the Bloodwood, the face of the Val Vallè princess, Seita.

Take up your cross and wield it in righteousness, for it is a blade sent from heaven. Only the three-fingered sign of the Laijon Cross over the heart can stave off the wraiths and the nameless beasts of the underworld. Only the three-fingered sign of the Laijon Cross over the heart can stave off Laijon's wrath, those Lightning Spears of Heaven. So let the sign of the Laijon Cross be like a sword unto you.
—THE WAY AND TRUTH OF LAIJON

CHAPTER FORTY-FIVE
TALA BRONACHELL

19TH DAY OF THE MOURNING MOON, 999TH YEAR OF LAIJON
AMADON, GUL KANA

Glade crawled into the small, dark chamber, letting the tapestry fall into place behind him. He wore all black—boots, pants, jerkin, and belt—with a shortsword at his side.

Tala felt along the stone wall until she located the wooden door above her head, pulled the Bloodwood dagger from her belt, and slipped the black blade into the crack. She heard a click and the door retreated inward with a rasp. With great effort, she pulled herself up and into the opening. A short corridor was disclosed before her with a ladder at its far end. She pulled herself the rest of the way through, dusting off her tan leather pants and maroon woolen shirt. She had been in these passages before, with Lawri, the day that she had first met the Bloodwood. "Follow me," she said.

"Whatever you say, m'lady." There was a hardness in Glade's voice.

Tala knew that Glade Chaparral, of all people, did not like being ordered about, especially by her.

She heard him climbing, and he was soon right behind her. "I only follow you on this fool's quest to see the humiliation on your face when there is naught to it, Tala."

He had been curt with her since she had sent him false word that Jovan wished to see him in Sunbird Hall, only to show him the latest note from the Bloodwood once he'd arrived. Reluctantly he read the note. After perusing its contents, he made her show him the black dagger mentioned in the note. "And you will come with me," she'd insisted. The dagger was tucked into her belt now.

Just this morning, Tala had found the note from the Bloodwood in her room. After praying over Lawri in Lindholf's chamber, she had stepped into her own rooms and immediately sensed something amiss. The shard of mandolin that Seita had given her under the Swensong Spire three days ago—the shard that she had so carefully placed in the center of the stone mantel shelf—had been moved. It had only been moved a few inches from where she had set it— enough to get her attention. When Tala had plucked the shard of wood from the mantel, she found the Bloodwood's note scratched in tiny letters onto the back side.

The note had read:

> *Before the light of day fades away, return my black*
> *dagger to the red room with the cross-shaped altar.*
> *There you will be given one last task. You will know it*
> *when you see it. Your clue to accomplishing the task is*
> *hidden in the verse I asked you to study. You will know*
> *that the task is complete when you've found the antidote*
> *for Lawri. Once you have the antidote, make haste, for*
> *Lawri's time of Absolution is near. Give the antidote to*
> *her and she will become as new. She will become even*

*more than she was before, ready for the greatness that is
her destiny.*

*Bring Glade Chaparral. Now that you have divulged
our secrets to him, I am forced to give him a part to play in
our game. He should play it well.*

Leave my black dagger at the foot of the altar.

It didn't take Tala long to recall the room with the cross-shaped altar. She remembered it from her foray into the secret ways with Lawri a moon ago. But it was the holy book that still vexed her; chapter twenty, verse thirty-one of the Ember Lighting Song of the Third Warrior Angel. It read, *And it came to pass that at the time of final Dissolution, he died upon the tree, nailed thusly, purging all man's Abomination, the sword of Affliction piercing his side. Thus all was sanctified. Upon the altar they laid his body in the shape of the Cross Archaic. And as prophesied in all Doctrine, she took up the angel stones. And it came to pass, the five stones of Final Atonement she placed into the wound manifest.* The verse made no sense to her, especially in the context of procuring the antidote for Lawri's poison.

Tala feared all she'd done for her cousin so far amounted to nothing but a sordid culmination of failures. Lawri was near death, each breath slower than the next.

Tala imagined the days a little more than a moon ago when her own cares had been relatively simple ones. She wondered whatever happened to those I-lost-my-shawl, should-I-stay-in-bed-a-little-longer days, those what-to-have-for-breakfast conundrums, those all-important should-I-scrub-my-hands-before-dinner questions, those don't-forget-to-say-my-prayers nights, those runny-nose, bad-hair days. Lawri's plight had certainly put her life into perspective, though. *My life before seems so ridiculous.* She knew she could no longer live in blissful ignorance again. Not after seeing Jovan and Leif together, not after seeing the grand vicar blessing Lawri.

Glade was staring at her in the dark. Just the sight of him could fill her heart with all kinds of terrible, conflicting emotions. Mostly loathing, even though his auburn hair glowed beautifully in the narrow ray of sunlight streaming down from a crack high above.

"Up there." She pointed down the narrow hallway toward the wooden ladder at the far end. Together they crossed the length of corridor. Glade examined the ladder, which rose up and disappeared into a dark hole in the roof. It was rotten, but Tala climbed anyway, knowing from her previous venture here that it was safe. Glade followed, mumbling his displeasure with the entire journey.

The ladder emptied them out into another room, more of a crawl space really, and dark. Kneeling, Tala bumped her head on the ceiling anyway but located the trapdoor in the floor with its bolt cut off. Together she and Glade lifted the wooden door up and over and descended a cramped circular staircase and through a series of dimly lit rooms lined with wood-plank boxes and piles of discarded, moth-eaten clothes and rusted pottery. Tala felt rat droppings crunch under her feet. She had to duck scores of hanging spiderwebs. The stench of dead mice permeated the air. The dreary squalor of the unkempt place nauseated her. They came to another wooden door, also with a broken lock, and they both slipped through into a much wider and well-lit hallway. Pink light filtered in at regular intervals through the arrow slits in the walls. She knew there was a spectacular view of Amadon through those slits, but she passed them by without a second thought.

Their journey through the dank air of the secret ways passed in silence, a silence laced with fear. Tala now had the sense that they were being followed as they traveled through a few more dark, narrow corridors, down a twisting stair, and into the glowing room she sought. She opened the door to the red-hazed chamber.

Tala stopped in her tracks. Glade bumped into her from behind, cursing softly. But she paid him no mind; her eyes were focused on the naked man lying faceup on the altar before her. Her heart felt like a lump of cold wax in her chest when she realized who it was. "Bloody Mother Mia," Glade muttered, and shoved his way past her. "It's Prentiss."

Sterling Prentiss lay on his back, arms spread in the shape of the cross, chains binding both wrists, the ends of both chains bolted to irons in the floor. The Dayknight captain was staring straight up, mumbling. A wild thatch of dark hair covered his chest and stomach all the way down to dark, curly hair around the flaccid stub of his groin.

"His tongue is cut out," Glade said, leaning over the altar. "And look at these other marks on him. Rotted angels of the underworld."

A small puncture wound was just discernable through the chest hair above Sterling's heart. On the mound of his belly there was a three-inch vertical slit in his stomach. Blood welled from the sliced flesh.

"We must unchain him," Tala said, swallowing the awkward lump in her throat.

"Certainly so," Glade said, and for a fraction of a second, the tone of hardness that had been in his voice earlier was absent and a momentary glint of compassion shone in his eyes. "Actually"—he wiped the expression away and his demeanor changed abruptly— "why should we?"

"How can we not?" Tala answered, confused. Clarity seemed far beyond her reach. She had trouble focusing on what he was saying. "If we do nothing, he will die."

"I doubt anyone even knows he is in here."

Tala caught the dismissal in his tone. "The person who did this to him knows that he is here," she said. "We could be implicated in the crime."

Glade studied her in a distracted way—a contradiction somehow only he could pull off. "Whoever did this will not confess, and neither will I say anything, or you. There is nothing to be done for him."

Tala could tell that even now he was working out some plan in his head. In the dim red light of the room, the purity of conceit and callousness in his eyes now burned like hot coals.

"It is time for my brother to be the Dayknight captain," he said. "I say, the quicker Sterling dies, the better."

Tala looked at him aghast—unbelieving. "How can you be so unfeeling when a man is dying right in front of us?" she asked, her fingers searching for the Bloodwood's black dagger at her hip, her fingers curling over its hilt. She kept a tight grip on the knife—if only to steady her quivering arm.

"Leif is meant to be the leader of the Dayknights." The words were coming out of him husky and feverishly ripe with bloodlust. "Your own brother wants it. Jovan only waits for this doddering fool to die before he makes the move, and now here he is, lying in chains before me, all but dead."

"He's not dead yet."

"True." Glade said, pulling a dagger from the folds of his own jerkin. "He is not dead yet." Then, gripping the blade tight, Glade bent over Sterling and drew the edge forcefully across the man's heaving neck, opening it wide.

Tala gasped, her eyes afire with the insanity of it all. Dark blood bubbled from Sterling's lips and poured from the new wound spanning the width of his throat to cascade down over the altar.

The directness of Glade's sudden, murderous act stole her breath. Frozen in immobility, she could do naught save watch in terror as the last of Sterling's life flowed away. Her body was tense at first, and then it shook with nerves, as if her muscles were trying to crawl from under her skin. Her first indrawn breath was congealed agony, thick and rancid and clawing up her throat like wraiths from the underworld seeking escape. *He's more like Leif than I'd ever imagined. Could this Glade Chaparral before me really be the same person I knew as a child?*

"What have you done?" The words slipped through her pursed and pallid lips. Her head hammered whilst sparks of rage formed behind her eyes.

"I've just secured a future for my brother." Glade swiped the dagger over Sterling's hairy chest, wiping away the blood. As he did so, Tala's heart thundered. She had a strange aching to touch Sterling's dead face. It was a morbid yet powerful desire that pulled at her. She had to take a step back to break the spell.

Glade rammed his dagger back into the sheath at his hip. "Now, let's find this magic antidote for Lawri and leave this damnable place behind."

Tala just stared at him, watching in sick fascination as he searched around the altar. He looked under all the benches, crawling, scouring the floor with his eyes, even folding back the Mia tapestry on the wall and looking there.

"There is nothing here," he said. "Have you led me into some trap, Tala?" Glade's eyes roamed the room almost frantically.

Tala's mind raced. *What do I do?* The air she breathed was so stuffy, cloying. She felt as if she were sinking under water. *Laijon forgive me. Lawri forgive me. I have failed.* She closed her eyes and silently prayed, making the three-fingered sign of the Laijon Cross over her heart. And when she opened her eyes, there was something that flitted at the edge of her mind, a sudden understanding.

"'And it came to pass that at the time of final Dissolution.'" The first words of the Ember Lighting Song of the Third Warrior Angel leaped from her mouth. But she stopped there, clamping her mouth shut. Still, she knew that in those words lay the answer to the Blood-wood's final riddle, right at the edge of her grasp, unreachable.

"You can stay here and pray to Laijon all you want," Glade said. "I'm leaving."

Tala grabbed the sleeve of his shirt and held him fast, not wanting him to go, the answer so near. She recited the rest of the passage. "'He died upon the tree,'" she quoted, looking at Glade, "'nailed thusly, purging all man's Abomination, the sword of Affliction piercing his side.'"

She released Glade and whirled to face the altar. "'Upon the altar they laid his body in the shape of the Cross Archaic.'" Her eyes went to Sterling's arms, spread wide upon the cross-shaped altar, and then to the three wounds in the man's body: the severed throat, the puncture just above his heart, and the small slit in his stomach. . . .

"'And as prophesied in all Doctrine, Mia took up the angel stones. And it came to pass, the five stones of Final Atonement she placed into the wound manifest.'"

Her eyes focused on the three-inch slit in Sterling's belly. The room now hummed with a music that would not quite form into melody—or was the sound only in her mind? Could Glade hear it too? It was hard to tell. He made no movement behind her.

"'She placed into the wound manifest,'" Tala repeated the last line to herself, almost in a whisper. And then it hit her. The horror of what she now must do sank in.

She placed into the wound manifest!

The Bloodwood had hidden the antidote inside Sterling!

The castle shivered beneath her boots. Sickness and fear threatened to overwhelm her. It seemed the room was too loud and red and bright, although she knew that it wasn't the case at all. The place was deathly silent. Sudden exhaustion hit her with force. She wanted to simply lie down and rest.

"Are you done praying?" Glade still watched her, his eyes silver glints against the darkening red haze of the room. "What are you waiting for?" he asked. "Let's go."

Tala stepped closer to Sterling and reached out her hand, running her fingers over his chest hairs to the slit in his belly. The hole in the flesh of his stomach was just large enough for someone to slip a hand into.

But dare I? Lawri's life depended on it. So, closing her eyes, bracing for it, Tala plunged her right hand into the wound.

"You fool," Glade muttered. "What wraiths possess you, girl?"

Wraiths indeed. Holding her breath, she began probing the steaming stew of Sterling's guts. It was warm inside the man's stomach, hot even, so hot she nearly jerked her hand right back out. But gritting her teeth, she resolved to finish the job. As she worked the hot, squirming lumps of his intestines and vitals aside, she was glad Sterling was dead. The Bloodwood had obviously planned for her to attempt this gruesome search whilst the man was still alive.

After several excruciating moments stirring Sterling's guts, a growing feeling of dread began to grow within Tala. The futility of what she was doing hit her. Despair crept upon her with the swiftness and ease of a serpent. And just when she was about to abandon her search, she felt it—a solid tubular object. At first she thought it was just another bone, a rib, perhaps. But this bone was not attached to anything and fell into the palm of her hand so snugly it nearly made her shout in surprise.

She pulled the object forth almost triumphantly and held it out for Glade to see, arm slick and steaming with globs of red. The thing in her hand glowed green through all the blood, and for a moment Tala thought she had pulled forth one of the fabled angel stones itself. But as she uncurled her fingers, she could see that it was not a bone, nor a stone, yet rather a small vial filled with a green, luminescent liquid. It was then that Tala felt the unseen eyes greedily boring into her from all around. She turned, pulling the Bloodwood dagger from her belt with her left hand, brandishing it. But there was no one in the room with her save Glade.

He was looking upon her with utter disgust. "What have you have involved me in?" he asked, eyes on the glowing vial. "I will not easily forgive you for making me a party to it. Only one overcome by the wraiths would behave so. You are no lady."

"It was you who killed Sterling," Tala said abruptly, disappointed in the meekness of her own voice. Feeling as drained as an empty wineskin, she just couldn't muster up anything in the way of emotion. "Who will forgive murder?" she tried more forcefully, holding up the vial. "You slit a man's throat in cold blood and you're disgusted by this?"

"Lest you forget, it was you who brought me here." He stepped up to her, anger and desperation in his voice. "We keep this a secret." His hand lashed out, grabbing her chin in a viselike grip. "All of it. Secret. Neither one of us speaks of it. Ever. Not Sterling's death. None of it. Do you understand?"

The pain where his hand tightened on her chin was intense. Anger filled her now. Rage. Fury. She struck at him with the dagger, but he effortlessly knocked it away with his free hand. It spun to the floor, clattering softly against the base of the altar. He whirled and snatched it up in a flash. She backed away, turned, and tried to run, but he was on her quickly, latching onto her arm, spinning her around.

Gripping her chin again, Glade forced her face up to his, black blade at her throat.

"Let me go," she demanded.

For a moment his eyes bored into hers with malice; then they traveled down to the green vial still clenched in her hand. "I helped you find that for Lawri. So now you will do as I say." He leaned into her until their faces were no more than a hand span apart. "Aye, I killed Prentiss," he snarled, pressing the blade against her flesh. "He was a useless fool. He needed to die. Your own brother would agree. I did Gul Kana a great service today." His lips brushed her trembling cheek. "But if you tell anyone that it was I who killed Sterling, then I will kill you as easily as I killed him."

He released her, shoving her back roughly. "And I will kill Lawri, too."

"You will not touch her," Tala growled as she slipped the green vial into her tunic. She hadn't journeyed this far for her cousin just to have this spoiled brat threaten to kill Lawri.

"And I suppose you think you can stop me?" Glade thrust the dagger out threateningly between them. "I will have no problem gutting her like I just—"

Tala clapped as hard as she could. She connected perfectly. The dagger spun from his hand and to the floor and skipped across the room.

Both surprise and pain filled his eyes as he drew his own blade and lunged for her.

It was instinctive, a reflex, swift and brutal: her right knee flew straight up between his legs with crushing force as she ducked his blow. His eyes bulged as her knee knifed into his groin like a thunderbolt and lifted him off the ground. Just as quickly, he folded to the floor, curling into the fetal position, gulping for air, his dagger no longer in hand. "Bitch," he managed to spit out between heaving gasps, and then a stream of vomit splattered the floor under him.

He tried to stand, clutching at the altar for help.

"You can find your own way out of here." She spun and made her way to the door alone, a throbbing pain in her knee, a sweetly satisfying pain that dulled by the second as she hurried from the room.

"I will kill her," he gurgled as she left him there. "Tell anyone, I swear it, and I will kill her."

† † † † †

But Lawri was already dead when Tala returned to Lindholf's room— dead from the Bloodwood's poison.

"She just stopped breathing," Lindholf cried breathlessly, devastation on his face. "I'm sorry, Tala, I didn't know what do to. I watched over her like you asked, wiped her forehead with the cool rags. I didn't know how long you'd be gone. I've been sitting here in despair watching her breaths become more shallow. Jovan will have us hung for this."

Panic hammered Tala's heart as she rushed to her cousin's side. When she felt Lawri's cold, sunken skin, anguish settled over her like a wintry blanket. *Dead! It couldn't be! After all I've been through . . . so much . . .*

She pulled the vial from her pocket. The liquid inside still glowed with a feverish green light. Tala uncorked the vial and poured a dab of the serum on her fingertip, its touch cool against her skin. She brushed her finger over her cousin's pale lips. The green potion instantly dissolved when it touched Lawri's flesh, then disappeared, drawn down into her skin, leaving behind the fresh, healthy color of life.

"Help me, Lindholf." Hope roared through Tala's veins as she wiggled her fingers into Lawri's lips, prying her mouth open. "Hold her head still."

Lindholf grabbed his sister's face with both hands and held her chin up as Tala emptied the Bloodwood's antidote down her cousin's throat.

Tala sat back, empty vial clutched in her hand.

Lawri's eyes flew open, and she sat bolt upright in the bed, coughing. "I had a dream!" she blurted excitedly.

Lindholf was wide-eyed. To Tala's astonishment, all color had returned to Lawri's flesh, and she looked almost completely healthy, if a bit meager and starved.

Lawri's willowy arm lashed out, and she grabbed Tala by the hand, lively eyes boring into hers. "I had a dream about you, Tala."

"Are you okay?" Tala could feel the warmth of life's blood pulsing through the palm of her cousin's hand. She was too stunned to cry.

"I'm fine," Lawri said, eyes darting around the small gray room and its chipped, broken mortar held together with cedar planks, brow furrowing when she spied the chains and irons and hooks high on the walls. "Where am I?"

"In a storage room just off your brother's chamber," Tala answered. "Are you sure you feel okay?"

Lawri looked around the room, confused. Her gaze lingered on her twin for a moment, and then she addressed Tala again. "I had a dream about you. You were married to Grand Vicar Denarius."

"But vicars and bishops can't marry," Lindholf said.

"That's exactly what Denarius said in my dream." Lawri kept her eyes fixed on Tala. "But Jovan claimed it was high time vicars and bishops be taken in marriage. And then he promised you to Denarius. In my dream you were betrothed to the grand vicar, Tala. I attended your wedding."

How art thou fallen from such lofty grace, O Laijon, father of all Mourning? What a great travesty that the hordes of the deceived think thy Mantle of Atonement lies in Amadon with wretches and fools, when it was so clearly bestowed upon your One and Only beloved son, Raijael, your true and pure Dragon Claw.
—THE CHIVALRIC ILLUMINATIONS OF RAIJAEL

CHAPTER FORTY-SIX

GAULT AULBREK

20TH DAY OF THE MOURNING MOON, 999TH DAY OF LAIJON
SOUTH OF RAVENKER, GUL KANA

Ava Shay bade him come in. At first he refused. Then, seeing the sober expression of fear and worry on her face, he'd reluctantly pulled open the folds of Aeros' tent and slipped inside. It was the first time Gault had been alone in the tent with the girl.

She walked in front of him now, leading him into the center of the entry room. The wind of the girl's passage brought a faint scent to Gault's nose, the enticing perfume of young womanhood and a freshly washed body. It also carried the smell of recent sex—a familiar aroma that hit him in the chest like an ax. She had lain with Aeros.

The Angel Prince had just received word from Spiderwood that the scouts he'd sent into Ravenker had reported a small band of Gul

Kana knights bearing King Jovan Bronachell's standard camped north of the town. At the news, Aeros had left, taking the Blood-wood with him, leaving Gault alone at his post in front of the tent.

Ava's sleeve brushed his hand. He jerked away as if stung, then realized she'd been watching him intently from the corner of her eye. Despite his best efforts to remain indifferent to the girl, some-thing about her was growing more alluring every day; his undeni-able attraction to her now extended beyond the notion that she was naught but a curious reminder of his dead wife, Avril. His attraction was now approaching lust. He knew he blushed whenever her eyes met his. She was not just watching him now but staring at him with an anticipation of some sort that he could not quite identify.

"What is it?" he asked, wanting to look away from her yet unable to.

She faced him, eyes deep green, eyes that one could get lost in and never desire to be found. She wore a white shift tied about her waist with a thin, black cotton sash, accentuating the suppleness of her figure. Blond hair flowed down her back. In the torrid glow of the tent's many candelabras, the silken curls about her face danced like flame. "I must warn you," she blurted in a rush of breath, "as we camped on the outskirts of Tomkin Sty, Aeros and the Bloodwood, they talked of you and me."

Gault's blood turned to ice. Tomkin Sty—the village they had destroyed after Gallows Haven. The Sør Sevier army had swelled in ranks to over ten thousand. And more ships would be arriving from Wyn Darrè by the time they reached Ravenker on the morrow. Still, despite all of his success, Aeros was showing signs of impatience. In Wyn Darrè, the Angel Prince's army had killed only those soldiers who'd fought against them, never women or children. However, Aeros' siege of Gul Kana was an all-out slaughter. Anything and everything in his way was crushed underfoot, leaving few alive, and those remaining were now his slaves.

His eyes narrowed of their own volition. "And what did they say?"

"Aeros cares not for the way you look upon me." She dropped her eyes. "Nor I you."

Gault cursed himself for not being more circumspect in how he had handled himself around Ava. He had never blatantly gawked at the girl in Aeros' presence, never spoken to her more than briefly. But Aeros had sharp eyes and even sharper instincts. He would be quick to pick up on even the smallest of clues, especially if he had caught the girl looking at Gault in the same way.

She continued tentatively, "Aeros said that you are not a full-blooded Sør Sevier man and your mother was a witch from Adin Wyte. He said that you were less than a bastard. He deemed you unholy. He thinks you will steal the helmet and angel stone from him. He is afraid you might find out the plans a man named Black Dugal has for your daughter."

Black Dugal! Gault felt all the color drain from his face. He took a step back from the girl and felt his eyes bore into hers. Plans for his daughter? The last image Gault had had of his stepdaughter was of her waving to him from the battlements of Rokenwalder Castle as the armies of the Angel Prince sailed from the shores of Sør Sevier toward Wyn Darrè. He remembered King Aevrett's promise to keep her safe. She had been scarcely twelve at the time. But those days were over and almost beyond recall, and allowing himself to dwell on them would only ruin the edge he needed to remain alert and alive in the coming days—that is, if what Ava told him was true. Longing for the past was an indulgence best left to the small-minded. He closed his eyes and cleared his head, breathing deep. When he reopened them, Ava's face was clear as crystal before him.

"How is it you heard them discussing me?" he asked.

"They speak freely in front of me. I fear the Bloodwood plans to kill you."

"Kill me?"

"I swear it."

"Perhaps you imagine things," he said. "A dream, maybe."

"The wraiths put no such imaginings in my head," she said with fierceness. There was something dark in her face, a look of rage, perhaps, or cruelty. "I only chose to warn you because I cannot bear the thought of your death." His questioning her brought genuine hurt to her eyes and genuine concern, too. She had exposed herself to him as a friend. She had wanted to help him. That he acted distrustful had disturbed her.

"You're right," he said. "For only the wicked can be deceived by the wraiths."

She seemed to retreat inward at his words.

"And you above all are not wicked." He lifted his hand and touched her hair. She didn't flinch, except perhaps around the eyes. "I wish to believe you. At the same time I hope that there is no truth in what you say. I thank you for risking so much to warn me."

"I risk nothing," she said. "I am already dead. I ask only that you kill Aeros for me. But if you cannot slay him, I understand. However, you should at least try to escape from this place. And if so, you should take me with you."

Gault found that his fingers were still entwined within the blond curls of her hair. But his body went rigid at her words. In all the battles he'd fought these last five years, nothing had prepared him for this. The very thought of Aeros plotting his death stung. But what stunned him more was the last wish of this girl. Fleeing in fear of his own life was something he had never contemplated.

"Aeros showed me the green stone." She pointed to the gold-filigreed chest set on a rug in the corner of the room. "And the helm. The White Prince thinks you will steal them anyway. So take them now. And take me with you when you escape."

Ava wanted him to abandon the Angel Prince—abandon his lord. To steal from him too. He could feel the stone pulling at him now. *And it's right there in that chest!* He'd felt the stone's glamour and lure ever since he'd first seen it. *But to gain it, this waif wants me to become a deserter, the lowest form of man.* And she wanted him to take her with him. But what shook him to his core was the fact that he was now contemplating doing just such a thing. He cursed himself for his own weakness. *Is it the striking look of her face and perfection of her body that has bewitched me?* He let her hair drop from his fingers, never more ashamed of his own lust.

Then he kissed her. She flinched away at first. But then her lips were pressed into his, soft and warm and open. His tongue searched her willing mouth, finding hers, curling together. Then, realizing what he was doing, he pushed away from her as if bitten. *She's scarcely seventeen!* He walked ten paces from her and poured himself a cool cup of water from the basin on the far side of the draped room. He drank deep, heart pounding. *Krista's age!* He looked at the girl and saw the hurt and confusion. *She's but a child.*

There was a stirring of the air and a flash of light. Gault's eyes flew to the entry of the tent. Aeros stood in the canvas doorway. The sunlight from outside grazed his shoulders and hair, the glint in his eyes like piercing hailstones. Silhouetted against the brightness of the sun, his face appeared absolutely bloodless.

"You are excused now, Gault," Aeros said, holding the flap of the tent open.

I have witnessed the folly of men. Trying to save your own skin will not make you a hero. For every soul has an instinct to survive. Even the starving rat slinking in the sewers of Amadon will fight the mangy cat that stalks it. You are only a hero when you risk your own life to save another. But man is stupid and filled with pride. I have seen men throw away their lives just to prove they were tough or, Laijon forbid, right.
—THE MOON SCROLLS OF MIA

CHAPTER FORTY-SEVEN
JONDRALYN BRONACHELL

20TH DAY OF THE MOURNING MOON, 999TH YEAR OF LAIJON
RAVENKER, GUL KANA

Jondralyn sat on a lichen-coated rock next to Culpa Barra. Her ears were alert to the cries of the gulls skimming the ocean below. Leif Chaparral stood near them in his leather armor, a black shard against the moonlight, the hilt of his sword a barely visible gleam at his hip. Leif held the king's standard in one arm, tip planted in the turf, his body leaning against it. The crescent moon was a sharp scythe poised over him. A soft light misted the jagged edge of the cliff not fifty yards from Leif. The cliff overlooked Ravenker and Autumn Bay. The sheer drop plunged heedlessly to the rocks and breakers below. Foamy waves crested the sea in the distance, glinting with a moon-washed glow.

The king's standard—a banner with a silver tree on a black background—snapped to life in the wind. The small gust also bent

and swayed the top of the few gnarled trees that shimmered along the cliff's edge. The gust was stout enough to pull the spring leaves from the branches and send them spinning away in silver twinkles. Sixty of Kelvin Kronnin's Ocean Guard stood at ease not a hundred paces behind Jondralyn, Leif, and Culpa. The three of them had ventured to this spot high atop the bluff on the western side of the bay for good reason. Even though it was well past midnight, they'd come here to scout the terrain, looking east over Ravenker and the looming mountain range beyond. More importantly, they were now looking across the bay at the White Prince's army, camped under the Autumn Range a mile south of town.

"We needn't risk discovery," Leif said. "We've satisfied our curiosity and seen Aeros' armies with our own eyes, Jon. I say we make haste to Lord's Point. We've brought too few men. The White Prince must know that we watch him. His scouts are clever. I worry for your safety. We should leave now."

From their vantage point, they could clearly see the army of Sør Sevier spread south of Ravenker. It looked to be over ten thousand strong. Ravenker itself was a town of surprising size, holding two thousand people at least, with outlying farms and steadings that spread out along the lowlands on either side of the bay. But it was dwarfed by the vastness of the army camped to the south of it. Good portions of the inner town itself were encircled by a high ancient stone wall, a crumbled-down affair filled with more holes than not. A bulky bell tower marked the northernmost inland curve of the wall, whilst two squat towers sat at either end of the wall flanking the bay.

On their journey to Ravenker, they had passed by many who were fleeing the southern coast northward. Many had heard of the White Prince's slaughter at Gallows Haven and Tomkin Sty. They were learning of Aeros' brutality and wished to avoid it, so they were all now heading to the safety of Lord's Point and places beyond.

"We shall meet with the White Prince at first light," she said.

Leif seemed bemused. "That would be suicide with no army of our own."

"We need not delay in delivering Jovan's terms of war."

"It seems like madness to me, m'lady. Your safety is of utmost importance."

"I will meet with the White Prince on the morrow."

"Aeros would kill you and the sixty knights with us."

"He will not," she said. "We will go under a banner of truce. Aeros asked that my brother come to him and swear fealty. And that is what he will be expecting. We are being invaded, Leif. We must show our quality at some point. Why not on the morrow? We cannot stand about tremble-footed forever."

"Let us wait until Aeros advances on Lord's Point before offering the king's terms of war. At least then you will have the entire army of Gul Kana behind you."

Jondralyn looked to Culpa for help, but the blond fellow sat on the rock, the point of his Dayknight sword buried in the turf between thick leather boots, the black opal atop the weapon resting against his face. The young Dayknight just sat that way, staring across the bay at the Sør Sevier army. Jondralyn looked back up at Leif, whose dark-rimmed eyes were like black pits in the night. Though Leif's thin lips were visible, they were pursed in a tight smile as he said, "We should retreat to Lord's Point and make preparations there, I beg of you."

"I disagree," Jondralyn stated. "Meeting with the White Prince here and now is the proper thing to do."

Leif did not relent. "What of Kronnin's Ocean Guard? You have to understand, Jon, that when one of royal blood, one who commands even a bit of power over them, shows up on the battlefield, hardened battle commanders with years of experience will sense the futility of their position and the common soldier grows wary. They all of them wonder, will I be needlessly sent to my death now on the whim of a woman, a princess? I sensed this very thing in Kronnin not four days ago."

Jondralyn winced at his words. Leif just stared at her, unblinking. Those painted dark eyes of his cut through the night, sharp as knives. She gave him a cold stare back. *He is trying to help me here. His advice is sound. Yet he does not know the things I know. He is not part of the Brethren of Mia.*

"I appreciate your forthrightness, Leif. And I see there is wisdom in your words. And I know it is no small favor I ask of them. But my mind is set. I will take Lord Kronnin's knights and venture into the White Prince's camp at first light and offer Jovan's terms of war."

"There must be another way, m'lady," Leif said. "Will you let me think on this a while alone? I must take a piss." He bowed. "By your leave, of course."

Jondralyn nodded and Leif excused himself, the king's standard now planted in the ground. He walked alone down the slight incline toward the gnarled trees and cliff's edge, not fifty yards away, limping through the grass as he went.

"If it were anyone but Leif"—she turned to Culpa—"I would simply order him to do as I wished. But I do want him to feel like he is part of this. He has swallowed his pride, accepted me as his leader, and made himself an asset to our venture. I know that initially he harbored scant respect for my position over him. "

Culpa Barra said, "I would consider it an honor to ride into the camp of the White Prince with you. I know who you are. I know the prophecies hidden within the scrolls of Mia. Leif does not."

"You will have ample opportunity to prove your loyalty," Jondralyn said. "That both Roguemoore and Squireck hold you in such high esteem is no small thing."

"Squireck, Roguemoore, your father, all of them have taught me much of the Brethren." Culpa lifted his sword and pulled out a whetstone, running it along the edge. "Did I tell you my father was a swordsmith in Port Follett?" he asked.

"You did not." Jondralyn shook her head. "Roguemoore mentioned your father was the greatest swordsmith ever. That he was friends with Roguemoore's brother."

"A fine-honed blade is a beautiful thing," Culpa said, holding up his sword in the moonlight. "This sword is my life." He paused a moment, a reflective look in his eyes. "I gazed upon *Afflicted Fire* but the once, when Ser Roderic and I found it at Deadwood Gate. What must it have been like to wield such a blade? Magnificent, I assume. The sword of Laijon. Hawkwood and Roguemoore go to get it. We will have it with us again soon, and *Blackest Heart* as well."

Afflicted Fire. We will have it with us again soon. Jondralyn thought on Culpa's words. Did she really believe Culpa had seen it, had been witness to its rediscovery, then left it where he and Ser Roderic found it? *We have found the five,* Roguemoore had said. *The Princess, the Gladiator, the Assassin, the Thief, and most importantly the Slave. Each a descendent of one of the Five Warrior Angels, each tied to one of the Five Isles by blood, each ready to play a part in summoning forth the true heir of Laijon and bringing about his return as the* Moon Scrolls *have foretold.*

Jondralyn pulled out her own sword—the standard-issue Amadon Silver Guard blade. "Not much of a weapon here." She bemoaned the simplicity of the thing, with its flat blade and standard cross hilt. "Perhaps *Afflicted Fire* is different, like you say. Val-Draekin told me how the Vallè believe that their souls are in their swords. I fear there's naught but poorly forged iron in this blade. This weapon is not my life, Culpa. And I don't know why you're so enamored of yours. They are all of them the same."

"You have it wrong." With great care Culpa ran the whetstone down the length of his blade again. "A sword is a symbol of justice. A symbol of authority. A sword will survive long after its owner is gone. It can be handed down through generations of warriors. My son will one day own this blade. I should be proud of it. It is an honor to carry the steel of the Dayknights—standard issue or not."

"A sword is naught but a damn fine way to kill a man," she said, "or oghul."

Culpa rubbed his hand over the black opal atop the pommel of his weapon. "My father used to quote verses from the Book of the Cross in *The Way and Truth of Laijon*. My favorites were, 'Nothing can set Laijon's honor more right than the cut of a sword.' And 'With the sword, wipe away moral stain and achieve perfection in the spirit.'"

Jondralyn liked those verses. And hearing them recited by Culpa, a man so full of conviction, made her think upon the subject more deeply. There was a verse in *The Way and Truth of Laijon* she had always fancied that had to do with swords. But at the moment, the sense of it eluded her. She racked her brain, wishing to recall it, hoping, by doing so, that the measure of her quality as a fighter would go up in Culpa's eyes. But the passage would not reveal itself. And most knights worth their salt memorized every scriptural reference to swords in *The Way and Truth of Laijon*. But the verse that eluded her would just not come to mind. She cursed herself, knowing how her fickle brain worked sometimes. She knew that when she least expected, or least needed it, the passage she was looking for would thrust itself into her head for no reason.

Frustrated, she looked out into the darkness at Leif under the gnarled trees at the edge of the cliff. Silhouetted against the moonlit sky, Leif's back was arched as he pissed with the wind. It was no simple task undoing even the leather armor of the Dayknights to urinate, then doing it back up again. In full Dayknight battle armor, complete with black-lacquered breastplate and greaves, some knights were known to go without food or drink for days just to avoid the inconvenience of their bodily functions. Her own armor had rubbed her raw in places she wished she could forget. Riding as hard and swiftly as they had to reach this spot had been a cruel lesson in torture for her. Battle armor and horse riding did not make a perfect match.

Culpa spoke again, his tone reverent. "My father said that the finest swords are forged under a full moon, thus endowing them with the powers of the stars. I was lucky to have grown up by the glow of the forger's fire. The very best swords my father ever made were those he made for the Dayknights. He would test each sword's sharpened edge by dipping it into a river and slicing floating lily pads in half as they drifted by."

"Why did you not take up the craft?" she asked. "You seem to love the art."

"Hadn't the talent. But I cut a good figure with a blade at my hip, my father said."

It was true. Culpa could handle himself well with a blade. And there was nothing like the lethal beauty of a sword to enhance one-self. Someday Jondralyn now hoped there would be a special weapon for her. *Afflicted Fire*. It wouldn't be the clunky Silver Guard blade she was forced to wear now—or the clunky blade that had acciden-tally skewered Anjk Bourbon. The fact that she hadn't been affected by killing the oghul surprised her none. It had been like killing a chicken, or a dog, nothing more. She wanted to know what it felt like to really take a life, a human life, in battle, of course, for a purpose—an enemy's life, the life of a Sør Sevier soldier. After all, her brother had. At Oksana, Jovan had fought alongside their father during Sør Sevier's initial invasion of Wyn Darrè. So had Leif.

Her gaze again traveled to the edge of the cliff where Leif was in the process of fastening up his armor. Perhaps they should do as Leif advised. Perhaps they should just turn back their army and wait in Lord's Point. *But that is not the way a person of destiny would think. It is not what my mother would do.* Culpa Barra was still working his sword with the whetstone. The concentration and care the fellow displayed were truly astounding. He stroked the blade back and forth with a certain tenderness, as if the Dayknight sword meant as much to him as a person would . . . as a lover would.

Even Culpa has killed. It seemed that any normal man would be racked with guilt at what Culpa had done to his four fellow Dayknights in Black Glass Courtyard. Yet Culpa had remained stoic in following Jovan's orders. She had always meant to ask the young Dayknight about his involvement in the events of that day, but there had never seemed an appropriate time to broach the subject.

Culpa looked up, not at her, but outward, out toward the cliff edge, his eyes tightening. Jondralyn followed his gaze. Leif stood facing them now, stretching—as much as he could in his armor— his back to the cliff, the moon hovering just over his head, the tree branches looming above the moon like crooked claws.

At first Jondralyn hadn't seen the crows, still and soundless in the trees, but when Leif turned, they all leaped skyward, branches rustling and creaking in the night. They were everywhere, hundreds of them, filling the already black sky. Their flapping wings sent a fright through her. But soon the night settled again around her as Leif returned.

"I see some wisdom in what you say, m'lady," Leif began, kicking at the dirt under him with his steel-toed riding boots. "We may as well get this war started. It's not as if the White Prince has been dallying about these last ten years. He is on our shores and conquering our villages. I agree. We should meet with Aeros on the morrow and tell him that Jovan will not surrender at Lord's Point. There is bravery in your course of action, Jon. We need to show our enemies that we will not break before them, nor cower to their will. Your bold valiance in the face of overwhelming odds does great honor to your father." Leif then bent his knee to her.

Jondralyn stood and placed her hand on Leif's shoulder. "Thank you," she said, almost in tears. She had hoped this journey that Jovan had sent her on would satiate her unsatisfied yearning for validation in everyone's eyes. If she could show some measure of courage before Aeros Raijael here at Ravenker, she knew she would be looked upon as a more than just a beautiful face on a coin. "Stand, Leif," she commanded. He stood and she continued, "The history books will speak of this day when we faced the White Prince together, Leif Chaparral and Jondralyn Bronachell."

"Indeed," Leif said, yet his eyes held a haunted look. "I just ask of you one thing. I think it unwise for us to go riding into the camp of the White Prince with but sixty knights, even under a banner of truce. I think it more prudent I go to the White Prince tonight, alone. Not to deliver the king's terms of war by myself; no, that is your rightful task and I do not wish to strip you of that honor. I do, however, think it best that Aeros agree to meet with you on equal terms. I shall but arrange a meeting between you—our sixty knights along with sixty of his in the center of Ravenker. That he should agree to. That way, my mind will be at ease. If we meet with him on equal terms, we do not place ourselves at undue risk of being killed or, worse yet, captured."

"It is a good plan," she said, clasping his shoulder again. "And you risk much by volunteering to go alone. Do you wish Culpa to accompany you?"

"This task I take upon myself. I shall go alone. And if I do not return by first light, know that I am dead. And I beg of you, Jon, if I do not return, ride back to Lord's Point with all haste, for I fear if Aeros will kill me, your messenger, then he will kill you, too."

The merfolk and grayken and sharks of the ocean are likened unto to
the nameless beasts of the underworld. Man's continued dominance over
them is as man's continued dominance over the lord of the underworld.
Therefore, I prophesy to you with an eye toward truth: the return of
Laijon, as Laijon of old, will be born and raised by the sea. He will become
like a torch unto mine path, leading all toward that Fiery Absolution.
—THE WAY AND TRUTH OF LAIJON

CHAPTER FORTY-EIGHT

NAIL

21ST DAY OF THE MOURNING MOON, 999TH YEAR OF LAIJON

AUTUMN RANGE, GUL KANA

Lightning flashed all around, hitting the water with thunderous claps. Nail felt his lungs ravished of what scant air
remained. Red-glowing symbols swirled in the deep: circles,
crosses. Then his head broke the surface of the sea. Mermaids surrounded him on every side. "Come this way," they whispered with
liquid voices. "No, this way," they prodded, circling in the fiery water.
Nail floundered, thrashed. "Come this way." The mermaid nearest
him reached out her delicate pale hand, lifting his chin, turning his
face. Nail saw Stefan, sitting against a white birch, dead, rough-hewn
arrow piercing his chest. A blue angel stone lay at his side. Above
Stefan, Liz Hen was hanging from the tree. Her hands and feet had
been severed. A potato sack, painted black, hung around her neck.
Somehow, Nail knew beyond a shadow of a doubt that Jenko Bruk

was responsible for the dismemberment of the girl. Jenko stood beside Liz Hen, grinning, sword stained red. "She *is* more important than you, Nail," Jenko said. "She had to die." The bottom of the potato sack tore free, and Liz Hen's hands and feet spilled forth.

Nail looked away. When he looked again, Liz Hen's feet and hands were being sewn back on with glowing blue thread by a sad blond girl with a metal claw for a hand. In Liz Hen's own hands was an ornate dagger. Nail watched as she ran her fingers over the intricate Vallè scrollwork of the knife's cross-guard and the sleek texture of its ivory-covered hilt. She carved the word *dragon* into the white bark of the birch. Suddenly her brother Zane was there, standing on the edge of an icy glacier crevasse. He had the dagger now. He raised the bright blade slowly to Nail's forehead, pressing the tip gently against his flesh with both of his hands. Two big tears squeezed out from the red-haired boy's eyes and trickled down his cheeks. "You should have tried harder to save me." Then Zane sliced into Nail's forehead twice, once crosswise, once down, then peeled back the skin. Blood oozed out, then congealed, then flaked from Nail's skin and floated away over the edge of the glacier like soot.

Then Zane did something truly awful. He plunged the dagger into his own chest right where his heart would be. He rooted the blade around and, with the tip of the knife, pulled forth his still-beating heart. It dripped blood and was covered in bright-glowing blue granules of sand. Zane's tongue flicked out hungrily, licking the sand from his heart as if he were licking the sugar from a candied apple. "Who are these men you follow, Nail? Who?" Zane then crammed both the heart and dagger back into his chest. "Death is your heritage. . . ."

And with a crack of thunder the glacier gave way around Zane and he was plunged into the icy depths of the bottomless crevasse. All that remained of his passing was a broad bloody smear that led over the lip of the ice to the darkness below.

† † † † †

Nail could not identify the clattering noise that woke him, and for a span of a few heartbeats he lay confused, dizzy, not knowing where he was, eyes cracked open. It was as if the world was tilted alarmingly. His head swam with panic. When his vision cleared, he found he was looking straight up at the dark spindly pine boughs overhead and the stars twinkling between them.

He could feel the warmth of the campfire on the side of his face. Hawkwood, Godwyn, and the dwarf sat around the fire, talking. Nail rolled over, placing his back to the fire, breathing heavily, trying to repress the dream he'd just had. It was way past midnight.

It had been a long day of hard travel from the abbey. He'd grown exhausted within the first half day of riding: sore, unaccustomed to the feel and motion of Godwyn's piebald pony, Dusty. After the long day of riding he both appreciated and hated Dusty. Stefan, Dokie, and Liz Hen struggled with their ponies too.

"I'd sooner stay here for a time," Liz Hen had said when Godwyn first told her of their plans to leave the abbey. "I can tend the goats and ponies for you, bishop, while you and the others go back down to the coast."

"And I'll help her," Dokie piped up. "I dare not venture far from here, specially any place near the army of the White Prince, you know, lest they toss me in with the sharks and I dump in my britches again."

But the bishop would have none of it. "You will be safer with us, young Dokie. The abbey will be boarded up and the sheep and goats can roam for the summer. The ponies will bear us to Ravenker quickly. Fear not, Liz Hen, you will be given a stout-enough mount. You won't have to hoof it yourself down the mountain. We will see you to safety at Lord's Point and elsewhere. The abbey is not the place to stay."

Stefan was overly protective of the bow Shawcroft had given him. When Godwyn had tried to secure the bow onto the back of Stefan's pony, he snatched it from the bishop's hands roughly. "I will carry it."

Nail knew the bow meant a great deal to Stefan. Especially ever since his friend had carved Gisela's name into its wood.

For the journey, Shawcroft's satchel had been tied to the back of Dusty along with the battle-ax. But he couldn't search the satchel for Shawcroft's note without drawing attention to himself. Since the start of the journey from the abbey, it was what he'd desired most. To see what was written there. To see if it answered any more of his questions that the men had failed to answer earlier. *And if I ask Godwyn to just show it to me, I'm sure to get a lecture on faith or some such.*

Every time he'd tried to slow his mount and let the others pass him on the trail so he could read the note, something would foil his plan: Beer Mug would bound off into the woods after a fox, causing a commotion, or Dokie would stop and stare at one of the many standing-stones they passed. The bishop had given the boy a small sketchbook. Dokie had taken up the habit of sketching each new symbol he saw on the stones during their breaks from riding. Dokie was not an artist at all. But Liz Hen would flaunt his drawings in front of Nail, claiming with each one that Dokie was far better than he. Nail wasn't sure if he had the stomach to ever draw again. Each standing-stone that they had passed was like another dagger in his heart. The ominous markers, with their familiar carvings sheathed in lichen, had seemed to call out to him. If he lingered near them, nausea soon overcame him. He could find nothing good or noteworthy about the stones or their carvings. They were home to the wraiths, he'd decided, wreathed in a thick pall of evil, dead set on making him ill—dead set on making him recall images best forgotten: bloody shark-infested water, mermaids, lightning, slave brands, a Vallè Bloodwood murdered by Shawcroft. There were still just too many things out of his control. Like a leaf fallen into a raging current, he was just spinning with the roiling waters into the vast unknown.

Now they were camped for the night, and Nail couldn't sleep more than a few winks without his dreams morphing into horrid, disturbing things.

He tried to concentrate on sleep. But the men talking so near made it difficult.

"It's what was done to Alana Bronachell that I cannot forgive," he heard Godwyn say, his voice filled with something not far from panic. Nail's heart beat faster.

"Leave it alone, Hugh," the dwarf said.

"I've paid my penance for past sins," Hawkwood said.

"I won't have us bicker over the past, which cannot be changed." The dwarf lowered his voice. "We are who we are. All of us."

"I fear for the lives of the young folk with us," Godwyn said, "especially Ser Roderic's ward. He is a danger to the others, a danger to us."

Nail's ears perked up, straining to hear the men talk over the crackling campfire.

"I see great strength in him," Hawkwood said.

"I do not share your optimism," the dwarf said. "He is teetering on the brink."

"Shawcroft did not raise him to be weak," Godwyn said. "Don't forget, he has been told his entire life that he was nothing. A bastard. And now we've hinted that he can be part of something far greater than anyone could have ever imagined. What is the precedent for such a thing? How should he react?"

"I sense his eagerness to pledge loyalty to us is but an act," the dwarf huffed.

Hawkwood interjected, "I have always respected your instincts when it comes to assessing one's character, Roguemoore. But with Nail we should reserve our judgment for a while. The bishop is right. How should the boy react to all we've said? Let him make his own decision. It is only fair. I say we tell him *exactly* why we need him."

"Keeping secrets may be a mistake, yes," the dwarf mumbled. "But I fear all would come to ruin if we were to tell him everything now."

"Ser Roderic was a hard, unfeeling man," Godwyn said. "He never wanted Nail. Never thought the charade was a good idea. Roderic resented the Brethren's decision and how it placed such strain on his life. As a result Nail has been treated with one part kindness and two parts meanness. The boy knows not what to believe. He has calluses on his heart that may never heal."

"He longs for friendship," the dwarf continued. "More than anything, I sense that in him. And it is just that kind of loyalty and longing for acceptance that could prove to be our biggest quandary. He wishes for the well-being of his friends. But someday he will come to know just how much of a danger he has always been to them . . . and to us. In knowing the truth, he may very well walk away from us without suffering a moment of remorse. One thing is certain. If his friends stay, they will all die because of him."

An ominous pall hung over the camp at the dwarf's statement. The campfire popped and hissed. For Nail, Roguemoore's last words were like a knife plunged inside of him, twisting and ripping at his innards. His heart burned with anger, yet he lay there under his blanket as cold as a rock, the dwarf's words sounding over and over in his head.

Even these men hide secrets from me. . . .

He was truly lost and alone. *I was responsible for the slaughter of Gallows Haven.* His mind spun. What crushed his soul the most, though, was the thought that he had finally found a place for himself in the Five Isles with these men, a cause to believe in. But during today's travel with them through the Autumn Range, he now felt a fool for his want to become a member of the Brethren of Mia. These men who he had pledged loyalty to had not been honest with him. So soon they had betrayed him. Now they claimed he was truly a danger to his very own friends. *Shawcroft never wanted me.*

The dwarf was right, Nail could walk away from his pledge to them without a moment's remorse, and, he vowed, on the morrow he would.

† † † † †

The wind's soft breath drifted from the ocean and up the mountainside. Nail, Stefan, Liz Hen, Dokie, even the dwarf, the bishop, and Hawkwood watched in dismay as the morning sun danced off the rippling waters of the bay like polished gold. Ravenker lay far below, nestled between the Autumn Bay to the east and the Autumn Range to the west. To the south of Ravenker along the coastline, the White Prince's army had destroyed all. Farmhouses were smoking ruins, fields trampled under by horse and soldier. It was a wasteland.

North, as far as the eye could see, unspoiled farms and cottages and hamlets dotted the landscape, random as seeds scattered in the wind. Patches of lush meadows, woodlands, and rock-fenced fields bordered the farms. A broken wall circled the northern half of town. Villagers streamed in lines from it, many leading oxcarts loaded with possessions, many walking singly and in groups. The mournful hymns they were singing floated with the breeze, high up the slope to where Nail sat atop Dusty. But he saw little meaning in their sad song. Too many dead spots were taking root in his emotions now. That the townsfolk below were about to lose their homes barely pierced his sense of sorrow. *Their deaths are probably my fault too.* The bishop had been correct. Shawcroft had raised him to be unfeeling and hard as nails inside. *And everyone is full of lies.*

The Swithen Wells Trail from the abbey to Ravenker was wide enough for wagons, as it was here. In the short time the piebald had lumbered down the trail since they had awoken and tore down camp near an hour ago, Nail's legs, still unaccustomed to riding, had begun to burn. His thighs were already tight and cramping. He brooded in the saddle, unhappy about a great many things.

"We dare not risk taking the stone and ax so near the army of the White Prince," Godwyn said. For the journey, the bishop had again forsaken his cassock and robe for knee-high boots, leather breeches, and a woolen shirt. With his Dayknight bow strapped across his back, he now looked the part of a deadly archer. It was hard for Nail to imagine the man had ever worn a bishop's cassock at all.

Roguemoore, face gruff and weather-beaten under his bushy beard, sat atop his swaybacked pony. Mountainous peaks still crowned with snow rose high over the dwarf's shoulder. "We may have no choice," he said.

Their road, now skirting an overgrown limestone quarry, dropped down abruptly into a series of steep switchbacks to Ravenker below. Nail's own mount shuffled sideways along the rutted-clay road. He pulled the reins, calming Dusty before she bumped into the back of Godwyn's taller draught mare.

Stefan, Dokie, and Nail had kept their own Gallows Haven armor for the journey. Nail somehow felt the old scrap of metal had just become a part of him. He wished he had a sword. Underneath, all three of them wore shirts and tan leggings of good wool edged with dark leather that the bishop had given them. They were all four wrapped in warm fleece-lined cloaks, also gifts from Godwyn.

Now here they sat above Ravenker, looking down upon the White Prince's army again in dismay. Stefan, Dokie, and Liz Hen looked ill. This was what they'd feared most. Stefan held his bow in anxious hands, fingers nervously caressing Gisela's name carved there.

"I see the king's banner." A stout wind lifted dark hair off Hawkwood's shoulders. He sat atop his roan between the bishop and Dokie. "North of town, I see it. But there seem to be only about fifty or sixty Gul Kana knights, all in blue livery."

"Lord Kronnin's Ocean Guard, no doubt." The dwarf looked at Hawkwood. "We risk capture if either Jovan or any of Sterling's men are down there with them."

"Our trail leads straight through Ravenker," Godwyn said. "I do not like this."

"There is no other road north," Roguemoore said. "It would take us a week to skirt around Ravenker through the cliffs and mountains. They are too rugged and steep. Our only path is through Ravenker."

"We can still slip through unseen," Hawkwood added. "We can easily pass ourselves off as just another group of fleeing villagers."

The dwarf nodded. "That would work, if we stow our weapons. Cover the ax. Stefan, you'll have to hide your bow."

Stefan's eyes widened in fear; whether it was fear of giving up his bow for a while, or fear of journeying so near the armies of Aeros Raijael again, Nail couldn't tell.

"Laijon be with us," the bishop said. "I still do not like the idea of traveling through that town, lest we become separated."

"If we become separated," the dwarf said, looking at them all one by one, "make your way to the Turn Key Saloon in Lord's Point, where my brother, Ironcloud, is to meet us. It will be our rendezvous point."

Luck lasts not. Skill endures. Laijon is on the side with the strongest warriors.
Laijon is on the side of those willing to look into the eyes of the men they
kill. For death cannot get more personal than face-to-face and blade to blade.
Laijon is on the side of those who do battle in the name of his son Raijael.
—THE CHIVALRIC ILLUMINATIONS OF RAIJAEL

CHAPTER FORTY-NINE
GAULT AULBREK

21ST DAY OF THE MOURNING MOON, 999TH YEAR OF LAIJON

RAVENKER, GUL KANA

It was first dawn now, but Leif Chaparral, the prince of River-meade and son of Lord Claybor Chaparral, had come to them in the middle of the night, bearing a banner of truce along with news from Jovan Bronachell. Leif claimed it was he himself who had escorted Baron Jubal Bruk from Lord's Point to Amadon. He'd assured Aeros that Jubal had delivered the Angel Prince's message to the king. Then he'd told them that Jovan had been sorely injured in an assassination attempt and could not meet them in Lord's Point as requested, saying, "In his stead, he sent his sister, Princess Jondralyn. She desires that you meet her at noon in the center of Ravenker. She has traveled with but sixty knights to show her good faith. She asks that you bring sixty of your own knights. There, she will deliver you Jovan's terms of war."

"Jovan does not wish to surrender?" Aeros asked.

"Jondralyn will answer to the particulars of that. She seems eager enough to. And I would hate to spoil her moment." Leif had appeared almost bored with the whole conversation. "I would take my leave now." He bowed. "I ventured into your camp at great risk to myself. If I do not return by first light, Jondralyn will make haste back to Lord's Point and you will not get to speak with her."

Aeros had studied the prince of Rivermeade with an amused glint in his eye. The prince of Rivermeade appeared unruffled. He was a long-haired, athletic-looking, and confident fellow with dark-rimmed eyes. Aeros said, "Before I grant you leave, Ser Leif, answer me this. What happened to the three knights I sent with Jubal Bruk: Marcus, Patryk, and Blodeved? Will they be returned to me?"

"They accompanied the baron to Amadon, true. From there I know not where they went. My king did not detain them, if that is what you are asking."

And that was the extent of the conversation before the prince of Rivermeade was escorted back to his camp by the Bloodwood.

Now, at the break of dawn, all five Knights Archaic stood in front of Aeros' tent: Gault, Spades, Hammerfiss, Spiderwood, and even Aeros' newest bodyguard, Mancellor Allen. Plus one unexpected soul, Jenko Bruk, there at the behest of Aeros.

The flaps of the Angel Prince's tent folded back and Aeros stepped out into the cool morning air. Gault and the other Knights Archaic bowed before him. Jenko Bruk even dipped his head slightly. As Aeros drew closer, his pace almost a saunter, he twirled a thin gold chain in his hand, his skin, as always, cold-looking and pale. His mouth quirked slightly as he spoke. "I am most unhappy about the coming meeting with this princess."

Spiderwood said, "I talked to the prince of Rivermeade at length as I escorted him back to his camp. I got the sense that Gul Kana has little will to fight. And Leif claimed Jondralyn Bronachell is ill equipped to deal with much of anything. Meeting with her would accomplish little in Leif's eyes . . . and mine."

"I imagine she is meek in spirit." Spades smiled, fingering the copper coin in her hand—her Gul Kana trinket with the image of the woman she so hated minted upon it. "Let me crush this princess and her sixty knights."

Gault knew Spades was like a coiled spring, ready to leap from Aeros' tent and pounce on this Gul Kana princess who had stolen Hawkwood's heart. She hadn't carried the coin with Jondralyn's likeness across the breadth of Wyn Darrè for nothing.

"Jovan's weakness is an affront," Hammerfiss snarled. "He could not even bother to come meet with you himself. Instead he sends his *sister*. I beg of you, let me parley with this Gul Kana bitch. I will gladly send her back to her older brother in a hundred finely carved pieces fit to barbecue."

Aeros paced before them, gold chain still twirling, faster now. Gault knew Aeros loathed trifling matters. And this meeting with the princess was clearly a trifle to him. Whenever the Angel Prince's eyes met his, Gault tried to read what he saw there. But Aeros' eyes were stone. Gault wondered if the guilt for what he'd done with Ava Shay was written all over his own face.

"That Jovan has not come himself is indeed an affront." The weblike veins under Aeros' pale, stretched skin pulsed in anger. He looked at Spiderwood with cold eyes. "Leif spoke of an assassination attempt on Jovan. With that I am most displeased. The king was not to be touched by any in Black Dugal's Caste."

"If there was an attack on Jovan, it was not the Bloodwoods' doing."

Aeros' face grew taut, veins now swelling along his neck and forehead, the chain still twirling in his hand. "If the king of Gul Kana cannot speak with me himself, why should I bother speaking with one of his underlings, one of his siblings?" Having seemingly asked the question of himself, Aeros looked to the ground, not expecting an answer. "I will send one of you in my stead." Again, he shot icy eyes at the Bloodwood.

"Send me," Spades growled, fist tightly clenched over the coin now, as if she meant to crush the princess of Gul Kana's image into pulp.

"That," Aeros said, watching the coin spin in Spades' hand, "I most certainly will *not* do. I do not want Jondralyn killed, leastways, not yet. And you would likely gut her from navel to throat and then slice her face off and send it back to Hawkwood in a box."

Fire burned in Spades' eyes. "Do not deny me this honor, my lord."

"I cannot risk her being killed. Not now."

Spiderwood bowed. "I will speak to Jondralyn for you. I harbor her no ill will. Plus, no use you falling prey to some foul trap this princess may have planned."

Aeros studied the Bloodwood, chain no longer twirling in his hand. "You will wear my armor, don my helm, and bear my sword, Sky Reaver. This princess must be convinced that it is indeed me she parleys with."

Everything the Angel Prince was saying had a strange sordidness that Gault couldn't quite place. For his part, something about this hastily thought-out plan did not feel right.

"As long as I'm allowed to ride my own horse, Scowl," the Blood-wood added, "if it pleases my lord."

Aeros raised his brow at that, a rueful smile playing at the corner of his mouth. "It would certainly unbalance Jondralyn to see the White Prince atop such a demon steed."

"I beg of you, my lord," Spades said, eyes aflame. "Let me do this. Do not send the Spider."

Aeros turned to his newest Knight Archaic, Mancellor Allen. "You will go too, Mancellor." Then his gaze fell upon the Gallows Haven lad, Jenko Bruk. "And you shall accompany the Bloodwood also. Get a look at your princess's face. I hear she is most beautiful. If it comes to battle or treachery of some kind, and she is captured, it will be you, Jenko, I give her to. What do you say to that? Would you like a chance to rut with the famed Jondralyn Bronachell?"

Enna Spades stormed away. Gault knew nothing good could possibly come of her being kept from this parley with Jondralyn Bronachell. *Nothing good could possibly come of her going, either.* Aeros was right to keep her out of it.

The Bloodwood stepped toward Jenko Bruk and whipped out a handshake, quick and firm. "Welcome to the adventure," he said.

With some hesitation, Jenko shook the Bloodwood's hand. With that one gesture, it was now clear: Jenko was slowly being welcomed into their fold.

"Make your preparations." Aeros motioned for Spiderwood to enter his tent. "Gather sixty Knights of the Blue Sword. You know my armor. Put it on. And find some Sør Sevier colors for Jenko Bruk."

As the Bloodwood vanished into Aeros' tent, Gault bowed to his lord and prepared to follow Spades back into camp. But Aeros latched onto his cloak and pulled him aside.

"Prepare yourself," Aeros whispered. "I am sending you, too, with the Bloodwood. I do not fully trust him. And get a sense of Jenko Bruk for me. See if he is made of the same material as Mancellor. I've a premonition he can become a great warrior for Raijael someday."

Gault could not rid himself of the vague aura of anxiety he felt under Aeros' immediate scrutiny. His mouth filled with a bitter taste. He did not want to go on this mission. None of it sat right with him. He could not stop thinking of those things Ava Shay had told him.

"Rest easy." Aeros let go his cloak. "The Bloodwood will not know you are there. You will go disguised as a Knight of the Blue Sword. I've already commandeered a suit of armor your own size. The armor awaits you in Hammerfiss' tent. You are my eyes and ears, Gault. I fear that Black Dugal and his gaggle of Bloodwoods have been meaning to betray Sør Sevier for some time now. This is why I have kept the

Spider so close." Aeros' eyes were narrowed, unblinking. "But Dugal forgets who I am. I can sense when those nearest me plot betrayal."

† † † † †

Ravenker. The view of it was desolate, empty. The roadway into the village was a patchwork of cobblestones and dirt. The streets of this strange place were lined with buildings, two, three, sometimes four stories high, most built of thick stone and wooden gables, leaning walls crawling with blossoming ivy. High, jagged cliffs and steep, mountainous terrain rose above the town for miles both north and south.

As he rode, Gault's visor was down, as were the visors of the other sixty Knights of the Blue Sword with him. They were all of them indistinguishable. Ahead, atop the black stallion with the glowing red eyes, rode the Bloodwood. He was dressed as Aeros Raijael: white cloak, shimmering pearl-colored chain mail, silver helm, Sky Reaver sheathed at his hip. Riding next to Spiderwood at the head of the column were both Mancellor Allen and Jenko Bruk. The Gallows Haven lad also wore the armor of a Knight of the Blue Sword. He bore the standard of Sør Sevier—the white flag with the blue cross. Gault had positioned himself in the middle of the column of sixty knights, uncomfortable on a horse not his own, a dun-colored destrier. He missed the reassurance of having Spirit under him.

A few Ravenker banners flapped wildly from atop the buildings round about. The gray flags with a black raven in the center were the only moving things in sight. The silence of the place was unnerving. Gault's skin crawled. A phantom sensation coiled around him like smoke; he felt someone was watching them from the windows above. But when he risked a glance upward, there was nothing. That he should be so wary in an abandoned town was odd. Gault detected some nervousness among the other knights too. Why? He did not know. They had sacked hundreds of such towns in Wyn Darrè. Still

Gault's eyes continually looked up, checking every nook, his trained eyes surveying every building for hidden archers. But for all intents and purposes, Ravenker was vacant.

The Bloodwood marched them down a long and winding street and into the center of town, where he held up his hand, bringing the column to a stop. The town square was an open space devoid of trees, with a ten-foot-tall statue of Laijon leaning on a grayken spear in its center. Directly across the square were sixty or so silver-and-blue-clad knights of the Lord's Point Ocean Guard, several bearing banners of blue, a group of squires huddled behind the knights. Before the sixty in silver and blue were three knights in the silver and black of Amadon, one bearing the black flag of Amadon with the crest of the silver tree, and a fourth in the silver armor and blue livery of the Ocean Guard.

It didn't take long before one of the three in silver and black removed his helm. It was a woman. In fact, it was the most beautiful woman Gault had ever seen—Princess Jondralyn Bronachell. No wonder Hawkwood had fallen in love with this Jondralyn. Even astride a lightly armored bay palfrey, with hair fresh tousled from under a helm, she radiated beauty.

The Gul Kana princess motioned for the three knights next to her to remove their helmets. They followed suit. And the three rode out to the center of the square behind her, stopping in the shadow of the Laijon statue, waiting.

The Bloodwood, atop his red-eyed steed, unmoving, looked high and regal in Aeros Raijael's armor. He wheeled his black steed around, facing the column of Sør Sevier knights. He raised his hand and pointed directly at Gault, motioning him forward.

Gault froze, his legs and heels unable to spur his mount. Sweat rose on his brow under his helm.

"Damn it, soldier," Spiderwood snarled from under the silver helm. "Come forward. We can linger no more. Four of us must ride out to parley with the enemy—me, Mancellor, the standard-bearer, and one other—come!"

The Bloodwood whirled his mount and rode up beside Jenko Bruk and Mancellor Allen. Gault reluctantly spurred the unfamiliar mount forward. There was a bitter, hollow feeling in the pit of his stomach. He reined his warhorse up beside those of Spiderwood, Mancellor, and Jenko.

The Bloodwood reached up and removed Aeros' helm, revealing his face and short-cropped black hair to all. There was darkness living in the Bloodwood's eyes as he stared at Gault. "They do not wear their helms," he said, his hard expression melting into a wry smile as he spoke. "We too must remove our helms here as a sign of good faith."

Good faith? Mancellor and Jenko removed their helms as ordered. *You deceive the Gul Kana princess by pretending to be Aeros.* Gault remained motionless. *And I deceived my lord Aeros by falling in love with his slave.*

"Off with it," Spiderwood commanded.

Gault's heart pounded. The warhorse, sensing nervousness, shifted under him. With a jerk of the reins he brought the unfamiliar beast under control. He was bristling with disgust and rage now.

"Off with it, soldier," the Bloodwood hissed.

Gault reached up and removed his helm. Spiderwood favored him with a cordial smile, eyes boring into Gault's.

"Let us go then and meet with this princess." The Bloodwood whirled and spurred his mount forward. Mancellor followed, as did Jenko, the Sør Sevier standard snapping in the wind. Gault allowed himself a tight grin. Cursing inwardly, he set spurs to flanks.

When the four of them reined up in the center of the square, the four from Gul Kana gaped at the Bloodwood, their eyes transfixed on his ghastly mount with its oily coat and demonic eyes.

"Where is the White Prince?" Jondralyn broke her gaze from the horse and asked.

Up close she was young and more sullen-looking than Gault had first imagined—still utterly gorgeous, though. She wore silver armor of a fine polish, far brighter than the black-lacquered armor of the two to either side of her. The fourth man, clearly a knight of Lord's Point, was just a few steps behind the others.

The Bloodwood answered flatly. "Much like your brother, Jovan, our Angel Prince could not find sufficient reason to attend this meeting."

"This is a disgrace." She turned to Leif. "This is not what was agreed upon."

"Who is to say what is disgraceful and what is not?" Leif answered. "He is an emissary of the White Prince. You are Jovan's emissary. What would you have me do about it?"

A breeze, stiffer than before, washed over them, ruffling Jondralyn's dark, lustrous hair and making Gault blink away dust and grit.

"Who are you?" Jondralyn asked the Bloodwood. "You've a familiar look about you. I don't like it."

"I am the emissary of the Angel Prince," Spiderwood answered. "Who are you?"

"I am Jondralyn Bronachell," she answered impatiently, then nodded to the long-haired man with dark-rimmed eyes to her left. "This is Ser Leif Chaparral, prince of Rivermeade, to whom your White Prince has already spoken. My standard-bearer, Ser Culpa Barra of Port Follett." She nodded to the stern blond fellow to her right. "And Ser Revalard Avocet of Lord's Point." She motioned to the man in blue.

Of the four, Gault judged the one named Culpa Barra to be the real fighter. There was a cold detachment in the eyes of that one. Leif looked the same as last night, capable but overconfident. Ser Avocet looked fierce. Jondralyn Bronachell, the princess of Gul Kana, though stunning to behold, was nothing as a fighter. He could see that. He'd always assumed that the women of Gul Kana were forbidden to learn sword craft and fight in the armies, yet here this princess was, armored up and looking serious.

Jondralyn demanded, her brow furrowed, her voice rising in pitch, "Introduce these men with you."

The Bloodwood did not answer her. He turned to Mancellor. "Go back," he ordered. "Tell the knights they must retreat to Aeros' camp, tell them that Jondralyn Bronachell has refused to negotiate with me."

"I've said no such thing," Jondralyn said, her voice more strained. Confusion covered her face as she watched Mancellor turn and ride away.

"Go with him." The Bloodwood slapped the flanks of Jenko Bruk's mount. With a lurch it bolted, galloping away. Gault watched the Gallows Haven captive race across the square and rein up before the Knights of the Blue Sword with Mancellor.

"What is the meaning of this?" Jondralyn spurred her mount forward, facing Spiderwood. "Where is the White Prince? Why did you give those two orders to send all your knights away? I mean you no harm."

But the Bloodwood held up his hand, hushing the Gul Kana princess, eyes still trained on Mancellor, Jenko, and the Sør Sevier knights in the distance. It wasn't long before the sixty Knights of the Blue Sword wheeled their mounts and followed Mancellor and Jenko back up the street around the corner and out of sight.

"What are you doing?" Gault's voice was a menacing whisper.

The Bloodwood whirled his black horse around. "As we agreed earlier?" he addressed Leif Chaparral. The prince of Rivermeade nodded.

There was a sudden iciness breeding in Gault's muscles. His hand gripped the hilt of the unfamiliar sword at his side. He felt a queasy rumbling in his stomach as he looked at Spiderwood coldly. The Bloodwood's eyes appeared aloof and vaguely amused as he said, "As I promised you, Leif, I bring you one of Aeros' own Knights Archaic for your king to slake his lusts upon."

Then a black dagger was in the Bloodwood's hand, the blade slicing through the straps of Gault's saddle, then sweeping up, burying itself into his warhorse's eye. As the saddle slid from the destrier's broad back, Gault lost his balance. He tried to right himself, but the horse, now dead, dropped out from under him. At the same time, Spiderwood whirled his own black mount and raced away.

Gault, now plummeting to the ground, lost sight of the fleeing Bloodwood as the destrier crashed down on his left leg and rolled up his body. And just like that Gault found himself trapped, staring up from under the dead horse at the Laijon statue above and the few white, fleecy clouds passing by beyond it.

As he struggled to crawl from under the dun-colored destrier, Gault realized the Gallows Haven girl, Ava, had been right all along, and the Bloodwood had indeed been quick about his betrayal, brutally efficient, even.

Both man and woman and Vallè alike will ascend into heaven to sit
upon the heights of the stars and exalt Laijon's throne. Thus I, your
Blessed Mother Mia, do promise the truth in all things, for I knew
Laijon Autour De Lukè and Dashiell Dugal and Morgand Raybourne
and Jabez Van Hester and Savon Bronachell. I will tell you everything
that I know of them, for I also knew them as the Five Warrior Angels.
—THE MOON SCROLLS OF MIA

CHAPTER FIFTY
JONDRALYN BRONACHELL

21ST DAY OF THE MOURNING MOON, 999TH YEAR OF LAIJON

RAVENKER, GUL KANA

As the dark-haired man and his red-eyed stallion disappeared around the corner, Jondralyn could do nothing. Rage clawed its way from deep inside her, emerging from her mouth in a torrent. "What is the meaning of this?" she shouted at Leif.

Leif, a smug smile on his face, looked down at the Sør Sevier knight trapped under the dead destrier. "Looks like your countrymen have abandoned you, Ser Gault."

The bald man continued to struggle under the horse.

Leif barked an order and the sixty knights behind Jondralyn trotted their mounts forward, their swords now drawn.

The Sør Sevier knight freed himself from under the dead horse and lurched to his feet, sword out, unbridled anger on his face. But it was too late. Sixty mounted Ocean Guards surrounded him. His skin was tan and his eyes icy as they ranged over those who now held him captive. He did not launch an attack. It looked as if he desired to but had weighed the odds and had wisely chosen against it.

"May I introduce Ser Gault Aulbrek!" Leif's shout echoed in the somber air. "Knight Archaic and bodyguard of the White Prince! Our king will soon do unto him what those Sør Sevier bastards did to Jubal Bruk!"

Jondralyn knew the name Gault Aulbrek. The Sør Sevier knight's eyes scanned the surrounding Ocean Guards, sword still poised in front of him.

"Are you truly Gault Aulbrek?" Jondralyn asked, her mind traveling back to Rockliegh Isle. "Roguemoore mentioned you—" She stopped talking, realizing she could not remember exactly what it was the dwarf had told her about this man Gault.

"Why was Aeros not here?" she demanded of Leif through gritted teeth. She sat atop her horse, motionless. Her fists, she noticed, kept clenching and releasing, clenching and releasing. She shouted the question at Leif again. "Why was Aeros not here?"

Leif gave her something approaching a defiant smile. Disgusted, confused, she looked down at the Sør Sevier man and snarled, "I say, is your name Gault Aulbrek?" But the bald knight's steely eyes remained fixed on Leif.

Then she remembered: the dwarf had claimed Gault was Squireck's cousin. "Are you Aeros' bodyguard, Ser Gault? Are you the cousin of Squireck Van Hester?"

Again, Gault just stared at Leif, who drew back his own palfrey a few steps. "I think he means to kill me," Leif chuckled. "Protect me, princess. I beg of you."

"You made a deal with death," the bald man said calmly, unamused eyes fixed on Leif. "That Bloodwood is not your friend. In time he will kill you."

"I doubt that." Leif's laughter rang through the square.

"He will kill you and take back the gold he must have paid you to take part in this ruse. I doubt you will live long enough to spend it."

Leif shrugged. "Someone must really dislike you, Ser Gault Aulbrek. The Bloodwood was quick to betray you. But you are correct on one account. He indeed paid me handsomely to deliver you to Jovan."

Jondralyn raged at Leif. "You arranged with our enemy for this man's betrayal?"

Leif's wide grin was long in fading. "What would you have done?" he asked. "A hundred lifetimes' worth of gold to do this one small task that will please Jovan greatly. What have I to lose?"

"Only your life." Gault's mouth curled in a mirthless smile. "If Spiderwood doesn't kill you, I soon will."

Leif raised his brow. "You're in no position to threaten me."

"I could kill you before your men could even draw their swords."

"I welcome you to try."

"Enough!" Jondralyn shouted, glaring at Leif. "Whatever the White Prince has against this man matters not. What you've done is dishonorable, Leif. We will let Gault go. Let him settle his own disputes with Aeros. I want no part of it."

"He is your prisoner now, princess," Leif said. "A gift to send to your brother. He is one of Aeros' most celebrated warriors. You will be hailed as a hero after such a grand capture. Is that not what you seek? Heroism? Adventure? He shall be tortured as was Baron Bruk. Jubal Bruk's shame will then be made right and his honor duly satisfied."

"And what of your honor?" Jondralyn's mount shifted under her. She clutched the reins. "I will be no party to a scheme cooked up behind my back."

"What's done is done," Leif said. "This is how war is waged. We cannot just release him."

"He has a right to his freedom."

"He has taken part in slaughtering our people!" Leif shouted, disgust for her alive and livid behind his eyes.

Jondralyn knew she had been played for a fool. *He's never been concerned for my well-being, or the success of this mission.* She had endured enough impertinent looks from those dark-rimmed eyes in the past. She would endure them no longer. "Then you, Leif, will duel him for his freedom," she said.

"A duel?" Leif's voice simmered. "To satisfy the whim of a princess?"

Jondralyn pulled her sword from its scabbard with a ring. Her mount shuffled under her again. "Then I will duel him," she said, trying to gather her balance atop the horse, sword held high. Unable to completely bring her horse under control, she simply dismounted; awkwardly, though, and nearly falling. The flesh under her armor was rubbed so raw in places it stung with a fury with every move she made.

She tossed the reins to Culpa. Concern was etched on his face. "You should not make such a decision in the wake of emotion, Jon."

"Worry not for me." She turned to face Gault, standing squarely before him now.

Culpa said, "The man is a battle-tested knight."

Jondralyn whirled, eyes flashing with anger and boldness. "I killed Anjk Bourbon," she said forcefully. "I too am battle-tested." She knew that despite her gender, she cut a sharp figure in her armor. She looked every bit the warrior dressed in full battle gear. She made the three-fingered sign of the Laijon Cross over her heart and looked heavenward. She felt the strength of Laijon and the Blessed Mother Mia infuse her as she stood under the impassive gaze of the Laijon statue in the center of the town square so near. Laijon was watching over her now and approved of the rightness of her resolution.

The Sør Sevier man had roaming eyes, always watchful. But Jondralyn knew she could conquer this enemy. A glint of something approaching fear now appeared on the man's face. What would they say about her in Amadon when she brought back the head of one of

Aeros' Knights Archaic? She would be hailed as a hero. She would have her sword swathed in real blood, drenched in glory. This man had taken part in the ten-year slaughter of two kingdoms. Many innocent deaths could be laid at his feet. Deaths that she could now avenge. The words of the Fourth Warrior Angel spoke to her now, the verse she was trying to think of last night. *There is absolution in the lonely sword that slays.* She held her sword up before Gault, motioning with it—motioning that the man should prepare for death.

"Jon." Culpa tried to get her attention. "You have no helm."

"Neither does the man before me. I fight as he fights. We are equal."

"Let me fight in your stead."

It wasn't that Culpa offered to fight for her—it was the real tone of concern in his voice as he made the offer that stabbed at Jondralyn's pride. She lowered her sword. *I have trained with Hawkwood and Val-Draekin and the greatest oghul gladiator trainer in all the Five Isles.* She looked up to the Laijon statue for reassurance. *My destiny has already been laid out before me. I am one of the Warrior Angels! The Princess! The Harbinger!*

"Let me fight in your stead," Culpa repeated.

"Let her fight if that is what she wants, Ser Culpa," Leif interjected. "Let Jondralyn Bronachell show her own quality before her brother's army. It is what she has desired from the start. It is why she led us down here to begin with, to show her quality. Let her show us what grit and bravery are in her. Let her show us the hero she is."

Jondralyn tore her eyes away from the statue. Nervousness gone, she cast a quick glance at Lord Kronnin's Ocean Guard gathered around. Did they all think her incapable? She could read nothing in their posture, their eyes hidden within the dark chasms of their narrow eye slits. Only her own blank stare reflecting off their polished silver helms answered back. She had mustered the courage, steeled herself for this very moment. She looked back up to Laijon and the unquenchable, unconquerable fire in her bosom grew. *I am one of the Five Warrior Angels and this man, this killer in Aeros' army, this Gault Aulbrek, Knight Archaic of Sør Sevier, deserves a swift death!*

"Clear a spot!" she shouted. "Form a circle around us!" As the knights backed their mounts away, forming a shallow ring, Jondralyn stood taller. The sword felt featherlight and finally fit her hand. She knew it would slay like crushing thunder. Her father would be proud of her now—prouder than he had ever been of Jovan. Like a bonfire, the spirits of both Laijon and the Blessed Mother Mia were burning in her bosom as never before. Confidence had never manifested itself so strongly within her as it was now.

She looked at Gault squarely. "I am Jondralyn Bronachell. I am in command of these men. It is clear that injustice has been done you. It is clear that that your fellow man, in conjunction with Leif, schemed to betray you. We will fight to settle the matter honorably. You have my word. My soldiers will let you go free if you are victorious. You will be allowed to go back to your own countrymen, go back to deal with those who've betrayed you in what manner you see fit."

She turned and looked up at Leif atop his horse and said, "If I am killed, let no man lift a hand against this man." Leif nodded, as did Culpa, the latter looking a bit pale.

She turned back to Gault. The bald man's armor was well made, his sword long and steady in his hand; the sun gleamed off its edge with a brilliant flash of sunlight. He looked confident. Jondralyn shifted her own sword from hand to hand, now squaring up to the Sør Sevier knight, preparing herself—her sword melding with her hand, both becoming one instrument. In a way, Culpa was right about the power of a sword's allure. *There is absolution in the lonely sword that slays.* Jondralyn repeated her favorite passage from *The Way and Truth of Laijon* in her mind again—words of the Fourth Warrior Angel. That the verse had come to her twice now after plaguing her all night was a telling sign. Laijon and Mia would guide her sword. Indeed, her standard-issue Silver Guard sword, as plain and utilitarian as it was, felt like lightning in her hand. *Bow down thine merciful ear, dear Lord,* Jondralyn repeated in her head. Other passages from *The Way and Truth of Laijon* now came to her in a flood. She recited them to herself. *Wash me of mine iniquity. Cleanse me of mine own sin. Forgive all transgression. In thee, O Laijon, I place my trust. My rapturous sword is yours. It is bathed in glory.*

Jondralyn struck first, aiming her initial blow at Gault's head. But she was met by a stout parry that knocked her off balance. In a flash, the bald man's sword bit through the air, slicing into the back of her neck.

She tried to duck aside, but found her armor splashed with blood. And when she put her hand to the back of her head, her fingers came away red and sticky. *This wasn't how it was meant to be.* Despite the wind, the courtyard seemed unnaturally hot.

She didn't even see the blow that ended it, but felt the impact of steel against the top of her forehead . . . and a flowering, tiny echo inside her brain that swallowed her up.

She knew she must be falling but never felt herself hit the ground.

There is but one Savior of our souls, Laijon. He it is who paid the butcher's bill. He it is who paid for our sins on the Tree. He it is with whom we covenant to keep ourselves pure of all abominations, lest the wraiths and winged demons arise up again from the underworld and bring about our ruin.
—THE WAY AND TRUTH OF LAIJON

CHAPTER FIFTY-ONE

NAIL

21ST DAY OF THE MOURNING MOON, 999TH YEAR OF LAIJON

RAVENKER, GUL KANA

I t was noon, and Ravenker was a windy place, frightening and vacant.

Beer Mug, panting, tongue drooping lazily from his open mouth, padded along beside Nail. Scattered clouds painted parts of the town dark with eerie shadow. The crumpled wall that circled the inner part of town had a moat filled to the brim with marshy grass. Nail lagged behind the others, leading Dusty by the bit. Cantering along about a hundred paces ahead was Rogue-moore, followed by Godwyn, Stefan, Liz Hen, and Dokie. Last was Hawkwood. All were cloaked and hooded, pretending to be villagers fleeing the might of the White Prince's armies. None had noticed Nail falling behind, none but Beer Mug, who had joined him. Shawcroft's satchel was still secured to Dusty's back. The battle-ax, too. It clanked now and then under the canvas that covered it.

As he lumbered on, Nail noted that the streets of this strange new town were bounded on both sides by buildings, two, three, four stories high. Many were slender, crammed side by side, others separated by narrow alleys. Other than the Gallows Haven chapel, he'd never seen buildings so tall.

He untied Shawcroft's satchel, fumbling at the leather ties and flap of the hidden compartment containing the note. Finding the note, he read:

> *The boy now bears the mark of the cross, the mark of the slave, and the mark of the beast. He has bathed in scarlet, bathed in blood.*

That was it. Nail looked for something else, anything. *The mark of the cross, the mark of the slave, the mark of the beast.* He already knew about those. He looked at the scars—the mark of the cross on top of his right hand, the broken *S* brand of the slave on the underside of that same wrist. He pulled up the sleeve of his shirt, adjusted his plate armor, and examined the scars, from the mermaid on his bicep to the tattoo next to it—the tattoo Stefan had given him after the grayken hunt. Either of those could be the mark of the beast.

He has bathed in scarlet, bathed in blood. That made little sense. He was disheartened that the note offered no information on his parents.

He placed the note back into the satchel. A handful of dusty curs playing in the roadway stopped and watched as Roguemoore and the rest passed by. One dog barked. Soon all barked. Beer Mug's ears pricked up. Nail noted a rumbling in the distance. The pack of dogs began running toward him. Chickens squawked as the dogs tore through their midst. The distant rumbling sound grew louder. Nail was familiar with the sound. Charging horses! *The White Prince attacks the town and we're in the middle of it!* Beer Mug's hackles bristled, and a low growl issued from somewhere deep within him as the rumbling cacophony of horses' hooves grew deafening.

It sounded like Hawkwood was yelling his name as a mass of warhorses came boiling from a side street to his right—straight at him, all wearing the blue and white of Sør Sevier.

Dusty broke and bolted. Nail, reins wrapped around his hand, was hurled sideways as the pony ran off with a shambling gait. Over fifty war chargers thundered by, dust billowing in the wind. As Nail scrambled for safety, he lost hold of the reins, and the piebald barreled away with the pack of barking dogs, chickens squawking and flapping in their wake, satchel and battle-ax bouncing wildly. Dusty disappeared around a corner out of sight. Beer Mug took after her. Nail stumbled back as the last of the knights in blue and white went pouring around him.

One knight peeled away from the main group, doubled back, and now drifted toward Nail at a loping gait. A second knight also disengaged from the group, turning toward him too.

For all the dust swirling around, Nail couldn't see any of his companions. He whirled and ran after Beer Mug and the pony. The two knights set heels to flanks and gave chase. Nail's legs, stiff and sore, churned under him, the soft dirt of the roadway kicking up behind. His tattered breastplate clanked against his chest as he flung himself around the corner and saw Beer Mug and the piebald bolt down another side alley not fifty paces away. Nail sprinted. He rounded the bend after them and found himself in a small market square, a large sculpture of a raven above a dry fountain and pool at its center.

Ahead, in the roadway near the fountain, stood Dusty, a touch of wind stirring the dust under her legs. Beer Mug was there too. The piebald looked spooked, jittery. Nail lumbered forward, gasping for air, trying to calm her with a soft word as he approached. He caught a flash of blue and white from the corner of his eye.

The two Sør Sevier horsemen had caught up to him.

He scanned the small square for something to hide behind or a doorway to dash into. Beyond a few rocks and wooden planks lying against the fountain, there was nothing. The street was clear and all buildings boarded up.

One of the knights charged toward him. Fear fluttered in Nail's chest. Dusty shambled away. Nail lurched after her, reaching for the battle-ax tied to her back. Seeing the pounding hooves of the warhorse bearing down, Nail dug under the canvas and pulled the ax free. Pain flared from somewhere deep within him, along the scars on his flesh.

Once again the surface of the ax seemed to cast a foggy blue glow. Wisps of smoky light leached from the metal in bright blue tendrils. It felt right in his hands—light as goose down floating.

In one smooth motion he whirled to meet his foe.

And felt a white-hot pain thunder through his shoulder as the flat of the knight's longsword smashed into him, sending him sprawling to the ground, battle-ax spinning away. Dirt clawed at his face and arms as he rolled.

Beer Mug danced away from the charging horseman, slavering teeth striking at the knight's steel-toed boots. Frightened, Dusty skittered down the road a ways and stopped. Nail tried to stand. Entangled in his own wobbly legs, he scrambled over the roadway for the ax on hands and knees.

The warhorse turned, dust puffing beneath its hooves as it trotted back toward Nail and reined up. A pole bearing the blue-and-white standard of Sør Sevier was in one of the knight's hands, a longsword in the other. The Sør Sevier rider threw the standard to the ground and dismounted.

Weariness tore at Nail's every limb as he crawled toward the ax.

The knight planted the standard into the ground and brandished his sword, stalking toward Nail. Beer Mug snarled a challenge. Tall and ominous, the Sør Sevier man soon stood over Nail, armor glimmering in the sunlight. His face was hidden behind a war helm with unholy eye slits that bred darkness and death.

Nail gathered what strength he had and picked up the ax, climbed to his feet, and faced the knight. The weapon again felt unnaturally light in his hands.

What was natural, though, was the way his fingers felt at home gripped around the haft, perfectly balanced. And his feet were naturally braced in one of the many stances Shawcroft had drilled into him over the years.

The second knight reined up. Nail backed away, blood crawling through his veins. Ax at the ready, feet steady.

Beer Mug snarled menacingly. The first knight leveled his sword at the dog, reached up, and removed his helm. And Nail found himself face-to-face with Jenko Bruk.

At the sight of the baron's son wearing the colors of the enemy, it was as if a great bloody ocean wave passed over Nail, spun him back in time within its whirling, frothing waters, and plopped him back down again roughly amongst the grayken bile and sharks and merfolk. Everything seemed changed, as if he were now seeing the world through completely different, red-hazed eyes.

"You're wearing Sør Sevier armor?" The words spilled from his mouth in a rush.

"You left me to rot and die." Jenko tossed the helmet aside. There was a glint in his eyes that was not welcoming. In fact, those eyes were dark, staring, and full of malice.

Nail wanted to ask about Ava, but Jenko's sword was already slashing toward his head. Nail swung up with the massive blade of the ax and parried Jenko's blow with ease. Jenko was thrown off balance while Nail set his stance again firm—the earlier red-hazed confusion instantly gone, replaced with a crystal-blue focus. He could feel something from the ax transferring into him, some familiar rush of power.

When the baron's son charged in again, Nail was ready. Footwork practiced and impeccable, he stepped into Jenko's hurried blow and met it headlong with a perfect, crushing swing. Jenko's sword was turned aside with a hollow clang and the follow-through brought Nail's battle-ax arcing up and around high and to the left. Like he'd performed a million times in the mines, he brought the ax swinging back around to the right, crashing into Jenko's return attack mid-swing, making the sword in the baron's son's hands quiver. Just like swinging a pick in the mines, only Jenko's sword wasn't unyielding stone.

Nail pressed the attack. One perfectly placed swing and he sent the biting blade of the battle-ax past the guard of his foe, sinking it into the heavy armor just under Jenko's ribs. The blade lodged there in the iron plate at least an inch or two deep.

As he would do with a pickax sunk in stone, Nail twisted the ax and raked back with all his might. The pointed horns of the curved ax head caught the hilt of Jenko's sword and ripped it violently from his hands.

Jenko looked at once horrified and stunned, sword now lying in the dirt at his feet, a gash in his armor. Whether the baron's son was bleeding underneath, Nail couldn't tell. But Jenko's eyes were now fixed on the gleam of the glorious weapon in Nail's hand. Nail noticed it too. The fog of light emanating from the ax seemed to mist and flow in sinuous blue tendrils up his arms.

What he failed to notice was the other knight who had dismounted and was now joining the fray. Nail threw himself to the side as the second knight's blade glanced off his iron chest plate. The ax was jarred from his hands as he fell heavily to the dirt, body numb with pain, breath now gone. The knight quickly kicked the ax away from Nail's reaching hand. Then his sword seemed to quiver and sing with a thin, keening noise as he brought it up for another blow.

"Mancellor, stop!" a commanding voice yelled.

Cursing himself for losing the ax, Nail, flat on the ground, saw a third man, a dark-haired man in pearl-colored armor, riding up behind Jenko on a stallion made of midnight. The steed's cold black coat glistened with an oily sheen, and the red of its eyes seemed feverish. Beer Mug cowered from the black horse. The man atop the beastly stallion wore a thin, cruel smile, his armor colorless A sword at his side was of a deep blue hue. It was like the armor and weaponry the White Prince had worn during the siege of Gallows Haven. But this man was not Aeros Raijael.

Still, there was something familiar about him. Nail had seen him before, somewhere. *In the muddy dreams of my youth?* Or more likely through a thin red film of his own blood whilst standing on a corpse-strewn beach. *A Bloodwood!* The newcomer's eyes raked over him, the dark gaze burning with intensity. *The Bloodwood who killed Shawcroft!*

"Who is this you torment?" the Bloodwood in pearl armor asked Jenko.

"Nail." Jenko faced the dark-haired fellow.

"Ah, yes." The Bloodwood narrowed his eyes, studying Nail. "A face I have not seen in over fourteen years. Older. But yet the same."

"The boy Aeros hunts for?" The second knight removed his helm. There was a familiar, animal-like bearing about this young Sør Sevier knight that Nail recognized. He had squinting eyes that were dark and fierce, with thick smears of blue war paint under each. Carefully pressed russet braids draped down his back in long cornrows. This was the young knight who had struck him down on the Gallows Haven beach.

"Ser Mancellor, unstrap that leather satchel from Nail's pony and go straight back to camp," the Bloodwood ordered the second knight. He then pointed to the ax on the ground, and to Dusty. "Make sure both the battle-ax and satchel reach Aeros. I trust you with this task. That ax is a priceless treasure." He turned to Jenko. "And you go with him."

Living in Jenko's dark-amber eyes was a sizzling rage. "Not before I kill Nail."

"Aeros wants him alive." The Bloodwood pulled a thin black rope from the folds of his white cloak. "Do as I say, Jenko Bruk, and follow Mancellor if you wish to live out the day." He leaped from his devilish steed and drifted silently toward Nail.

Nail scrambled back, feet kicking up dirt, butt sliding along the roadway. But the Bloodwood was fast. In two loping strides he circled behind Nail. In one slick motion he wrapped the rope around Nail's neck and pulled with such force that Nail's legs jerked straight out and all air was sucked from his lungs. "Do not worry," the man whispered in his ear. "I do this for the sake of my horse. Scowl does not suffer strange riders unless they are unconscious or dead . . . or very pretty girls. So give in. Let the darkness take you."

Nail had never known such pain. His lungs refused to breathe as the rope cut into his flesh. He clawed at it with his hands. But the Bloodwood only increased the pressure.

Beer Mug let out a short, sharp bark and lunged at the man, mouth pulled back, bearing daggerlike teeth. The man's stallion, braying more like a saber-toothed lion than any horse Nail had ever heard, blocked the dog's attack, front hooves lashing out, raking Beer Mug's hindquarters, sending the dog tumbling away. The black stallion reared, pawing at the air above Beer Mug, stomping down. The dog darted backward, barely escaping the beast's crushing hooves. The horse, undaunted, forced Beer Mug back even more. Blood matted the dog's haunches from where the stallion had first struck.

Through blurry eyes, Nail looked beyond the dog and horse. The Sør Sevier knight named Mancellor trotted down the roadway on his stout destrier, untying Shawcroft's leather satchel from Dusty's back. Jenko Bruk followed on his own mount, Sør Sevier standard in one hand, battle-ax in the other. Nail's vision soon faded and a bleak darkness engulfed him, blackness swimming at him from the very air. His lungs screamed in protest. Slaver and foam gurgled from his mouth as he choked and choked.

"Let the boy go, brother."

From a vast distance, Nail heard a familiar voice. "I said let the boy go."

The rope eased up on his neck. He could see again, but through a haze darkly.

"You can save either the boy or the stone," the man strangling Nail said. "The choice is yours, Hawkwood. Two Sør Sevier knights carry the stone and ax to Aeros. If you take off after them now, you might catch them. Kill them. Take back your treasure. The boy or the stone, brother? Answer me now. My blade grows thirsty."

Hawkwood stepped smoothly into Nail's line of sight, both of his curved swords drawn, his roan horse just behind him. "I said let him go, Spiderwood."

The man strangling Nail let out a shrill whistle. At the piercing sound, the demon-eyed horse backed away from Beer Mug, red eyes now fixed on Hawkwood. The roan behind Hawkwood appeared to offer challenge, then trotted back in defeat.

The man named Spiderwood released Nail, but in the same motion threw a black knife straight at Hawkwood. With a spontaneous ease, Hawkwood casually deflected the flying dirk with one of his swords. The clash of metal on metal rang sharp in Nail's ear. Freed now, Nail found he was not so much breathing the air but gulping it down, his hands gingerly feeling the torn flesh of his throat. There was blood there, warm and wet to his fingers.

His vision still faded in and out of focus. He saw naught but red fog. The town was turned sideways. His head was lying on the ground. His neck hurt, his legs hurt, his entire body hurt. Even his eyes hurt. He blinked madly to sooth the burning, catching glimpses of the men before him, both now fully engaged in battle.

Hawkwood launched the first attack, flashing a right-handed strike that thundered toward Spiderwood's face. The Bloodwood reacted with an upward slash of two black knives that hammered like lightning toward his opponent's belly. But Hawkwood danced away, feinting to the right and striking again, fast and furious. The Blood-wood backed away, not even bothering to unsheathe the bright long-sword at his side.

They circled each other like saber-toothed lions, their movements graceful, liquid, and refined. *Where is Roguemoore? Bishop Godwyn?* But there was no one else, nor any sound save the soft crunch of the two combatants' feet in the dirt road.

Spiderwood attacked. Hawkwood swayed back, then stepped in quick with a combination of strikes that drove his opponent away. The Bloodwood counterattacked, the black glint of his whirling knives severing the air with a flowing hum, every move of his arms blindingly fast. This man needed no sword. Daggers were clearly enough. The two circled again, each man testing the other.

Nail pressed his hands to the ground and tried to rise. Beer Mug was at his side, whimpering, tugging at his plate armor with his teeth, trying to drag him from harm's way. Nail rose to his knees, dizziness nearly toppling him again.

"Aeros' armor slows you considerably," Hawkwood said, circling.

"You've let your hair grow," Spiderwood countered. "You look like Leif Chaparral now. Like a Gul Kana woman."

Hawkwood surged forward, ducking under a murderously wicked strike, catching Spiderwood under the arm, his curved cutlass graz-ing the other man. The Bloodwood seemed unfazed, yet his daggers seemed to do little more than lick and graze over Hawkwood's back and left shoulder. But when Hawkwood danced away, his black boiled leathers were slashed open, glistening red with blood.

Still, Hawkwood glided forward and struck back just as quickly. But Spiderwood spun, sending a stinging slash upward. Hawkwood lurched back awkwardly, bicep sliced open, spraying blood over the dirt roadway. He dropped one of his swords.

Nail's body felt leaden, as if his knees had been sewn to the ground. He fell, rolled onto his back, and took a deep breath. Beer Mug's tongue licked at his face, the wetness of it awakening him. *Blue tendrils of mist rising up from the ax blade . . .*

"You fight with swords now," Spiderwood said. "Black Dugal will be most disappointed to hear that you've given up the knives."

"Black Dugal and his poisoned knives and his twisted honor can rot. I haven't given up much."

"Today you give up your life."

"Is Father still swallowing the Blood of the Dragon? Have you too taken up the habit, *older* brother? I see the streaks of red alight in your eyes."

Spiderwood struck again, exploding with a flurry of strikes, sending Hawkwood tumbling unceremoniously to the ground, bleeding from more wounds. Hawkwood rolled, many cuts now opened up in his torso, arm shredded, holding aloft his remaining sword in feeble defense. But it was too late. Spiderwood was on him, slashing, stabbing.

Nail levered himself to his knees. His mouth tasted of dirt and his eyes were full of dust and grit. He stood, rubbing his fists in his blurry eyes. He searched the ground for a weapon, but there was none.

"You have grown weak in your skills, brother," Spiderwood said as he halted his attack. "Is one beautiful princess worth betraying your country?" he asked, one booted foot now planted atop Hawkwood's chest. "Is Jondralyn Bronachell worth betraying your own father? There are many beautiful women. One is much like the next. Even Spades is beautiful. And she is the vilest creature in the Five Isles. How the shame of your weakness must eat at you."

"There is no weakness in falling in love," Hawkwood said, his voice strained from the pressure of the other man's boot on his chest. Scarlet pumped from his wounds all over the roadway as redness welled from a dozen different slashes and holes in his chest.

"Women carry naught but weakness in them," Spiderwood said. "It infects all whom they touch."

Nail saw the stack of wooden planks lying against the fountain not ten paces away. Hawkwood's roan lingered there with Dusty, head lowered. Nail took a step toward the wood planks, legs sore, injured neck and scorched lungs heaving for air. Spiderwood's stallion watched him with naked red eyes. The sound of the crunching dirt beneath Nail's uncertain feet whispered promises of safety if he just ran and saved himself. What did he owe this man Hawkwood? He scarcely knew him. He *could* run. By all rights he should run. There was nothing to panic about now. He was alive at least. He had survived. He had come through almost unscathed. If he just fled, nobody would know of his lack of bravery but for Dusty, Beer Mug, Hawkwood's roan, and the red-eyed horse.

The black stallion was pawing at the ground now, looking ready to charge at him at any moment and crush him underfoot. *You can save either the boy or the stone*, Spiderwood had said. The words rattled in Nail's head and gave him pause. Hawkwood had let the angel stone go with Jenko. Hawkwood had chosen to save him over the battle-ax and stone. Determination in every painful step, he stumbled toward the wood. The first board he grabbed was about four paces long, heavy, with half a dozen rusty nails jutting from one end like crooked little spikes. Wielding it like a club, he advanced on the man looming over Hawkwood.

The stallion charged. Nail kept moving, eyes focused on the two men before him. Through the thunder of hooves, he heard Spiderwood say, "I will look into your eyes as I kill you, brother." The Bloodwood knelt on Hawkwood's chest, black dagger poised over his throat. "I will look into your eyes so you will know there was never any weakness in me." And his knife slashed toward Hawkwood's throat.

Nail swung the plank with all his might. Like a pickax on rock. It smashed into the back of Spiderwood's head with a wet slap. The Bloodwood spun away and folded to the ground, legs and arms stiff, clenching, then twitching. Globs of scarlet flowed from the Bloodwood's ears. He coughed blood over his shiny armor. "That was for Shawcroft," Nail muttered.

Then the demon-eyed horse reached Nail. Bellowing in rage, it reared up on its hind legs, pawing at the air with its razor-sharp hooves. Beer Mug was between Nail and the stallion again, lunging high, snapping at the horse's neck. Nail cursed and swung at the beast with the wood. The black monster leaped aside as his swing connected, the nails of the board raking into the horse's flesh. Beer Mug leaped for the beast's throat again, but the stallion flicked the dog aside with a wide sweep of its body. The horse bucked and snorted, a raspy bellow escaping its maw. It lunged and feinted at the dog again, pawing at the dirt with its hooves, positioning itself over its fallen master, eyeing the dog with two danger-filled orbs, blood streaming down its chest and forelegs with each beat of its evil heart. Seeing that the stallion was not going to attack again, Nail dropped the length of wood and slumped down beside the inert form of Hawkwood. The man was dying; blood poured from a dozen or more wounds.

"What is happening?" Nail mumbled, voice hoarse, barely audible even to himself. "Who are you?" he asked a little louder.

"I'm nobody." Hawkwood struggled to sit up but fell back, eyes now closed. Nail tried to rouse him but could not. He turned toward Spiderwood. The man lay in the pearl-colored battle armor of the White Prince, blood pooling on the roadway around his head.

"Why did Aeros want me?" Nail murmured, knowing that the one man in the Five Isles who might know the answer to that question he had just bludgeoned with a stout length of wood and rusty nails.

"Wyn Darrè, boy," Hawkwood mumbled, voice slurred.

"Sit up." Nail propped the man's head up with his hand. "You must sit up."

Hawkwood struggled to sit, arm dangling uselessly at his side. He looked only slightly more lucid now than he had a few heartbeats before. He crawled forward and snatched his own two curved blades, and then pulled the longsword from the sheath at Spiderwood's belt. He slowly sheathed his own swords.

"Nail," he muttered, examining the other sword, which gleamed blue in the sunlight; its gleam reminded Nail of the ax. "There may be other . . . Sør Sevier knights around. And my brother's horse . . . it has been injected with rauthouin bane, a serum that can turn a horse rabid as a dog. I would not trust it to remain still for long. . . . Lift me to my feet."

Nail helped Hawkwood to a sitting position, eased his neck under the man's uninjured shoulder, and lifted him. Hawkwood stood, one arm around Nail's neck, the other using Spiderwood's sword as a crutch, trying to talk, each of his words struggling to the surface. "That . . . that my brother . . . was attempting to strangle you tells me that he . . . that he needed you unconscious quickly. It tells me the poison on his blades is of a kind that works slowly. I know not how long I will last . . . I have never before suffered the bite of his blades. Have to find the dwarf. Get me over there to my horse, my . . . my . . . saddlebag . . . poultice kit . . . if I'm to have a chance."

Bearing the weight of them both, hesitant and uncertain, legs so weary he feared they might just drop out from under him, Nail led Hawkwood toward the roan and Dusty. Beer Mug followed.

The red-eyed horse stood guard over the Bloodwood.

† † † † †

Though he'd taken some medicines for his wounds, Hawkwood sat like an awkward, burdensome weight atop his horse when they rode into the courtyard with the Laijon statue. Spiderwood's sword was cradled in his lap, his own two curved blades again strapped to the baldric crisscrossing his back. Gul Kana knights in bright-silver-and-blue livery were near the statue. Banners, also blue, rippled above. Warhorses milled about. These warriors, sixty or so, gathered near a litter bearing the body of a long-haired knight in silver and black.

The dead knight's head was cut from forehead to chin, face peeled back from the wound. Above one eye was pale bone and skull, nasal cavity partially exposed, chopped white and ragged. One eye gazed up vacantly; the other was hidden under a mess of blood and skin that was twisted, wrinkled, and shrunken, no longer completely stretching around the head but crawling away from the huge gashing wound that stretched from forehead to cheekbones to chin. Like a hunk of meat, it was just another poor dead fellow who would never again breathe or love or ride a horse, Nail figured. The sight of the knight with the destroyed face was merely one more horrible image in a lifetime's worth of horrible images Nail had suffered through. *Jenko Bruk was wearing the colors of the enemy!* The thought curdled his blood. *Is Ava one of the enemy too?*

Then the knight moved, and Nail realized that the injured fellow might still live.

Another knight with darkened eyes was silently tending to the faceless knight on the litter. He wore black-lacquered armor and made the three-fingered sign of the Laijon Cross over his heart.

"Ocean Guard," Hawkwood muttered. "And Leif Chaparral with them."

A blond knight in similar black armor stood near Leif. The blond fellow had a very familiar look to Nail.

"We must go." There was urgency in Hawkwood's voice.

"Who lies on that litter?" Nail muttered.

"I can't quite . . ." Hawkwood swallowed. "My vision plays tricks on me." His dark eyes struggled to focus on the litter bearing the knight with the destroyed face. "I'm afraid . . . *no*." Hawkwood's face looked pained beyond measure as he slumped low in his saddle. "Leave me, Nail. Flee! At once!"

Leif and the other knight in black armor were now staring at Hawkwood and Nail with purpose. Some of the blue-clad knights beyond them were taking an interest in them too, moving slowly around the litter. Dusty nickered and shuffled aside. Nail regained his balance on her. Beer Mug let out a sharp bark.

A fearsome-looking bald knight, sitting in the dirt at the foot of the litter and wearing the colors of Sør Sevier, looked up at the bark. Rope bound his wrists and ankles. A heavy rope drooped from around his neck down to the ground and back up again, connecting to a stout iron ring tied to the litter.

"That's Gault Aulbrek in chains," Hawkwood hissed. "A most dangerous man."

"All men prove dangerous," Nail said.

He detected rage simmering behind Hawkwood's next words. "A grand day for Leif Chaparral to capture Gault Aulbrek along with the turncoat Hawkwood. And . . . and *Jondralyn*." He went limp, nearly sliding off his horse. Nail moved Dusty next to the larger roan and helped Hawkwood stay upright in the saddle.

The two knights in black, Leif and the familiar blond, were now striding toward them. "I know that man," Nail said, an undertone of puzzlement in his voice. "He is Shawcroft's friend. It is Culpa. He is a *knight*?" The last time Nail had seen Culpa Barra, it was at Deadwood Gate and Culpa was no older than Nail was now. But it was certainly his master's friend who approached.

Hawkwood wobbled in the saddle again. The sword with the sky-blue blade slipped from his lap to the ground with a clank. Nail tried to right Hawkwood, but a firm hand stopped him. "Go, Nail. Run. Now." Hawkwood drew him close. "Remember Lord's Point. The Turn Key Saloon."

Nail's eyes flew to Culpa and the other black-clad knight, Leif, thirty paces away and drawing near. Beer Mug growled.

Hawkwood peered woozily from under dark locks of hair. He took Nail's hands in his. "You and your sister were kept from each other for a purpose—"

"Where is she?" Nail's heart raced, mind suddenly spinning with confusion.

"Listen, boy." Hawkwood gripped his arm. "Your mother is dead. I wish it were otherwise. They will say she was Cassietta Raybourne, the younger sister of King Torrence Raybourne of Wyn Darrè . . . and Shawcroft your uncle. They will say you are from Wyn Darrè. That Raybourne blood flows in your veins, mixed with . . ."

"Who will say?" Nail demanded through gritted teeth.

Hawkwood's eyes were glazing over quickly. "They will say your father is King Aevrett Raijael of Sør Sevier . . . that you are King Aevrett's *youngest* son. And that only the . . . only the *youngest* Raijael can claim ownership . . . of the title . . . Angel Prince."

Hawkwood's eyes rolled up. "But your . . . your destiny," he mumbled, falling forward into Nail's legs, clutching at him for support, "even they cannot fully fathom."

He thrust the reins of his roan into Nail's hands. "Don't let them . . . take my horse." And with that, Hawkwood crumpled into unconsciousness and dropped to the ground. He landed with a thud between the blue-bladed sword, his horse, and Dusty, who stepped aside. Nail backed both animals away from Hawkwood. The two knights had reached them, Leif kneeling, rolling Hawkwood over onto his back, Culpa Barra gawking at Nail in mute wonder.

And Nail stared back at Culpa. Here was Shawcroft's young friend from Deadwood Gate, dressed in ominous black armor, a huge sword with a thick, leather-wrapped hilt and a black-opal-inlaid pommel sheathed at his side. *Like Baron Bruk's sword. Just like Shawcroft's Day-knight sword.*

"Nail?" Culpa asked, a quizzical look on his face.

Leif, Spiderwood's sword now in hand, gazed up at Nail too. And what Nail glimpsed in Leif's dark-rimmed eyes made him tremble with bitterness. He had seen the look before—in Jenko Bruk's eyes that night not so long ago when they had agreed to spar in the Grayken Spear Inn. It was the look that men of station frequently gave him, that look that said, *Whoever you are, you are of no account to me*. With that one look from Leif Chaparral, Nail knew what he must do.

He wheeled Dusty around, set heels to her flanks, and galloped away as fast as the piebald would take him, Hawkwood's roan trailing.

And with a short, sharp bark, Beer Mug raced after.

Behold Laijon whom you seek, whom you delight in. He shall come suddenly to the place of his death, that place where he banished the demons and winged serpents into the underworld. And the tree that he was hung upon shall become like unto a pillar of fire, and those five once hidden from sight will finally be revealed.
—THE WAY AND TRUTH OF LAIJON

CHAPTER FIFTY-TWO

AVA SHAY

21ST DAY OF THE MOURNING MOON, 999TH YEAR OF LAIJON
RAVENKER, GUL KANA

In the waning light of the tent, Ava heard Jenko's shaking voice. "We bring you treasure from Ravenker, my lord."

Ava carefully eased her way through the room toward the tied flaps of canvas that separated Aeros' bedchamber from the rest of the tent. She set her eye to one of the narrow slits between the canvas drapes. Jenko Bruk, Mancellor Allen, and Aeros Raijael stood in the section of tent adjacent to the Angel Prince's bedchamber. Jenko was handing Aeros a gigantic double-bladed battle-ax. Its edges gleamed in the faint light.

To Ava, the monstrous thing looked sharp enough to cleave through someone's leg just by dropping it. The ax had a thick haft of steel wrapped in black leather interwoven with Vallè runes and silver thread. Though beyond murderous-looking, the ax was the most magnificent thing Ava had ever laid eyes on. Its haft seemed to fit perfectly in Aeros' two pale hands.

Neither Jenko's nor Mancellor's eyes left the ax, even as Aeros spoke. "You've damage to your armor?" he addressed Jenko.

"A scratch," Jenko answered. Ava saw it—a long gash in his plate armor just below the ribs—and gasped. It appeared some blood had leaked from it.

"I send you two off on a fool's errand of the Bloodwood's making, and you return bearing one of the five greatest gifts known to mankind." Aeros leaned the magnificent ax against his divan. He then took up the leather satchel at Mancellor Allen's feet.

The satchel was dark umber. A flap wrapped over the top and buckled on the side. The scrollwork inlays decorating the leather were of a unique design entirely—of Vallè workmanship, Ava surmised.

Aeros opened the satchel's flap and pulled forth an old collection of bound scrolls and an ornate prayer book. He gave them only a cursory glance and set them aside. The object he took from the satchel last was a black swatch of silk. Aeros unwrapped it. Buried within was another brilliant stone—an exact replica of the stone he had shown her and the Bloodwood before, but this one was a radiant, sparkling blue. It rested graceful and perfect in the White Prince's hand. Mancellor Allen's eyes widened at the sight.

Aeros held the stone out for Jenko. But Jenko recoiled as smoky waves of dazzling blue color passed over the stone's smooth surface.

"You're lucky." Aeros wrapped the stone into the black silk. "For your feeble wit comprehends none of what you've seen."

"What are they?" Jenko asked with a blank-faced stare.

"Plunder. That is all. May I ask where you two found such treasures?"

"We took them from a boy," Mancellor Allen answered.

"I took them from Nail." Jenko looked at Aeros with some emotion now.

"The boy is with the Spider," Mancellor finished.

Aeros' eyes were alight. "You bear most excellent news. For the gifts, and the tidings you bring, I offer you both anything you desire."

With Aeros' words, hope was not lost in Ava. This was what she had prayed for all along. Jenko would now demand her freedom. He would demand freedom for them both. After the other day, she knew that Gault was not her savior. But now, finally, she and Jenko could escape this nightmare and be together forever. They would travel back to Gallows Haven and start anew. She would finally have her husband and family.

Yet it was Mancellor Allen who answered first. "I need no further gifts. For I have seen the truth and desire to grow in the ways of Raijael. I am your Knight Archaic. I serve you. Beyond that I have no other desire."

"Surely there must be one thing," Aeros said, placing the stone back into the satchel. "Not one?"

"Not one, my lord." Mancellor bowed.

"And you, Ser Jenko Bruk?"

Ava's hopes rose—it was now that Jenko would demand her release.

"I felt something when I held the ax." Jenko was staring again at the large weapon leaning against the divan. "There is some power within it."

"You felt something?" The Angel Prince's eyebrows rose. "Only those most loyal can know the secrets of the ax."

"I wish to wield it in battle." It seemed Jenko wanted to devour the double-bladed weapon with his eyes.

"Only those most *loyal*, Ser Jenko."

"I wish to fight alongside you, my lord." Jenko bowed. "I desire to prove my loyalty. I wish to be made a Knight of the Blue Sword." As he spoke, his eyes never once strayed from the battle-ax.

"You are an opportunist, for sure." A curving smile was playing over Aeros' lips. "But you have not even taken the oath of the Hound

Guard, or blooded yourself as a Rowdie. Yet you still want to be made a Knight of the Blue Sword?"

"I mean to prove myself."

"Of that, I have no doubt."

A rising tide of both panic and deep sadness filled Ava's soul. To her, Jenko was now wreathed in total darkness. She had prayed day and night he would not succumb to this evil. But now it appeared those prayers were going to go unanswered.

Throughout her torment of the past weeks, the one hope she had clung to was that Jenko would one day rescue her from the demon, Aeros. Instead Jenko offered him allegiance. The wraiths now assailed her from every side. They wailed in horrific song, tightening their grip around her soul. She had never felt such despair, such absolute hopelessness. She had never dropped so far down into the darkness with the wraiths and known, deep in her heart, in her soul, that it was never, ever going to get better.

Hope had been lost forever. It was never coming back. And she wasn't sure that she cared. She was so tired. So bruised and exhausted.

It was dark. Everything was dark. Everything was naught but darkness and despair.

But who am I to be worthy of such despair? Who am I?

Woe unto Amadon, O Amadon, dread city where Laijon was slain.
Wilt thou be distressed with heaviness and sorrow during your
final Absolution? Wilt thou be smote with pillars of fire and rivers
of blood? Only Laijon can return to save thee, O Amadon.
—THE WAY AND TRUTH OF LAIJON

CHAPTER FIFTY-THREE

TALA BRONACHELL

21ST DAY OF THE MOURNING MOON, 999TH YEAR OF LAIJON

AMADON, GUL KANA

There was one last note from the Bloodwood on her mantel.

Bravo! You succeeded in every task.
Thanks to your devotion, the downfall of Gul Kana and
the entire Five Isles is now underway. Just a few more tasks
and Lawri's transformation will be complete. And only then
will your destiny also be secured.
Do any of us ever truly show our true selves?
Here is what I need you to do—

Tala stopped reading and crumpled the paper, stuffing it into the
folds of her cloak as Lawri entered the chamber. She was flanked by
both Seita and Val-Draekin.

The two Vallè had shown much concern over Lawri as of late, practically fawning over the girl since her sudden recovery. And Lawri reveled in their company.

At the sight of the three, Tala's heart hammered in dismay. Her mouth was unexpectedly dry and her heart clogged her throat. She swallowed, feeling the pulse in her temple increase. *I saved Lawri!* But this new note swept away all pleasure and sense of accomplishment that was hers. *What have I done?*

"Everything okay?" Seita asked.

No! She wanted to slap the Vallè princess. *Things are not okay!*

Tala searched her cousin's pale, innocent face in the pitiless torchlight of her room. *She is so beautiful.* But Tala knew the game was not over. *What foul green potion did I feed her?* The game had just begun. She could see it in Lawri's eyes. *Those eyes!*

Those once wide, dark, dark Le Graven pupils, they were lit luminescent jade from inside, as if some cursed magic had been let loose in Lawri's brain, and her eyes were crystal windows to the raw green mayhem within. *Or was it some trick of light?*

No. Tala studied Lawri's smiling face. It was no trick of light. She could clearly see . . . the flecks in her cousin's dark eyes were mostly green. . . .

Oh, that I were once again pure Vallè and could recapture the dreams of mine heart. Oh, what did I give in exchange for mine own heritage? Behold, I confess unto you now my greatest wish. For I desire that the Adversary of Laijon, that Assassin, that Fifth Warrior Angel, that great Betrayer, whoa, even that Last Demon Lord, had not taken up quill and ink and written that dread tale, that Book of the Betrayer. *For some things best hidden may soon be discovered before that last fiery day of Absolution.*
—THE ANGEL STONE CODEX

CHAPTER FIFTY-FOUR
LINDHOLF LE GRAVEN

21ST DAY OF THE MOURNING MOON, 999TH YEAR OF LAIJON

AMADON, GUL KANA

Lindholf felt the rough scars on his own left ear with trembling fingers, wishing he were whole. The burns and scars were a plague and a curse. But they had brought him here today. He had dreamt of this moment, glimpsed it within those fleeting and foggy images always hiding near the darker places of his mind.

He gazed up at the statue of Laijon and remembered his own words. *Tala, know that I would defile a thousand Laijon statues at your whim.*

Even now, his hunger for Tala's affection burned in his soul as fiercely as ever. Even now as he stood before the statue, caressing the thin black dagger buried deep in the pocket of his cloak—caressing it as a man would caress the delicate hand of a lover—he thought of her. *Tala.* He thought of what she had done. Sterling Prentiss had not been seen for days. But Lindholf knew where the Dayknight captain was.

He was dead. Rotting on a cross-shaped altar.

How Sterling Prentiss had come to be there, Lindholf would not hazard a guess.

But there were a few things he knew for a fact. Glade had killed Sterling—he had run a knife across the man's throat—and then Tala had reached her hand into the man's guts and pulled forth a vial of glowing green liquid.

After Tala and Glade had left Sterling, Lindholf had slipped from his hiding place into the hazy red room. Moving silently, he had drifted warily toward the altar and snatched up the black dagger—the strange weapon that his darling cousin had knocked from Glade's hands when he had threatened her. He fondled the thin blade now. It was his prize, his evidence against the two of them. He had followed Tala and Glade into the secret ways and had watched Glade murder the captain of the Dayknights and then threaten Tala.

He was conflicted. His sister was again alive and healthy. The green vial Tala had pulled from Sterling's guts had saved Lawri. He'd been there. He knew shortcuts through the secret ways. He'd hurried from the room with the cross-shaped altar and been there in Lawri's room waiting, breathless, for his cousin. He'd watched Tala's eyes grow cloudy with tears as she'd fed Lawri the strange green serum. And somehow, his sister's sickness had vanished. Some witchcraft was now at work within Lawri, even within Tala, within Glade, too, and Lindholf meant to find out what.

Tala wasn't alone in her skulking through the secret ways. Despite his cousin's warnings, Lindholf had done his share of sneaking about the castle too. Val-Draekin and Seita had been tutoring him in the ways of pickpocketing and thievery and creeping about unseen. Alone, he'd snuck into places he shouldn't have. Heard secret conversations, too. Words not meant for his ears. Things said between Hawkwood and Roguemoore, things about the Brethren of Mia and angel stones hidden under Amadon. He was privy to events and matters even Tala and Glade were not.

But Hawkwood, Roguemoore, Tala, hidden treasures; those were not Lindholf's concerns today. Today was for Laijon. Lindholf's eyes wandered about the Temple of the Laijon Statue. The domed interior blazed with the light of a thousand candles. Worshippers prayed at Laijon's feet, their eyes gleaming in the shimmering light.

As Lindholf looked at the statue, his heart pounded.

Upon a dais of pale gray stone stood the great Laijon, carved of Riven Rock marble, one muscular arm held aloft, great silvery sword in hand pointing skyward. His face was surrounded by bright, dancing motes of dust that filtered through the sunlight beaming down from the stained-glass windows high above. His intricately carved chain-mail armor glittered, sending sparkling shards of glorious light raining down upon all. A wreath of heather crowned his head, and his gaze was fixed forever heavenward. This was the statue of the great One and Only.

And it was curiously flawed.

Lindholf stared up at the exquisitely carved face of Laijon; so aesthetic it was, so precise in its symmetry and elegance. To behold Laijon's peerless physique was an honor. This spectacular perfection in marble was, Lindholf believed, why men followed Laijon, why soldiers and gladiators were inspired to hone their own flesh in his likeness and perfection. For this massive sculpture was, indeed, *almost* perfection.

Lindholf studied Laijon's squared yet supple chin, the smooth lines of his sublimely carved mouth and nose and the fine lines of his jaw. The subtly aquiline, beautiful features were unmistakable now. They stood out so strongly, so overwhelmingly. Laijon's marble eyes, though they gazed toward the dome of the ceiling, emanated softness and caring and bravery at the same time. Lindholf looked upon the graceful sweep of Laijon's brow leading to the wreath just above the flaw. . . .

His heart skipped a beat as he spotted it there again.

That he knew of the hidden blemish—when nobody else did— filled him with a silent, almost panicked pleasure. And he only knew of the flaw because he had been atop the statue. He had climbed its smooth surfaces, stood on those broad shoulders and felt the perfectly sculpted marble face of Laijon with his own hands. Felt the nose, the eyes, the hair . . . and the ears that bore that one mysteriousness of which no one knew.

Lindholf had felt the chisel marks atop those ears—ears that used to be pointed.

So it was: he alone knew that this glorious likeness of the great One and Only—this holy visage of Laijon that all humankind throughout the breadth of the Five Isles had bowed down before in supplication and flagellation and then prayed to—was a fraud.

Only he knew that it was no likeness of a human at all.

It was the likeness of a Vallè.

† † † † †

TO BE CONTINUED IN
THE BLACKEST HEART,
VOLUME TWO OF
FIVE WARRIOR ANGELS

APPENDIX

Seasonal Moons of the Five Isles

A year is 360 days.

There are fifteen moons (months) per year.

A moon (month) is twenty-four days long.

A week is eight days long. There are three weeks per moon (month).

Afflicted Moon . . . . Winter
Blackest Moon
Shrouded Moon
Mourning Moon
Ethic Moon . . . . Spring
Angel Moon
Fire Moon
Blood Moon . . . . Summer
Heart Moon
Crown Moon
Thunder Moon . . . . Fall
Archaic Moon
Lonesome Moon
Forgetting Moon
Winter Moon . . . . Winter

Five Tomes of Ancient Writings

The Way and Truth of Laijon
The Chivalric Illuminations of Raijael
The Moon Scrolls of Mia
The Book of the Betrayer
The Angel Stone Codex

Five Weapons of Laijon

Forgetting Moon: battle-ax. Angel stone: blue for the Slave.
Blackest Heart: crossbow. Angel stone: black for the Assassin.
Lonesome Crown: helm. Angel stone: green for the Gladiator.
Ethic Shroud: shield. Angel stone: white for the Thief.
Afflicted Fire: sword. Angel stone: red for the Princess.

Timeline of Events Leading up to *The Forgetting Moon*

5000–6000 Years Before: Humans arrive on the shores of Gul Kana.

1000 Years Before: Thousand Years' War of the humans, dwarves, oghuls, and Vallè begins.

Year Zero: Laijon is born.

18th Year of Laijon: Laijon is thrown into the slave pits.

19th Year of Laijon: Rise of the Five Warrior Angels and rise of the Demon Lords.

20th Year of Laijon: Laijon unites all races against the Fiery Demons and Demon Lords (some call this the War of Cleansing, some call it the Vicious War of the Demons).

21st Year of Laijon: Death of Laijon and banishment of all demons to the underworld.

21st Year of Laijon: Raijael, son of Laijon, is born to the Blessed Mother Mia.

22nd Year of Laijon: Church of Laijon formed by the last three Warrior Angels in Amadon.

40th Year of Laijon: Raijael banished from the church and flees Amadon to Sør Sevier.

40th Year of Laijon: Raijael begins his twenty-year war to reclaim his crown as Laijon's heir.

60th Year of Laijon: Death of Raijael in war, after having conquered Adin Wyte and Wyn Darrè.

200th Year of Laijon: The Church of Laijon retakes Adin Wyte in war from Sør Sevier.

220th Year of Laijon: The Church of Laijon retakes Wyn Darrè in war from Sør Sevier.

300th–400th Years of Laijon: Sør Sevier slowly retakes Adin Wyte and Wyn Darrè in war.

500th–900th Years of Laijon: The Church of Laijon reclaims Adin Wyte and Wyn Darrè.

900th Year of Laijon: The Brethren of Mia formed by a secret group of scholars.

900th–985th Years of Laijon: Battles continue between Sør Sevier, Adin Wyte, and Wyn Darrè.

985th Year of Laijon: Shawcroft fights two Bloodwood assassins atop a Sky Lochs glacier.

986th Year of Laijon: Shawcroft and the boy, Nail, arrive in Deadwood Gate.

989th Year of Laijon: Sør Sevier launches its final crusade against Adin Wyte.

994th Year of Laijon: Adin Wyte conquered by Sør Sevier.

994th Year of Laijon: Shawcroft and the boy, Nail, arrive in Gallows Haven.

994th Year of Laijon: Sør Sevier launches its final crusade against Wyn Darrè.

997th Year of Laijon: Squireck Van Hester slays Archbishop Lucas in Amadon.

999th Year of Laijon: Wyn Darrè conquered by Sør Sevier.

999th Year of Laijon: Sør Sevier prepares for the Final Battle of Absolution against Gul Kana.

ROKENWALDER, SØR SEVIER

Crest: the Blue Sword of Laijon
Colors: blue sword on a white field

KING AEVRETT RAIJAEL: King of Rokenwalder and Sør Sevier.

QUEEN NATALIA RAIJAEL: Wed to Aevrett. From Kayde, Sør Sevier.

AEROS RAIJAEL: 28, the Angel Prince. Son of Aevrett.

SPIDERWOOD: Aeros' Knight Archaic bodyguard. A Bloodwood assassin.

HAMMERFISS: Aeros' Knight Archaic bodyguard.

BEAU STABLER: Aeros' Knight Archaic bodyguard.

ENNA SPADES: 27, Aeros' Knight Archaic bodyguard.

GAULT AULBREK: 38, Aeros' Knight Archaic bodyguard.

AVRIL AULBREK: Wed to Gault. Mother of Krista.

KRISTA AULBREK: 17, Gault's stepdaughter.

AGUS AULBREK: Gault's father. Lord of the Sør Sevier Nordland Highlands.

EVALYN AULBREK: Gault's mother. Sister to Edmon Guy Van Hester of Saint Only.

MARCUS GYLL: a Rowdie.

PATRYK LAURENTS: a Rowdie.

BLODEVED WYNSTONE: a Rowdie.

RUFUC BRADULF: Hound Guard captain.

KARLOS: a Hound Guard.

ALVIN: a Hound Guard.

BLACK DUGAL: Head of the Bloodwood assassins.

MANCELLOR ALLEN: 22, Knight of the Blue Sword. From Wyn Darrè.

GALLOWS HAVEN, GUL KANA

BARON JUBAL BRUK: Baron of Gallows Haven and owner of the *Lady Kindly*.

JENKO BRUK: 18, Baron Jubal Bruk's son.

BRUTUS GROVE: works for Baron Jubal Bruk.

OL' MAN LEDDINGHAM: owner of the Grayken Spear Inn.

AVA SHAY: 17, works at the Grayken Spear Inn.

TYLDA EGBERT: 16, works at the Grayken Spear Inn.

POLLY MOTT: 16, works at the Grayken Spear Inn.

GISELA BARNWELL: 15, Maiden Blue of the Mourning Moon Feast.

SHAWCROFT: also known as Ser Roderic Raybourne.

NAIL: 17, a bastard boy under the care of Shawcroft.

STEFAN WAYLAND: 17, friend of Nail.

DOKIE LIDDLE: 17, friend of Nail.

ZANE NEVILLE: 17, Liz Hen's brother.

LIZ HEN NEVILLE: 19, Zane's sister.

BISHOP TOLBRET: Bishop of Gallows Haven chapel.

BISHOP HUGH GODWYN: Bishop of the Swithen Wells Trail Abbey.

AMADON, GUL KANA

Crest: the Atonement Tree
Colors: the silver Atonement Tree on a black field
Silver Guard. Silver Throne.
KING BORDEN BRONACHELL: Former King of Amadon and Gul
    Kana.
QUEEN ALANA BRONACHELL: Wed to Borden. Sister of Mona
    Le Graven.
JOVAN BRONACHELL: 28, Borden's son. King of Amadon and
    Gul Kana.
JONDRALYN BRONACHELL: 25, Borden's daughter.
TALA BRONACHELL: 16, Borden's daughter.
ANSEL BRONACHELL: 5, Borden's son.
DAME MAIRGRID: Tutor to Tala and Ansel.
SER STERLING PRENTISS: Dayknight captain.
SER CULPA BARRA: 28, a young Dayknight.
SER LARS CASTLEGRAIL: Commander of the Silver Guard.
SER TOMAS VORKINK: Steward of Amadon Castle.
SER LANDON GALLOWAY: Chamberlain of Amadon Castle.
SER TERRELL WICKHAM: Stable marshal of Amadon Castle.
DAME VILAMINA: Kitchen matron of Amadon Castle.
GRAND VICAR DENARIUS: Grand vicar in Amadon. Holy
    Prophet of Laijon.
ARCHBISHOP VANDIVOR: Quorum of the Five Archbishops in
    Amadon.
ARCHBISHOP DONALBAIN: Quorum of the Five Archbishops in
    Amadon.
ARCHBISHOP SPENCERVILLE: Quorum of the Five Archbishops
    in Amadon.
ARCHBISHOP LEAFORD: Quorum of the Five Archbishops in
    Amadon.

ARCHBISHOP RHYS-DUNCAN: Quorum of the Five Archbishops in Amadon.

DELIA: Barmaid at the Filthy Horse Saloon.

GEOFF: Patron of the Filthy Horse Saloon.

SHKILL GHA: an oghul. Gladiator.

ANJK BOURBON: an oghul. Gladiator trainer.

G'MELLKI: an oghul.

ROGUEMOORE: Dwarf ambassador from Ankar.

HAWKWOOD: from Sør Sevier.

ESKANDER, GUL KANA

Crest: the Saber-Toothed Lion

Colors: black lion on a yellow field

Lion Guard. Lion Throne.

LORD LOTT LE GRAVEN; Lord of Eskander. Lion Throne.

MONA LE GRAVEN: Wed to Lott. From Reinhold. Sister of Alana Bronachell.

LINDHOLF LE GRAVEN: 17, Lott's son, twin to Lawri.

LAWRI LE GRAVEN: 17, Lott's daughter, twin to Lindholf.

LORHAND LE GRAVEN: 12, Lott's son, twin to Lilith.

LILITH LE GRAVEN: 12, Lott's daughter, twin to Lorhand.

RIVERMEADE, GUL KANA

Crest: the Wolf

Colors: gray wolf on a maroon field

Wolf Guard. Wolf Throne.

LORD CLAYBOR CHAPARRAL: Lord of Rivermeade. Wolf Throne.

LESIA CHAPARRAL: Wed to Claybor. Sister of Nolan Darkliegh.

LEIF CHAPARRAL: 28, Claybor's son.
SHARLA CHAPARRAL: 23, Claybor's daughter.
JACLYN CHAPARRAL: 21, Claybor's daughter.
GLADE CHAPARRAL: 17, Claybor's son.

AVLONIA, GUL KANA

Crest: white with silver overlay
Colors: silver overlay on a white field
Marble Guard. Marble Throne.
LORD NOLAN DARKLIEGH: Lord of Avlonia.
ELYNOR DARKLIEGH: Wed to Nolan. Edmon Guy Van Hester's
    sister.
LESIA CHAPARRAL: Nolan's sister. Wed to Claybor Chaparral.

LORD'S POINT, GUL KANA

Crest: Blue of the Ocean
Color: blue
Ocean Guard. Ocean Throne.
LORD KELVIN KRONNIN: Lord of Lord's Point.
EMOGEN KRONNIN: Wed to Kelvin.
BEATRIZ VAN HESTER: Kronnin's sister. Wed to King Edmon
    Guy Van Hester.
RAYE KRONNIN: Kronnin's baby daughter.
SER REVALARD AVOCET: one of the Ocean Guard.

BAINBRIDGE, GUL KANA

Crest: Purple Stag
Colors: purple stag on a black field
BARON BRENDER WAYLAND: Uncle of Stefan Wayland.

SAINT ONLY, ADIN WYTE

Crest: two Crossed Spears
Colors: two white crossed spears on a field of red
Spear Guard. Throne of Spears.
KING EDMON GUY VAN HESTER: King of Saint Only and Adin
    Wyte.
QUEEN BEATRIZ VAN HESTER: Wed to Edmon. From Lord's
    Point.
SQUIRECK VAN HESTER: 28, Edmon's son. Prince of Saint Only.
    Gladiator.
EVALYN AULBREK: Edmon's sister. Wed to Lord Agus Aulbrek of
    Sør Sevier.
ELYNOR DARKLIEGH: Edmon's sister. Wed to Lord Nolan
    Darkliegh of Avlonia.
ELYSE KOHN-AGAR: Edmon's sister. Wed to Lord Nigel Kohn-
    Agar of Agonmoore.

WYN DARRÈ

Crest: the Black Serpent
Colors: black serpent on a yellow field
Serpent Guard. Serpent Throne.
KING TORRENCE RAYBOURNE: King of Wyn Darrè.

QUEEN BIANKA RAYBOURNE: Wed to Torrence. From
 Morgandy, Wyn Darrè.
KAROWYN RAYBOURNE: 19, Torrence's daughter.
SER RODERIC RAYBOURNE: Torrence's brother. Known as
 Shawcroft.
CASSIETTA RAYBOURNE: Torrence's sister.
IRONCLOUD: Dwarf from Ankar. Brother of Roguemoore.

VAL VALLÈ

VAL-KORIN: Val Vallè ambassador.
SEITA: Val-Korin's younger daughter.
BREITA: Val-Korin's older daughter.
VAL-DRAEKIN: was once betrothed to Breita.
VAL-SO-VREIGN: bodyguard of Val-Korin.
VAL-GIANNI: Vallè healer (sawbones).
VAL-CE-LAVEROC: a gladiator.
VAL-RIEVAUX: a gladiator.